Praise for *The Core*

"*The Core* is not just a fitting conclusion to The Demon Cycle, it is (by far) the greatest book of an already impressive saga. Peter V. Brett has saved the best for last in a story that is big, bold, and brilliant."
—Beauty in Ruins

"If I were making a Fantasy Rushmore for series that I love, it would be impossible for The Demon Cycle not to take up one of the few spots available."
—Total Inability to Connect,
Fantasy and Sci-Fi Book Blog

THE
CORE

BOOK FIVE OF THE DEMON CYCLE
PETER V. BRETT

DEL REY • NEW YORK

2018 Del Rey Mass Market Edition

Copyright © 2017 by Peter V. Brett
Ward artwork designed by Lauren K. Cannon,
copyright © Peter V. Brett

Published in the United States by Del Rey, an imprint of Random House,
a division of Penguin Random House LLC, New York.

DEL REY and the HOUSE colophon are registered trademarks of
Penguin Random House LLC.

Originally published in hardcover in the United States by Del Rey,
an imprint of Random House, a division of Penguin Random House LLC,
and in the United Kingdom by Harper Voyager,
an imprint of Harper Collins Publishers Ltd., London in 2017.

Map on page vii is reprinted by permission of Harper Voyager,
an imprint of Harper Collins Publishers Ltd., London.

ISBN 978-0-345-53151-3
Ebook ISBN 978-0-425-28579-4

Cover design: Elizabeth Shapiro
Cover illustration: © Larry Rostant

Printed in the United States of America

randomhousebooks.com

9 8 7 6 5 4 3 2 1

Del Rey mass market edition: August 2018

For Sirena Lilith,
who is already changing my life in countless ways.

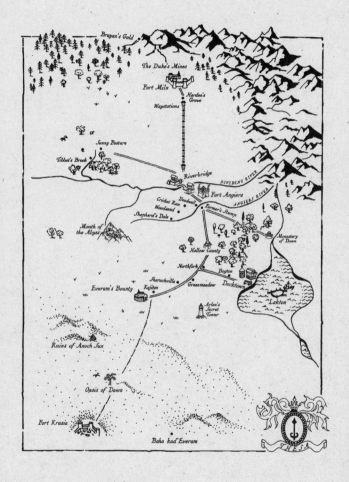

CONTENTS

x · Contents

THE
CORE

PROLOGUE

GAOLERS

334 AR

"There will be swarm."

Alagai Ka, the demon Consort, spoke with the lips of the human drone, the one they called Shanjat. The Consort lay bound within a circle of power, but he had shattered one of the locks and taken the drone before his captors could react.

His will crushed, Shanjat was little more than a puppet now, and the Consort took pleasure in the pain that caused his captors. He shifted the drone's feet, getting a sense of the body. Not as useful as a mimic, but strong, armed with the primitive weapons of the surface stock and an emotional connection to his captors the Consort could exploit.

"What in the Core is that supposed to mean?" the Explorer demanded. The one the others called Arlen or Par'chin. He held influence over the others, but it was not true dominance.

The Consort accessed the drone's language center, growing in fluency with the primitive grunts that passed for communication among humans. "The queen is close to laying."

The Explorer met the drone's eyes and crossed his arms. The wards inked into his flesh throbbed with power. "Know that. What's it got to do with a swarm?"

"You have imprisoned me and killed my strongest brethren," the Consort said. "There are none left in the mind court with power enough to keep the young queens from draining their mother of magic and maturing."

The Explorer shrugged. "Queens'll kill each other, won't they? Right there in the whelping room, with the strongest one taking over the hive. Better a hatchling queen than a fully matured one."

The Consort kept the drone's eyes fixed on the Explorer as he watched the auras of the others in the room with his own eyes.

Armed with the cloak and spear and crown of the Mind Killer, the Heir—the one called Jardir—was easily the most dangerous. Chained in a warding circle, the Consort had few options if the Heir decided to kill him, and the subjugation of Shanjat enraged the Heir beyond measure.

But the Heir's aura betrayed him. Much as he wanted to kill the Consort, he needed him alive.

More interesting was the web of emotions connecting the Heir to the Explorer. Love and hate, rivalry and respect. Anger. Guilt. It was a heady mix, and the Consort took pleasure as he studied it. The Heir was impatient for information. There was much the Explorer had not told him, and irritation crackled along his aura at having to follow another's lead.

Less predictable was the Hunter, the one called Renna. The fierce female was hot with stolen core magic, her flesh stained with wards of power. She was less skilled in the use of her power, apt to lash out unless kept in check. She was tamped down, weapon in hand, ready to spring at the first break in the stalemate.

The last was a female drone, Shanvah. Like the puppet, she had no great magic about her. If she had not killed a demon prince with her weapons, the Consort would have dismissed her as irrelevant.

But while Shanvah was the weakest of his captors, her aura was exquisite. The puppet was her sire. Her will was strong, keeping her surface aura still, but beneath, her spirit was wracked with pain. The Consort would savor the memory of it when he sliced open her skull and bit into the soft meat of her mind.

The Consort made the puppet laugh, keeping the humans' attention on the drone instead of him. "The young queens won't have a chance to fight. With none of my brethren strong enough to dominate the others, each will steal an egg and flee."

The Explorer paused at that, understanding dawning. "Start nests all over Thesa."

"No doubt it has already begun." He made the puppet wave its spear, and predictably the eyes of the humans followed. "You doom your own kind, keeping me here."

Delicately, the Consort shifted its chains, probing for a weakness. The wards etched into the metal burned, pulling at his magic, but the Consort kept a tight grip on his power. Already he had shattered one of the locks and freed a limb. If he could break another, the puppet might disable the circles enough for the Consort to escape.

"How many minds are left in the hive?" the Explorer demanded. "We killed seven so far, not counting you. Reckon that ent nothing."

"In the hive?" the Consort asked. "None, by now. No doubt they have already divided the breeding grounds and seek to pacify their new territories before the laying."

"Breeding grounds?" the Hunter asked.

The puppet smiled. "The people of your Free Cities will soon find their walls and wards less secure than they have been led to believe."

"Bold words, Alagai Ka," the Heir said, "as you lie bound before us."

The Consort found what he sought, at last. The tiny flaw in one of the locks, eroded slowly over the months of his imprisonment. Breaking it would allow the demon to slip the chain, but the power required would be bright, and his captors might notice before it was done.

"You were allowed your breeding grounds against this time." The puppet took a step to the side, and their eyes went with it. "Hunting preserves for my brethren. They will take their drones and crack your walls like eggs, stocking their larders to satiate their hatchling queens."

"And doom for Ala grows in their wombs," the Heir said. "We must not allow this."

"Free me," the Consort said.

"Not a chance," the Explorer growled.

"It is your only real choice," the Consort said. "My return can still prevent swarm."

"You are the Prince of Lies," the Heir said. "We are not fools enough to trust your words. There is another choice. We will go to the abyss and kill Alagai'ting Ka once and for all."

"You claim not to be fools," the Consort said, "yet you believe you can survive the path to the hive? You will not even get as far as Kavri before he broke and fled back to the surface."

The words had the intended effect as the Heir stiffened, tightening his grip on the spear. "More lies. Kaji defeated you."

"*Kavri* killed many drones," the Consort said. "Many princes. It took centuries to repopulate the hive, but his attempts to breach our domain failed. That is the best your kind can hope for. This is not the first cycle, nor shall it be the last."

"Said you'd guide us to the Core," the Explorer said.

"You might as well ask to go to the surface of the day star," the Consort said. "You would be consumed long before you reached it. You know this."

"To the hive, then," the Explorer said. "The mind court. The ripping whelping room of the demon queen."

"That will destroy you, as well." The Consort edged the puppet another step.

"Take our chances," the Hunter said.

At last, they were in position. The puppet raised its spear and threw it at the Explorer's heart. As expected, he dissipated and it passed harmlessly through, flying straight at the Heir, who spun his weapon to bat it aside.

The puppet flung the shield with all its strength, the hard edge shattering one of the wardstones keeping the Consort imprisoned. The Hunter was moving fast to attack, but the female drone gave a cry, blocking the Hunter's path to her sire.

It was time enough for the puppet to turn, taking the warded chain in hand as the Consort focused a burst of magic to shatter the weakened link. Like a spider picking apart a damaged web, the puppet unwove the chain. The silver wards burned the Consort's skin, but the pain was a small price to pay for freedom.

He flicked a claw, using a burst of magic to fling a tiny piece of the shattered metal link through the air, striking the Heir's crown and knocking it from his head, preventing him from raising the shield that had first trapped the Consort.

The Hunter cast the female drone aside, leaping to try to stop the puppet, but it was too late. The Consort dissipated even as she swung her weapons, leaving solid only a single claw to lay open her bowels as they passed. He slipped through the gap the puppet had made in the circle, rematerializing at the edge of the outer warding.

The Explorer rushed to his mate as she gasped, trying desperately to keep her intestines from spilling onto the floor. The Hunter did not have the focus to dissipate and heal herself, and the Explorer would waste valuable time and power healing her.

The Consort drew an impact ward in the air, and the stones at the Heir's feet exploded, sending him stumbling as he scrambled for his crown. The puppet kicked the crown across the room, then attacked to stall the Heir just a few seconds more.

Turning, the Consort raised the stub of his tail, sending a spray of magic-dead feces to disable the wards.

He was about to dissipate again when the Heir cried, "Enough!" He slammed the butt of his spear to the floor, and a wave of magic knocked everyone from their feet. The Consort recovered quickly, dematerializing and moving for the gap in the wards, but not before the Explorer threw magic of his own, pulling back a curtain to cast dawn twilight over the gap in the wards. The day star had not yet crested the horizon, but already the light burned at his magic—unspeakable agony. The demon dare not approach.

The Hunter dissipated, re-forming with her wounds healed. She and the Explorer drew wardings in the air with practiced hands, sending shocks of pain through the demon's cloud even as he fled the light. In his noncorporeal form, the Consort could not control the puppet, and the female drone quickly put him in a submission hold. The Heir recovered his crown, raising the shield, trapping the Consort once more.

There was no choice but to surrender and negotiate. They still needed him alive. The Consort solidified, claws retracted and teeth covered, arms held high in the human sign of submission.

The Hunter struck him hard in the side of his head, impact wards rattling his skull. She was impulsive. The others would be more restrained.

But as the Consort rolled with the blow, the Explorer struck him from the opposite side, cracking his skull and bursting an eye from its socket.

The demon stumbled, only to take a third blow from the shaft of the Heir's spear, striking harder than a rock drone.

The beating continued, and the Consort thought surely they would kill him in their primitive savagery. He attempted to dissipate, but like the Hunter moments before, he found it impossible to focus enough to trigger the transformation.

Then it became hard to focus on who delivered which blow, and there was only the sound and shock as each fell.

And then it became hard to focus at all. Blackness filled his vision.

The Consort woke in agony. He attempted to Draw power from his inner reserve to heal, but there was little remaining. Unconscious, he must have Drawn deeply to recover from the worst of his injuries. The rest would have to heal naturally.

He remained free of the cursed chain. Perhaps they were rushing to repair it, even now. Perhaps they expected him to remain disabled for longer.

If so, they were greater fools than even he had believed. The curtain had been drawn, and the Consort could sense the darkness beyond the thick cloth. Escape again felt within reach. He raised a claw, siphoning a bit of his remaining magic to power a ward he drew in the air.

But the power dissipated before it reached the tip of his talon, and a shock of pain ran through his body, causing him to hiss.

Again he Drew, and again the power failed, even as his flesh burned.

The Consort looked down at his skin, realization dawning even as he saw the glow of the wards.

They had inked his flesh with needles, much as the Explorer had done to himself. He was covered with wards.

Mind wards, keyed to his own caste. The symbols put him in a prison of his own flesh, preventing him from dissipating or reaching out with his mind. Worse, if the Consort—or one of his captors—fed the wards with enough magic, they would kill him.

It was worse by far than the chain. An indignity beyond anything the Consort could imagine.

But every problem had its solution. Every warding its weakness. He would bide his time, and find it.

CHAPTER 1

BOTH

334 AR

The cramping startled Leesha awake.

Ten days on the road with an escort of five thousand Cutters had gotten her used to discomfort. She could only sleep on her side now, something the carriage bench was not designed for. She had taken to curling on the floor like Amanvah and Sikvah in their carriage full of pillows.

Waves of pain washed over her as uterine muscles tightened and contracted, readying themselves for the task to come. Leesha wasn't due for another thirteen weeks, but it was common for women to experience this.

And every one of them panics the first time, Bruna used to say, *thinking they'll birth early. Even me, though I'd smacked dozens of squalling babes into the world before I grunted out one of my own.*

Leesha began breathing in a quick steady rhythm to calm herself and help endure the pain. Pain was nothing new these days. The skin of her stomach was blackened and bruised from powerful fetal blows.

Several times during her pregnancy, Leesha had been forced to channel powerful ward magic. Each time, the baby reacted violently. Feedback from magic could grant inhuman strength and stamina. It made the old young again, and brought the young to primacy before their time. It heightened emotions and lessened control. Folk in the throes of magic could be violent. Dangerous.

What might such power do to a child not fully formed? Not even at seven months, Leesha looked and felt full term. She anticipated an early delivery, even welcomed it, lest the child grow too large for natural birth.

Or punch through my womb and crawl out on its own. Leesha breathed and breathed, but she did not calm, nor did the pain subside.

All sorts of things can bring a set of contractions, Bruna taught. *Like the brat kicking a full bladder.*

Leesha found the chamber pot, but relieving herself did little to ease the spasming. She glanced at the porcelain. Her water was clouded and bloody.

She froze, mind racing as she stared at the pot. But then the baby kicked hard. She cried out in pain, and she knew.

It was coming.

Leesha was propped on the bench by the time Wonda came to report. It was nearly dawn.

Wonda handed off her reins, rolling off her horse nimbly as a cat. She landed on the lip of the moving carriage and opened the door, effortlessly swinging onto the bench across from Leesha.

"Almost home, mistress, if ya wanna warsh a bit," Wonda said. "Gar rode on ahead while ya slept. Just got word back."

"How bad is it?" Leesha asked.

"Bad," Wonda said. "Whole staff's turned out. Gar tried to stop it like ya asked. Said it was like trying to pull up a stump bare-handed."

"Angierians and their ripping ceremony." Leesha grimaced. She was beginning to understand how Duchess Araine could walk past a cloud of bowing and curtsying servants while pretending not to see them at all. Sometimes it was the only way to get where you meant to go.

"Ent just maids and guards," Wonda said. "Half the town council's turned up."

"Night." Leesha put her face in her hands.

"Give the word and I can have a wall of Cutters shuttle you

right inside," Wonda said. "Tell everyone yu'll see them when yu've had yur rest."

Leesha shook her head. "This is my homecoming as countess. I won't begin it by shunning everyone."

"Ay, mistress," Wonda said.

"I need to tell you something, Wonda," Leesha said. "But you must remain calm when I do."

Wonda gave a confused look, then her eyes widened. She began to rise.

"Wonda Cutter, you keep your bottom on that bench." Leesha swung her finger like a lash, and the girl fell back.

"The contractions are sixteen minutes apart," Leesha continued. "It may be hours before the baby comes. I'm going to be quite dependent on you today, dear, so I need you to listen carefully and stay focused."

Wonda swallowed heavily, but she nodded. "Ay, mistress. Tell me what ya want and I'll make it happen."

"I will exit the carriage at a stately pace and head for the door," Leesha said. "I will speak to one person at a time as I walk. At no time do we stop or slow."

"Ay, mistress," Wonda said.

"I will openly appoint you head of my household guard," Leesha said. "If everyone's mustered in the yard as you say, that should be enough for you to take command and send Cutter women to secure the royal manse. Once they have the royal chambers secure, no one gets in save you, me, and Darsy."

"Vika?" Wonda asked.

Leesha shook her head. "Vika will be seeing her husband for the first time in months. I won't take that from them. There's nothing she can do that Darsy can't."

"Ay, mistress," Wonda said.

"You're not to tell anyone what is happening," Leesha said. "Not the guards, not Gared, not anyone."

"But mistress . . ." Wonda began.

"No one." Her words came out in a growl as Leesha grit her teeth through another contraction. It was like a serpent wrapped around her belly, squeezing. "I won't have loose talk turning this into a Jongleur's show. I'm giving birth to Ahmann Jardir's baby. Not everyone will wish it well, and after the birth we'll both be . . . vulnerable."

Wonda's eyes hardened. "Not while I'm around, mistress. Swear it by the sun."

Wonda gave no sign anything was amiss when she exited the carriage, stepping easily into the stirrup of her moving horse.

The wardlight inside the carriage dimmed in the early-morning light, but it brightened as the door clicked shut. With it, the wards of silence reactivated, and Leesha let out a groan of pain.

She put one hand on the small of her back and the other under her heavy belly as she heaved herself upright. Heat wards had the kettle hot in seconds. Leesha poured steaming water on a cloth and pressed it to her face.

The reflection in the mirror was pale and hollow, dark circles beneath her eyes. Leesha longed to reach into her *hora* pouch, Drawing a bit of magic to give her strength through the ordeal to come, but it was too dangerous. Magic was known to send the child into wild fits. It was the last thing she wanted now.

She glanced at the powder kit, but she'd never had the skill painting her face that she had painting wards. That was her mother's talent. She made do as best she could, brushing her hair and straightening her dress.

The roads of Cutter's Hollow's outer boroughs twisted and turned, following the curving shape of the greatwards she and Arlen Bales designed. The Hollow had over a dozen boroughs now, an ever-expanding net of interconnected greatwards that pushed the demons back farther every night. Leesha knew the shape as intimately as a lover, not needing to glance out the window to know they were passing through Newhaven.

Soon they would enter Cutter's Hollow, the capital of Hollow County and the center of the greatwards. Just two years ago, the Hollow had been a town of less than three hundred souls—barely large enough for a dot on the map. Now it was equal to any of the Free Cities.

Another contraction took her. They were getting closer—just six minutes apart now. She was dilating and could feel the child sitting lower. She breathed. There were herbs that could ease her pain, but she dare not take them until she was safely ensconced in her chambers.

Leesha peeked from the curtain, immediately regretting it as a cheer went up in response. She'd hoped to keep her homecoming quiet by arriving before dawn, but there was no quieting an escort of such size. Even at the early hour, folk crowded the streets and watched from windows as the procession wound its way home.

It was strange, thinking of Thamos' keep as home, but it belonged to her now as Countess of Hollow County. In her absence, Darsy had turned Leesha's cottage in the Gatherers' Wood into the headquarters for Gatherers' Academy, hopefully the first of many establishments of learning in the Hollow. Leesha would rather be there training apprentices, but there was far more she could accomplish if she took up residence in the keep.

She wrinkled her nose as the fortress came into view. It was a blocky, walled structure, built more for defense than aesthetics—at least on the outside. The inside was worse in some ways, lavish as a palace in a land struggling to rebuild. Both problems would have to be addressed now that the place was hers.

The great gates of the keep were open, the road lined on either side by the remains of the Wooden Lancers, Thamos' cavalry. There were barely fifty of them now, the others lost with the count himself in the Battle of Docktown. They were resplendent on their great Angierian mustangs, man and horse equally stone-faced at attention. All were armed and armored, as if expecting Leesha to command them into battle at any moment.

The courtyard, too, looked mustered as much for a war as a homecoming. To the left, Captain Gamon was mounted with his lieutenants before hundreds of men-at-arms, straight-backed with eyes forward, heavy polearms planted on the ground, points all at precisely the same angle.

Courtyard right, the entire keep's staff—an army in its own right—lined up no less sharply than the infantry, uniforms clean and pressed.

It will be interesting to see what happens to those perfect ranks if I give birth in the courtyard. The thought was wry, but then the child kicked, and it ceased to amuse.

As Wonda warned, a knot of people stood at the base of the steps to the keep. Lord Arther was at their front, rigid in his dress uniform and spear. Beside him was Tarisa, the count's childhood nurse who had become lady's maid to Leesha. Gared was waiting with Rosal, his promised, and Rosal's mother. With him were Inquisitor Hayes; Gatherers Darsy and Vika; her father, Erny; and . . . night, even Leesha's mother, Elona, glaring daggers at Rosal's back. Leesha prayed the early hour would succor her from that demon, at least, but as usual it went unanswered.

Wonda poked her head in the door. "Ready, mistress?"

A fresh contraction ripped through her. She felt hot, sweating even in the cold winter air.

Leesha smiled, showing none of it. Her legs shook as she got to her feet, and she felt the child inch lower. "Yes, dear. Swiftly now."

Gamon dismounted as the carriage arrived. He, Arther, and Gared nearly tripped over one another in the scramble to offer their hands as she stepped down. Leesha ignored them all, clutching Wonda's arm as she carefully descended the steps. It would not do to fall in front of the entire assembly.

"Welcome back to the Hollow, Countess Paper," Arther said with a courtly bow. "It is a great relief to see you well. When we heard of the attack on Angiers, we feared the worst."

"Thank you," Leesha said as she steadied herself. All around the courtyard, there were bows and curtsies. Leesha kept her back straight, acknowledging it all with a dignified nod that would have done Duchess Araine proud.

Then she began walking. Wonda angled herself to take the lead even as she lent her support. Close behind, two meaty Cutter women followed.

Caught off guard, the men stumbled out of their path, but they recovered swiftly, scurrying after. Gamon was the first to match her pace. "My lady, I have prepared a roster of the house guards . . ."

"Thank you, Captain Gamon." Leesha's insides were churning. She clenched her thighs, terrified her water might break before she reached the house. "Be a dear and give it to Captain Wonda, please."

Gamon's eyes widened, and he stopped in his tracks. "*Captain* Wonda?"

"I hereby appoint Wonda Cutter captain of my house guard," Leesha said loudly, continuing to walk. "A long-overdue promotion."

Gamon hurried to catch back up. "If my command has been in some way unsatisfactory . . ."

Leesha smiled, wondering if she might vomit. "Not at all. Your service was exemplary, and your valor on behalf of the Hollow is without question. You will retain command of the Wooden Soldiers, but my house security will report to Captain Wonda alone. Order the men to fall out and return to their duties. We're not expecting an attack."

Gamon looked like he was trying to swallow a stone, but after months in Angiers not knowing if she was captive or guest, Leesha was tired of seeing Wooden Soldiers everywhere. Wonda had already hand-selected Cutters to take over the house guard, and signaled them to secure the entrance and sweep the manse.

Arther moved quickly to take the empty place as Gamon fell back, stunned. "The house staff . . ."

". . . looks crisp and ready to start the day," Leesha cut him off. "Let's not keep them." She whisked a hand, dismissing the assemblage.

"Of course, my lady." Arther gave a signal, and the crowd began to disperse. He looked ready to say more, but Leesha's mother pushed her way in front, Erny trailing after. Elona was six months pregnant, though she hid it well with low-cut gowns that masked her belly and drew eyes elsewhere. The men fell back like she was a coreling.

"My daughter, Countess of the Hollow!" Elona spread her arms, face glowing with . . . was that what pride looked like on her? It was terrifying if so.

"Mother, Father." Leesha allowed each a brief embrace, trying to keep from shaking.

Elona sensed it, but she had the decency to drop her voice. "You look terrible. What's wrong?"

"I just need to get inside and rest." Leesha gave Wonda's

arm a squeeze, and they started moving again. Others might fear to impede Elona, but Wonda was implacable as a falling tree. Elona moved to follow, but pulled up as Erny held her back. She glared at him, but like Wonda Cutter, Leesha's father was always on her side.

"Welcome home, Countess." Rosal dipped a practiced curtsy, her mother following suit.

"Emelia," Leesha said, careful to use the woman's proper name. "Mrs. Lacquer. I'm surprised to find you here at such an early hour."

Gared swept in, the three of them following Leesha up the steps. "Count had the ladies staying here in his keep on account of propriety. We can find another place . . ."

"Nonsense." Leesha winked at Rosal. "We've plenty of room. How would it look for an upstanding young woman like yourself to move into the baron's household before the wedding? A scandal!"

Gared blushed. "'Preciate it. Got some papers for you to look at when you have time . . ."

"Send them over in the morning." Leesha was almost to the steps now.

Inquisitor Hayes appeared next, bowing deeply. His acolyte Child Franq, usually inseparable from his master, was conspicuously absent. "Countess. Praise be to the Creator that you are well."

The next carriage in line pulled up and opened its door. Hayes' eyes widened as Tender Jona stepped out. Vika gave a cry, breaking from the receiving line to hurry down the steps to her husband.

Hayes looked at her in shock, but even shaking with pain, Leesha's smile was genuine. "You'll be pleased to know, Inquisitor, that your interim assignment to the Hollow has ended. Jona will resume leading services in Hollow County."

"Preposterous," the Inquisitor sputtered. "I'm not going to just hand my cathedral over . . ."

Leesha raised an eyebrow. "*Your* cathedral, Inquisitor? The one in *my* county?" She was still moving. The doors to the keep were closer, but still so far.

Hayes was forced to sacrifice dignity, lifting his robes to scuttle after her. "Only Duke Pether can relieve me . . ."

Leesha cut him off, producing a letter bearing the royal seal. "Your inquisition is over."

"The inquisition was about more than one heretic Tender," Hayes argued. "The question of Arlen Bales . . ."

"Is one you and the Council of Tenders can debate all you wish back in Angiers," Leesha said. "Shepherd Jona will minister to the Hollow's flock."

Hayes' gawp was greater even than Gamon's. *"Shepherd?!"*

"His Grace gave up the title when he became duke," Leesha said, "and there are more people in the Hollow than Angiers in any event. The Pact of the Free Cities gives our Tenders the right to form a new order."

Unsure how to respond, the Inquisitor took the letter and fell back from Leesha's determined march. The duke's decree gave her the power to choose the spiritual leader of Hollow County, but she was testing the limits by promoting Jona to Shepherd. It was a declaration of independence that would not please the ivy throne, but there was little they could do to stop it now that Leesha was ensconced in the Hollow once more.

Darsy moved in quickly at a signal from Leesha, the woman's bulk effectively dismissing the Inquisitor as she moved between them. "Creator be praised; it's good to see you, mistress."

"You have no idea." Leesha pulled her into an embrace, dropping her voice. "Contractions are coming every two minutes. If I'm not inside soon, I'll be giving birth on these steps. Wonda's sent women to secure the royal chambers."

Darsy nodded, not missing a beat. "Want me to go on ahead, or walk you?"

Leesha felt a rush of relief. "Walk me, please."

Darsy took her other arm, she and Wonda guiding Leesha along as the next carriage pulled up and Amanvah, Sikvah, and Kendall made their solemn exit. Darsy watched them curiously.

"Mistress," Darsy said. "Where's Rojer?"

Leesha kept her breath a deep, steady rhythm as she pointed to the coffin a group of Cutters were pulling from the carriage.

Darsy let out a strangled cry and pulled up short. Leesha would have overbalanced and stumbled if not for Wonda.

"Bottle it, Darsy," Wonda growled. "Ent got time right now." Darsy nodded, recovering herself and getting them back in motion.

Amanvah glided up the steps swiftly, ignoring the glares of Wonda and Darsy. One look in her eyes was all Leesha needed.

She knows.

"Countess Leesha," the *dama'ting* began.

"Not now, Amanvah," Leesha breathed.

Amanvah ignored her, stepping in close. Wonda reached out to bar her way, but Amanvah put a knuckle into the arm and it fell away long enough for her to pass.

"I must assist the birth," she said without preamble.

"Core you will," Darsy growled.

"I have cast the dice, mistress," Amanvah said quietly. "If I am not with you in the coming hours, you will die."

"That some kinda threat?" Wonda's voice was low and dangerous.

"Stop it, all of you," Leesha said. "She comes."

"I can do anything . . ." Darsy began.

Leesha groaned, feeling the need to bear down. "There's no time." She put a foot on the steps. Such a short climb, but it felt like a mountain.

Tarisa was waiting at the top. Leesha managed the climb unassisted, but still the woman needed only a glance to see what was happening.

"This way," she said, turning on her heel and opening the doors, snapping her fingers at a group of maids. They scurried to her as she walked, and like a general, Tarisa sent them running off with instructions.

Leesha knew word would spread quickly now, but there was nothing to be done for it. She kept all her focus on breathing and putting one foot in front of the other.

The moment they left the great hall, Wonda signaled the guards. They closed ranks as the big woman swept Leesha up into her arms like a child, carrying her the rest of the way.

———

"Push," Darsy said.

It was a pointless request. Leesha could feel the baby moving the moment they had her propped on the edge of the bed. It was coming whether she pushed or not. She was fully dilated, her water broken all over Wonda's fine wooden armor. It would be over in moments.

But then the child thrashed, and Leesha cried out in pain. Darsy, too, gave a cry, seeing Leesha's stomach distend as tiny hands and feet thrust into the lining. It felt like a demon inside her, trying to claw its way free. Fresh bruises were forming atop the faded ones all over her abdomen.

"Can you see it?" Leesha demanded.

Darsy sucked a breath and moved back in between the makeshift stirrups. "No, mistress."

Corespawn it. She was so close.

"Help me up," she said, gripping Wonda's hand. "It will be easier if I squat." She bore down, trying to squeeze the child free.

Again the child struck, hitting her like a horse's kick. Leesha screamed and stumbled, but Wonda caught her, easing her back to the pillows.

"It is as I feared," Amanvah said. "Mistress, I must cut the child free."

Wonda immediately interposed herself. "Not a chance."

Darsy rose, the large woman towering over tiny Amanvah. "Not if you were the last Gatherer in the world."

"Leesha vah Erny am'Paper am'Hollow," Amanvah said. "By Everam and my hope of Heaven, I swear to you, the only chance you have to survive this night is for me to cut you."

Wonda had her knife in hand now, and Leesha knew how fast the woman could use it.

But then Amanvah did something Leesha could never in a thousand years have imagined. She dropped to her knees, putting her hands on the floor and pressing her forehead between them.

"By the blood we share, mistress. Please. Ala needs you. Sharak Ka needs you. You must believe me."

"Blood you share?" Darsy asked. "What in the Core . . . ?"

"Do it," Leesha growled as the thrashing continued.

"You can't mean . . ." Darsy began.

"I can and I do, Darsy Cutter," Leesha snapped. "She's better with the knife than you and you know it. Swallow your pride and assist."

Darsy scowled, but she nodded as Amanvah produced stones from her *hora* pouch. "I will put you both to sleep . . ."

Leesha shook her head. "Calm the child, but I'm staying awake."

"There is no time to take herbs for the pain," Amanvah said.

"Then get me something to bite on," Leesha said.

Amanvah's eyes crinkled as she smiled behind her veil. She nodded. "Your honor is boundless, daughter of Erny. Pain is only wind. Bend as the palm, and let it blow over you."

The child's cries filled the room, the babe wrapped in swaddling and thrust into Wonda's arms while Amanvah and Darsy finished their work. Darsy was suturing the wound as Amanvah prepared *hora* magic to speed the healing.

Wonda stood stiff as any new father, terrified she might squeeze the child too hard and crush it. She looked down at the tiny olive-skinned face, and Leesha knew the young woman would die to keep the baby safe.

Leesha's arms twitched, wanting to reach out, but she needed to remain still until the work was done. For the moment, it was almost enough to know the child was healthy and safe.

Almost.

"What is it?" Leesha asked.

Wonda's head snapped up like an apprentice caught daydreaming. "Mistress?"

"My child," Leesha begged. "Is it a boy or a girl?" So much rode on the question. A male greenland heir to Ahmann Jardir might provoke outright war with Krasia, but a daughter would be no less a target. That the Krasians would come for the child was never in doubt, no matter what Amanvah swore. But *when* they came—now or over a decade hence—hinged on Wonda's next words.

Wonda cradled the babe in one arm as she opened the swaddling. "It's a b . . ." She frowned, looking closer.

At last she looked up, face twisted. "Core if I know, mistress. Ent no Gatherer."

Leesha stared at her, incredulous. "You don't need to be a Gatherer, Wonda, to know what parts a boy has and what parts a girl."

"That's just it, mistress." Wonda looked terrified.

"Babe's got both."

CHAPTER 2

OLIVE

334 AR

For perhaps the first time in her life, words failed Leesha. She stared openmouthed, mind racing as the child's screams rang through the room.

A babe born with both sets of parts was not unheard of. There were documented cases in her books of old world science, but it was another thing to find it in a live child.

Her child.

Tarisa peeked over Wonda's shoulder and gasped, turning away.

Leesha reached out. "Let me see."

Darsy caught her arm, pulling it back to the table. "Leesha Paper, you move again 'fore we're done and I'm strapping you down."

A shout came from the doorway, and Leesha looked up into a nightmare: one of Wonda's guards stumbling back to keep out of the path of a very angry Elona Paper.

"Ay, Bekka!" Wonda cried. "Said no one was to get in!"

"Sorry, Won!" Bekka cried. "She pinched my pap and shoved by!"

"I'll pinch more than that, you try to keep me away from my daughter," Elona warned. "Why wasn't I . . ."

The words caught in her throat as Wonda turned and Elona caught sight of the child in her arms. She ran to it, arms reaching, but Wonda deftly sidestepped. The glare Elona threw her would frighten a coreling, but Wonda bared her teeth right back.

"It's all right," Leesha said, and Wonda relented, reluctantly letting Elona take the child.

There were tears in her mother's eyes. "Skin like the father, but those eyes are yours." Elona pulled back the blanket. "Is it a boy or a . . ."

She froze, illuminated in the wardlight as Amanvah activated her healing magic.

The rush of power was like air to a drowning person. It jolted through Leesha's torso, repairing the damage and filling her with new strength. When the light died down, she began to rise.

"Now, don't go . . ." Darsy began.

Leesha ignored her. "Wonda, help me to the bed, please."

Wonda picked her up effortlessly, carrying her to the great feathered bed. Leesha reached out, and Elona slid the baby into her arms. It looked up at her with bright blue eyes, and Leesha fell in love so utterly it shook her.

Wonda Cutter's not the only one who would die for you, darling. Pity human and demon alike, if they try to come between us.

She kissed the beautiful, perfect face and freed the child from its swaddling, laying it skin-to-skin on her chest, sharing her warmth. The child began to root, and Leesha massaged her breast, readying it as the babe reached the nipple. The little mouth opened wide, and she pulled it in quickly to ensure a tight latch.

How many mothers had she guided through this milestone? How many newborns had she brought to the pap? It was nothing compared with experiencing it firsthand, seeing her perfect child begin to suckle. She gasped at the force of its pull.

"Everything all right?" Darsy asked.

Leesha nodded. "So strong." She felt herself express, and knew she could endure any pain to feed her child. So many times in recent months, she had feared desperately for the child's life, but now it was here. Alive. Safe. She wept for the joy of it.

Tarisa appeared with a damp cloth, blotting away the tears and sweat. "Every mother cries at first latch, my lady."

Her sobs were a needed relief, but there were too many unanswered questions for Leesha to succumb for long. When her breathing calmed, she let Tarisa clear her eyes one last time and drew back the swaddling.

Wonda hadn't been wrong. At first glance the child was a healthy boy, with fully formed penis and testicles. It was only when Leesha lifted the scrotum that she could see the perfectly formed vagina beneath.

She breathed, pulling back and beginning a full examination. The baby was large, too large to have passed through her birth canal without damage to her and risk to the child. Amanvah had been right. The surgery saved both their lives.

It was strong, too, and hungry. By all accounts, the baby was perfectly healthy, with no other distinct feature to mark it boy or girl.

She slipped on her warded spectacles, inspecting deeper. The child's aura was bright—brighter than any Leesha had seen short of Arlen and Renna Bales. It was strong, and . . . joyful. The child took as much emotional pleasure in nursing as she. Tears welled in Leesha's eyes again, and she had to brush them away before she could continue her examination.

A glance down confirmed her initial diagnosis. Male and female organs, both healthy and functional.

She gave Wonda a nod. "Both."

"How in the Core's that even possible?" Elona asked.

"I've read about it," Leesha said, "though I've never witnessed it. It means there were two eggs at fertilization, but one absorbed . . ." The words choked off as Leesha's throat tightened.

"It's my fault," she gasped.

"How's that?" Darsy asked.

"The magic." Leesha felt like the walls of the great chamber were closing in on her. "I've been using so much. Starting when Inevera and I fought the mind demon that first night after Ahmann and I . . ." Her face stretched as the full horror of it dawned on her.

"I fused them."

"Demonshit," Elona said. "Ent no way to know that. Said yourself you seen it in books."

"Ent every day I agree with Elona, mistress," Darsy said,

"but your mum has the right of this. Ent no reason to think magic had anything to do with it."

"It did," Leesha insisted. "I felt it happen."

"What if it did?" Wonda demanded. "Should yu've let yurself get et by a demon, instead?"

"Of course not," Leesha said.

"No point laying blame when you've a fever to fight, Bruna used to say," Darsy said. "Everyone's got perfect vision—"

"—when they're looking back," Leesha finished.

"I read the same books you did," Darsy went on. "There's notes on how to treat this."

"Treat it, how?" Elona asked. "Some herb is going to close its slit or make its pecker dry up and fall off?"

"Course not." Darsy shrugged as she stared at the child. "We just . . . pick one. A girl that handsome could easily pass for a boy."

"And a boy that pretty could pass for a girl," Elona countered. "That don't treat anything."

"Ay," Darsy nodded to the operating table where Amanvah still worked, "but that combined with a few snips and stitches . . ."

"Wonda," Leesha said.

"Ay, mistress?" Wonda said.

"If anyone other than me ever tries to perform surgery on this child, you are to shoot them," Leesha said.

Wonda crossed her arms. "Ay, mistress."

Darsy held up her hands. "I only . . . !"

Leesha whisked her fingers. "I know you mean no harm, Darsy, but that practice was barbaric. We will not be pursuing surgical options any further unless the child's health is in danger. Am I clear?"

"Ay, mistress," Darsy said. "But folk are going to ask if it's a boy or girl. What do we tell them?"

Leesha looked to Elona. "Don't look at me," her mother said. "I know better than any that we don't get a say in these things. Creator wills as the Creator will."

"Well said, wife of Erny," Amanvah said. She had come last from the operating table, hands still red with birthing blood. She raised them to Leesha. "Now is the time, mistress. There is no casting stronger than the moment of birth."

Leesha considered. Letting Amanvah cast her *alagai hora*

in the mixed blood and fluid of the birth would open her vision to the futures of Leesha and the child both. Even if she was fully forthcoming—something *dama'ting* were not known for—there would be too much for her to convey in words. She would always have secrets, secrets that Leesha might desperately need.

But Amanvah's concern for the child, her half sibling, was written in gold through her aura. She was desperate to throw for the child's protection.

"There are conditions," Leesha said. "And they are not negotiable."

Amanvah bowed. "Anything."

Leesha raised an eyebrow. "You will speak your prayers in Thesan."

"Of course," Amanvah said.

"You will share everything you see with me, and me alone," Leesha went on.

"Ay, I want to see!" Elona said, but Leesha kept her eyes on Amanvah.

"Yes, mistress," Amanvah said.

"Forever," Leesha said. "If I have a question twenty years from now about what you saw, you will reply fully and without hesitation."

"I swear it by Everam," Amanvah said.

"You will leave the dice in place until we can make a copy of the throw for me to keep."

Amanvah paused at this. No outsider was allowed to study the *dama'ting alagai hora,* lest they attempt to carve their own. Inevera would have Amanvah's head if she acquiesced to this request.

But after a moment, the priestess nodded. "I have dice of clay we can cement in place."

"And you will teach me to read them," Leesha said.

The room fell silent. Even the other women, unschooled in Krasian custom, could sense the audacity of the request.

Amanvah's eyes narrowed. "Yes."

"What did you see, when you cast the bones for the child in Angiers?" Leesha asked.

"The first thing my mother ever taught me to look for," Amanvah said.

Leesha set warded klats around the antique royal heirloom that had been used as an operating table. The wards activated, barring sound from both directions as she and Amanvah bent over the operating table, studying the glowing dice.

Amanvah pointed one of her long, painted nails at a prominent symbol. *"Ka."* The Krasian word for "one" or "first."

She pointed to another. *"Dama."* Priest.

A third. *"Sharum."* Warrior.

"First . . . priest . . . warrior . . ." Leesha blinked as her breath caught. "Shar'Dama Ka?"

Amanvah nodded.

"Dama means 'priest,'" Leesha said. "Does that mean the child is male?"

Amanvah shook her head. "Not necessarily. 'First Warrior Cleric' is a better translation. The words are neutral, that they might call either gender in *Hannu Pash."*

"So my child is the Deliverer?" Leesha asked incredulously.

"It isn't that simple," Amanvah said. "You must understand this, mistress. The dice tell us our potentials, but most are never reached." She pointed to another symbol. *"Irrajesh."*

"Death," Leesha said.

Amanvah nodded. "See how the tip of the die points northeast. An early death is the most common of the child's futures."

Leesha's jaw tightened. "Not if I have a say in it."

"Or I," Amanvah agreed. "By Everam and my hope of Heaven. There could be no greater crime in all Ala than to harm one who might save us all.

"Ala." She pointed to another die, angled diagonally toward the face with *irrajesh.* "Even if we risk she doom the world instead."

Leesha tried to digest the words, but they were too much. She put them aside. "What will your people do, if they learn the child is without gender?"

Amanvah bent closer, studying not just the large symbols at the center of the dice but dozens of smaller ones around the edges, as well. "The news will tear them apart. It is too dangerous to announce the child's fate now, but without it, many will take this as a sign of Everam's displeasure with the Hollow Tribe."

"Giving them excuse to break the peace Ahmann and I forged," Leesha said.

"The few who still need excuse, after the son of Jeph cast the Deliverer from a cliff." Amanvah bent to look closer at the dice.

"See here," she noted, pointing to a symbol facing into the cluster. *"Ting."* Female. She slid her finger along the edge of the die, continuing to show how the line intersected *irrajesh.* "There is less convergence if you announce the child as female."

The child was bathed and changed by the time Leesha and Amanvah finished. Elona dozed in a chair with the sleeping baby in her arms. Wonda stood protectively over her, while Darsy paced the room nervously. Tarisa had stripped the bloodied bed and put down fresh linens, now busying herself readying a bath.

"She," Leesha said loudly, stepping beyond the wards of silence.

Darsy stopped in her tracks. Elona started awake. "Ay, whazzat?"

Leesha squinted into her warded spectacles, searching the auras of the women as they gathered before her. "So far as anyone outside this room is concerned, I just gave birth to a healthy baby girl."

"Ay, mistress," Wonda said. "But said yurself, babe needs guards day an' night. Sooner or later, one'll catch an eyeful while we change the nappy." Her aura colored with worry. "Speakin' of which . . ."

Leesha laughed. "By order of the countess, you're relieved of nappy duties, Wonda Cutter. Your talents would be wasted wiping bottoms."

Wonda blew out a breath. "Thank the Creator."

"I will personally read the aura of every member of the house staff and guard with access to my daughter." Leesha looked at Tarisa. "Any who cannot be trusted will need to find employment elsewhere."

Her maid's aura flashed with fear, and Leesha sighed. She had known this was coming, but it made things no easier.

"We'll tell Vika and Jizell as well," Leesha said. "We'll all need to watch as she develops in case her condition causes unforeseen health problems."

"Course," Darsy agreed.

"You tell Jizell, you're tellin' Mum," Wonda warned. Jizell was Royal Gatherer to Duke Pether now, reporting directly to Duchess Araine.

Leesha met Tarisa's eyes. "I expect she'll find out, regardless. Better it come from me."

"That go for her, too?" Darsy jerked a finger at Amanvah.

"It does." Amanvah's aura stayed cool and even. It was a fair question. "I will not lie or withhold information from my mother, but our interests align. The Damajah will have a vested concern for the safety of the child, and will be essential in keeping my brother from trying to claim or kill her."

Elona opened her mouth, but Leesha cut off the debate. "I trust her." She looked back at Amanvah. "Will you and Sikvah stay here with us?"

Amanvah shook her head. "Thank you, mistress, but enough rooms have been finished in my honored husband's manse for us to move in. After so long in captivity, I wish to be under my own roof, with my own people . . ."

"Of course." Leesha put a hand on Amanvah's belly. Shocked, the woman fell silent. "But please understand that we are your people now, too. Thrice bound by blood."

"Thrice bound," Amanvah agreed, putting her own hand over Leesha's in an act so intimate it would have been unthinkable just a few months ago. It was strange, how sharing pain could sometimes do what good times could not.

"What's that supposed to mean?" Darsy asked when Amanvah left the room.

"It means Amanvah and Sikvah are carrying Rojer's children," Leesha said. "Anyone doesn't hop when one of them wants something had better have a good corespawned reason."

Darsy's eyebrows shot up into her hair, but she nodded. "Ay, mistress."

"Now if everyone will excuse me," Leesha said, "I'd like to put my daughter in her crib and have that bath."

Darsy and Wonda made for the door, but Elona lingered, her aura showing her unwillingness to let go of the baby.

"Night, Mother," Leesha said, "you've imprinted more on that child in an hour than you did in my entire life."

"This one ent got your mouth, yet." Elona looked down at the sleeping baby. "Lucky little bastard. Could've run this town, I'd been born with a pecker."

"You'd have made a wonderful man," Leesha agreed.

"Not a man," Elona said. "Never wanted that. Just wanted a pecker, too. Steave made me a wooden one, once. Polished it to a shine and said it was to do when there was no wood at home."

"Creator," Leesha said, but Elona ignored her.

"Meant it for me, but it was your father that liked when I . . ."

"Corespawn it, Mother!" Leesha snapped. "You're doing this on purpose."

Elona cackled. "Course I am, girl. Keeping the stick from your arse requires constant maintenance."

Leesha put her face in her hand.

Elona finally relented and handed Leesha the child. "I'm just sayin', Paper women are fierce even without peckers."

Leesha smiled at that. "Honest word."

"What are you going to call her?" Elona asked.

"Olive," Leesha said.

"Always wondered why that was a girl's name," Elona said. "Olives got stones."

CHAPTER 3

COUNTESS PAPER

334 AR

Tarisa was waiting when Leesha finally managed to pull her gaze away from Olive, fast asleep in her crib. The older woman's aura still looked like a rabbit backed into a corner, but she did not show it. "My lady must be exhausted. Come sit and I'll brush out your hair."

Leesha reached up, realizing her hair was still pinned from her homecoming, half the pins loose or missing. She wore only a sweaty and bloodstained shift with a silk dressing gown pulled over it. Dried tears crusted her cheeks. "I must look a horror."

"Anything but." Tarisa led her to the bedroom vanity, unpinning and brushing Leesha's hair. It was a ritual they had performed so many times, it gave Leesha a pang of nostalgia. These were Thamos' chambers, his servants, his keep. She had meant to share it all with him, a storybook tale, but her prince's part in the story was ended.

Everywhere, there were signs of him, active pieces of a life cut short in its prime. Hunting trophies and spears adorned the walls, along with ostentatious portraits of the royal family. Three suits of lacquered armor on stands like silent sentries around the room.

Leesha dropped her eyes to the floor, but her nose betrayed her, catching the scented oils the count had used, fragrances that triggered thoughts of love, lust, and loss.

Tarisa caught the move. "Arther wanted to sweep it all away so you wouldn't have to look at it. Spare you the pain."

Leesha's throat was tight. "I'm glad he didn't."

Tarisa nodded. "Told him I'd have his seedpods if he moved a single chair." Leesha closed her eyes. There were few pleasures in life as soothing as Tarisa brushing her hair. Suddenly she remembered how tired she was. Amanvah's healing magic had given her a burst of strength, but that had faded, and magic was no true replacement for sleep.

But there were matters to settle first.

Leesha cracked an eye, watching Tarisa's aura. "How long have you been a spy for the Duchess Mother?"

"Longer than you've been alive, my lady." Tarisa's aura spiked, but her voice was calm. Soothing. "Though I never thought of it as spying. Thamos was still in swaddling when I was brought in to nurse him. It was my duty to report on him to his mother. Her Grace loved the boy, but she had a duchy to run, and her husband was seldom about. Every night as the young prince slept, I filled her in on his day's activities."

"Even when the boy became a man grown?" Leesha asked.

Tarisa snorted. "Especially then. You'll see as Olive grows, my lady. A mother never truly lets go."

"What sorts of things did you tell her?" Leesha asked.

Tarisa shrugged. "His love life, mostly. Her Grace despaired of ever settling the prince down, and wanted an account of every skirt to catch his eye." Tarisa met Leesha's eyes. "But there was only one woman who ever held Thamos' attention."

"And she had a shady past," Leesha guessed. "Childhood scandal, and talk of bedding the demon of the desert . . ."

Tarisa dropped her eyes again, never slowing the steady, soothing stroke of her brush. "Folk talk, my lady. In the Corelings' Graveyard and the Holy House pews. In the Cutter ranks and, Creator knows, the servants' quarters. Many spoke of how you and the Warded Man looked at each other, and how you went to Krasia to court Ahmann Jardir. None could prove they'd taken you to bed, but folk don't need proof to whisper."

"They never have," Leesha said.

"Didn't tell Her Grace anything she wasn't hearing from others," Tarisa said. "But I told her not to believe a word of it. You and His Highness were hardly discreet. When your laces began to strain, I assumed the child was the prince's. We all did. The servants all loved you. I wrote my suspicions to Her Grace with joy, and waited on my toes for you to tell His Highness."

"But then we broke," Leesha said, "and you realized your love for me was misplaced."

Tarisa shook her head. "How could we stop, when our lord did not?"

"Thamos cast me out," Leesha said.

"Ay," Tarisa agreed. "And haunted these halls like a ghost, spending hours staring at his portrait of you."

A lump formed in Leesha's throat, and she tried unsuccessfully to choke it down.

"Some may be holding out hope you'll announce Thamos has an heir tomorrow," Tarisa said, "dreaming there might still be a piece of the prince to love and cherish in this house. But none of them will turn from you when they meet Olive."

"I wish I could believe that," Leesha said.

"I never knew my own son," Tarisa said. "I was kitchen maid to a minor lord and lady, and when she failed to give him children, they paid me to lie with him and give up the child."

"Tarisa!" Leesha was horrified.

"I was treated fairly," Tarisa said. "Given money and reference to take a commission from the Duchess Mum, wetnursing and helping rear young Prince Thamos. He was like the son I never knew."

She reached out, laying a gentle hand on Leesha's belly. "We don't get to say which children the Creator gives us. There's love enough in this house for any child of yours, my lady."

Leesha laid a hand over hers. "Enough with *my lady*. Call me mistress, please."

"Ay, mistress." Tarisa gave the hand a squeeze and got to her feet. "Water ought to be hot by now. I'll go see about that bath."

She left, and Leesha allowed herself to raise her eyes once more, taking in the reminders of her lost love.

And she wept.

Leesha kept the curtains pulled through the day, staring at Olive with her warded spectacles, glorying in the strength and purity of the child's aura. Olive ate hungrily and slept little, staring up at Leesha with her bright blue eyes. The magic in her shone with an emotion beyond love, beyond adoration. Something more primal and pure.

There was a knock at the door, startling Leesha from the trance of it. Wonda went over to answer it, and there was muffled conversation. The door clicked as Wonda closed and locked it again, then came back to the sleeping chamber.

"Arther's waitin' outside," Wonda said. "Been tellin' him yur busy, but he keeps coming back. Wants to talk to ya somethin' fierce."

Leesha pushed herself upright. "Very well. He's seen me in dressing gowns before. Tarisa? Please take Olive into the nursery while we talk."

Olive clutched Leesha's finger painfully in her little fist as Tarisa pulled her away. Her aura made Leesha's heart ache.

Lord Arther stopped a respectful distance from the bed and bowed. "I apologize for the intrusion, Countess Paper."

"It's all right, Arther," Leesha said. "I trust you would not have done so if it wasn't important."

"Indeed," Arther said. "Congratulations on the birth of your daughter. I understand this was . . . earlier than expected. I trust all are in good health?"

"Thank you, we are," Leesha said, "though I expect Wonda has already told you as much."

"She has, of course," Arther agreed. "I came with another rather urgent matter."

"And that is?" Leesha asked.

Arther drew himself up straight. He wasn't a tall man, but he made up for it in posture. "With respect, Countess, if my command of the house staff has been relieved and I am dismissed, I do not think it too much to ask that I be informed directly."

Leesha blinked. "Has someone informed you indirectly?"

"Lady Paper," Arther said.

"Lady . . . Night, my mother?" Leesha asked.

Arther bowed again. "Lady Paper moved into the keep a week ago, when news of your new title reached the Hollow. She has been . . . difficult to please."

"You don't know the half of it," Leesha said.

"It is her right, of course," Arther said. "Without word from you, she and your father are the ranking members of your household. I assumed you had sent them to ready the keep."

Leesha shook her head. "It meant only the keep has richer furnishing than my father's house."

"It is not for me to say," Arther said. "But this afternoon, after announcing your daughter's birth, she told me my services were no longer required, and that house staff would be reporting to her directly."

Leesha groaned. "I am going to strangle that woman." She looked at Arther. "Be assured the Core will freeze before I give my mother dominion over my household. I will make it clear to her before the end of the day."

"That is a relief," Arther said. "But with the dismissal of Gamon and Hayes, I cannot help but wonder if I am next in any event. Do you wish my resignation?"

Leesha considered the man. "Is it your wish to remain in my employ, with Thamos dead?"

"It is, my lady," Arther said.

"Why?" Leesha asked bluntly. "You've never approved of my policies, particularly entitlements for refugees."

Indignation shocked through the man's aura, but Arther only raised an eyebrow. "My approval is irrelevant, my lady. It was my responsibility to keep the prince's accounts balanced and see his funds spent wisely. I questioned every spending policy proposed by the council because I would have been remiss in my duties not to. Nevertheless, when His Highness made a decision, it was carried out diligently and without delay. You may have every confidence that I will do the same for you, if you will have me."

There was no lie in his aura, but her question remained unanswered. "Why?" Leesha asked again. "I expected you would volunteer your resignation soon after my arrival and return to your family holdings in Angiers."

An image flashed across Arther's aura. It was distorted, but Leesha could make out a once great Angierian townhouse, fallen into disrepair. It linked to Arther with shame, and with fierce pride.

"My family's holdings were mortgaged to buy my commission in the Wooden Soldiers," Arther said. "That and a bit of luck saw me squire for young Prince Thamos. My life was his. Gamon is no different."

Another image. Thamos, Arther, and Gamon, inseparable as brothers.

"But now the prince is gone." Arther gave no outward sign of the pain tearing across his aura. "As is the Angiers we left. Euchor's Mountain Spears occupy the city now, with their flamework weapons. The Wooden Soldiers will soon be relegated to policing the boardwalk, breaking up domestic disturbances and illegal Jongleur shows. There is no longer anything for us there, even if we wished to return."

Leesha had not considered that. "Where would you go, if I asked you to resign?"

"I remain quartermaster for the Hollow's Wooden Soldiers, unless you relieve me of that as well," Arther said. "I would return to the barracks while I sought employment among the barons. Baron Cutter, perhaps."

"I am still not certain of your loyalties, Arther. I fear I must be quite blunt," she tapped her spectacles, "and see the answers in your aura."

Arther looked at her a long moment, eyes flicking to the lamps and curtained windows, and then to her warded spectacles. His aura was active, but it was too complex for Leesha to read, as if he was still sorting his own feelings about this invasion of privacy.

At last he sniffed, pulling himself up straight. "You are forgiven, my lady, for any blunt questions you put to me. As it was my due diligence to question your policies, it is yours to question my loyalty before taking me into your service."

"Thank—" Leesha began.

"But," Arther cut in with a raised hand. "If we are to work in good faith, you must agree that you will never again subject me to this . . ." he waved a hand at Leesha's spectacles, ". . . undue scrutiny without just cause and evidence."

Leesha shook her head. "If you feel I have invaded your privacy I apologize, but my spectacles are a part of me now. I won't take them off every time you enter the room. There are going to be changes in the Hollow, Arther. If anyone in my employ is uncomfortable about ward magic, I will of course provide excellent references and generous severance."

"Very well, my lady. I shall inform the staff. As for myself, if you have additional questions regarding my integrity, pray ask and let us have it done." Arther's aura roiled with growing indignation. He considered himself above reproach and was offended by her mistrust.

Leesha knew she must step carefully. She might find Arther loyal, only to drive him away by refusing to give trust in kind.

Leesha crossed her arms. "The child is Ahmann Jardir's."

Arther's aura did not change. "I am not a fool, my lady. Even if my lord had not informed me months ago, your mother would be shouting it from the turrets if the child belonged to Thamos."

"And still, you would remain in my service?" Leesha asked.

"Ahmann Jardir is dead," Arther said. "Whatever might have gone before, I think any ties you had to the Krasians died with him. After the Battle of Docktown, there can be no doubt that the new Krasian leader sees the Hollow as his enemy, and I know you well enough to trust you will not surrender it to him."

"Corespawned right," Wonda said.

"My lord is dead as well," Arther said, the indignation in his aura gnawed away by a growing emptiness. "I know you loved him, and he you. Both of you were . . . free with your affections before you met. It is not my place to judge."

"You sent regular reports to Minister Janson," Leesha said.

"We all did, including His Highness," Arther said. "Thamos hid nothing from the ivy throne."

"Janson is dead now, too," Leesha said. "And the ledgers of the Hollow are closed. You said yourself, the Angiers we knew is gone. The Hollow must find its own path."

"You mean to be Duchess of the Hollow," Arther guessed.

"And if I do?" Leesha asked. "Is your loyalty to me—to the Hollow—or to the ivy throne?"

Arther took a step back, unsheathing the ceremonial fencing spear on his back. Wonda twitched, but Leesha stayed her with a hand as Arther laid the weapon on the floor before the bed and knelt. "To you and the Hollow, my lady. I swear it by the Creator, and will swear again in the sun."

Leesha held out a hand, and Arther took it. "And I swear to be worthy of your trust, First Minister."

Arther kissed her hand. "Thank you, my lady."

He rolled back on his heels, getting smoothly to his feet as he took a writing board from the satchel at his waist. "In that case, I've received dozens of requests for your calendar already, and there are a number of pressing matters . . ."

Leesha sighed, but felt much of her stress wash away with it. She glanced at the nursery. "You have until Olive begins to cry, Minister."

Leesha Paper, Mistress of the Hollow

Leesha's back spasmed as she scrawled the words for what seemed the thousandth time. Thamos' chair was a great carved monstrosity, chosen more for intimidation than comfort. Magic helped speed her recovery, but she did not want to grow dependent upon it, especially with Olive suckling hungrily a dozen times a day.

She put one hand on the writhing muscles at the small of her back and stretched. She'd been signing since midmorning. Outside the office window, the sky was darkening.

Minister Arther snatched up the paper, laying it atop the completed pile even as he placed another in front of her. "Fifty thousand klats for horse barding bearing Baron Cutter's arms." Arther swept the pertinent numbers with the end of his pen before drawing a quick X at the bottom. "Sign here."

Leesha scanned the page. "This is ridiculous. I'm not approving that. The baron can spend his own money dressing up his horses. There are hungry mouths to feed."

"Your pardon, mistress," Arther said, "but the order was

completed a month ago. The baron has his barding, and the
vendor is owed payment."

"How did it go through without approval?" Leesha asked.

"His Highness left Baron Cutter in charge, and the man
would rather box a wood demon than pick up a pen." Arther
sniffed. "Apparently among the Hollowers, spitting on your
hand is considered a binding contract."

"Most of them can't read, anyway." Leesha grit her teeth as
she bent and signed, then glanced at the tall, unruly stack of
papers the baron's clerk had sent over. "Are they all like this?"

"I'm afraid so," Arther said. "The people needed a symbol
to rally to in the absence of the count and yourself. Especially
after Mr. and Mrs. Bales disappeared. In that, Baron Cutter
was a great success. As an administrator, he . . . left much to
be desired."

Leesha nodded. She could not pretend this was news to her;
she had known Gared all her life. The people loved and trusted
him. He was one of them—first of the Cutters to answer Arlen
Bales' call to take their axes into the night. He'd put himself
between the Hollowers and the demons every night since, and
they all knew it. Folk slept better, knowing Gared Cutter was
in charge.

But he was much better at spending money than he was at
counting it. Leesha could stamp an endless number of klats,
but they were only worth as much as the people believed them
to be.

"Would you still seek his employ if I asked for your resignation?" Leesha asked.

Arther blew a breath through his nose. "That was an empty
threat, mistress. Baron Cutter goes through clerks faster than
mugs of ale. Squire Emet resigned after the baron threatened
to tear his arms off."

Leesha sighed. "And if I ordered you to go, and him to take
you?"

"I might break my oath and defect to Krasia," Arther said,
and Leesha laughed so hard it rasped her throat.

Her eyes moved back to the pile of papers, and the humor
left her. She rubbed her temple, massaging the dull ache that
would soon blossom into pain if she didn't have something to

eat and an hour alone in her garden. "Gared needs a clerk that's not afraid of him."

"I don't know where you'll find such a man, this side of Arlen Bales," Arther said.

"I wasn't thinking of a man," Leesha said. "Wonda?"

"Don't look at me, mistress," Wonda said. "I'm worse with papers than Gar."

"Be a dear and fetch Miss Lacquer, then," Leesha said.

Wonda smiled. "Ay, mistress."

"Thank you for coming, Emelia." Leesha swept a hand at one of the chairs by her desk. "Please, take a seat."

"Thank you, Countess." Rosal dipped a smooth, practiced curtsy, snapping her skirts as she rose so that when she seated herself, not a fold was out of place.

"Please just call me mistress," Leesha said. "Tea?"

Rosal nodded. "Yes, please, mistress."

Leesha signaled to Wonda. The woman could thread a needle with her bow, and she had an equally adept pour, carrying two steaming cups and saucers in one hand like a pair of klats.

"How have you found the Hollow thus far?" Leesha asked as she took her cup.

"Wonderful." Rosal dropped a sugar in her tea, stirring. "Everyone's been so welcoming. They're all excited about the wedding. Even your mother has offered to help with the planning."

"Oh?" This was the first Leesha had heard of it. It seemed unthinkable that Elona might offer to help anyone out of the goodness of her heart, Emelia Lacquer most of all.

Rosal nodded. "She's introduced me to the best florists and seamstresses, and offered some . . . interesting advice on the dress."

"My mother isn't one to waste excess cloth," Leesha said. "Especially on top."

Rosal lifted her cup with a wink. "I've worn worse than anything your mum can dream up. But not this time. Rosal was for other men. Gared's going to get a bride out of a Jongleur's tale."

"Gared's not getting anything until his paperwork gets done," Leesha said, indicating the pile on her desk.

Rosal nodded. "Papers aren't Gar's strength. After the wedding I can . . ."

"That's not going to do, dear," Leesha said. "Need I remind you of your debt to me?"

Rosal shook her head. Leesha had kept the Duchess Mum from throwing her in prison after the scandal at court. "Of course not, mistress."

"Good," Leesha said. "Amanvah's dice said I could trust you to be loyal to the Hollow, and I need someone like that on my side right now."

Rosal set down her saucer and sat up straight, hands in her lap. "How can I help?"

Leesha pointed to the stack. "Tell your promised he doesn't get his seedpods drained until you sit him down and make him balance his ledgers."

Rosal raised an eyebrow, a slight smirk twitching at her mouth. "Why, mistress, I have never once drained the baron's seedpods. We are unwed! Think of the scandal!"

The smirk spread into a smile. "But I keep his tree at attention. Told him I won't have it out of his breeches unless he's tied down. Now whenever we're alone he runs for the shackles."

"Creator," Leesha said. "You're as bad as my mother. Be careful he doesn't have his night strength, or he might break those shackles."

Rosal's eyes glittered. "Deep down, mistress, he doesn't want to."

"All right I wait outside, mistress?" Wonda cut in.

Rosal smiled at her. "Why, Wonda Cutter, you're blushing!"

"Like listenin' to you talk about my brother," Wonda said.

"I've two brothers myself," Rosal said. "I know more than I'd ever wish about their love lives." She winked. "But I won't say the information wasn't useful."

"Can I assume, then, you will quickly have the problem . . . ah," Leesha smiled in spite of herself, ". . . in hand?"

All three women shared a laugh.

"Think no more on it, mistress," Rosal said. "I'll put the shackles under his desk."

"The sun is set, mistress," Tarisa said.

Leesha pried Olive from her breast, handing her to Elona. "Is everyone arrived and given tea?" Tarisa moved to fix her neckline, adding deft pats of powder.

"Lot of 'em been waiting over an hour, now," Wonda said.

Leesha nodded. Keeping the councilors waiting was something Thamos had done to show his power, and it seemed apt to keep the practice for her first council meeting since she returned.

More, by calling the meeting late in the day, Leesha could wait out the sun, which flooded the western windows of the council chamber in the evenings. She slipped on her warded spectacles and rose, gliding out into the hall. She'd been home a week now and couldn't put this off any longer.

"Leesha Paper, Mistress of the Hollow," Arther said simply as he ushered her in through the royal entrance to the council chamber, all but hidden behind Thamos' monstrosity of a throne. Eventually Leesha meant to be rid of the thing, but for now it served its purpose well, looming over the council.

Leesha had purposely removed the title from her name. *Countess* was something given to her by the throne of Angiers, but she had no intention of remaining beholden to them. It was high time the Hollow stood on its own.

Everyone rose, bowing and curtsying. She nodded in acknowledgment and swept a hand for them to take their seats. Only Arther kept his feet, taking up position beside the throne.

Leesha looked over the councilors. Her father, Erny, spoke for the Warders' Guild. Smitt for the Merchants'. Shepherd Jona had taken Inquisitor Hayes' great wooden chair, but Hayes had found another nearly as grand and sat next to him. Likewise, Baron Gared had Captain Gamon beside him. Darsy and Vika had the far end of the table, Darsy in the great padded chair Leesha once occupied. Next to them sat Amanvah, Kendall, and Hary Roller, master of the Jongleurs' Guild.

"Thank you all for coming," Leesha said. "I know there are many preparations to make for tonight's ceremony, so we'll keep this first meeting brief. First, as you all know, Lord Arther will retain his position as first minister." She nodded to the man. "Minister?"

Arther stepped forward, writing board ready. "The Hollow has sixteen baronies now, mistress, not counting Gatherers' Wood. Eleven have active greatwards. Four have begun to pay taxes. The others remain . . . unstable as the people settle into their new lives."

Most of those baronies were formed of refugees from the Krasians, a steady flow over the last year. The Hollow had grown exponentially to accommodate them, printing klats to start their economies and providing structure and materials to rebuild their lives.

"All of 'em are sendin' folk to join the Cutters," Gared noted. "Got recruits comin' in every day, which is good. Demons are getting pushed out by the greatwards, but it ent thinnin' their ranks. Anythin', it's gettin' worse."

"We're using molds and stencils to ward their weapons and shields," Erny said. "Not as effective as those warded by hand, but it's allowed us to keep up with demand. We're working on bolts of cloth, as well, to mass-produce Cloaks of Unsight."

Leesha nodded. "What are we doing to rebuild the cavalry?"

"Jon Stallion has more horses coming," Smitt said. "The Wooden Lancers . . ."

"Hollow Lancers," Leesha said, looking at Gamon.

"Eh?" Smitt asked.

"The Wooden Soldiers are dissolved as of today," Leesha said. "Any who wish to join the Hollow Soldiers shall be automatically enrolled and keep their rank and pay, upon oath of allegiance to the Hollow. The rest . . ."

Gamon held up a hand. He and Arther had already discussed this. "I have spoken to the men, mistress. There are none who wish to return to Angiers."

Leesha gave a nod. "We will see them back to strength soon, Captain."

She looked to Jona, sitting with the rigid Inquisitor Hayes. "And your Tenders, Shepherd?"

"It will be some time before they are returned to strength," Jona said. "The Krasian invaders executed Tender and Child alike, whenever they found them. We have only a handful to minister to many. I wish your blessing to appoint Inquisitor Hayes to speak for the Hollow's first Council of Tenders."

Leesha and the inquisitor eyed each other. He, too, had worn spectacles to the meeting. Leesha could see wardlight dance across them, and knew he was watching her aura as she did his.

This, too, had been agreed in advance. A way for both of them to keep face as they followed their script before the council.

"How do you think Duke Pether will react," Leesha asked, "if you renounce the Church of Angiers and swear oath to an independent Church of the Hollow, with Jona as Shepherd?"

Hayes sketched a quick warding in the air. Leesha could see the script ripple across the ambient magic, impressed at his skill. His own eyes were drawn to it as well.

Leesha smiled at the dawning understanding in his aura. *The Tenders have more power than they know.*

Hayes shook off his surprise. "I trained Pether. He will take this as a personal betrayal. The Church of Angiers will declare me a heretic and likely issue a warrant for me to be burned alive if I set foot on Angierian soil ever again."

"And still you wish to do this?" Leesha asked.

"I was sent here to quell heresy," Inquisitor Hayes said. "To bring the Hollow back under the control of Shepherd Pether and the Church of Angiers. But in the months I have served here, I have seen people of tremendous faith and courage, and witnessed things the Angierian Council of Tenders can only imagine.

"I do not pretend to know the Creator's Plan, but I know that He put me here for a reason, to stand between these people and the Core. To let them know the Creator is watching, and He is proud."

His aura shone with conviction, and Leesha gave a bow of her head to Jona. "You do not need my blessing, Shepherd, but you have it."

"Thank you, mistress," Jona said. "We will begin promoting Tenders and bringing in new Children, but it may be years before our ranks are secure."

"Of course," Leesha said. "Perhaps it is time to promote Child Franq?"

The auras of both men colored. They cast nervous glances at each other, and Gared. Slowly the color rippled around the table, until it was clear everyone else knew something Leesha did not. Even Darsy.

"What?" she demanded.

"Franq's a small part of a bigger problem," Darsy said. "One growin' like chokeweed in the middle of the Hollow."

"The Warded Children," Leesha said.

"Can't tell 'em anythin' anymore!" Gared slapped one of his giant hands on the table, and the whole thing shook, rattling everyone's tea. "Don't show up to muster, don't listen to anyone but their own."

"They live in the Gatherers' Wood," Smitt said. "They refuse to sleep inside walls."

"Like they ent folk anymore," Gared said. "Becomin' . . . somethin' else."

It was Leesha's turn to slap the table. "Enough of that, Baron. These are not demons we're talking about. These are brothers, sisters, and children of the Hollow. We're talking about Evin and Brianne's son Callen." She looked to Smitt. "Your son Keet and granddaughter, Stela."

"Callen broke Yon Gray's arm," Gared said.

"I caught Keet and Stela stealing from one of my warehouses," Smitt said. "Food, weapons, tools. My own son knocked me down when I tried to stop them. I put a new lock on the warehouse, and the next time they came they kicked in the six-inch goldwood door like it was kindling."

"What does all this have to do with Child Franq?" Leesha asked.

"It came to my attention that the Children had begun to self-train, forming their own rituals," Hayes said. "Fearing a growing risk of heresy, I sent Franq to minister to them. Reports indicated they were hungry to learn warding, and Franq is a skilled Warder. He used it to gain access."

"And?" Leesha asked.

Hayes blew out a breath. "He has . . . joined them, mistress."

Leesha blinked. "You're telling me that Child Franq, a man made entirely of starch, has joined the Warded Children?"

Hayes nodded grimly. "The last time I saw him, mistress, he had taken to wearing a simple brown robe."

"That isn't unusual," Leesha said.

"His sleeves were cut away to show the wards tattooed on his arms," Hayes said. "And he stank of sweat and ichor."

"I'll need to meet with them," Leesha said. "And soon."

"Ent a good idea, mistress," Wonda said.

"She's right, Leesh," Gared said. "Children're dangerous."

"I trained 'em," Wonda said. "Listen to me. Know they will."

Leesha shook her head. "I need to see for myself. I assure you, we will go prepared and do nothing to provoke them until we have their measure."

"Must be someone you can send," Wonda said, "just to feel things out."

"Normally that would be a job for my herald," Leesha said, "but with Rojer gone, that position is empty." She looked to Kendall. "The job is yours, Kendall, if you want it."

Kendall blinked. "Me, mistress? Ent much more'n an apprentice . . ."

"Nonsense," Leesha said. "Rojer himself told me you are the only one he's ever met with his talent for charming demons. The Hollow needs that with him gone, and Rojer's word is more than good enough for me. Guildmaster?"

Hary Roller smiled, producing a scroll and handing it to the young woman. "Your Jongleur's license, Kendall Demonsong."

"Ay, like the sound of that," Kendall said, taking the scroll.

"So will you take the job?" Leesha pressed. "The license is yours regardless, but there is no one else I would have in the position."

Kendall looked to Amanvah, who nodded. "Yes, mistress, of course."

Hayes harrumphed. Leesha raised an eyebrow his way. "Something on your mind, Inquisitor?"

Hayes pursed his lips. "Only that your new herald appears to answer to an Evejan priestess first and her countess second."

Amanvah's brows knit together, aura spiking. Hayes saw it, too, and flinched. Leesha raised a hand before she could retort. "I trust Kendall implicitly, Inquisitor, which is more than I can say for your judgment at the moment. As for Amanvah . . ." She looked to the *dama'ting*. "You might as well tell them."

Amanvah drew a breath, returning to serenity. "Sikvah and I will be returning to Everam's Bounty after our husband's funeral. The *Damaji'ting* of the Kaji was slain in my brother's coup. I am to take her place."

There were gasps around the table. *"Damaji'ting . . ."* Jona began.

"'Shepherdess' is the closest translation," Amanvah said, "though it falls short, as it is a secular title as well. I will have direct control of the *dama'ting* and women of the Kaji, Krasia's largest tribe."

"Shepherdess and duchess both, then," Jona said, bowing to her. "Congratulations, Your Highness."

Similar sentiments echoed around the table. Amanvah acknowledged them with regal nods before turning to meet Leesha's eyes. "I cannot speak for my mother and brother, mistress, but know by the blood we share that you and the Hollow will always have an ally in me."

Leesha nodded. "Of that I have no doubt." She turned back to Arther. "What news from Lakton?"

Arther eyed Amanvah warily. "Mistress . . ."

"There's nothing you can say that Amanvah won't learn on her return, Minister," Leesha said.

Arther pursed his lips, choosing his words carefully. "The island remains free, though the waters now host a growing number of Krasian privateers."

"And the mainland?" Leesha asked.

"Still under Krasian control," Arther said, "but their positions are weaker. The remains of Prince Jayan's army have not returned. Half have deserted, preying like wolves on any settlements they come upon. The rest have taken refuge behind the walls of the Monastery of Dawn."

"And the refugees who took succor there?" Leesha had sent Briar Damaj to find any that may have escaped the slaughter.

"Briar's been in and out," Gared said. "Brought in a group already. Due this evening with the last of 'em, includin' a couple of Milnese dignitaries he wants you to meet."

Leesha took a sip of her tea. "Have rooms ready for them, and an invitation to call on me once they've had a day or two to refresh themselves."

She set down her cup. "Amanvah, let us discuss tonight's service."

Elona was pacing the hall outside when the meeting ended, but she wasn't waiting for Erny. Her eyes, and her aura, remained fixed on Gared as she gave her husband a peck on the cheek and sent him on down the hall with a shove.

None of the councilors noticed Elona's fixation, not even Hayes with his warded eyes. All were simply grateful she was not focused on them, and hurried past. But Gared lingered, talking with Arther and Gamon. When Elona entered the room, the two men scampered away as quickly as their dignity would allow. By the time Gared saw her, Elona had closed the door and he was trapped.

Elona turned to Leesha, who saw the same frightened urge to flee ripple through her own aura. She liked to think she had better control of her mother, but auras didn't lie.

"Bit of privacy, dear?" Elona's voice held a dangerous edge. Gared looked at Leesha in panic.

"Sorry, Gar, this is overdue. You and my mother have things to discuss."

Leesha turned and Wonda opened the door to the royal entrance. The two of them swept through, closing the heavy door behind them.

"That'll be all for now, Wonda," Leesha said.

"Mistress?" Wonda asked.

"I may need to step back into this," Leesha said. "Do you want to be anywhere near it when I do?"

The panic rushed through Wonda's aura now. Night, was there anyone in all the world not terrified of Elona? "No, mistress."

"Off you go, then," Leesha said. "Run and find Rosal. Ask her to fetch her promised from the council room." Relief flooded Wonda's aura as she turned and sprinted down the hall.

Since returning to the Hollow, Leesha had forgone wearing

the pocketed apron of an Herb Gatherer. Araine had told her it was not dignified or proper for a countess, and much as Leesha resented it, the woman was right.

But neither was it dignified or proper for Leesha to hide who she was. She had everyone address her as mistress, and her gowns were covered in stylish pockets, filled with herbs and warded items.

She selected a delicate warded silver ball dangling from the end of a fine silver chain. She set the ball into one ear, pulling the chain over and behind her ear to hold it in place. Inside the ball was a broken piece of demon bone. Leesha had left its twin on her throne, and through it she could hear everything occurring in the council room.

"Been avoiding me, boy," Elona said, but it wasn't the snappish tone she took with others. This was the purr of a cat sleeping atop the mousehole.

"Just been busy," Gared said.

"Ay, you were always busy," Elona agreed. "Until you had a stiff tree in your pants, and then you were at my door, beggin' like a wolfhound."

"Ent gonna do that anymore." Gared's words sounded more a plea than an order. "Promised Leesha and swore by the sun."

"Easy to make an oath like that," Elona said. "Lot harder to keep it—believe me. Easy now, with that Angierian skink draining your seedpods night and day. Always like that at first. Think you'll never need another woman. But she'll tire of the chore, and untie your breeches less and less. Then one day, when your pods are fit to burst, you'll come looking for me, knowin' I'll take you leaves-to-root and use tricks that young debutante of yours never heard of."

Gared gasped. Was she touching him?

"What do you think, boy?" Elona asked. "She empty you like I can?"

"W-we ent . . ." Gared stuttered, "done that yet."

"Must be backed up to your eyeballs!" Elona laughed, and it sounded triumphant. "What say I do your young promised a favor and skim some off the top for old times' sake?"

There was a sound of stumbling and shifting furniture.

Elona laughed. "Want me under the table, ay? Let me take care of you in secret while folk buzz about?"

More shifting furniture. "Ent happenin' again, Mrs. Paper," Gared growled. "Deliverer said I could be a better man, and I aim to."

"You're bein' an idiot, boy," Elona snapped. "You can do better than that girl."

"Ya don't even know her!" Gared said.

"Had enough tea with that simpering girl and her idiot mum to drown a water demon," Elona said. "She's got nothing to offer now that my daughter's single again."

Night, Mother! Leesha thought. *Still?!*

But Gared surprised her. "Don't want Leesha. Shined on her, I know, but that wern't ever gonna work."

Honest word, Leesha agreed.

"It's not just Leesha, you idiot," Elona snapped. "You marry her, you could be Duke of the Hollow. Night, one day you might be king of Thesa!"

Her voice turned back to a purr. "Now that she's had a few spears, she's ready for a real tree. And when she's not climbing it, I'll keep the fruit plucked."

"W-what about Erny?" Gared squeaked.

"Pfagh," Elona said. "He'll hide in the closet and pull at himself until you're gone, like always."

Leesha had enough, slipping off the warded earpiece and opening the door. Gared was using the council table like a shield, frozen as a deer on the far side.

"Creator be praised." Gared hurried over. Leesha wanted to laugh at the sight of Gared Cutter, seven feet of pure muscle, cowering behind her.

"Fine, keep it in your pants!" Elona growled. "That don't change what it's left behind!"

"Ay, what's that supposed to mean?" Gared asked over Leesha's shoulder.

"It means I've got your babe in my belly, woodbrain," Elona snapped.

"What?!" Gared demanded. "Just thought you put on a few pounds."

It was the worst thing he could have said. Elona's aura went red, her eyes bulging.

But then the council room door opened and Rosal stepped in.

"Night!" Elona threw up her hands. "Does everyone in this ripping keep have an ear to the door?"

Rosal smiled. "I was just looking for Gared." She threw him a wink. "He's got paperwork to do."

Gared looked pale as Rosal looked back to Elona. "It's not as if this is news to me. Gared has tells whenever your name is mentioned."

"I do?" Gared asked.

Rosal's eyes flicked over, holding his. "You're not in trouble for anything past, so be smart and keep quiet now. I'll handle this."

Gared blew out a breath. "Ay, dear."

Elona put her hands on her hips, fixed on Rosal now. "Smarter'n I gave you credit for, girl."

Rosal gave a mocking curtsy. "I know you're something special here in the Hollow, Lady Paper, but I went to school with dozens like you. I don't mind that you broke Gared in, but on our wedding night I'm going to do things that will make him forget all about your bumpkin wife's tricks."

Elona's hand darted out, reaching for Rosal's long, thick hair, but Rosal was ready for it, slapping the hand aside and stepping out of reach. She had a dancer's balance, and Leesha knew she could strike back if she wished.

But Rosal kept control. Her voice was quiet, smile still in place. "He's not yours anymore."

"Core he ent," Elona said. "Got his brat in me."

"You've got a child in you," Rosal agreed. "But is it Gared's? Who can say? You're a married woman."

"And when the babe don't look like Erny?" Elona asked.

Rosal shrugged. "I doubt any will be surprised. You have quite the reputation. 'What's Lady Paper done now?' is a drinking game among the servants, did you know?"

Elona's aura darkened again, but she stood frozen.

"But . . . what if it really is mine?" Gared squeaked. All eyes turned to him.

"Told the Deliverer I'd be a better man," Gared said, his voice slowly gaining strength. "Ent lookin' for scandal, but I ent any kind of man, I can't stand by my babe."

Rosal went over to him. He flinched as she reached for him, but she only laid a gentle hand on his arm. "Of course not, my love. I would never ask that of you. But there are many ways to stand by the child, if we learn it's yours."

"Ay?" Gared asked.

"By the time the babe comes, we'll be married," Rosal said. "And our marriage contract will put our issue first in your succession. After that, you're free to claim the child if you wish."

She put a hand on his face. "But you may find it easier for all to simply visit often and shower the child with gifts."

Elona crossed her arms. "And if I start the scandal, my-self?"

"You won't," Rosal said. "Not without proof, and likely not even then. You're not as smart as you think you are, Lady Paper, but you're smarter than that. You have more to lose than Gared."

Leesha spoke up at last. "I can call Amanvah if you wish, Mother. With a drop of your blood and a throw of her dice, she can give you proof. We can settle this all here and now."

"You, too, girl?" Elona spat on the rug, turning on a heel to storm from the room.

Gared let out a groan, and Rosal patted his arm. "Breathe, love. You did well. We haven't heard the last of this, but the worst is over. You just keep your distance and leave Elona to me."

She turned to him, catching his eyes and holding them with her own. "And come our wedding day, you'll never want her to climb your tree again."

"Don't want it now," Gared said.

Rosal caught his beard, pulling his face down for a peck on the cheek. "Smart boy."

Gared put his hand over hers. "Thought ya'd never under-stand, ya knew what I done."

Rosal smiled. "Past is past, we agreed. Yours and mine."

She looked to Leesha. "Thank you, mistress."

"Ay, Leesh," Gared said. "Came in like the Deliverer just then."

"Hardly," Leesha said.

"Demonshit," Gared said. "Ent the first time. Yu've always been there when folk need ya most, Leesh. You an' Rojer an' Arlen Bales. Came to the Hollow together when we were beaten, and turned it around. Ent no one whose life ent changed by ya."

"Now Arlen is gone," Leesha said. "And Rojer. People are going to realize I'm no Deliverer when they see the foolish choices I've made."

"Ent gonna see any such thing." Gared waved an arm dismissively. "Broken folk come to the Hollow, lookin' for the Deliverer, but the first thing they see is Leesha Paper, takin' care of 'em."

Leesha shook her head. "You're the first thing they see, Gar."

"Ay, on the road, maybe," Gared agreed. "Cutters make 'em feel safe, but safe don't give them a place to sleep and a full belly. Safe don't heal the cored. Safe don't put clothes on their backs and put 'em right back to work. Don't give 'em a new life before losing the old one even has time to set in. You do that, Leesh. Time ya stopped bein' so guilty about it."

"Guilty?" Leesha asked.

"That yur alive and Rojer ent," Gared said. "That ya had to kill those Krasians came to murder the duke. Poisoned them *Sharum* last summer so they couldn't turn on us. Stuck the demon of the desert. Ya done what ya done to help people, every time. Wern't selfish, or evil. Quit tellin' yurself otherwise."

Leesha looked at Gared, trying to peel back the years to their childhood romance, or the young man she had hated for so many years. The man who had ruined her reputation and arguably her life. The man in front of her was both those men, and neither. The mistakes of youth had cast both of them onto new paths.

Those paths had been difficult, but they'd led inexorably to them becoming the most powerful people in Hollow County.

And somewhere along the way, he had become like a brother to her. He was a woodbrained oaf even now, but he was a good man, and she loved him still. Leesha reached out, taking Gared's and Rosal's hands in hers. "I am truly happy for the two of you."

CHAPTER 4

RAGEN
AND ELISSA

334 AR

"Night." Ragen pulled up short as the thick woods to either side of the warded Messenger road ended abruptly. It was nearing dusk, but there was light still. "We passed through less than a year ago, and this was miles of woodland."

"Cutters' axes swing day and night," Briar said. The boy was on foot, somehow keeping pace with the horses.

Even atop his saddle, Ragen could smell Briar. Elissa had him bathing now, but all the hogroot the boy ate had gotten into his sweat. The scent protected him from demons at night, but it made him stand out to everyone else.

"They didn't just clear the land," Elissa said. "There are entire towns that weren't there before."

"Greatwards, too," Briar said. "Cories can't touch the Hollow."

"Creator be praised." Elissa blew out a breath. "I set out from Miln to have a taste for once of the naked night. Now I've had my fill. I'm ready for walls, a bath, and a feathered bed."

"Walls make you soft," Briar said. "Forget what's out there."

"I daresay I'll have no trouble remembering," Ragen said. They had been making their way out of Lakton for weeks via ill-used Messenger ways. Ragen had maps, but since the great Messenger road was built, many of the old trails had been reclaimed by the wetlands.

But the road was too dangerous. After the Battle of Docktown, the Krasians sent an army to take the Monastery of Dawn. The monastery was the most defensible spot Ragen had ever seen short of Lakton itself. He and Shepherd Alin had thought to hold out for weeks, but even those great walls were no match for Krasian laddermen. There was handfighting on the walls the first day, and they had been forced to flee to the docks.

Krasian privateers harried them for miles, but could not keep pace with Captain Dehlia and the *Sharum's Lament*. They lost sight of the pursuers long enough to send boats out to a tiny fishing village to the north where they could begin the trek back to Miln.

The Krasians were conquering every village near the Messenger road, so Ragen had taken his charges overland, through out-of-the-way hamlets and along trails that were little more than dim memories of a path. They made valuable contacts along the way, and sent Euchor reports whenever possible, though Creator knew if any of them made it to him.

Ragen shook his head as they approached the first greatward. "I remember when Cutter's Hollow was a hamlet with less than three hundred people. Now it's home to a hundred thousand, by some estimates."

"All because of Arlen," Elissa said.

"You really knew him?" Briar asked. "Warded Man?"

"Knew him?" Ragen laughed. "We practically raised him. Like a son to us." Briar looked up at him, and Ragen reached down, squeezing the boy's shoulder. Briar tended to flinch at intimate contact, but this he allowed, even leaning into it a bit. "Like you've become, Briar."

"In another life, you might have called him brother." Elissa choked on the words. "But now Arlen is gone."

"Ent," Briar said.

"What's that, boy?" Ragen asked.

"Folk saw him," Briar said. "When Krasians first came. He was on the road, helping."

"There were rumors," Elissa said.

Ragen reached over to take her hand. "People tell ale stories, Briar."

Briar shook his head. "Different folk, different places, same story. Drew wards in the air and cories burst into flame."

"Do you think . . ." Elissa asked.

"Wouldn't surprise me," Ragen said, though he hadn't dared believe it himself. "Boy's too stubborn to die."

Elissa laughed, sniffling.

She looked up suddenly. "Do you hear singing?"

"There." Ragen had the distance lens to his eye, whatever he saw lost in the gloom to Elissa.

"What is it?" Elissa asked.

Ragen passed Elissa the lens. "Looks like a funeral procession."

In the lens, Elissa could see a fiddle-playing Jongleur, flanked by two singing Krasian women in bright, colorful robes. Behind the Krasian women were a Tender and a finely dressed woman, followed by their attendants and six Cutters bearing a wooden litter on their wide shoulders.

Hundreds followed in their wake, voices joined in song. They were led by a bright patchwork troupe of Jongleurs.

"The Jongleur at the lead," Elissa said, moving the lens back to the front. "Might that be Arlen's friend? The fiddle wizard, Rojer Halfgrip?"

"Not unless Arlen didn't notice that Halfgrip is a woman with two hands," Ragen said. Elissa looked closer and saw he was right. The three in front were all women.

Elissa studied the women. Their music was eerily clear, carried on the night air as if by magic. "Why would a funeral procession be heading to the edge of the greatwards?"

"Kill seven cories," Briar said.

Elissa looked at him. "Whatever for?"

"It's a Krasian ritual," Ragen said. "They believe killing seven demons—one for each pillar of Heaven—honors and guides a departing spirit down the lonely path."

"The lonely path?" Elissa asked.

"Path that leads to the Creator." Briar's voice tightened. "And His judgment."

They stepped off the road as the procession reached them, blending into the crowd as it passed. The Mistress of the Hollow held a rod in her hand that looked to be a slender bone covered in gold plate, etched with wards. As they went, she used it to draw light wards that hung in the air like silver script. Then she gave a flick of her wrist and they shot high into the sky and burst into brilliance, hanging in the air to illuminate the procession.

"Ragen," Elissa said quietly.

"I see." Ragen had heard of the demon bone magic of the Krasians, but didn't truly understand it until now. If demon bones held magic after the coreling died, it meant any skilled Warder could do what the mistress just did.

And few in Miln were as skilled as the Warders' Guildmaster and his wife.

The procession stopped at a great clearing, and the trio at the lead left the road, going to stand at its center. They changed their song, and demons appeared at the outskirts, drawn to the sound. Elissa gripped Ragen's arm with sharp fingernails, but neither of them could utter a word.

A few in the crowd cried out when the corelings were almost upon them, but again the music shifted, and demon claws dug great furrows in the ground as they pulled up short.

The fiddler kept her tune, holding the center of the clearing free of demons as the Krasian women circled, driving some of the demons away with shrieks, even as they kept others bound in place until there was only one of each breed.

It was incredible, the level of control the players had. Elissa had never seen anything like it. Even Arlen's stories of Halfgrip the fiddle wizard paled in comparison.

"We must take this power to Miln," Elissa said.

"Ay," Ragen said.

"Halfgrip wrote music on paper," Briar said. "Seen Jongleurs with it."

Elissa nodded. "I'll find the Jongleurs' Guildmaster and pay whatever it takes to get a copy."

"Ent s'posed to charge," Briar said. "Halfgrip said all could share."

"You don't suppose . . ." Elissa's eyes flicked to the pall, seeing a crossed fiddle and bow embroidered on the cloth.

"Night," she whispered.

Leesha's eyes were drawn by the sound of thundering foot-falls. A twenty-foot rock demon appeared on the far side of the clearing, brushing winter-barren trees aside like reeds as it stepped from the woods.

The Cutters closed ranks behind the demon, trapping the seven demons in the clearing and preventing others from en-tering. Their warded cutting tools hung over their shoulders, unused this night. They stood guard with voices alone.

The song was *Keep the Hearthfire Burning,* an old wood-cutting chantey every Hollower knew. *Hearthfire* was meant to keep cutters' tools in sync while they worked. Leesha re-membered the night Rojer first heard it. He hummed the tune for days after, working the melody on his fiddle. The changes he made were subtle, but somehow her friend worked his spe-cial magic into the music.

Now the first verse of *Keep the Hearthfire Burning* kept the Cutters marching in step while keeping demons at bay. The second drew the enemy in close, and the third disoriented core-lings as the axes fell upon them.

"Still keeping us safe," Leesha whispered.

"What's that, mistress?" Wonda asked.

"Rojer's protecting us, even now," Leesha said.

"Course he is," Wonda said. "Creator wouldn't have taken Rojer if his work wern't done."

Leesha had never been comfortable with the idea of a Creator so involved in who lived and who died. What was the point of Gathering if it were so? Nevertheless, the thought of Rojer in Heaven was a comforting one.

There were seven demons in all, one for each pillar in the Krasian Heaven. A flame demon danced around the rock's feet. There was a spindly-armed bog demon and a long-limbed wood demon. A field demon, sleek and low to the ground. A squat stone demon lumbered, and above in the sky a wind demon circled.

Amanvah and Sikvah ceased their singing, and Kendall lowered her fiddle. The priestess raised a hand. "Jaddah."

"That's my cue." Wonda passed Leesha her bow, rolling her

loose sleeves as she strode to the center of the clearing. The wards stained onto her arms glowed softly.

Wonda chose the bog demon, skittering in before it could snatch her in its arms. The demon was not flexible enough to strike in close, and she landed a series of blows, accentuated by the impact wards on her fists and elbows. A warded boot heel sent the demon stumbling back, and she moved in quick, stomping the demon's knee and putting it on its back.

She moved in close again, falling atop the coreling and pinning it, raining blows down upon its head. The demon flailed, but after a time its movements were only reflex responses to her continuing blows. Her wards glowed brighter and brighter until the demon's head cracked open.

"Avash," Amanvah said when Wonda at last stepped back, covered in ichor that sizzled on her wards.

Gared stepped forward then. His axe was slung, but he wore his great warded gauntlets, and he chose the ten-foot-tall wood demon as his gift to Heaven. He wasn't as graceful and quick as Wonda, but the demon was immediately on the defensive, stumbling back under his thunderous blows. It lasted less time than the bog demon.

"Umas." Amanvah named the third pillar of Heaven as she called Rojer's apprentices, led by Hary Roller, into the clearing. The Jongleurs chose the field demon, driving the coreling into a frenzy with their music before setting it on the stone demon.

The field demon leapt upon the stone demon, claws raking, but they could not penetrate the heavy armor. The stone demon batted the field demon to the ground and smashed its skull with a heavy talon.

Amanvah caught Leesha's eye. "Rahvees."

Leesha drew a breath, stepping forward and raising her *hora* wand at the stone demon. She drew silver wards in the air with quick, sharp script. Cold wards froze it in place, ichor turning solid in the demon's veins. Lectricity wards shocked through the beast, racking it with pain.

"For you, Rojer." Leesha drew impact wards, and the demon shattered.

"Kenji."

Kendall stepped forward, raising bow to string. She drew the flame demon to her effortlessly, coaxing the beast to draw firespit into its mouth. Then she changed her song, forcing the demon to swallow it.

Flame demon scales were impervious to heat, but the same could not be said of their insides. The demon choked and fell onto its back, thrashing as its insides burned.

Kendall picked up the tempo as she circled the coreling, notes becoming hard and discordant. The flamer whined and cried, curling into a protective ball as Kendall played faster and faster. Her bow became a blur as she raised her head away from the fiddle's chinrest. The music grew so loud, Leesha's eardrums throbbed even beneath the wax she and the other mourners wore.

At last the flame demon gave a final throe and lay still. Kendall let her music die away as Amanvah pointed to the wind demon in the sky. "Ghanith."

Sikvah took her turn, calling to the demon. It circled down, talons leading to snatch the tiny girl up and sweep away into the sky with her.

But as it drew close, Sikvah touched her throat and gave such a cry the demon pulled up short, flapped wildly, and then fell to the ground, dead. Sikvah turned to her sister-wife, bowing. "Horzha."

Amanvah's colored silks billowed in the breeze as she sauntered up to the rock demon, beginning to sing the *Song of Waning*. Her voice rose alone in the night, holding the rock demon in its grip.

Louder and louder she sang as she circled the rock. She had a hand to her throat, working the magic of her choker. It grew so loud that Leesha had to cover her ears, and she saw folk half a mile up the road doing likewise as they watched. Leesha felt she could almost see the vibration in the air as the resonance grew.

And then, abruptly, there was a great crack, and the rock demon fell, striking the ground with a boom.

"Honored husband, Rojer asu Jessum am'Inn am'Hollow." Amanvah's voice carried unnaturally far. "Rojer of the Half Grip, disciple of Arrick of the Sweetest Song, let our sacrifice summon a seraph to guide you on the lonely path to Everam, where you shall sup at His table until there is need for your spirit to return to Ala once more."

Leesha walked beside Amanvah as they entered the Corelings' Graveyard. Sikvah and Kendall were two steps behind them, followed by Tender Jona and Cutters bearing Rojer to the pyre.

The Straw Gatherers had done their work well. Rojer's handsome face was serene, showing nothing of the violence of his death. He was clad in bright silk motley and looked as if he might leap to his feet at any moment and begin playing a reel.

He lay on a bed of axe handles crossed over the broad shoulders of Gared, Wonda, and half a dozen handpicked Hollowers. Dug and Merrem Butcher. Smitt. Darsy. Jow and Evin Cutter.

Folk filled the Graveyard, packing the cobbles before the pyre and stretching down the road in every direction. All roads in Cutter's Hollow led here, to the center of the greatward.

The pyre had been built in front of the bandshell that had been Rojer's place of power. Gared and Wonda were weeping openly as they laid Rojer on the great platform over the pile of kindling.

Amanvah, Sikvah, and Kendall fell to their knees on the stage, wailing and sobbing with dramatic flair as young Krasian girls scraped the tears from their cheeks into tiny bottles of warded glass.

Leesha wanted to weep. She had often sought solace in tears, and wept over Rojer many times in private over the last few weeks. But now, before all the gathered people of the Hollow, she felt as if she had nothing left to give. Thamos, dead. Arlen gone, and Ahmann's fate uncertain. And now Rojer. Would it be her fate to bury every man she loved?

After a time, Amanvah recovered herself and got to her feet, looking out over the crowd as she activated her choker. "I am Amanvah vah Rojer vah Ahmann am'Inn am'Hollow, First Wife to Rojer asu Jessum am'Inn am'Hollow. My husband was son-in-law to Shar'Dama Ka, but there was no denying that he, too, was touched by Everam. We burn his body according to your custom, but in Krasia, *sharik hora,* the bones of heroes, are honored above all others. My honored husband's bones will be taken from the remains, lacquered, and encased in warded glass to consecrate the new temple to the Creator here on the sacred ground of the Corelings' Graveyard."

Kendall began a slow, mournful song, and Amanvah began to sing. Sikvah joined her, the trio wrapping the crowd in their music as easily as they charmed corelings.

As she sang, Amanvah produced the tiny skull of a flame demon and pointed it at the pyre, fingers sliding across the wards to activate the magic. A blast of flame shot from the jaws, setting the wood beneath the pyre alight. The Straw Gatherers had filled the body with chemics and sawdust, and it blazed quickly, shining over the crowd as they stood entranced by the Krasian funeral song.

When it was over, Leesha took the stage, clearing her throat. She did not have a choker like the princess, but there was magic in the bandshell as well, carrying her words far into the night.

Still Leesha's tears would not come, and no doubt the mourners were wondering at the sight. *Why isn't she crying? Didn't she love him? Doesn't she care?*

She took a deep breath. "Rojer made me promise that if this day ever came, I'd have singing and dancing, and toss the speeches in the flames with him."

There was scattered laughter.

"It's honest word." Leesha produced a folded paper. "He even wrote it down." She opened the paper, reading.

Leesha, I plan to live long enough to dazzle my great-grandchildren with magic tricks, but we both know life doesn't always go according to plan. If I should die, I'm counting on you to make sure my funeral isn't some boring, depressing affair. Tell everyone I was great, sing a sad song while you light the pyre, then tell Hary to spin a reel and order folk to shut up and dance.

Leesha folded the paper, slipping it into a pocket of her dress. "I wouldn't be here if not for Rojer Halfgrip. I daresay many of us wouldn't. More than once, his music was the last line of the Hollow's defense, giving us time to regroup, to find our feet, to catch our breath.

"When Arlen Bales fell from the sky at new moon, it was Rojer's fiddle that lured the coreling hordes into ambush after ambush, allowing us to hold the night.

"But that's not how I remember him best," Leesha went on. "Rojer was the one who was always ready with a joke when I was sad, or an ear when I needed one. He could be my conscience one moment, and turn a backflip the next. When problems mounted and everything seemed too much to bear, Rojer could just take out his fiddle and soothe it all away.

"That was his magic. Not drawing wards or throwing lightning. Not seeing the future or healing wounds. Rojer Inn saw into hearts, human and demon, and spoke to them with his music. I've never known anyone like him, and I don't expect I shall again.

"Rojer was great." She choked, putting a hand to her mouth, and suddenly found her tears. Amanvah herself rushed forward, catching the drops before they fell from her cheek.

Leesha took a moment to compose herself, then turned to the leader of the Jongleurs in the bandshell. "Hary, it's time for that reel."

Elissa drank and danced with the Hollowers all night. Ragen swung Elissa about like he hadn't since they courted, and even Briar took a turn—the boy surprisingly light on his feet and quick to pick up the steps. The three of them laughed until their faces hurt, feeling safe and joyful for the first time in Creator only knew how long.

As the night wore on, Jongleurs broke off, luring revelers back to their own boroughs just as Halfgrip once lured the corelings, and there was cheer and laughter throughout the Hollow.

There were groans throughout the taproom of Smitt's Inn as dawn light filtered in the windows. There were trays piled high with eggs, bacon, and bread, pitchers of water, and a bucket at the end of every table for retching. One patron was not quick enough, emptying his stomach onto the floor. The sight of it made Elissa's own stomach roil, but she took deep breaths, focusing on the water pitcher until the room stopped spinning.

Stefny, the innkeeper's wife, was there before the man finished with a damp cloth to wipe his mouth and a mop to shove in his hands when he was clean. The man wisely set to cleaning his mess.

"You all right?" Stefny asked Elissa. "I know the look. See one lose it and others are quick to follow."

"I'll manage," Elissa said, sipping at her water.

Stefny nodded. "Ent much business getting done today. Mistress Leesha sent word she'll receive you on the morrow." She sniffed, eyes flicking to Briar. "Time enough to rest up and have a proper bath before going to court."

Briar frowned. The boy, bless him, had the resilience of youth, and looked fitter than the rest of them. He'd finished two helpings of breakfast and now got to his feet. "Come find you tomorrow morning."

"There's room—" Stefny began.

"Don't like walls," Briar cut in. "Got a briarpatch in the Gatherers' Wood." Without another word, he was out the door.

The water had long since cooled, but Elissa was still soaking in the bath when Ragen returned to the room the next morning.

"Turns out Smitt's the local banker, as well," Ragen said. "Once he sobered a bit, our name was enough to get a line of credit to fund our journey back to Miln. Be a few weeks before we can hire hands and get supply, but things should go smoothly from here."

"From your lips to the Creator's ear," Elissa said. "I was beginning to think the children would be grown by the time we returned."

"Hard to plan for an invasion," Ragen said. "If there's a Creator, I'd say He's done His part just seeing us through."

As promised, Briar was waiting on the porch when they had readied themselves. He still smelled of hogroot, but the dirt was gone, at least. Elissa had seen him swim in freezing ponds and streams without so much as a shiver, but it saddened her nevertheless to see him this way. Ragen had hoped to take the boy back home with them, and Elissa dreamed of teaching him the pleasures of a bath and a clean set of clothes, but both of them knew now it was only a fantasy. Briar was Briar, and that wasn't going to change. The path that made him who he was could not be unwalked.

There were guards everywhere in the countess' keep, a surprising number of them female, though no less armored and intimidating than the men. Milnese were tall, but Hollowers tended to be broad, as well. Their fine clothes walked them past the outer security, but surprisingly it was Briar that got them into the inner chambers.

"Briar!" There was a shout, and all three of them spun to see the Baron of Cutter's Hollow looming over them. Briar tensed, but he accepted the hand the giant man stuck out at him. The baron yanked, pulling him into a great bear hug.

Briar scrambled back out of reach when he let go, and the man turned to Ragen and Elissa, staring openmouthed at the scene. "Boy saved my life. Night, lost count of the lives he's saved."

"You'da killed that corie," Briar said.

The baron shrugged. "Ay, maybe, but it would've taken a chunk of me with it."

"For a boy that lives in the woods, he seems to make a lot of powerful friends." Ragen put out a hand, and he and Gared clasped forearms. "Ragen, Warders' Guildmaster of Fort Miln." He swept a hand next to him. "This is my wife, Mother Elissa, daughter of Countess Tresha of Morning County in Miln, and head of the Milnese Warding Exchange."

Elissa couldn't remember the last time she'd needed to curtsy, but the move was ingrained still. "A pleasure to meet you, Baron."

"Lord Arther's got his hands full today," Gared said. "Sent me to fetch ya for Mistress Leesha." He led them through a series of halls, past the formal receiving rooms, and into a residential wing. "Mistress had a babe this past week. Likes to keep it close."

"I'm surprised she's seeing us at all, if it's been just a week," Elissa said.

"Briar says yur important, so yur important," Gared said as they came up to a door guarded by one of the biggest women Elissa had ever seen. Even indoors, she had a bow over her shoulder and a small quiver of arrows on her hip.

"'Scuse me a minute. Need to make sure she ent . . ." His face reddened. "Feedin' or anythin'."

Elissa swallowed her smile. Men could face demons and Krasians and everything else the world could throw at them, but a suckling babe was still too much for many of them to bear witness to.

He spoke to the guard, and she slipped inside, returning a moment later with permission to enter. The office was spacious, with great windows, their heavy curtains thrown back to let in the morning sun. The Mistress of the Hollow was seated on a throne behind a gigantic desk of carved and polished goldwood, but she rose as they entered, coming around to embrace Briar, heedless of his dirty clothes and everpresent smell. She held him a long time, kissing the top of his head, and Elissa knew then this was a woman she could trust.

Briar looked up as they parted, seeing the cradle in the back corner of the room behind the desk. "That . . . ?"

"Olive," the countess said. "My daughter."

A wide smile broke out on Briar's face. "Can I . . . ?"

"Of course," the countess said. "But quietly now. I've only just gotten her to sleep." She turned to the others as Briar crept over, silent as a cat.

"Welcome to the Hollow, Mother, Guildmaster. Will you take tea?"

"Thank you, my lady," Elissa said, reaching for her skirts.

The countess waved dismissively as she led them to couches around a tea table. "Please, call me Leesha. Briar's told me what you've done for the Laktonians. There's no need for formality here."

"We did what any in our position would have," Ragen said, "for all the good it did."

"Most in your position would have fled home, not spent the better part of the year helping refugees and the resistance," Leesha said as a servant poured the tea. "And I think the folk building the borough of New Lakton would say you did quite a bit of good."

"You've done your research, mistress," Elissa said.

"I like to be informed," Leesha said.

"Our condolences for your loss," Ragen said. "Halfgrip's fame extended to Miln and beyond. The power your people held in the night with his songs was . . . staggering."

"We would like to take the music back to Miln," Elissa said. "It could safeguard travelers, caravans . . ."

Leesha nodded. "Of course. Nothing would honor Rojer's memory more than spreading his music far and wide. We'll send written music back with you for your Jongleurs."

Elissa bowed. "Thank you, mistress. That is most gracious."

"It's the least we can do, considering our friend in common," Leesha said.

Elissa raised an eyebrow. "Briar?"

Leesha shook her head. "The boy Ragen found on the road many years ago, and you raised as your own. Arlen Bales."

Gared dropped his teacup, and it shattered on the floor.

"Do you think he's still alive?" Elissa asked.

"Course he is," Baron Cutter said. "Deliverer, ent he?"

"No one in all the world loves Arlen Bales more than I," Elissa said. "He was a brilliant boy, and he grew into an amazing man. But I've dried his tears and cleaned his sick. Argued when he was stubborn and seen him err. Saw the hurts he carried and how he blamed himself for them. I don't know if I can ever see him as the Deliverer."

"It's irrelevant in any event," Leesha said. "Deliverer or no, he's set the world on a path we all need to walk."

"That ent the Deliverer's job, dunno what is," Wonda said. "I'll eat my bow and the quiver besides, he ent alive. Folk seen him on the road, helping those fleeing Lakton."

"No one saw his face," Leesha said. "That could as easily have been Renna."

"Arlen's wife," Elissa said. There were many regrets in her life, but missing the wedding cut deep. If any man deserved a bit of happiness in his life, it was Arlen Bales.

"Night, that's right," Ragen said. "Didn't think any woman could settle that boy down. What's she like?"

A pained look flickered over Leesha's face, and Elissa gave him a subtle kick. Arlen had spoken of Leesha and what they shared—a spark doused by fear and panic.

Ragen lacked subtlety, but he wasn't wrong. It wasn't the first time Arlen Bales had fled a woman offering something too joyful for his tortured soul to bear. What kind of woman had finally reached him?

"Renna Bales saved my life," Gared said. "Saved us all, when the Deliverer fell."

"Fell?" Ragen asked. "Over the cliff with the demon of the desert?"

The baron shook his head. "'Fore that. When the minds came for the Hollow on new moon. Went out with Rojer and Renna to scout, and we found a world of trouble. Mind demons were digging greatwards of their own."

"Night," Ragen said. "Corelings can ward?"

"Only the minds, it seems," Leesha said, "but their warding makes ours look like a child's scrawl."

"Fought like mad, but there were too many of 'em," the baron went on. "Only made it back slung over Renna's shoulder. Rojer told Mr. Bales what we saw and he jumped into the sky."

"What?" Elissa asked.

"Took off like a bird," Wonda said. "Thousands saw him, floating in the sky, throwin' lightning at the demons like the Creator Himself."

Ragen looked to Elissa. "How's that possible?"

"He was Drawing off the greatward," Leesha said. "Pulling massive amounts of power and throwing it at the demon wards before they could activate fully. But even a greatward has limits."

"One moment he was glowin' like the sun, then . . ." Wonda blew a breath. "Out like a candle. Fell and cracked like an egg on the cobbles."

Elissa gasped, covering her mouth with her hands.

"Thought everythin' was lost then," Gared said. "No one was givin' up, but there wern't much hope. But then Renna Bales stepped up. Held the last line when every defense was broke. Held it until Mr. Bales came back to us. Two o' them held hands as the tide came in, and threw it back into the night."

"Ent dead," Wonda said. "Man who can walk away from that . . ."

Leesha pursed her lips, then nodded to herself, getting to her feet. "Bar the door, Gar. Wonda, the curtains."

Ragen, Elissa, and Briar watched in confusion as they were locked into the room and cloaked in darkness. Leesha unlocked a drawer in her desk, producing what looked like a large piece of obsidian, but they could well guess what it was, even before she fitted it into a slot on the wall and a wardnet sprang up around them. It circled the room and crisscrossed the ceiling and floor, casting them all in gentle wardlight.

"No sound will escape the room." Leesha returned to her seat, taking her teacup and sipping thoughtfully. "What I say here must never be repeated."

"Swear by the sun," Gared said.

"Course, mistress," Wonda added. Briar grunted his agreement.

Ragen took Elissa's hand. "You have our word."

"Renna Bales came to me the night we learned the Krasians attacked Lakton," Leesha said. "She told me Arlen is alive."

"Knew it!" Wonda burst, even as Gared roared a laugh, bringing his hands together in a resounding smack.

"Creator be praised," Ragen whispered, but Elissa said nothing, knowing there was more.

"She also told me they would not come again," Leesha said. "They'd become too powerful, and were drawing the minds' attention to the Hollow, just as Ahmann was doing in Krasia. We needed time to grow our defenses, and so he left to give us that."

"Said it himself," Gared said. "Told Jardir he was the last piece of business before he took the fight to the Core."

"What does that mean?" Ragen asked.

"Arlen can mist as the demons do," Leesha said. "Renna, too, the last time I saw her. He told me he could hear the Core calling to him, could slip down into it like a coreling at dawn."

She shook her head sadly. "But he didn't seem to think much of his chances if he tried."

"Better chance'n any of us," Gared said.

Ragen kept his composure, but he was squeezing Elissa's hand so hard it hurt. She laid her other hand gently atop his, and his tension eased. "Gared's right. How many times has Arlen cheated death? He'll turn up again, just when we've given up, and start the worry afresh."

Ragen laughed. "Ay, that's my boy."

"In the meantime, we need to do as he asked, and grow strong," Leesha said. "Not something we can do if we're more concerned with killing one another than the corelings."

"We didn't bring that fight, mistress," Ragen said. "The Krasians believe Sharak Ka is coming, and the Evejah tells them the only hope mankind has to survive is for all the world to kneel before the Skull Throne."

"They brought the fight," Leesha agreed, "but it's been brewing for years. Euchor didn't build his flamework weapons and train men in their use overnight."

"No," Ragen agreed. "He's long had his eye on subjugating the ivy throne and reuniting Thesa under his rule, but he would never have struck first."

"The question then," Leesha said, "is will he be content to stop at Angiers now that he has it, or will he use the Krasians as an excuse to press south and claim all the Free Cities as his own?"

Elissa exchanged another look with Ragen. "He will press. And expect you to follow and thank him for the privilege. The Hollow is too powerful for him to suffer at his doorstep when Angiers gives him a claim to it."

"Gettin' tired of folk who ent ever bled for the Hollow marchin' in and expecting us to bow and scrape," Gared said.

"You won't have to," Leesha said. "Euchor's weapons won't work as well here as he thinks."

"Because of you," Elissa said. "Because of your magic."

Leesha nodded. "I have wardings that can render their chemics inert. Flamework weapons are not welcome in my lands."

"Will you teach us something of this bone magic, and how the *hora* is preserved?" Elissa asked.

Gared and Wonda looked to their mistress, but Leesha did not hesitate. "Of course. After all, who do you think taught me?"

She looked to Ragen. "I know you have retired as a Royal Messenger, Guildmaster, but I beg you take one last commission and act as my voice in Miln before His Grace, Duke Euchor."

Ragen bowed. "I would be honored, mistress. His Grace will be expecting a full report from us upon our return. You have my word I will hold secrets given me in confidence, and negotiate in good faith on your behalf."

Leesha bowed in return. "The honor is mine. We can discuss details in the coming days. For now, I invite the three of you to transfer your belongings here to my keep."

"Thank you, mistress," Elissa said. "We gladly accept."

"S'fine," Briar said. "Got a briarpatch in Gatherers' Wood."

Leesha looked up at that. "You're sleeping in my wood?"

"Ay," Briar said.

"Do you know my Warded Children?" Leesha asked.

Briar nodded. "Seen 'em lots of times. Live in the night like me. Brave, but . . ." He searched for a word. "Angry."

"Will you look in on them for me tonight?" Leesha asked. "I've been away some time, and would like to know what I can expect when I visit them."

Briar nodded. "Ay."

CHAPTER 5

THE PACK

334 AR

Briar padded on bare feet through the Gatherers' Wood. The soft leather boots he wore out of respect for Mistress Leesha's carpets were laced together and slung over his shoulder under his father's battered shield.

Bare feet told much that boots could not. Where footing was sure and silent. The residual warmth where prey had been. The rush of nearby water. The thrum of hurried feet. Things that made you part of the night, instead of something clumsily passing through it. Things that could mean your life.

Briar loved the Gatherers' Wood. Too vast to conform to magic's shape, it was one of the few places in Hollow County not protected by a greatward. After dark, wood demons roamed the boughs and prowled the forest bed. Water demons swam its ponds. Wind demons skimmed the wider paths and circled above the clearings.

But even amid the wild nature, Briar could see how Mistress Leesha was shaping the wood from within. Some changes, like warded crete walkways and posts, were obvious to all, safe as sunlight. Others, their power shaped by natural features and cultivated plants, were so subtle the unwary might never know they were under the mistress' protection.

It was why Briar trusted Mistress Leesha so implicitly. She had taken the time to understand the cories. How a certain slick moss on the branches could make wood demons avoid a copse of trees, or a patch of dry ground limit how far a bog demon might range. How fruit and nut trees drew cories in search of prey, and other plants urged them away.

Briar helped as he wandered the wood, cutting hogroot stalks and planting them in strategic places. There was a wild patch growing in a ring around an ancient goldwood tree, limbs hanging over the stalks like a parent bending to embrace a child. A half-frozen stream ran through the patch, eroding beneath the thick roots. It created a small hollow Briar could widen and expand, the moist soil pungent enough to drive off demon and human alike.

He grew the wood's protections with love and harmony, leaving no sign of his shaping hand. The wood returned his love, providing sustenance and shelter from the cories.

The Warded Children were less delicate. Here and there Briar found signs of their passing, scattered like trash in the street. Broken limbs, trampled plants, wardings carved into the living bark of great trees. Some of their traps were cunning enough to catch a demon, but most were so obvious even cories could spot them.

Still, Briar had seen them fight. For all their clumsiness, the Children had power in the night. It would be foolish to underestimate them. Mistress Leesha was wise to want to learn more.

Briar drew near his patch, but he never went directly to the entrance. He circled, checking the defenses. Like Mistress Leesha, he preferred stinks to snares, urging demons gently away. A few shoots of hogroot, transplanted and allowed to grow wild, were enough to turn a stalking demon onto another path.

Other scents had a similar effect on humans. Even the brave souls living in the Gatherers' Wood hesitated to step into a patch of skunkweed, or a place reeking of rot. In one place, a diverted stream turned the path into sucking mud that woodies and humans alike would avoid.

Everything seemed in order, until he found a fresh snare. It was an area he'd littered months ago with animal carcasses stuffed with hogroot. Unlike plants and diverted streams, some deterrents had to be maintained. The carcasses were gone and Briar saw signs demons had returned to the area.

The trap was a good example of the craft, evidence that at least one of the Warded Children had claimed this place as a hunting ground. The child knew enough to use the deterrents around the Briarpatch to herd the demon into the path of the hidden snare. The loop lay in a shallow groove dug into the soil, covered lightly with the natural detritus of the forest bed.

The rope had been rubbed with sap and dirtied, leaved twigs stuck along its length to give the impression of natural vine as it disappeared into the branches of a wintergreen tree. Briar had to climb the boughs to find the net holding the counterweights.

Even the wary might be caught in so cleverly hidden a trap, but Briar knew this part of the wood intimately, and the snare stood out to him as if ablaze. It was discomfiting—so close to where he laid his head—but it made Mistress Leesha's request all the easier to fulfill. At dusk, the hunter would be positioned and waiting. All Briar had to do was watch.

Briar woke to darkness in his sleeping hole, but after a decade living without wards, he could sense the approaching night like a chill.

It was no great space, but every time he returned, Briar dug a little more, added a vent, or shored the packed dirt. The walls and floor were lined with tough, dried hogroot stalks—comfortable to lie upon and resistant to water. Even if the entrance was discovered, the scent would keep cories from investigating further.

Stretching, he listened carefully, checking his spyholes one by one. When he was confident no one was about, Briar lifted the trap just enough to slither into the center of his hogroot patch.

As its name implied, the roots of the plant were aggressive, knitting a thick sod that pulled up like a carpet. He quickly and carefully smoothed the trap back down, strewing leaves to obscure the faint impression.

Here and there Briar snapped off leaves as he made his way through the patch, leaving minimal sign of his harvest. Some he ate, filling his pockets with the rest. There was another trapdoor away from the sleeping den where he made his water and squatted out his night soil.

Making his way to the snare, he was surprised to see the hunter in plain sight, not bothering to hide as she waited by the rope with a ready knife.

Mistress Leesha said Stela Inn wasn't much older than him, but she was taller, looking more a grown woman than he felt a man. Magic had made her body hard, and she wore little to cover it. A loincloth. A binding around her breast. A leather headband.

Her bare skin was inked with wards. The pattern started on her feet, winding up her calves and thighs, twisting about her midsection, then slithering down her arms. Looking at her, Briar felt his chest tighten and his face heat.

He shook it off, circling the area. He expected to find other hunters in hiding to assist, but after several minutes he became convinced Stela was alone.

It was curious. In his experience, the Children hunted as a pack. This was something new.

Slipping quietly behind her, Briar shimmied up the far side of the tree holding the counterweights. From its boughs he could study Stela while keeping view of the surrounding area.

She carried neither spear nor shield, though a number of pouches and ornaments hung beside the knife sheath on her belt. Stela froze as full dark fell, but made no other effort to conceal herself.

There was an unmistakable crunch as the wood demon that claimed this part of the forest lumbered down the path Stela had laid with fresh carcasses. Briar kept expecting her to hide, but she remained in plain sight. Did she mean to use herself to bait the trap?

But as the corie approached, it showed no sign it saw her. The wards on Stela's flesh had taken on a soft glow, and the demon's eyes slid past like she wasn't there.

It was a good trick. The corie moved past her, oblivious as it stepped into the snare.

Stela moved fast, kicking the back of the corie's knee, driving it into the ground. She spun like a dancer, whipping her knife through the rope that held the counterweight. Laden with heavy stones, the net dropped and the noose caught the woodie at the knee, yanking it to swing upside down. Stela had measured well. The demon's flailing talons scraped the air just above the ground.

Stela tamped down as the corie's body swung her way, eyes hard as she watched its claws. When it swung back in, she shot forward, slapping its branchlike arm aside to step inside its guard. Close in, she delivered a quick combination of punches and elbows, blows flashing with magic. Before it could recover, she push-kicked it back out of reach.

She skittered back and forth three more times, controlling the battlespace fully as she kept the corie disoriented, hitting it again and again.

But wood demons were strong, their armor thick. She could cause the demon pain and some temporary hurt, but its magic would heal those quickly unless she brought her endgame. Briar glanced at the knife, still sheathed on her belt.

She's charging her wards, he realized. The symbols glowed a little brighter each time she struck, and instead of tiring, Stela seemed to get faster, stronger. She floated in, changing her combinations and skittering away before the demon could land a blow in return. She treated it like the practice dummy Briar's father had built in their yard to train his sons in *sharusahk.*

Patterns began to emerge, telling Briar much about Stela. Her reach, how she moved, the language of her body. Useful to know if he ever needed to fight her.

Everam, never let it be so, he prayed. Stela grew fiercer with the brightness of her wards. Soon each blow lit the darkness like a bolt of lightning, the thunderous report echoing through the trees.

It seemed she would beat the woodie to death, but the demon still thrashed when the light and sound drew unwanted attention. Briar watched as a field demon clawed its way up into one of the surrounding trees with a vantage not much different from his own. Its eyes tracked her movements as Briar had, seeking the pattern.

The corie tamped its haunches. Briar knew well how far fieldies could leap. In one bound it could be on her back.

As the demon sprang, Briar gave a cry, throwing his shield. The corie looked up at the sound a split second before the shield struck, wards flaring as it knocked the demon away. Stela looked up, too, eyes widening as she saw Briar drop from the tree.

Stela stepped out of reach of the swinging wood demon. The snared corie took the opportunity to swipe at the rope, but there were tiny wardplates tied along its length, sparking to deflect its talons.

The knife was in Stela's hand now, but again she froze in place, wards glowing. The demons blinked at her, eyes unable to focus. After a moment she took three quick, sliding steps to the left. The cories' eyes searched where she had last been.

But while Stela was safe, the demons had no trouble seeing Briar, who had foolishly dropped into their midst, meaning to rush to her aid.

The field demon pounced, and Briar didn't have time to bring the point of his spear to bear. He gave the corie a good whack with the shaft, knocking it aside as he rolled out of the way.

The demon leapt again, but stumbled as Stela stomped a foot on its tail. A sweep of her knife severed the appendage, covering Stela in a spurt of black ichor.

The demon's ichor sparked and sizzled when it touched the wards running over her skin. Power flickered through the net, and her face turned feral. As the demon whirled on her she kicked it in the face, knocking it aside. "Who in the Core are you?!"

Briar had no time to answer. He pointed with his spear. "Look out!"

With a mighty heave, the wood demon had reached high enough to sever the rope. It tumbled down with a crash, even as the field demon shook itself off and began to circle.

Stela was on the woodie before it could recover, impact wards on her palms flaring with a boom as she boxed its ears. Discombobulated, it could not stop her from quickstepping behind its back. She whipped a string of warded beads around its neck, pulling tight. The demon surged back to its feet, Stela's feet swinging in open air, but she kept the hold, cord wrapped tight around her fists.

A growl brought Briar's attention back to the immediate danger as the field demon stalked in. Briar growled back and the demon hissed at him, eyes wide as Briar spit juice from the hogroot leaf he'd been chewing in its face.

The fieldie fell back shrieking. Briar raised his spear to finish it off, but he was checked by a cry from behind. The wood demon stumbled back and smashed Stela into a tree, knocking her breathless to the ground.

The field demon would recover quickly, but Briar turned and ran for the woodie as it raised a talon to slash at the helpless woman. He gave a cry, distracting it just long enough for him to put his spear into its back.

The wards on the weapon flared and magic rushed into Briar, thrilling him from fingers to toes. The demon lashed out, but already Briar was faster. He sidestepped one blow, raising the shaft of the spear, its tip still embedded in the demon, to bat another aside. Still the magic flowed, draining the corie's strength even as it made Briar feel invincible. He pulled the spear free then thrust it again, ducking a return blow and stabbing a third time. His face twisted into a snarl and he shouted unintelligible things, reveling in the demon's pain as its life-force flowed into him.

Stela's cry brought him back. She and the field demon rolled in the dirt, locked in fierce combat. Her sides were streaked with blood from its raking talons, and she held its jaws at bay with one hand, warded thumb sizzling in its eye socket, as she punched with the other.

Briar ducked another swing of the woodie's arms, coming up fast to thrust under the demon's chin and up into its brain. It jerked and thrashed, pulling the spear from his grasp as it fell to the ground, dead.

Briar whirled to help Stela, but she had rolled atop the demon now, accepting its raking claws as she stabbed repeatedly with her warded dagger. Soon the corie lay still.

Briar rushed to her side, examining her wounds.

He met her eyes. "Cut up bad."

Stela shook her head, putting a hand under her. "Just scratches. Magic'll close them up." She made it halfway to her feet, then hissed in pain, stumbling.

Briar slid under her arm, catching her.

She turned to face him. "You're the Mudboy, ent you? The one that guided the count to Docktown." She spat on the ground, and Briar wasn't sure if it was meant for him or Docktown, the place now synonymous with failure and loss.

"Briar," he growled. "Don't like *Mudboy.*"

Stela wheezed a chuckle. "Ay, don't bite my head off, I didn't know. We all get saddled with nicknames we hate. If I snapped at everyone called me Stelly, my brothers and sisters would only do it more."

"Ay." Briar's siblings had been no different.

"Know a place we can rest a bit, Briar?" Stela asked.

Briar nodded. With Stela hunting so close, he was going to have to abandon his Briarpatch in any event. No harm taking her there now. "Safe place. Ent far."

Stela's eyes widened as he led her into the hogroot patch. "There's paths." She looked back. "You'd never see them from the outside."

"Cories won't come in," Briar said. "Hogroot makes 'em sick up."

"That what you spit in that demon's face?" Stela asked.

Briar nodded.

"No wonder your breath smells like an Herb Gatherer's farts," Stela said.

Briar laughed. It was a good joke.

"Thought you found my hunting spot," Stela said. "Guess it was the other way around."

Briar shook his head. "Don't hunt cories. Only bother 'em when they bother me."

"You bother pretty well when they do," Stela noted.

Briar shrugged, setting her down before disappearing into his hole. He returned with his herb pouch to clean the wounds, but Stela was right. Her superficial scrapes had healed, and the shallower cuts had scabbed over. Only a few needed stitches. When it was done, he ground a hogroot paste to spread on the wounds.

"Night!" Stela barked. "That stings!"

"Better'n demon fever," Briar said. "Long night, even if you fight it off."

Stela grit her teeth, allowing him to continue. "Must be lonely by yourself. No Pack to hunt with and keep you warm at night."

"Got family," Briar said.

Stela looked about dubiously. "Here?"

"In town," Briar said.

"Then why ent you with them?" Stela asked.

"Don't like walls."

"Arlen Bales said they make folk forget what's out in the night," Stela agreed.

"Can't forget," Briar said. "Never forget."

"I've got family behind walls, too," Stela said. "Love 'em, but they ent Pack. Maybe after I rest a bit, you'll come meet them."

"They're so great, why do you hunt alone?" Briar asked.

Stela chuckled. "Pack's like brothers and sisters. Die for 'em, but sometimes they drive you rippin' crazy."

It was more than ten years since Briar lost his family to the night, but he remembered. How his brothers and sisters tormented him. How he hated them. How he would give anything to have them back.

"Corespawn it!" Stela hissed as she looked down at his stitches. "Just had those inked, and already I need them retouched." She pushed her loincloth down for a better look at the damage to the tattooed wards, and Briar felt his face heat. He turned away.

Stela caught his chin, turning his face back to hers. She was grinning like she knew a secret. "Got anything to eat? Killing demons always makes me hungry." She winked. "Among other things."

Briar broke off some hogroot leaves, offering them to her.

Stela's eyes rolled. "Please tell me that ent all you got. Din't even wash it."

Briar popped one of the leaves into his mouth. "Good for you. Fills your belly and keeps the cories away."

Stela looked doubtful, but she took the leaves. "Mum always said, *Only way to kiss a man who eats garlic is to eat some yourself.*"

She bit into one and grimaced. "Tastes like a bog demon's spunk."

Briar laughed. "Ay."

"Gets in the nose." Stela swallowed and popped another leaf into her mouth. "Can't smell much else."

"Get used to it."

"Better'n a lot of the Children. Half the Pack ent bathed in a month, and fighting demons works up a stink." Stela pointed to the uneven sod of Briar's trapdoor. "That where you sleep?"

Briar nodded.

"Big enough for two?" she asked.

Hogroot stalks crunched as Briar pressed himself against the wall, but however far he backed away, Stela snuggled closer. She faced away, round hips pressing against him. The air in the den was hot despite the night's chill.

Not knowing what to do with his arms, he put them around her, hands thrilling at the feel of her skin. She shifted, giving him a noseful of hair. He inhaled reflexively, and the scent of her was overwhelming. He felt movement in his breeches and tried to pull back, lest she notice.

But Stela gave a sound that was part chuckle, part growl, grinding her bottom into it. Briar groaned, and she rolled suddenly to face him.

"You don't hunt," she said, reaching down between his legs and squeezing, "but killin' demons gets you stiff as any man."

She pushed him onto his back and Briar froze, not knowing what to do. If there had been room he would have fled into the night, but the den was cramped, and she had him pinned. He did nothing as she pulled the ties on his breeches and set him free. Before he realized what was happening, she raised her hips and took him in hand, sitting down hard.

He gasped, grabbing her hips, but Stela was in control and it was all he could do to hold on as she began grinding.

"Ay!" Briar cried, his limbs going rigid.

Stela kissed him, biting his lip. "Don't you dare!" she growled. "I ent there yet!"

Briar squealed as something uncontrollable came over him. He thrashed, bucking and kicking, spurting inside her.

He expected Stela to be angry, but she gave that laughing growl and pressed down harder as he spasmed. "Ay, I can work with that. Hold on tight." She gripped his shoulder, putting her full weight on him. She scratched and bit, but it seemed right somehow, and he held her tight as she bucked against him.

They lay panting and clutching at each other, the air thick and stifling. Stela wriggled, feeling him still inside her, still hard.

She kissed him. "Creator be praised. Ent done by a long sight. Put me on my back."

Briar swallowed. "I . . . I don't . . ."

Stela laughed and grabbed him, locking him with her legs and rolling until he was atop her.

"Relax." She kissed him again. "Take your time. Both got a good dose of magic in that scrap. Gonna be hard and wet all night. Might as well make the most of it."

It was some time before they finally began to drift off. Stela clutched Briar's arm, keeping it around her like a blanket as she snored. They lay curled together, skin melded by sweat, and Briar felt something he had all but forgotten.

Safe.

He remembered sleeping in his parents' bed, six years old, nestled warm between them. The night he had woken and thought there was a coreling in the house. The night he stoked up the fire to drive the shadows away, forgetting to open the flue.

The night his family burned.

Briar remembered the black silhouette of their cottage, outlined in bright orange. The billowing, choking smoke that filled the air as he cowered in the hogroot patch.

Demons flitted about in the firelight, waiting for the wards to fail. The Damaj family was already screaming when they broke in the door.

Briar jerked awake, thumping his head against the ceiling of his den.

"Whazzat?" Stela moaned, but Briar couldn't breathe. The walls were closing in on him. He had to get out. Get out or die.

He pulled away while Stela was still confused, grabbing at his clothes as he scrambled out the trap.

Outside, he could breathe again. He filled great lungfuls with the cold night air, but it never seemed to be enough. His chest constricted, muscles knotting. He paced around, swinging his arms about to reassure himself there were no walls around him.

His senses were on fire, taking in every sight, every sound. The breeze on the leaves and stalks. The quiet rustle of nocturnal life. The distant cries of demons. He was aware of everything, ready to react in an instant to any threat. His fists were bunched, and he almost wished there was a threat just so he could release the tension, building and building until he thought he would tear himself apart.

He heard the trap open and considered running into the night before Stela found him.

"Briar?" she called. "You all right?"

"Ay," Briar said, though he felt anything but.

"It's all sunny," Stela said. "Don't need to explain. Know how you feel."

Briar put his back to her, peering into the night. "No one knows."

"Started to relax, ay?" Stela asked. "Then remembered what happens to folk that relax. Chest got tight. Hard to breathe. Maybe felt like the walls were closing in. Had to get out into the open air, and been pacing like a chained nightwolf."

Briar looked at her. "How could you . . ."

"Got the flux last year," Stela said. "Half the town was falling down with it. Folk dropping candles and knocking over lamps. Fires everywhere."

"Fire brings the cories," Briar said. "Watch and wait for the wards to fail."

Stela nodded. "Stayed in Grandda's inn till smoke filled the room, then stumbled out into the night with my little sister and my uncle Keet. Keet was half carryin' me, and we were slow. Demons would've had us . . ."

She turned away, breathing hard, and Briar went to her. He reached out, not knowing what to say, and she leaned into him.

"But my sister stumbled," Stela went on. "Got her instead."

She looked back at him, eyes wet. "Ent just you that hates walls, Briar. Ent just you that wakes with a jump and can't seem to breathe. Arlen Bales talks of it in the New Canon."

"New Canon?" Briar asked.

"Brother Franq's been talking to everyone ever met Arlen and Renna Bales," Stela said. "Making copies of their teachings so we don't ever forget again."

She turned in his arms. "Ent alone, Briar. Everyone in the Pack feels it. We've all lost someone, all seen up close what the night can do. Makes us different from folk in town, but we're there for each other. Can be there for you, too, you let us."

Briar nodded. He could not imagine wanting anything more.

Briar knew the way to the Warded Children's camp, but he let Stela lead, drifting along in her wake. It was still dark and the magic tingled inside him, his senses on fire. He floated along, following her as much by scent as sight.

Stela. He felt drunk at the thought of her.

Briar could hear the camp a mile off. By the time they were close, the chatter of it filled the woods. There was a bark ahead, and Briar saw a huge wolfhound leap atop a stone on the path. Moments later a guard appeared.

All the Hollowers were taller than Briar, but this one towered nearly a foot over him, with biceps the size of Briar's head. He wore wooden armor—helm, breastplate, gauntlets, and greaves, warded and lacquered. At his waist hung a three-foot spear, demon ichor still smoking against the wards on its broad silver blade.

"Ay, Stela!" the giant cried. "Nearly dawn! Where in the dark of night you been?"

Stela laughed, shoving him aside. "Needed a few hours away from your donkey smell, Callen Cutter." Callen gave the ground, if grudgingly. Briar could see with his night eyes that she was dominant.

"Who the Core's this?" Callen slapped a hand at Briar as he followed in Stela's wake. Briar seized his wrist and pulled, twisting the blow into a throw that flipped the larger man onto the ground. The wolfhound growled, crouching to spring, but Briar met its eyes and growled right back, checking it.

There were close to a hundred people in the camp. A few were children and elders, but most were of an age with

Briar—not yet twenty. Briar saw Milnese faces and Angierian, Rizonan, Laktonian, even Krasian. Some wore robes or
bits of armor; others bared warded flesh to the limits of decency.

Now every eye was on Briar, pinning him with the weight
of their collective stare. He wanted to flee, but Stela took his
hand and gave a reassuring squeeze. Callen got back to his
feet, face a thundercloud, but Stela snarled and he held back.

Stela cast her eyes over the crowd. "This is Briar Damaj!
The one Gared said saved His Highness on the road."

"Then led him to his death." A bearded man stepped forward, his thick brown hair pulled back to show a mind ward
tattooed on his forehead. He wore a Tender's brown robes
covered in needlepoint wards, and carried a carved crooked
staff. "I remember him. Mudboy. The Krasian traitor."

Briar bared his teeth. "Ent a traitor. Laktonian. Ent my fault
I look like them."

Stela gave his hand another squeeze. "Mudboy," she confirmed loudly. "But anyone other than me calls him that,
they'll be doing it with missing teeth. We shed ichor together.
He is Pack."

Pack. The word sang to him, but looking at the staring
faces, he knew it would take more than words to make it so.

"That how it works now?" The speaker wasn't as tall as
Callen, lanky instead of broad. His armor was lighter as well,
wards burned into boiled leather. He and Stela shared a resemblance. He pointed at Briar with his short spear, wards on
its blade glowing with inner power. "You decide who's Pack
and who's not?"

Stela put her hands on her hips. "Keep pointing that spear
at me, *Uncle* Keet." She used the honorific mockingly. "Everyone's here to see me shove it up your arse."

Keet hesitated. His eyes flicked about for support, but there
was little to be had. Few in the camp wanted anything to do
with this confrontation. They kept their eyes down, though all
were watching with interest. Callen still glared at Briar, but
even he seemed unwilling to challenge Stela directly.

Stela leaned in, and Keet reflexively leaned back. "Briar is
Pack."

After a moment, Keet dropped his eyes. "You want to make him a Wardskin, ent my business."

"We'll initiate him," Stela agreed. "But he can find his own path after that. Once folk see what Briar can do, might be some folk start calling themselves Mudboys."

Briar scowled, and Stela winked. "Better than Hogbreaths."

Briar laughed in spite of himself.

"We all must find our own path." The man in Tender's robe stepped up to Briar. Stela's grip on his hand tightened painfully, but the man only bowed.

"Welcome, Briar. I am Brother Franq."

Stela's grip on his hand eased, and the rest of the Warded Children followed suit. Callen and Keet might not have been able to challenge Stela, but this man could. "You're the one writing New Canon."

Franq dismissed the thought with a wave. "The words belong to Arlen and Renna Bales. I merely record them."

"And help us find their meaning," Stela said.

Franq bowed to Briar a second time. "I apologize for calling you traitor. The Tenders of the Creator taught me to judge, but Arlen Bales has shown us a better way. All who stand together in the night are brothers and sisters. We are all Deliverers."

All around the camp, people drew wards in the air, echoing his word. "All Deliverers."

"Mistress Leesha had us split into three groups at first," Stela said as she walked Briar through the camp. "Strongest were training to join the Cutters one day. Mistress gave them all specially warded spears, short to make the Draw more efficient. We call 'em gut pumps, because you stick one in a demon's gut and it pumps magic into you. Callen leads the Pumps."

Briar turned his head slightly, examining Callen's faction as Stela gestured to another cluster. "Keet's group was runtier—most of them tried out for the Cutters and got passed over. Call them Bones, because the mistress put slivers of demon bone in their spears. Makes up the difference in muscle, and to spare.

"My group were folk who had no illusions about being fit to fight demons." Stela nodded to another cluster, mostly young women dressed as sparsely as Stela. "Not strong enough to swing an axe or wind a crank bow like Wonda's set." She held up her warded hand. "Mistress honored us most of all. Warded our very skin."

"Mistress Leesha tattooed you?" Briar asked.

Stela shook her head. "Drew them on with blackstem, but then she went away. When the stain started to fade, I asked Ella Cutter to take a needle and ink them on permanent before they were lost."

Briar watched how the others in the camp gave the Wardskins a respectable berth. Though generally smaller in stature, they moved like predators, even here.

"Children have grown since then," Stela said. "Widows and heirs of the *Sharum* lost at new moon." She gestured to the tents and water well used by the Krasian faction. They were not in battle, but every one of them had their night veils up, even the men. Briar noted on closer inspection that several of them had the light skin of Northerners, but had adopted Krasian dress and manner.

"Then Brother Franq joined us and started training Siblings." She gestured to a smaller group, all in plain brown robes.

A tall woman stepped to the front of the cluster of Krasians, waving to them. The hair that fell from her headwrap was streaked with gray, her eyes full of wisdom, but she did not move like an elder. She was strong.

Stela led Briar to her, bowing. "Briar, this is Jarit, First Wife of Drillmaster Kaval. She leads the Pack's *Sharum*."

The woman studied Briar, trying to peel away the dirt and hogroot resin to see the features beneath. "What is your name?" she asked in Krasian.

"Briar asu Relan am'Damaj am'Bogger," Briar replied.

"*Damaj* is a Kaji name," Jarit noted. "Yet you claim not to be one of us?"

"Born and raised in Bogton," Briar said.

Jarit nodded. "I remember when your father went missing. The men of Kaji searched for him in the city and Maze, not knowing if he had died on *alagai* talons or fallen to a Majah blade. Who could have guessed he fled to the North?"

"You knew my father?" Briar asked.

Jarit shook her head. "No, but my husband was the Kaji's greatest drillmaster. I learned much in his house."

"Jarit and her granddaughter Shalivah started teaching us *sharusahk*," Stela said, "after Wonda Cutter left with Mistress Leesha." At the comment a girl of ten appeared. She seemed more like Jarit's daughter than her granddaughter, but Briar knew how magic could shave years from a person. He looked around the well, realizing how many of the Krasians were children. Two young Krasian men wore the brown robes of Siblings with added night veils.

"Tender converted you, like my father," Briar guessed.

"We still pray to Everam," Jarit said.

Briar nodded. "My father said Everam was the Creator, and the Creator was Everam."

Jarit smiled. "Your father was a wise man. We have not been converted by Tenders, or they by us. All of us saw Arlen Bales cast lightning from the sky when Alagai Ka came on Waning. If there remained any doubt, it vanished when Arlen Bales cast Ahmann Jardir down in *Domin Sharum*. The son of Hoshkamin was a false Deliverer. The son of Jeph is Shar'Dama Ka, and we must be ready for his call."

Briar grunted, having no real response. He nodded to the rising sun. "Why do your men keep their veils up?"

"Everam commands modesty in His light," Jarit said. "Arlen Bales showed us that it is when we face Nie that we must bare ourselves and stand proudly against Her."

"Don't let the modesty fool you," Stela said as they walked back to the Wardskins' camp. "Pity the corelings when Jarit and her *Sharum* drop their veils."

Briar spat. "Ent got pity to spare, comes to cories."

"Honest word." Stela gave his hand another squeeze, sending a thrill through him. "Come on. We've got work to do, if we're going to initiate you tonight."

"What work?" Briar asked.

They came up to a blond girl weaving her long hair. She could not have been much older than Stela. Like the other

Wardskins, she was clad in little more than a few scraps of leather, tattoos twining about her limbs and body.

"This here is Ella Cutter," Stela said. The young woman gave Briar an appraising glance but kept her nimble fingers about the braiding. "Ella's our best tattooist."

Ella smiled. "Bath and a shave first. Need a clean canvas."

Stela waved a hand before her nose. "First on my list. Got a cake of soap?"

"Not sure about this," Briar said.

He felt strange after the bath. Stela had found a stiff brush and scrubbed every inch of him while some of the other Wardskins laughed and jeered. His skin tingled, dry and raw in the cold morning air.

Stela ignored the comment. "How in the Core do you still smell like hogroot?"

"Sweat some, you eat enough," Briar said. "Keeps the cories away, even when someone forces you into the bath."

Stela laughed at that, giving him a clean robe and bringing him to the tent where Ella knelt by a small fire with her implements. "Show Ella your hands."

"Not sure about this," Briar said again. "Said I'd come to camp. Din't say I'd get inked."

"Arlen Bales says yur body is the only weapon yur never without," Ella said.

"Just your hands for now," Stela said. "Every Wardskin does it. Gives us weapons we can't ever lose."

Briar couldn't deny he liked the sound of that. He didn't resist as Ella reached out to him. Her hands were soft as they took his, turning them over to inspect the palms.

"Blackstem first," Ella said, taking a brush and inkpot. "Hold still." With a quick, bold hand, she drew an impact ward on his right palm, and a pressure ward on his left.

"Offense and defense," Stela said. "The first tools of *gaisahk*." The word was Krasian, meaning "demon fighting," but Briar had never heard it before.

Ella finished her work, glancing at Stela. "What do you think?"

"Perfect!" Stela said. "Do it."

Ella put a small table between them. "Arm here." The table had straps on it, and when Ella reached for them, he snatched his hand away. The last time he saw a table like that, it was an instrument of torture.

Stela steadied him. "Just to keep you from flinching. Even the best of us do sometimes. I'm right here, Briar. Ent gonna let anyone hurt you."

Briar met her eyes and took a deep breath, putting his arm on the table, palm up. Stela pulled the straps tight as Ella took up what looked at first like a small brush. It wasn't until she began passing it through the fire that he saw the bristles were needles.

"What do you think?" Ella asked, wiping the blood from his left hand. His right was already poulticed and wrapped in a bandage.

Briar flexed his hand, watching the ward conform. He straightened the palm and curled his fingers and thumb in tight around it in the proper form his father had taught for an open-hand *sharusahk* blow.

"Beautiful," he said. A weapon he could never lose, a part of him, even more than his hogroot sweat. The thought made him hopeful in a way he had never known. As Ella wrapped his hand he looked down at her long legs, covered in wards, and envied her their protection and power.

Stela gave him a smack on the back of the head. "Ay, that's enough of that. Go have a bite and a rest while I talk with Ella a spell."

Briar nodded, leaving the tent. The sun was high in the sky, and most of the people in camp were asleep in the shade. Still, enough moved about that he felt crowded. He needed time to himself.

He circled behind the tent before anyone noticed him, meaning to make his way out of the Warded Children's camp and back into Gatherers' Wood.

"Honest word?" Ella's voice was clear even through the tent wall. "Ya stuck that filthy little bugger?"

"Didn't just stick him," Stela said. "Took his first seed."

"No!" Ella squealed. "Ya sure?"

Stela laughed. "Didn't have a clue what he was doing." Briar felt his face heat at the words. Her laugher, so beautiful a moment ago, cut at him.

"Bad, then," Ella guessed.

"Didn't say that," Stela said, and Briar perked up. "Little stinker made it up in enthusiasm. Popped quick the first time, but I wasn't far behind. Then it was popping all over."

Briar smiled from ear to ear.

"Do all Krasian men have small cocks?" Stela asked, freezing the grin on his face.

"Not ones I been with," Ella said. "Not as big as Cutters, but bigger'n most."

"Briar's half Laktonian," Stela said. "Maybe that's why."

"How small are we talking?" Ella asked. Stela must have shown with her hands, because her squeals of laughter followed Briar as he fled the camp.

Briar cleared the few possessions from his hideaway, returning to the hollow he dug beneath the goldwood tree, far from the Warded Children's hunting grounds. He didn't know how to feel about Stela anymore, but he knew he would never be able to sleep with the Pack nearby.

His thoughts were still in chaos when he made his way to Mistress Leesha's keep. There were guards on patrol, but they never saw Briar slip over the wall and through the courtyard, scaling a shadowed wall of the manse.

His bandaged hands were a hindrance in the climb, both for the loss of grip and for the reminder of all that had transpired in the past day. For better or worse, a simple scouting mission had changed his life forever.

He ran across the roof, crouched too low for any to see, until he came to the spot above the mistress' office window and clambered down to the sill.

Careful not to be seen, Briar checked the hall window first. Two of Wonda's guardswomen stood at the chamber doors, attention outward. He moved to Leesha's office window.

The mistress was on the office divan, Olive in her arms. Her back was to the window, and Briar could not see or hear anyone else in the room. He reached out to knock.

"Come in, Briar." Leesha spoke before he could make a sound. "Close the window quick. Cold as a demon's heart out there."

Briar slid a wire between the panes, tripping the lock. Warmth from the roaring fire engulfed him as he slipped inside and shut the pane. Cold seldom bothered him, but few things did. He adjusted easily to the heat, stepping carefully to avoid leaving dirt on the warded floor.

The mistress' dress was unlaced, the babe latched at one breast. A day ago, Briar would have thought little of it, but now he felt himself flush, casting his eyes down.

"No need to look away," Leesha said. "Nothing to be ashamed of, using them for the purpose the Creator meant for them. Folk are going to have to get used to the sight."

She gestured to the laden tea table. "Help yourself to tea and a bite."

Briar's mouth watered when he saw the sandwiches on the table. Not the delicate crustless fingers Duchess Araine served, these were thick brown bread with generous cuts of meat. He stuck one in his mouth, holding it while he took a handful of dried hogroot leaves from his pocket, crumbling them into a cup and pouring hot tea over it.

Briar glanced warily at the empty couch across from the mistress. He was freshly bathed but still felt too dirty to sit on such fine material.

"Sit, Briar," Leesha said. "Elissa told me they didn't want you muddying the furniture in the Monastery of Dawn, but here you are my guest."

Briar sat stiffly, legs tight together to put the least surface of his backside possible on the couch. He hunched, gnawing on his sandwich while the tea steeped.

Leesha cleared her throat. "That doesn't mean you don't need a napkin."

The scolding was one his mother had given a thousand times, and Briar quickly snatched a napkin off the table, laying it across his knees.

"What happened to your hands? Let me look at them." Olive began to thrash and cry as Leesha broke the latch.

Briar raised his hands to forestall her. "S'fine. Just scraped. Washed and wrapped."

He meant to tell her about the tattoos, but when the moment was upon him the lie came easily. He didn't know himself what the ink meant, and had no desire to share the question before he thought it through.

Leesha looked ready to insist, even as she allowed Olive the nipple once more. "You're not the clumsy type, Briar. What happened?"

"Found Stela Cutter fighting cories and threw in," Briar said, skipping the details. "She brought me back to the Children's camp."

"Stela Cutter was out hunting alone?" Leesha demanded. "Does she have a night wish?"

"Safer'n you think," Briar said. "She's strong. Leads the Children."

"Stela?" Leesha gaped. "She's the sunny side of a hundred pounds and eighteen summers old."

"Everyone's afraid of her and the other Wardskins," Briar said. "Act like they're not, but I can tell."

"Afraid why?" Leesha asked.

Briar shrugged. Stela changed dramatically when they were no longer alone. There was still so much he didn't understand about her and the other Children.

"How many are there?" Leesha asked.

"Hundred, at least," Briar said. "Wardskins, Bones, Pumps, *Sharum,* and Brothers. Call themselves the Pack."

Olive fell asleep at the breast. Leesha pried her gently away and rose, throwing the babe over a shoulder. Olive gave a contented burp, still sleeping as Leesha glided to the crèche and laid her down.

She returned a moment later, dress laced tight, and sat across from Briar. Her eyes, the color of sky, pierced him.

"Tell me everything."

The sky was darkening when Briar returned to the Warded Children's camp. He'd told Leesha everything about the Children, but kept private the details of his own interactions with them. Wasn't her business.

The Children bustled about, preparing for the coming night. They mended and folded nets of wardplates, sharpened blades and painted wards on their skin. The young Krasian girl Shalivah was teaching *sharusahk* to a large class with all factions of the Pack in attendance. The girl looked like a snake, flowing from pose to pose with impossible grace.

Briar moved close, mesmerized.

"Everam blessed my granddaughter," Jarit said, moving to stand next to him. "She used to watch Kaval train her brothers. One time he caught her practicing the moves and struck her. *If you dare take the sacred poses, you had best do them properly!* he cried. *If a man who is not your husband lays hands on you, will you shame the house of Kaval, or will you break his arm?*"

Jarit smiled. "My honored husband made her repeat the move a hundred times, and set her to endlessly cleaning in the training room."

"Fifty miles in any direction is Sharak Sun." Briar used the Krasian term for the Daylight War, the conquest of humanity that the Evejah taught was necessary to win Sharak Ka. "What side will you take, when it reaches you?"

"The Pack will not fight in Sharak Sun," Jarit said. "As the son of Jeph revealed to us, *There is no honor in shedding red blood.*"

"Honest word," Stela said, coming to stand with them. She slapped Briar on the back. "Starting to worry you weren't coming back."

"Like to be by myself," Briar said.

"Ay, I get it," Stela said. "But the light's fading. Time we went to the initiation ground."

Briar looked at her curiously but followed as she led him to where the Wardskins were mustered. There were more than twenty of them, dressed in scraps and covered in wards. They were often small and thin, but with predator's eyes. Brother Franq stood with them, clad only in a brown bido. His thickly muscled body was covered in tattoos, but he kept his crooked staff as well.

They ran into the night, coming to a high bluff, warded with pillars on all sides save the path upward.

"Wait here," Stela told Briar. Without waiting for him to respond, she gave a whoop, thrusting an *alagai*-catcher into the air, then ran off with the others.

Briar itched to follow the sounds of battle and flashes of wardlight that followed, or to flee them, but he waited patiently as it went on, noting after a time that the sounds and flashing grew closer.

Soon the Wardskins came back into sight, led by Stela and Franq. Between them they dragged a struggling wood demon, bent almost double by the *alagai*-catcher's cable and crooked staff hooked around its neck. Behind, the other Wardskins jeered, kicking and punching to keep the corie off balance as it was dragged into the warded circle where Briar stood.

The sight answered any questions Briar might have about his "initiation." He began unwrapping the bandages on his hands as the Wardskins formed a circle around them. His palms were a little tender, but the impact and pressure wards were sharp and clear.

Stela looked at him as she and Franq dragged the demon to the center of the bluff to stand before Briar. "Initiation's over when it's dead."

Briar nodded, and she pressed a button on her *alagai*-catcher, releasing the cable even as Franq unhooked his staff. He drew a ward in the air over Briar. "Blessings of the Deliverer upon you, Briar Damaj." Then the two of them stepped back into the ring of onlookers.

The wood demon shook itself off with a roar, hauling in great breaths and scratching at its throat. It was not seriously injured, and in moments its magic would restore it to full combat ability.

Briar never gave it time, leaping in close and driving his open right palm into its knee. The impact ward flared and the demon toppled with a shriek as a rush of power rocked up Briar's arm. While the demon was prone, Briar spit hogroot juice in its eyes, blinding it. The Wardskins cheered.

Briar gave ground as the corie lurched back to its feet, seven feet tall with arms long enough to drag talons on the ground. It tried to pinpoint Briar by sound, but the shouts of the Pack drowned its ears. It sniffed for him, sneezing at the scent of hogroot.

Like humans, demons closed their eyes and clenched up when they sneezed. Briar used that moment to step in, catching the woodie's arm in his left hand. The pressure ward smoked against its skin, flooding Briar with strength as he shattered its wrist with the impact ward.

The demon howled, clutching at its limp talons as Briar slipped back out of reach, circling.

Wisdom dictated he take his time. He was growing stronger with every blow, delivering harm quicker than the demon could heal, especially with Briar draining its magic. That kind of caution was why Briar had survived so many years, living in the naked night since he was six summers old.

He struck again, hitting the corie in the back and knocking it off balance. It swept its good arm at him. Briar ducked back, then shot forward, delivering an open-palm blow to its snout.

His mind told him to retreat again, but the demon seemed to have slowed. It was vulnerable as it reeled back, and Briar kept the offensive, landing blow after blow. He forgot caution. Forgot defense. He sensed the kill.

A wild swing of the wood demon's great gnarled arm took Briar in the stomach, cracking ribs and launching him through the air. He hit the ground hard several feet away, and the crowd, cheering a moment ago, gasped.

Coughing blood, Briar shook himself off, rolling to his feet. Already the magic was healing him, but the world spun as he tried to take a step, and the recovered demon leapt at him.

The Wardskins shouted encouragement, Stela loudest of all, but none of them moved to help him. This was part of the initiation. Either the initiate killed the demon, or the demon killed them.

Wood demons' arms were long and powerful, but they were not nimble. Too dizzy to fight, Briar fell flat on the ground. The talons whiffed overhead as the demon passed.

Briar kept prone, letting the magic rushing through his body do its work. The world had stopped spinning by the time the woodie pulled up short, talons tearing the soil atop the bluff in great clumps.

It roared, rushing him again. Briar rolled away at the last moment, throwing a pouch into the demon's gaping maw. The woodie snapped at it instinctively, filling its mouth and nostrils with powdered hogroot.

While the demon choked and retched, Briar got back to his

feet. He watched for a moment, then saw his chance and rushed in, using the woodie's gnarled knee as a step to climb onto its back. He put a leg into its armpit, hooking it around the corie's good arm to lock it in place as he caught its throat with his left hand. The pressure ward smoked and burned, Briar's grip growing strong enough to crush steel. The demon's neck was filled with powerful corded muscle and sinew, but it was only flesh.

Briar put his right hand against the back of the woodie's neck. The impact ward flared, pushing forward even as Briar's other hand pulled back. Slowly, his hands moved closer together.

The demon thrashed wildly, stumbling around the bluff. It drew close to the onlookers, but the crowd only jeered, shoving it back toward the center with warded kicks and punches.

The demon threw its free arm at its back, but with the wrist broken, it could not bring its talons to bear. Briar accepted the blows, keeping his hold. The more the magic built, the stronger he felt.

The woodie threw itself to the ground, rolling to try to dislodge him. The wind was knocked out of him, but Briar sensed desperation and tightened his grip. The Wardskins stood silent, holding collective breath until the corie's neck broke with an audible snap.

The crowd erupted in cheers, everyone rushing in as Briar lifted the huge demon clear over his head and threw it off.

Then he was up in their arms, bounced above the crowd as they carried him about the bluff chanting, "Wardskin! Wardskin! Wardskin!"

Briar had never felt so alive.

One of the girls produced a pipe, playing a lively song, and the crowd began to dance.

Briar tired of being tossed about, slipping down to his own feet right in front of a beaming Stela Inn.

"Knew you could do it!" Stela kissed him, his lips still tingling from magic. "That was the fastest kill yet, and I didn't pick a little one." She winked. "Wanted to show you off."

Briar knew he should say something, but no words came. He just stood there, stupidly grinning at her.

Stela drew her knife and flipped it in her hand, holding it

out to him handle-first. "Ent over. You have to cut out its black heart."

Briar stared dumbly at her for a moment, then shook himself, taking the knife. He strode over to the demon, catching one of its armor plates and prising the knife underneath. Cutting wards flared as Briar yanked on the plate, half cutting, half tearing its chest open.

Black ichor covered the wards on his hands. They glowed, leaching its magic, making him strong beyond belief. He dropped the knife, ripping the next armor plate off with his bare hands. He weakened the demon's rib cage with the pressure ward, then struck hard with the impact, shattering bone.

Briar thrust his hands inside the creature. In a moment he held up its heart, and the Wardskins cheered again. They had produced a great barrel of ale and were passing sloshing cups.

"My uncle Keet didn't think Mudboy had it in him!" Stela boomed to the crowd. "Said Briar Damaj wasn't good enough to be Pack."

There was jeering in response, and Stela put her hands on her hips. "What do the Wardskins say?"

"Pack!" the others shouted, punching fists in the night air. "Pack! Pack!"

Stela stepped up to Briar, putting her hands on the heart. They came away black with ichor. "Pack." She wiped the fluid across her breast, gasping in pleasure as her wards glowed, absorbing the power.

"The Deliverer is strong within you," Franq agreed, stepping up next to touch the heart. Like Stela, he wiped the blood across his tattoos, shivering as they brightened. Then he turned to Briar, reaching out a black finger to trace a ward on his forehead. "Pack."

The Wardskins formed a queue, each touching the heart and wiping ichor across their wards. "Pack," they whispered.

"Want another taste," Stela said, giving the heart a squeeze, rubbing ichor onto her warded arms like lotion.

"Ay, you going to take a bite of it, next?" Ella Cutter jeered.

"Don't think I won't!" Stela said.

"Hear that, Wardskins?" Ella cried. "Stela's going to take a bite of the demon's heart!"

"Do it!" someone shouted from the crowd.

"She ent got the stones!" a girl cried.

"You'll slosh for sure!" a gangly young man added, laughing.

"Gatherers say ichor's poison!" someone said.

Stela looked at Franq, but the Brother did not try to stay her. Indeed, he eyed Stela and the heart intensely. Hungrily.

"Eat it!" the crowd boomed. "Eat it! Eat it! Eat it!"

Stela gave a wild smile, chomping down and tearing free a chunk of demon flesh. Her mouth ran black as she chewed, a mad look in her eyes. She retched once, but managed to swallow the mouthful.

"Tastes like a coreling shat in my mouth!" Stela cried, and the crowd laughed. She turned to Briar, offering him the heart. When he balked, she grabbed the front of his shirt and pulled him in, kissing him wetly on the mouth.

The ichor was foul on his lips, clinging and noxious, but he felt its power, even so. He felt his bile rise and swallowed hard, feeling the ichor burn its way down into him.

Franq strode at them as she pulled away. Briar half expected him to condemn them as corespawned. Instead the man stepped up and kissed Stela, tasting the ichor from her lips as Briar had.

Briar expected her to push him away, but Stela seemed to welcome the kiss, ecstatic in the rush of magic.

Briar lost sight of her as the other Wardskins swarmed forward to take their own bites from the heart. Soon the heart was consumed, everyone retching and laughing, faces black with demon blood. Unsatisfied, some went to the demon's body, tearing into its chest and pulling out gobs of meat.

More of the Wardskins began kissing, rubbing ichor over one another's faces and bodies. Briar saw Ella and the gangly young man move away from the demon, smeared with ichor. Ella laughed at Briar, wiggling her littlest finger at him as the man laid her back in the dirt.

Briar felt his face heat, turning away, but it was becoming a common scene atop the bluff, the few scraps of cloth the Wardskins wore being pulled away, wards glowing brightly in the night.

Stela had vanished. Briar wandered through the cavorting Pack looking for her. The chaos was surreal amid the magic flooding his senses. Stela was nowhere to be found atop the bluff. He moved down the pathway into the woods.

He heard her grunting and picked up his pace, not knowing what he would find. He burst through the trees to see Stela naked on all fours, growling. Brother Franq knelt behind her, bido pulled aside to reveal a cock thrice the size of Briar's. His hands were on her hips, pulling her onto it.

Briar clenched his fist, every instinct screaming at him to strike the man. To kill him. To tear open his chest as he had the demon's and feast on his heart.

But then Stela looked up. "Briar! Don't be shy! I've openings for two."

She beckoned, and Briar froze, terrified. The thought of joining them was horrifying. A perversion of the beauty they shared. He was repulsed, but his cock betrayed him, hard in his breeches.

He shook his head sharply, turning and running into the trees.

"Briar, wait!" Stela cried. He heard Franq's bellow as she threw him off. He picked up speed at the sound of her feet, pounding across the forest bed after him.

Briar zigzagged through the trees, but while Franq's angry shouts receded into the night, Stela kept pace. "Corespawn it, Briar! Will you please stop and talk to me?!"

He kept running, but he had no plan. The territory was unfamiliar, his thoughts still reeling. Stela gained ground until she could reach out and catch his arm. "What in the dark of night's gotten into you?!"

Briar whirled to face her. "You were . . . You . . . !"

Stela crossed her arms. "Ay, I was what? Don't belong to you, Briar Damaj, just because you stuck me."

Briar shook her arm off. "Din't say you did! Know you want more than the little stinker with the small cock."

Stela's expression softened. "Heard me and Ella, din't you? Night, I'm sorry, Briar. Din't mean it cruel."

Briar barked a laugh. "Else could it be?"

"Just girl talk," Stela said, giving him that wicked smile. "Don't mean you won't still get your turn."

"What?" Briar stumbled back as Stela stalked in.

"Like you, Briar," Stela said. "Din't lie about that. Felt safe with you at my back last night."

Briar backed into a tree and she was against him, still wearing nothing but tattoos and ichor. His heart thudded in his chest.

She put a hand between his legs, squeezing. "Did good work on my front, too, when the scrap was over. Small cock or no, I ent letting go a man who can kick a demon's arse and curl my toes when it's done."

She kissed Briar again, breath still hot with magic and hinting at the noxious ichor of the corie.

Stela took his chin in her free hand as their lips parted, turning him to meet her eyes. "We don't own each other in the Pack. I'll stick who I want, when I want, and you should, too. Ella may joke, but don't think she ent curious after what I told her."

She undid the laces of his breeches, freeing him. Everything seemed to be spinning, but in that one place he felt rigid—ready to explode. "But not tonight." She took him in her hand, skin on skin. Briar shut his eyes and grit his teeth to keep from crying out. "Tonight is your night, Wardskin. Let's get the first one out of the way, and then you can have me as you please."

She pushed him back against the tree, mounting him standing. She ground her full weight down on his crotch, reaching back between their legs to fondle his seedpods. Briar howled, and Stela gave a whoop of delight, picking up the pace as they gripped and scratched at each other.

Stela slipped off him when it was done, taking a few unsteady steps before turning around and kneeling on all fours. She turned to look him in the eye, smiling. "This is what Franq wanted. Now he's pulling himself and it's yours."

The words teased a primal hunger—the exquisite pleasure of thrusting aside a rival and taking what was his. And why not? Dominance was the natural order of the world. Wolves did it. Cories did it.

Gonna be like them now?

He looked at Stela, covered in ichor, beckoning, and something churned in him. Was this the life he wanted?

He shook his head, reaching down to pull up his pants. "No."

Stela threw him an angry look. "No? What in the Core do you mean, no?"

Briar finished lacing himself up. "Last night in the Briarpatch, I thought . . ."

"What, Mudboy?" Stela snapped, springing to her feet. "That we were one spirit the Creator tore in half?"

"That you understood," Briar said.

"We killed two demons and stuck each other," Stela said. "What's there to understand?"

"World's bigger than this," Briar said. "Folk struggling for their lives outside Gatherers' Wood, and all the Pack are doing is . . ."

"Hunting and killing the demons that prey on them," Stela growled.

Briar shook his head. "Prey on them yourself. Stealing ale and supplies, even from your own family. Ent looking to protect them when night falls. You just want . . ." He swept a hand at her.

Stela put her hands on her hips. "Just want what, *Mudboy*?"

There was danger in her eyes, but now that he had started talking, Briar was past caring.

"To bathe in ichor and rut," he said. "And corespawn any that ent Pack."

Stela lashed out at him. The magic made her fast, but Briar had tasted it, too. He took a quick step back, avoiding the slap.

"So what, you're just gonna walk away?!" Stela demanded. "No one walks away from Stela Cutter, you quickshooting little stinker, least of all you."

She snatched at him, and Briar batted her arm aside with his right hand. There was a flare of power as the impact ward struck, throwing her off her feet.

Briar looked at her in horror. Stela wasn't a demon, but covered in ichor, the wards reacted as if she were. He could still taste it in his mouth, and spat.

Then he turned and ran into the night.

Briar returned to Mistress Leesha's keep, slipping unseen past the night guards and into her private garden. If Stela or the other Warded Children were hunting for him, this was the last place they would think to look.

The hogroot patch looked inviting, but sleep was far from Briar's thoughts. Just the opposite, his limbs shook with unreleased energy.

So he paced until he knew the garden intimately. There were three entrances—two grand and inviting, and one carefully hidden against one of the manse walls, obscured by flora.

Briar dug a small burrow in the hogroot for future use. He practiced *sharusahk*. Anything to keep his thoughts from drifting back to Stela Cutter.

Leesha had shown an affinity for Duchess Araine's gardens, walking the rows at least twice a day. Sure enough, while the sky was still brightening, the hidden door opened and the mistress slipped out among the herbs.

When he was certain she was alone, Briar stepped out to face her. "They're dangerous."

Leesha's hand snapped into one of the many pockets of her dress, but then recognition caught up. "Night, Briar! One of these days you're going to end up with a faceful of blinding powder."

Briar nodded at the distance between them. "Can't throw powder that far."

Leesha tsked. "Are you all right, Briar?"

He didn't know how to answer. He'd washed every inch of himself, but still he felt the ichor on his skin, tasted it in his mouth. Stela's scratches had already healed, but he could still feel them itch.

"Who's dangerous, Briar?" Leesha asked.

"The Children," Briar said. "Ent fighting to keep the wood safe. Fighting because it feels good to fight. Magic makes us feel unbeatable."

"Us?" Leesha asked. She stepped close, taking one of his hands and turning it over. She gasped at the ward there.

Briar pulled his hand away. "Thought they were like me. Ent. Ent like me at all."

"Briar, what's happened?" Leesha asked.

"Ate a coreling's heart tonight," Briar said. "Made'm . . . drunk. Wild. Only going to get worse."

Leesha looked taken aback. "Idiot girl," she muttered to herself. "Told us himself! Said he ate them." She growled, clenching her fists.

"Ay?" Briar asked, confused.

"The tattoos are only half the reason Arlen Bales can ripping fly," Leesha said. "It's the corespawned meat!"

Briar looked at her dumbly, having no idea what she meant. After a moment she collected herself, looking back at him. "I need you to go back, Briar. I need you to convince them to meet with me."

Briar shook his head. "Ent going back. Not now, not ever. Going home."

"Home?" Leesha asked. "Elissa and Ragen won't head north for weeks yet."

"Not north," Briar said. "Home. Lakton."

CHAPTER 6

EVERAM IS A LIE

334 AR

Renna grit her teeth, watching as Shanvah spoon-fed a thin gruel to her father. Shanjat swallowed mechanically, eyes straight ahead, staring at nothing. His aura was bright with life but flat and unmoving. Auras showed emotions, but Shanjat had none to show.

The sight sickened her. Two days ago, Shanjat had been a powerful man in the prime of his life. A better fighter by far than Renna. Now he had all the will of Renna's old milking cow. He could walk a path if led, squat in the privy and wipe himself when told, even spoon his own gruel if it was placed before him. But if left to his own devices, he would stand in his stall staring at nothing until he dropped.

It didn't help that Arlen and Jardir were shouting at each other on the tower's next level. In some ways, that was the worst of it. Shanvah, usually so calm and detached, was weeping openly, and flinched at every angry sound from above.

"Be strong," Renna said. "They'll find a way to bring your da back to us."

"Will they?" Shanvah asked, using the edge of the spoon to scrape a dribble of drool from her father's lip. She kissed his cheek and moved away, Renna following.

"Not all will make it to the end of Sharak Ka," Shanvah's voice was low, "if indeed any do. It is an honor to die on *alagai* talons. But this . . ." she gestured to her father, staring at nothing, ". . . half life? Alagai Ka made a mocking shell of my father to whisper his evils. If the Deliverer cannot restore him, I will kill him myself."

Renna's throat was heavy, and she found herself blinking back tears of her own. She and Shanvah were hardly friends, but that no longer mattered. The Krasians believed that all who shed blood together against the night were family, and for better or worse that was what they were now.

Shanvah was watching her, eyes daring Renna to argue. "Time comes," Renna said, "I'll be there to catch your tears."

Shanvah wept anew, throwing her arms about Renna. Renna fought the instinct to pull away, holding the girl tight and patting her back.

When she was finished, Shanvah pulled back, sniffling as she undid her scarf and moved to the basin to wash. When she looked up at her reflection in the silvered mirror, there was grim determination on her face.

She turned to Renna, producing a small, sharp knife. "I won't share my father's fate."

Renna eyed the blade warily. "Don't know yet that they can't save him, Shan. Ent time yet."

"It is not for him." Shanvah flipped the knife in nimble fingers, handing it to Renna hilt-first. "It is for me. I want you to cut mind wards into my forehead."

Renna shook her head. "I can paint them with blackstem . . ."

"Blackstem fades," Shanvah said. "And our supply may dwindle as we walk the road to the abyss. You heard the father of demons. *The journey is long, and you are mortal. The time will come when your guard grows lax, and then I will be free.*"

Renna blinked. "Ay, you may be right about that. We can tattoo . . ."

Shanvah shook her head. "The Evejah commands we not profane our bodies with permanent ink. I will follow the example set down by the Shar'Dama Ka."

Renna looked at her, seeing the strength and determination in the girl's aura. "Ay, all right." She took the knife, laying Shanvah on her back. "Need something to bite on?"

Shanvah shook her head. "Pain is only wind."

"Ent no choice but to stick to the plan," the Par'chin said.

Jardir looked at him incredulously. "Of course there is a choice, Par'chin. There is always a choice. You had a choice when you broke into Sharik Hora and started us on this path, and there is a choice now. Do not let the honeyed words of Alagai Ka blind you. The very fact that he endorses your mad plan is reason to reconsider. He seeks to lure us into forgetting our true responsibility."

"And that is?" the Par'chin asked.

"To lead our people in Sharak Ka, vanguard in the battle between Everam and Nie."

"Night." The Par'chin rolled his eyes. "You still spouting that nonsense? Everam is a lie, Ahmann. Nie is a lie. Demon said it himself. Fiction to keep folk from fearin' the dark."

The blasphemy no longer surprised him, but still Jardir marveled at how stubborn the Par'chin could be. "How can you say that after all we have seen, Par'chin? How many prophecies must come true before you begin to have faith?"

The Par'chin closed his eyes. "I can see the future now. The sun will . . . rise tomorrow." He smirked as he opened his eyes. "Gonna think I speak to the Creator when that comes true?"

"You were not so insolent when I was your *ajin'pal*," Jardir said. "Mocking what you do not understand."

"Ent," the Par'chin said. "Mocking stories *you* make up to explain what we *both* don't understand. We're cattle to these things, Ahmann. Sharak Ka means no more to them than a bull stirring up the cows, and we've started a stampede. It will happen now whether we're there or not. I trust my people to stand against the night. Do you?"

"My people stood in the night long before yours, Par'chin," Jardir reminded him.

"Then let them!" the Par'chin cried. "While they hold the surface, we have this one chance to take it downstairs."

"To Nie's abyss," Jardir said. "Yet you deny Kaji's divine instruction, set down in the Evejah . . ."

"The Evejah is a book," the Par'chin said. "A book that's been rewritten over the years, and never had the whole story anyway."

"And how do you know this story, Par'chin?" Jardir asked.

"How do you, an infidel, know more of Kaji than his sacred order of scholars?"

"The *dama* are political creatures," the Par'chin said. "Corrupt. Said it yourself. That's why you cast the Andrah from his throne. The Evejah bends to suit their will, selectively enforced. The real version is painted on the walls of Anoch Sun. Or was, till your diggers knocked most of them down."

Jardir crossed his arms. "So we should put our faith in the Father of Lies, instead?"

The Par'chin laughed. "Don't trust that demon farther than the reach of our spears. But I had a look in the head of the mind demon it sent to kill me. With both sides of the story, it's easier to tell fact from fiction."

"So what *truly* transpired, three thousand years ago?" Jardir asked. "What great secret have the *dama* hidden?"

"That Kaji failed," the Par'chin said. "Din't make it all the way. Din't get to the queen. We wouldn't be in this fix if he had."

"He gave us millennia of peace," Jardir said. "And it was only when we forgot his teachings that the *alagai* returned. Did Kaji fail us, or did we fail him?"

The Par'chin rubbed his face in frustration. "What does it matter? Creator or no, a hatching is coming up. We either let it happen and lead our armies against hives popping up all over our lands, or we try to stop it and maybe, just maybe, accomplish what Kaji never could."

Jardir scowled. "You think we can control Alagai Ka?"

The Par'chin shrugged. "Gonna need to talk to it again."

"How?" Jardir asked. "With its flesh warded, Alagai Ka cannot touch Shanjat's mind, and without him it cannot speak."

"Wards keep it from striking at a distance," the Par'chin said, "but it can still enter an unwarded mind if it makes physical contact."

"So you wish to deliver my *kai* to Alagai Ka's talons once more," Jardir said. "To make him a puppet to spread the prince of demons' lies. A weapon to use against us."

"What choice we got?" the Par'chin asked.

Jardir had no answer.

Renna held Shanvah's face with her left hand as she worked. The knife was steady in her right, cutting flesh away from the girl's forehead in ribbons, ensuring a keloid scar that would Draw and hold a charge.

She let magic flow through both hands, activating the cutting wards on the already razor-sharp blade, and speeding the healing. Scabs formed in seconds in the blade's wake.

Shanvah did not flinch at the cuts, but there was fear in her aura.

"Nothing to worry over," Renna said. "Know what I'm doing. Still be pretty when I'm done."

"The scars of *alagai'sharak* are an honor to carry," Shanvah said.

"Then what's got you tenser than a pig at the chopping block?" Renna asked.

Shanvah's eyes flicked to the stairs. "They've gone quiet."

Renna paused in her work, realizing for the first time that the shouting from above had stopped. In her concentration she hadn't noticed.

"I thought nothing could be worse than the sound of my uncle and the Par'chin shouting," Shanvah said.

"But 'least we knew they weren't choking each other," Renna agreed. "Gotta hold faith they were gonna do that, they'da done it months ago."

"Our faith is tested daily, with Sharak Ka approaching." Shanvah relaxed, aura cooling with acceptance.

"There," Renna said, making the last cut. She looked at the ward this way and that, paring away a last bit of flesh before she set the knife aside.

"How does it—" Shanvah began, but her words were cut off with a gasp, her eyes widening. Renna turned to see Arlen and Jardir descending the stairs.

"What are you doing?" Jardir demanded.

Shanvah scissored her legs for momentum, rolling off her back into a kneeling position facing Jardir. She put her hands on the floor and pressed her face between them, the scabs on her forehead touching the wood. "Mercy, Deliverer! The daughter of Harl wards me at my request."

Jardir reached down, putting a finger under the girl's chin to tilt her face upward. "Your mother used to brag of your beauty, and the ease with which she could find you a husband."

"No doubt a husband for the Deliverer's niece would be easy enough to find, beauty or no," Shanvah said. "But there will be no husbands in the abyss. No beauty. There will only be *alagai,* and *sharak.*"

Jardir nodded. "You are as wise as you are brave, Niece. Your honor is boundless."

Shanvah gave no outward sign, but her aura lit with pride at the words. "May I ward my father next?"

Jardir shook his head. "I fear we will need him again. We have more questions for the Prince of Lies."

The pure gold that had been Shanvah's aura again became a swirling mix of colors—anger, frustration, humiliation. They all saw it, but she kept her composure, flicking her gaze back down.

"Speak," Jardir commanded. "I can see the question in your heart, and we cannot afford to let it fester."

"Is my father's shame not great enough," Shanvah asked, "left trapped in a body without will? Must we permit Alagai Ka to violate him further? My father's honor was boundless. I beg you, if he cannot be healed, let me send him on the lonely path."

"Not all warriors get the fortune of a quick death on *alagai* talons, Niece," Jardir said. "Heroes beyond count, great men like Drillmaster Qeran, who trained your father, have lived on with injuries they believed would forever put them from *alagai'sharak.* We must honor these men no less for their service to Everam than those that walk the lonely path."

Shanvah shifted. "By your own words, Deliverer, those crippled in battle are put from *alagai'sharak.* You send my crippled father back into battle."

"It is not without precedent," Jardir said. "Countless crippled warriors have volunteered as Baiters in the Maze, dying in glory as they led the demons to their doom."

"Of course your words are true, Deliverer," Shanvah pressed, "but my father has no will to volunteer. I cannot believe he would have wanted this . . . abomination."

Renna saw growing frustration in Jardir's aura. He was not used to being questioned by any of his people, especially one who had barely seen eighteen summers. But he breathed, and his aura cleansed again. Arlen had tried to teach Renna the trick, but it never worked for her.

"You do your family honor, Shanvah vah Shanjat," Jardir said. "But I knew your father better than you. We fought in the *nie'Sharum* food lines and bled together in the Maze. Such was his honor and loyalty that I gave him my own sister, your honored mother, as his First Wife."

He gestured with the Spear of Kaji, always in his hand, and the weight of it washed over Shanvah's aura. "I tell you here with Everam my witness, if I told Shanjat asu Cavel am'Damaj am'Kaji that to win Sharak Ka I needed him to be the voice of evil, he would not refuse me."

Shanvah put her face back to the floor, weeping openly. "Of course the Shar'Dama Ka is correct. My father's honor was boundless, and I shame him with my doubts. I will not question you again, Deliverer, and should you require any sacrifice of me, know that my spirit will always be willing to serve you in Sharak Ka."

"I never doubted it, Niece," Jardir said.

"It may be that Alagai Ka sends my father against you, as he did last night," Shanvah said. "I beg your permission to stand guard when the Prince of Waning touches him. If my father must be put down, it should be I who does it."

She looked up, surprised to see Jardir bow in return. "Of course. I have never met a warrior, Shanvah vah Shanjat am'Damaj am'Kaji, who carried greater honor than you. Your father's spirit sings with pride. When he is at last untethered and walks the lonely path, his steps will be lighter knowing he has left a worthy successor to carry on his blood."

The words cleansed Shanvah's aura once more, washing away the swirling colors with a pure white light.

Shanjat's hands and feet were manacled. A short chain between them would allow him to sit but not to stand. The Par'chin warded the bindings himself, and Jardir could see the power in them.

If the *kai'Sharum* felt any discomfort at being so bound, he gave no sign as Jardir carried like a child up the steps to

Alagai Ka's prison. But for his breathing Shanjat might have been dead, eyes staring blankly.

The demon looked up as they entered, tilting its head as Jardir crossed the wards, Shanvah covering his every step with her spear. He laid Shanjat in the center of the room, then retreated outside the circles that held the demon prisoner.

But the demon did not move toward Shanjat, simply watching them with huge, inhuman eyes. Jardir could see the endless dark of Nie in those black pools, thoughts unknowable.

The Par'chin and his *jiwah* pulled open the heavy curtains. Night had fallen, but it was not the dark of Waning. Moonlight streamed through the windows and Alagai Ka hissed, scrambling to the center of the room.

Jardir felt his skin crawl as the demon wrapped itself around Shanjat. Shanvah tightened her grip on her spear, aura like a taut bowstring. She ached to strike, killing demon and sire both, but she was one of Everam's spear sisters, sprung of Jardir's own *Sharum* blood. She embraced the pain and mastered it.

Shanjat looked up, eyes bright and alive once more. He turned to Shanvah, lip curling. "Everam curse me, to have sired such a pathetic excuse for a daughter. It would have been better for all if your Tikka had married you off before you could be sent to the Dama'ting Palace. Better if I had crushed your head when I saw you were only a girl."

Shanvah kept her spear steady, but Jardir could see how the words tore across her aura.

"Your brother would have saved me," Shanjat said. "Or at least done the honor of killing me."

Shanvah's tears glistened in the moonlight, but she held steady.

"Do not listen to these poisonous words, Niece," Jardir said. "It is not your father speaking."

"Oh, but it is," Shanjat said, laughing. It was so much like his friend's great bellow that Jardir's heart ached. "That is what makes it so delicious! This drone boasted to his brethren of the strong son growing in his mate. His first thought at the sight of you was disgust. He imagined killing you to save face."

"Stop it." The Par'chin's *jiwah* stepped forward. "Need you alive, but that don't mean we can't cut a few bits off now that you can't grow 'em back."

The demon tilted its head, studying her. "What will your egg be?" Shanjat asked. "Will your consort allow you to walk the path before us, once he learns you carry it?"

"What's he talkin' about, Ren?" the Par'chin asked.

"Core if I know," Renna said.

"Humans are so inefficient in their mating." Shanjat clicked his tongue. "Ten cycles of vulnerability for a single egg. But do not fear. We will keep you alive until the birth. The mind of a child is a delicious morsel—like the bird eggs you consume."

Renna snarled, drawing her knife.

Jardir moved to block her path to the demon, but the Par'chin was faster. He blurred into mist, flowing across the room to re-form in her path. "Tryin' to get a rise out of us, Ren. Tryin' to get us mad enough to cross the wards, give it a chance to escape. Long as they hold we gotta stand fast, no matter what it says."

Renna panted, struggling to master the rage boiling in her aura.

"The Par'chin speaks true, sister," Shanvah said. "You told me yourself the princelings steal our thoughts, but speak only those that cut."

Renna blew out a breath, glaring at the demon. "Odds are you taste like shit, but don't think that means I won't eat your brains, too."

She meant the words. Jardir could see it on her aura, and knew the demon could, too. The creature seemed to think better of goading her further.

"Ask your questions," Shanjat said. "This drone will serve as mouthpiece and mount as we travel the dark paths below."

The Par'chin stepped forward. "Where is the surface entrance to the path?"

"North and east," the demon said. "In the mountains not far from where you and the Heir held your primitive submission duel."

"Lands unclaimed by either side," Jardir said. "That is fitting, for such a quest."

"Unclaimed by you," Shanjat agreed, "but not unclaimed."

"Who, then?" Jardir demanded.

"The factions of your surface stock are meaningless to me. They provided fresh minds for my larder on my last visit."

Jardir clenched a fist but did not take the bait. "Is the path guarded?"

"Magic flows to the surface strongly from a vent that size. Drones are drawn to the area, but they do not truly understand what they protect."

"How far to demon town once we find this cave?" the Par'chin asked.

"Weeks even for a mimic drone," Shanjat said. "Whole cycles for the slow and clumsy limbs of humans."

"There food on the way?" the Par'chin asked. "Clear water?"

"So much power, and not the slightest idea how to use it. The energies of the Core can sustain you without need for feeding."

"You don't need to eat?" Renna asked. "Then why keep a larder? Why raid the surface?"

Shanjat smiled. "Why do your kind drink fermented fruit and grain? Why do you sing and dance?"

The Par'chin shook his head. "More than that. Can't make something from nothing. Might not need food often, but you need it. Queens most of all."

Shanjat nodded. "My brethren can exist without, but none of us does so willingly. Queens at laying must feed—and our hatchlings. Those most of all. Soon hives will fill your lands, each springing forth thousands of hungry hatchling drones to pick the surface clean."

Renna grit her teeth. "That a long way o' sayin' we don't need supplies?"

"We will bring them, regardless," Jardir said. "I do not trust the demon's words."

"Why not?" Shanjat asked. "Have you not spent your life a pawn to the dice your females carve from our bones?"

It surprised Jardir how deeply the words cut. "They speak with the voice of Everam."

Shanjat laughed. "They are a Jongleur's trick! A primitive glimpse at a minuscule fraction of infinite possibility."

"Those primitive glimpses have led us to victory after victory against your kind," Jardir noted.

"Perhaps," Shanjat said. "Or perhaps we play a larger game, and even in your minor 'victories' you are only pawns."

"Pawns that caught you with your pants down," the Par'chin said. "Pawns that got you locked up sweatin' the sun. Pawns that could kill you on a whim. Tellin' me that's all part of your game?"

"In every game there is risk," Shanjat said. "Play is far from over."

"It is for tonight," Jardir said. He raised the Spear of Kaji and drew a ward in the air, sending power into the tattoos on the demon's knobbed flesh. It gave a howl, falling back from Shanjat and thrashing on the floor. The others advanced on it while Shanvah crossed the wards to collect her father.

"Corespawned thing wasn't lying." Arlen knelt in front of Renna's belly, studying her aura. "Barely a spark, but it's there."

"So much for pullin' out," Renna said.

Arlen stood, meeting her eyes. "Creator knows we wern't perfect about it." He shook his head. "Should've been more careful."

"Why?" Renna asked. "I'm your wife. Supposed to carry our babes. Creator knows you ent able. Sayin' you don't want it?"

"Course not," Arlen said. "Ent a thing in the world I want more. Just mean timin's bad."

"Timin' ent ever gonna be good, long as demons come out at night," Renna said. "Don't mean we stop livin' our lives."

"Know that," Arlen said. "But you can't go down to the Core carryin' our baby."

"Can't?" Renna crossed her arms. "You think, Arlen Bales. Ever have a talk you started with *can't* go well for you? Can and will."

"Night, Ren!" Arlen shouted. "How am I supposed to keep my mind on this job I got to do if I'm spending the whole time worrying over you?"

"What, you're the only one with feelin's? You'll do it the

same rippin' way I do every time you run off and do somethin' dangerous."

"Ay, but now I'm worrying for two," Arlen said.

"So. Am. I!" After months of eating demon meat, Renna was nearly as quick as Arlen, and he didn't see the slap coming. The blow knocked him back a step, echoing off the stone walls of the tower.

Arlen pressed a hand to his cheek, looking at her in shock.

Renna leveled a finger at him. "You're not the one carryin' this babe, Arlen Bales. Part of me. Say again I ent lookin' to its best interest and that slap'll seem like a kiss."

"Then how can you mean to take it to the heart of demon town?" Arlen asked. "You seen what just one of the minds can do. What chance we got inside the rippin' hive?"

Renna shrugged. "What chance we got if I stay up here and have our baby with new hives poppin' up all over Thesa?"

"Don't know that for sure," Arlen said. "Demon could be lyin', playing us to let him go."

"Already gambling the world that it ent, if we go through with this."

"How's it supposed to work?" Arlen said. "We gonna take an Herb Gatherer with us?"

Renna bared her teeth. "You even say her name . . ."

"Why not?" Arlen asked. "She's carryin', too. You can set up a nursery in the Core."

"Don't need a Gatherer," Renna said. "Got two Deliverers with me."

"Ent funny, Ren."

"Said yourself the babe's little more'n a notion right now," Renna said. "Ent gonna slow me for months. By then either we'll have won, or it won't matter."

"What if you get morning sick?"

"Can't be worse'n chokin' down demon meat," Renna said. "I'll manage. You need me."

"I . . ." Arlen began.

"Don't deny it," Renna cut in. "Jardir means well, but he's got a different way of lookin' at the world. Threw you in a demon pit once. Don't think he won't do it again if he thinks it's the Creator's will."

Arlen blew out a breath. "Don't think I forgot that."

"Shanjat's an empty shell," Renna said. "He may still be breathin', but he ent coming back, and I wouldn't trust it if he did."

"Honest word," Arlen said.

"Shanvah's as good as any can get in a fight, but she can't dissipate, and she ent as strong as the rest of us," Renna went on. "You want any chance of making this work, you need me. World needs me. Gotta put that first, just like we asked her to with her da."

Jardir watched Shanvah, marveling at what his niece had become. It seemed just days ago he saw her newborn and squalling in his sister's arms. In Krasian fashion, he had seen little of her in the ensuing years, and nothing since she went into the Dama'ting Palace as a child.

Now she was a woman grown, carrying a weight of honor that could break the strongest *Sharum*. Shanjat was not capable of shame, so she carried it for them both, locked inside an iron will.

"Come and sit with me, Niece." Jardir disdained the Northern chairs, sweeping his robe back to sit cross-legged on the bare floor. While he did, he concentrated, activating one of the powers of the Crown of Kaji. As Shanvah took a spot facing him on the floor, he put a bubble of silence around them, keeping their words from Shanjat's ears.

Shanvah knelt before him, bending to put her hands on the floor. "Raise your eyes," Jardir commanded. "I am Shar'Dama Ka, but I am your uncle, as well. With your father . . . absent, I would speak to you as both, while we walk the path to the abyss."

Shanvah sat back on her heels. "You honor me beyond my worth, Deliverer."

Jardir shook his head. "No, child. This is but a fraction of the honor you are due for service given, and nothing in the face of what I must ask of you."

"I understand, Uncle," Shanvah said. "Alagai Ka cannot guide us to Nie's abyss without my father's voice."

Jardir nodded. "Nor can we allow the demon free movement. He must be chained."

Shanvah closed her eyes, breathing. "Alagai Ka said he would make a mount of my father."

"Indeed, I think it must be so. Imagine the damage Alagai Ka could do if it took over my mind, or that of one of the *chin*? We cannot risk touching it in anything but battle."

"Nor can you allow it to control my father without constant guard," Shanvah said.

"We will separate them whenever possible," Jardir said, "but must assume that every time the Prince of Lies touches your father's mind, it will learn all Shanjat has seen and heard. We can no longer speak freely in his presence. Nor can you let your guard down around him. There is no telling how much of Alagai Ka's influence remains when they are apart."

Shanvah placed her hands on the floor and bent to touch her forehead between them. Then she sat up and met his eyes again. "I understand my place in things, Uncle. I will not fail you."

In her aura he saw it was true. She would carry this burden atop a broken heart all the way to the Core. He opened his arms, and after a moment Shanvah moved awkwardly into his embrace until he pulled her tight. "Of that, I have no doubt."

The Par'chin noted Jardir's sphere of silence as he and his *jiwah* returned to the group. He nodded, moving to sit between Jardir and Shanvah on the floor. Renna took up a place opposite him, all of them facing one another.

"Gonna do this, it needs to be soon," the Par'chin said.

"Agreed," Jardir said. "But not too soon."

"Ay, what's that mean?" the Par'chin asked.

"It means I will see my *Jiwah Ka* before I go to the abyss," Jardir said. "I will hold her in my arms again, and have her cast her dice in my blood."

"Ent got time—" the Par'chin began.

"This is not a request, son of Jeph!" Jardir made a lash of his words. "We must claim every advantage in this endeavor, and the dice can do much to counter the Prince of Lies."

"And if the dice conveniently tell her she ought to come along?" the Par'chin asked.

"Then she will come," Jardir said. "As your *Jiwah Ka* does.

She will not dissemble with all Ala in the balance. Everything Inevera does, she does for Sharak Ka."

He could see in the Par'chin's aura that the man wanted to argue further, but he checked himself. "Fair enough. Ren and I should make a few stops, too. Let folk know what's coming, we don't find a miracle."

CHAPTER 7

THE EUNUCHS

334 AR

A stab of pain between his legs woke Abban from one of the rare lapses of consciousness that passed for sleep in his new reality. He sat up from the cold ground with a start, his foot joining the agony as he squinted in the firelight.

Hasik took his cock first. Abban had steeled himself, knowing it was coming, but nothing could truly prepare a man for that. He did it with his teeth, and made Abban watch.

Abban begged Everam to let him bleed out, or take a fever and die, but warriors of Hasik's experience knew their way around wounds. He'd tied it off first, and burned the end.

Dampness between his thighs made Abban think the wound had reopened. His chains clinked as he scrambled to undo the drawstring of his ragged pants and check.

Abban might have prayed for death while it was going on, but now, cock or no cock, he meant very much to live. He pulled back the cloth. There was no fresh blood on the bandages, but they were stained yellow and soaking.

It was nothing new. Abban now pissed through a hollow needle punched into the charred flesh. He had no control, bladder draining steadily throughout the day. He was always wet between the legs now, and stank of piss.

Hasik laughed from the other side of the fire. "You'll get used to it, *khaffit*. So used to wet pants they will grow as comfortable as dry. So used to the smell of your own piss you will sniff the air and smell nothing even as everyone around you complains of your stink."

"That's hopeful, at least," Abban said, retying his pants. It wasn't as if he had anything to change the dressing with. For now he would have to endure the wet.

"Enjoy it while you can, *khaffit.*" Hasik waved at the lightening sky. "The sun will rise soon. How many has it been?"

Abban grit his teeth, but he knew better than to fail to answer. Hasik fed on his pain and anguish like *Sharum* fed on magic. But while a certain amount of torture was inevitable, there was nothing to be gained in making it worse.

"Fourteen," Abban said. "A holy number. Fourteen days since you murdered the Deliverer's son."

Hasik laughed. He did so often now, his mood more jovial than Abban had ever seen. "And yours. No doubt you thought the poisoned blade at the end of your crutch was clever. How did it look shoved up Fahki's ass while he foamed and shook?"

He chuckled again as Abban swallowed, uncharacteristically finding himself with no reply.

There was a crackle of magic and a flash of light. A lone wood demon paced the perimeter of their circle, searching for openings where none were to be found. Even the dimmest *Sharum* had the basic circle of protection beaten into his head by the time he earned his blacks, and Hasik was turning out to be brighter than he let on.

Hasik lay back on his saddle, hands behind his head. An empty bottle of some *chin* spirit lay beside him. His cold eyes followed the demon as it paced.

"Why not kill it and have done?" Abban asked. "Isn't that what *Sharum* live for?"

Hasik spat in the demon's direction. "All those years in *sharaj* and you never learned anything about us, did you, *khaffit?*"

"I learned that you love carnage more than you hate the *alagai,*" Abban said. "That you prefer weak foes to strong, particularly the soft *chin*. But drunk or not, I did not think you a coward, afraid of a single demon."

He expected the words to get a rise from Hasik, but the warrior was unmoved. "I fear nothing, but I am through with Everam's foolish war."

"Now, with Sharak Ka nigh?" Abban probed. Hasik seemed to be in a rare moment of introspection. Perhaps he might learn something of use. Crippled, he could not flee Hasik. His only choice was to find a way to manipulate the warrior into keeping him alive until new opportunities presented themselves.

"The Deliverer was to lead us in Sharak Ka," Hasik said. "But Ahmann was cast down in shame, and his son was pathetic. Who does that leave? Even if the rumors are true and the Par'chin is still alive, I'll go to the abyss before I follow him."

He swept a hand at the demon, watching their words with the blank stare of a camel. "I will fight demons when there is something to gain, but I am through killing them for Everam's sake. What has the Creator ever done for me?"

Abban shook his head. "If the Creator exists, He is not without humor, that only now should we begin to understand each other."

"Perhaps it is because we both lack cocks now." Hasik smacked his lips. "I tell you, *khaffit,* that was the sweetest meat I ever tasted. I'm tempted to carve off more."

"No doubt it's all the pig I've eaten," Abban said. "If you've truly turned your back on Heaven and look to the pleasures of Ala, there is none greater."

Hasik laughed. "Bold words, *khaffit.* I doubt any meat can give greater pleasure than I had atop your wives and virgin daughters."

"As you say, those days are behind us both," Abban said. "We are eunuchs now, and must take pleasure where we can. Find me a pig, and I will prepare a meal you will never forget."

"You've tried to poison me for years," Hasik said. "What makes you think you'll be more successful now?"

It was true. When they were boys together in *sharaj,* Hasik beat Abban regularly. Once, Abban paid him back with a drop of sandsnake venom in his gruel. Not enough to kill, but Hasik spent a week embracing pain above the waste pits.

There was no proof it was Abban, but Hasik was no fool. The beatings worsened. After that fateful week, Abban tried countless times to poison Hasik in a more permanent fashion, but the big warrior had learned his lesson. He ignored the food lines, simply picking another warrior at random and taking his bowl at mealtime.

Even among the *dal'Sharum,* where pride often took the better part of good sense, few dared rise to the challenge. Those who did—often at a bribe from Abban—were gleefully broken in front of the other men.

"You have always been difficult to kill," Abban admitted. "But that is no reason to stop trying."

"You are not utterly without spine, *khaffit,* even if you fear to strike at me yourself." Hasik spread his arms. "When you are ready, come at me. I will allow you one free blow. You may even poison it, if you wish. I will still have time to gouge your eyes and feed them to you. Still time to suck the tongue from your mouth and bite it off."

Abban turned out his damp pockets, chains clinking. "I have no poison in any event. But Everam my witness, I can roast a pig that will dizzy you and set your mouth to water at just the smoke. Pigskin hardens into a cracking shell, slick with grease, and the flesh beneath will make you wish you had renounced Heaven sooner."

"Everam's beard, *khaffit!*" Hasik cried. "You've convinced me! Today we will find a pig and roast it to commemorate our first fortnight together."

Hasik reached into his wide belt, producing a small hammer. "But first, there is our dawn prayer."

The wood demon faded to mist and slipped back to the abyss as they talked. Now the sun crested the horizon, and Hasik at last got to his feet.

The hammer—no *Sharum* weapon—was a simple worker's tool stolen casually as they fled the ruin of Jayan's army after the Battle of Angiers. A lump of iron at the end of a stout stick.

But Hasik wielded that hammer like a *dama'ting*'s scalpel. He twirled it absently in his fingers, limbering them as he came to kneel by Abban's feet.

"Please," Abban said.

"What will you offer me today, *khaffit?*" Hasik asked.

"A palace," Abban said. "One to put the greatest *Damaji* to shame. I will empty my coffers and build towers so high you can speak to Everam."

"I speak to Him daily," Hasik said.

The foot of Abban's crippled leg still had its boot, but the other was long gone, his foot too swollen to fit the leather. Hasik had wrapped the foot in rags to keep it from freezing, though Abban welcomed the numbness of cold over the fresh pain each morning.

"Everam, giver of light and life," Hasik drew a ward in the air, "I thank you this and each day forward for delivering my enemy unto me. I sacrifice him to you as I promised long ago, one bone at a time."

Abban howled as Hasik grabbed the purple, bloated appendage, pinning it while he searched for an unbroken bone. He had crushed the toes, then moved on to the bones of Abban's instep, slowly making his way toward the ankle. Abban never dreamed there were so many bones in a human foot.

"Quit whining, *khaffit*," Hasik said with a grin. "*Sharum* break toes every day with little more than a grunt. Wait until I start on your leg. Your hip. Wait until I take your teeth."

"It would be more difficult to have these lovely conversations," Abban said.

Hasik laughed as he brought the hammer down. The pain was unbearable, and as his vision began to close in, Abban welcomed oblivion like a lover.

Abban slowly regained consciousness, slung over the back of Hasik's great charger like a sack of flour. The beast's every step sent waves of dizziness and nausea through him to accompany the ever-present pain.

He gave in to it for a time, weeping. He knew the sounds were like music to Hasik, but Abban had never embraced pain as easily as a *Sharum*.

Still, even the worst pains became bearable over time, especially in the numbing cold. Eventually, the nausea subsided and Abban came back to himself enough to feel the sting of a snowflake striking his cheek.

He opened his eyes, seeing flurries blowing in the wind.

North of them great clouds were gathering. There would be a storm soon.

They were making their way along the Old Hill Road, a paved Messenger road that once connected the Free Cities of Thesa to the *chin* city of Fort Hill, lost nearly a century ago to the *alagai*. Prince Jayan had used the highway—abandoned for most of its length—to move his warriors north to attack Fort Angiers.

It felt like riding through a tomb. Jayan sacked the Angierian hamlets and farms along the road, their burnt remnants standing in judgment over Abban, who had encouraged the foolish prince in his mad plan.

Hasik spat. "Pigs everywhere in the greenlands, until you want to eat one."

"Turn left at the next fork," Abban said.

Hasik looked back at him. "Why?"

Chains clinked as Abban gestured at a distant line of smoke drifting above the trees. "Jayan kept his foragers within a mile or two of the road, but my maps show Messenger paths to hamlets and isolated farmsteads beyond his reach."

"Good news," Hasik said. "I may not need to cut anything off you for my supper."

"I fear you would find it all marble and little meat in any event," Abban said.

Hasik chuckled as he turned his charger onto the dirt path leading into the woods. Trees were thick on either side, and even in daytime they rode in shadow deep enough to have Abban wary of *alagai*.

They encountered several farms along the way, oases of cleared land amid the forest. Each was a wreckage, burned out and abandoned, livestock taken and fields picked clean.

Abban was not surprised. Thousands of *dal'Sharum*, Jayan's finest, were lost in the slaughter at the gates of Fort Angiers. When the defeat became known, the *chi'Sharum* turned on their masters or fled, and the remains of Jayan's army, perhaps ten thousand *Sharum*, scattered to the wind. Everam only knew if they would re-form into any sizable force, but there were doubtless enough deserters to plague the *chin* lands for years.

"The *chin* flame weapons allowed them to hold the gate,"

Hasik said, "but they do not have the strength to guard their lesser wells."

"Yet," Abban said.

"Today is all that matters, *khaffit*," Hasik said. "Tomorrow I may yet see how much meat is truly on your bones."

The next farm they came upon was not deserted. Abban smelled smoke, but it was not the acrid stench of all-consuming flame. This was sizzling fat and Northern spices, woodsmoke from a warm hearth.

But it was not Northerners they encountered. At least not entirely. Two *Sharum* moved along the fences protecting the fields and yard, keeping the wards clear of snow. Others stood over a handful of *chin* working in the yard. They leaned casually on their spears, but the greenlanders were wise enough not to test how quickly they could be put to use. There was noise from the house and the stables.

"They look to be settling in," Abban said.

"We were not made for these Northern winters, *khaffit*," Hasik said, though Abban had never seen him show the slightest bother at the cold.

"Perhaps it would be wise to . . ." Abban began, but Hasik ignored him, kicking his charger into a trot.

Hasik had opened the gate and ridden into the yard before there was a shout. Nine *Sharum* came running out to surround his horse, a circle of spears pointed inward.

Hasik spat on the ground. "No one on watch. Who leads this rabble?"

"We'll have your father's name first, warrior," one of the *Sharum* said. He was bigger than the others and had an air of command about him, though the veil around his neck was as black as any other.

"I am Hasik asu Reklan am'Kez am'Kaji."

"Jayan's dog," the lead warrior said, "left with no one to heel." The others laughed.

Hasik joined their laughter. "True enough, though I have my own dog now." He swept a hand over Abban.

All eyes glanced his way, and Abban wilted further under the collective stare. No doubt the men had only just noticed him, *Sharum* focused foremost on potential threats.

"The Deliverer's *khaffit*," the first warrior said. "Not so proud anymore. Is it true he can turn sand and camel shit to gold?"

"Indeed he can," Hasik said. "He can sell water to the fish men, and wood to cutters."

The warrior tilted his head, meeting Abban's eyes. "It did not save him."

Hasik showed his teeth. "Nothing could, on my day. Now we have given our names. I ask again for yours."

"Orman asu Hovan am'Bajin," the man said. "Welcome to my *csar*. It is no prince's palace, but there are slaves and food is plentiful."

"The Bajin are not returning to Everam's Reservoir?" Hasik asked.

"Not these Bajin," Orman said. "Who leads there, now? Qeran? I've no desire to become a privateer and spend my life on the water."

"The monastery, then," Hasik said. "Dama Khevat still rules there?"

Orman shook his head. "For now, perhaps, but he hasn't the men to hold it. The fish men will be eager to reclaim the monastery with Jayan's forces broken. It is the key to striking at Everam's Reservoir. Why spend a week walking that freezing, demon-infested highway to join a hopeless battle when there is warmth and comfort here? The greenlands are soft and ripe for plunder."

"Wise words." Hasik glanced about the yard. "Do you have pigs?"

Orman nodded. "The *chin* slaves eat them. Need to feed your *khaffit*?"

"He can feed off his fat," Hasik said. "I thought I would taste one, myself."

"If that is your wish," Orman said, "providing you can pay. We have women, as well. *Chin* women, not much to look at, but under the veils one is as good as any other, yes?"

One of the men whispered in Orman's ear. The warrior tossed his head and barked a laugh, then met Hasik's eyes. "They remind me Jayan's dog was gelded. Women not much good to you, are they?"

Abban tsked, shaking his head. "You will regret that, son of Hovan."

The man glanced at him. "What . . . ?"

But then he was gasping and doubling over, grasping at the handle of the knife Hasik had thrown, embedded now in his crotch.

The other warriors surged in. They speared Hasik's charger in the throat, but Hasik wore armor of warded glass beneath his robes, and their weapons skittered off. He was rolling off the beast, spear in hand, even as it reared. Abban was thrown clear, landing heavily on the ground in a blast of pain.

Hasik was a blur amid the warriors. Then the warriors were a blur.

Then everything went dark.

Abban woke on a hard wood floor. A fire burned in the hearth a few feet away, stealing the numbness from his wounds and bringing back the pain afresh. There was a woman bent over him, wiping his forehead with a damp cloth.

"You're alive."

"I am alive," Abban agreed. "Though at the moment I wish otherwise."

"Well I thank the Creator for it," the woman said. "The new master said any who die will be guided on the lonely path by my family."

Abban squinted in the light. "New master? Hasik?"

The woman nodded. "He killed three of the Bajin. Cut the stones from the rest." She spat. "No less than they deserve."

"The change in rule may seem a relief now," Abban said, "but you may come to think the Bajin a blessing by comparison."

"There are no blessings left for us," the woman said, "in this age of false Deliverers. All we can hope for is to survive."

"There is always hope in survival," Abban said. "I have glimpsed the lonely path more than once, but here I lie, still breathing on Ala."

"The master says you are his chef," the woman said. "The men will slaughter a pig for you to roast. A celebration for his new tribe."

"A tribe of eunuchs." Abban attempted to sit up. "I don't suppose you have something I can use to poison the meat?"

"If we had, I'd have used it long ago." The woman held out a hand to pull him to a sitting position. "I'm Dawn."

"A beautiful name," Abban said. "I am Abban asu Chabin am'Haman am'Kaji. I'll need your help if I am to prepare a feast. I fear I will not be able to stand without crutches, and poorly even then."

"We have a chair with wheels my grandfather used before he passed," Dawn said.

"Creator be praised," Abban said. "If you can help me into it, I would thank you. If Hasik wants a feast, we would be wise not to keep him waiting."

Dawn nodded, leaving the room briefly and returning with the wheeled chair. It was handmade and crude, but sturdy enough to hold Abban's considerable bulk.

"How many warriors does Hasik have now?" Abban asked as she wheeled him to the kitchen. Three women, one older and two younger, were already at work preparing the evening meal. A few had bruises, and all kept their eyes down.

"Six still able to fight," Dawn said, "though all walk tenderly now. Two more with broken bones. Three left out in the snow."

A shriek and a flash of light drew Abban's attention to the window. It was dark, with snow blown up against the panes. No doubt the *Sharum* were out clearing the area of demons, eager for the healing magic to soothe their wounded groins.

They won't grow back, Abban wanted to tell them. Magic would heal the wounds and broken bones, but it would not grow back what was severed.

"And your family?" Abban asked.

"Seven." Dawn nodded to the other women. "My mother and daughters, my son-in-law, my husband and father-in-law."

"Did the Bajin kill anyone?" Abban asked, reaching out to sniff at the spices on the rack.

Dawn shook her head. "They didn't speak a word of Thesan, but it was clear they wanted slaves, not killing." One of the younger women sobbed at that, and her sister moved to comfort her.

"Survival is hope," Abban said.

"You're not like the others," Dawn said. "You and the new master speak our language, and they treat you . . ."

"I am *khaffit*," Abban said. "A coward. In the eyes of warriors, I am worth no more than you. It will be all our lives if the feast is not satisfactory. Let us look at the pigs."

Abban shivered as Dawn wheeled him out into the evening snow, crossing the lamplit yard to the slaughterhouse. *Sharum* flitted about in the darkness beyond, illuminated here and there in a flash of wardlight.

The Bajin had killed most of the other animals, but the pigs they disdained. There were seven of them, fat and healthy. Abban's mouth watered at the sight.

These will sell for a thousand draki apiece, to the right buyer. He shook his head at the useless thought. The bazaar was far away, and it was *inevera* whether Abban would ever see it again.

Live in the now, he reminded himself, *or there will be no future.*

Three *chin* men were in the slaughterhouse, all of them bruised and moving stiffly. Two were in their prime, the other older but still sturdy.

"That one." Abban pointed to the best of the lot. The plump young hog squealed as the *chin* men slaughtered it. Abban left the men to the work, Dawn pushing him back to the kitchen that they might plan a menu.

Hasik found them in the yard. "It is good to see you awake, *khaffit*. I have not forgotten your promise to me." He seemed almost jovial, as if every man he gelded lessened his own shame that much more.

"I always keep my promises," Abban said. "It will take a night and a day to roast the pig properly."

Hasik nodded, touching the diamond in the center of his *kai'Sharum* turban. There was a kernel of demon bone within, and when next he spoke, his voice boomed through house, yard, and barn. "The Eunuch tribe fasts until sunset! Any caught touching food before I give word at tomorrow's feast will lose his tongue as well as his cock."

"You'll recall how such taunts ended for me," Abban noted.

Hasik shrugged. "One day I will be weak, and man or *alagai* will kill me. Until then, I am strong, and will taunt as I please." He looked out into the night. "Already the wounds to their flesh have healed. A fast and a feast will help them begin to accept their new lives."

Abban nodded. "The *kai* is wise. It will be a meal they never forget."

"It had better," Hasik said, "Or the *chin* women will roast *you* next."

Abban passed out in the barn, cradled by the wheeled chair, basking in the heat of the coals and the scent of roasting pig. It was the closest he'd been to comfortable in all the weeks of his captivity.

Which only made the white-hot spike of agony that woke him all the worse.

His eyes snapped open to see Hasik kneeling before him with his small hammer, dawn light coming through the barn door. While Abban slept, he had freed the *khaffit*'s foot from the chair, placed it on a block, and broken another bone for Everam.

Hasik laughed as Abban screamed. "I never tire of that sound, *khaffit*! I want you to know what it means to wake in anguish every day."

"You . . ." Abban coughed.

"What was that, *khaffit*?" Hasik asked.

". . . didn't . . ." Abban labored for breath, every word heavy on his tongue. ". . . even . . . let . . . me . . . offer . . . my . . . bribe."

Hasik smiled. "Was it a good one?"

Abban nodded. "A . . . pleasure even the . . . *Damaji* fear to . . . indulge."

Hasik stood, crossing his arms. "This I must hear."

"A dozen *heasah*," Abban said. "Chosen because they look nearly identical to the Damajah, to pillow dance for you."

Hasik grew red in the face, and Abban realized his mistake. "And what am I to do with *heasah*, without my cock?"

"There are straps *heasah* sometimes wear, to simulate having a man's spear," Abban said. "I did not lie when I said I could give you a cock of gold, smoother, larger, and stiffer than the real thing ever was."

"If I wanted to shame myself with such a harness, it would

not be the Damajah I would wish to fuck." Hasik leered at
him. "No, it would be you I make howl, *khaffit*. Louder even
than your daughters and wives."

He stuck the hammer back in his belt. "Now get back to
making my feast."

Everam, if I but had a drop of tunnel asp venom, Abban
thought, but he knew it was a lie. Here, crippled deep in the
greenlands with *Sharum* deserters looting and pillaging, he
would be a fool to poison Hasik. The powerful *kai'Sharum*
was his only hope for survival until they reached Krasian
lands or Abban's network in the Hollow.

"Better a bone at a time than a spear in the back, or a *chin*
noose around my neck," he muttered.

And so he roasted the pig with utmost care, glazing the skin
to a hard, delicious shell connected to the moist, hot meat by
a melted layer of fat. He directed the women as well, teaching
them to roll couscous and prepare dishes suited to Krasian
palates. There was a Bajin pea dish that could be reasonably
approximated with Northern corn, and Abban had them make
it in plenty to honor Hasik's new men.

Hasik was in good spirits throughout the day. Abban made
sure the *chin* fasted as well, and the smells teased everyone at
the farm. By sunset, even the Bajin seemed eager when they
were called to the table.

The *Sharum* had taken a pair of Northern feasting tables
and cut the legs short, laying them end-to-end. Hasik was already kneeling upon a bed of pillows at the table's head when
the others arrived. "Orman." He gestured to the single pillow
to his right. The Bajin leader glared at him but wasn't willing
to challenge Hasik again. He knelt, eyes down. The other
warriors followed suit, kneeling on the bare floor four to a
side.

When the warriors settled, Hasik pointed to the foot of the
table. *"Chin."*

The three Angierian men kept their distance, circling out of
reach until they knelt together at the foot of the table, tense
with fear.

The Bajin scowled, and Orman spoke up. "We are to sup
with *chin*?"

Hasik's hand was a blur, gripping the warrior's beard and

pulling hard, smashing his face into the table. He roared and struggled, but Hasik kept the thick hair in his fist, holding him prone until he calmed.

"Perhaps you thought kneeling at my right gives you leave to question me." Hasik said. "Do you still succor such foolish thoughts?"

Orman shook his head slowly. "No."

"No?" Hasik asked.

"No, master," Orman said.

Hasik grunted, letting go his beard and acting as if nothing had happened. "*Sharum* sit."

The warriors shifted from kneeling to sitting with military skill. How many hours had they spent drilling it in *sharaj*? The *chin* stayed on their knees as Abban had instructed, setting them apart. The Bajin seemed mollified at this.

No place for me, Abban noted, pleased to be relegated to the kitchen, invisible. He sent the women back and forth, filling the table with steaming platters that held the attention of the hungry men. They inhaled deeply, tasting with their noses as mouths began to water.

At last they wheeled the animal out, still dripping on the spit. The melting fat pooled in a tray beneath the succulent beast.

"Prepare your bellies for a wonder you have never dreamed of," Abban said, smiling at the looks the men cast the pig. Even mighty *Sharum* could be ensorcelled by the scent of pork. His own belly groaned and grumbled, desperate to partake.

"Come and sit behind me at my left while I taste this wonder, *khaffit*," Hasik said.

"The *kai* honors me," Abban said.

"Nonsense," Hasik said. "I merely wish to ensure you continue your fast. You are too fat, Abban. You will see it is for your own good."

Abban was so hungry he would have sacrificed another bone for a taste of pork, but it was pointless to argue. Orman, Hasik would settle for humiliating. If Abban questioned him in front of the men, Hasik would have no choice but to kill him.

Or worse, Abban thought. He took a deep breath. For now,

he was worth less than a warrior, but once Hasik tasted the pig, Abban knew his value would soar.

Still Hasik did not give permission to eat. He clasped his hands and closed his eyes. The others at the table immediately did likewise.

"Blessed Everam," Hasik said, "He who honors the strong. We thank you for the feast before us. It may be against your law to sup on the flesh of pigs, but you have shown me your laws are for the weak."

He paused. "I was weak, once. Driven by pleasures of the flesh even when they brought pain and misfortune upon me again and again. I made the weakest part of me my ruler." He straightened. "Now that part of me is severed, and I am free at last. Free to see the world around me without weakness. I see for the first time the grains in the dunes, and know I am stronger for it."

He looked at the Bajin. "No doubt you would all put a spear in me given the chance, but you will see now how you, too, are free. How we have become strong."

He looked to Orman. "Are there other *Sharum* in the area?"

Orman nodded. "A dozen Khanjin have taken a farm down the road."

"You and your men will soon have a chance to visit your shame on your night brothers." Hasik smiled. "You will find nothing eases your torment like sharing it."

The Bajin remained grim-faced, but Abban could see the words stoked a new hunger in their eyes. Hasik was not wrong.

Hasik looked at the *chin,* switching to their language: "Everam smiles on you, *chin.* In the new order, even you may claim honor. The choice is yours. You can be slaves, or you can learn to fight and join us."

The younger men froze, turning to look at their patriarch. He hesitated, but only for a moment. He bowed as Abban taught him, placing his hands on the floor and touching his forehead between them.

"We will fight."

"Then let us seal it with a feast!" Hasik called. He lifted the haunch Abban had carved him, and the skin crackled as he bit into it and tore away a mouthful of flesh. His eyes widened, and then it was chaos as the men tore into the food.

Abban watched in pain as they stuffed themselves, but he kept his mask in place, giving Hasik a look pathetic enough to satisfy him as he mocked the starving *khaffit* with his glistening fingers and lips.

There was Northern ale, and it flowed freely as they ate. Soon the Bajin were laughing, and even the *chin* seemed to relax. When the plates had been emptied and filled and emptied again, they began to slow, eating more for pleasure than hunger. Hasik lounged back on his bed of pillows as they sang warrior songs.

At last the women cleared the empty bowls and carcass from the room, and Hasik looked at the *chin*.

"You have eaten of my pig," he said. "There is only one more thing keeping you from joining the Eunuchs."

The *chin* looked at one another in confusion as Orman laughed, drawing a knife.

CHAPTER 8

MONASTERY

334 AR

"A dozen fat slaves, dressed as me," Abban promised. "One delivered the first day of the month to torture until you kill them in a new and inventive fashion on Waning and begin anew."

"I admit, that is a good one," Hasik said.

"Spare me, and I can make it reality," Abban said.

Hasik clicked his tongue. "There is where it fails, *khaffit*. What good is pretending vengeance for a year when true vengeance escapes?"

"Then I will lease my life," Abban offered. "One slave dressed to look like me each Waning until you collect in full."

Hasik pursed his lips. "The idea has merit. I will take a few months to consider."

Then he swung the hammer, and Abban screamed.

The Eunuchs and slaves were used to it now, ignoring Abban's wails and whimpers. Once, when a blood fever from his shattered bones had threatened to kill Abban, Dawn had begged on his behalf.

Hasik had warded Abban's leg and smeared it with stinking *alagai* ichor. The demon blood activated the wards and healed Abban. His strength and vigor returned, sweeping away the pain, but the shattered bones of his leg and foot fused into a twisted ruin. Abban doubted even a healer as powerful as the Damajah could make him walk again.

Then Hasik cut the noses from Dawn and her daughters, a permanent warning to all that might take pity on him again.

Hasik was gone by the time Abban mastered his pain enough to crawl into his chair. The camp was full of activity as Abban wheeled to Hasik's tent, slaves rushing to and fro to service the warriors.

In the past five weeks, the Eunuchs had swollen massively in number. First in fits and starts as Hasik hunted *Sharum* deserters, catching warriors sometimes in ones and twos, and other times in sizable bands. The freshest recruits were always the most eager to capture and castrate new members, as if cutting off another man's cock somehow helped their own healing.

They sacked farms and hamlets as their numbers grew, growing heavy with supply. Then, impossibly, men began to come to them. *Sharum* that had set off in search of plunder and found ill fortune begging to join, willingly surrendering their genitals in exchange for full bellies and the sense they were once again part of something powerful.

The growth had come with a positive change in Abban's circumstances. Hasik healed him regularly now, needing Abban's eyes sharp and his mind unclouded. Once relegated to cook, the *khaffit* was back on familiar ground, keeping Hasik's ledgers and acting as quartermaster for his troops and caravan of slaves.

Hasik was lounging on the pillows in his pavilion, eating eggs and bacon.

"Nie's black heart, *khaffit*," Hasik said. "Had I known the flesh of pigs was so delicious, I would have turned my back on Everam's law long ago."

"It is a great burden lifted," Abban agreed, "setting aside the Evejah to eat and drink as you please."

Hasik tore another bite off the rasher, his lips shiny with grease. "Read me the tallies."

Abban grit his teeth, wheeling over to his writing desk. "You have . . . three *kai'Sharum,* one hundred seventy-two *dal'Sharum,* eight hundred seventeen *kha'Sharum,* two hundred and six *chi'Sharum,* and four hundred thirty-six slaves. We have seven hundred forty-two horses . . ."

Hasik put his hands behind his head and closed his eyes as

if listening to music. The tallies were a burden to a good leader, as Ahmann had been, but to a man like Hasik it read as a list of his personal wealth, and Abban could not deny that in a very short time that wealth had become considerable. So considerable that all the Eunuchs had a taste of the largesse. There were no hungry in the caravan, and all had proper clothes to ward off winter's chill. The *Sharum* were well equipped and obedient. Even the *chi'Sharum* conscripts had weapons to go with their ongoing training.

The canvas flap opened, admitting Orman, now wearing the white veil of a *kai'Sharum* around his neck. Orman had remained Hasik's second in command and was, so far as Abban could determine, quite loyal and competent. The Bajin was a small tribe, and Orman would likely never have risen as high there as he had in the Eunuchs.

Orman bowed. "Eunuch Ka, there is a messenger. He claims to know you."

"A messenger?" Hasik asked. "From who?"

"From Dama Khevat!" a *kai'Sharum* boomed, pushing past the door guard.

Abban immediately recognized the man by the scars on his face, a faded remnant from the night a quarter century ago when he had taken a swipe of a sand demon's claws in the village of Baha kad'Everam. Magic had kept the man young, but he was an honored elder of their fathers' generation.

Jesan, Hasik's *ajin'pal.*

Among the *Sharum,* the bond between *ajin'pal* was as strong as family. For those near in age it was a sibling bond, but more often it was one of father to son. Nightfathers, they were sometimes called, with a relationship no less complicated than fathers and sons of blood. They were mentors and authority figures.

The two were close when Hasik was the Deliverer's brother-in-law, a respected member of the royal family. They had not spoken since Hasik's disgrace.

"Jesan." Hasik got to his feet. The men didn't reach for weapons as they moved in to each other, but they didn't need to. Both had been Spears of the Deliverer and were more than capable of killing with their bare hands.

Instead they gripped each other's shoulders and laughed, embracing.

"*Khaffit!* Brandy for my *ajin'pal*!" Hasik called, leading Jesan to the pillows. Hasik took the center, where the pile was thickest, gesturing for Jesan to sit at his right and Orman at his left.

Dawn appeared, silently filling a tray and laying it across the arms of Abban's chair. It was a small blessing that she kept her eyes down, that Abban did not have to meet them as he looked into the gaping hole where her nose had been. She vanished as quickly as she had appeared, and Abban wheeled over to the pillows with the tray.

Hasik took a glass, handing it to Jesan. "There is no couzi this far north, but I've found the *chin* distilleries even better."

"Just water, thank you." Jesan's voice was tight.

"Some bacon, perhaps?" Hasik swept a hand to the plate. "Everam could not have made a food so delicious if it was not meant to be eaten."

Jesan stiffened. "Perhaps that is exactly why we were commanded not to eat it."

"Oh?" Hasik's question seemed casual, but there was challenge in his tone.

Jesan met Hasik's eyes, breathing deeply. The familiar rhythm was an easy tell that the *Sharum* was attempting to remain calm. "To remind us everyone has a master."

"You think I need a reminder of who my master is?" Hasik asked quietly.

"I am not the Creator, Hasik," Jesan said. "Nothing happens, but that Everam wills it. I do not care that you drink couzi. I do not care that you eat pig. I have shed blood with you in the night and that is all that matters. I do not come as some glowering elder, but as your *ajin'pal*. There are pressing matters to discuss."

"Of course." Hasik leaned back in the pillows, sipping the brandy he had offered to Jesan. "Please go on."

"Dama Khevat congratulates your successful efforts in recapturing deserters from the Battle of Angiers," Jesan said.

That's one way of putting it, Abban thought.

Hasik nodded. "The men lost heart when the Sharum Ka and his finest warriors were killed storming the gates of Angiers." The lie came easily to his lips. Abban, the only living witness to the truth—that Hasik killed Jayan himself—was wise enough to keep silent on the matter.

"Your honor was taken from you unfairly, brother," Jesan's eyes flicked to Abban with disgust, "but you can restore it. The Monastery of Dawn is under renewed attack from the *chin*. We cannot hold without aid."

"How is this possible?" Hasik asked. "Khevat had a thousand warriors, not to mention the remnants of the Sharum Ka's forces."

"Twenty-five hundred made it back from the Battle of Angiers," Jesan said, "but it was deep in the cold months. With the lakeshore frozen solid, we did not have sufficient supply. Dama Khevat sent them on to Everam's Reservoir.

"But then came an unexpected thaw. *Chin* saboteurs opened the main gate for a secret raid by the fish men, who braved the icy waters under cover of darkness to land a sizable force."

"Everam's beard," Abban breathed. The monastery was built on a great bluff, with only one narrow land route to the main gates and treacherous stairs leading up from the docks. The walls were nearly impregnable, but if the gate had been opened . . .

"By the time we discovered the treachery, we were outnumbered," Jesan said. "But the Deliverer's son Icha rallied the men and we threw back the foe, reclaiming the gates and docks."

"Of course." Hasik sipped his brandy. "They are only *chin*."

"But the attacks did not stop," Jesan continued. "The fish men stole our ships, sailing out of range of the stingers and rock slings. Khevat put all the *chin* slaves to death, but still the fish men found allies within our walls. *Chi'Sharum* from Everam's Bounty snuck hundreds through a hidden tunnel in the basements, starting fires and opening the gates again."

"The greenlanders are tenacious," Hasik said.

"Khevat had all the *chin* put to death," Jesan said, "*Sharum* and slave alike. The walls still hold, but there are less than three hundred *Sharum* left, half of them too injured to fight."

"Can they not speed their healing killing *alagai*?" Orman asked.

Jesan shook his head. "The *chin* Holy Men did their warding too well. *Alagai* avoid the place."

Jesan offered a scroll, sealed with the wax stamps of Dama Khevat and Ahmann Jardir's third son, Icha. The two were the ranking Krasians north of Everam's Bounty. Hasik took the scroll and handed it to Abban, for of course he could not read.

Abban unrolled the parchment. "Greetings Hasik asu Reklan am'Kez am'Kaji, in the year of Everam 3785, from Dama Khevat asu . . ."

Hasik whisked a hand. "I know who Khevat and that snot-nosed brat are. Get to the meat of it."

Jesan bristled as Abban scanned the page, quickly filtering out the endless formalities. "You and your men are ordered to abandon your lawless ways and return to Sharak Sun. Your sins will be forgiven, and your status restored."

"Ordered?" Hasik asked.

"That is what it says," Abban said.

Hasik looked to Jesan, who swallowed, breathing steadily. "Ordered by who, Jesan? As you say, I have forgotten my master."

"The Deliverer . . ." Jesan began.

"Chose loyalty to a *khaffit* over loyalty to me," Hasik said. "And soon after was cast down by the Par'chin. His heir was an idiot who treated me as a dog. *Chin* threw him down, as well."

"Prince Asome is Shar'Dama Ka now," Jesan said. "He slaughtered the *Damaji* and killed Ashan for the Skull Throne."

"To the abyss with them, and Asome, besides. All of them turned their backs to me." Hasik bent in close. "Even you, *ajin'pal.*"

Jesan did not flinch. "Your answer is no, then?"

Hasik relaxed, leaning back with a grin. "I never said that. I tire of sleeping in tents. I think a walled fortress would suit the Eunuchs much better."

He looked to Orman. "Send scouts to the monastery. See how much of this tale you can verify."

Orman punched a fist to his chest, getting immediately to his feet. "Immediately, Eunuch Ka."

"Your deserter army will not follow you as you spit upon the Skull Throne," Jesan said.

"My men are loyal, as you will soon see." Hasik's grin widened as he drew the sharp, curved blade from his belt. "Be honored, nightfather. As you brought me into the ranks of *Sharum,* I welcome you into the ranks of the Eunuchs. You will be given a place of honor. I have need of more *kai.*"

Jesan's calm finally shattered. He screamed and fought, but in the end it made no difference as the men held him down and yanked off his pantaloons.

It would be days before Orman's scouts returned, but Hasik ordered them to break camp immediately. Everything save the tents was packed by dawn, slaves pulling up the stakes even as Hasik raised his hammer.

The target was Abban's smallest toe. Each night, Hasik healed it with *alagai* ichor, and each morning he broke it again. The appendage was a gnarled, misshapen thing now, more grotesque each day.

And try as Abban might, there was no getting used to the pain.

"Bottom feeders!" he shouted.

Hasik paused. "What?"

"The *chin* lake is so wide and deep, it is filled with armored fish," Abban said. "Bottom feeders."

"What of it?" Hasik said.

"Meats forbidden by the Evejah," Abban teased. "But I have tasted them, Eunuch Ka. Spiced and dipped in fat and lemon, they tear like flesh but melt in the mouth. Even bacon pales in comparison."

Hasik crossed his arms. "Bold words, *khaffit.* And an easy lie to test."

"And if it proves no lie?" Abban asked.

"Then I will break one of Dawn's bones, instead of your own, to buy back the one I break today."

It was a horrifying thought, but after a moment Abban decided it was progress he could live with. "I will prepare the feast myself, when you take the monastery. You will see."

"Perhaps," Hasik raised the hammer and quickly brought it down, too fast for Abban to prepare himself.

He screamed.

Soon after, the caravan was on the move, crawling at a snail's pace down the Old Hill Road toward the Monastery of Dawn. It would be a week or more before they arrived, but riding hard, the five hundred men in Hasik's cavalry could cover the distance in less than a day.

"You ride with us." Hasik held out the reins to a strong Krasian charger.

Abban looked dubiously at the animal. "I am not one for horses, Hasik. Now, if you have a camel . . ."

"I once shared your dislike of horses," Hasik said. "They were a liability in the Maze, and it wasn't until we invaded the greenlands that I knew the pain of a day in the saddle." He smiled. "But you will find it easier to ride without balls."

"No doubt," Abban said. "But surely I would only slow you. Would it not make more sense for me to remain with the caravan, to rejoin you after the walls are secured?"

"Your crippled legs will not slow you atop a charger," Hasik said. "I am not such a fool as to let you out of my sight, *khaffit*. If I am brought down in battle, you will walk the lonely path at my side."

"Everam grant me such fortune." Abban clambered painfully atop the beast, where he strapped himself into the saddle. As Hasik promised, the riding was easier on his crotch than he remembered.

"Small blessings," he breathed as they moved south, the light-footed chargers quickly leaving the caravan behind. Late in the day they caught up to one of Orman's returning scouts.

"It is everything the kai told you, and more," the Bajin said, nodding at Jesan. Hasik kept his former *ajin'pal* close—as he did Abban—as if daring the man to attempt vengeance.

"The monastery is under renewed assault, even now," the Bajin said. "The *chin* have laid siege to the main gate, even as their ships crowd the harbor. If they do not take the city today, it will surely fall tomorrow."

"Nie's black heart," Hasik growled. "Signal the men. We ride hard."

Abban was thankful for his lack of balls by the time Hasik called a halt. The horses were lathered in sweat, but they had a high vantage, giving clear view of the monastery in the distance.

With the sun setting, battle had ended, the *chin* retreating to their tents and ward circles.

They could afford to wait. Thousands of men choked the narrow road that climbed the great bluff, the only means by which a land force could make the gate. At the base of the hill they made camp, one prepared to remain as long as necessary.

"They know the defenders are weak," Orman said.

"And that help from Everam's Reservoir is not forthcoming," Hasik agreed. "Their rear defenses are pitiful."

Jesan nodded. "We can take them at dawn."

"Dawn?" Hasik asked.

"The sun is setting," Jesan said. "We cannot attack men in the night."

"I have no master," Hasik said. "None to tell me what I cannot do. It is no less than the fish men did to us at Waning."

"We need not fall into all the infidel ways of the *chin*," Jesan said.

"There are no infidel ways anymore. We are free." Hasik turned to Orman. "Give the men an hour to rest their mounts, then we move in."

In the dark of night, with the *chin* all in their tents or huddled around fires for warmth, unarmed and unarmored, five hundred of Hasik's best men struck.

The enemy camp was destroyed in the slaughter that followed, but Hasik was wiser than Prince Jayan had been, keeping the fires and carnage away from the enemy stores.

They cut a swath through the fish men, never slowing as they broke through their lines and ascended the hill. The *chin* had built progressive fortifications, but all were aimed at an assault from the monastery walls, not one from behind. Soon the Eunuchs controlled the road fully, guarding Hasik's back as he, Jesan, Orman, and Abban rode up to the gate.

Hasik drew a breath, but it was unnecessary. With a great clatter of chain and counterweight, the portcullis was raised to admit Hasik's forces.

Dama Khevat and Kai Icha were waiting in the courtyard. Both were bloodied, the *dama*'s white robes stained red. If the old cleric had been drawn into the fighting, things were dire, indeed.

Khevat gave the shallow, superior bow of a *dama* to a *Sharum*. "Everam sent you in our darkest hour, son of Reklan . . ."

Hasik ignored him, turning to Orman and pointing. "Put a hundred fresh men on the walls. Another fifty to secure the courtyard."

"I need men in the basements, as well," Icha said. "There are *chin* gathered in the caverns below, forcing at the door . . ."

"Another fifty to the basement," Hasik told Orman, not sparing him a glance. "Ready the rest to ride out again now that we control the gate."

Icha clenched a fist. "We will crush them at dawn."

Hasik deigned to look at him. "No, boy, we will crush them now, while they are scattered and bloody. Now, before they can flee with their supply, or dig in and hinder our rear guard."

"It is night . . ." Khevat began.

Abban rolled his eyes. "Dama, please. You've already lost this argument once."

Khevat's eyes flicked to Abban, quivering with rage. "Why is this piece of offal still alive? I would have expected you to kill him long ago."

"You have always been low in your expectations," Hasik said.

"He cut off your cock," Khevat growled.

"And I ate his," Hasik agreed. "And then I cut the cocks from all my men, that none might think himself my better."

Khevat paled. "That is an abomination . . ."

Hasik smiled, drawing his curved knife. "Pray to Everam you get used to it, Dama."

CHAPTER 9

THE MAJAH

334 AR

"The blood, Damajah."

Inevera took the uncorked vial Ashia offered, decanting a few precious drops onto the dice in her palm. She closed her fingers, rolling the smooth, polished bones with practiced skill to coat them evenly.

Kept sealed and cold, away from sunlight, the thick fluid still held a touch of magic, a fragrance of the owner's soul. Enough to focus her dice and perhaps pry a few secrets from Everam, helping put order to the swirling chaos of futures before her.

It was a ritual Inevera performed daily, in the full dark before sunrise. Some futures were unknowable, too many convergences and divergences for her to glean a sense of likelihood. Others cut off abruptly, signifying her own death.

"May I ask a question, Damajah?" Ashia asked.

Inevera's eyes flicked to the girl in annoyance. Ashia had changed in the weeks since Prince Asome's coup—the Night of Hora. Having her own brother try to strangle her while her husband watched was enough to change any woman's perspective on the world.

Even standing guard in her mistress' pillow chamber, the Sharum'ting Ka wore her infant son, Kaji, slung across her belly. She would not be parted from the child for any reason, even in her sacred duty.

It was no great hindrance to performance, Inevera had learned. The bodies Ashia left in her wake during the coup attested to that. Like his mother, Kaji could be preternaturally silent when he wished. Inevera had looked into his aura and seen how the slowing of his mother's heart affected his own. He would be a great Watcher one day.

At times of his choosing, though, Kaji could make his voice known throughout the Damajah's chambers. His laughter made feet laden with duty step lighter, and his screams could jar even Inevera from her center.

But even as he took on some of his mother's traits, she was taking on his. Ashia would never have dared interrupt Inevera's casting ritual before.

"Ask," Inevera said. Ashia had risked everything in bringing Kaji and his grandmother Kajivah to her on the Night of Hora. Inevera's eunuchs and spear sisters were perhaps the only people in Krasia she trusted completely, and Ashia knew it. With her child's fate tied to her own, it was not surprising she had begun to assert a voice in it.

"Why do you waste time seeking the *khaffit* when enemies mount in this very palace?" Ashia asked.

Because my husband is dead, Inevera thought, but didn't say. Nie had piled many stones atop her, but all of them came from the foundation broken by Ahmann's fall. The Par'chin's unforeseen challenge had created such a divergence as to throw decades of careful planning to the dogs. Inevera had tied her fate too closely to Ahmann, certain that he was the Deliverer. Certain that, in the end, he could not fail. Together, their power had been absolute.

Now he was dead, along with so many others. Now there were spears everywhere, pointing at her heart, the heart of everything she and Ahmann had built.

Even her *Jiwah Sen* could no longer be trusted. All save Belina now had their sons in direct control of their respective tribes. They had their own wealth, their own power. They had become willful, and Inevera's tools to bring them in line were few.

—Your fates are intertwined— the dice said of Inevera and Abban. They needed to pool their strength to bend with the wind of Ahmann's passing.

"Because Everam does not care what weights we bear," Inevera said. "Everam cares about one thing, and one thing only."

Ashia nodded. "Sharak Ka."

"Something your husband has forgotten," Inevera said. "His efforts in the night were for political gain. He has the throne, but no strategy in the First War. Someone must keep focus on that. The *khaffit* is an advantage, and every advantage must be seized. If Abban does not return soon, I fear he will find his nephew has taken everything from him and given it to Asome."

And with that, she closed her eyes and whispered her prayer to Everam, feeling the *alagai hora* warm her fingers as their power was called forth, tuned to Abban's aura.

She threw, watching the wards of prophecy flare, twisting the dice into a glimpse into the unknowable.

—The man who is not a man has him.—

Inevera breathed, keeping her center. If Hasik had Abban, the *khaffit*'s prospects were grim, but Hasik took no greater pleasure than in the suffering of others. He would not want to kill Abban right away. He would hurt him, over and over, until Abban bled out from a thousand cuts.

Perhaps there was time.

"Hasik," Inevera said. Ashia needed no further instruction, moving quickly to the cold room where Inevera stored the blood of almost every man, woman, and child of note in Krasia.

Normally, Inevera would cleanse the dice between throws, but since Abban's and Hasik's fates were now tied, she left his essence to help the spell. Ashia returned with Hasik's blood, and Inevera fell into her breath, relaxing as she freshly coated the sticky dice.

"Everam, giver of light and life," she prayed. "Your children need answers. I beg you for knowledge of Hasik asu Reklan am'Kez am'Kaji, former brother-in-law to Shar'Dama Ka. Where can he be found?"

—Spreading like poison in the North.—

—Nie's power grows in him.—

—He has turned from Sharak Ka.—

"Shar'Dama Ka!" The guards stamped their spears as Asome entered the throne room.

Inevera lounged on her bed of pillows atop the dais beside the electrum-coated Skull Throne. Her pose was practiced, artfully appearing relaxed, disinterested, and submissive when she was anything but.

Inevera could not deny her second son looked the part. Like his father, he now wore a warrior's black under his white outer robe. He carried expert forgeries of the Spear and Crown of Kaji. From a distance, they were indistinguishable from the originals, lost when the Par'chin carried Ahmann into darkness.

The Evejah forbade male clerics from blade weapons, and none save the Deliverer had worn a crown in centuries. They were a message to all that Asome had transcended.

At his back was Inevera's third son, Hoshkamin the Sharum Ka, followed by their ten *Damaji* brothers, each fifteen years old and commanding an entire tribe. All of them looked worshipfully at their elder brother.

As he drew closer, Inevera could see his spear and crown didn't have a fraction of the wardings engraved into the originals, but she had observed them in Everam's light, and they glowed with power not to be underestimated. Made from electrum and priceless gems with cores of *alagai hora,* they were covered in the familiar fluid scripts of Melan and Asavi. A betrayal months in the making.

The *Damaji* wore a single warded gemstone in their black turbans. Gems were effective for conducting and focusing magic, and each had been warded by his *Damaji'ting* mother to give him some small powers.

But Asome's crown—like Ahmann's—had nine horns, each set with a different gemstone. Even Inevera could not guess the full extent of Asome's magic when he wore it, and she had never seen him outside his wing of the palace without it.

Likely she could still overwhelm him in a battle of magic, but not easily or without risk, and Asome knew it. He was careful not to test his magic against his mother.

Ahmann, confident in his powers and position, had kept his courtroom shielded from sunlight, that he and Inevera might use magic freely. Asome had torn down the thick fabric blocking the great windows of the Deliverer's court, bathing it in light from east and west and proclaiming court only be held in Everam's light.

She wanted to believe it was because he feared her, but in her heart Inevera knew it was wisdom, not fear that guided his actions.

There is too much of me in you, my son, Inevera thought sadly.

"Mother." Asome reached the top of the steps and gave a slight bow.

"My son." Inevera extended a hand.

Asome could not in politeness refuse, but he was careful as a snake handler as he took her hand and bent to kiss the air above it, offering her no advantage in grip or balance.

"If I meant to throw you from this dais, I would have done it weeks ago." Inevera's voice was too low for others in the court to hear.

Asome gave her a peck and pulled smoothly back. "Unless the dice told you to wait." He turned and went to his throne. "They have ever been more important to you than blood."

Below, similar gazes crossed the aisle as the new *Damaji* and their *Damaji'ting* mothers met eyes. For centuries, they had been groups of twelve, but since the Night of Hora there remained only ten of each.

Dama Jamere stepped forward from the writing podium Abban had occupied for so long. Since the disappearance of his uncle, the young *dama* had been left in full command of Abban's vast holdings and inherited his uncle's place in the Deliverer's court.

Jamere knelt before the steps, putting his hands on the floor and his head between them. "You honor the court with your presence, Deliverer."

Like Abban, Jamere was utterly corrupt. But where his uncle had been corrupt in ways Ahmann and Inevera could use, Jamere's loyalties were unreadable, even when she peered into his aura in Everam's light.

And Asome knew Jamere from Sharik Hora. They were of an age, and Inevera hadn't needed to see his aura to know they had been lovers. Asome and Asukaji were infamous in their class of *nie'dama,* and there were few boys unwilling to lie with them in hope of finding favor with their powerful families. With Asukaji dead, how long before Asome resumed his ways?

Her eyes flicked to her son, watching the richest man in Krasia prostrate himself. There was a slight quirk to Asome's lips. Perhaps he already had.

I must find Abban, and soon.

"Rise, my friend," Asome said, beckoning with his spear. "Your presence is a vast improvement over the court *khaffit*."

"Few can abrade like my dear uncle," Jamere said. "*Inevera,* he will return safely to us."

Asome nodded. "Or if he was lost on my brother's ill-fated attack on the forest fortress and you are now a permanent member of my court, then that, too, is *inevera*. You may take the sixth step."

Jamere rolled smoothly to his feet, smiling as he climbed the steps. He stopped at the sixth, a step below the dais. His head was well below Asome's, but close enough to whisper words so softly even Inevera strained to catch them without magic.

"What is our first order of business?" Asome asked.

Jamere consulted papers on his writing tablet, but it was all for show. Like his uncle, he had every word memorized. "The Kaji, Shar'Dama Ka."

The Kaji, the largest and most powerful tribe in Krasia, had lost both its leaders in the coup. Asome and Inevera, both Kaji themselves, had taken direct control of the tribe in the interim, but it weakened their ability to be impartial, especially with the Majah in rebellion.

Asome turned to Inevera, but his words were loud enough for the entire court. "Mother, when will my sister return from the greenlands to take up the black turban of *Damaji'ting*?"

"The summons has been sent," Inevera said. "Your sister will not forsake her responsibilities."

"Then where is she?!" Asome demanded. "We should have had an answer by now."

"Patience, my son," Inevera counseled. "It is not as if you have produced a new *Damaji* for the Kaji."

"My son will be *Damaji*," Asome said.

"Your son is an infant," Inevera reminded. "Patience."

Asome smiled. "Indeed. And so I have decided to appoint an interim *Damaji,* to hold the turban and speak for the council until my son earns his robes."

Jamere gave a signal, and the guards opened the doors to admit a small group of men. At their head was Dama Baden. A man of more than seventy, the *dama*'s paunch rounded the front of his robes like he carried a child. He leaned on a staff as he walked, but his eyes remained sharp, the look on his face triumphant as he moved to stand before the steps.

Behind him walked two men. Shar'Dama Raji, Baden's grandson and heir—another from Asome's generation—and their *kai'Sharum* bodyguard.

Cashiv.

Inevera's blood went cold at the sight of him. For years, Inevera had depended on anonymity to shield her family in the bazaar. The *dama'ting* wore veils to hide their identity, after all, and many women were named Inevera.

But like Asome and Jamere, Cashiv and Inevera's brother, Soli, had been lovers. He was one of the only people left alive who remembered the girl she had been, and who her family were.

Her father, Kasaad, had slain Soli on learning he was *push'ting,* and while Cashiv had not dared defy the *dama'ting* and taken his revenge, he had not forgiven.

Cashiv met her eyes, and she knew.

"Baden has ever been a thorn in the side of the council," Inevera said quietly for her son's ears only. "He is greedy and power-hungry. He cannot be trusted."

Asome was unperturbed. "He has proven trustworthy to me."

"And what did he give you in return for his seat at the head of the council?" Inevera asked.

Asome smiled. "Something beyond price."

Before Inevera could react, he turned back to Jamere. "Now that the council is complete once more, you may send in the Majah."

Baden's entourage bowed and took their place at the head of the young *Damaji* as Jamere signaled the guards once more. The doors opened, and in stormed Damaji Aleveran. The man was not yet sixty, robust and dangerous.

When Asome's Majah brother Maji failed to kill Damaji Aleverak, Asome executed the *Damaji* personally, breaking the pact that had held peace between the Kaji and Majah since Ahmann took the throne. Asome had no other Majah *dama* brother to install as leader, and with the overwhelming support of his tribe, the black turban fell to Aleverak's eldest son, Aleveran.

Immediately Aleveran left the council, imprisoning Belina and reinstating the former Majah *Damaji'ting,* the ancient but formidable Chavis. The old woman walked at his back, every bit as angry. Aleverak's honor had been boundless, and his murder had all the Majah sharpening their spears.

They were shadowed by a small army of *Sharum* bodyguards. They were outnumbered by the Spears of the Deliverer lining the walls of the courtroom, but the men were alert, ready to fight and die to protect their leaders.

"Damaji Aleveran!" Asome called without preamble. "I call upon you and your *Damaji'ting* to kneel before the Skull Throne and take your rightful places on the aisle. Do this, and all will be forgiven."

"Forgiven?" Aleveran snarled. "I am not the one who has committed a crime, boy. I am not the one who sullied this council chamber."

"Ware your words, *Damaji,*" Hoshkamin warned, and around the room warriors tensed. "You stand before Shar'Dama Ka."

Aleveran looked ready to spit on the ground, but Chavis laid a hand on his shoulder, and he thought better of it.

"Shar'Dama Ka is dead," he said. "The Majah will not bow before a usurper who uses *hora* magics to murder in the night."

Hoshkamin's eyes narrowed, but Asome was wise enough to keep things from escalating. "Stand down, brother."

"Sharak Sun still rages, *Damaji,*" Asome said, "and Sharak Ka looms. Krasia must be unified if there is any hope of victory. I wish no further bloodshed over the matter. Stand for your tribe as your father did."

"How can I stand before the man who murdered him?" Aleveran demanded.

"How, indeed?" Inevera asked, drawing all eyes to her. It was known in the palace, if not beyond, that Asome had attempted to kill her, as well. "You would not be the first *Damaji* to lose his father in the struggle for the throne. We are all bound to serve Everam's will."

Damaji'ting Chavis stepped forward. "In that we agree. But Everam's will has always been a mystery. I have consulted the *hora,* and the Creator has given me an answer to our problem."

Inevera's eyes narrowed, wondering what the old woman was playing at. She wished she could pull the curtains shut, that she might view Chavis' aura. "The *hora* have said nothing of the sort to me."

"Fortunate, then, there remain some with more experience." Chavis' smile was benevolent condescension. Inevera smiled in reply, wishing she could simply take out her *hora* wand and blast the woman from existence.

"What do you propose?" Asome asked.

Aleveran's next words shocked the court into silence.

"That the Majah take their spoils and return to the Desert Spear."

Inevera and Asome knelt on the pillows of her private casting chamber off to one side of the throne room. Two curtained doorways separated the chamber from the bright sunlight of the throne room. Bathed in darkness, Inevera relaxed slightly at the restoration of her powers.

The relief was short-lived as she looked at her son, glowing in Everam's light almost as intensely as his father had. His aura was flat and even, the result of a lifetime of meditation training. *Dama* grandmasters deep in meditation presented an aura of flat white, but even the most skilled practitioners could not entirely control the emotions running along their surface aura during periods of activity. There would be flares as he absorbed new information.

She wondered what he saw when he looked at her, how skilled he had become at reading the constantly shifting colors and patterns for secrets others wished to keep hidden.

"Where is my family?" Inevera demanded.

"I don't know what you mean," Asome said. His aura

showed the lie, but she could not tell if it was a loss of control at her sudden demand, or if he allowed her to see it.

Inevera Drew on the magic of the large *hora* stone hidden in the flooring beneath her pillow. Asome squinted as her aura brightened, and though he kept it from his face, she saw a flare of fear across his aura. "Do not lie to me, boy."

The fear left his aura as Asome glanced around the room. "This is the room where Father lay with Leesha Paper, is it not?"

Inevera blinked as Asome looked down at his pillow. "Perhaps he took her on this very spot! She was a filthy *chin,* of course, but comely enough, if one likes that sort of thing. I hear you redecorated with fire when they were done."

He knew how to cut at her. Inevera gave him credit for that. She bent against wind of it, face serene, giving him nothing. "And where did you kneel, when you sucked Cashiv's cock?"

Asome's grin was wicked. "I won't be sucking Cashiv's cock. That will be Grandfather Kasaad's duty, if you do not return Kaji to me. At least, until Cashiv decides to kill him."

For a moment Inevera lost her center. An instant only, but Asome did not miss it, his aura showing satisfaction at the tiny victory.

"Your father forgave Kasaad's sins," Inevera said. "He will go clean to Everam."

"He murdered your brother for being *push'ting,*" Asome said. "Perhaps that is why you hid them from us. You knew I might not be as forgiving as Father."

"Shar'Dama Ka must be merciful," Inevera said.

"Only Everam's mercy is infinite." Asome shrugged. "You have kept our families so separate that I will not weep at the loss."

Inevera herself had only recently reconciled with her father over the crime. It weighed on her, but there was never a choice. Her prisoners were her strongest leverage against Asome, and she could not give that up, even for her father's life. "And Manvah?"

"Will be kept safely in my custody," Asome said. "Accorded every courtesy befitting the mother of the Damajah. As I trust my Tikka is."

Inevera gave a shallow nod. "Of course. Now let us discuss

your failure to bring the Majah into the fold as you stumbled up the seven steps."

Irritation pricked Asome's aura even as he smiled. "How is it different from Father's own rise? Father, too, was unable to quell the Majah fully. They have been a plague on unity since Kaji defeated Majah in *Domin Sharum* three thousand years ago."

"If you had waited until Maji was older . . ."

Asome waved the idea away. "I knew my brother better than you, Mother. I grew up with him in Sharik Hora. He was never going to grow enough to defeat Aleverak, *hora* stones or no. It was *inevera* he fail."

"And what was your plan in that eventuality?" Inevera asked.

"There are only two choices," Asome said. "Find something that will appease them into accepting the new order, or force them into submission."

"At what cost?" Inevera asked. "The Majah are too numerous. Open war will destroy our forces just as Sharak Ka is nigh."

"We could let them go," Asome said, "but that weakens us as well. The greenlanders already outnumber us."

Inevera reached into her *hora* pouch, producing her electrum-coated dice. "These are questions for Everam."

Inevera raised her curved knife. "Hold out your arm."

Aleveran's aura was stone, but his eyes flicked to Chavis. The *Damaji'ting* gave a slight nod, and Aleveran rolled his sleeve, arm steady as he extended it.

She made a quick, shallow cut, enough blood for the spell and not a drop more. No need to antagonize the Majah any further.

"Everam, Creator of Heaven and Ala, Giver of Light and Life, your children need guidance. Should Damaji Aleveran lead his people back to the Desert Spear?"

The dice flared as she shook. She and Chavis leaned in the moment the dice settled from her throw. Their eyes flicked from symbol to symbol, taking in the orientation of the dice to one another and to due east, where Everam's light was born each day. Even then, there were many interpretations, all potential futures. Reading the most likely was an art *dama'ting* spent lifetimes perfecting, and even the most skilled often disagreed.

"If the gates of the Desert Spear close behind the Majah, they will not open again without bloodshed." Inevera glanced at Chavis to see if she would dispute the reading, but the old woman only grunted in assent.

"It is *inevera,*" Chavis said. "Ahmann Jardir was a false Deliverer, and his armies are destined to fail. The Desert Spear is our last hope."

"I do not know what they taught in the Chamber of Shadows when you were young, *Damaji'ting,*" Inevera said, "but we teach *nie'dama'ting* not to assume what the dice do not tell."

"Perhaps our armies risk failure because the Majah desert in our hour of need," Asome noted. "Slinking away to hide like *khaffit* as all mankind unites against Nie."

"No one is uniting behind you, boy," Aleveran said. "Already your army is a fraction of your father's, eroding more each day. Would you add warring in the streets to the attrition?"

"I will make you leader of the council of *Damaji,* as your father was," Asome said. "You will stand above all save the throne."

Aleveran shook his head. "To the abyss with your council. I will not bow to a man who broke sacred law to murder my father in the night."

Inevera looked to Chavis. "Let us consult the dice again."

"You have had your question in Aleveran's blood," Chavis said. "Now Asome will surrender his arm for a question of mine."

Asome stiffened, pulling up to his full height. "I am Shar'Dama Ka. You presume to ask for my blood?"

"Your blood now may spare the blood of many of our people," Chavis said. "If you are Shar'Dama Ka, you are wise enough to see that."

Doubt flickered across Asome's aura. He started to look to Inevera for advice, but thought better of it. He rolled his sleeve and held out his arm as Aleveran had.

"Everam, Creator of Heaven and Ala, Giver of Light and

Life," Chavis shook the dice after coating them in his blood, "your children need guidance. Should Damaji Aleveran bow before Asome asu Ahmann am'Jardir am'Kaji?"

She threw, and again the women bent together, studying the dice. As before, one answer was stronger than the others.

"No."

Inevera nodded to Asome, confirming the word as Chavis spoke it, but she could see he did not trust her.

"If you cannot stay, take your people to Everam's Reservoir," Asome said. "Fine lands, rich with water and as green as the Bounty. I give you those lands, to claim for Everam."

Aleveran shook his head. "Take the land just as the waters of the fish men thaw and they renew their assaults? I will not be your buffer against the greenlanders after they scattered your brother's armies. Take it yourself, and leave us Everam's Bounty."

"I would sooner have your head," Asome growled.

"Try and take it now," Aleveran dared. "Or let us go in peace, a last bulwark against the forces of Nie."

CHAPTER 10

FAMILY MATTERS

334 AR

Beware, sister, Jarvah's fingers said. *I have never seen the Damajah so angry.*

Ashia found her center in the comforting weight of Kaji sleeping in his sling as the Damajah stormed into the room. With the windows covered, she glowed and crackled in Everam's light.

"He has my family," the Damajah growled.

Ashia tilted her head. *Her* family? Ashia and her spear sisters were Inevera's nieces after all. The Deliverer was lost, Jayan was dead, and Asome sat the throne. Who was she referring to? "Apologies, Damajah, but I do not understand."

Inevera's eyes found hers. The Damajah's gaze was unnerving under any circumstances, but now it burned with such intensity, Ashia wished she could look away.

"My mother and father, Manvah and Kasaad, yet live," the Damajah said. "Until recently, they remained anonymous in the bazaar. Even the Deliverer himself did not learn of them until just before his fall."

Ashia blinked. She and her spear sisters followed the Damajah everywhere, but even they barely knew her, it seemed.

"Asome discovered and hostaged them," Ashia said.

"Dama Baden's bodyguard Cashiv knew of them." Micha jumped as the Damajah spat. "I should have killed him long ago."

The Damajah shook her head. "This cannot stand. As soon as the sun sets, take your spear sisters to my son's wing of the palace and find them."

Ashia put a protective hand over Kaji at her breast. "I cannot take my son into Asome's wing. Micha and Jarvah . . ."

The Damajah's eyes flared, and her aura brightened until it became difficult to look at her. Ashia put up a hand, lest she be blinded.

"They. Have. My. Mother." The Damajah bit the words off, each striking like a lash. "I have tolerated your insolence long enough, Sharum'ting Ka. You will not send your little sisters into danger alone. You will do as I command. Kaji will be safe with his grandmother in the Vault."

Ashia slipped down to her knees, putting her hands on the floor. She bowed, touching her forehead between them. "Yes, Damajah."

"Asome gave reason to believe they were in the royal suite," the Damajah said. "No doubt he wishes to know his grandparents better. Begin your search there, and plant a *hora* stone in his chambers to give me an ear there."

Ashia nodded. "Of course, Damajah."

"When you have their location, bring it to me and I will retrieve them myself."

Ashia looked up at that, horrified. Inevera still flared bright with power, and she closed her eyes against it. "Damajah! You cannot expose yourself so."

"It is *inevera*," the Damajah said.

Ashia made her way through a series of hidden passages down into the Damajah's underpalace, only recently cut into the bowels of the hill beneath the greenland duke's palace.

The smooth rock walls glittered with wardlight, the symbols running along them proof against demon and mortal intrusion both. Here, the Damajah worked her deepest magics and secured her most precious treasures.

"Nie's black heart!" The words echoed in the hall. "Is there half a mind among you? Apple juice, I said!"

One of her moods? Ashia's fingers asked the eunuch guarding the door.

She only has one, the eunuch's fingers replied.

Ashia sighed, finding her center before she pushed open the door. Kajivah's chambers were large and lavish, with servants to attend her every need. At the moment all of them were on their knees, auras ripe with fear.

"Holy Mother," one of the servants said. "The greenland fruit is not in season. There are none to be had in all Everam's Bounty."

Kajivah drew breath to shout what would no doubt have been a terrible reply, but she caught sight of Ashia in the doorway and the rage dissipated with her exhale. She strode over, arms extended. "Give him to me."

Ashia's jaw tightened beneath her veil, but she undid the fastenings, catching the sleeping Kaji in the crook of her arm long enough for Kajivah to take him.

The woman's whole demeanor changed the moment she held him, and Ashia knew that whatever came to pass, Kajivah would never harm her great-grandson—would stand between him and all the demons of the abyss.

"Will you take him for the night?" she asked. It would be Ashia's first night apart from her son since the Night of Hora when they walked the edge of the abyss together.

"Of course, of course." Kajivah did not take her eyes off the child.

"Thank you, Tikka," Ashia said.

Now the woman looked up. "Do not call me that. Not ever again."

Ashia swallowed. Once, she had been the favorite of Kajivah's many granddaughters. It was Kajivah's own insistence that sent Ashia and her spear sisters to the Dama'ting Palace, putting them on the path to *Sharum'ting*. Now they were nothing to her.

She dropped her eyes, bowing. "As you wish, Holy Mother."

She turned on her heel, striding quickly from Kaji lest she lose her resolve and rush back to him.

Even at night, infiltrating Asome's wing of the palace was difficult. The new Shar'Dama Ka had found and sealed the secret passages the *Sharum'ting* used to move unseen about the palace. Guards and armed *dama* patrolled the halls, eyes warded to see in Everam's light. Tapestries, rugs, and tiles were warded against *alagai,* but Ashia could see, too, wardings much like those the *dama'ting* used. Symbols to raise alarm if even a human were to cross them, and to seal this part of the palace from prying eyes. The *hora* stones the Damajah hoped to use to eavesdrop would be of little use, their magic blocked.

But Ashia, Micha, and Jarvah were clad in their *kai'Sharum'ting* robes, embroidered in electrum thread with wards of unsight. Whether in human sight or Everam's light, they blended with their surroundings as easily as a sand demon in the dunes. It was only when they moved swiftly that they could be seen.

Their jewelry was similarly magicked, rings and bracelets on their hands and feet allowing them to cling to walls and ceilings like spiders. Slowly they slithered deeper and deeper into her husband's sanctum.

Check the lower levels, Ashia told Jarvah when they were past the barriers. *Asome will have an underpalace of his own. Find and penetrate it if you can.*

Yes, Sharum'ting Ka.

Jarvah disappeared as Ashia and Micha made their way up to the residential floors. The palace had seven levels, one for each pillar in Heaven, but the outer stair only went to six, landing doors guarded by an alert *kai'Sharum,* bright in Everam's light.

The sixth floor was reserved for the royal family, a place Ashia knew well. She and Kajivah both had chambers there. Technically they had been Asome's chambers, but her husband had only seen the pillows there once.

The Damajah believed her blessed mother would be housed on the sixth as well.

The topmost floor, Asome's private level, could only be reached by an inner stair, no doubt guarded as well.

The young women paused, clinging to the ceiling as the door guard came into clear view. Even with his white night veil in place, Ashia recognized her cousin Iraven, the Deliverer's firstborn Majah son. Stripped of rank by Damaji Aleveran, he was now relegated to guard duty for his elder brother.

Micha took one hand from her hold on the ceiling, making the sign for the sleeping potion they carried. Applied to a cloth and forced over the mouth and nose, it could render even a large man unconscious for some time, waking with only fuzzy memories of his last moments. Her littlest finger curled, indicating a question.

Ashia shook her head. *Too slow,* her fingers said. *Precise Strike.*

The Precise Strike, their master Enkido's school of *sharusahk,* targeted the natural convergences in the body. Places where muscle, vein, and nerve met. The targets were small and always in motion, each unique as their owner, but a sharp, precise blow could temporarily cripple an opponent, or knock them out instantly.

They edged slowly into position, clinging to the ceiling directly over their cousin. Micha would hold him, and Ashia would strike. But before Ashia signaled the drop, a pair of *nie'dama* carrying food trays ascended the steps. She could tell from body language that Iraven recognized them and would let them pass unhindered.

Micha needed no orders as they opened the doors, following instantly as Ashia sprang through. They landed in identical rolls on opposite sides of the hall, warded bracelets absorbing the sound. Their robes blurred for a moment, but they were effectively invisible again by the time the boys passed through the door.

The floor was warded, a puzzle of steps that would sound an alarm if crossed improperly. Ashia memorized the path the boys took, but she and Micha followed along the walls, blending perfectly with the paint. They reached an inner stair guarded by a pair of clerics with warded staves, and the *nie'dama* split up, one continuing down the hall as the other ascended to the seventh floor.

Follow. Ashia used a finger to indicate the first boy. Her mission was to find the Damajah's parents, but this close, Ashia could not resist looking in on her treacherous husband. She followed the second boy up the stairs, slithering along the ceiling faster than he could climb. She was his shadow as he passed guards and doors, coming at last to an anteroom where the boy laid the tray on a table, knocked at the far door, and then quickly scurried out, closing the hall door behind him.

Ashia was ready to leap when the door opened, but when

she saw Asome, her breath caught and she nearly missed her opportunity. In their entire marriage, had she ever seen her husband answer a door? That was a task for women and servants.

Then Asome did the unthinkable. The Shar'Dama Ka, supreme leader of all Krasia, bent and picked up the tray himself. Ashia slipped in while his back was turned, thoughts reeling. Had Asome become a recluse since Asukaji died? A haunted shell of a man? Part of her hoped it was so. A taste of the judgment he would find in Heaven.

"Dinner, my sun," Asome called, and Ashia blinked. His wife and lover murdered, and he had already found another? Anger threatened her center, but she brushed it aside, skittering along the ceiling to follow her husband to the pillow chamber. Who would she find? Dama Jamere? Cashiv? One of Asome's half brothers?

The last person she expected was her brother, Asukaji, whose neck she had broken.

"I am not hungry." Asukaji's voice was a harsh whisper. "Take it away."

Asome set the tray by the bedside. Asukaji lay prone, his body unmoving, its aura flat. Not dead, but not truly alive.

That changed at his neck. The aura about her brother's head was hot and raw, his eyes focused and his face full of emotion.

Paralyzed, Ashia realized with horror. For a warrior, it was a fate worse than death. Even now after he had tried to strangle her, she did not wish this upon her brother. They had been close when they were young, and part of her loved him still.

"You must eat, my love," Asome said. "You cannot feel your hunger, but it is there. Without food, you will waste away."

"And what if I do?" Asukaji demanded. "Better I eat, and lie helpless as I shit the bed an hour from now? I could have died with honor. Instead you force me to linger, a prisoner in this worthless shell."

Asome sat on the edge of the bed, taking one of Asukaji's limp hands. "I cannot do this without you. Half my plans and stratagems are yours."

"That is not what you thought when you fucked that *heasah*." Asukaji's head lolled with the force of his snarl.

Asome was quick to steady him, kissing his forehead. "She is your sister, whom you yourself insisted become my *Jiwah Ka*."

Ashia's cheek twitched. She fell deeper into her breath, silent as stone.

"*I* am your *Jiwah Ka*!" Asukaji's cry was hoarse. "She was a womb to carry the son I could not."

Asome lifted the cover from the tray, steam rising off a bowl of thin gruel that was likely all her brother could swallow. Asome blew on a spoonful like a mother preparing to feed an infant. "We needed her trust, cousin. For her to believe me loyal to her and humble before my mother. And if I'd created another son for us, so much the better."

Asukaji spat at the spoon as it came near, but it came out as a dribble on his chin. "I am not a fool, Asome. Sons and plots were not on your mind when you bent her."

"What does it matter?" Asome took a silk napkin, wiping Asukaji's mouth. "She could never replace you in my heart. No one can. She could have been a valuable *Jiwah Sen* but for your jealousy. You insisted on killing her."

He took Asukaji's jaw in his hand, squeezing until his teeth opened enough to admit the spoon.

"But you were not her match, were you, sweet Asukaji?" Asome forced the gruel into his mouth. "Nor Melan and Asavi together a match for my mother. Now they are on the lonely path, you lie frozen, and my mother has hostaged half the throne." Asome massaged Asukaji's throat until he swallowed.

"Soon Amanvah will return to control the Kaji *dama'ting*, bringing with her a *Jiwah Sen* no doubt as deadly as your sister, and a husband blessed by Everam."

"A *chin* and *khaffit*," Asukaji growled. "Amanvah should have been mine, as Ashia was yours. That was our bargain."

"*Khaffit* or no, his power over the *alagai* is undeniable," Asome said. "What could I say when Father gave her to him? Mother's power will grow when they return. We must balance the scales now, while there is still time."

Asukaji stopped resisting, eating in silence. Asome was

tender and attentive, massaging every swallow until the bowl was empty.

"I am sorry, cousin." Asukaji looked pitiful as Asome wiped the last smudge from his lips. "I failed you. Everam judged me and found me unworthy."

"You yet live," Asome said. "We will find a way to heal you. Already the *dama* make great strides with *hora* magic. Soon we will unlock all the secrets of the *dama'ting*. You will be restored and given another chance at glory."

"The Damajah could heal me now," Asukaji rasped. "We have her parents. She would not dare refuse."

"We should not underestimate what my mother will dare," Asome warned. "Who knows what this *dal'ting* and a *khaffit* are truly worth to her?"

"Surely not as much . . ." Asukaji's face reddened with the exertion of speaking, ". . . as Tikka or Kaji, or you would have them in the underpalace."

Asome shook his head. "I do not trust them down among the *dama*'s experiments. An explosion in Dama Shevali's laboratory killed one of his *nie'dama* and cost another his eye."

"They had best be worth something," Asukaji wheezed. "You traded my black turban for the hostages. If they cannot buy back our son, then let it be my limbs."

"We cannot reveal such a weakness to my mother," Asome said. "She will find a way to twist it against us. The turban will be returned to you when you are healed. Baden thinks he is holding it for Kaji. He knows he cannot keep it forever."

"Do not underestimate Baden," Asukaji whispered. "I know how you get around Cashiv. He makes you stupid."

"I can handle Cashiv," Asome said.

"That is what worries me."

"What does it matter?" Asome growled. "We have gone to Baden's parties with oil on our belts since we were in *sharaj*. You've lain with Cashiv as many times as I."

"It matters because I could please you, then," Asukaji said. "Because I was your *Jiwah Ka*, the first sheath for your spear."

"You still are," Asome said.

"Then take me."

"Eh?" Asome's face slackened.

"Now, before that cursed gruel runs through me," Asukaji begged. "Roll me onto my stomach and have me."

"Asukaji . . ." Asome said.

"No!" There were tears in her brother's eyes. "I cannot stop you lying with others, but I swear by Everam I will never swallow another spoonful if you cease to lie with me."

Asome took a deep breath, blowing it out slowly. Ashia could not bear to watch as he took oil and began to work himself for the deed. She fled the chamber while her brother and husband were too occupied to notice.

Micha was waiting when Ashia made it back to the stairs, a welcome distraction from her thoughts.

Report, Ashia's fingers commanded.

I have found them, Micha replied. *There are guards, but together we might . . .*

Ashia made the sign for Nie. *Our duty is to report to the Damajah.*

Jarvah joined them as they descended. *Asome's underpalace is protected by* hora *magic. I could not penetrate it.*

Irrelevant, Ashia told her. *We have intelligence the Damajah needs.* The three *Sharum'ting* slipped past the guards and out of Asome's wing.

CHAPTER 11

SORCERERS

334 AR

"Nie's slimy cunt!" Inevera scooped up the dice. They had not warned that her mother was in danger, and now they brought nothing but bad news and vagaries.

She breathed, trying to find her center, but peace eluded her. Had she fallen from Everam's favor? How could He let this happen to Manvah, as honorable a woman as any alive? Always before He had warned her when her family was threatened.

But now her husband was dead, and the dice betrayed her.

She rolled back on her heels and stood, feeling the vibration in her earring. The connection with Ashia and her spear sisters had been severed when they entered Asome's wing of the palace. A bad sign. Melan and Asavi had given Asome and his brothers the secret of *hora* magic, and it seemed they were quick studies.

"Damajah," Ashia whispered in her ear from the other side of the palace. "We have found them, but there is more. We must speak immediately."

"The west passage." Inevera was already moving for the door. She was bedecked in warded jewelry, her *hora* pouch laden with spells. She had been overconfident, spoiled by the strength of her wand, when Melan and Asavi came to kill her. She would not make that mistake again.

She wore opaque robes of crimson silk, embroidered with

wards in electrum thread. Like the robes of Everam's spear sisters, all eyes—human and *alagai*—would slip from her when she wished it. At her belt was the curved knife she used to draw blood for her foretellings. It was not meant as a weapon, but the edge was razor-sharp and would do if all else failed.

The *Sharum'ting* were waiting for her in a hidden tunnel leading to the west wing. The Damajah had claimed the east wing to face the dawn, the Shar'Dama Ka west to face the sunset.

"Asukaji is alive," Ashia said.

Inevera scowled. Another thing the dice had failed to tell her, though in fairness she had not asked. "You told me you killed him."

"I snapped his neck," Ashia confirmed. "But he clings to life, unable to move, hidden in Asome's chambers. He wants to trade Manvah for you to make him whole again, but Asome does not trust you."

"Nor I, him," Inevera said. "This changes nothing. We go now to free my parents."

Ashia stepped in front of her, kneeling with hands on the floor. "It is not necessary for the Damajah to expose herself. We have penetrated my husband's defenses. Everam's spear sisters can effect the rescue."

Inevera shook her head. On this, the dice had been clear. "You will die if you go without me, and the rescue fail."

The women's auras clouded at that. They were the finest warriors she had ever known, but their pride was as boundless as their honor.

"Will it succeed if the Damajah accompanies us?" Ashia asked.

Inevera blew out a breath. "Unclear."

"Damajah, you must . . ."

Inevera clapped her hands, cutting the young woman off. "You do not tell me what I must, *Sharum*. Your duty is to be silent and obey."

Inevera let the spear sisters surround her, Ashia in front and Micha and Jarvah to either side. All of them skittered quickly and quietly along, robes blending with the ceiling tiles. They penetrated the outer halls, making their way unseen to the sixth-floor stairwell were Iraven stood guard.

As Ashia warned, the boy was alert, clad in impenetrable armor of warded glass that glowed brightly in Everam's light. She could see the demon bone cores of his weapon and armor, enough to give him inhuman strength and speed.

Inevera slipped her wand from her belt. Made from the arm bone of a demon prince coated in electrum, it had power enough to blow the entire roof from the palace. Still clinging to the ceiling, she drew a quick series of wards in the air, Drawing and shaping her spell before flinging it toward the unsuspecting warrior.

Ahmann might forgive her killing his son if there were no choice, but Iraven was the last hope of bringing the Majah tribe back to heel. Inevera's spell would put him into a deep, dreamless sleep.

Yet the moment she cast the magic, the wards on Iraven's armor flared bright with magic. Instead of passing out, he set his feet, holding his spear defensively.

"Come out, servant of Nie!" His eyes scanned the walls, searching.

Inevera gave him no time to find them or raise the alarm, dropping down to stand before her son-in-law.

"You think the Damajah a servant of Nie?"

Iraven's eyes widened. "What are you doing unannounced in Shar'Dama Ka's wing of the palace?"

"A mother needs permission to visit her son?" Inevera asked.

Iraven did not lower his weapon. "Visitors do not skulk along the ceiling and cast spells at guards. If you have business, state it."

"You know my business," Inevera said. "The Majah hostage your mother, my sister-wife Belina, yet here you stand, gaoler to my own."

Iraven was unimpressed. "Your words would hold more weight, Damajah, if you yourself did not hold Tikka captive."

"It is my duty to protect the Holy Mother," Inevera said, "not let her be drawn into the crossfire of a political scheme to supplant me."

Iraven was unconvinced. "No doubt Asome seeks to similarly protect your mother."

"We all want what is best for our mothers," Inevera said. "You should go to yours now, before she is taken from Everam's Bounty."

Iraven's aura colored at that. An image of Belina floated over the young man, tethered by countless strands of emotion, as any mother to her son.

"I may no more see her than allow you entry here," Iraven said bitterly. "I cannot free her alone, and Asome will not commit to a rescue that would result in open war."

"Demon's piss," Inevera said. "That is what Asome would have you believe."

"Then where is the Damajah's support? Why are you here, and not in Aleveran's palace rescuing your sister-wife?" There was a spark in his aura. One she might fan to a flame.

"Because it is a task for you, Iraven asu Ahmann am'Jardir am'Majah," Inevera said. "Did your father cower before every problem he could not solve with his spear? The *Damaji* has taken your birthright, but that does not mean you cannot win it back."

Iraven paused. The fire in him was growing, but cautiously. "How?"

"Go to Aleveran," Inevera said. "Submit to his rule, and he will take you with him when the Majah depart Everam's Bounty. Win glory, and the warriors will whisper your family name. One by one, they will follow you."

A new image appeared over Iraven, an idealized version of himself standing tall as his pride grew with the fire in his heart.

But then he shook his head, dispelling the image. "My brother said words are your weapon, Damajah."

"I speak only the truth," Inevera said. "I pulled you from between your mother's thighs myself, and cast your future before the cord was cut. There is glory still for you, if you are man enough to seize it."

"Perhaps," Iraven said. "But I seize no glory by turning from my duty this night. No doubt your *Sharum'ting* skulk about, ready to kill me if I refuse, but no words or threats will make me leave my post." With that, he slammed the butt of his spear down upon a warded tile, one Inevera knew would activate a wardnet running through the thousands of tiles around the doorframe, raising an alarm.

She raised her *hora* wand, Drawing the power away before the wards could activate. Iraven's eyes widened.

"*Acha!*" he cried. "Intruders!" The sound should have echoed in the stairs, but a few quick wards in the air stopped it as easily as the alarm.

Inevera advanced upon him. "I do not need Everam's spear sisters to pass, Iraven. It is written in the Evejah that it is death to strike a *dama'ting* or hinder her in any way. How will Everam judge you if you strike the Damajah herself?"

Her senses afire with the magic coursing through her, Inevera smelled the sweat even before it broke on the boy's brow. She pitied him, torn between duties—another innocent in the crossfire.

But her family was on the other side of those doors, and every second this continued, the danger to them was greater.

Iraven closed his eyes. "Everam forgive me."

Then he struck.

Inevera met him head-on, diverting the thrust of his spear with a hooked wrist. She caught the shaft and pulled as she punched.

The inflexible plates of warded glass in Iraven's robes were too rigid to cover the convergence point at the base of his neck. The flexible armor there was meant to turn a spear point, not block the single raised knuckle on Inevera's fist. Her blow was a blur, aided in strength and speed by *hora* magic.

But Iraven seemed to know her target, turning his head to take the blow on his jaw, instead. He rolled with it, using the momentum to turn a circuit, spear swinging low to sweep her feet.

Inevera was surprised but never lost control, bending back and putting hands on the floor, kicking him in the jaw a second time as she avoided the spear and came back to her feet.

Iraven reeled, but he, too, kept control, spinning the spear behind him and coming back in. He glowed bright with magic, fast and strong. The spear like a feather in his hands.

Ashia and her spear sisters dropped to the floor, but Inevera stayed them with a hiss and the back of her hand.

Inevera had never held much respect for *Sharum* fighting styles, but Iraven had been trained by her husband and Damaji Aleverak, the two greatest *sharusahk* masters in Krasia. He worked his weapon and feet in perfect harmony, giving her little free energy to turn against him as he picked off the most dangerous of Inevera's return blows and let others skitter off his armor. All the while he herded her with his spear toward kicks and leg locks that could easily cripple.

Fast as he was, Inevera was faster, bending away from thrusts and kicks, diverting others with minimal contact. She ducked under a sweep of his spear, leg curling around to kick him in the back. He pitched forward, tripping as she hooked his ankle with her support leg.

That should have ended it, but again he surprised her, turning the fall into a somersault and redirecting that energy back in at her. Inevera caught his spear shaft, and he push-kicked her dead center, slamming her back into the doorframe.

Inevera knew then she had been too merciful, meeting him with *sharusahk* instead of magic. Thousands of wards on the tiles of the doorframe came to life on contact with the *hora* about her person, filling the landing with light and setting off alarms throughout the palace.

Inevera snarled as Iraven thrust again, kicking the point of his spear down and running up the shaft to hook a leg around his throat, bearing him to the floor.

Still the warrior thrashed and fought, but Inevera accepted the minor blows, striking convergence points to break the lines of power in his limbs even as she cut off the blood to his brain.

"Leave Everam's Bounty with the Majah," she told him as his aura began to darken, "or I will have your head mounted above the city gate."

"Damajah, we must flee." Ashia reached out to help her to her feet when Iraven slumped unconscious to the floor.

Inevera ignored the words as she studied the magic flowing through the tiles. She drew an intricate script in the air, and the flare of the wards began to dim even as her wand brightened. She pointed at an inert tile. "Break it."

Ashia did not hesitate, shattering the tile with a punch. Inevera drained two more wards for Ashia to break, then lifted her wand and drew an impact ward, blowing the doors from their hinges.

"Kill any who stand in our way," Inevera commanded, and the *Sharum'ting* went for the short spears on their backs, warded glass infused with electrum, razor-sharp and indestructible.

Guards were rushing down the hall as the women darted through. Inevera reached into her *hora* pouch, flinging a handful of black marbles their way, the glass formed around bits of lightning demon bone. Sparks flew as the guards' muscles seized, and her bodyguards knocked them down like game pieces. Their spears flashed, and Inevera knew the men would not rise.

Up ahead, a group of *kai'Sharum* clustered by the door to where her parents were being held. Behind them, two *dama* stood with staves glowing bright in Everam's light.

Ashia and her sisters flung sharpened glass into the cluster, but one of the *dama* raised his staff, and a great gust of wind blew the weapons back at them. Most skittered off the women's armor, but one embedded in a gap between the plates on Jarvah's thigh. The girl made no sound, keeping pace with Ashia's charge, but Inevera could see the wound ripple through her aura and knew it was serious.

Before the women could reach the guards, the other *dama* raised his staff, sending forth a crude but powerful blast of fire. It expanded quickly, catching two of the guards as it filled the hall.

Ashia and her spear sisters did not hesitate, ducking behind their glass shields and wading in. The wards on the shields absorbed the demonfire, and then they were amid the warriors.

There was a shriek as Micha crippled one of the *Sharum* with a spear thrust to the leg. A spatter of blood as Ashia spun her two-headed spear through a *kai'Sharum*'s throat. A grunt as Jarvah found a seam in the glass armor and ran another through.

The walls and carpets were ablaze now, but Inevera did not feel the heat, her warded jewelry absorbing the energy. The first *dama* sent another blast of wind at her as she advanced, but she parted it with a flick of her wand, collecting it behind her and throwing it back at the cleric.

They raised their staves defensively, wards flaring to part the wind much as Inevera had, but she followed the wind with a spell of her own, impact wards blasting apart the floor and knocking them from their feet. One lost his grip on his staff, and Inevera sent it spinning down the hall out of reach. The other held his tightly, fingers running like a flutist to manipulate the wards along its surface. Inevera raised her wand to kill him before he could release the gathering energy.

But then the door opened, and Inevera saw her mother. Asome stepped out behind Manvah, a hand around her throat.

"That's far enough, Mother."

Inevera froze. The *hora* wand was warm in her hand, slick with her sudden sweat. Its power dwarfed that of even the great staves the *dama* carried—no doubt with demon bone cores of their own—enough to kill everyone in the palace.

But not enough to free her mother. Not before Asome snapped her neck.

"I must say I'm surprised you took the bait," Asome said. "Did you really think it would be so easy?"

"Let her go," Inevera said. "That is your grandmother, not some *chin* slave."

"Neither of you made the effort for her to know me," Asome said. "Why should I care if she dies? But I will let her go when you return my son to me. When you return my true grandmother." He tilted his head, eyeing Ashia. She was veiled, but though he had been a poor excuse for a husband, there was no mistaking her. "My 'dead' bride."

"Three hostages for one?" Inevera asked. "Your *dama* make poor sorcerers, but I thought they taught simple arithmetic in Sharik Hora."

Asome smiled. "Enjoy the advantage while you can, Mother. Melan and Asavi taught us much about *hora* magic, if unwittingly. We narrow the gap each day. Magic is no longer the sole purview of the *dama'ting*."

"Against the direct teachings of the Evejah," Inevera said. "*Suffer no sorcerer to live,* Kaji told his people."

Asome shrugged. "I am Shar'Dama Ka now, Mother. It's time those passages were updated."

"Murdering your way atop the dais does not make you Shar'Dama Ka, boy," Inevera said. "You have betrayed all Krasia, put Sharak Ka itself in jeopardy, all for your own ambition."

Inevera met her mother's eyes. "Forgive me, Mother. The First War must come before even family."

"You are my daughter," Manvah said. "I would love you if you put out the sun."

Asome's aura spiked hot with anger. He jerked his head and Kasaad was shoved into the hall, stumbling on his peg leg. Behind him Cashiv grinned, a knife at her father's throat. His exposed forearm was armored, and he was careful to keep the heavier Kasaad in place as a shield.

"Let us start small, then," Asome said. "Surrender my *jiwah,* now, or Cashiv will open your father's throat."

Inevera's fingers itched to raise her wand, but it would do little good. She could not strike at Cashiv without risking her father any more than she could kill Asome without risking her mother. Down the hall, she heard reinforcements coming. They would arrive soon, *dama* wielding *hora* staves and many, many *Sharum.*

"Do not, daughter," Kasaad said, drawing a sharp breath as Cashiv pressed the blade to his neck. "The Deliverer forgave me. My soul is clean."

Inevera looked into her father's aura and knew it to be true. In his *Sharum* days, he had been a drunk and a coward, but now he was ready for death and Everam's judgment. His spirit looked to the lonely path, ready to walk it for his family's sake. He knew Asome saw him only as *khaffit*—expendable. Manvah had true value. His grandson would never kill her.

"It will never be clean after what you did to Soli!" Cashiv's muscles bunched, but Asome threw out a hand, staying him.

"I will go, Damajah," Ashia said.

Inevera fell deep into her breath and shook her head. Sharak Ka must come first. The dice said Ashia still had a part to play. Kasaad did not. "You tried to murder your wife once already, my son. You will not have another chance."

Asome dropped his hand and Cashiv's blade flashed, drawing a hot line of blood across Kasaad's throat. Inevera screamed as her father fell, choking on his own blood. The moment Cashiv lost Kasaad's body as a shield, Inevera raised her wand, blasting the life from him. The warrior was thrown down the hall to land in a smoking ruin, but the damage was done.

Manvah made a choked sound as Asome pulled her in close, shielding himself with her body as he dragged her back inside. His men closed ranks to cut off pursuit.

"Kill them!" Asome shouted, kicking the door shut.

Inevera let them go, glad to have Manvah out of harm's way as she raised her *hora* wand. With her free hand, she spoke to her *Sharum'ting*.

Leave no survivors.

I am a fool, Inevera thought as they returned, singed and bloody, to her wing of the palace.

They had taken a heavy toll, leaving a trail of dead *Sharum* and *dama* throughout Asome's halls, but it was nothing compared with the numbers at her son's command. Already his guard would be tripled. There would be no second chance, now that his trap was sprung.

Only Asome, Manvah, and the spear sisters lived to bear witness to what happened, but it made Inevera's failure no less complete. She had been arrogant, letting anger guide her instead of the cold reason of the dice.

Now her father was dead, and it was doubtful she would see her mother alive again. Asome had confirmation of something he already suspected—that Ashia was alive.

And in return, what had she gained?

Nothing.

"Damajah." Ashia bowed as they returned to her private chambers. "May I go to my son?"

Inevera's eyes flicked to the girl, not yet twenty years of age, and saw the fear in her. Not for herself—she had been willing to die this night, in battle or in sacrifice. But the encounter with her husband had her worried over her son. Inevera could see Asome's image, hovering over her like a haunting spirit. Ashia knew he would willingly kill every man, woman, and child in Krasia to have Kaji back.

Inevera reached out and Ashia stiffened, her aura shocked. Did the Damajah mean to embrace her?

But Inevera did not put her arms around the girl, instead pressing her hand against Ashia's robe where it had been cut by a *Sharum* spear in their escape. The wound beneath had healed, but Inevera's hand came away wet with blood.

She knelt, drawing free her dice and rolling them in her palm, coating them in her niece's essence before she cast.

"Everam, giver of Light and Life, your children need guidance. How can I best protect your honored son Kaji asu Asome am'Jardir am'Kaji, that he and his mother might serve you in Sharak Ka?"

The glow of the *alagai hora* brightened, and she threw, watching coldly as they fell into a complex pattern. It took her long moments to decipher it.

—She must seek the *khaffit* through the father of her father, and find your lost cousin.—

Inevera blinked. That Abban still had a part to play was no surprise, and sending Ashia out of Everam's Bounty might well be the only way to keep her and Kaji safe. Ashia's father's father was Dama Khevat, who had once been in command of the monastery, and was likely there still.

But cousin? What cousin?

She cut herself this time. The dice said *her* cousin, not Ashia's. Perhaps her own blood might provide answers where Ashia's could not.

But as ever, the dice raised more questions than they answered.

—She will know him by his scent.—

"You will slip out in the hubbub as the Majah prepare to leave," Inevera said. "Asome won't expect me to send you away. Make for Everam's Reservoir. Jayan's defeat has left many widowed mothers there. Another will not draw scrutiny, and no one will recognize you or Kaji outside the capital."

"And once there?" Ashia asked. "How will I find the *khaffit*?"

"Seek out Qeran," Inevera instructed. "The drillmaster commands the town now, and his privateers dominate the waters, at least until spring. If any can aid you in finding his lost master, it is he. I will cast daily and update you if I have any more information. It should be days before the *hora* stone in your earring is out of range. After that, you will be on your own."

"And this lost cousin?" Ashia asked.

Inevera shrugged. "You will know him by his scent."

"That is little to go on," Ashia said.

"We must trust in Everam," Inevera said. "The dice were clear. You must find them, if you are to do your part in Sharak Ka."

Ashia touched her forehead to the floor. "As you command, Damajah." She rose and left to say her goodbyes to her spear sisters waiting silently outside. They knew she would be leaving, but none save the two of them would know where, or for what purpose.

"Niece," Inevera said, pulling Ashia up short. She turned to meet Inevera's eyes.

"Know that I could not be prouder of you if you were my own daughter. If any shoulders can bear this burden Everam has set, they are yours." Inevera held her arms open, and Ashia, stunned, fell into them for the first time in her adult life.

CHAPTER 12

DRAINED

334 AR

"Bekka's got 'em in her sights." Wonda's head was tilted, listening to the broken piece of demon bone resonating in her helmet. "Stela and Keet, skulkin' down the road toward Smitt's storehouse."

Leesha nodded. They always came when the storehouse was restocked, even if Smitt changed the schedule. Someone was feeding them information.

She pulled on her cloak and gloves. "Let's go. Tell Bekka and the others to stay on the rooftops and keep fingers off their triggers. I see a stray bolt and someone's out of a job."

"Ay, mistress," Wonda said. "But they make a move at ya an' I'll feather 'em myself. Not takin' any chances with yur safety."

Leesha gave her *hora* pouch a reassuring squeeze. "Neither am I."

Bruna had taught her it was undignified to run, but Leesha had long legs and put them to use, setting a brisk pace. The Warded Children could move swiftly at night.

Wonda touched her helmet again. "Ay, got it." She turned to Leesha. "Ent in a hurry. Strollin' like they own the whole town."

Leesha pursed her lips, seeing Smitt standing in front of the heavy storehouse doors with his arms crossed. They were warded now, reinforced with unbreakable glass.

"Try not to provoke them," she said, coming to stand beside him.

"Them?!" Smitt asked. "My son and granddaughter rob me every fortnight, but you worry *I'll* provoke *them*?"

"Man's got a point," Wonda said.

"Ay," Leesha agreed. "But they're drunk on magic, and we don't want a fight. Just here to talk."

"Hope they feel the same way," Wonda said.

Just then, Stela and her uncle rounded the corner, pulling up short as they spotted the trio waiting for them. Both of them shone with power, but Stela was brighter. Not as bright as Renna Bales, but brighter than anyone else Leesha had seen, short of Arlen and Jardir. All this, in half a year.

And it's my doing, she admonished herself. *Arlen warned me. Begged me. But I was so sure I knew better.*

Keet at least had the decency to look chagrined. Stela only snickered.

"Think this is funny?" Smitt demanded. "I put a roof over your head and food in your bellies your whole lives, and you pay me back by robbing me?"

"Oh, come off it, Pappy," Stela said. "Creator knows you can afford it. We're out bleeding in the night while you get fatter every day."

"Lot of folk out bleeding in the night," Wonda said. "Ent no excuse to turn bandit."

"Never hurt anyone," Keet said. "Just a few sacks and kegs. You rather we go hungry?"

"Used to earn your keep," Smitt said.

"Still do!" Stela argued. "Now more than ever! Keepin' folk safe."

"Demonshit," Smitt said. "You're not out there for anyone but yourself."

"Your grandfather has a point," Leesha said. "I didn't ward your skin so you could get magic-drunk and stick each other out in my wood."

"No, you just gave us a taste, then abandoned us!" Stela snapped. "Arlen Bales said we were all Deliverers, but you just want to keep the power all to yourself!"

"Ay, don't you talk to Mistress Leesha like that," Wonda growled.

"C'mon, Stel. Let's just go," Keet said.

Stela ignored him, crossing her arms and setting her feet as she met Wonda's eyes. "Or what?"

There was a creak of armor as Wonda clenched her fists. "Or I'll give you a spankin', ya little pissant."

An image flashed over Stela, Wonda putting her on the ground in training. The girl was eager for a rematch. "Try it, you ugly skink. Think you're so special because you're Leesha's attack dog. Time someone put you back in your kennel."

Wonda's aura was blazing as well. Leesha laid a hand on her arm, calming her. "I didn't abandon you," she told Stela. "The duke commanded I go to Angiers. What was I to do? Rules are what keep us civilized. Something you seem to have forgotten."

"Ay, rules," Stela said. "Like you've ever let that stop you doing whatever you like."

"Everything I've done, I've done for Hollow County," Leesha said.

"Ay?" Stela countered. "That why you got the demon of the desert's baby up in your keep?"

Wonda growled, and Leesha had to put a hand on her chest to hold her back. "Yes, even that. Would you have preferred his army came through the Hollow like they did Rizon and Lakton?"

Stela laughed. "Tellin' me you didn't like it a bit, playin' the bad girl? Didn't curl your toes while you were at it?"

"I don't have to explain myself to you," Leesha said.

"Course not," Stela said. "Leesha rippin' Paper doesn't need to explain herself to anyone. Leaves town for seven years and comes back orderin' folk around like someone made her duchess."

"Enough," Leesha said. "There were conditions when I warded your skin and gave your people weapons. You have broken them, and the laws of Hollow County. You will be taken into custody to answer to the magistrate for your crimes."

Stela barked a laugh. "By what army?"

Leesha pointed, and the two looked back to see Cutters blocking egress from the alley. They had kept their distance as Leesha instructed, but there was no way out for the pair.

Stela had a wry smile as she turned back. "Ent enough. Not by a long sight." She leapt, easily clearing the thirty feet between them.

But as fast as she was, Wonda Cutter was faster. She stepped in front of Leesha, immovable as a rock demon, and struck Stela an open-handed blow to the chest that stopped her short, blowing the wind out of her and knocking her to the ground.

The wards tattooed all over Stela's skin flared to match the anger in her aura. She put her hands under her, not seriously injured.

Wonda gave her no time to recover, kicking her onto her stomach and torquing back one of her arms. Stela screamed, but it was short-lived as Keet stepped in, cracking Wonda across the head with the shaft of his *hora* spear so hard the strap broke and her wooden helm was sent tumbling away.

"Let's go!" Keet shouted, pulling Stela to her feet as the Cutters charged.

Stela threw off his arm. "Not until I put this ugly skink on the ground!" Wonda was stumbling to her feet as Stela came in, impact wards flaring on her fist as she punched Wonda square in the jaw.

Had Wonda been a normal person, even a Cutter, the blow would likely have killed her. But Wonda's flesh was warded as well, and her wooden armor was infused with *hora*. Even so, Leesha heard the crack of bone.

Leesha pulled her wand, but Wonda wasn't down yet. She sidestepped the next blow, catching Stela's wrist and using her own momentum to pull her into a body blow that cracked ribs.

Keet had seemed unwilling to fight, but now that it was upon them, his aura flared nearly as hot as Stela's. He push-kicked one of the charging Cutters into the woman next to him, cracking a third across the face. A year ago he had been a harmless boy, innocent and a bit simple, but now he moved like a predator, striking where his foes were weakest, never losing track of them as they tried to surround him.

Stela had been right. They hadn't brought enough warriors.

Stela and Wonda fought like demons, exchanging heavy blows. In the thick of battle, much of the artistry fell from *sharusahk,* leaving only a brutal melee of kicks, punches, and twists. Wonda put them on the ground, wrestling her way toward a hold, but Stela put an elbow into her, impact ward flaring. Wonda was knocked back and Stela tried to reverse the hold, but Wonda got a foot between them, kicking her off.

"Enough!" Leesha shouted, lifting her wand. Stela turned to her, eyes like a coreling, and started to move her way.

Leesha wrote a practiced series of wards in the air as easily as she might sign her name. She could have used the magic to strike at Stela, but this wasn't the girl's fault—at least, not entirely. Instead Leesha formed a Draw.

Stela screamed as the magic was torn from her. Her wards dimmed as the wand grew warm in Leesha's hands. Wonda reached for her, then shouted and pulled her hand back as she was caught in the Draw.

"Stop Keet!" Leesha shouted. "I have this!"

But it didn't seem like she had it. Stela found her feet, stalking in, eyes ablaze. Smitt took a step back as his grand-daughter drew close.

The wand was hot now, but Leesha grit her teeth and stood fast, even as she felt the feedback passing through her specially warded gloves and up her arm. It made her strong, but only increased her anger and frustration.

"How dare you!" Leesha shouted. "You were nothing! A mouse scurrying in my hospit! I gave you power to stand up in the night and this is what you do with it? This is how you repay me?!" She wrote more wards in the air, increasing the pull.

And then, suddenly, Stela's aura winked out, snuffed like a candle. She collapsed to the ground, lifeless.

"Night!" The sight brought Leesha back to herself. She stopped the Draw and ran to the girl, panic screaming through her as the magic heightened that as well. She had not meant to drain so much. Not meant to kill her.

Stela was still warm, but she wasn't breathing, her heart still and her aura dark. The wand was still hot in Leesha's hand, and she touched it to the keyword on Stela's breast, giving back a touch of what she had taken.

Leesha saw as the ward greedily drank the magic, sending a spark through the net, racing throughout Stela's body. The girl jolted, eyes wide as she pulled in a gasping breath, then fell back, panting. Her aura was dim, but Leesha could see her heart beating again, and knew she would survive.

By then Wonda and the Cutters had Keet pinned, stripping him of weapons and armor. Wonda looked to be healing, but her jaw was crooked. Leesha might need to break it again to set it properly.

"Keet and Stela Inn, you are under arrest," Leesha said. "I'd hoped never to use the dungeons Count Thamos built, but you leave me no choice."

Stela coughed, spitting blood, but she was smiling. "Not for long. Pack's gonna hear about this. They'll come for us."

"Then they'll share your cells." But if the rest of the Warded Children were eating demon meat, Leesha knew it wouldn't be so simple.

Things would get worse before they got better.

"Don't see the need for all this, mistress," Darsy said as she and Leesha sipped tea, watching Hollow Soldiers march onto Gatherers' Academy grounds.

They were in what was once Leesha's cottage, now the seat of Headmistress Darsy's administration. It was odd, being a visitor in her old home.

"I pray there isn't one," Leesha said, "but the Warded Children's camp is only a few miles away, and it's only a matter of time before they realize we have Stela and Keet locked away. With magic amplifying their emotions, they may want to strike back, and not be picky about where."

Darsy gave her a knowing look. "Ent your fault, Leesha. You didn't know what would happen."

"Didn't I?" Leesha asked. "Arlen told me not to ward flesh. Night, he begged me not to! He knew what it did to folk's minds. I told myself he wasn't giving us enough credit, but I think now I wasn't giving enough to him. The will to resist power like that . . . what kind of person does it take?"

Darsy blew out a breath. "Thought Renna was bad at first, but she came out the other side, didn't she?"

"I suppose, but she had Arlen Bales with her, day and night. Children just have each other." Leesha sipped her tea.

Melny came out of the kitchen with a tray. "Cookie, mistress?"

"Thank you dear." Leesha took a cookie. "They smell delicious."

Melny's smile lit her face. She was a beautiful young woman, swollen bosom and belly barely contained by her homespun dress, but seeing her tending Darsy's house, no one would ever guess she was the Duchess of Angiers, snuck out of the city with Leesha's apprentices when her husband was killed in a Krasian attack.

"Can I get you anything else, mistress?" she asked.

"Tea's a bit sweet," Leesha said. "No need for sugar in mine next time."

"I can bring another cup . . ."

"That's all right, dear," Leesha said. "How have you been?"

"Very well, mistress. Headmistress Darsy's taught me so much."

"Not enough about baking," Darsy muttered as the young woman swept out of the room, humming to herself.

Leesha looked at the cookie. It was burnt around the edges, the center too thick. She took a bite and sure enough, it was raw in the middle.

"Most of the apprentices you brought back have done well." Darsy shook her head. "That one . . ."

"I watched her husband die," Leesha said. "She has no one, and I promised to keep her safe." It was true, if not the whole truth. Should Duke Pether fail to produce an heir with Princess Lorain of Miln, the child Melny carried was next in succession.

Leesha knew she might one day need to use them both as political tools, and hated herself for it. "Thank you for taking her in."

Darsy shrugged. "Girl ent too bright, still learning her way around the kitchen and a broom, but she's a good hand with a needle, and always sunny. Throws that pretty smile at everyone, and they all dote on her, especially with the babe in her belly."

"And how are our Milnese guests faring?" Leesha asked.

"Learning more from them than they are from us," Darsy admitted. "Guildmaster Ragen and Mother Elissa have been giving guest lectures on warding all week." She shook her head. "Doesn't seem right, though, teaching bone magic to a man."

"You're going to have to get used to it, Darsy," Leesha said. "Just as the men are getting used to women taking up the spear. Olive has me thinking a lot about the lines we draw for ourselves. Why shouldn't a man be allowed to Gather, if he has the aptitude and desire?"

"Core if I know." Darsy blew out a breath. "Just strange, is all. Next thing we'll be teaching them the secrets of fire."

"You heard the news from the Battle of Angiers," Leesha said. "The men of Miln already have the secrets of fire, but all the flamework weapons in the world aren't going to save them if a mind demon targets them on new moon. Guildmaster Ragen raised Arlen Bales. If he can't be trusted, we might as well give up hope."

CHAPTER 13

THE LAST WILL
AND TESTAMENT OF ARLEN BALES

334 AR

"She's gonna be steamed," Renna warned.

"Ay, you don't know the half of it," Arlen agreed. "But she's got a right."

"Sure you don't want me to come along?" Renna asked. She didn't say it, but the image of Arlen and Leesha in passionate embrace flashed across her aura. She didn't believe it was a real risk now that they were man and wife, but neither could she forget it happened.

"Be back for you soon enough, Ren," he said, "but Leesha's earned herself a shout, and I'm better equipped to weather it alone."

"Long as that's all it is," Renna said. "No one gets to slap you but me."

"Ent I fortunate." Arlen winked at her, drawing a deep breath and letting himself dissipate as he blew it back out. The demons called this the between-state, where they existed only as energy, subject to the currents of magic all around them, with only will to hold them in place.

He reached out with his will, finding a tendril of magic venting up from the Core and using it as a guide as he slipped deep beneath the surface. Other paths opened to him, converging in a complex maze, but he didn't hesitate in choosing his course. Even hundreds of miles away, he could sense the current of the Hollow greatwards, Drawing all magic in the area into a great vortex.

He let it Draw him until he was inside the net, then exerted his will and fell into orbit around the greatward's center, lest it pull him apart.

Knowledge opened to him once he was on the greatward, and he drank it in, absorbing much of what had transpired in his absence as he sifted out a single aura and skated toward it with the speed of thought.

The wards Leesha had laid about the count's keep were formidable, but they were meant to repel demons and, in some cases, humans. Arlen was neither, slipping between the cracks, invisible to the unwarded eye. Even those with wardsight would only see an increase in ambient magic, drawn to the pull of the wards on the walls.

Arlen skated along these as easily as the greatward. He taught wardcraft to Leesha; knew her script like none other. Running along it was like caressing a part of her, reminding him of caresses they shared in what felt like another life. He was thankful Renna was not with him. When they dissipated together, their emotions were laid bare.

He found her sitting in the count's office. Arlen materialized in the shadows, releasing some of his inner magic into the wards of unsight tattooed along his limbs.

Hidden from sight, he Drew a touch of ambient magic from the room, Reading. Not the count's office anymore. Thamos hadn't been here in months, and one glance at Leesha's aura told him she was countess now. Power—and the burdens it brought—radiated like heat around her, images dancing around her like demons.

Arlen remembered to breathe, letting the pain wash over him. Count Thamos, for all his bluster, had been a good man, and those were ever in short supply. His death did the world no favor.

Leesha was not alone. Wonda stood guard, blackstem wards peeking out from the rolled sleeves of her blouse. She shone with power, and it was beautiful to see. Arlen had looked into thousands of auras, but few were as pure and uncomplicated as Wonda Cutter's.

But even that was nothing compared with what radiated

from the cradle. The child of Leesha and Jardir, burning like a miniature sun. He swallowed a lump in his throat, reaching up to brush a tear from his eye.

There were inert wards of silence around the room. Arlen sketched a ward in the air, activating them.

Leesha stiffened, sensing the change. Her hand darted to her belt, where a gold-plated wand of demon bone hung.

Ever alert, Wonda put a hand to the knife at her hip. "Everythin' all right, mistress?"

"Check the door," Leesha said. "Take your bow."

"No need for that, Won." Arlen stepped from the shadows.

Leesha was on her feet in an instant, drawing a mimic ward in the air.

"Ent a demon, Leesh," Arlen said. "It's me. Honest word."

"Deliverer." Wonda dropped to one knee.

Arlen rolled his eyes. "How many times I need to tell you to knock that off 'fore you start listening, Wonda Cutter?"

Wonda shrugged, getting back to her feet. "'Bout a million, I reckon."

"Halfway there, then," Arlen said.

"Good to see ya, sir," Wonda said. "Knew ya wern't dead."

"Good to see you, too," Arlen said. "Got words for you and a few others, soon. Proud of you. But right now, be obliged if you stand outside the door and make sure we don't get any accidental visitors."

"Ay, sir." Wonda took her bow and quiver, heading for the door.

"Not a word to anyone, Wonda," Leesha said.

"Ay, mistress." Wonda closed the door behind her.

"Countess Paper," Arlen said. "Do I bow, or . . . ?"

Leesha clipped the wand back on her belt and opened her arms. "Shut it and hug me."

Arlen embraced her tightly, and she him. Her scent filled his nostrils—herbs and soap, the sweetness of her milk, and that smell that was hers alone. He resisted the urge to put his face in her hair and breathe as he once had.

They let go only reluctantly, but once his grip loosened, Leesha shoved him back. "Corespawn you, Arlen Bales! You gave us all a deathly fright! You and your ripping secret plans! Is Ahmann alive, too?"

Arlen rubbed at the back of his neck. "Course he is, Leesha. Didn't kill anyone. Renna told you that."

"She didn't." Leesha practically spat the words. "She said he wasn't coming back, same as you."

She smacked at his chest. He could have stopped her, or moved, or dissipated and let the hand pass through him, but he let it happen. "Get it all out, Leesh. Know I got it comin'."

"Corespawned right!" she growled, but his passive stance took some of the wind from her. Leesha's emotions could boil over now and again, but at heart she was a creature of logic. She had questions, and they couldn't be asked while she was shouting.

There was a cry from across the room as the baby stirred.

"Now look what you've done," Leesha said. "I only just got the baby to sleep."

"I ent the one shouting." Leesha moved toward the crib, but Arlen was faster. He scooped the child up, unable to keep the smile from his face.

He looked back, and there was panic in Leesha's aura. She was terrified by him touching the child, but she kept it in check, saying nothing. Arlen put out a finger and the babe took it, cries forgotten as the tiny eyes stared up at him.

Looking closer into the child's aura, he saw what Leesha feared. "Ay, don't see that every day."

Leesha's aura became guarded. "That all you have to say?"

Arlen ignored the question. "What's her name?"

"Olive." Arlen could see the image of an olive floating above Leesha, half bitten with the stone showing.

He laughed. "Olives got stones."

Leesha crossed her arms. "My mother said that."

"It's a good name," Arlen said. "She'll like it."

Leesha's aura shifted from guarded to curious. "What makes you think Olive's a she?"

Arlen looked back at the child, wondering that himself. He probed deeper, pulling a touch of magic through Olive and absorbing it, Reading the imprint she left. All around her, images danced in her aura. More than he had ever seen. They weren't her thoughts or memories; she was too young for those. They were what might be.

"Don't know," he said at last. "But I know I'm right. Olive'll answer to *she*, but always know she's neither."

Pain lanced across Leesha's aura. Her eyes teared, and she put a hand to her mouth to stifle a sob.

Arlen cradled Olive in one arm, reaching a hand out to squeeze Leesha's shoulder. "Don't matter. She'll be Olive, too big to fit in any box. World's just gonna have to get used to her."

Leesha let out a choked laugh. "My mother said that, too."

"Smarts like a whip, your mam," Arlen said. "Olive's got hard times ahead, but she's as special as her parents. Maybe more. Ent nothin' the world can throw at her she can't handle."

Leesha looked up at him, eyes still wet with tears. "How can you know these things?"

Arlen looked back at the swirling images around Olive and shrugged. "See things, now. Sometimes what folk are thinkin', and sometimes . . . something else. Like the dice, I reckon. Not what will be, but what might. Odds are good none of us has much future left, but if we get through what's coming . . ."

"Where's her father?" Leesha asked.

"On guard duty till I finish up here," Arlen said. "Then he's got his own business to settle in Everam's Bounty. After that, we'll be away again."

"What business?" Leesha demanded. "Guarding what? Away where? What's coming?"

Arlen blew out a breath. "Stirred up the hornet's nest, Leesh. Gonna be a swarm, and it's kind of my fault."

Arlen saw the flash of pain behind Leesha's eye even before she pressed the heel of her palm into her temple, easing it. "That sounds like the Arlen Bales I know." She strode back to her chair. "Tea?"

"Ay, thanks," Arlen said. Olive closed her eyes, and he eased himself gently onto the couch across from Leesha so as not to wake her. Leesha poured, and he took the cup with his free hand. It was bitter, but that was no surprise. Leesha didn't withhold sugar on purpose; it just never occurred to her that anyone would want it.

She squinted at him through her warded spectacles. "Night, Arlen. If you want sugar, all you have to do is ask."

He smiled. "You're better'n you let on at reading auras."

"Doesn't take a mind demon," Leesha said. "I can see a ripping sugar pot floating over your head."

"Don't start to make out images till you've got the hang of it," Arlen said.

Leesha waved a dismissive hand, but he could see she was pleased. "Does this mean you've been wanting sugar all this time and never said a word?"

Arlen shrugged. "You never set it on the table unless someone asks, and I ent one to cause a fuss. Drank worse'n bitter tea in my time."

"Ichor?" Leesha asked, and Arlen felt his blood turn cold. He kept his haggler's mask in place, probing her aura to see how much she knew.

He blew out a breath, setting down the drink. "How'd you figure it out?"

"I didn't," Leesha said. "Stela Inn did. Now she's locked in the dungeon in a warded cell, and dozens of magic-drunk teenagers are eating demon meat out in Gatherers' Wood."

"Night." Arlen put his face in his palm.

"You could have told me," Leesha said. "You could have trusted me."

"Like I trusted you not to go warding folk's skin?" Arlen asked. "Like I trusted you to take my word that too much magic's dangerous? You saw what I was like, Leesha. Livin' in the wild like an animal, forgettin' what it meant to be a man. Nearly left you and Rojer for dead on the road, and you caught me on a good day."

Leesha crossed her arms. "But it was all right for Renna?"

Arlen scowled. "Renna din't give me any more choice in the matter'n you, Leesh. Surrounded by women who won't do what I tell 'em."

She smirked at him. "Maybe that's what you need to keep you from acting the fool."

Arlen chuckled in spite of himself. "Ay, maybe."

Leesha got up, striding to a side table with a simple clay tea service. No fancy silver for this duchess. She returned with the sugar pot, taking the tongs and dropping two cubes into his cup. She set the pot down and returned to her seat. "Now tell me what you've gone and done."

"Trust you, Leesha Paper," Arlen said. "Always have. But just like you din't hand me the secrets of fire when I asked, I kept some things. We all got a right to our own counsel."

Leesha pursed her lips but didn't argue.

"Now . . ." He sighed. "Don't know I'm gonna live to see you again, so there ent much point in holdin' secrets. Tell you everything you want to know, but I need your oath, out loud, to keep it quiet. Someone gets wind of what I'm about to tell you, and a mind catches 'em, whole world's in jeopardy."

Leesha didn't hesitate. "I swear on the child sleeping in your arm. Your secrets are safe with me."

Arlen nodded. "Minds didn't come after me and Jardir by accident. They take this Deliverer business even more serious than the Tenders. Call us Unifiers. Minds to stir the drones into a real resistance. Long as we were around, they were going to keep coming."

"Renna said as much when you sent her," Leesha said.

"Thought we could fight 'em, like they did in the old days," Arlen said. "Then they caught me in that trap on new moon and went through my mind like a rummage trunk. Could hear 'em, chattin' in my head. Looked at my life and plans and laughed at what a joke it all was.

"But then," he tapped his temple, "they let slip one little thing."

"What?" He could see her resisting the urge to lean in.

"Saw where I got the wards from," Arlen said. "Saw Anoch Sun, and swore to go back there the next new moon and obliterate the place."

Leesha's eyes narrowed. "You knew where they'd be."

Arlen nodded. "Knew then I couldn't kill Jardir. Demons saw that plan in my mind. Had to do something they didn't expect."

"*Domin Sharum* was a ruse from the start," Leesha guessed. "You kidnapped Ahmann and took him there."

Arlen nodded. "And Renna, Shanvah, and Shanjat."

Leesha clenched a fist, aura spiking hot with anger. "But not me. Not Rojer or Gared or . . ."

"Couldn't risk it," Arlen said. "Whole thing hinged on hiding in a tiny burial chamber until the minds came to shit in

Kaji's sarcophagus. Every added body increased the chance they'd spot us and run before we struck."

"So what happened?" Leesha demanded.

"Jardir's crown projects a warding field in a sphere," Arlen said. "Demons can't get in, and they can't get out. We killed some of the lesser minds, and trapped the big bad in with us."

Leesha's eyes widened. "You mean . . . ?"

Arlen nodded. "Alagai Ka. He's real as you'n me."

"Did you kill him?" Leesha asked.

Arlen looked around, checking to see that the wards of silence were still active. He drew a few extra, just in case. Unsight. Confusion. Leesha watched patiently.

"Corespawned bastard wiped the floor with us," he said. "Literally. Took me, Jardir, and Renna, with all our tricks and traps, to finally beat him down and chain him up."

Leesha gaped. "Chain?"

"He's alive," Arlen said. "That's what Jardir's guarding."

"But why?" Leesha asked.

"Ent gonna like the answer," Arlen warned.

Leesha scowled, crossing her arms. "Out with it, then."

"Gonna make him take us to the Core to kill the demon queen."

"Night." Leesha's aura showed she had been readying a scolding, but as the enormity of his words sank in, she deflated. "And the demons are going to swarm to stop you?"

Arlen shook his head. "Not exactly."

"Night," Leesha said again, when Arlen finished explaining. She always knew he was crazy, but this . . . "Do you still think going down to the hive is a good idea?"

"Got a better one?" Arlen asked.

Olive remained asleep in the crook of his arm, looking so peaceful. His aura enveloped her protectively. What would it be like for her to grow up never knowing him? Without ever having met her father? Leesha was not as skilled as them at reading auras, but even she could see that Arlen saw this as a mission they would not return from.

"You say the lesser mind demons are already nesting," Leesha said. "You could kill the demon king and hunt them down, one by one. Fight the demon war the old-fashioned way."

"There were a lot more folk back then," Arlen said. "Kaji's army numbered in the millions. We ent got spears enough now, much less if the queen squirts out a hundred thousand fresh demon eggs."

He blew out a breath. "But maybe this *is* the old-fashioned way, give or take. Evejah says Kaji took the fight underground, and Alagai Ka confirms it."

"Kaji killed the demon queen?" Leesha asked.

"Tried to," Arlen said. "Got close. But something happened in the last press. Creator only knows."

"Since when do you believe in the Creator?" Leesha asked.

Arlen shrugged. "Know what I mean."

"How do you know this demon isn't leading you into a trap?" Leesha asked.

He shrugged again in that infuriating way he had. "Probably is. But the corelings don't know we're coming, and thanks to your cloaks they ent likely to see us. With the demon daddy tattooed and chained, there's a limit to the damage he can do."

"Sounds like he's already shown you that limit is more than you expect."

Arlen nodded. "Won't take any chances we don't have to, but can't just sit here and wait for night to fall for good."

"No," Leesha agreed. "No, you can't."

"Minds are going to try to crack the Free Cities open like eggs," Arlen warned. "They'll need fresh meat to feed the hatchling queens. Every major settlement is going to get hit as they stake out their territories."

"What happens when they kill us all and run out of food?" Leesha massaged her temple.

"Then they expand their reach," Arlen said. "We ent the only people in the world, Leesha, and this hive ent the only one."

"So what?" Leesha asked. "You kill the queen and we withstand the swarm and it's all just a temporary fix?"

Arlen shook his head. "Not if we keep building greatwards. We last through the next year, a generation from now corelings won't be able to materialize anywhere in Thesa."

"You really believe that?" Leesha asked.

"Much as I believe anything," Arlen said, and there was no lie in his aura. "When I was little, folk didn't think demons could be fought at all. Proved 'em wrong, and then folk didn't think Krasians and Thesans could work together. Proved them wrong, too. Write our own destinies, Leesh, long as we got the stones to do it."

Olive burbled, shifting to nestle further into him, and Leesha clenched a fist. "Then that's what we'll do. What do you need?"

"Gonna have to get word to the other cities," Arlen said. "Can you handle Angiers? Euchor ent going to listen, but I've got some other friends in Miln—"

"You don't," Leesha cut in.

"Ay?" Arlen asked.

Leesha savored the moment. "Elissa and Ragen are here, in the Hollow."

Arlen's eyes grew wider than teacups, and she smiled. "They were in Lakton when the Krasians attacked. They're staying in this very keep while they gather supply for the trip home."

"Saves me a trip then." Arlen regained control of his expression, but she could see the pleasure her words brought.

Creator, let him have this bit of joy. If anyone deserves it, it's Arlen Bales.

"Can you ask Wonda to fetch them here while I skate back to get Ren, please?" Arlen asked. "Rojer and Gared, too."

Leesha froze, keeping her expression calm, but it didn't matter. Arlen saw right through her. His eyes flicked above her shoulder, seeing the ghost that no doubt hovered there. Any touch of elation vanished from his aura.

"Rojer's *dead*?!"

In his arm, Olive began to cry.

Arlen was still brushing away tears when he and Renna rematerialized in Leesha's private office. Leesha had gathered Ragen, Elissa, Derek, Wonda, and Gared as he'd asked.

"Night," Gared muttered to Wonda. "Coulda gone my whole life without seeing the Deliverer cry."

Leesha glared at him, but it was too late. Arlen had ears like a bat.

"Human as you are, Gar," he snapped. "Ent got a right to a few tears for my friend?"

"Course ya do," Gared said. "Only meant—"

"Only meant you're still stuck on this rippin' Deliverer nonsense when there's wood to chop!" Gone was the serenity they were accustomed to seeing on Arlen's face. His eyes were afire, like Stela's had been. His aura burned a hot red, and everyone in the room could see it.

Arlen advanced, and Gared shrank back. His knees buckled, and Arlen's aura blazed. "So help me, Gared Cutter, you try and kneel and I'll . . ."

Leesha started forward, but it was Renna, her own eyes wet and swollen red, who put a hand on his arm, checking him.

"Breathe," she murmured.

Arlen pulled up, drawing a deep breath. The anger flowed out of his aura with the exhale, and everyone in the room joined in a sigh of relief.

"Sorry, Gar," Arlen said.

"Had it comin'." Gared blushed and waved a hand to dismiss it. "Might need a change o' shorts, though."

"Din't," Arlen said. "Ent you I was mad at. Should've been there. Should've . . ."

"Ay," Gared said. "Think that every night. Never should've left the city with him locked up."

"We all do," Leesha said. "None of us imagined Janson could be so bold."

Now it was Renna's aura that reddened. "Take it this Janson ent breathin' anymore?"

Leesha glanced around the room. With Rojer's wives returned to Krasia, the secret didn't really matter anymore. "Sikvah slit his throat in a palace lavatory."

Gared blinked. "Li'l Sikvah? That can't be right."

"Believe it," Wonda said. "Got in her way that night. Put me down like she was spankin' a toddler."

"Good riddance." Renna spat on the floor, and Leesha bit her tongue.

"Sorry for missin' the service," Arlen said. "Leesha says it was somethin' to see."

"Whole Hollow came out," Wonda said. "Tens o' thousands, singin' Rojer's songs and beggin' the Creator's blessings for him in Heaven."

"We came to the Hollow right in the middle of it," Ragen said.

"I've never seen anything so beautiful," Elissa added.

Arlen swallowed a lump in his throat. "Least I had family there, then." He and Ragen started to put hands out, then thought better of it and had a brief hug, slapping each other on the back.

Men. Leesha fought the urge to roll her eyes.

Elissa put her arms out, and Arlen fell into them. He shuddered, and everyone's eyes dropped, allowing them a moment's privacy. Renna spied her bubbled spit on the floor and sketched a ward with her finger, evaporating it.

When at last they drew apart, Elissa produced a silk kerchief, gently wiping Arlen's eyes. It was hard to imagine the Arlen Leesha knew letting anyone do that, but he just sniffed until Elissa finished and gave him a kiss.

Arlen turned to extend an arm to Renna. "This is my wife, Renna Bales."

Renna took a step forward but kept her eyes down. Shame flared in her aura as images flickered around her. A proper dress. A bathtub. A memory of herself from before she cut her hair with a knife to keep it out of the way as she fought.

Creator, she's changed so much in the last year. Leesha gave her head a tiny shake. *Night, we all have.*

Renna's feelings were understandable, especially in the presence of Mother Elissa, who wore nobility like a robe. But there was no sign in aura or expression that it mattered a whit to the woman. She held her arms open to Renna just as she had to Arlen, and pulled the reluctant young woman in tight.

"Have you been taking care of my boy?" Elissa asked quietly.

Renna sniffed and nodded. "Doin' my best." She pulled back, and their eyes met at last. "I was there when Arlen lost his mam. Told me how you and Ragen were there for him, even when he din't know he needed you. Thank you for that."

And then it was Elissa who teared, and they held each other again.

Derek stepped forward next, staring at Arlen, trying to see past the tattoos on his face. Images flashed above him—Arlen as a young man, sandy-haired and smooth-cheeked, not a ward on his skin. He was beautiful, and Leesha's heart ached at the sight.

Derek put out a hand. "Been a long time."

Arlen slapped it aside, pulling the man into a rough hug. "Too long. And you a Messenger, now! Who'd have thought?"

Derek grinned. "Just needed a kick out the door. Still be rotting up in Brayan's Gold, but for you."

Arlen waved the thought away. "How are Stasy and Jef?"

"Well enough, when I get to see them," Derek said. "Count Brayan's got 'em locked up in his keep, and after a fortnight's visit I outstay my welcome."

"Get your own house, then," Arlen said.

"Easier said than done," Derek said. "Stasy and Jef got royal blood, and I ent. I can't give them a life like Count Brayan can, if he'd even let them go. All I can do is keep workin', maybe one day earn enough to get them back for real."

Arlen clicked his tongue. "Core with 'one day.' Sortin' this right now. Din't risk our necks getting you to Miln so Brayan could snub you. Worth ten o' him." He looked to Leesha. "Mind if I use your desk?"

Leesha nodded, and Arlen took a seat and fresh parchment, dipping the pen with a practiced hand. He looked to Ragen. "What was it Cob left me in his will again?"

"Fifty-one percent of the warding business," Ragen said. "And two of the five seats on the Ward Exchange, yours and his. We've been renting them. You're worth millions of suns, if you ever come claim it."

Arlen nodded, bending and writing across the top of the page in his beautiful, flowing script.

The Last Will and Testament of Arlen Bales

"Cob's seat will go to you and Elissa," Arlen told Ragen, "along with thirty of my fifty-one percent." He looked to Derek. "My seat, and twenty-one percent of the business, will go to you."

Derek's eyes grew wide, and his aura turned white with shock. "You can't be serious."

"Serious as nightfall," Arlen said. "You left the wards to find me when you thought I needed help. Now you need help, and I'm happy to give it."

"Ay," Derek sputtered, "but millions of suns? What if you need it one day?"

"Ent likely, where I'm goin'," Arlen said. "Sides, got gold aplenty stashed all over Thesa."

"It's true," Gared said. "Seen the barrels."

"You keep it in barrels?!" Derek gaped.

"Can't just leave it on the floor, can I?" Arlen asked. He finished writing, blowing on the ink to dry it. "Needs witnesses. Leesha? Gar?"

Leesha took the pen, signing her name, and handed it to Gared. He furrowed his brow, hand shaking a bit, but managed to write his name. Rosal's lessons were progressing well.

"There," Arlen said, blotting the paper and rolling it up. "Let's see Brayan try and keep you down now."

"But you ent dead," Derek said.

"Far as the world knows, I am," Arlen said. "Ent got to look over your shoulder, Derek. It's yours, now."

"I . . ." Derek shook his head. "I don't know what to say."

"Say *thank you*," Elissa suggested.

Derek pulled Arlen into another hug. "Thank you."

"Congratulations, partner!" Ragen slapped Derek on the back. "Lucky to have you!"

It was a few minutes more before Leesha had everyone seated for tea. She made a point of putting the sugar pot in everyone's reach.

Arlen produced a letter, handing it to Ragen. "For Tender Ronnell. He's another one got this Deliverer business stuck in his head, but it means he'll listen where Euchor might not."

Ragen took the letter. "Do you want us to tell him you're alive?"

"No one outside this room needs to know that." Arlen's eyes drifted to meet those of everyone in the room as he spoke. "You and Elissa left Miln not long after I disappeared. Easy enough to say you picked that and my will up when you first passed through the Hollow, and been carryin' 'em ever since."

"We've exchanged many messages with Miln in recent months," Elissa noted.

Arlen shrugged. "Tell him Rojer gave it to you, with instructions not to trust it to anyone else."

"A secret message sent just before your mysterious disappearance?" Elissa asked. "That won't do much to dispel his belief that you're the Deliverer."

"Don't think anything will," Arlen said. "Belief is stubborn as a rock demon."

"Ay," Elissa agreed. "Like your belief that you're not."

Arlen rolled his eyes. "Night, not you, too."

"There's no test to know if someone is the Deliverer or not," Ragen pointed out.

Arlen looked at him, incredulous. "Taught me yourself Deliverers don't exist."

"I taught no such thing," Ragen said. "I said when humanity needed them, great generals rose to lead us. Their existence is documented, Arlen. It's a fact. The Creator didn't come down from Heaven to confirm it then, and I don't expect He will now, but that doesn't change the fact that our whole world has shifted because Arlen Bales had a stubborn streak."

"Corespawned right," Gared said, and even Leesha could not help but feel the power of the argument. Was Arlen Bales the Deliverer? Was Ahmann? Did divine blessing matter, if they were to walk that path?

"Can't have people waiting for me to save them," Arlen argued.

"Gettin' tired o' hearin' that," Wonda said. "Believed in you from the start. Din't stop me from fightin'."

"Or me," Gared put in.

"Or most of the Hollow," Leesha added. Arlen frowned at her, turning to Renna.

"What's it matter?" his wife asked. "Doesn't change what anyone's got to do."

Something softened in Arlen's aura at that, a stubborn streak turned contemplative. "Belief of Ronnell and the other Tenders might be all that saves Miln in time. Trouble's comin', and fast. Euchor's put all his faith in his flamework weapons, but they ent gonna be enough by a long sight. Holy Houses are going to be the safest places in Miln once the demons breach the walls."

Ragen and Elissa looked at each other, paling.

"Do you think it will get that far?" Ragen asked.

"Miln's walls hold because they've never really been tested," Arlen said. "If One Arm could breach them, the minds'll have no problem. Church wards are stronger, but still no match for rock demons with stones to throw. Hiding ent gonna be enough. Folk need to be ready to fight."

Quickly, he relayed much of what he had told Leesha—the capture of the demon king, the coming swarm, and his plan to attack the hive.

Gared got to his feet at that. "Goin' with you."

"No, you ent," Arlen said.

Wonda stood as well. "Can't let the two of you go down there alone."

"Ent alone," Renna said. "Jardir and Shanvah are comin', and they know their way around a fight. Two a' you can do more up here than you can down there."

Gared shook his head. "Bad enough, what happened to Rojer—"

"Gonna happen to Hollow County, they don't have Gared and Wonda Cutter around when new moon comes again," Arlen cut in. "Means the world to us you're willing to go, but Renna's right. Ent your fight."

"Could use your help with Promise, though," Renna said. "Don't reckon I want to take her down into the dark with us."

"Course," Wonda said.

"Promise needs a firm hand," Renna's voice tightened, like a parent giving up a child, "but she won't shy from a fight."

"Take good care of her," Wonda said. "Swear by the sun."

"Gonna need all the help you can get," Arlen said. "Minds are coming in hard. You'll need to fight smart and take every advantage. Keep the Hollow safe, but find the hive ground and take it out if you can. It'll be somewhere with surface access to an underground cavern. Close enough for them to direct the drones attacking the Hollow, but far enough you won't find it by accident."

"I'll send out survey teams first thing tomorrow," Leesha said.

"Be better if you still had Amanvah and her dice," Arlen said.

"Amanvah's returned to Krasia, but she's promised to send another *dama'ting* to liaise with us," Leesha said.

"Barely trusted Amanvah, but at least she was married to Rojer," Gared said. "Now we're gonna put our faith in some priestess with no stake in the Hollow?"

"Know how you feel, Gar," Arlen said. "Honest word. But we gotta start trustin' sometime. Ent got time to fight among ourselves anymore. If there's a demon prince out there, it's the last thing any good Evejan would lie about."

"Next new moon is in less'n a week," Renna said. "She gonna be here by then?"

Leesha shook her head. "In the meantime, Amanvah taught me something of reading dice, and I've been making a set of my own. Perhaps I can help point the way."

"You know what you're doing?" Arlen asked her.

Leesha smiled. "Do you?"

Gared and Wonda seemed scandalized at the question, but Arlen laughed. "Fair and true."

"That's well enough for the Hollow," Ragen said, "but there are a thousand caves in Miln for a mind demon to hide from the sun."

"Miln doesn't have a Deliverer . . . yet." Arlen winked. "Minds are going to underestimate you. Might be fool enough to show themselves."

"And if not?" Elissa asked.

"Leave me a vial of your blood," Leesha suggested. "Perhaps I can cast the dice, or persuade the *dama'ting* to do it for you."

Arlen nodded. "Good thinkin'. I'll have a word with Jardir before he heads back to Krasia. See if he can get you some help on that front."

"What about Angiers?" Leesha asked. "And Lakton?"

"Lakton's in less danger," Arlen said. "At least the city proper. Water ent a good conductor for magic, and minds can't control drones all the way out on the lake from shore.

Krasians will have to do for any in their inland territory. As for Angiers . . ." He shrugged. "Can't say I know much of anything about Duke Pether, and I doubt he'll be inclined to listen if I skate into his office like I did yours."

"You're right about that," Leesha said. "He sees you as a threat and is actively inciting his Council of Tenders against you."

Arlen blew out a breath, looking to Ragen. "You spent more time there than anyone. Know any who'll listen?"

"Most of my business was with Rhinebeck and Janson," Ragen said. "I've been hunting a few times with the royal brothers, but each had his own entourage, and Pether was the one I knew least. He'd remember me well enough to secure an audience, but I doubt I can sway him with unprovable portents of doom. We've done a lot to line the pockets of the Warders' Guildmaster, but the Tenders have their own Warders, and with Pether on the throne, the guild is out of favor."

Leesha looked to Elissa. "You'll need to meet with Araine."

"The Duchess Mum?" Arlen asked. "How's that dim old bird going to help?"

"Mum ent dim." Wonda's measured tone was respectful, but Leesha could see fierce loyalty in her aura, and knew Arlen must, as well. "Done nothin' but right by the Hollow."

"Cannier'n she looks," Gared agreed, "but she ent gonna be much help in a war."

Leesha sighed. If things were as dire as Arlen was saying, there was no point in keeping secrets anymore. "Up until Rhinebeck was murdered and Sikvah killed Janson, Duchess Araine was the real power in Angiers."

Arlen blinked. "How's that?"

"You always said the royals couldn't tie their shoes without Janson," Leesha said. "It was truer than you know. What you and everyone else were in the dark about was that Janson reported directly to Araine."

Arlen's eyes were on her, reading her aura, and she knew he could see the truth in her words. "When I 'disappeared' for your audience with the duke, it was to meet with her and negotiate terms for the Hollow. Everything that happened in your meeting was orchestrated by Araine. Rhinebeck had as much say in where things went as a Messenger's horse deciding where to ride."

"Huh," Arlen said. "And now that Rhinebeck and Janson are dead?"

"I don't know," Leesha admitted. "Duchess Lorain was on the rise when we left, and Pether convinced the Creator put him on the throne."

"Will she be any more inclined to believe us without evidence?" Elissa asked.

"I'll pen letters," Leesha said. "My old teacher Jizell is Royal Gatherer now. She's been to the Hollow and seen what we're up against. She'll listen, I hope."

"Night," Arlen said. "Ent got time for politics and whispers. Need every ally we can get."

"We could use your help with allies closer to home," Leesha said. "I need you to speak to the Warded Children."

Arlen shook his head. "Absolutely not."

"You said we need every ally," Leesha pressed. "Every advantage. They're strong, Arlen, and they worship you. You're the only one who can guide them."

Arlen shook his head again. "Didn't fake my own death and hide out in a tower all these months to go and parade around in front of a mob. More people know I'm alive, more we risk everything. This is your mess, Leesha. Need to clean it up yourself."

"What's all this?" Renna asked.

Arlen turned to her. "Leesha took it on herself to paint blackstem wards on a bunch of kids. They got crazed and stopped listening to sense."

"Dun't sound so bad," Renna said.

"Then one night they ate a demon's heart on a dare," Arlen said.

"Night," Renna muttered.

Gared looked green. "Ent that poison?"

Arlen blew out a breath. "That's what I wanted everyone to think. Ever wonder why Ren and I got powers in the day? Why Evin's hound Shadow grew big as a nightwolf?"

"Arlen . . ." Elissa began.

Arlen met her eyes, and pain lanced across his aura. "Didn't have a choice. Krasians left me to die in the desert. Nothing else to eat. I thought, *They take so much from us, why not take something back?*"

"Think I'm gonna slosh," Wonda said.

"Hush," Leesha told her.

"It's all right," Arlen said. "Don't blame you, Won. But you've felt what warding your skin is like."

"Makes you crazed," Wonda agreed. "Ent in your right mind."

Arlen nodded. "I'd just discovered the fighting wards. Right or wrong, wasn't thinkin' about anything 'cept living long enough to bring them back to the world."

"But if you think wards on your skin make you crazed, ent nothing compared with eatin' demon," Renna said. "Started doing it to keep up with Arlen, just 'fore we came to the Hollow. Remember what I was like then?"

"Scary." Gared shrank back as Renna turned to him. "No offense."

Renna smiled at him. "Scared myself. Still do, sometimes. New struggle, every day. But I had Arlen Bales to pull me through it."

"Stela and the others need you, too," Leesha told Arlen.

"Can't hold everyone's hand," Arlen said. "Far as the world knows, I'm dead. Needs to stay that way."

"Stela's in the dungeon right now," Leesha said. "Sooner or later, the others are going to come for her, and we'll have civil war, right when we most need to unite."

Arlen turned his back, fists clenched.

Renna turned to Leesha. "Know it's your office, mistress, but I'd like a few minutes alone with my husband."

Floating above her was a ghostly image of Renna slapping the back of Arlen's shaved head. It was so comic Leesha had to fight back a smile. "Of course."

Arlen didn't need to see Renna's aura to recognize her tone when she asked the others to leave. He made her promise to slap the fool out of him when it was warranted, and it was a promise she'd never failed to keep. He turned, ready to bat the hand aside.

But Renna stood calmly, arms crossed. There was no anger

in her aura, only disappointment. "Turnin' your back on folk in need? That ent the man I married."

He grit his teeth at the sting of the words. "What am I supposed to do, Ren? Barely kept you in check when you turned feral. To hear Leesha tell it, there's dozens of them now. Ent got time for this."

"So we're gonna give up on 'em?" Renna demanded. "Hollow folk? Stela Inn? Callen Cutter? You an' I were worth savin', but they ent?"

"Ent as simple as that," Arlen said.

Renna jerked her head from side to side. "All Deliverers, you said. You mean that, or was it just words to trick a bunch of scared woodcutters out into the night?"

"Course I meant it," Arlen said.

"Then we need to make time," Renna said. "You can spare a couple hours."

Arlen scowled. "Couple hours ent gonna do it. I been gettin' help for two years now, and I still nearly ripped Gared Cutter's head off when he struck a nerve. You heard Leesha. Franq's got their heads spinnin' with this Deliverer nonsense. Already twistin' our words to suit himself. Anythin' I say's gonna get turned around once I go."

"Then he needs a spankin'," Renna said. "Front of everyone. An' words he can't twist. Creator knows I don't shine over Leesha Paper as much as the rest of this town, but even I can see the sense in tellin' the Warded Children to mind her until this swarm business is done."

Arlen blew out a breath. "Say I do that. Take Stela an' Franq an' anyone else needs it to the woodshed. Tell 'em to stop stealin', mind the Hollow's leaders, and keep the fight to the demons. For the sake of argument, say it even works.

"Then say just one of them runs their mouth in town about me bein' alive, or gets caught by a mind. Our whole plan falls apart. Everything we sacrificed, all these months. Demon princes ent dumb, Ren. They'll figure what we're aiming for and be ready for us."

Renna put her hands on her hips. "Ay, then. I'll do it."

Arlen shook his head. "It's too dangerous . . ."

Renna spat on the floor. "Kids don't know their own strength yet. Took me months and my life on the line to learn to mist.

Now's the time to get 'em to eat a little dirt and set 'em back in the sun."

She grinned. "Think the minds were scared of us? What're they gonna do when there's dozens out there?"

Slowly, Arlen too began to smile. "Keep their eyes on the surface. Stop lookin' for us."

CHAPTER 14

SPANKIN'

334 AR

Shanvah was right where Renna expected, meditating outside her father's cell.

Shanjat, his mind corrupted by the demon, could no longer be trusted. He was chained inside a cell, fed and cleaned thrice a day by his daughter. The cell door was kept locked at all times.

Shanvah had come to make the hall outside the cell her home, furnishing it with a small mat where she could kneel and meditate, practice *sharusahk,* or polish her weapons. Whenever not otherwise occupied, she could be found there.

The girl's eyes were closed when Renna silently materialized, but Shanvah sensed her anyway, eyes opening.

She was on her feet immediately, coming to Renna's side. "Sister, are you all right?"

Renna shook her head. "Ent. Got any of them tear bottles?"

"Of course, sister." She went to the satchel lying by her mat, producing a tiny glass vial, mouth raised on one side and sharpened to scrape moisture from a cheek.

Shanvah knelt at one end of the mat, gesturing for Renna to join her. "It is my honor to assist you in your mourning prayer. Who has taken the lonely path?"

"Ent much for prayin'," Renna said, but she knelt anyway, knees weakening. "Got this thing I need to do, an' it's important, we want anyone left alive up here when our job's done."

"Your honor is boundless, sister," Shanvah said. "You will be victorious."

"Ay, maybe," Renna said. "But right now, all I know is my friend is dead, and I don't . . ."

Shanvah said nothing as Renna choked and tried to compose herself. Her eyes itched. "Don't want him thinkin' that I was too busy to cry for him."

"Of course," Shanvah said.

"But I thought, if I had one o' them bottles in my pocket . . ."

"You could carry his honor with you as you face the trials to come," Shanvah said.

"Ay, that's it," Renna said.

"Speak his name, so that Ev . . . ah, the Creator, can hear." Shanvah held up the bottle.

"Rojer," Renna said. "Ah, son of . . . Jessum of the Inn family of Hollow County."

Shanvah's hand dropped. "Rojer Inn, the jongler?"

"Jongleur, yeah," Renna said. "You know him?"

"He is my cousin by marriage," Shanvah said, "wed to my spear sister Sikvah and my cousin Amanvah. Are they well?"

Renna blinked. After all this time together, how could she not have known that? She and the *Sharum'ting* spoke often, but suddenly she realized how little they really knew about each other.

"Amanvah and Sikvah are all right," Renna assured her. "Both pregnant with Rojer's kids. Headed back to Inevera now."

"Thank you," Shanvah produced another bottle. "I only met my Rojer once, but I will cry with you."

"How you gonna cry over someone you barely knew?" Renna asked.

"Oh, sister," Shanvah said sadly. "Tears are never hard to find. Tell me of the son of Jessum."

"Put out a bad foot, I first got to the Hollow," Renna said. "Drunk on magic and angry, I can't blame folk for not takin' to me, 'specially since they all wanted Arlen to marry prissy Miss Paper."

"Leesha Paper?" Shanvah asked. "The Northern whore who seduced my uncle?"

Renna laughed out loud. "Girl, we need to talk more." Then

she remembered why they were kneeling, and felt a wave of guilt wash over her.

"Everyone in the Hollow was giving me side eye," Renna went on. "Everyone but Rojer Inn. Kissed my hand, first time I met him. Treated me like a person, even while Leesha and the others acted like I was shit on a boot."

She shook her head. "Saved my life so many times at new moon, I lost count. Not just me. *Song of Waning* protected thousands, on the field and off. Hollow County would have been lost, not for Rojer Inn."

Renna started. "You and Sikvah are sisters?"

Shanvah nodded. "Cousins, but trained together in the Dama'ting Palace."

"Leesha said she was a warrior," Renna noted.

"A great one," Shanvah agreed.

"Din't know that," Renna said. "Never saw her fight, but the demons all ran scared of her. Said you trained together. That mean you can sing?"

"Of course I can sing."

"They sang the *Song of Waning* at his funeral," Renna said. "Wasn't there for it, just like I wasn't there when he needed me most."

Shanvah reached out, placing one of the tiny vials in Renna's hand. "Sing it with me, sister, that we may guide the son of Jessum on the lonely path."

All the talk had calmed her so much Renna feared she could not bring herself to tears on command, but then Shanvah opened her mouth and began to sing.

Renna pressed a finger against her chest, feeling the tear bottle nestled there on its leather thong. She moved slowly in Wonda's wake as the big woman relieved the dungeon guards. Feeding a steady stream of power to the wards of unsight on her skin, Renna was like a raven in the night sky, invisible to all who did not look closely. With Wonda to draw attention, none did.

"Down there," Wonda said, unlocking the heavy goldwood door, banded with warded steel. Inside, rough stone steps led down out of sight.

"Thanks, Won," Renna said.

"Sorry this is on you," Wonda said. "Trainin' Stela and the others was my job." She dropped her eyes. "Scarred those wards pretty bad. Girl was ready to kill me when we brought her in last night."

"Ent your fault," Renna said. "Tried to kill Arlen more'n once, when the magic was up in my blood."

Wonda gaped. "Honest word?"

Renna nodded. "He coulda killed me, when it happened. Night, sometimes I wished he had. But it wasn't me. Got control of it. Stela can, too, she's strong enough."

"And if she ent?" Wonda asked.

Renna gave her a hard look. "If she ent—if any of 'em ent—I'll handle things, and leave your mistress with a clear conscience."

There was no pleasure in Wonda's aura at the words, but there was a relief of sorts. She could see Wonda loved Leesha, but knew her mistress didn't have it in her to execute anyone, even when it was needed.

Renna padded down the stone steps, feeling the hairs on the back of her neck stand up as she heard the door shut and lock behind her, leaving her in the dim wardlight.

She immediately felt the pull of the wards glowing on the walls and floor. There was no ambient magic, all of it Drawn into the powerful net that kept the prisoner drained. Renna quickened her step. If she did not keep a tight rein on the magic stored within her, Leesha's wards would suck that away, too.

Even for a dungeon, the place felt unfinished. Count Thamos had built the walls and floor of hewn stone to prevent corelings from rising inside, but as with much of the keep, he had died before it was complete. Not the sort to imprison folk in the cold and dark, Leesha had clearly left it that way until recently. The stone was rough, and most of the cells did not have bars. The wardnet was painted rather than carved. Temporary at best.

"Who's there?" Stela called from down the corridor. Her voice had changed from the timid thing Renna recalled from just half a year gone. It was deeper now. Confident. "Told you before I got nothin' to say till the Wardskins come and fetch me."

"Ay, think you'll talk to me," Renna said, moving to stand before the bars of the girl's cell.

Stela squinted, no doubt seeing Renna's bright glow in her own wardsight. She was dirty, but larger and more muscular than Renna recalled. Tattooed flesh peeked out from the utilitarian smock she had been given. Her aura was weak, drained, but Renna could see how the demon meat had changed it, perhaps forever.

Was a fool to think I could hide it from Arlen, Renna thought.

The cell looked comfortable enough, with a curtain for the privy and a clean cot, but nothing that could be used as a weapon or a means of escape. The bars were thick iron, set deep into the stone.

"Renna Bales." Stela gaped and fell to one knee.

"Cut that demonshit right now." Renna was amazed at how much like Arlen she sounded. "Hear tell you Children wrote down everything me and Arlen ever said, but I don't recall either of us ever tellin' folk to kneel. Or to steal. Or to turn on kith and kin."

Stela got to her feet, aura unsure. "They don't understand us."

"Don't understand yourselves!" Renna snapped. "Actin' the fools, drunk on magic, behavin' more like demons than people!"

Stela shrank back into her cell, and Renna could see how the words stung. Her aura filled with shame, and fear.

Good. Renna stepped forward and gripped the bars, again Drawing on the power stored within her. They bent like supple branches, allowing her to step through.

Stela froze as Renna passed by her to sit on the cot. She patted the space beside her. "Come sit with me a spell. Creator knows you and your friends've been askin' for a belt across the backside, but I ent here to give you one, 'less you make me."

Tentatively the girl came forward, taking the offered seat.

"Been where you are now," Renna said. "First started warding my skin, killin' demons was all I could think about. Started seein' day folk as weak. Had nothin' for 'em but contempt. Cut a man's hand off in a tavern when he put it up my leg."

Stela spat on the floor of her cell. "Had it comin'."

"Ay, maybe," Renna said. "But I din't do it 'cause he had it comin'. Did it 'cause all I could see was red. 'Cause I was so drunk on magic I couldn't think."

Renna put a finger under Stela's chin, lifting until their eyes met. "That's how animals act, Stela Inn. That's how corelings fight. All passion and no thought. And that's why, at the Battle of Cutter's Hollow, a bunch of scared woodcutters beat 'em down and sent 'em runnin'."

She let her finger drop, holding the girl's eyes. "But demons din't fight stupid when the minds came at new moon. Fought smart, like we gotta. Because the minds are comin' back, sure as the sun rises."

Stela's eyes began to tear. "I tried, Mrs. Bales. I tried, and it all went to the Core. Met a boy. A good boy, and I shined on him like I never knew I could. But I was so drunk on magic I hurt him without a thought. And when he turned his back . . ."

"All you wanted to do was pounce," Renna finished.

"Ay," Stela said sadly.

"He still alive, this boy?" Renna asked.

"No thanks to me," Stela sniffed.

"You kill anyone else?" Renna asked, peering deep into her aura. "Don't lie to me."

"Haven't," Stela said, and her aura confirmed it. "Wanted to sometimes. Broken a few bones, but ent killed anyone."

"Ent too late, then," Renna said. "Ent too late to come back and get it under control. Ent never gonna be normal, now that you et that demon's heart, but you can get a handle on it, like Arlen and I did."

Stela looked at her with wide eyes. "Deliverer used to lose control, too?"

"Dun't like to be called that, and you know it," Renna said. "But ay. Never really control it completely, but that's okay. Sometimes you need the passion. The aggression. Sometimes, when it's you against a demon's talons, it's all that keeps you alive. But you gotta remember who the real enemy is, Stela Inn. Can't ever forget."

"Demons," Stela said.

"Ay," Renna agreed. "You turn your night strength on day folk, and you become no better'n them. That what you want?"

Stela shook her head. "No, ma'am."

"And the others?" Renna asked.

Stela slumped. "They're lost, Mrs. Bales. Like I was. Got some of my senses back when Mistress Leesha drained me, but they're all still full of ichor. Don't know if they'll listen, even to you."

Renna put a hand over hers. "Then we'll make them listen."

Wonda stiffened when she opened the door to see Stela standing behind Renna on the stairs, but she said nothing, stepping back to let them pass.

Stela looked at her, pain lancing through her aura. "I wasn't myself, Wonda. I know it doesn't make it better, but . . . I wasn't myself, and I'm sorry."

Wonda pursed her lips. "Know what it's like, Stel. I do. But my da used to say, 'Sorry's only halfway to makin' things right.'"

"On our way to work on the other half," Renna said. "Let Leesha know I'll drop in after I give the Children a talkin'-to."

"Ay," Wonda said.

"What about Keet?" Stela asked.

"He can wait," Renna said. "Insurance on good behavior. Sides, got a trick to play that won't work on him."

She took Stela's hand, wards on their skin touching. There was a tingle at the connection. Renna fed a bit of power into the girl, then Drew it back, Reading her. The change was in her blood. Maybe not enough for her to control it—yet—but perhaps enough . . .

She dissipated, and pulled Stela along with her as she slipped down into the greatward, skating toward Gatherers' Wood.

They materialized a moment later just outside the wood. Leesha and Arlen had designed the net of Hollow greatwards to leave a gap for the wood, in part because of the difficulty of shaping so many trees, and in part so they could experiment freely with demon magic within.

"Gonna slosh." Stela stumbled away, falling to hands and

knees as she heaved. It was long moments before she caught her breath and wiped her mouth.

"Always like that?" she asked.

Renna shrugged. "Never bothered me, but I'd been eatin' demon a lot longer'n you before I tried it. Prob'ly easier when you're at the reins."

"Ay," Stela agreed. "Felt like a windie swept out of nowhere, caught me in its talons, and dragged me through the air. Only, there was no air."

"Get your feet under you and Draw a bit of power," Renna said. "You'll feel better."

"Draw?" Stela asked.

"Like you're suckin' air through your feet," Renna said. "Take a deep breath and pull a bit of magic from the greatward. Not too much."

Stela raised an eyebrow, then scrunched her eyes shut and grit her teeth, pulling in great gasps of air. It was almost comical. There was no Draw, and her aura remained dim.

"Not like that," Renna said, coming over to take her hand again. "Like this." She Drew, pulling magic up from the greatward through Stela. Immediately her aura brightened and she straightened.

Stela gasped. "I feel strong again. How'd you do that?" There was eagerness in her aura now, an addict's craving reawakened.

"Teach you, and the others, they get in line," Renna said. "Need to take care, though. Greatwards hold a lot of power. Get greedy an' take too much, you'll go up like oil in a fire."

Stela swallowed, fear flashing in her aura.

"Now show me where the Children make camp," Renna said.

The trees blurred as they ran, magic granting them inhuman speed. Renna had spent a fair bit of time in the wood, but Stela knew it intimately, like the common room of her own home. In minutes, Renna could see the knot of brightness in her wardsight and knew the camp was close.

She caught Stela's arm, pulling her up short. "Hold out your arms."

Stela's aura was confused, but she did not hesitate, and Renna traced wards of unsight on her limbs and breast, imparting a bit of power to them. She energized her own wards, and the two of them faded into the night. She reached out and took Stela's hand before she became too difficult to see, and the two moved forward at a slower pace.

The Children were not on guard as they entered the camp, clustered around a podium, eyes on Brother Franq as he paced back and forth, shouting. Half a dozen young Siblings clustered before the pulpit, steely glares scanning the crowd.

The Holy Man was very different from the stiff Child Renna remembered from previous meetings. His neatly trimmed beard and hair had grown wild, fine robes exchanged for a rural Tender's homespun brown, dirty with the sleeves cut away to reveal his tattoos. They glowed with power, and his aura was bright. Brighter than any single other out of the dozens standing around the platform.

"Do we let this stand?" Franq demanded. "Let them hold our brother and sister in chains for nothing more than wanting to run free in the naked night?"

"No!" the Siblings shouted on cue, and many in the crowd joined them, auras red with anger. It was easy enough for Renna to pick out the Wardskins, their auras almost as bright with power as Franq's, and the Bones, with their demon bone weapons. They had lost their leaders and boiled with rage. Images floated above them, Children storming Leesha's keep and kicking in the doors. Considering the power massed in those groups, Renna thought they might well manage it.

But not all were convinced. The *Sharum* stood apart, Jarit and her granddaughter at their forefront, auras calm as they watched the crowd. They didn't seem likely to be swayed, but neither were they inclined to intervene.

The Pumps, however, looked like they might be convinced. Callen Cutter stood at their forefront with Jas Fisher, arms crossed. They were angry, too, but not so far gone as the others, having tasted less of the magic than the other groups. They did not join in the shouting.

"Brother Callen!" Franq called, knowing who he must convince. "You doubt our righteous course?"

"Want Stela and Keet back much as any," Callen said. "But that don't mean I'm ready to kick in Mistress Leesha's door."

"There are times men and women of conviction must stand

against injustice," Franq shouted. "I was there when Arlen Bales himself told Inquisitor Hayes, *You stake a fornicator, and I'll break the stake over my knee and shove half through your door and the other half through the count's.* It was the Deliverer's way of telling us those who stand against the night are not subject to the laws of men."

Renna remembered the words. Arlen had spoken them in anger, part of an argument that began, ironically, with Franq mocking her lack of refinement as he served fine wine in crystal stemware. Now he was the unrefined one, pacing like an animal as he attempted to incite the crowd to violence in her husband's name.

Enough, she thought, cutting the power to her wards of unsight.

"I was there, too!" Renna shouted as she strode into the crowd. Faces turned to her, eyes widening. The Children fell back, stumbling over those behind as they made room for her to approach the podium.

"Renna Bales," folk whispered all around her, but Renna ignored them, eyes locked on Franq.

"Behold!" Franq gestured to her with a Jongleur's flourish. "Renna Bales, Bride of the Deliverer, returns to lead us on our righteous path!"

"Ent nothin' righteous in attackin' the Hollow!" Renna barked back.

Franq hesitated, but only for a moment. "Do you deny the Deliverer's own words? *You've been taking liberties,* he said, *and need to know where the wards end.*"

Renna misted, materializing an instant later on the podium beside Franq. She gripped his robes and twisted, throwing him from the platform to land on his back at the center of a widening ring of onlookers.

"Wards end with you tellin' me what my own husband meant!" Renna said. "Usin' words from a fight *you* started!"

She moved to the steps, eyes angrily locked on Franq, but his young acolytes barred her way. Confusion roiled in their auras. They had been taught to worship her, but it was Franq who knew them, trained them, commanded their loyalty. It was Franq who had given them power.

They would need to be dealt with, and perhaps others, too,

but first things first. She drew an impact ward in the air, scattering them from her path as she stalked their leader like a nightwolf.

Brother Franq had risen to a crouch. He was unhurt, his ample magic strengthening his body, his aura seething with rage.

Good. Renna dropped her guard as she approached, inviting attack. Franq took the bait, springing forward in a rush to try to tackle her. She sidestepped easily, catching his arm and turning a circuit to use his own momentum against him as she threw him across the ring.

Franq remained unhurt, but that give little concern. Much as she wanted to deliver a beating to the man, the show was more important. The onlookers needed to see a fair fight, and to see her dominate.

Franq's aura was bright with magic, and he outweighed her by close to a hundred pounds, but his *sharusahk* was still rudimentary. Renna had fought like him once, trusting in sheer ferocity to power through. Against mindless demon drones, it was often enough.

But Renna's training with Shanvah had broken her of that. The *Sharum'ting* had humiliated her in much the same way until she had learned respect for defense and the mind of her foe. More, she had taught Renna about convergences, the places where the lines of energy in a body met and branched. It was the secret to *dama'ting sharusahk,* and Renna, with her wardsight, could see the bright points in Franq's aura like stars in a night sky.

His rage doubled, Franq came at her again. His guard was up now, but his punches caught only air as Renna bent her torso back and heel-kicked the convergence in his hip. He folded like paper as Renna snaked an arm over his right biceps and back under his arm, twisting it behind his back. A kick to the back of his knee brought him down as she torqued the arm up until it broke with an audible snap.

Franq roared in pain, but she could see in his aura the fight wasn't over. He shoved hard against the ground enough to get a foot under him, and with his arm broken, much of Renna's advantage was gone. *Sharusahk* relied on the weight and le-

verage of the combatants, but with the magic Franq was holding, Renna weighed little more than a doll.

She let him go, putting her hands on her hips and smirking
as he crouched and grit his teeth, pulling his arm straight for
the magic to heal. In moments he would be back to combat-
readiness.

Renna moved to finish him before that could happen, but
there was a shout, and the Siblings charged her. Their surprise
was over, and they moved like a pack of drones to protect
their mind.

Renna took a deep breath, finding her center as she focused
on the convergences in their auras. One young woman tried a
kick, and Renna caught it, punching two knuckles into her
thigh, collapsing the leg. Another swung a fist and found himself flying through the air. She dropped as she continued the
circuit, spinning to hook the leg of a boy she was sure she had
seen mucking stables in town.

The last was a young Krasian man who fought with more
skill than the others, but he wasn't nearly as fast. Renna
backed up two steps, blocking his punches and kicks, until he
was in position, then shattered his pelvis, removing him from
the fight.

And then once more there was a clear path to Franq, now
recovered. His aura was burning with anger, but he knew better than to try hand combat now. Instead, he raised a hand,
drawing a glowing impact ward in the air. His control was
rudimentary at best, and he powered it with more than was
needed.

Renna collapsed into mist as the concussive force hit, blasting through her to fling one of Franq's own acolytes to the
ground, a twisted ruin.

That's torn it.

Like a gust of wind, she blew across the ring. Franq flinched,
punching wildly through the mist, but he might as well have
struck air. She materialized behind him, an arm around his
throat and the other up under his armpit, locking her wrist.

In a normal fight she might have choked him, but Franq
was too strong, and it was not the message she wanted to
send. Instead she reached out through the wards on her skin,
connecting with those on Franq's. But she did not feed magic

into him, as she had with Stela. Rather, she Drew hard, sucking the power from him.

Franq's muscles seized, bucking as if he'd been spat on by a lightning demon. Renna kept control and held tight, increasing the pull. The wards on her skin began to glow, then flare until she could feel the heat of them. Her eyes, throat, and nasal passages dried out, burning. Still she pulled, watching Franq's aura as it dimmed. The pain increased, until she felt like her entire body was aflame, but she held until his aura was about to wink out.

Renna let the man go with a kick to his backside, and he collapsed limply to the ground. The pain was unbearable now, and she threw as much magic skyward as she could, drawing a light ward that turned night into day.

Still bursting with power, she misted over to the Krasian acolyte whose pelvis she had broken, looking into his aura as she pulled the bones straight and imparted a portion of her magic to fuse them back together. She flitted to the young acolyte struck by Franq's impact ward, but he was dead, his aura snuffed like a candle.

Corespawn it.

She played another of Arlen's tricks then, misting only partially as she leapt skyward, floating above the awestruck Children, backlit by her light ward. They squinted and put hands before their eyes, trying to look at her in the glare.

Night, she thought. *They're all so young.*

"Arlen Bales din't say nothin' about robbin' folk!" Renna sketched wards to amplify her voice until it shook the trees. "About bustin' criminals out of prison! He demanded respect, ay, but he gave it first!

"And he trusted in Mistress Leesha! More than any, she's stood by the Hollow in its time of need. More than any, she's led the way. Arlen knew it, I know it, and it's time you knew it, too. Anyone here don't hop to her word is gonna get a spankin' that makes what I did to Franq look like a pat on the bum!"

There was a stunned silence as dozens of faces looked up at her, illuminated in the wardlight.

"If you hear me, say ay!" she barked.

"Ay!" they shouted. "Ay! Ay! Ay!"

Renna pointed, drawing a smaller ward to illuminate Stela, who entered the circle to help Franq to his feet. "Stela Inn, say ay!"

Another quick ward, and Stela's "Ay!" sounded louder than any other.

Renna made a fist, the wards on her hand burning with power. "Brother Franq, say ay!"

Franq looked up at her, his dim aura cowed at last. "Ay," he croaked, but Renna made sure his word was clear to all.

She slowly drifted down to the ground, softening her voice as she let the light behind her dim. "Know what you're feelin'. Magic makes it hard to think. Makes your every emotion into a storm. Been there. Arlen, too."

Her feet touched the ground. She turned slowly as she spoke, meeting the eyes all around her. "But now more'n ever, can't forget you're human. The Core's about to rise up again, and you need to be ready to fight, not just for Hollow County, but for the entire human race. Ent gonna get another shot at this."

She caught Jarit's eye. "Sharak Ka ent comin' anymore. It's here."

She spread her hands. "You got powers now, but ent one of you got a clue how to control 'em. Things get bad," she gestured to the crumpled body of the acolyte, "when you can't. I can help, but in the end you need to help yourselves."

Renna could see Leesha's aura, relaxed at first, tense when she saw it was Renna, not Arlen, materializing in her office.

Good. Don't want her gettin' too comfortable.

The two women eyed each other for a moment, but Leesha was quick to break the stare. "Thank you for coming. Tea?"

"Ay, thanks," Renna said. "Can't stay long. Need to skate back to Arlen before sunup." She flopped in one of the countess' fine chairs, putting her feet on the table. Leesha's eyes flicked to them, but she said nothing as Wonda poured the tea.

"Did you see them?" Leesha asked.

"Ay," Renna said.

"And?" Leesha prompted, when she was not forthcoming.

"Stela was right," Renna said. "They were ready to march into the Hollow and kick your gate in."

"Night," Wonda said. "How many? When?" Images floated above her, the walls of Leesha's keep lined with women aiming crank bows.

Renna waved for her to calm. "Settled 'em down like I promised." She turned back to Leesha. "Still be a headache, but that's on you."

"What did you do, if I may ask?" Leesha looked like she had eaten a lemon. Renna didn't smirk, but no doubt Leesha could see the feeling on her aura, and that was all right.

"Franq was the biggest rabble-rouser," Renna said. "Delusions of grandeur. Turnin' Arlen's words to his own ends. Took him to the woodshed, and let the others watch. Put the fear of the Creator into 'em. Can't promise they'll stay pliant, but they'll fight for the Hollow when night comes, and the raids will stop."

"What can we do to ensure it stays that way?" Leesha asked. "Do they have demands?"

Renna shook her head. "Still changin' their shorts after my little display, but that ent gonna last. Aim to visit a few more times, try'n make things stick. Be a sign of good faith, you release Keet in the morning. Gonna want to break the Pack up if you can. Find places for the Pumps and Bones with the Cutters, maybe get Franq a seat on Jona's new Council of Tenders."

"Ya just said he was the one stirrin' things up!" Wonda said.

But Leesha nodded. "All the more reason to keep him somewhere we can see him. I'll speak to Jona, and ask that the council meet under the sun."

"Smart," Renna agreed. "Wardskins are going to be a problem no matter where you put 'em. Keep 'em in sight, but I wouldn't want them inside your walls."

"We'll think of something," Leesha said.

"Not sure what you can do with the *Sharum*," Renna went on. "Could ask Jardir for his thoughts before he leaves to see his wife."

Leesha flinched at the words, and Renna cursed her own stupidity. There was a time she might have thrown them as a purposeful barb, but . . .

"Sorry," she said. "Din't mean . . ."

"It is what it is," Leesha said. She put a hand in one of the many pockets of her gown, pulling forth a sealed letter. "Will you give this to him, when you see him? If he's to learn of the babe, I'd rather it be from me."

Renna nodded, taking the envelope. "Course."

"Thank you, Renna," Leesha said. "I know we haven't always . . ."

Renna smacked the air. "Tired of you slingin' that line, Leesha. You ent fond o' me and I ent fond o' you. Don't mean we're not on the same side. Not gonna get in the way of you doin' right by your child."

Reflexively, Renna brushed her fingers over her still-flat belly, thinking of the life growing there.

"Fair and true," Leesha said, but her head tilted suddenly, studying Renna's aura. It went on a little longer than Renna liked, until she felt her skin begin to crawl.

"What?" she snapped.

"Wonda, dear," Leesha said. "Will you excuse us, please?"

"Ay, mistress," Wonda said, taking her bow off the wall and heading for the door.

The moment it closed behind her, Leesha activated the wards of silence around the room, and Renna got to her feet, unable to stand sitting a moment longer. "What?!"

"You're pregnant," Leesha said.

Renna went cold. She Drew her aura in tight, breathing to remain calm. Should she deny it? Argue? Tell Leesha it was none of her corespawned business?

It wasn't, but neither was Leesha's child, yet half a year ago Renna had been happy to rub Leesha's indiscretion in her face.

She blew out a breath. "Married woman, Leesha. Don't owe you any explanations."

"You don't." Leesha got to her feet, coming over to her. Her hands were spread, eyes calm, voice soothing. Her aura was tense, worried. "But using magic while I was pregnant affected my child. Please, for the sake of the baby, let me examine you."

Renna felt her muscles tighten. Her hands clenched into fists, and it was a sheer act of will to straighten the fingers again. She'd just finished preaching to the Warded Children, but now the magic in her blood was screaming, amplifying her own emotions, telling her to flee, or to attack Leesha, silencing her before she could tell anyone else. It was all she could do just to stand there, breathing.

Leesha no doubt saw much of it, no matter how hard Renna tried to hide her aura, but she weathered it calmly, keeping still and saying nothing.

"Ay," Renna said at last. "Think that's a good idea."

"How'd it go?" Arlen asked as Renna materialized in the kitchen of their tower. He, Jardir, and Shanvah sat at the table having breakfast.

"Broke a few bones and did a little flamework display," Renna said. "Put the fear o' the Creator back in them and got 'em on track, but they need lessons, they want to be in control when the swarm comes. Goin' back a few more times before we leave."

She looked to Jardir. "There's Krasians among them. Widows and children of Leesha's escort. They're painting their skin with blackstem and ent eaten demon that I seen, but they're lost, Ahmann. Hollow's their home, but they don't fit in."

"I don't imagine they would," Jardir said. "But neither are they likely to leave the ground their husbands and fathers hallowed with their blood."

"Leesha said she'd be obliged, if you had advice on it," Renna said.

"Who leads them?" Jardir asked.

"Jarit," Renna said.

Jardir nodded. "Kaval's *Jiwah Ka*. I have looked into her soul, and it is pure. She has done well in holding her people together. I will speak of her to Inevera. She will need to send *dama'ting* to the Hollow, and *Sharum* to escort and guard them. Our brothers and sisters in the Gatherers' Wood will not be forgotten."

"There's more," Renna said, producing the letter. "Leesha asked me to give this to you."

Jardir's eyes widened, and he took the paper, immediately

bringing it to his nose and inhaling. "Thank you, Renna *jiwah* Arlen am'Bales am'Brook." He bowed once, then quickly left the room.

Renna shook her head. "Talkin' about his wife in one breath, and inhalin' Leesha's perfume with the next."

"We do not see marriage as you greenlanders do," Shanvah said. "The Evejah tells us love is boundless. It does not dishonor the Damajah to share. A portion of infinity remains infinite."

"That go both ways?" Renna asked. "Love infinite enough for a woman to have two husbands?"

"Got someone in mind?" Arlen asked.

Shanvah said nothing, but her face made it clear she was scandalized at the very notion.

"Thought not," Renna said.

Renna watched as Ragen rode Twilight Dancer awkwardly around the practice yard, trying to get a feel for him. He was a big man, and an expert rider, but Dancer was no ordinary horse. He stood a head taller than other mustangs, they in turn giants compared with even the heavy destriers Milnese Messengers favored. Arlen had pondered long and hard, but in the end there had been no one he trusted more to take his precious stallion—his friend—than Ragen, the man who taught him to ride.

Promise was her engagement gift. Their intention had been to breed the horses, expanding their family in more ways than one. Arlen had tears in his eyes when Renna left the tower with the horses. Seeing Wonda approach, Renna understood how he felt. She stroked Promise's neck, gripping tight to her mane.

The horse seemed to sense her tension, snorting and stamping. Renna laid her head against her, and did not fight her tears. "Come back for you. Swear it by the sun. Wonda'll be good to you. Ent no woman more suited to ride you while I'm gone."

Wonda moved confidently as she approached the horse, but Renna caught a hint of fear in her scent. Arlen and Renna's horses were legends in the Hollow.

"Won't take a bit or saddle," Renna said. "Got a harness to hold bags and help you keep your seat, but she ent much for reins. Don't be afraid to give her mane a good yank, she tries to throw you or go her own way. She can take it."

Wonda swallowed, but she nodded. "Da used to have a workhorse. Din't have money for a saddle. Learned to ride bareback."

"Don't take any of her demonshit till she learns to respect you," Renna said, "and you'll be all right."

Promise eyed Wonda coolly, but allowed the woman to lay a hand on her neck. Something about the gesture made it real, and the lump in Renna's throat grew.

"Likes green apples the best," she choked. "Sour, like her disposition."

"Buy a barrel of 'em today," Wonda said.

"Ent too good for honey in her oats, though," Renna said.

"Got bees right here in the keep."

Renna couldn't stand it anymore. She sobbed, giving Promise one last embrace, then fled the yard.

"Greatward's our strongest asset, and worst enemy," Renna said loudly, pacing the floor of the lecture theater at Gatherers' Academy. The floor was painted with a miniature greatward, powered by *hora* stones set around the walls.

Leesha and Wonda stood to the side, observing with crossed arms. Both glowed bright with power, unmistakable to the gathered Children seated around the theater. Renna had guaranteed their safety, but they were taking no chances.

"Remember Arlen floatin' in the sky?" Renna asked the crowd. "Throwin' lightning at the demons?"

Several of the Children cheered and applauded. Renna nodded, waiting until it died down. "Remember how he fell?"

There was no applause at that. It had been the Hollow's darkest hour.

"Wards Draw magic and hold it," Renna said. "Directing it depending on their shape. But when you're standing inside the lines," she stepped onto the greatward on the floor, "you can tap into them by sheer will." She Drew, and grew brighter and brighter, until some of the observers had to shield their eyes. The point made, she let the power drain back into the symbol.

"Hollow greatwards got power enough to make you feel like the Creator Himself, but we ent built to channel power like that. Not me, not even Arlen Bales. He pulled too much and burned out. Came crashin' down to the cobbles, broke like an egg." Renna pointed to Leesha. "Mistress Leesha din't come runnin' to put him back together, he wouldn't've made it."

Leesha acknowledged the words with a nod, a purposeful reminder to the gathering of her power.

"Stela Inn," Renna called. "Come down here and Draw some power off this ward."

There was fear in Stela's aura, but she came, tentatively stepping onto the theater floor.

"Sandals off," Renna said. "Gonna want to put your wards right on the lines at first."

Stela kicked off her sandals and stood on one of the thicker lines, closing her eyes.

"Like I taught you," Renna said. "Draw nice and slow. Careful, not too much."

Stela's breathing was even, but her heart was thudding in her chest, trying to contain the pleasure and ecstasy flooding her. "How much is too much?"

"That's enough for now," Renna said as Stela's wards began to glow of their own volition, visible to the unwarded eye. "More, your insides will start to itch. Eyes and throat and nose will dry out, and you'll have trouble concentratin'. More'n that, you'll start to ache, and it'll be hard to think straight. Keep goin', and you'll lose control and burn yourself alive."

"How do I let off the excess?" Stela sounded worried, the fear in her aura reflected in the onlookers.

"Greatward's pullin' at it even now," Renna said. "Only your will keeps it in you. Drain it out slow and steady, like pouring boilin' water from a kettle."

Stela shut her eyes, willing the magic to drain away, but she was too eager, pushing the magic from her instead of letting the ward do the work. The powerful greatward greedily drank it in, and Renna had to grab her hand and stop the Draw before the girl was sucked dry.

"Good try," Renna said. "Go an' take your seat. Ella Cutter, step down and give it a try."

She sniffed as the next girl approached. The Wardskins were still eating demon meat, but she didn't tell them to stop. They'd need the power soon enough.

If she could teach them to control it.

CHAPTER 15

SISTERS RETURN

334 AR

One of Inevera's many earrings began to vibrate. She ran a finger along the cartilage of her right ear to find it. The second from the top.

The Damajah blew out a breath. At last.

She twisted the ring until the wards aligned and the vibration ceased. "Daughter."

"Blessings of Everam be upon you, Mother," Amanvah said. "It is good to hear your voice again."

"And yours," Inevera said. "Everam has been watching over you."

"Perhaps," Amanvah said. "I return to Everam's Bounty less than a year after I left, already a widow."

"It is *inevera*," Inevera said. "The dice tell me you bear the son of Jessum's heir."

"As does Sikvah," Amanvah said, "though it is early for us both."

"All the more reason you return to the fold," Inevera said. "Sikvah is with you?"

Immediately one of the rings on Inevera's left ear began to vibrate. "I am here, Damajah," Sikvah said when Inevera turned it.

"How soon will you return?" The earrings did not work over great distances.

"Another day," Amanvah said. "Two at the most."

"I will send an escort," Inevera said. "Jarvah will lead them. Accept no other."

"Are things so dire that I cannot trust an escort from my brother?" Amanvah asked.

"So dire, and worse," Inevera said. "Asome attempted to have Ashia killed in his coup."

"No!" Sikvah gasped.

"Ashia proved the stronger," Inevera said, "leaving Asukaji crippled."

"At least Asome will cease his attempts to force me to marry my cousin," Amanvah said.

"Perhaps," Inevera agreed, "but that was your greatest value in his eyes. Do not think he will hesitate to kill you, if it will weaken me."

"No harm will come to Amanvah while I live, Damajah," Sikvah said.

"You may find yourself a target as well, Niece," Inevera said. "Ashia has been sent from Everam's Bounty, and Shanvah has not returned. You are now Sharum'ting Ka."

There was silence as the words sank in. At last, Amanvah spoke. "Congratulations, sister. Everam's blessings upon you."

"I am not worthy," Sikvah said.

"It is good to be humble before Everam," Inevera said, "but you are the ranking spear sister now. I have seen you grow, and know your worth."

"I failed to protect my husband," Sikvah said. "His blood stains my honor."

"Nonsense," Amanvah said. "I was there, sister. There was nothing more you could have done. It is by your skill that we lived to carry his heirs and avenge his death."

"The dice have spoken," Inevera said. "Micha and Jarvah will pledge their spears to you when you see them. This is not a mantle you can lay aside, Niece. Sharak Ka is nigh, and all must stand when Everam calls."

"Yes, Damajah," Sikvah said. "I will strive to be worthy."

"You already are," Inevera said.

"Does this mean we may drop the ruse that my sister-wife is some weak *dal'ting*?" Amanvah asked.

"Immediately," Inevera said. "Few in the court are fools enough not to have deduced it by now."

"Good," Amanvah said. "I will be more comfortable with armor protecting our husband's heir in her belly."

"What other news from the Hollow?" Inevera asked. "The baby Mistress Leesha carries?"

Amanvah did not ask how she knew. The girl was wise enough to know her mother's Sight.

"The child is born," Amanvah said. "I delivered it personally."

"So soon?" Inevera could not contain her surprise. "It has been but six moons . . ."

"Mistress Leesha has been channeling powerful magics," Amanvah said. "They accelerated the pregnancy. Something my sister-wife and I must be careful of."

It was a danger, but the furthest thing from Inevera's mind. This was a development that could change the course of the war.

"And the child?" she demanded. "A boy or a girl?"

"Nie'Damaji'ting Amanvah vah Ahmann am'Jardir am'Kaji, firstborn daughter of Shar'Dama Ka and Damajah, Princess of all Krasia," Dama Jamere called as Amanvah was presented before the Skull Throne.

Amanvah was clad in the white silk of a *dama'ting,* floating about her like smoke, but clinging enough to her femininity to remind all that she was Inevera's daughter. Asome still held court in the sun, and the golden light glittered across the electrum wards embroidered on the cloth.

Her white veil had been exchanged for one of black, evidence of what all in attendance already knew. At the tender age of eighteen, she was to take her place as leader of the Kaji *dama'ting.*

"Kai'Sharum'ting Sikvah vah Hanya am'Jardir am'Kaji," Jamere went on, "firstborn of Princess Hanya, third sister of Shar'Dama Ka." Hasik's name—and the dishonor that came with it—had been stricken, but its absence was a reminder of her father's crimes.

Still, Sikvah cut an impressive figure, white-veiled in her *Sharum* blacks. Twin spears crossed on her back in easy reach, harnessed beneath a great rounded shield, all made of indestructible warded glass inlaid with electrum. She moved with predatory grace, glass armor plates in her robes adding bulk to her tiny frame, especially a step behind Amanvah in her thin silk.

"Blessings upon you, sister, cousin," Asome called from the throne, though his face was sour at the sight of Sikvah clad as a warrior. Inevera watched from her pillowed dais, making no effort to hide her smile.

As the assembled court looked on, the two women knelt, putting their hands on the floor and their foreheads between them. They rolled back in unison, gazing up the seven steps to the dais.

Amanvah touched a finger to her throat, and her words, soft and melodious, echoed throughout the chamber. "We come at the summons of the Skull Throne, honored brother, to take our rightful places in the Deliverer's Court."

"The women of the Kaji are in need of your wisdom and leadership, sister." Asome actually sounded convincing. He glanced to Sikvah. "But I did not summon you, cousin."

"I did," Inevera broke in, using her warded jewelry to amplify her voice, much as Amanvah had. Much of her magic was denied in the sunlight, but it was good to remind him that she and the other *dama'ting* were not entirely powerless. "With the death of your honored wife Ashia, and the disappearance of Shanvah, the white headscarf of Sharum'ting Ka will go to Sikvah."

Asome scowled, and Baden stepped forth from the assembled *Damaji* to bow to the Skull Throne. "With respect, Damajah, there is no precedent for this. The Shar'Dama Ka's honored cousin has killed no *alagai* in battle. She has not earned the right to carry the spear, much less command Everam's spear sisters."

Amanvah looked at him like an insect to crush. "With respect, *Damaji,* you are not known for walking the night, even now, in the time of shar'dama. Who are you to bear witness to the deeds of my *Jiwah Sen* in *alagai'sharak*?"

She swept her gaze over the assembled court, again activating her choker to carry her words to every ear. "On my honor and hope of Heaven, I testify before Everam and the Skull

Throne that Sikvah vah Hanya am'Jardir am'Kaji has shown more *alagai* the sun than any *Sharum* in Krasia."

"A preposterous claim." There were murmurs of agreement to Baden's words throughout the chamber. "There are *Sharum* throughout the Deliverer's army who were fighting and killing *alagai* fifty years before this girl was born. You dishonor them all with your claim."

Asome stamped his spear. "Apologize, sister."

Amanvah raised her eyes to meet her brother's. "Even you, Shar'Dama Ka, may not command me to bear false witness before the Skull Throne. In trio with our husband, my sister-wife and I marched *alagai* by the legion mindlessly into the weapons of the Hollow Tribe. Even the changeling that killed Drillmaster Enkido quailed before our sound, allowing our companions to destroy it."

Asome paused. Many warriors in Everam's Bounty had witnessed the son of Jessum's fiddle magic, and how it could lead *alagai* to slaughter like lambs. It was power Asome coveted, and only Amanvah and Sikvah could provide the keys to unlock it.

"Perhaps," Baden allowed. "But a *Sharum* fights with the spear, not magic."

Amanvah smiled. "Do you wish to test my sister-wife's skill with the spear, *Damaji*?"

Baden scoffed. "Are you asking me to strike a woman in the Deliverer's Court?"

"Of course not, venerable *Damaji*," Amanvah said. "I invite you to choose a champion. One of these men whom you claim have killed more *alagai* than my sister?"

She turned, scanning the crowd. "Or your famed grandson, Shar'Dama Raji, perhaps?"

All eyes turned to Raji. The young *shar'dama* was just a few years Sikvah's senior. A warrior-cleric known for his fearlessness against the *alagai*. He was armed even in the day, wearing warded fighting silvers across his knuckles, leaning ever so slightly on the warded whip staff he was famous for. A barbed *alagai* tail hung coiled at his belt. He was a big man, dwarfing tiny Sikvah, but she did not hesitate, turning and crossing fists over her heart, giving him a warrior's bow.

Raji smiled and took a step forward, eyes flicking to his

grandfather for permission to crush the upstart girl. The *Damaji,* however, sensed the trap. For decades, Baden had worked closely with the *dama'ting,* and he knew better than any not to underestimate them. Ashia's fighting prowess was already legend in the palace. If Sikvah proved equally formidable and his heir was put down in front of the assembled court, he risked a loss of face.

He hesitated, and every moment cost him a bit of the dignity he sought to preserve.

Asome saw it, too. "Enough. My father did not tolerate violence in his court, and neither will I. Dama Baden is correct. None question the power of this . . . spellsinging, but Sharum are raised by the spear. Whatever her skills, Sikvah has not killed a demon in battle before witnesses."

"Tonight, then," Amanvah volunteered. "How many witnesses would you like?"

"Even if she succeeds, killing a demon armed in the Damajah's invincible spears and armor is no great feat of glory. The Sharum'ting Ka must be worthy to lead warriors in Sharak Ka. The throne will not recognize Sikvah."

"What feat of glory would satisfy the Shar'Dama Ka?" Amanvah asked.

"She must do it as true *Sharum,*" Asome said. "Like our father did, a boy in his bido with an unwarded spear, fighting to earn his armor."

"The Shar'Dama Ka has spoken," Inevera announced, "and the Pillow Throne agrees. Tonight Sikvah will enter *alagai'sharak* in her bido with an unwarded spear. Tomorrow at dawn she will present the throne with an *alagai* head to burn in the sun, or we will find another to lead Everam's spear sisters."

There were gasps from the assemblage, particularly the *Damaji'ting,* offended at the thought of forcing a woman to abandon modesty in front of male warriors.

Sikvah gave them no time to protest, returning to her knees and putting her forehead to the floor. "By Everam, it will be done, Shar'Dama Ka."

———

Inevera studied the dice Amanvah had cemented in place, a marker on the slate noting direction and time. "Are you sure this is precise?"

Irritation rippled across Amanvah's aura, the abrasion of a child struggling to escape her parent's shadow. It was something Inevera would need to be careful of, if her daughter were to be an effective *Damaji'ting,* but this was too important to spare her pride.

"Yes, Mother," Amanvah said.

"You know what this means." Inevera was careful to make it a statement. Her daughter was no fool.

"It means Asome will stop at nothing to kill the child, if this is ever revealed," Amanvah said. "It means in the eyes of Everam, Olive Paper is the true heir of Ahmann Jardir. It means the child has the potential to be the Deliverer reborn."

It was a bitter truth. Inevera had lain with the Deliverer countless times, given him four sons and three daughters, none of them with such potential. The Northern whore dallied with him for a week and gave birth to the first potential Shar'Dama Ka in a generation.

Inevera shook her head. "Deliverers are not born, daughter, they are made."

Amanvah tilted her head. "If that were the case, why not make an army of them, as Arlen Bales purports to do?"

"Would that we could," Inevera said. "With your father and Arlen Bales missing, this child is the only potential Deliverer we know of. Perhaps the only one in the world."

"It must be protected," Amanvah said.

"She," Inevera corrected. "You were correct in your advice to Mistress Paper. The child is safer if all believe it female. Asome's sorcerers will find no lie in this, even if they have mastered some form of foretelling."

"She," Amanvah agreed.

"What did Mistress Paper demand, in exchange for your casting?" Inevera asked. The dice had told her to ask the question in person, when Amanvah was alone. They told her she would not like the answer.

Indeed, Amanvah's aura went cold, like a pickpocket caught with purse in hand. She closed her eyes and fell into her breath, finding her center before replying.

"I cast with Mistress Leesha's blood before the child was born," Amanvah said. "I knew then the birth would be difficult, and the child special. Perhaps what you taught me all those years ago to search for."

"You're stalling," Inevera said.

Amanvah breathed again. "Mistress Paper demanded I teach her to read the *alagai hora.*"

"What?!" Inevera shouted.

Amanvah kept her composure, eyes still closed, breathing even, hands folded on her lap as she knelt in the pillows of Inevera's private chamber.

"I know you have cause to hate Leesha Paper, Mother," Amanvah said. "Did I not put blackleaf in her tea on your command?"

She opened her eyes, meeting Inevera's. "But you were wrong about her. She is an enemy of Nie, and has done as much as any I have ever seen to ready the world for Sharak Ka—even before she gave birth to this child. If the First War is to be won, she must have every advantage."

Inevera breathed hard through her nose, the only outward sign of the anger boiling within. Amanvah had overstepped herself in teaching *dama'ting* secrets to the greenland witch, in challenging her authority as Damajah.

But she was also right. As she bent against the wind of her own emotions, Inevera saw the truth of it in her center.

"Again you are correct, daughter," Inevera said. "I feared you too young to take the black scarf, but I see that fear was misplaced. You will make a fine *Damaji'ting.*"

Pride flushed through Amanvah's aura, but she simply bowed. "You honor me, Mother."

"Mistress Leesha could not have learned much in the short time before you left the Hollow," Inevera said.

Amanvah nodded. "I left her the relevant sections of the Evejah'ting, but she will need a proper instructor. I promised to send a *dama'ting* to take my place in the Hollow. Jaia, perhaps, or Selthe."

Inevera pursed her lips. "They are too inexperienced. One of them may assist, but we must send someone wiser for such an important task."

"Who can be trusted?" Amanvah asked. "Most of the

dama'ting would as soon slit the mistress' throat and abscond with the child, styling themselves the next Damajah."

"It is a danger," Inevera agreed. "We will need to cast on it. I would kill the mistress and steal the child myself, but the palace is not safe so long as your brother sits the throne. The farther Olive is from him, the more likely she will grow old enough to take up the mantle of Shar'Dama Ka and save Ala."

"Or destroy it," Amanvah said.

Inevera nodded. "Such is the weight upon the Deliverer's shoulders."

Sikvah knelt before the Skull Throne, naked but for her bido, a simple strip of black cloth wrapped around her breasts and crisscrossed between her legs. Her face and hair were uncovered, and she wore none of her warded jewelry, not even her famed choker. Next to her lay a spear of plain wood and steel, unwarded, yet coated in ichor that sizzled in the morning sun.

It was scandalous by anyone's standard. Inevera relished how it put the men off balance. Half were unsettled, averting their gazes. Others stared openly. None was thinking clearly.

Seven black-veiled *Sharum'ting* knelt behind her, each bearing a bag of thick black velvet.

"You did not specify which type of *alagai* would bear me the greatest glory, Honored Shar'Dama Ka," Sikvah said, "so I brought one for each pillar of Heaven."

On cue, her warriors opened the bags, dropping the severed heads of wind, flame, rock, field, bog, stone, and bank demons onto the marble floor.

The moment sunlight struck the heads, they burst into flame.

If the display rankled Asome, he gave no sign. "Rise, Sharum'ting Ka."

Amanvah stepped forward with a helm wrapped in a white turban, placing it on Sikvah's head as she rose to her feet. Sikvah was given a simple black robe, donning it unhurriedly.

"Enough *ting* politics." Asome gave a sweep of his spear, dismissing them. "It is time we attend to the Majah."

Guards opened the chamber doors to admit Damaji Aleveran and his entourage. Chavis was with him, followed meekly

by Belina, once again in the white headscarf and black veil of
nie'Damaji'ting. Iraven was with them as well, his eyes on
the floor. Everam only knew what oaths Aleveran and Chavis
had extracted to restore him to some semblance of status in
the tribe, but it was a good sign, if the Majah were to have any
hope of returning to the fold.

As agreed in advance, a table was set on the courtroom
floor, Asome and Inevera descending to meet the Majah delegation. Asome looked regal with his crown and spear, but
Aleveran seemed unimpressed, impatient to get on with the
proceedings.

Jamere presented the contracts, two copies of a lengthy
document granting the Majah rights to leave Everam's Bounty
and return to the Desert Spear.

Inevera hated Asome for forcing them into this, but there
was nothing for it now. Asome and Aleveran pierced their
fingers, squeezing till blood welled and dipping pens in the
drops to sign in blood.

The other *Damaji* followed suit, including the Majah's pro-
tectorate tribes, which would remain in Everam's Bounty to
serve Asome. The lesser tribes, such as the Sharach, were no
great loss, but the Nanji Watchers had served the Majah for
centuries. Aleveran's face was bitter as Asome's Nanji brother
signed his name and sundered that alliance.

"This concludes our business," Aleveran said, rolling his
copy of the document and securing it in a warded tube. "We
part in peace, but not forgiveness. Ala is wide and varied.
Everam grant we never meet again."

He strode to the door, snapping his fingers. Belina and
Iraven cast one last glance at Inevera, then followed with the
rest of his entourage as he left the room.

The days that followed were long, with endless lines of sup-
plicants to the throne, some vying for positions to fill the
vacuum left by the Majah, others seeking protection, or the
renegotiation of land rights. The Majah had stripped their territories, but the lands they controlled were vast, full of the
rich, arable soil that had made the greenlanders so soft.

At first, Asome adjourned an hour before the call to sunset

prayer, but as the days wore on he worked later and later, until finally the sun set with court still in session. Inevera thought it might have been a simple oversight, but as her jeweled headpiece activated and she began to see in Everam's light, she knew it was no accident.

The *Damaji* all glowed with power now, warded jewels on their fingers and in their turbans, gold-coated rods and *hora* pouches at their belts. *Dama* sorcerers walked openly, their heavy demon bone staves providing great wells of power.

Asome caught her looking, giving his mother a predatory smile. *Dama'ting* mastery of the night was fading. How long before he decided he no longer needed her at all?

Inevera breathed, struggling to find her center. It was she who had begun the gender imbalance, giving women the spear, but it had never been her desire to replace the men of the tribe.

Asome might not feel the same. There were many in his court who believed they should return to the old ways, when women were silent. Obedient.

Slaves.

She shuddered. Enough that it was a moment before she noticed one of her earrings was buzzing.

She reached up, sliding a manicured nail down the cartilage, counting to see who was attempting to contact her. It would have to be important, to disturb the Damajah while court was in session.

It wasn't one of her sister-wives, or the *Sharum'ting*. It wasn't one of her daughters.

At last her finger came to rest on the lobe, and her heart froze in her chest. That earring had not vibrated in many months.

Not since Ahmann fell into darkness.

CHAPTER 16

BELOVED

334 AR

The Par'chin walked Jardir out to a clearing from the tower. "Think you got the hang of it?" Concern showed in the Par'chin's aura, and it was touching. Twice now, Jardir had tried to kill him, and still his greenland brother fretted for his well-being.

"I will be fine, Par'chin," Jardir said, quelling his own doubts.

"Gets windy, gotta be ready . . ." the Par'chin began.

Jardir chortled. "Enough, Par'chin! I have a doting mother and fifteen wives. I don't need you trying to suckle me as well."

"Had to make it awkward." The Par'chin put out a hand, but Jardir disdained it, wrapping his *ajin'pal* in a tight embrace.

"Time's against us," the Par'chin said. "Take care of your business, but don't get pulled in."

"And you, Par'chin," Jardir said. "Take care with your *jiwah* away. Shanvah's honor is boundless, but her love for her father is a weakness Alagai Ka will exploit, given the chance."

The Par'chin nodded. "Got this. Just . . . hurry back, ay?"

"Ay," Jardir said, taking the Spear of Kaji from his back and holding it crosswise like a *dama's* whip staff. There were thousands of wards etched into the weapon's electrum head and shaft. As with the crown, Jardir had come to understand the purpose of many of them, but others remained a mystery, and some he had only just discovered.

He laid his thumbs on wards of air and gathered his will, calling forth the power contained in the ancient weapon as he leapt, winds gathering to lift him high into the sky.

He climbed higher and higher, laughing aloud as he watched the land shrink beneath him. The wind on his face was exhilarating, fresh and cold in his lungs. The stars of the night sky brightened, and he felt at one with the beauty of Everam's creation as never before.

As the Par'chin warned, the currents were stronger in the sky, but he compensated well until he entered a low patch of cloud. Suddenly blinded and lashed with water and ice, Jardir lost his concentration, plummeting toward the *ala*.

He managed to gather the power again, buffeting the ground, but while it blunted the impact it did not keep him from tumbling into an open field, tearing through the tall, half-frozen grass.

He got to his feet, cursing and spitting straw as he attempted to brush the filth from his robes. The power gathered in his body kept him from harm, but Leesha's Cloak of Unsight was dirtied—a sully to her honor that pained him. He sent power through the cloak's wards, burning away the stains like water from a pan.

At least I am too far for the Par'chin to have seen, he thought.

He began to gather his will for another attempt, but checked himself at a low growl. There was only an instant's notice before the field demon pounced, but Jardir, trained by decades of fighting *alagai,* needed no more. He spun, impaling the beast on the end of his spear and Drawing its magic like sipping through a straw.

Again he leapt into the sky, wobbling slightly as he gained altitude and speed, but eventually leveling off. It was cold up in the clouds, but he Drew more power, warming himself as he streaked northwest toward Everam's Bounty.

A shriek rang out in the night, and Jardir turned to see three wind demons following him, their great leathery wings beating hard as they sought to close the gap.

He could have increased his speed, but it felt beneath him to flee the beasts, leaving them to prey on Ala. He pulled up instead, climbing higher and looping back to put the demons in front of him. Careful not to upset the delicate interplay of wards and Draw that kept him aloft, he pointed the Spear of Kaji at one of them, sending a blast of magic that streaked the sky, only to miss the speeding creature. He fired again, and again, before finally puncturing its wing and sending it tumbling through the air. The *ala* was more than a mile below them. Even the powerful healing magic of the *alagai* could not recover from such an impact.

The other demons caught sight of him again, banking in opposite directions to circle back and come at him head-on, wing talons extended. Speeding toward them, Jardir did not trust his aim for another blast, nor did he relish attempting to absorb the impact of a direct clash and remain airborne.

But there were other options at his disposal. He sketched wards of cold as one of the demons passed through a patch of cloud. The moisture clung to its leathery skin, freezing into a coating of ice that dropped it like a stone.

The last demon was coming in fast, and Jardir made no attempt to strike or flee, simply hovering as best he could in place, an easy target. As he did, he called upon the power of his crown, forming a shield around himself, impenetrable to the servants of Nie.

The demon struck the barrier with such force, its hollow bones shattered like a bird striking a thick glass window. Ichor spattered, leaving a black smear as the *alagai* fell away. The ichor blew away as Jardir dropped the shield, resuming his flight.

In control now, he flattened himself to minimize resistance to the wind as he caught sight of the Messenger road, a tiny thread far below, leading him inexorably home.

He waited until he was far from the tower before attempting to contact Inevera, lest he risk servants of Nie spotting the resonance in the air. The last thing he wanted was to lead them to Alagai Ka's prison. He and the Par'chin had agreed an hour should be enough, but time was difficult to gauge in the sky, and it was a guess in any event.

Everam's Bounty was still hundreds of miles distant, too far for the tiny *hora* stone in his earring to reach, but Jardir was fully in control of his power for the first time in his life, and understood intimately how the delicate bit of magic worked. He needed only to concentrate, boosting the ring's power with his crown to set its twin buzzing in his *Jiwah Ka's* ear.

No doubt she would be furious, but Jardir could not help but smile at the surprise in store for her, nor keep his heart from beating faster in anticipation of hearing her voice.

It was long moments before he felt the connection open, the magic flowing freely through Inevera's ring and back into his own. "Who is this?" she demanded angrily. "Who dares . . . ?!"

"Peace, Jiwah," Jardir said. "Whom did you expect, if not your husband?"

"Ahmann Jardir is dead," Inevera rasped. "I will not be fooled by some changeling speaking in his voice."

Jardir frowned. He had anticipated many reactions, but outright denial was not one of them. "It is I, wife. We met in the *dama'ting* pavilion, the day Hasik broke my arm. You taught me to embrace my pain. You were beautiful, and I carried your face in my mind's eye for years, until I saw it again on our wedding day."

There was a pause, then a whisper more timid than Jardir had ever heard from his fearless bride. "Ahmann?"

Jardir felt his throat tighten. "Yes, beloved."

"What is that sound?" Inevera's voice was shaking. "Do you speak to me from Heaven?"

It took a moment for Jardir to realize what she meant. He laughed. "No, *jiwah*. That is only the wind, rushing by as I speed my way to you."

"How can it be?" Inevera asked. "The dice said you were dead."

"Did they?" Jardir asked. "You taught me the *alagai hora* do not lie, but sometimes they do not mean what we think."

"They said the *alagai* went to desecrate the corpse of Shar'Dama Ka, half a year ago."

"That is true, but it was not me they sought to defile," Jardir said.

"It cannot have been the Par'chin," Inevera said. "If you had defeated him, you would have returned."

"It was not the Par'chin," Jardir agreed. "The *alagai* princes went to Anoch Sun, to lay waste to the city of Kaji and shit upon his bones."

Inevera's gasp was nearly lost in the rush of wind in his ear. At the sound of her voice, he had instinctively put on speed, desperate to have her in his arms once more.

"You could not allow that," she guessed.

"No," Jardir agreed. "And yes. Knowing where the *alagai* princes would strike, this once, forged an alliance that might have been impossible otherwise. The Par'chin and I traveled to Anoch Sun together, and were waiting when they came to the resting place of Kaji."

"What happened?" Inevera asked.

"I cannot speak of it until we are together, safe within the protection of the crown," Jardir said. "Tell me of you. The months of my absence must have been difficult, but there is no one in all Ala more able to bear such burden. Are you well?"

"My heart was broken, but I remain unbent." Jardir breathed in relief at Inevera's words.

"Your glory is boundless," Jardir said. "Did you put Ashan on the throne?"

There was a long pause. Enough that Jardir sent a touch of magic through the earring to assure himself the circuit remained.

"Wife?"

"Perhaps that is best spoken of when we are together as well," Inevera said at last.

Inevera was waiting on the rooftop when Jardir soared to his palace atop the great hill at the center of Everam's Bounty. Diaphanous red robes billowed in the night air, illuminated by the glow of her jewelry. He could see the curves of her body silhouetted in the silk, leaving little to the imagination.

He'd hated those scandalous robes once, a reminder that his power over his First Wife was by no means absolute. But now, after months apart, all he could think about was her beauty. He inhaled, tasting her perfume on the night air, and felt himself stiffen.

She fell into his arms as he landed, and he crushed her to

him. Her body was soft against his, but there was strength as well. He knew how hard her muscles could be when taut. There was so much to say, but he pushed the thoughts aside for a moment, putting his nose into her oiled hair and relishing the scent of her.

They drew apart just enough to press their mouths together hungrily. Jardir felt his heart pounding and pulled back. With a thought, he cast a sphere of silence around them with the powers of the crown.

"The Majah fill the roads," he said. "What . . . ?"

"Later," Inevera said, pressing her soft lips against his as she pulled at his belt.

"Here?" he asked. "Now?"

She pulled his belt sash away with a snap. "I will not wait an instant longer." She pulled Mistress Leesha's Cloak of Unsight from his shoulders, casting it to the roof like a blanket in the sand.

With a growl, he took her by the waist and kicked her feet from under her. She did not resist as he guided her to lay on the cloak, ripping at her silks when they did not pull away easily enough. She was shaved and oiled, her sex slick as he thrust into her.

There were no *dama'ting* tricks to their coupling, no pillow dancing or seven strokes. It was fierce, animal passion, venting months of frustration. Biting and bucking, scratching and slapping, communicating needs and desires with growls and shoves. Jardir knew his return should be secret, but in the moment there was nothing but Inevera, his First Wife, and passion ruled.

When it was over, they lay sweating in the cold night air, curled together in a nest of torn clothes. Jardir kept his eyes on her face, drinking it like a man dying of thirst. He brushed his fingers against her cheek and down her ear, feeling the connections of each earring as he did. His other wives. His nieces. Now that he understood their power, he could not believe he had not sensed it before.

"I should be angry at you for keeping the earrings a secret," he said.

Inevera smiled. "It is the duty of a First Wife to watch over her husband. Had you known, you would have found a way to silence what you did not wish me to hear."

"Like my time in the pillows with Leesha Paper," Jardir said.

Inevera kept her composure, but she could not hide the feelings in her aura. He peered into her soul, seeing the pain there.

"You listened to every moment," he said.

"How could I not?" Inevera said. "I was losing you to that . . ."

Jardir took her face in both hands, kissing her again. "Never, beloved. We are bound, in this life and the next. I understand now why you lay with the Andrah. I forgive you, though you need no forgiveness for putting Sharak Ka above all else."

Inevera sobbed, and he held her to him. "I need you, wife. Now like never before, we must be united. No more secrets. No more lies and half-truths. All Ala hangs in the balance, and there is none I trust more than you."

She kissed him, pulling back to meet his eyes. "I understand why you lay with Leesha Paper. I forgive you, though you need no forgiveness for putting Sharak Ka above all else. I am yours as you are mine. The dice foretold that your return would herald Sharak Ka, and we will weather it as one mind and one heart. No more secrets. No more lies and half-truths. I swear it before Everam on my hope of Heaven."

She reached out, touching the ring on his ear. "Why wasn't I able to hear you after you fell?"

"The Par'chin saw the connection in the earrings before I did," Jardir said. "He blocked their power, and we were soon out of range."

"The Par'chin," Inevera spat. "I should have killed him when I had the chance."

Jardir shook his head. "And perhaps doomed Ala. It was he who taught me to use the Crown of Kaji to boost the signal and contact you from hundreds of miles distant."

Inevera's eyes widened. "You can do that?"

Jardir nodded. "A simple matter. I can teach you to do it as well. The Par'chin taught me much while he held me prisoner."

"Prisoner?" Inevera growled. "He dared . . . ?"

Jardir held up a hand. "Peace, wife. The son of Jeph did what he must to gain advantage in Sharak Ka. As you have always done."

"I do not believe that," Inevera said.

Jardir took her gently by the arms, looking into her eyes. "Look into my soul, *jiwah*. If you believe nothing else, believe me when I tell you the Par'chin looks to nothing more than Sharak Ka. I would have killed him in *Domin Sharum*, but that was never his intent. He had greater plans. Glorious plans."

"Attacking Nie's princelings in Anoch Sun," Inevera said.

Jardir smiled. "Oh, *jiwah*. That is only the beginning."

"Damajah," Micha said, as Inevera opened the door to the rooftop stair. "Your robes . . ."

Indeed, they were torn, but holding her top closed with a fist did nothing to lessen Inevera's regal bearing, her air of command. "It is nothing. Clear the path to my chambers."

"Yes, Damajah," Micha said. Jardir was proud to see his daughter moving with easy grace in her *Sharum'ting* blacks, but he kept Leesha's Cloak of Unsight about him, boosting its power with his own. Micha, and his other warrior daughter, Jarvah—who fell in behind them as they descended into the halls—did not see him as he followed Inevera to their private chambers.

"See to it I am not disturbed," Inevera told them, closing and locking the chamber doors, activating a wardnet that would stop an army—human or *alagai*.

She turned, embracing Jardir once more. "Alone again. We will have complete privacy until we decide how best to announce your return."

Jardir sighed. "I am afraid that is premature, beloved. I cannot reclaim the Skull Throne yet. Perhaps not ever. None save you must know I have returned, and I must leave before dawn's light binds me to Ala."

"Impossible," Inevera said. "You have only just returned."

"Nevertheless, it is so."

"You do not understand," Inevera said. "So much has happened."

"Whatever it is, it pales against the path before me," Jardir said. "The weight of Sharak Ka is upon us."

Inevera breathed, her aura growing calm as she reached out, taking his hands. "Ashan is dead."

Jardir blinked. "What?"

"And Jayan," Inevera went on, clutching his hands tight at the name of their firstborn. "The entire council of *Damaji* as well, and your son Maji. All murdered in the night by Asome in his ascent to the Skull Throne."

Jardir opened his mouth, but no words came out. Any of those deaths would have been a blow. Together, it was stunning. He embraced it all, squeezing Inevera's hands in return. "Tell me everything."

He listened in disbelief as Inevera related the events in Krasia since his disappearance. He knew his coalition of tribes was fragile, but never dreamed it would dissolve so quickly without his unifying hand.

"It was a mistake to make Asukaji heir to the Kaji," Jardir said. "It left Asome with no path save to reach higher."

Inevera shook her head. "It was the right decision, husband. You could not have known he would hold such murder in his heart."

"To use *hora* in the night to take the throne," Jardir clenched his fist, "he dishonors everything we stand for."

"At the cost of one of our most powerful tribes," Inevera said. "But now, with you returned, perhaps the Majah can be brought back."

Jardir shook his head. "I cannot bring them back without revealing myself, beloved, and that I cannot do."

"Why not?" Inevera demanded. "What could possibly be more important than keeping your forces together with Sharak Ka approaching?"

"Sharak Ka is not approaching, beloved," Jardir said. "It is here. Now. Already the *alagai* are massing, establishing hives all over the greenlands. I must go to the source and stop them."

Inevera looked at him, incredulous. "You cannot mean Nie's abyss?"

Jardir nodded. "It was not to stop the *alagai* from desecrating our ancestors that we traveled to Anoch Sun. Indeed, we let it happen."

"Why?"

"We went to capture Alagai Ka," Jardir said. "And, beloved, we were victorious!"

"Impossible," Inevera said.

"Nearly," Jardir said. "Our combined power, along with that of the Par'chin's *Jiwah Ka,* Shanjat, and Shanvah, was barely enough."

"Shanjat and Shanvah found you?" Inevera asked.

"Indeed," Jardir said. "Thank you, beloved, for sending them. If not for them, we might not have succeeded. Their honor is boundless. Shanvah now claims an *alagai* prince among her kills."

"And Shanjat?"

Jardir sighed, telling her of Alagai Ka's attempted escape, and the crushing of their brother-in-law's mind. He related the interrogation, and the Par'chin's plan.

"Madness," Inevera said.

"Beautiful madness," Jardir said. "Glorious madness. Madness worthy of Kaji himself. It is a bold plan, but it strikes at the very heart of Nie."

"You will take the Prince of Lies at his word?" Inevera demanded. "Everam's balls, husband, are you such a fool?"

"Of course not." Jardir rolled his sleeve, exposing his forearm. "It is a gamble with all Ala in the wager." He held out the arm, streaked with countless scars from Inevera's curved blade. "I traveled all the way back to Everam's Bounty that the Damajah could cast the bones against its success."

Jardir resisted the urge to scratch at his arm as he healed Inevera's latest cut. She seemed determined to drain him of blood as well as seed, casting the bones again and again, seeking answers. The cuts were superficial, easily healed now that the Par'chin had taught him the knack, but the skin itched as it knit back together. For some reason, that was harder to erase than pain.

"What do you see?" he asked when he could take it no more.

"Death," Inevera said, still staring at the dice, her face illuminated in their eerie red glow. "Divergences. Deception."

"These words are not helpful, beloved," Jardir said. "Does the Par'chin's plan have a hope of success?"

"Scant," Inevera said. "But you must go, nevertheless."

The words surprised him. He thought she would say anything to keep him in Krasia.

Ah, beloved, he thought. *Again, I underestimate you.*

"There are futures where all of you die in the abyss, far from your goal," Inevera went on. "Others where you find Alagai'ting Ka, only to be overwhelmed. Some where you arrive too late, and the laying is done."

"But success is possible." Jardir clenched a fist.

"Possible, as finding a particular grain of sand in the desert is possible," Inevera said. "And even in that infinitesimal possibility, you will not all survive."

"Irrelevant," Jardir said. "Our lives are nothing against this cause."

"Do not be so quick to martyr yourself," Inevera said. "You must be vigilant. I see treachery at every turn."

"But I must go?" Jardir asked.

Inevera nodded. "If you do not . . . you doom us all. The Par'chin has freed a river, and it will not stop until it reaches the sea."

Jardir reached into a special pocket in his robes, withdrawing four vials and laying them on a pillow before her. They were filled with a deep red liquid, clinging to the glass. "Blood from the Par'chin, his *jiwah,* Shanvah, and Shanjat."

Inevera reached eagerly to snatch them up. "Bless you, husband."

Jardir reached into his robe, producing a fifth vial. Unlike the others, the liquid inside was black as tar.

Inevera's eyes flared, her aura going cold. "Is that . . . ?"

"Ichor," Jardir confirmed, "taken forcibly from Alagai Ka."

Inevera's hand shook just a little as she took the last vial. "I will need time, to prepare the dice for new castings, and to formulate questions."

Jardir nodded. "There are matters I must attend in the meantime."

"I believe I should go with you when the time comes," Inevera said. "Like the Par'chin's *jiwah*."

"Absolutely not," Jardir said, perhaps too quickly. Inevera's eyebrows narrowed. "Krasia needs you now more than ever." It was truth, though perhaps not the whole truth, and no doubt Inevera saw it. "The forces of Nie mount, and it will be up to you to keep our people unified for the fight. I have never been the politician you are."

"Perhaps," Inevera said. "I will cast on it. But if my presence adds a single divergence where you find victory . . ."

"Then we will consider it against the divergences where we return victorious to find our people slaughtered for lack of leadership," Jardir said.

Inevera clutched the vials to her and nodded sadly. Then she laid them aside, going to a polished wooden box and returning with a needle and tube. "I will need more blood. For now, and for when you are gone."

Instinctively, Jardir scratched at his arm.

She took him again when the bloodletting was done. Unlike the rutting under the stars, this was gentle lovemaking in the silk pillows they had shared for years as man and wife. She began by pillow dancing for him, slipping away her scarves until she was clad in nothing but her jewels, then took kanis oil and performed on his spear all seven sacred strokes laid down in the Evejah'ting.

Only then did she sheathe his spear, bouncing to an ancient rhythm and bringing them both in sight of Heaven before drifting back to Ala.

Jardir's stomach growled as they lay entwined in the perfumed pillows. "I can heal the cuts, beloved, but the magic cannot make flesh and blood from nothing."

Inevera nodded. "Of course. But while magic cannot make flesh and blood from nothing, it can make food and drink from anything."

"Eh?" Jardir asked.

"One of the first spells a *dama'ting* must master before taking the robe," Inevera said. "One that will be invaluable on your quest."

She went to a great clay urn, scooping fine white sand into two large bowls. Smoothing the surface, she drew wards in the sand with one of her manicured nails, a complex net that Jardir watched closely.

A moment later one bowl was filled with clear, cold water, the other with steaming couscous. Jardir took a bite, eyes widening. "I have never tasted anything so . . ."

"Perfect," Inevera said. "If drawn incorrectly, the food and drink are poison, but done properly they are sustenance as pure as Everam's light."

Indeed, famished a moment ago, a single bite and a swig of water left him satisfied. "The Par'chin says the path to the abyss may take us weeks to traverse. I feared we would have to carry supply for the entire journey."

Inevera shook her head. "With Everam's blessing, all things are possible. Now come and strip away those shameful robes. If you go to the abyss, it must be done in raiment befitting Shar'Dama Ka, to cast fear into the hearts of Nie's servants."

Jardir looked down, having forgotten the *khaffit* tan the Par'chin clothed him in during his imprisonment. It was an attempt to humble him—perhaps deserved—but there was no need for it any longer.

And there were other reasons to don his true robes.

Jardir put his hand against the Vault door, feeling the bracelet Inevera had given him warm. The great door, several tons of raw stone reinforced with wards drawn in electrum, swung open with just that touch, silent as a tomb. The hall before him was bathed in wardlight, barren save for the symbols etched onto the walls.

Jardir wrapped his Cloak of Unsight about himself as the door closed behind him and moved quickly down the tunnel until it branched. There was a guard outside the door he sought, a tongueless eunuch in *Sharum's* black, wrists and ankles shackled in gold. The eunuch guards were masters of *dama'ting sharusahk,* quick and deadly.

Jardir traced a series of wards in the air with a finger, powering them with the crown. In moments the eunuch's eyes began to droop. He fought valiantly, shaking his head to clear it, but the power could not be denied. He put his back to the wall, bracing himself with his spear, and fell asleep on his feet.

Jardir used his crownsight, peering through the heavy wooden door like a pane of glass. His mother was awake within, lecturing her daughters-in-law, Jardir's wives Everalia and Thalaja, as they dressed her hair. The chamber was richly appointed, but a prison still.

"Not so tight, stupid girl," Kajivah snapped at Everalia as she wove a perfect braid. "How many years will it take you to get it right? And you." She half turned to Thalaja, who had brushed her hair to a flawless sheen. "A hundred strokes, I told you. I counted ninety-seven. Begin again."

It saddened Jardir that his *dal'ting* wives must share his mother's imprisonment—slaves in all but name—though no doubt Kajivah's ordeal was more bearable for it. There was so much about his people, even his own family, that he had been willfully blind to. Could he have done more to stop the cancer growing within his house if he had been sensitive to the trials his mother put his wives through, or to his sons' ambition?

He shook his head. There was nothing to be gained in looking back. Now was the time to look ahead. He drew more wards, putting Everalia and Thalajah to sleep much as he had the eunuch guard.

Kajivah felt the women's work cease, looking back to find them breathing peacefully, eyes closed. She let out a shriek. "Insolent girls! You have the audacity to sleep while the Holy Mother speaks?!"

Jardir raised his hand, and the bar on the other side of the door lifted. He entered as Kajivah was about to slap Everalia.

"Do not lay hands on my wife, Mother," he said. "She cannot hear you. I have put my *jiwah* to sleep so we may speak privately."

Startled, Kajivah turned at the sound, letting out another shriek. "Ahmann, my son! My son! You have returned from the abyss!"

She ran to him, weeping with joy, and he returned the embrace as she threw her arms around him. For a moment, he allowed himself to forget his purpose, to be her son one last time, safe in his mother's arms.

But then she spoke.

"Thank Everam you have come, my son," Kajivah wept. "That *heasah* you married has been keeping me prisoner like a *khaffit* caught stealing bread. You should whip her for her insolence. I've always thought you took too lax a hand, letting her dress like a pillow dancer at court and . . ."

Jardir took her arms, thrusting her back enough to look at him. "Enough, Mother! You speak of the Damajah of Krasia, not one of your *dal'ting* servants! Every moment of every day, she stands fast against the forces of Nie, while you do nothing but complain and berate the servants and women of our house! You shame our family with your behavior!"

Kajivah's eyes grew wide with shock. "But—"

"I do not want to hear it," Jardir cut her off. "You say I have taken too lax a hand, and you are right. But it is you I should have been more firm with."

"Do not say such things!" Kajivah cried. "I have always been loyal to you!"

"It was I who put Inevera on the dais of the Skull Throne," Jardir said. "I who left her to choose my successor. I who trusted her with the safety of our people in my absence. But where has your support been?"

"I supported your sons and heirs," Kajivah said.

"My sons are too young for the weight of rulership!" Jardir snapped. "Even after Asome murdered his brother and half the council, you think he serves Krasia better than Inevera?"

"What has that woman done but take you from me?" Kajivah asked. "Taken my daughters and nieces, given women the spear—"

"Nie's black heart, Mother!" Jardir cried. "Can you think of no one but yourself? Sharak Ka is at my heels, and you would poison my court with womanly squabbles? It was I who gave women the spear, not Inevera, and if she had not 'taken' Shanvah from you, the girl would have been vapid and worthless. But Inevera has been given the Sight by Everam Himself. She saw my trials, trained the girl, and sent her to me when I needed her most. Without her and her father fighting side by side to shield my back, I would have been overwhelmed these past months. Might have fallen, and all Ala fallen with me."

"But Ashia struck me," Kajivah protested. "Killed *Sharum* and stole my grandson."

"Ashia is that boy's mother, not you," Jardir said. "She cannot steal what is already hers. That girl carries more honor than the greatest Spears of the Deliverer, and because of you she and her child have been forced to flee Everam's Bounty."

Kajivah's aura went cold. "Kaji is gone?"

"He is gone," Jardir confirmed. "It was the only way to keep Asome from using the boy as a pawn, as he would have used you. A tool to oust Everam's Damajah and replace her with a foolish old woman who does not understand what it means to rule."

"Never have you spoken to me this way," Kajivah said. "I who gave birth to you. I who suckled you at my breast. I who supported you after your father walked the lonely path. What have I done to deserve your wrath?"

"It is my own fault," Jardir admitted. "I was so focused on our enemies without, I gave no thought to the affairs of the court's women. I let you lord yourself over them, shrieking at everyone who dared bring you the wrong nectar or braid your hair too tightly. To think that because you were in the palace, it was the duty of all to serve you, and not the other way around."

Kajivah shrank further and further from him with the words, and he could see in her aura how they pained her. Still he pressed. Their relationship would never be the same, but it could not be helped. This might be his last chance to get through to her—to make Kajivah the ally and leader Krasia needed her to be.

"Listen to my words, Mother, and mark them well," he said. "All Ala hangs in the balance, and I must know I can count on your support in my absence. I need you in this. Krasia needs you."

Kajivah fell to her knees. "Of course, my son. That is my only wish. Tell me what to do and it will be done."

"Every time you vex the Damajah, all Krasia suffers," Jardir said. "I will leave again on the morrow, and may not return for many months, if at all. You will obey Inevera until I return. Not Asome. Not my sons and grandsons. Inevera."

"And if you do not return?" Kajivah asked. There was anguish in her aura at the thought, but he had no time to coddle it.

"Then you will obey her until you die," Jardir said.

Jardir lifted the spear of Kaji, laying it on her shoulder. "Swear it. Before me, and before Everam."

"I swear," Kajivah said.

Jardir deepened his voice. "What do you swear, Mother?"

She looked up at him with tear-filled eyes. "I swear, before Everam, before my son the Shar'Dama Ka, to obey the Damajah, Inevera vah Ahmann am'Jardir, in all things, from this moment until your return, or unto my death."

She clutched at the hem of his robes. "But you must return, Ahmann. I could not bear to lose you as I did your father and Jayan."

"It is *inevera,* beloved Mother," Jardir said. "You must hold faith in Everam's great plan. I will not spend my life cheaply, but if I am meant to martyr myself for the sake of Ala, I will not refuse."

Kajivah wept openly at the words, and Jardir dropped to one knee, holding her as she sobbed. When it was finished he rose, lifting her with him and setting her on her feet. "I must leave you here now, to be freed when I am gone. No one, not even my *Jiwah Sen,* must know I have been to see you."

"But why?" Kajivah asked. "It would give our people such hope, to know you are alive."

"Because even now, Nie's forces hunt for me," Jardir said. "Word of my return would endanger you, and draw the eyes of Her princelings when I wish for them to be fixed elsewhere."

He went to Thalaja and Everalia, kissing them as they slept. "Blessings upon you, my sweet wives." He turned to his mother one last time as he headed for the door. "From this day forth, you will show my wives, daughters, and nieces the respect they are due."

Kajivah bowed. "Of course, my son."

He stared into her aura a long time, weighing a boy's adoration against an adult's wisdom. It pained him to see they were not the same. "I love you, Mother. Though I walk the depths of Nie's abyss, never doubt this."

"Never," Kajivah promised. "Nor you doubt that your mother's pride and love are greater than those of any who ever lived."

He nodded and was gone.

Jardir left the chamber, Drawing behind him the magic that kept his wives and the guard asleep. By the time they woke, the Vault door was closed behind him.

Once again wrapped in his Cloak of Unsight, he moved through the palace until he came to an unguarded window, slipping out and taking flight. The power exhilarated him, cold wind rushing his face as the moon and stars lit the night sky. He had to remind himself that flight was a gift of Everam, a holy tool, not a plaything for his pleasure. He flew to the opposite side of the palace, to chambers that had once been his—now claimed by his upstart son.

The windows were well warded and barred against unwanted entry. No doubt Asome feared assassins, and not without cause. He'd angered many of the most powerful in Krasia with his dishonorable rise to power. Instead Jardir chose an outer wall he knew faced a seldom-used corridor, drawing a series of wards he learned at great cost while battling Alagai Ka. The stone of the wall melted away into mud, opening a portal large enough for him to pass through. Once inside, he drew a ward in the air, securing the opening against *alagai*. Even here, in the center of Krasian power, he would not risk a weakness against the night.

Inside, he once again powered the cloak, moving silently down the hall into his son's chambers. There, to his sorrow but not surprise, he found what Inevera had told him to expect—Asukaji bedridden, his aura flat and lifeless, and Asome, still wearing his replica crown, tending his lover personally. There were no servants, and for that Jardir was thankful.

Despite Jardir's camouflage, Asome sensed something amiss. His aura showed it first, then he stiffened slightly, ears perking. He turned, slowly scanning the room, his crown glowing fiercely. The boy had grown adept in its use, as Inevera had warned, and if the circlet had less power than Jardir's own, it was formidable nonetheless.

"Who is there?" Asome demanded, his eyes drifting over the wall Jardir stood against, struggling to fix on him. He stood, reaching for his spear, another replica bright with power.

Seeing no reason to continue hiding, Jardir threw back his cloak. "Hello, my son."

He expected surprise, even fright. What he did not expect was for Asome to attack. Like a tunnel asp, he struck, thrusting with his shining spear.

"Impostor! My father is dead!"

Jardir barely had time to get his spear up, batting the point aside. Asome was undeterred, working his weapon with blinding speed as he thrust again and again, each time from a different angle, seeking a hole in his father's defenses.

It was not surprising that this warrior had fought demons unarmed in the night—had killed his way up the seven steps of the Skull Throne. Jardir trained the boy himself, teaching him and his brothers a blend of the deadliest *sharukin* of the various tribes. Jayan had been larger, stronger, taking after Jardir himself. For a time when they were young, it was a telling advantage, but Asome had thrown himself into his studies in Sharik Hora and found his own style. He was quick, tireless, and deadly. The spear and crown energized him, giving him strength beyond strength.

An errant blow Jardir diverted struck a marble pillar, thicker than a man could wrap his arms around, sending a spiderweb of cracks clear through to the other side.

Shocked at the sudden ferocity, Jardir struggled simply to defend himself, unprepared to kill his second son, especially after just learning of the death of his first. As his father taught, Asome was careful not to repeat a pattern, his feet in constant motion, next moves unguessable to a common warrior.

But Jardir was no common warrior. He, too, had fought his way to the Skull Throne, and while Asome had grown in skill using crownsight, he had not achieved his father's mastery. The boy's aura was steady, but there were ripples along its surface as he sent energy to his limbs. After a moment of adjustment, Jardir knew his son's moves before they began.

When Asome's next thrust began, Jardir was already moving. He slipped to the side of the blow, taking one hand from his own spear to grip the shaft of Asome's. He kicked out hard, and Asome, anchored by his own grip on the weapon, took the full blow on his hip, folding in half as he was knocked back to slam into a wall, leaving Jardir holding both weapons.

"Asome!" Asukaji cried, but it was a hoarse thing, barely audible. His aura writhed in anguish, trying to force a broken body to go to his lover's aid.

"Now will you speak, my son?" Jardir asked, but again Asome came at him, fearless.

Jardir threw the weapons aside, out of easy reach. He could call the spear back to him with a ward if needed, but if they were to fight, better it be with hands and feet alone, lest he accidentally kill the boy before they had words.

"Begone, specter!" Asome cried as he struck. "Haunt me no more!"

Jardir wasn't able to catch the punch, but he followed the circle of energy, giving his son no advantage in his next attack. The words gave him pause, and even as they fought he peered into his son's spirit, seeking their source. Images rose at the beckon of his crownsight—Asome tossing and turning in his sleep, crying out and coming awake in violence. Once he had struck Asukaji in his half-woken state, and they had since slept apart. Another night, he had nearly killed Jamere, choking him naked in the pillows before the young *dama* had woken him fully.

Indeed, Asome was haunted, seeing his father's disapproving face whenever he closed his eyes.

As he should, Jardir thought. He accepted a glancing blow to get in close, grabbing Asome's robe and push-kicking his thigh, forcing his knee to hyperextend. Even Asome's perfect balance faltered at that, and Jardir used the momentary shift to take him down. They wrestled in close now, too quick and furious to read auras and react accordingly. It was a primal struggle for dominance—the kind of struggle Jardir had known his entire life. Asome was no stranger to such fighting, but as a prince of Krasia he had always known his opponents would fear to kill him.

Jardir had experienced no such luxury in his rise to power. It was what had allowed him to defeat so many *dama* in his conquest of the Desert Spear, and the key to victory here.

Inch by inch, he worked his way to a dominance hold, controlling his son's midsection to make his legs useless, pinning one arm beneath him and immobilizing the other as he forced his forearm against his son's throat.

He could have forced the boy's head aside. Denying an opponent sight of you was a powerful advantage, but Asome's greatest fear was his father's disapproving face, and Jardir showed it to him now.

"I am no specter. You are not asleep. I have returned to find the faithless ruin you have wrought upon my court in the short months of my absence."

Asome's struggles increased, sheer panic and stark terror giving him new strength, but Jardir had the hold and would not let go. Asome's blows and thrashes had no leverage behind them, and Jardir was larger, heavier, and stronger. He eased back a moment and Asome rose with him, then he thrust back down, bashing his son's head against the floor.

"I did not come to fight!" Jardir barked. "I do not seek to kill my son, though I have just cause." He slammed Asome's head down again, cracking floor tiles. "But I will, if you leave me no choice."

At last, Asome's struggles eased, though if it was submission or lack of air, Jardir could not be sure. He kept the press, waiting until his son's aura dimmed and his eyes fluttered. Then he let go, standing quickly and stepping back. He drew a ward in the air and the Spear of Kaji flew to his grasp as Asome choked and gasped, putting a weak arm under himself as he struggled to rise.

"Choose," Jardir said. "Remain on your knees and accept my judgment, or come at me again, and I will send you along the lonely path to be judged by Everam Himself."

Asome's aura swirled, and even Jardir could not guess what he would do. He could see the boy had come to realize it was indeed his father, but he had stepped too far in taking the throne and knew there might be no turning back.

At last, he put his hands on the floor, shaking as he pressed his forehead between them. "What will you do with me, Father?"

"That remains to be seen," Jardir said. "You must answer

for your crimes, but it may be there is use for you yet, in Sharak Ka."

"What crime have I committed, Father?" Asome raised his eyes to watch his father's aura as they spoke. He was Drawing on his crown, healing quickly. In moments, he would be back to fighting strength. Jardir readied himself in case he was fool enough to attack again.

"Need you ask that, my son?" Jardir asked. "You betrayed your brother, sending him to his death, and killed your uncle to take the throne he had been rightfully given."

"How does that differ from your glorious example, Father?" Asome asked. "Did you not betray the Par'chin, sending him to his death? Did you not kill Damaji Amadeveram, who trained you in Sharik Hora, and all his sons, on your path to the Skull Throne? Did you not spear the Andrah like a *khaffit* spitting a pig?"

"That was different," Jardir said, but whether he was saying the words to his son or himself, he could not be sure.

"How?" Asome pressed.

"It was *inevera*," Jardir said.

"Everam's will?" Asome asked. "Or my mother's?"

"Both," Jardir said. "The Andrah was corrupt. His foolishness was killing our people. Amadeveram was a good man, but he was a part of that broken system and would not stand aside. There was no dishonor in his death."

"My brother was corrupt," Asome said. "His foolishness was killing our people, forcing us into war before we were ready to slake his lust for conquest and desire to prove himself a worthy successor to the throne. If he had been allowed to succeed, Krasia would have suffered under his rule."

"Perhaps," Jardir said.

"And perhaps the Par'chin would have led us to glory when he carried the spear in the Maze," Asome said. "We make the choices we think best for the good of our people, Father. You taught me that. I took no pleasure in killing my uncle, but he was part of a broken system, and there was no dishonor in his death. I used no *hora*, and challenged him and the *Damaji* openly, in accordance with our law."

"In the night," Jardir growled. "When all men are brothers.

And you goaded my other sons to cheat with *hora* in their sacred challenges."

Again Asome shrugged. "Was the Par'chin lying when he spoke of your betrayal before *Domin Sharum*? Did you not turn on him in the night, throwing him to the demons?"

Jardir grit his teeth. "I did. And it is my greatest shame. Had the Par'chin not proven stronger than I believed, all Ala would have suffered."

Asome tilted his head. "How?"

"The Par'chin and I have forged a peace. Together we have captured Alagai Ka, and will take him back to the abyss as a hostage."

· If the words surprised Asome, he gave no sign. "To what end?"

"To gain passage through the maze of the abyss and Nie's endless legions, until we stand before Alagai'ting Ka."

Asome blinked. "Can even you accomplish such a thing?"

"The *alagai hora* say I am the Deliverer," Jardir said, "or the Par'chin is. If any can do this, it is us, united."

"You may not return," Asome noted.

"You think to keep the throne you stole," Jardir said.

Asome met his eyes. "We have established no crime, Father."

Jardir nodded. "You gave honorable deaths to the *Damaji* and Andrah. Your brother died of his own foolishness."

Faster than even Asome could counter, he seized his son by the throat. With his free hand he plucked the crown from Asome's brow, throwing it across the room. Asukaji gave a hoarse cry as Asome struggled helplessly against his father's iron grip.

"But there is one crime we have not accounted for," Jardir growled. "One crime I cannot forgive."

He pulled Asome so close their noses touched. "You tried to kill your mother." Jardir lifted his son from the floor by the throat, slamming him against a marble pillar. "That is crime enough to damn any man to the abyss. But Inevera is Damajah, *Jiwah Ka* of Everam himself." He tightened his grip, Asome's face purpling as he struggled for breath. "For that, it would be a mercy to strip you of the white and cast you from the window to your death. It would be a mercy to chain you naked in the bazaar for *khaffit* to piss upon and use your body as fuel to roast a spitted pig."

Asome's hands slapped ineffectually against Jardir's arm, his last throes. Jardir had meant this as an act, but in that moment he found his rage was true, and was tempted to kill his treacherous son before he could further shame the Skull Throne and its people.

With a roar, Jardir threw his son onto the pillows beside the prone Asukaji. "But you are needed, if you have it in you to find honor once more."

Once again, Asome was left choking and heaving, struggling for breath, but this time he did not have the crown to Draw upon, and he was slower to recover. Jardir waited patiently, though the night grew long.

"You were not ready for the throne, my son," Jardir said when Asome's eyes became lucid. "Your treachery proves it. But for better or worse, Sharak Ka is upon you. The *alagai* gather. Soon Alagai'ting Ka will lay, and the surface come alive with swarm. Even now, Nie's princelings seek to form hives across the land, and will muster their legions to defend them. Krasia needs a leader."

Asome stumbled in his attempt to leave the pillows, falling clumsily to the floor. He struggled, forcing breath through his crushed throat as he knelt, putting his forehead to the floor. "I live to obey, Father."

Jardir peered into his son's aura. The truth of those words was unreadable, but he could see already the images forming of Asome out in the night, hunting *alagai* princes. The boy was hungry for the glory. Hungry for redemption. Hungry to prove, at last, that he was his father's son.

Jardir drew a ward in the air, calling Asome's spear to his hand. He set it over his shoulder in the harness for his own spear, then called the crown to him, tying it to his belt sash.

"Tomorrow, before the entire court, you will ascend the seven steps and fall to your knees before the Damajah's pillows. You will beg her forgiveness for your crimes and pledge to serve her as you would me, in letter and spirit, until your death. Do this with truth in your heart, and she will return the spear and crown to you. Fail, and Heaven will ever be denied you."

Asome's aura swirled at that, doubt returning. Jardir demanded he shame himself before the entire court. "She is holding my son, and your mother."

"Kaji is with his mother. Your *Jiwah Ka*." Jardir turned to stare at crippled Asukaji, whose aura colored with shame. "The elder sister you tried to murder."

He looked back at Asome. "Your claim to the child is denied. Your plan to force an heir upon your cousin was without honor, and I should never have allowed it. Only Ashia can return your rights, and for that you will need her forgiveness, a boon not easily won."

Asome's aura darkened, and Jardir knew he might be demanding too much. But the boy touched his forehead to the floor again. "As you say, Deliverer."

"My Holy Mother will regain her freedom," Jardir said. "I have already seen to it. Neither you nor Inevera may detain her again. Manvah will be similarly released, and presented to your mother at court when you beg her forgiveness."

"Of course, Father," Asome said.

Jardir turned again to Asukaji. "And you, nephew? You who bid to murder your own blood, your father and sister, leaving my eldest sister a widow. Would you continue to lie there, bitter and wretched, as your soul shrivels like Nie's black heart?"

Asukaji embraced the turmoil in his aura. "No, Deliverer," he whispered. "I am ready to walk the lonely path and face Everam's judgment."

Jardir peered into his nephew's spirit, rifling through the boy's hopes and dreams like the robes of his wardrobe. His desire for glory, for greatness, was no less than his lover's. Asome and Asukaji had played equal part in the treachery on the Night of Hora.

But Asukaji had been humbled that night. The image of his defeat at his sister's hands was burned into his spirit, a scar that might never heal. Months spent crippled had driven him to the brink of despair. If there had been a way to take his own life, he would have done it long ago.

But deep within, there was a spark of light. He spoke truth regarding his readiness to face Everam's judgment, understanding at last how he had failed. Born to privilege, he and

Asome had taken their right to rule as a given, but still they meant to stand against Nie.

Jardir crouched beside the pillows where the boy lay. "It will not be so simple, nephew. Do you swear to renounce Nie, in this life and the next?"

"I swear it, Deliverer," Asukaji said.

"Do you swear to serve the Damajah?" Jardir asked. "To beg her forgiveness as Asome must?"

A tiny candle flame of hope lit in Asukaji's spirit. "I swear it, Deliverer."

"Will you serve your people, rather than expect they serve you?" Jardir demanded. "From the *dama* to the lowliest *chin*?"

It was a question too big for the boy's mind to comprehend, but he did not hesitate. "I swear it, Deliverer."

Jardir laid a hand on Asukaji's forehead, sending his own spirit into the boy, seeking that convergence where his lines of energy had been shattered. He found it, a knot of scars and broken connections, a chasm between mind and body.

With a push, Jardir shattered that wall, rejoining that which was severed. Asukaji cried out, first in pain, and then in ecstasy. He began to laugh, weeping as he flailed his weakened limbs.

Jardir let go and stepped back. Asome rushed to his lover and embraced him, tears mingling on their cheeks. Jardir nodded, wrapping himself in his cloak and activating the wards of unsight. Before they had eyes for anything but each other, he had already stepped into the night and flown back to Inevera's wing of the palace.

Jardir stepped through the window to Inevera's chambers, breathing deeply of the perfumed air. He savored the scent, committing it to memory. The Evejah told of the abyss stinking of sulfur, death, and despair.

He went to her perfume table, lifting the delicate vials and inhaling their scents until he found the one he had come to most associate with his *Jiwah Ka*. He pocketed the vial. In the endless night of Nie's depths, it would be a defense as strong as any ward.

He found Inevera deep in meditation, staring at the dice

scattered before her, aura flat and even. He could tell she was aware of his presence, but he made no sound, waiting patiently until she sat back on her heels, thin silks pulling tight.

Even after their night's passion, the sight stirred him. He had been too long without her for any one night to sate.

Inevera looked back at him and smiled. "Soon, my love. I will have you again before you leave me."

Jardir felt his pulse quicken. "You no longer believe you must come?"

Inevera glanced back at the dice sadly. "As you feared, your chances of victory below increase slightly if I come, but even if victorious, we would return to find our people destroyed. Nie waxes strong, my love. All Ala will tremble at Her wrath."

"What else have you learned?" Jardir asked.

"Alagai Ka is ancient," Inevera said. "The Prince of Lies spoke true when he claimed to have lived in the time of Kaji."

"He is the father of demons," Jardir said. "Perhaps he always was, since Nie's foul taint first seeped into Ala."

Inevera shook her head. "He was little more than a hatchling in Kaji's time, by the measuring of his kind. There have been many fathers of demons, since the coming of Nie."

"The Par'chin believes there are more," Jardir said. "That even if we should prove victorious, Nie's taint will live on. Across the sea, perhaps. Over the mountains. Beyond the Northern snows."

"Everam and Nie struggle eternally," Inevera said. "And as above, so below."

Jardir nodded. "Nothing is as precious, or fleeting, as peace. So Alagai Ka became Consort to the Mother of Demons after the time of Kaji. What else can you say of him?"

"With such a long life, only the barest glimpses can be seen," Inevera said. "But he is afraid. Perhaps for the first time in his existence."

"Afraid for himself?" Jardir asked. "Or for Alagai'ting Ka?"

"Himself," Inevera said. "He cares nothing for the Mother of Demons, apart from the station and power that comes from being her Consort. He fears death at your hands, or the machinations of rivals in his absence."

"Can we trust him to guide us to Nie's abyss?" Jardir asked.

"Trust?" Inevera laughed. "You must doubt every word

from Alagai Ka, every motive. There is treachery there. Of this there is no doubt. But he will take you to the abyss, if for his own purposes and not yours."

"A trap," Jardir said.

"Perhaps," Inevera said. "Or a trick. Alagai Ka lies with truths, and does not tell all. You must be ready for anything."

Jardir pursed his lips. It was good advice, but as vague as it was obvious.

"I wish I could tell you more, beloved," Inevera said. "But the divergences before you are many. You walk a shallow line in the sand amid a storm."

"You have spoken of pillars in the sand," Jardir pressed. "Constants amid the future's chaos."

"You will find a piece of Kaji," Inevera said. "A gift from your ancestor to guide you in the dark."

Jardir leaned in eagerly. "What piece? Where?"

"I cannot say," Inevera said. "It is not for you to seek. It is fate for you to find. Perhaps the Deliverer, in his wisdom, saw the possibility of his own failure, and left some sign for his successor?"

"Three thousand years ago?" Jardir asked.

"Time means nothing to Everam," Inevera said. "He exists beyond such things, and speaks to His prophets."

"And the Par'chin?" Jardir asked.

"He must make a choice," Inevera said. "Between his *jiwah* and his duty. Everything is balanced upon it."

"She carries a child," Jardir said.

Inevera nodded. "A boy of limitless potential, and a future of despair. He will be born in darkness, and will carry it inside him."

"So he will live," Jardir said. It meant Renna would survive long enough to deliver him, and that, at least, was something.

"Perhaps," Inevera said. "If Renna vah Harl am'Bales am'Brook accompanies you into the darkness below, there are futures where her son lives, and others where he dies. Some where he is born in captivity, mother and child food for Alagai Ka's table. Others where he is born an orphan, cut from her cooling body."

Jardir clenched his fist. The Par'chin's *jiwah* was brash and disrespectful, but she carried greater honor than any woman he had ever known short of Inevera herself.

"And if she remains behind?" he asked.

"You will fail," Inevera said flatly, "and all Ala be consumed."

"Then we must hold faith in her," Jardir said. "I have looked into the daughter of Harl's spirit. She will not falter."

"We must pray not," Inevera agreed.

"The Par'chin, too, will hold the course," Jardir said. "Even if the price be his wife, his child, he will strike a spear into the heart of Nie Herself."

"Do not trust in that," Inevera said. "Whatever your feelings for him, whatever you have seen when you peer into his spirit, he is a man, and men are fallible, especially when their mates are concerned."

Asome's face flashed in Jardir's mind's eye, purpling as his father strangled him for daring to strike at his *jiwah*. "There is wisdom in your words, beloved. I will be there to keep the Par'chin on his path. Is there more?"

"Nothing else yet," Inevera said. "I will cast again when I have some time to meditate upon what the dice have already shown."

"With the amplified power of the earrings, you should be able to speak to me until we reach the mouth of Ala and travel into the dark below," Jardir said. "The magic will interfere with the resonance once we are beneath the surface."

"In the meantime, there are other matters to discuss," Inevera said.

Jardir produced Asome's spear and crown. "Asome and Asukaji will kneel before you on the morrow, to beg forgiveness and ask you to restore their power. All will know they are yours, if they should convince you."

Inevera blew a breath, making her veil dance like smoke. "My mother?"

"She will be released to you at the same time." Jardir gave her a hard look, brooking no debate. "As will my mother. Neither of you will detain her again."

"Of course, beloved. I spoke the truth when I said it was for her own protection. I would never have harmed her." Inevera's bow seemed sincere, but there was dissembling in her aura.

"I thought we were past lies, beloved," Jardir said.

Inevera met his eyes. "I put Sharak Ka above all else, husband. I detained Kajivah so I would not be forced to harm her should Asome attempt to supplant me."

Jardir's teeth clenched, but he embraced the feeling. He could not fault his wife for that. He loved his mother, but she was in no way qualified for the burden of the seventh step.

He switched topics to break the tension. "Where is Abban?"

"Alive, the dice tell me," Inevera said. "I believe Hasik killed Jayan to get to him, and stole the *khaffit* away. Ashia hunts for them even now."

Jardir scowled. "I was a fool to leave Hasik alive. Every time I have shown him mercy, I have regretted it."

"Mercy should never be cause for regret," Inevera said. "It may be that Hasik yet has a part to play in Sharak Ka."

"Perhaps," Jardir conceded. "My time grows short. What else is there to attend?"

In reply, Inevera touched one of her bracelets, and there was a sound of a latch turning behind them. The door opened to admit Amanvah and Sikvah.

Jardir looked back at Inevera in irritation. "I said to tell no one." Despite the words, he could not deny his pleasure at seeing his eldest daughter clad in a black headscarf, and his niece in a white. Gentle Sikvah looked fierce in her armored robes, armed with spear and shield, and the sight filled him with pride.

"Amanvah and Sikvah have vital news," Inevera said. "You will want it directly from their lips."

"Father." Amanvah knelt before him, putting her hands on the floor. "My heart sings to see you returned alive. I had judged the Par'chin a man of honor. I am glad to see that faith was not misplaced."

Jardir opened his arms. "Rise, beloved daughter, and embrace me."

Amanvah flew to his arms faster than might be considered proper, but Jardir only laughed, crushing her to him. When was the last time he held her thus? Before she was sent to the Dama'ting Palace, a decade and more ago. He and Inevera spent so much time grooming their children to lead, they neglected to show them a parent's love.

It was too late for many of his children now, but for one moment he allowed himself to set aside the mantle of Shar'Dama Ka and be a father. "I am proud of you, daughter. Never doubt this."

"I will not, Father," Amanvah said, drawing back as reluctantly as he. Her eyes were wet.

Jardir did not pull away completely, keeping an arm around her as he reached out to Sikvah. "And you, Niece. I mourn your loss. The son of Jessum carried boundless honor. Ala is darker without him, but no doubt Heaven shines brighter than ever."

The fierce façade fell away, and she was gentle Sikvah again, joining her sister-wife in his embrace, the two of them weeping openly. In his crownsight, Jardir could see the ambient magic drawn to their emotion, imprinting upon the tears. They ran like streaks of light down their cheeks, beautiful beyond words.

Inevera produced a tear bottle, collecting the precious drops. When it was full she stoppered it and held it out. The vial glowed with power, much like the *hora* jewelry she wore.

"A keepsake to carry next to my perfume as you journey to the abyss." Her smile was wry. "A reminder of love, in that place of endless despair."

Jardir took the bottle reverently, bowing as he slipped it into his pocket.

"Is it true that Shanvah will travel into the dark below with you, Uncle?" Sikvah asked.

"It is, niece," Jardir said. "Your spear sister carries untold glory. A demon prince fell to her spear, and for a time she stood alone against Nie's hordes while the Par'chin and I fought to subdue Alagai Ka."

Sikvah knelt again, slipping the bright spear and mirrored shield from her back. They were glass treated with electrum, forged and warded by Inevera herself. Sikvah stripped herself of rings and bracelets, anklets, necklace, and choker. All of them shone bright with power, the intricate script of his wife and daughter glowing white in crownsight.

"For such a quest, my spear sister must have the finest weapons and equipment, Deliverer," Sikvah said. "I would be honored if you would give these to her with my love and blessing."

Jardir laid a hand on her shoulder. "With pride, Sharum'ting Ka, it will be done."

"Tell her the *Song of Waning* will protect her in the night," Amanvah said. "If her voice is strong, it will protect you all, as you walk the path to Nie's abyss."

Jardir nodded. "The son of Jessum saw what we had forgotten. Preserved in the ancient songs of prayer to Everam is true power against Nie. When we join him in Heaven, we will find your husband seated at Everam's table."

Fresh tears met the words, but there was little time for weeping. They all knelt on pillows in a ring facing one another. Inevera's wards were strong, but Jardir took no chances, raising the crown's protective field as well.

"Mistress Leesha has given birth to your child, Father," Amanvah said. "I delivered the babe myself."

Leesha's letter told him of the child, but this was news. His eyes flicked to Inevera, but her aura remained serene.

"I cast the dice in the child's birthing blood, Father," Amanvah said.

Jardir clenched a fist and had to embrace the sudden tension. He had dozens of children. Why did the fate of this one matter so much to him? "What did you see?"

"Potential," Amanvah said.

"All Everam's children have potential," Jardir said.

"Potential to be Shar'Dama Ka," Inevera cut in. "Potential to save the world, or doom it."

Jardir looked from Inevera to Amanvah and back. "You're certain?"

"As certain as anything the dice can tell," Amanvah said.

"Our daughter has a keen eye, beloved," Inevera said. "I examined the pattern myself. The child is like you—like the Par'chin."

"A Deliverer," Jardir said.

"Deliverers are made," Inevera said. "The question is, can we trust your *chin heasah* to teach the child what it must know?"

"Do not call Leesha Paper that," Jardir snapped. The words struck Inevera's aura like a lash, but it could not be helped.

"She is the mother of my child, a worthy foe of Nie, and has stymied your attempts to kill or silence her more than once. You need not show her love, or kindness, but by Everam she has earned your respect."

Inevera's jaw tightened, but she bowed. "I apologize, beloved. When it comes to your greenland *jiwah* . . ."

Jardir held up a hand. "I understand, beloved. You have no reason to feel otherwise. But Sharak Ka is upon us, and we must rise above such things and forge peace with our Northern cousins, if humanity is to survive."

"Of course." Inevera breathed deeply, her center returning. "I will make peace with my Northern . . . *zahven*, even as you have with yours."

Zahven. The word meant "rival," but it meant "equal," as well. It was the first time Inevera had acknowledged Leesha Paper as such, and he knew the admission cost her deeply.

"A child belongs with its mother," Jardir said. "And Olive will be safer away from Krasian scheming. Even if Asome finds his honor again, there would be many who would seek to exploit the child."

"Or slay it," Inevera agreed.

"But that does not mean we cannot send tutors," Jardir said. "And bodyguards. Those the dice tell you can be trusted to know the honor they carry."

"Olive will be raised a girl," Amanvah said. "We can plant a *Sharum'ting* in disguise by her side, a secret guardian much as Sikvah served for me."

Jardir looked to Sikvah. "Who do you recommend?"

"Micha," Sikvah said without hesitation. "She is eldest, next to me, *Sharum* blood of the Deliverer and half sister to Olive Paper. She will guard the child with her life, and teach her to defend herself."

"Very well." Jardir nodded, looking to Inevera. "And to cast for her?"

"We will send three *dama'ting* to the Hollow Tribe," Inevera said. "A maiden, a mother, and a crone."

"Who will lead them?" Jardir asked.

"Ancient Favah's skill with the dice was revered when I still wore a bido," Inevera said. "She will be strict, and not bow before the *chin*, but a child needs that."

Jardir knew the old woman. Her stare could unnerve even him, but her spirit was true. "And the mother?"

"Dama'ting Shaselle, who studied with me in the Dama'ting Palace," Inevera said.

Jardir nodded. Shaselle had served as one of Inevera's closest advisors during his rise to power. "The maiden?"

Inevera turned to Amanvah, and the girl considered. After a moment, she reached into the pouch at her waist and cast the *alagai hora,* studying them carefully.

"Dama'ting Jaia," Amanvah said at last. "She has only recently taken the white, and has yet to produce an heir. The dice foretell she will find a worthy father in the greenlands and further cement our ties to the Hollow Tribe."

"Very well," Jardir said. "Dawn approaches, and there is one thing left to discuss."

"The Majah," Inevera said. "They return to the Desert Spear."

Jardir paled. "What?"

"*Inevera,*" his wife said. "It was the will of the dice."

"Unacceptable," Jardir said.

Inevera shrugged. "No doubt if you fly into their midst and seize Aleveran as you did your son, you can turn them around."

Jardir shook his head. "That I cannot do without jeopardizing everything we fight for."

"Then we must trust in Everam's will." Inevera turned to the other women. "Leave us."

Jardir looked to the window as his daughter and niece left, seeing color wash across the horizon. "You have kept me until dawn."

Inevera smiled. "A day to rest in safety is no small thing, husband, before you march to the abyss."

Cold wind blew across Jardir's face as night fell and he took off from the palace roof. He meant to return immediately to the tower, but found himself turning north instead, flying fast for the Hollow. He had no plan for his arrival, but his failure with his sons weighed heavily upon him. If they did not succeed, Olive might be Ala's last hope, and he did not think he could bear going into the abyss without at least holding her and whispering a blessing.

The Hollow was alive at night, but—secure in their greatwards—the Hollowers were not in the habit of looking upward. Jardir found the keep Amanvah described easily enough, wrapping himself in his cloak as he peered in crownsight through window and wall alike until he found the room he sought. Within was a cradle, the pure aura of an innocent glowing brightly within.

The wards around the room were powerful, but meant to keep *alagai* at bay, not humans. Jardir used a flick of magic to trip the window latch and slip inside. He left his sandals by the sill and padded silently to the cradle, careful not to wake the child.

He needn't have bothered. As he looked down upon her, Olive's eyes stared back at him, wide awake as if he had been expected.

Her aura was as bright as any Jardir had seen short of the Par'chin and his *jiwah,* but . . . clean. Unburdened by compromise, failure, or shame.

And then, shamefully, Jardir's eyes flicked down.

What he saw surprised him. On hearing of Olive's condition, Jardir assumed it a weakness she would need to overcome, as if being half of each gender made her less than either.

But as he peered deeper with his crownsight, images beyond count danced about Olive, more than he had ever seen in a single aura. Ghostlike impressions of what she might become. Rather than being halved, Olive's possibilities were doubled.

Olive cooed softly as he lifted her from the crib. Tears filled Jardir's eyes at the beauty of the sound. He cradled her in his arm. "Blessings of Everam upon you, daughter."

She wrinkled her nose, yawning as she snuggled close to him. For a moment, he did not know what to do. He had never held his other children with such tenderness.

Perhaps if he had, things might have gone differently.

"Your mother believes I have been a poor father," he whispered, "and perhaps, if I am honest, she is correct. Always, my attention was fixed on Sharak Ka instead of my own family. I failed my eldest sons, barely knew my daughters."

Olive reached up, fingers twining into his beard and pulling with surprising strength. "I cannot promise it will be better with you, Olive vah Ahmann am'Jardir am'Hollow. I walk a path I may not return from, but I do it out of love. For you, and all the people of Ala. I pray you never know this burden, but if one day it fall to you, Everam grant you the strength to bear it."

"Am'Paper," a voice said behind him.

Startled, Jardir spun into a defensive pose, blocking the child with his body as he snatched up his spear.

Leesha Paper stood with arms folded into the wide sleeves of her dressing gown, offering no threat. She was just as he remembered, beautiful as the dawn, proud as a mountain. "We are not married, Ahmann. Her name is Olive Paper, not Jardir."

"She is mine, Leesha," Jardir said. "It is written across her aura. You would deny my claim?"

"Of course not," Leesha said. "I will not hide who she is, but your name will draw assassins' blades every time one of your heirs feels threatened."

"Asome is cowed," Jardir said. "He will not . . ."

"You have over seventy children, Ahmann. Can you speak for every one, in all the years to come?"

"I cannot speak for the *alagai,* either," Jardir said. "Nie will strike at one such as Olive all her life. *Inevera,* she will prove the stronger. That is no excuse."

"I do not need an excuse," Leesha said. "We are not married, and the law is clear. She is Olive Paper. And why should she not be? It was I who made her. I who carried her in my own body, nursed her on my own milk. It is I who protect her. I who will raise her."

"My name and blessing are the only gifts I have to bestow before I go to the abyss," Jardir said.

Leesha smiled at last. "A middle name, then. Olive Jardir Paper."

Jardir accepted the concession, looking back into the child's eyes. "Blessings of Everam upon you, Olive Jardir Paper."

Leesha came to him, kissing him softly on the cheek. "We made a beautiful child."

Olive tugged at his beard, trying to pull it into her mouth. "Indeed, we did."

"Am I right in assuming you would not have come to me, next?"

"In truth, I did not know if I was welcome," Jardir said. "Your letter did not say. I meant only to bless the child."

Leesha laid a gentle hand on Olive's head, stroking her fine black hair. "You already have."

"Then blessings upon her mother," Jardir said, "still lovely as the bluest sky."

Leesha laughed. "Ever the charmer. Don't think you'll be putting another in me before you go. One was enough."

Jardir felt his face heat. "I . . . did not mean . . ."

Leesha laughed, cupping his chin. "I am teasing, Ahmann."

Jardir longed to take her into his arms, and quickly turned his eyes back to Olive. "Inevera will send three *dama'ting* to the Hollow to advise and teach. With them will be my daughter Micha. She will be in *dal'ting* robes, but like Sikvah, she studied under Enkido. She will keep her half sister safe. You can trust her in this."

"I will," Leesha promised. "Thank you."

Jardir gently set Olive back in her cradle, disentangling her tiny fingers from his beard. "I must go."

He turned away, but Leesha caught his arm, pulling him into a tight embrace. He held her one last time, breathing the scent of her hair. She laid her head on his chest. "Be safe, Ahmann. Come back to see your daughter grow."

"I will not spend my life cheaply," Ahmann promised. "Everam's blessing upon you, Leesha vah Erny am'Paper am'Hollow."

He kissed her. A feather-light touch of her lips that lingered even as he pulled away. He stepped back to the window, slipped on his sandals, and leapt out into the night.

CHAPTER 17

FOREST FORTRESS

334 AR

Ragen tightened his grip on Twilight Dancer's reins as the sun began to dip below the horizon. He could feel the massive animal tensing, powerful muscles readying themselves for battle Ragen prayed was not to come.

"Strange feeling, to keep riding as the sun sets." Derek's warded armor was in fresh repair and polished to a shine, but he kept his hand close to the spear harness on his horse's flank.

"Yu'll get used to it." Yon Gray was the leader of their Cutter escort. He was a huge man, thick with muscle. "Roads're warded and yu've got a score o' Cutters at yur back."

"How long will it take to reach the city, if we can push on after dark?" Elissa wore a warded cloak she'd purchased in the Hollow, and fresh riding leathers. Ragen could not recall seeing her in breeches once in their first twenty years together. Now they looked as natural as the expert way she handled her mare.

"Don't rightly know," Yon admitted. "Lived eighty years without going more'n a couple miles from where I was born. Tomorrow we'll pass farther'n I've ever been."

Ragen blinked. Yon was over eighty? The man looked younger than he was.

"Then why volunteer to take us all the way to Miln?" Elissa asked.

Yon stroked his long beard, dark hair close to his face streaking to iron gray and then to pure white. "Son and grandsons are grown. Laid my wife on the pyre sixteen summers ago. Magic got me a second chance at life. Aim to see a bit more o' the world this time round."

"You want to be a Messenger, I know an opening," Derek said. "Spent twenty-two years in Brayan's Gold. Weren't more than sixty in the whole town, and you could walk from one end to the other in a quarter hour."

He blew out a breath. "But now I've seen as much of the world as I care to. Servants know my son better than I do. My wife's family would as soon I stay away, but when I get back to Miln, I don't mean to leave again."

"Ay," Ragen agreed. "Past time we were all back home, but there's miles to go. I used to make this run every year. Alone, I could make it back to Miln in two weeks from this point. A group our size will take a month if we don't push a bit. There's a campsite just a few hours up the road. If we stop there, we can shave off half a day's ride."

Elissa kept her expression calm. Half a day didn't seem like much, but faced with another month on the road, any savings was worth a few hours in the dark.

The children need you. Marya. Little Arlen. What must they be feeling after their parents disappeared for nearly a year? Letters assured everyone of mutual well-being, but it was no substitute for a mother's guiding hand, a father's love.

To return to them, she would ride all night.

She stroked the velvet pouch hanging from her belt, comforted by the presence of her silver stylus.

The tool was the result of their studies in the Gatherers' Academy and Hollow Warders' Guild. The Hollowers used *hora* wands to draw wards in the air, but Elissa found it clumsy and imprecise. She preferred to ward with a pen.

When Mistress Leesha generously provided materials for *hora* wands of their own, Elissa, Ragen, and Derek made styluses instead. The pens had demon bone cores in their thick handles, coated in warded silver and tipped with an electrum nib. By manipulating wards along the handle, Elissa could adjust the Draw of power into the nib, giving each ward as much or as little power as desired.

But there was a difference between drawing practice wards in the air in the safety of the academy and drawing them at a charging demon. A coreling shrieked somewhere in the distance, and Elissa clenched her thighs so tight she felt she might squeeze the breath from her mare.

They rode for three more hours, twilight deepening into full dark. The wardposts cast a dim light that ended at the brush on the roadside. Beyond, there were shrieks, growls, and sounds of movement in the darkness, but no demons tested the wards.

Twilight Dancer stomped and snorted as Ragen struggled to control the mighty stallion. Derek had his shield on his arm. Even Yon looked tense, hand drifting to the long handle of his axe, harnessed in easy reach on his saddle. "Corelings're out in force this soon after new moon."

New moon. Elissa felt a chill run down her spine. Arlen said the normally mindless corelings could act in concert when the more powerful mind demons were about. She reached up to touch the golden circlet she wore, running a finger over the mind wards. The others had the symbols on their helmets.

Creator, let them not be necessary.

"Let's pick up the pace," Ragen said. "Campsite can't be much farther."

They fell into a grim silence against the backdrop of shrieks and roars, moving as fast as the carts in their train would allow. As her eyes adjusted, Elissa began to see shapes flitting in the darkness along the side of the road. Were they being followed?

At last she could bear it no longer. She reached into her pouch and drew out the silver stylus, eyes scanning the darkness. She saw movement and drew a light ward in that direction, tapping the ward to let just a flash of power into the nib.

Light flared, and Elissa immediately regretted the move.

They were surrounded. Dozens of corelings scattered from the light, and no doubt there were many more out of sight.

"Cutters!" Yon called. "Axes out! Crank bows at the ready, but don't waste yur bolts unless there's a breach!"

Fear gave them speed as they hurried down the road, and

soon the caravan circle came in sight. It was occupied, but there was room enough for their carts and horses. Elissa began to breathe easier.

But then, the ground began to shake.

Yon spat. "Rock demons. Everyone into the camp! Bows around the perimeter! Now!"

The Cutters moved with calm efficiency, but it did little to quell Elissa's mounting fear. She dared another light ward and saw two fifteen-foot rock demons, their armor like granite. One held a pine tree in its talons like a club. Clumps of loose soil still clung to its roots, and broken branches jutted from its length. Behind them, scores of corelings gathered.

The other held a stone the size of a rain barrel.

Creator. The realization barely sank in before the demon's long arm swung like a catapult, launching the stone at the camp.

It arced high in the air, and Elissa watched, transfixed, for a long moment before remembering her stylus. She drew a hurried impact ward. With no time to calculate how much force it would take to stop the stone, Elissa opened the nib fully to power the symbol.

The resulting blast shattered the stone, but the recoil knocked her from her horse. She hit the ground hard, stylus flying from nerveless fingers as dust and pebbles fell on the camp like sleet.

"Elissa!" Ragen leapt from Twilight Dancer's back, running to her side as she struggled into a sitting position.

She waved him off. "I'm all right. See to the demons!"

Derek took out his own stylus, drawing careful light wards in the air to illuminate the enemy. Cutters loosed crank bows at the rock demons, but the tiny bolts did little more than anger the corelings as they stalked in.

"Gonna have to step off the wards to take 'em down." Yon readied his axe. "Jase! Lary! You're with me!"

"Wait!" Ragen called. "There's too many! Stay inside the wards!"

"Wards ent gonna last with two rockies swingin' trees and throwin' stones!" Yon shouted back. "Let us do our business."

"Corespawn it." Ragen ran to head the Cutters off. The rock

demon carrying the tree drew it back for a swing at the ward-posts. Ragen pulled out his own stylus, drawing a heat ward.

There was a flash and a *whump!* as he powered the symbol, but the results were less than impressive. One side of the tree blackened and charred, a few embers flying, but it did not hinder the coreling.

"Demonshit!" Ragen growled, trying again. This time he used too much power. The tree exploded in flames that engulfed the demon and lit up the night.

The other rock demon had its clawed hands in front of its face as Cutters renewed crank bow fire, but then it laced its talons together and brought both stony fists down hard on the ground. Elissa stumbled as she tried to get back on her feet, and around the campsite she saw others off balance as well. Crank bow bolts flew wide of their targets.

Elissa searched frantically in the dirt for her stylus. If the rocks managed to breach the wards, demons would swarm the camp. After a moment she found it, brushing the dust from the wards. She rushed to the wardposts and drew a careful impact ward, giving it moderate power. The recoil wasn't as bad when she was prepared for it, and the ward flared to life, punching the ground-shaking demon in the chest.

The demon was knocked onto its back, but seemed unharmed. Derek drew cold wards and fed them deeply with power. He hissed, dropping his stylus from numbed fingers, but the prone demon's legs turned white with rime.

Ragen drew a series of thick impact wards, hammering at the frozen limbs. With the third strike there was a great *crack!* and one of the demon's legs shattered.

The flames from the burning pine tree died away, leaving the immolated rock demon unharmed. It came at the wards, but Elissa, Ragen, and Derek were ready now, and drew wards in sync. Elissa knocked the demon down; Derek froze its chest. Superheated from the flames, the sudden shift cracked armor plates. Ragen followed quickly with another series of impact wards, caving in the demon's chest and crushing its heart.

The other demons retreated at that, drifting back beyond the edges of the wardlight.

"Fightin' smart." Yon spat on the ground. "Demons shun't

know enough to use weapons unless a mind's about, but new moon's three days past."

"There's still a lot we don't know," Elissa said. "Mistress Leesha said mimic demons could lead drones as well."

"Ay," Yon agreed, "but if there's a mimic about, ent willin' to show itself."

"Perhaps," Ragen said.

"No more pushin' our luck," Yon agreed. "Now on we make camp a'fore dark, and keep guards all night."

"We've gotten more used to worrying about the Krasians than the corelings," Elissa said.

"Think it's comin' around again," Yon said. "Night's getting stronger."

Ragen led them into Farmer's Stump a few days later. None had slept well, but now that they were taking an hour each evening to reinforce the wards, the demons did not test them again. They stopped at Ragen's favorite inn for supper and a full night's rest, pressing on in the morning to reach Fort Angiers by lunchtime.

The great wooden gates were mismatched, patched with fresh lumber where the Krasians broke through. There was scaffolding everywhere—the new duke making improvements along with repairs.

"They're thickening the walls," Ragen said. "That's a good sign."

"Against Krasians, maybe," Yon said. "Get a few rock demons with stones to throw, those walls won't last long."

Mountain Spears, clad in the familiar uniforms of Ragen's homeland, patrolled the walls and guarded the gate. Their bayonets were wicked as any spear, but largely decorative. None would dare challenge them now that the destructive power of their flamework weapons was known. Angierian Wooden Soldiers, the fencing spears over their shoulders looking quaint by comparison, did the more menial work of questioning travelers and searching carts.

"Name and business," one of them said, coming up to Ragen at the head of the procession.

"Ragen, master of the Milnese Warders' Guild," Ragen said,

producing papers sealed by Euchor himself. The guard's eyes widened, and he moved to consult his superior, one of the Mountain Spears.

"Angierian soldiers answer to the Milnese, now?" Elissa asked.

"Rhinebeck's brother may have held the throne," Ragen said, "but it seems Euchor is now the real power in Angiers."

"We'll need to take care," Elissa said. "There's bound to be resentment at court."

By the time they made it through the gate, the captain general of the Mountain Spears was waiting for them atop a spotless white destrier. "Ragen!" His booming voice was a welcome sound. "I thought I smelled a foul wind blowing from the south!"

"Bruz!" Ragen cried, dropping from his saddle as the man mirrored him. "I didn't know it was your ugly face Euchor sent to Angiers!" They embraced roughly, breastplates striking each other as they laughed and slapped backs.

"None other, to guard the princess." Bruz was one of Euchor's closest military advisors. Ragen had known the man for decades.

Ragen tapped the epaulet on Bruz's shoulder. "And a promotion, I see."

Bruz nodded. "After we broke the Krasian assault, Euchor sent another three thousand Mountain Spears south, along with the proclamation and a chest of gold that nearly broke the mule's back."

"Impressive," Ragen said.

"No less than I can say of you!" Bruz said. "All the North owes you and Mother Elissa a debt for sending news from behind the Krasian lines. No doubt Euchor will reward you upon your return. In the meantime, you'll take your ease at the palace. Stay as long as you like."

"Not long, I'm afraid," Ragen said. "I've messages to deliver at court, but Elissa and I are eager to be back home with our children."

"Of course, of course," Bruz said. He gave a whistle, and an escort of Mountain Spears began shouting and shoving to clear the road of traffic.

"This isn't necessary," Elissa said as one guard pushed a

vendor to the ground when he did not clear the way quickly enough.

"Nonsense," Bruz said. "These woodbrains need to learn to move when the Mountain Spears whistle. They'd all be dead or Krasian slaves if not for us."

Ragen pressed his lips together and met Elissa's eyes, shaking his head. Thankfully, she let the matter drop.

"I'm here in a more official capacity," Ragen said. "It's been some time since I was a Royal Messenger, but Countess Leesha persuaded me to come out of retirement one last time to speak for the Hollow in Duke Pether's court."

Bruz raised an eyebrow. "A Milnese guildmaster speaking for an Angierian countess? Is that not a conflict of interest?"

Ragen shrugged. "Desperate times, my lord. One cannot blame her for not wishing to send Halfgrip's successor to Angiers so soon after her master's death."

"Euchor won't like it," Bruz noted.

"It won't be the first time His Grace was vexed with me," Ragen said.

Bruz laughed. "Ay, that's undersaid!"

They reached the palace, where another familiar face was waiting in the entrance hall.

"Creator spare me," Ragen muttered as Keerin, Euchor's idiot herald, came rushing up to greet them.

"Ragen!" Keerin called, arms wide as if to greet an old friend, though they were hardly that. The two men worked together on a single Messenger run fifteen years past, but there was no love lost between them. Most of Keerin's fame was built off taking credit for Arlen's deeds, and he once had his apprentices beat Arlen and his friend Jaik when Arlen dared protest in public.

Keerin recovered smoothly as Ragen sidestepped to avoid his touch. "It's good to see you, old friend."

Ragen tightened his jaw. "What can I do for you, Keerin?"

"I was hoping to find a place in your caravan back to Miln," Keerin said.

Ragen shook his head. "Euchor sent you here as his herald, and until such time as he requests and provides for your return, it's not my place to get involved."

"Oh, by all means." Bruz was struggling to keep the laugh

from his voice. "Master Keerin's duties have long since been fulfilled. We simply haven't had resources to escort him home, and despite his *legendary* bravery, he's been unwilling to make the trek alone."

Keerin swallowed at that, but he did not argue, lowering his voice for only Ragen to hear. "You heard him. I'm not wanted, and this court has a way of getting Jongleurs killed. First Jasin Goldentone and his apprentices slaughtered in the lower hall, then poor Master Halfgrip, slain in the South Tower. I don't care if Euchor fires me. I want to go home."

Ragen glanced at Elissa. She was no fonder of Keerin than he was, but she put a hand on his arm. "I know what it's like to be desperate to go home. Of course you can join us."

The Jongleur's face lit up, and he took Elissa's hand in both of his own, kissing it repeatedly. "Thank you, Mother. Creator bless you! I will start packing immediately." He gave a yip of glee, doing a backflip in a flash of motley cloth as he ran down the hall.

"We're going to regret that," Ragen said.

"Perhaps," Elissa said. "But after all these months, I won't stand in the way of someone who wants only to go home."

A page appeared, and Bruz swept a hand his way. "You'll forgive me, but I have matters to attend. Their Graces will receive you at evening court. In the meantime, the Little Minister will see to your needs."

"Little Minister?" Ragen asked.

The boy bowed. "Pawl is my name. The captain general calls me that because my father was First Minister Janson."

"I hardly started the name, but it's apt." Bruz tousled the boy's hair. "He's the only one who can make anything of his father's ledgers. We'd be lost without him."

"This way." Pawl led Elissa, Ragen, Derek, and Yon down a long hall. "Your chambers should be ready shortly. In the meantime, we've prepared a sitting room for you to refresh and take your ease."

"Know yur rich, when you have a room just for sittin'," Yon said.

The room was lavish, with a laden buffet and steaming tea

service. There was water, wine, even a pitcher of ale. After days on the road, it looked so enticing it was a moment before Elissa noticed the old woman enjoying her tea by the couches.

One glance at her jewels and silk, and Elissa dropped into a curtsy.

She elbowed Ragen, who made a hurried leg. Yon and Derek, halfway to the buffet, froze awkwardly.

The Duchess Mother gave an irritated wave. "Enough of that! I won't keep hungry men from their food. On to it, boys."

"I know when I'm dismissed." Ragen and the others gave quick bows and hurried to the meat and ale.

"Come and let me have a look at you, dear," the Duchess Mother said. "My eyes aren't what they used to be."

Elissa went over, resisting the urge to curtsy again as Araine got to her feet to receive her. "Your Grace."

"We can leave the titles at the door, Elissa," Araine said. "I've been corresponding with your mother since before you were born. Countess Tresha and I are old friends. Surely she's mentioned me."

The words caught Elissa off guard. Mention of her mother had a way of doing that. "The countess and I do not speak often."

Araine snorted. "That's undersaid. Something to discuss over tea." Pawl pulled a chair for Elissa, serving tea and a sampling of delicate sandwiches from the buffet.

"I have a letter for you," Elissa said when the page retreated to the wall.

"Right to business," Araine said. "You've more in common with your mother than you think."

The comment nettled Elissa, but she swallowed her retort, producing the envelope with Leesha's message for Araine. The Duchess Mum popped the seal with a sharp fingernail, scanning the pages quickly.

Araine sighed. "I'm afraid I can't offer much more than advice."

Elissa blinked. "Leesha said you were the true power in Angiers."

"Once," Araine said. "Before Janson was murdered. Before Euchor bought the ivy throne at the price of our lives. What little power Lorain hasn't stolen from me, Pether has claimed for himself. All Angiers used to run through my embroidery room. Now it's just a collection of unfinished hoops."

"That may be a problem," Elissa said. "Lorain and I . . ."

"Haven't gotten along since that spat when you were children," Araine said. "Young Lord Sament asked you to the Equinox Ball?"

"Solstice," Elissa said. "And I declined."

"Leaving the Duke of Miln's daughter feeling second best."

"How do you know this?" Elissa said.

"Tresha's been telling tales of you since she fired your first wet nurse," Araine said. "She's quite proud of you."

This time Elissa could not resist. "If you think that, you don't know my mother as well as you believe."

"Don't be so sure of that, dear," Araine said. "You caused quite a scandal, running away from Sunrise Hall to marry a Messenger. She only wanted the best for you."

"I don't see how disowning me was wanting the best," Elissa said. "Thankfully my sisters were more dutiful in marrying the barons Mother paraded through our gardens."

Araine waved a hand. "She'll never admit it, but Tresha admired how you stood up to her. It was a feat your spineless sisters never managed. All you have to do is ask and she'll have you back."

"Have me back." Elissa ground her teeth. "As if marrying the best man I've ever known is some crime to atone for. I don't want 'back.' My mother can keep her court politics and whispers."

Araine gave a bemused sniff. "You may not have much choice in that regard. You've seen and done too much to go back to sweeping the floor of a warding shop. I expect you'll be called before the Council of Mothers on your return for a full account of your adventures in the wetlands. I know that pack of mean old women well. Whatever your feelings about her, your mother leads the council. She's a better ally than enemy."

Elissa swallowed. The Mothers' Council of Miln was nearly as powerful as Duke Euchor, responsible for most of the day-to-day operations of the city. Much as she hated to admit it, if she and Ragen were to effect any change in the city before it was too late, she would need the council on her side.

"You may be right. Thank you for your counsel." The words were sour in her mouth, but she managed to deliver them with a polite smile.

"Of course, we all know your mother isn't the most interesting of your family issues." Araine took a tiny sandwich from the table, eating it in two quick, efficient bites.

"Oh?" Elissa asked.

"I met young Mr. Bales last year," Araine said, "before all that business with the demon of the desert. He was shorter than the tales tell, but he seemed a good boy. Idealistic, perhaps, but the young always wear that well."

"He was a good boy." Elissa chose her words carefully.

"A good boy who made Euchor look the fool," Araine said. "Now that it's known your young stray grew up to be the Warded Man, there are questions at court about what you knew and when you knew it. If you're wise, you'll ware your words and ensure you and your husband follow the same script."

"They can ask whatever they wish," Elissa said. "We have nothing to hide."

"Of course." Araine tapped Leesha's letter against her teacup. "You believe this, girl? The demons are going to swarm?"

"I do," Elissa said. "The corelings are increasing in numbers, even as the Hollowers and Krasians kill them by the thousands. They were hunting us on the road." She quickly explained about the rock demons striking at the wards.

"A pair of demons testing the wards doesn't prove the demons have some hidden agenda. We've seen no sign of a change in their behavior here. Perhaps this is what comes of the Hollow provoking them."

"Do you wish to take that chance?" Elissa asked.

"The Krasians are the real enemy," Araine said. "They killed three of my sons. Pether's brothers. Lorain's husband. And thousands of husbands, wives, and children throughout the Free Cities—more by far than the demons over the same time. Now deserters from the Battle of Angiers have formed into roving war bands, committing horrible atrocities. They castrate the men and boys, taking them as levies, and leave nothing but blood and ash in their wake. None of the eastern hamlets is safe."

"And they keep Euchor from declaring himself king," Elissa said.

"I don't know anything that can stop that, now," Araine said. "Euchor has played his hand too well. He'll keep feeding Mountain Spears south along the way stations until he has enough men to go south and join the men Pether levies from the Hollow to crush the Krasians once and for all."

Elissa sipped her tea, keeping her eyes down. "Countess Paper is unlikely to commit her warriors to attacking their neighbors while she believes the demon threat is growing."

"She's learning the dance," Araine agreed, "but she may not have much choice. You have your own problems. Step carefully, when you return home."

"Aaaand thaaaat's why it's called coooorling's knoooooooooob!" Keerin finished with a final, flourishing strum of his lute, and Elissa let out a breath. The Jongleur was so happy to be out of Angiers, he hadn't put his lute back in its case in days.

Thank the Creator. Their audience with Pether and Lorain had not gone well, and Araine's warning kept nagging at her. *Step carefully, when you return home.*

No sooner had Elissa given praise for the silence than Keerin struck up another song.

Elissa resisted the urge to cover her ears. "I'd pay a thousand suns to shut that man up."

"I warned you," Ragen said.

"Ent so bad." Yon and the other Hollowers were enjoying the singing, joining the choruses as they rode. "He's no Half-grip, but we're fond o' red-haired Jongleurs in the Hollow. Had a pint or seven in that tavern in Riverbridge. Feller told me Keerin cut the arm off a rippin' rock demon. Din't even use his music. Imagine that little feller standin' toe-to-toe with a rock."

"Ridiculous," Ragen agreed.

Yon gave a wistful grin. "Wish I coulda been there to see it."

Ragen gaped. "You actually *believe* that story?"

"Ay, why not?" Yon said. "Seen things these past couple years that put every ale story and tampweed tale I ever heard to shame. Don't expect the got to be royal herald by lyin'."

Stunned, Ragen took a moment to formulate a response. Before he could speak, Elissa laid a hand on his arm, and he calmed.

"We couldn't have just left him," Elissa said. "That city is readying for a war, and you and I know Keerin's no fighter, whatever his reputation in the taverns."

"Lucky for him, Euchor built way stations to supply his Mountain Spears in Angiers," Ragen said. "The Hollowers need not see his mettle at night."

Indeed, their last few nights were spent safely behind the way stations' powerfully warded walls, each well supplied and garrisoned with Mountain Spears armed with flamework weapons.

Elissa longed for the sight each dusk. There hadn't been a hamlet or town in days, and it was reassuring to see warded walls each night, and be surrounded by Milnese accents again after so long in the south.

Already they could see the next one ahead, high on a hill for vantage. Its thick walls and smoking chimneys promised a warm night away from the demons.

But then they drew closer, and Elissa saw the break in the walls. A scent wafted to her on the wind, and she realized the smoke coming from the station wasn't nearly so inviting.

CHAPTER 18

HOMESTEAD

334 AR

Jeph Bales sucked his pipe in his favorite rocking chair as he watched the yard. His children lined the porch rails, eyes scanning every direction as the sun dipped in the sky. Inside, he could hear Norine and Ilain bustling in the kitchen, readying supper.

Shadows lengthened across the yard, and Jeph resisted the urge to check the wards again. He leaned back, drawing the embers in his pipe bowl to brightness.

His control surprised even him. Sunset had a way of exposing all the fears folk kept bottled during the day, and Jeph had always been a coward. Not a year ago he'd have been pacing the house, checking locks and wards over and over.

Fifteen years ago, he watched from this very spot as his wife Silvy was cored, unable to do more than clench his thighs and hope not to piss himself.

But last summer Renna Tanner appeared in his yard screaming, and years of shame and tension inside him snapped. He picked up his axe, stepped off the porch, and did what he should have done for Silvy all those years ago.

Then came the tattooed Messenger with his warded weapons. Jeph had killed or helped kill thirty-seven demons since then. His favorite method—the safest—was a heavy blow before they could solidify, holding the warded weapon in the wound as its magic drained the demon's power.

Demons came in two types. The first, Regulars, always rose in the same spot, hammering at the same wards with the patience of an immortal, waiting for that one inevitable night when maintenance failed and the forbidding could be breached.

The other type, Wanderers, moved from place to place in search of prey. They shied from places claimed by Regulars unless drawn in by a commotion.

Not long ago, the yard would have been full of misting forms at sunset. But the Messenger scoured it with warded arrows, killing most of the Regulars. Jeph had done for the other Regulars on his land slow and steady, like weeding a field.

His land had been clear for weeks now, but places like Jeph's farm, isolated and stinking of humans and livestock, drew Wanderers that could become Regulars if left unchecked.

"There!" Silvy squealed, pointing to the pigs' day pen. A telltale blurring, like smoke or a summer haze, signaled the rise of a demon not ten feet from where her namesake was cored.

Jeph spat, knocking the burning dottle from his pipe into it, crushing them underfoot.

"Corespawned things're worse'n voles," he said. "Every time I start to relax . . ."

Jeph Young lifted his bow, fitting a warded arrow. "I got it, Da."

"No, you don't." Jeph reached for the handle of his heavy axe mattock. "You stay on the porch and keep an eye for others. Got this."

Jeph admired the boy's spirit, but at fourteen Jeph Young wasn't as good a shot as he liked to think. Demons healed quick. If he failed to kill it, the coreling might flee and return with a will.

He strode into the yard, still marveling how things changed. Striding beyond the wards with a demon materializing in the yard used to mean certain death. Now it was another chore. Dangerous, but so were many tasks on the farm, if you weren't careful.

Jeph was always careful. He kept watch over the forming demon, but scanned the rest of the yard as well, making sure the coreling had not brought friends.

The mist coalesced into the shape of a field demon by the time Jeph reached it. It opened its mouth to hiss at him, but no sound came; the materialization was not yet complete. For a few seconds more, it could not harm him.

But he could harm it. With practiced ease, Jeph swung the mattock up over his shoulders in a smooth arc, letting the heavy blade at the end do most of the work as he brought it down on the demon's head with force enough to split a log.

A normal blade would have bounced off the demon's armored skull, angering it without doing real harm, but Jeph had warded the mattock himself. The symbols flared to life as it struck, sending a jolt of magic up his arms as the blade bit deep and stuck.

He shivered with something akin to pleasure, something akin to lust. Power rushed through him, making him feel strong, invincible. He was nearing fifty, but felt stronger than he had at thirty. His senses came alive, hearing clearly the voices of the children on the porch, the women inside, even the animals locked behind the heavy barn doors across the yard.

He listened for sounds of other demons. For a moment, he even hoped there were more, just so he could feel the rush of power again. So he could take something back, for all they had taken from him. He bared his teeth.

Get hold o' yerself, Jeph Bales you fool. The voice in his head belonged to his father, always speaking common sense. *What kind of idiot hopes for demons in his yard?*

He shook himself, coming back to his senses. He killed demons, but unlike many in the Brook, he hadn't grown to like it. The jolt of power was pleasure like nothing he had ever known, but it was not worth the loss of control. Control was what kept folk alive when others went to the pyre.

"Da! Look out!" Jeph Young called.

Jeph turned to see another form materializing barely a few feet away. Usually the rising occurred right at sunset. *This'n must've slept in,* he thought as it coalesced. Upright and bipedal, it was probably a small wood demon.

He moved quickly to pull this weed as well, but as he raised his mattock, a second demon began to form next to the first. He hesitated.

Ent a match for two, his father said in his head. *Run. Run now.*

Jeph Young shared his father's fears. "Da! Get down!" The boy drew back an arrow and loosed just as the closer of the demons leapt at Jeph, solidifying faster than he would have believed possible. There was a hiss, and the sound of the arrow shaft quivering.

Jeph blinked, seeing the Messenger standing before him, face grim as he held the quivering arrow inches from where it would have struck Jeph's head.

Gone were the Tender's brown robes he had worn on his last visit, though there was no mistaking the Messenger's tattoos. He wore an open-collared shirt of faded white cotton and denim trousers, cuffs rolled away from bare hands and feet.

The Messenger turned to glare at the porch. "You ent learned not to shoot when folk're in the way, Jeph Young, then you got no business holding that bow!"

"Messenger?!" the boy cried. "Thought you was a demon!"

"Boy's got a point," Jeph said, turning back to the man. "You misted like they . . ." His words broke off as he took in the woman who materialized by the Messenger's side. He almost didn't recognize her. She had hacked her long hair away, cut her dress down to almost nothing, and covered herself with painted wards, but the eyes, the shape of her face, so like his wife's, were unmistakable.

"Renna?" he asked. "Renna Tanner?"

"Renna Bales, now," the Messenger said.

"Eh?" Jeph asked, turning back to the man.

The Messenger glanced at the warding on the arrow and grunted. He put a hand on Jeph's shoulder and met his eyes. There was something familiar about that look, but Jeph couldn't place it until the man spoke again. "Got a lot to talk about . . . Da."

Jeph stood there, staring. The yard was dark, but his mattock still tingled with magic that ran up his arm, and his night vision was strong. He peeled away the wards with his mind as he had with Renna, seeing in the man's face an echo of his mother, killed fifteen years past on this very spot.

His knees buckled, and the mattock blade dropped to sink

into the ground at his feet. Suddenly dizzy, he leaned on the handle for support. The air felt thick, the night closing about him like water.

"Arlen?" He couldn't breathe. Couldn't stand.

The Messenger caught him as he stumbled. "Ay, Da. It's me."

Jeph was numb as he escorted his son and—What was Renna to him now? Sister-in-law? Daughter-in-law?—onto the porch.

"Inside and wash up for supper," he told the children. "Tell your mam to set two extra places at the table." They stood their ground, staring at the newcomers, until Jeph clapped his hands. "Go on!"

Jeph couldn't blame the children as he watched them scamper into the house. He moved aside to let his guests enter first, staring at the man his son had become. He could forgive himself for not seeing it before, but now that he knew, the resemblance was unmistakable, wards or no.

Arlen was alive.

His boy had come back a man.

The air at the supper table felt fragile, as if speaking would shatter the dream and the pair would mist away like they had never been there at all. Norine led a brief prayer and they set to eating in silence, even the children sensing the tension. There was none of the usual squabbling, no pinches under the table, no tall tales of the day's work.

"Pass the taters, please?" Arlen asked Cholie, and the boy jumped like he'd seen a ghost. In a way, he had. The ghost of his elder brother, now returned and asking for taters.

Finally Ilain could stand it no more. "Gonna take some gettin' used to, Ren. You bein' my daughter-in-law."

"Shun't be hard. Been acting like you was mam for years." There was something about the way Renna said the words, like there was a barb to follow. Creator knew, there were plenty to throw. Their mother had died when Renna was young, and Ilain ran off with Jeph only a few years later, leaving her sisters to the care of their coreson of a father.

Ilain tensed, waiting for the slap, but whatever she might have said, Renna swallowed it, painting a smile on her face.

She looked at the children. "Goin' by my niece and nephews, looks like you've got a knack for the job."

Ilain let out a breath, returning the smile. "Been blessed to learn from my mistakes." She turned to Arlen before either of them could muddy the waters. "Guess you kept your promise after all, comin' back for Ren like that."

Jeph grit his teeth. Couldn't the fool woman leave well enough alone? Was she determined to drive them away again?

But Arlen seemed to seize on the words as a lifeline. "Din't come back for Ren. Came back to see home one more time, and to make sure you had the wards to protect yourself. To make sure what happened . . ." He paused like Renna had, thinking better of his words. ". . . to so many families in the Brook," he nodded to Norine, "never had to happen again. But when I saw Ren there, staked . . ." He shook his head. "Couldn't just stand by, could I?"

There was an awkward silence around the table, for standing by was what they—what the entire town—had done.

"Course not." Jeph found his voice at last, meeting his son's eye. "That ent ever been your way, thank the Creator. Shamed the whole town, but we needed shamin'."

Arlen gave an almost imperceptible nod. "Remembered Ren. Thought of her some nights while I was . . . away. Kiss she gave me that last night before Mam died." He shook his head. "Din't believe a handshake between das made us promised, really. Figured a woman like her would've found someone else." He turned, taking her hand and looking her in the eyes. "Been to Miln and the Krasian desert. Seen most everyplace worth seein' in between. Lot of folk tried to find me a wife and settle me down, but it never took. Who knew the one for me was waitin' back at home all along?"

"I knew." Renna squeezed his hand. "But Arlen Bales has always been stubborn."

"Ay, that's undersaid," Jeph agreed, and the laughter about the table seemed almost at ease.

"Think it's romantic," Jeni Tailor said, taking Jeph Young's hand. They were promised, no doubt in much the same way, though it would be years yet before they were old enough to marry. "Would you cross the world and back for me, Jephy?"

Jeph Young looked green, coughing something that approximated assent. Jeni seemed not to notice his discomfort, smile undiminished.

"You two back for good, then?" Ilain asked. "Come home to start a family? We been talkin' about buildin' a new house—takin' on hands. Folk're flocking to the Brook from Sunny Pasture. Things're better all around, even with the troubles."

Arlen looked up at that. "Troubles?"

"Cholie, Silvy," Jeph said. "Clear the table and put on the kettle, then run off and play a bit."

"Made a sweet cake this morning," Norine said. "Savin' it for after Seventhday service, but this is a special occasion. Jeni? Why don't you and Jeph Young slice it up and bring the tea?"

"I want to stay," Jeph Young whined.

"You and Jeni can come back to the table when the tea and cake are ready," Jeph allowed. "Now scoot!"

The children scurried off, and Jeph got up from the table, taking his time fetching his pipe and weed pouch. He offered the pouch to his son. "I've a spare pipe . . ."

"S'all right," Arlen said, waving a hand. "Used to smoke sometimes, when I was a Messenger. Made me think of home. Now I'm here . . ." He shrugged. "Don't feel right."

Jeph nodded, grateful for the excuse to drop his eyes as he packed the bowl and took a taper to light it. He puffed a moment, bringing the weed to a glow and surrounding himself with a fragrant cloud before returning to his seat. "Things been . . . messy since you left. Brook's prospering, but folk're . . ."

"Harder," Ilain supplied.

"Folk found the stones to fight corelings," Norine said, "but some . . . got to like it."

Arlen nodded. "Ent unexpected. They causin' trouble?"

"Nothin' Selia can't handle," Jeph puffed his pipe. "She put a militia together—cleared most of the demons been hauntin' Town Square and Boggin's Hill. Brine's got things harder in the Cluster by the Woods, but the Cutters took to choppin' wood demons like it was second nature."

"Not surprisin'," Arlen said. "Bet they're turning out more lumber than they have in years."

"Ay." Jeph set the pipe in his teeth. "Most everyone's yield is up. Ent no empty bellies in the Brook."

"Good news," Arlen said. "You'll be needin' lumber for your new fence."

"New fence?"

"Gonna show you a new kind of wardin' we tested out in Cutter's Hollow," Arlen said. "Put an end to demons on your land once and for all."

Jeph took the pipe from his mouth, exhaling a cloud of sweet smoke. "Sounds too good to be trusted."

"Plenty o' bad news to go with it," Arlen said. "Get to that. Want to finish hearin' about things in the Brook. Fishin' Hole still givin' you trouble?"

"Bit, at first." Jeph leaned back. "But without wards for their fishing spears, other folk got . . ."

"Stronger," Arlen supplied. "Killin' demons does that."

Jeph nodded. "Fisherfolk couldn't push people around after that. Raddock kept tryin' to hold firm, but folk wanted protection from the militia and voted him down. He's still Speaker, but ent got the pull he once did."

"Don't approve, what they done," Norine said. "But Creator my witness, ent a good time to be a Fisher. Militia bullies 'em somethin' nasty, and takes more'n a fair share o' fish."

"Need to put a stop to that, 'fore it gets worse," Arlen said.

"Reckon they got it comin'," Renna said. Fishing Hole led the mob that staked her out for the demons after her father killed Cobie Fisher.

"Raddock Lawry's got it comin', Ren," Arlen agreed. "Garrick Fisher, maybe. But they been shown the error of their ways. Ent no good can come from punishin' the rest of the borough for a couple waterbrains. We're all on the same side against the demons."

Renna looked ready to argue, but she only nodded. "I'll skate over and talk to Selia about it after cake."

"Skate?" Jeph asked.

"Bit of a . . . magic trick I picked up in my travels," Arlen said. "How Ren and I got here."

"You misted," Jeph said. Night, he had almost forgotten. "Rose up like demons, steada comin' in on that big scary . . ."

He trailed off, but Arlen only chuckled. "Ay, Dancer can be

intimidatin' when he's not kickin' in a demon's skull. Faster'n any horse you ever seen, but even that's a crawl when you can mist down underground and ride the currents."

"Currents?" Ilain asked.

"Magic currents," Renna said. "Run up from the Core like streams from a pond. Learn how, and you can ride 'em like a paper boat."

"Nonsense," Norine said.

"Show you later," Arlen said. His matter-of-fact tone quieted her. No attempt to convince—he spoke of something impossible like it was a new plowshare he'd show off after tea. "That the worst of the Brook's troubles? Folk pickin' on the Fishers?"

Jeph shook his head. "Jeorje."

Arlen frowned but kept his peace as Jeni and Jeph Young brought out the tea and cake. Jeorje Watch, Speaker and Tender for Southwatch, had stood as magistrate when the town council decided to put Renna out in the night.

Arlen held Jeph's eyes, waiting. When the plates and cups were settled, Jeph Young and Jeni back in their seats, Jeph could hesitate no more. "Southwatch seceded from the Brook once they got the fightin' wards."

Arlen took a spoonful of honey and put it in his tea. "Wern't much part o' things to begin with."

"I was a girl," Norine put in, "Watches were as much part o' the Brook as any borough. But then Jeorje got in a feud with the Town Speaker, Selia's da, after one o' his granddaughters got cored in Town Square. Watches stopped comin' round after that, 'cept once in a while to trade or answer the great horn. No one talks about it, but they say both sides hold a grudge."

"How long ago was that?" Arlen asked.

Norine shrugged. "Fifty years, give or take."

"Long time to carry a grudge," Arlen said.

"Hard feelings only get heavier with the years," Jeph said. "Till the weight of it breaks you, and you snap."

"What did he do?" Arlen asked, cutting the sweet cake with his fork.

Jeph forced himself to lean back and take a puff of his pipe. "Annexed Soggy Marsh."

Arlen had just taken a bite of cake when his eyes snapped up. "Say again?"

Jeph pulled on his pipe. "Marshes were always queer folk. Kept to themselves, had their own ways. Din't like their young'uns coming to Town Square—too many wanted to stay once the mud on their clothes dried off. And they got their own demons in the Marsh. Ent like the ones out here."

"Ay," Arlen nodded. "Swamp demon spit can eat through iron, and they run across branches like coons. Bog demons are slow, but they blend into the trees and got terrifyin' reach. And that's not even gettin' to the ones in the water . . ."

Jeph swallowed. "Ay. Well the Marshes were having a harder time than any, clearing their lands of corelings. Lost some folk and turned resentful. That's when Jeorje made his offer."

"What offer?" Arlen's voice had gone cold.

"Protection, same as Selia's militia gives the Fishers," Jeph said.

"And in exchange?" Arlen pressed.

"They convert," Jeph said. "Accept Jeorje as Tender and Speaker, both. Give him young wives and a weekly tithe."

Jeph met Arlen's eyes. "Thinks he's the Deliverer."

"Corespawn it!" Arlen threw down his fork.

"Ent no one to blame but yourself," Norine said. "You put that fool notion in his head and it took."

"That was rippin' sarcasm," Arlen growled.

"I know it," Norine said. "Everyone north o' the Marsh knows it. But they got different notions in Southwatch."

"What if he is?" Jeph Young asked.

Jeph looked at his son. "Eh?"

"What if he really is the Deliverer?" Jeph Young asked again.

"He ent," Arlen said.

"He's a hundred and eleven," Jeni put in. "But they say he's got black hair, and leads the fighting. Ent a demon left alive in Southwatch."

"Magic can do that," Arlen said. "Killin' demons can make

old folk young, make you stronger, but that don't make you the Deliverer."

"Selia's hair has gone yellow at the roots," Norine said. "And she's older'n me. Don't make her the Deliverer."

"Creator, I'm feeling it, too," Jeph said. "Back used to hurt so bad on plow days I couldn't move. Now I'm pushin' the corespawned thing without a horse."

"You listen to me, Jeph Young," Arlen said. "As your brother and your elder. Ent no such thing as a Deliverer. That's work every man and woman's got to do for themselves. Can't count on someone to save you from the demons. Learn to save yourself—and others, when you can."

Jeph nodded. "Good advice, your brother's got."

"This is goin' to mean trouble for the Brook, you don't put a stop to it," Arlen said. "Corelings ent all brainless. Tend to notice when a leader organizes folk to kill off all the Regulars. Draw attention the Brook ent ready for."

"Maybe we can set him straight," Renna said.

"Too risky," Arlen said. "Watches think too much of Jeorje. Liable to backfire, you try and spank him like you did Franq."

Jeph felt a growing dread in his stomach. "What kind of attention will it draw?"

Arlen looked around. "Got paper?"

Jeph shook his head. "Hogs got it at a premium, these days."

Arlen looked at the table, then to Ilain. "Know it ent good manners, but I need to paint on the tablecloth. Wouldn't ask, it wern't important."

"Ay, that's all right," Ilain said, though the cloth had been a gift from Selia when their first child was born. She looked at it sadly as Arlen unrolled his warding kit, selecting a worn brush and a jar of black ink.

"Mind demons can only rise at new moon," Arlen said. "Night before, night of, night after." He painted a large ward on the tablecloth. "Need this ward to keep 'em out or they can rummage through your thoughts and memories like an old drawer."

"How does it connect to a circle?" Jeph asked.

Arlen showed how to link the ward to others, his hand

steady as ever. Jeph had taught him personally, and always been proud when his young son's skill began to exceed even his.

"Don't take chances," Arlen said. "Start watching the calendar, and on new moon nights put the ward on a necklace, band of your hat, even a strip of cloth around your forehead. Kids, too."

"Demons get smart, when a mind's around," Renna said. "Start workin' together, usin' weapons an' tools, throwin' stones."

"Night." Jeph had to squeeze his legs together to hold his bladder. "What do you do against that?"

"First step is to banish them from your property." Arlen began a new warding, this one much larger and more complex than any Jeph had ever seen. "This is a greatward." He continued drawing as he spoke. "Need to shape your property with it."

Jeph gaped. "How's that?"

"Fences and walls, mostly," Arlen said, waving a hand over the jagged edge of the symbol. "House and barn are here." He sketched little buildings inside the ward. "Lay stone paths for the inner lines, or plant shrubs." He pointed with the brush handle. "Maybe build a funny-roofed shed over here. You can plant right up to the fence. Closer the better—it'll strengthen the ward."

"Back aches just thinkin' about it," Jeph said.

"Ay, it's a lot of work," Arlen agreed. "But not so much when you never have a demon on your land again. Kids can walk the yard after dark. Animals won't need to go in the barn every night."

"How do you make a ward that big without mistakes?" Jeph asked.

Arlen took a straightstick from his kit and began drawing a measured grid over the ward. "Make a grid outside and match. Build a little tower on the roof, so you can look down on it."

Jeph considered the drawing. There were familiar wards contained within, overlaying one another. "Say you've tried this elsewhere?"

Arlen nodded. "Whole towns being built to shape in Angiers. Streets themselves are the lines of protection."

Arlen reached out, putting a hand on Jeph's shoulder. It was a fatherly gesture, something he never expected to get from his own son. "Need you to do this, Da. Need you to do it quick as you can, and show it to others. Call a council meetin', and give out the mind wards, as well. Could mean the life of every man, woman, and child in the Brook."

Jeph laid a hand over his son's. "Get it done. Swear it by the sun."

Selia Barren still felt the tingle in her fingers as the militia rode back into Town Square, heading home after a quiet patrol. The town's Regulars had long since been killed off, and these nightly patrols did for most of the Wanderers. They only found one demon tonight, and Selia speared it personally.

The skin on her hands was smoother now, wrinkles all but gone. Even her face had lost its lines, save for a few creases at the eyes and mouth.

"Ready to call it a night, that's all right with you, Speaker." Lucik Boggin fingered his spear wistfully as they approached the road to Boggin's Hill. Like many of the others, he'd grown to crave the thrill of magic.

"Ay, go on home and get some rest," Selia said. "And be thankful for the quiet nights. Creator knows they aren't all so."

"We've prayed for three hundred years to have a night so quiet." Tender Harral didn't carry a spear, but his crooked staff was carved with impact wards and defenses. A big man, he could hook a demon by the throat, pull it from its feet, and bash its head in. But for all his ferocity, the Tender never seemed taken with ichor lust.

"Ay, quiet night does us all good." Lucik turned his horse up the road, followed by Harral and the other men and women from Boggin's Hill.

"Be takin' our leave, too," Ferd Miller said. "Got to report in."

"Can't keep old Hog waitin'." Selia dismissed the men with a nod. Rusco Hog seldom rode out with the militia, but he hired men to bolster the ranks in his name.

"Wonder if they get a cut in pay, they don't bring back a coreling to hold down for him," Coline Trigg mused.

It was a fair question. Hog didn't fight, but he'd grown as addicted to demon magic as any. It was no secret his men brought him demons to spear, so he could steal a bit of their power. It was dangerous work, but Hog paid well for it.

"Hog's shed almost as many gray hairs as I have," Selia said. "Can't put a price on that."

"Yet somehow, Hog managed to find a way." The Herb Gatherer's words were only a little bitter. Coline never fought, still burdened by weight and age even as the new combat wards restored others to their physical prime. Still she rode with the patrol each night, ready with her needles and poultices when one of them was injured.

"Want us to hold down a coreling for you, mistress?" Lesa Square asked. The girl was barely twenty, but magic had made her strong. Muscles rippled along her bare arms. The hands that held her spear were crisscrossed with tiny scars. But there was a softness about her, too. A roundness in her pretty face that . . .

Selia shook her head, turning away before she was caught staring.

Coline sniffed, turning up her nose. "Ent natural. We're born, we grow old, we die. That's the way o' things. Maybe the Creator wants you fighters stronger—I'm no Tender to guess His plan—but holdin' a coreling down so I can suck it like a skeeter? Ent for me."

"Don't know what you're missin'," Lesa said.

"Enough of that," Selia said loudly. "Rest of you head on to your beds. Got work to do under the sun, no matter what the night brings."

The remainder of the patrol broke off for home as Selia headed down the road alone. Not long ago such a ride would have been fraught with fear, but Selia was alert, her senses alive with the rush of magic. Her spear was in easy reach, and the wards cut into her horse's hooves could break demon bones.

The safety of the town center should have relaxed her, but it served as a reminder that bigger questions loomed. The outer boroughs and farms still had demon problems, not to mention the looming threat of Southwatch and Jeorje.

For everyone's sake, her father and the Tender from Southwatch kept the scandal quiet, all those years ago. But Jeorje hadn't forgotten. He wouldn't rest until everyone in Tibbet's Brook was dressed in black clothes buttoned tight, following his strict interpretation of Canon.

Preferably with me staked out in Town Square.

She reached her property, crossing the wards and taking her mare to the stall behind her cottage. She lit a lantern and brushed the animal down, giving it water and grain, then headed for the house.

Lesa stepped from the shadows, grinning like she'd just stolen a cookie. She was quick, grabbing Selia by the back of her neck and pulling her close. Her lips were soft, slick with scented wax. It tasted of honeysuckle and made Selia's mouth water.

She pushed Lesa back, drawing a breath she hoped sounded more dignified than a gasp. "Fool girl! What in the Core you think you're doing?! What if someone saw?"

"Don't care." Lesa reached for her again.

Selia batted the hands away. "Course you don't. Ent got a notion what we're in for, word gets out."

Lesa's smile didn't waver. "Circled the block before I came. Mam won't know if I take an extra hour. I could come inside . . ."

She moved in close again, and Selia felt her heart thudding in her chest. Vitality thrummed in her, her senses alive. She could smell Lesa's sweat, the scent of her arousal. She felt her own as well, slick between the legs like she hadn't been in thirty years.

"Can't keep takin' you to bed," Selia said. "Night, girl, I've fifty summers on you!"

Lesa shrugged, putting hands around Selia's waist and pushing her against the wall of the stall. "Can do it here, you prefer. No one'll see." She reached down, tugging at Selia's skirt.

In a moment, she would squat down, and Selia, corespawn her, wouldn't stop her. She glanced at the house, and Lesa's nose crinkled in victory. But then Selia's sharp eyes caught a movement in the shadows. She stiffened, pushing Lesa back as she searched in the dim light for the source of the movement.

Lesa was immediately on guard, hand dropping to the warded knife at her belt. "What is it? Coreling?"

Selia shook her head. "Jumpin' at shadows. Run on home now."

"But . . . !" Lesa whined. The tone was a reminder of her youth, and only hardened Selia's revolve.

"Another time," Selia said. "Scoot!"

Lesa's shoulders slumped, but she left. Selia waited till she was gone, then turned to the shadowed porch and crossed her arms. "Might as well come on out."

She didn't recognize the young woman at first, seeing only the bare arms, legs, and midsection, covered with painted wards. Her hair was roughly cropped from her face, with a long braid in back. She had the look of the Messenger—not just the warded flesh, but the predatory look in her eyes. From there, it took only a moment to guess.

"Renna Tanner, come back to Tibbet's Brook," she said.

Renna stepped further into the lamplight. "Ent a Tanner no more. Got married."

"Congratulations," Selia said. "The Messenger, I take it?"

Renna nodded. "Renna Bales, now. Folk used to call you Selia Barren, but tonight's got me wonderin' they got it wrong. Maybe you ent barren after all."

Selia put her hands on her hips, foot tapping. "Gonna tell folk?"

"Ent my business who kisses who," Renna said. "Sure as sunrise ent the business of the town. I should know."

"Thank you," Selia said.

"Don't owe me thanks," Renna said. "Other way 'round. Night take me 'fore I turn on you, Speaker. Wern't in my right head, but I remember what you did for me. Stood by me when my own kith an' kin din't have the stones."

Selia's throat tightened. "I failed you."

Renna moved close, and Selia saw again how pretty she was. The wards and cropped hair gave her a fierce look not unlike Lesa's.

"Din't," Renna said. "Gave me time to pull my head back together. Time for Arlen to come and fetch me."

Selia started, all thoughts of Renna's beauty forgotten. "Arlen? Arlen *Bales*? Are you tellin' me that rippin' Messenger who turned the Brook on its ear is Jeph Bales' boy?"

"Ay," Renna said. "And that ent all, by a long sight."

Selia sighed. "Come inside, girl. I'll put the kettle on."

Jeph and Arlen sat on the porch with a pitcher of Boggin's Ale. The whole scene felt like a dream, even if they hadn't just watched Renna turn into mist and vanish.

The children whooped at the sight and were a terror getting to bed after, but now all was quiet save for the crickets and the sound of Jeph's rocking chair.

"Strange, settin' on this porch again after so many years, starin' at the yard like nothin's changed," Arlen said.

"But they have," Jeph said. "Remember you used to peek through the shutters every night, lookin' for corelings. Won't find those in my yard anymore."

"Ay, for now." Arlen sipped his ale, eyes distant.

Jeph cleared his throat. "Might as well talk about the coreling in the common. Can't be easy, lookin' out at the place your mam got cored. Settin' in the spot I was rooted to, tryin' not to piss myself while you ran out to save her."

"Ent," Arlen agreed, taking another sip. "Older now, though. Seen more o' the world. Seen what the demons done to folk. Made 'em feel helpless, like there was no point in fightin' back."

"But you did," Jeph said. "Eleven years old, you fought the demons and won."

"Din't win," Arlen said. "Just managed not to die."

"Stopped 'em killin' your mam," Jeph said.

Arlen sighed. "Din't do that, either. Bought her a couple days, but wern't any stoppin' it."

"Might have been," Jeph said, "I'd had the stones to press on to Old Mey Friman."

Arlen shook his head. "Thought that back then. Thought it for years after, and blamed you. Hated you."

Jeph grit his teeth at the words. He'd imagined his son's

spirit telling them to him for fifteen years, but it was another thing to have him there in the flesh, saying them.

"But I seen a lot of folk cored since then," Arlen said. "We'd had a Hollow Gatherer here on the farm that night, Mam might've made it. Even if Coline Trigg had known her business the next day like a proper Gatherer in the Free Cities. But by the time we'd of made it to Mey . . ." He spat over the porch rail. "Too late."

"Wasn't too late when your mam called me for help, though," Jeph said.

"Ay." Arlen kept his eyes on the yard, taking another sip of ale.

"Ent got any excuses," Jeph said. "Ilain's been a good wife. Love her and the young'uns. But I could go back, I'd undo it all to have your mam back, even if it meant taking her place on the claw. Loved her all my life. Used to break my horseshoes on purpose . . ."

"Just for an excuse to see her at the farrier shop," Arlen finished. "Mam loved tellin' that'un."

Jeph choked, clenching his throat and squeezing his eyes. His son had a right to hate him, and he wasn't about to try to guilt him to sympathy with tears.

"Failed you both, that night," Jeph managed when he had recovered himself.

"Ay," Arlen said. "Won't lie. Carried a lot of anger at you on my travels. Used to hear you in my head, times I was thinkin' of doing somethin' foolhardy. Hated that voice. Used to do fool things, just to spite it."

Jeph snorted, and Arlen looked at him in surprise.

"Ent funny," Jeph said. "Only made me think how I hear my da's voice in my head, same way. Callin' me fool, every time I try'n screw my courage up."

Arlen sat back, taking another drink. "Ay. Maybe it's just the way o' das and their boys."

"Ay," Jeph said.

"Meant to have a reckoning, I came back to the Brook last year," Arlen said. "Out of my head, back then. Convinced I'd become somethin' . . . inhuman. Ready to die, and wanted to settle accounts 'fore I let the night take me."

"Creator." Jeph wanted to reach out to his son, but his hand betrayed him. If he reached out and Arlen pushed him away, he didn't think he could bear it.

"Don't care what you done," he said instead. "What you become. Seen what you done for your mam. What you done for Renna. What you done for this town. You ent human, what hope the rest of us got?"

"All have our low moments," Arlen said. "Things we carry even when folk around us forget, or never knew."

"Honest word," Jeph said. "Carried those few days with me like they just happened, even as the years blew by."

"Know you did," Arlen said. "That night made the world clear to both of us, in our way. Took a while, but when the night came callin' in the yard again, you din't set on the porch. Expected us to fight, I came back, but then I heard what you done for Ren, and realized what a fool I been."

"Had every right to carry a grudge," Jeph said.

"Ay, maybe, but grudges never made anyone a better man," Arlen said.

"Honest word." Jeph eased a bit, taking a long pull of his ale. "Any chance you two come home for good, like Lainie hopes? Be good for the young'uns to get to know their brother."

"Like to," Arlen said. "Creator, dunno anything I'd like more. But it ent in the dice. Truer is, come back to say goodbye."

Jeph blinked. "Goodbye?"

Arlen rubbed the back of his neck. "'Fraid I might've . . . started a bit of a war, when I brought back the fightin' wards. Time's come to settle it, and things're apt to get ugly. Wern't right, not tellin' you who I was last time. Needed to set that right."

Jeph had begun to relax, but the tension returned. "Ugly, how?"

Arlen blew out a breath, then raised a finger, drawing wards in the air. Jeph found himself clutching his cup and had to force his hand to unclench as he waited.

"Like I said," Arlen said when he was done, "fightin' back draws attention from a particularly nasty breed o' demon. They came at us, got a kickin' for it, and now they're plannin' to come back in force. Got this crazy plan to meet 'em on their own ground before it goes down."

Jeph felt his face go cold and his bladder strain. He clenched tight, hoping Arlen didn't notice. "Own ground?"

Arlen tilted his head toward the ground. "Downstairs."

"Creator," Jeph said. "How's that even possible?"

"Can't say," Arlen said. "Mind demons can pinch your thoughts like a carrot from a field. More I say, more I endanger the plan."

"Ren's all right with this? You going off . . . below?" The idea was still numbing to Jeph, almost too big to grasp, but he'd watched Renna turn into mist and slip into the ground. This wasn't much harder to believe.

"Don't go tellin' her sister, but Ren's comin', too," Arlen said. "And a couple others."

"Take an army," Jeph said.

"Armies draw notice. Takin' just enough to get the job done, but few enough to sneak." Arlen took another drink. "Least, I hope I am. Truer is, dunno if I'm pullin' out a rotten stump or breaking open a hornet's nest."

Jeph wanted to argue. To convince Arlen to abandon this path, to come home and be safe. Looking at his son, he knew that was what he expected, the father's voice urging caution to the son.

The look hardened him to the fear. There was never any turning Arlen from a path once he set his mind to it, but perhaps Jeph could ease his doubts. "Never know what you're gettin' with either, son. Had stumps give me such trouble I'd welcome a stingin', and hives that dropped into the sack and tied up neat as can be. But you can't leave either one on your property without regrettin' it."

"Ay," Arlen said. "Thanks, Da."

"Sounds like we both got our work cut out for us," Jeph said. "You really think one o' them mind demon's going to try and nest in the Brook?"

Arlen shrugged. "Sooner or late. Might be next month, might be in a decade, but you keep killin' demons and one's sure to check in. Too many folk in the Brook, and they know from my memories you're here, far from help."

"What're we supposed to do about that?" Jeph asked.

"Just demons, Da," Arlen said. "Smarter'n most, and got their tricks, but I killed more'n one. Renna, too. We ent the Deliverer. Just Brook folk like you and everyone else in town. We could do it, so can the rest of you."

He finished his ale. "No more standin' still. Night's gonna come get us, we don't get it first."

CHAPTER 19

HUNTED

334 AR

"We're going to die," Keerin whined, looking at the smoking ruin of Euchor's way station. The walls were smashed, deep claw marks visible on the stone, and coreling prints covered the hard ground around the ruined structure. The air was thick with the acrid stink of burning flesh and the noxious tang of demonshit.

Elissa opened her mouth, but Ragen was faster, reaching out to grab the front of the Jongleur's motley. He nearly pulled Keerin from his horse to face him nose-to-nose. "Say that again and you won't have to worry about being cored. I'll kill you myself and no one under the sun will miss you."

"Jongleur ought to know better'n to talk like that," Yon said. "Yur job to stoke us up, not start a panic. Best get that lute ready. Gonna be a long night."

Keerin looked at the man as if he were mad. "Just what in the Core is my lute going to do in the naked night?"

"Ay, Core if I know." Yon made a vague strumming motion. "Rojer could charm demons so they'd never know we was there."

"Well it didn't keep Halfgrip from getting killed, did it?" Keerin snapped.

Yon balled a heavy fist. "Keep talkin' like'at, ya little pissant, Ragen's gonna have to get in line."

Keerin eased his horse away from the men, but others were

watching the exchange and casting nervous glances at the devastated way station. Hollowers expected more from their Jongleurs, it seemed.

Elissa nudged her horse his way, rooting in her saddlebag until she found the leather case from Hary Roller.

"The Jongleurs' Guildmaster in the Hollow gave us these." She handed a sheaf of papers to Keerin. "Music he claims will allow any skilled Jongleur to influence the corelings."

"Ridiculous," Keerin said, but he took the papers and flipped through them. They were covered with lines and symbols Elissa could not read, but hoped would make sense to the man.

"These are no simple songs." Keerin glanced at the setting sun. "Am I supposed to master them in two hours?"

Elissa kept her face serene, but Ragen could tell even she was losing patience. "Unless you want to end up in a demon's belly. I suggest you start practicing."

Keerin pulled hard on his reins, turning his horse sharply away, but he pulled the lute from his saddle and led his horse to a broken bit of stone wall where he could sit while the others inspected the wreckage.

"That was well done, my love." Ragen slipped from his saddle, handing off the reins.

"I don't know how you expected to inspire the man by threatening to kill him." Elissa dismounted as well, accepting the kiss he planted on her cheek.

"I wasn't looking to inspire," Ragen said, "only to shut him up. Things are grim enough without that kind of talk."

"They are," Elissa agreed. "If you want to live to tell the tale, you'd best stop threatening and start inspiring."

Ragen stared at her in surprise, but after a moment he nodded. "Wise words, Mother."

Elissa winked as they made their way into the way station. Inside, the smoke and reek were so overpowering they had to wet a cloth and tie it over their faces, but Ragen insisted on a full sweep of the place, looking for survivors.

There were none. Blood spattered the stones, and here and there lay piles of white human bones jutting from dark, oily excrement. They found charred remains of a handful of corelings, but the station's complement had been thirty men, all of them armed with flamework weapons.

"It seems Euchor's weapons don't work as well against the demons as he hoped." Ragen didn't sound terribly surprised.

"Ay," Yon said. "Even caught by surprise, thirty men with warded weapons should've given better'n this."

Ragen glanced at the shattered walls. "No point staying here. We're not going to repair the wardnet before nightfall."

"We could use it to hide," Elissa suggested. "If the demons already think the place destroyed, and we draw a few wards of confusion and unsight . . ."

Ragen shook his head. "If there were only a few of us, perhaps. But our group is too large, and this place is about to be swarmed, come sunset. They'll have our scent even if they can't see us."

"Perhaps they moved on," Elissa said.

"Dun't work like that," Yon said. "Cories rise in the same place they misted the last dawn, and it looks like they stuck around to eat."

"Demons are known to haunt settlements they destroy," Ragen added, "in hope more humans will be drawn there. Best ride fast as we can for an hour, then circle the wagons and set wards before nightfall."

"Forward or back?" Yon asked.

Ragen scowled. "If the demons are attacking way stations, neither is safe. I mean to get home, Yon."

"Ay, and we'll get ya there," Yon said.

"Ragen." Elissa's voice was tight. "What if this wasn't an attack on the station? What if they know we're on the road, and they're cutting off our succor?"

"Well past new moon," Yon said. "Ent any minds about."

"They didn't need minds to hunt us on the road to Angiers," Elissa said.

Yon shuddered, dropping a hand to his axe handle.

Ragen turned to Elissa. "You're right, but I don't see how it changes anything. Ditching the wagons and trying to make a run for it is premature. I know a spot up the road where we'll be able to see them coming."

Ragen could hear the cries of the coreling for miles as they raced up the road. There could be little doubt now that the demons had been lying in wait.

"You were right, Liss. We're being hunted."

"This is one time I would have been happy to be wrong," Elissa said.

Ragen ran his eyes over their camp. They had chosen the best available spot, with clear visibility for the Hollowers' crank bows and few trees or stones for demons to use against them. The wards on the ring of wagons were strong, and Ragen, Elissa, and Derek supervised staking the wardposts of the outer ring personally.

But if there was truly an intelligence behind the attack, even those protections—which had seen Ragen through thirty years of night travel—might not be enough.

"Maybe we should have abandoned the wagons and ridden hard for the next station," Ragen said. "Or hired a larger escort after the attack on the road to Angiers."

"You might as well wish we never left home in the first place," Elissa said.

Ragen's smile was humorless. "It wasn't as if Briar actually needed us to rescue him."

Elissa took his hand. "Mistakes are easy to see, when you look back."

Inside the ring of wagons, the animals made nervous sounds as the demons grew closer, mingling with the increasingly desperate twangs of Keerin's lute as the Jongleur struggled with Rojer's music sheets. The sounds had little effect as the faster demons began to appear, field and flame demons circling, eyes aflame in the darkness.

"Sing!" Yon shouted to the Cutters positioned along the perimeter of the outer circle. The men and women of their escort stood with a calm Ragen envied, crank bows ready, and lifted their voices in *Keep the Hearthfire Burning*.

The demons were not swept up by the song as they had been in the Hollow, but neither did they like it. Flame demons spat fire at the singers, the burning droplets skittering across the web of magic from the outer wardnet. Field demons shrieked and threw themselves at the net, rebounding as the magic flared.

Normal demons instinctively stepped back when a wardnet flared and hurt them. They would growl and cautiously circle the wards, probing only now and then.

But these demons were different. They struck hard, again and again, moving incrementally along the net, searching aggressively for gaps in the protection.

Ragen could see the web every time the wards activated. Its interlacing protections were tight and regular. They wouldn't get in that way, but too many corelings could short out the web. It would take dozens of demons striking in unison, but more arrived every moment, surrounding their camp. Ragen could see them flitting just beyond the wardlight.

"Thin 'em out!" Yon called, and the crank bows twanged, sending heavy warded bolts thudding into the nearest demons at point-blank range. Corelings dropped to the ground, some killed outright, others convulsing as the warded bolts lodged in their bodies continued to turn their own magic against them.

It was a satisfying moment, but it didn't last as the ranks were immediately filled with new demons. Cannibal by nature, they even ignored their fallen to resume testing the wards.

"Light!" Ragen raised his stylus, Elissa and Derek mirroring him at even intervals around the circle. As one they set light wards hanging in the sky, bright as day around their camp. Wind demons, circling silently above, shrieked and veered away.

Ragen's heart sank as the horde surrounding them was revealed. In addition to field, flame, and wood demons, stone demons were coming up the road, hauling rubble from the ruined way station. The ward circle would prevent the demons from entering, but it would do nothing to slow thrown rock, and if they should strike the wards and mar the circle . . .

"Bows!" Yon cried, and the Cutters raised their heavy crank bows. "Chip away at the stones!"

Ragen hesitated, trying to gauge the range of the weapons against how far the demons might throw. Stone demons were terrifyingly strong, but they couldn't throw farther than Hollow crank bows.

Neither, it seemed, could the crank bows keep them from

getting into range. Bolts that skewered lesser demons skittered off or were caught in the outer layers of stone armor, angering the demons more than harming them.

One of them came into range with a bristle of sizzling bolts across its chest, drawing back a great arm to fling a rock the size of an apple crate.

Ragen drew heat and impact wards, but again he overpowered the spell, and the silver stylus flew from his hand. The stone was shattered to pebbles, taking one of the demon's hands with it. It clutched the crippled limb, screaming, even as Ragen turned and began frantically searching the ground for his stylus.

Another stone demon readied a throw, but Derek drew a deft impact ward that batted the stone from its hand like a ball.

More stone demons were coming up the road, even as Ragen got to hands and knees, pawing through the sod for his stylus. A third readied a throw, and Elissa drew a cold ward that struck it in the shoulder. When it brought its arm forward in the throw, there was a great *crack!* and the limb broke off, falling to the ground alongside the hunk of rubble.

Ragen found his stylus and used his fine warded cloak to clean the mud from it, turning to see a stone strike Gema Cutter full in the chest, knocking her out of line and throwing her back to crash through one of the carts, opening a gap in the inner circle.

Night. How old was Gema? Younger than Arlen. Her warded armor might have withstood the blow, but even so, no one could survive an impact like that.

"That tears it!" Yon cried. "Cutters! Tools out!"

The men began to swing their axes, picks, and mattocks, splitting any demon fool enough to draw close to the wardnet like cordwood. The women continued to shoot, covering the men.

Two more chunks of rubble smashed into the Cutter ranks. Lary Cutter struggled back to his feet using his long-handled axe as a crutch. His brother Fil remained on the ground, convulsing in his smashed armor.

Demons concentrated fire on that spot, and finally a stone smashed one of the outer wardposts, opening a breach. Field and flame demons raced for the spot, and were met by a wall of Cutter shields. Yon and his men threw them back, hewing limbs and bodies with their axes.

Ragen drew more wards, shattering the chest of a stone demon. The rock it lifted fell upon its dead body, but Ragen's momentary satisfaction vanished when another demon picked up the stone and hurled it at him. He barely threw himself aside in time, and the stone blasted a hole in one of the wagons. On the far side he heard an animal scream.

A field demon leapt from the shadows, throwing itself at Yon. Elissa drew a field ward and the coreling slammed into the forbiddance like a bird into a window, giving Yon time to split its skull.

A wood demon reached for Lary, and she set it ablaze with a heat ward. The coreling stumbled, setting the scrub and grass alight, scattering its fellows. She drew a cold ward before the flames could spread, and the fire winked out, the demon crashing stiff to the ground, white with hoarfrost.

The hairs on her arm stood on end as she drew the lectric ward, arcing lightning through a group of field demons racing toward Ragen, dropping them twitching onto their sides. The effect was temporary, but it bought them a few moments.

But then she fell into shadow, and looked up to see a huge chunk of masonry arching toward her from above. She shrieked and threw herself to the ground as the masonry smashed the wardpost in front of her and bounced past, missing her by inches. She felt the wind as it passed.

A field demon raced through the breach at her, so fast she barely drew a forbidding in time. The coreling's slavering jaws were inches from her face when the ward activated. She was still linked to the script, and the rebound struck the stylus from her fingers even as the demon was knocked back.

She struggled to get her hands under her. *I'll have to make a wrist thong, if I live to see the dawn.*

More demons poured through the gap in the wards. Elissa clutched at her pockets and found her purse, clawing open the knot. She scattered the ground around her with wooden Hollow klats, each with a ward circle stamped around its edge.

Alone they were too small to make much difference, but together, perhaps they could buy her a moment to find her stylus.

A wood demon stalked her, raising one of its arms like a great cudgel, but it stumbled as the klats sparked and jumped beneath its feet, knocking it over onto a field demon. The two landed in a tangle, clawing at each other.

The outer circle had multiple breaches now, demons flooding the first ring. The Hollowers dropped their bows and it was close-quarters fighting, axes and spears and shields against a foe that only seemed to grow in number.

A rock demon charged one of the breaches, swinging a full-grown tree like a club. Elissa found her stylus and drew another cold ward. The tree turned white with frost and shattered on the next swing, though it did little to save Amee Planter, who took the crushing blow on her shield.

The demon was disoriented at the sudden loss of its weapon, and Yon Gray did not hesitate, leaping in close and burying his axe in the back of its knee. Men rushed in to surround the rock demon's legs, some hacking while others used the defensive wards on their weapon hafts to block its blows and provide cover for their fellows.

Another field demon came at Elissa, and she drew a forbidding, but the lines in the air were dim as the last of the pen's charge was expended. The demon was slowed but not stopped, knocking her to the ground. Elissa had no armor like Ragen and Derek, and she screamed as talons raked her flesh.

She had no weapon, so Elissa did the only thing she could think of, sticking her stylus into its eye. It was a desperate move. She could not hope to kill the creature with a pen, but perhaps she could slow it a few seconds—time for one of the others to reach her.

But then the wards along the stylus' length, inert a moment ago, flickered to life as ichor spilled over them. Instinctively, she thrust deeper, moving her fingers to the wards that would activate a Draw.

The wards flared so brightly she needed to shut her eyes. Power flooded into the stylus, filling its reservoir, flowing into her when the *hora* inside could contain no more.

Her wounds began to close. The ringing in her ears stopped.

Strength like she had never imagined jolted through her muscles. She reversed the hold and kept the demon pinned until its thrashing began to die away.

Then the stylus grew hot, and her eyes began to burn. She pulled back, kicking the demon's lifeless form away. She lifted the stylus, scattering a reap of demons moving her way.

There was a growl, and Ragen turned just in time to see a wood demon swipe at him. Defensive wards flared on his armor, but the rebound knocked him from his feet and he hit the ground hard, landing on the shield slung on his back. His warded spear was out of reach, stuck in the ground where he had been standing, and his stylus, for all its power, seemed scant defense in close as the demon swiped again.

Ragen rolled, letting the demon's talons deflect off the warded shield, and kept rolling, working the shield off his shoulders and slipping his left arm through the shield straps.

The demon snarled, showing rows of bladelike teeth. Ragen's every instinct was to run, but there were people counting on him.

He was ready when the wood demon struck again. He hooked its leading talons with the edge of the shield, then push-kicked it in the belly, creating space to draw a quick impact ward that knocked it onto its back. A wood ward pinned it on the ground, out of the fight.

A field demon clawed at Nona Cutter's shield nearby. Ragen drew a cold ward and Nona didn't hesitate, swinging her shield to shatter frozen scales and crack the demon's sternum.

Panting, Ragen scanned the scene, his heart pounding. Gaps were opening all around the circle, too many for the Cutters to seal with their shields. Their formations were gone, too busy gasping to sing. Everyone was fighting for their lives.

"Fall back into the carts!" Ragen drew a sound ward to amplify his voice over the din. The inner circle was already compromised, but perhaps they might shore the defenses long enough to regroup.

The Cutters complied as they were able, falling through the

gaps in the wagons into the inner circle. The women went first, and once protected they readied their bows. Charged with magic from fighting, they needed no cranks, pulling back the heavy strings with a flex of corded muscles to provide cover for the men's retreat.

As Ragen feared, the protection didn't last. A stone demon caught one of the damaged carts in its talons, lifting the heavily laden wagon and hurling it aside. Twilight Dancer pulled his stake and leapt at the demon, spearing it on his great warded horns, but field demons leapt into the gap.

Keerin appeared, playing desperately on his lute, but it seemed to have no effect on the charging demons. A pair of Cutters charged in front of him to hold them back. A wind demon swept down, taking one of the men in its talons and carrying him off.

Ragen stuck a foot in Twilight Dancer's stirrup and swung up into the saddle. "Those that are able, mount up and flee! I will clear a path to the road!"

It was a desperate ploy, but perhaps a handful might outrun pursuit until dawn or the next way station.

Then he saw a demon charging Keerin flinch and veer away. Oblivious, the Jongleur continued to play, but the sounds of battle were too great for his lute to overcome. There was little effect outside his immediate vicinity.

Ragen lifted his stylus, drawing sound wards around the herald. Suddenly the discordant sounds of his instrument shook the night air, and the demons shrieked.

The effect was so powerful and immediate that none could miss it. The demons backed away from the Jongleur, and the Cutters formed a ring around him, filtering the injured to the back of their ranks as Keerin's music rang out into the darkness.

Flame and field demons scampered off at speed. Stone demons put talons to their ears, howling as they stumbled back, easy prey the skilled Cutters took quick advantage of. In the sky, wind demons shrieked and banked away.

Keerin's confidence grew as he played, and his song changed, drawing the fleeing demons back just enough to put them in range as the Cutter women began to pick targets with their powerful crank bows. When they drew too close for his comfort, Keerin changed his tune again, driving them back.

Elissa was already seeing to the wounded while Ragen and Derek used their styluses to shore up the gaps in the circle of protection. It began to look like they would survive after all, if not find outright victory.

But then a boulder came crashing through their ranks, scattering warriors and forcing Keerin to tumble out of the way. He managed to hold on to his instrument, but the music stopped, and the corelings shook themselves, returning to their senses.

Into the gap charged a massive field demon, big as a horse and running faster than even Twilight Dancer in open gallop. Its head was earless and smooth, and it seemed unaffected as Keerin resumed playing and other demons began to shriek again.

A Cutter moved to block it from the Jongleur's path. Jase was quick and agile as he timed the swing of his axe, but the demon barely slowed, its flesh flowing from the path of the strike. The demon stepped to the side and stood on its hind legs, sweeping a razor talon that grew two feet in length in the time it took to strike. Jase's head flew from his body as the demon carried on, making for Keerin.

His confidence vanished, Keerin stopped playing and tried to flee, but it was hopeless; the demon was too quick.

Fast though it was, Elissa was faster. She raised her stylus, silver script tracing lectric wards in the air. She powered the spell, and lightning arced through the creature, knocking it from its feet. It melted away from the blast and re-formed, resuming its charge.

"Corespawn you, Keerin!" Ragen screamed as the other corelings began to converge again. "Keep playing!" As he shouted, he raised his stylus, knocking the mimic demon from its feet with an impact ward, then powering a cold ward to freeze it.

Hoarfrost gathered on the demon's scales, but its eyes began to glow like a flame demon's, and the rime began to melt.

Elissa added her power to his, both circling the demon and drawing cold wards, even as Keerin resumed his song. Derek amplified Keerin once more, then drew an impact ward that shattered the mimic demon like glass.

Just like that, the battle ended. The shattered bits of demon melted to ichor, lifeless and reeking, and Keerin's music sent the lesser corelings running.

Keerin continued to play long after the ward circles had been repaired. He played until his fingers bled, bandaged them, and played on.

He played until the sun rose, then crawled into one of the remaining wagons and collapsed.

"Lay the dead in the ruined wagons, and we'll set them ablaze."

Yon looked at Ragen skeptically. "Don't seem right, leavin' 'em."

"Nothing about this cursed journey is right," Ragen said. "But if the demons are on our trail, we can't allow the dead to slow the living."

Yon spat in the dirt. "Ay, all right."

By midmorning they were on the road again, abandoning all the carts save the one where Keerin slept amid chests of precious *hora* from the Hollow. The rest of the company was still charged from killing demons, alert despite the lack of sleep and wounds mostly healed.

They could see the smoke long before the next way station came into sight late afternoon. There was less than the total destruction of the last station, but the broken wall said enough.

"Night," Derek breathed.

"Ay, the caravan!" a familiar voice called from the watch-tower.

"Ay, the way station!" Ragen kicked Twilight Dancer into a gallop, quickly leaving the others behind as he raced to the gate.

The guard met him at the gate, and Ragen was surprised to find he knew the man. Sergeant Gaims, who once worked the Miln city gate.

"Guildmaster Ragen!" Gaims cried. "Thank the Creator! Have you a Gatherer in your company?"

"We don't," Ragen said, "but I've some Gathering training, and many of the Hollowers in our escort have experience with demon wounds. What happened here?"

"Corelings attacked the station just before dawn," Gaims

said as Elissa, Derek, and Yon caught up. "We weren't expecting it. Demons attack at sunset or deep in the night, not as the sky lightens. Before we knew they were there, the wall was cracked open and corelings were flooding the yard. We fired on them, knocking some of the lesser demons from their feet, but most shook the wounds off. Bullets didn't even slow the larger demons."

"Creator," Elissa said.

"We barricaded ourselves in the station, but the corelings had a shape changer with them. Punched a hole in the wall and poured through it like cake batter. Then it was in among us . . ." Gaims shuddered.

"How many survivors?" Ragen asked.

"That's the thing," Gaims said. "It didn't kill anyone."

Ragen blinked. "No one?"

Gaims shook his head. "Broke our weapons. Bit and sliced and bashed. Crippled a few men, and others hurt real bad. Everyone is on their back, but so far no one's died."

"How come you're all right?" Ragen asked.

Gaims paled, and Ragen didn't need an answer. "You ran."

The guard looked at his feet. "Hid in the cold cellar."

"Why you little . . . !" Yon balled a fist, but Ragen held up a hand.

"Any man with a lick of sense will run from a mimic demon, Yon. We're not here to judge."

Yon eased his hand open. "Ay, fair and true. Leave judgment to the Creator."

"Who's in command?" Ragen asked.

"Lieutenant Woron," Gaims said, "but he's in a bad way."

"Run and tell him help's arrived," Ragen said. Gaims backed quickly away from Yon and ran inside the station. The doors had been bashed in, but the walls were mostly intact.

"Expected more from the Mountain Spears, after all the ale stories in Angiers," Yon said when the man was gone. "Mark me, there's somethin' that little pissant ent tellin' us. Corelings don't leave folk alive."

"Nor do they attack just before dawn," Elissa put in.

"Unless they were the same demons that fled Keerin's music," Derek said. "It would have taken most of the night to reach the next station and try to deny us succor."

"Dun't explain leavin' survivors when they had the walls down," Yon said.

"Because they're not just denying us succor," Ragen realized. "It's a trap."

Elissa nodded. "Twenty wounded men in a station already breached. They know we can't just leave them."

"Can't we?" All eyes turned to Derek.

Yon's hand curled again. "Just once, gonna pretend ya din't say that, boy."

Derek held up his hands. "I want to help these men as much as you, but if the demons want us to do something, we should at least *consider* not doing it."

"Consider all ya like," Yon said. "But ya wanna run, yu'll do it alone. Cutters don't leave folk to the demons."

Elissa laid a hand on Derek's arm. "Yon's right."

Derek blew out a breath. "Ay, all right. What do we do?"

"Bring everyone inside and patch the breaches in the wall with wardposts," Ragen said. "Make sure to create fallback positions. Wake Keerin and put him in the watchtower. Elissa and I will go talk to the lieutenant."

"Ay, we'll see to it," Yon said.

Elissa looked at the wounded in horror. She'd seen blood aplenty in the last year, a stark reminder that humans were fragile things of meat and bone.

"Good to . . . see you . . . Guildmaster." The words seemed to exhaust Lieutenant Woron, and he lay back against the wall, drawing a slow, wheezing breath. He'd taken his own mountain spear in the midsection, the bayonet's point jutting from his back. He was pale, bathed in sweat. Elissa marveled that he was still alive.

"I was afraid to pull it out." Gaims pointed to the weapon.

"If you had, he'd be dead," Ragen said, and Elissa couldn't help wondering if the demon had intentionally left the man impaled to prolong his death. Were they that intelligent?

"What do we do?" Gaims asked.

"Not sure there's anything we *can* do," Ragen said. "I can stitch a wound or poultice a burn, but this . . . this needs surgery."

"Please," Gaims said. "Can't just let him die. Woron and I been together fifteen years now."

"Perhaps we can use *hora* magic," Elissa said.

Gaims gaped. "Honest word?"

Elissa nodded and Gaims forgot himself, wrapping her in a hug. "Creator bless you, Mother!"

Ragen cleared his throat, and the guard backed away quickly. Ragen leaned in so only she could hear. "Are you sure you're not giving the man false hope?"

"False hope is better than none at all." Elissa pulled out the grimoire of healing ward circles they were given at Gatherers' Academy.

"If we yank that spear out and mix up our lessons, he's going to die," Ragen said.

"He's going to die anyway," Elissa said. "Along with the rest of us, if we can't find a way to get these men on their feet."

They covered the windows, then cut Lieutenant Woron's clothes and armor away. Ragen detached the bayonet from the barrel of the mountain spear, leaving the blade in as Elissa cleaned the skin around the wound.

She set the book open in front of her and took her silver stylus, drawing each ward with precision as she worked her way around the entry and exit wounds. She imparted only a trickle of magic from the nib until the circles were complete.

"Ready?" Ragen asked.

"No," Elissa said, "but yes."

"Hold him still," Ragen told Gaims and yanked the bayonet out.

The moment the blade pulled free, Elissa opened the nib of her stylus and fed power into the circles. They glowed and seemed to swirl around the wounds, the wards drawing hungrily at the stylus' magic. Before long the item had nothing left to give and the wards faded, leaving an angry scar.

"Incredible." Strength returned to Woron's voice.

"Don't . . . !" Gaims said, but he steadied Woron as he grit his teeth and rose.

"Thank you, Mother Elissa," Woron said.

"You're welcome, Lieutenant." Elissa slipped *hora* stones into a silver box and slipped the nib of her stylus into a slot, activating a Draw to refill the item's reservoir. "Now let's see about getting the rest of your men on their feet."

Elissa could hear Keerin tuning his lute as she climbed into the watchtower. It was nearing dusk, and she had depleted much of the *hora* they brought from the Hollow, but all twenty of the station guards were again contributing to the defense.

"Master Keerin, how are you feeling?"

"Wretched, if I'm to give honest word," Keerin said.

"It's going to be another long night, I'm afraid." Elissa looked out from the watchtower to the men and women moving about the walls and yard.

"I'm no stranger to sleeping through days and performing at night." Keerin rubbed at his bandaged fingertips. "You can count on me to do my part."

"I never doubted it," Elissa said. "Last night was the performance of a lifetime, but you must outdo yourself tonight." She produced a thin piece of demon bone etched with sound wards and slipped it into the sound hole of Keerin's lute.

"Is that . . ." Keerin began.

"Ay," Elissa cut in. "Do not expose it to sunlight. It will lose its charge, and likely burst into flame."

Keerin gaped, looking at the lute like a loved one. "Maybe I shouldn't . . ."

"We're all taking risks tonight, Keerin." Elissa handed the Jongleur a velvet pouch. "So you remember to fish it out and tuck it in here before sunup. Now play."

Keerin strummed the instrument, and the sound shook the very air. He nearly dropped his precious instrument in surprise, and Elissa had to cover her ears.

"I have some wax," Elissa said, "to plug our ears while you play."

"Our?" Keerin asked.

"Of course." Elissa took out her stylus. "Someone has to keep you safe."

The repaired wardnet forced the demons to rise outside the walls, and the Mountain Spears opened fire as they did. Ragen warded many of the rounds personally, watching with satisfaction as they flared on impact. The lesser demons put down did not heal as they had the night before.

Even rock demons avoided concentrated fire. They could only throw at a third the range of the flamework weapons, and learned quickly they could not survive long in the kill zone.

Those demons quick or lucky enough to get past the missile fire were turned back by Keerin's music. For hours, they held a stalemate with the corelings.

But then a rock demon came charging into range, moving too quickly for the Mountain Spears to track. More shots than not missed the mark, and Ragen saw the great stone clutched in the crook of its arm like a tackleball.

He raised his silver stylus, but Elissa beat him to it. There was a flare of magic from the tower, and the ground exploded at the demon's feet, tripping it. The rock demon tumbled hard into the ground, the stone falling harmlessly from its grip.

"Now, while it's prone!" Ragen cried, but the Mountain Spears knew their work, concentrating fire on the demon's head and chest. The demon tried to claw its way back out of reach but soon kicked its last.

"Mother Elissa!" Ragen cried, and the men gave a cheer.

Another rock demon rushed the wall with a huge stone held overhead. This time Ragen was quicker, drawing a deft rock ward in its path. The demon struck the ward like a man running full-speed into a wall. Magic flared at the powerful impact, and the demon was knocked onto its back, the heavy stone landing hard on its head.

"Ha!" Ragen heard Elissa laugh from the tower. "Guildmaster Ragen!" The men cheered.

"Next one's mine!" Derek called, and Ragen began to hope they might last the night without close fighting.

But the next one proved to be six, and it was all the three of them could do to halt the onslaught. Their script, so smooth and precise before, became sloppy and desperate, trying to keep up.

Stones began to breach the defenses. Some smashed into the wall, and others arched over it into the yard, but Ragen quickly saw they were concentrating fire. He drew a sound ward. "Abandon the watchtower!"

Keerin's music cut off abruptly, and a moment later a stone smashed into the top of the tower. "Elissa!" Ragen screamed, but there was no reply. Had they made the stairs in time?

Ragen and Derek warded with new desperation, knocking away some stones before they struck, but another slipped through, hitting the base of the tower. The structure seemed to fold on itself, and collapsed.

Ragen screamed a mindless fury, drawing heat and impact wards that exploded in the demon ranks, but the enemy was moving in unison, charging the walls now that the music had stopped. So many that the protections overloaded and the demons pushed through, climbing the walls and squeezing through the breaches.

Ragen was almost glad to have to abandon his stylus for his spear and his shield. Rage gave him power as he skewered, kicked, or shield-bashed any demon that showed its face over the walltop.

All along the wall, Mountain Spears lost time to reload and resorted to bayonet fighting, bolstered by Ragen, Derek, and the Cutter women.

In the yard, Yon led men with axes to hold one of the breaches. Woron and a group of Mountain Spears held another. There was blood and ichor in equal measure, but the corelings had the numbers, and Ragen knew it was only a matter of time.

An explosion in the yard caught Ragen's attention, and he feared flame demons had gotten into the ammunition bunker. He saw instead a smoking hole in the rubble of the tower, and Keerin emerged. His head was wrapped in a bloody bandage, but he began to play, and the demons in the yard screamed.

Elissa emerged at the Jongleur's back, stylus aglow, and Ragen breathed for what felt like the first time since the tower fell.

"We can't keep that up night after night." Lieutenant Woron was pale and sweating.

"We won't," Ragen said. "At dawn, we head to the next station."

"And if the demons have hit that one, too?" Derek asked.

"Then we keep moving," Ragen said. "I won't be trapped like a nightwolf in its den."

Woron nodded. "I'll give the order to my men to load as much ammunition and supply as we can carry." He got to his feet but grimaced and clutched at his side. Gaims hurried to support him.

"Were you wounded in the fighting?" Elissa asked.

Woron shook his head. "Not done healing, I suppose. I can still feel the bayonet."

"Let me have a look," Elissa said, and the lieutenant opened his breastplate and lifted his shirt. Woron's abdomen was distended, the scar angry and red, but it had not ruptured. It was nothing like the complete healings she had seen the Hollow Gatherers perform, but she had only studied with them a few weeks. She painted a fresh set of wards and fed them from her stylus, easing the swelling. "Rest as you can today."

Woron nodded. "Thank you, Mother."

Again Keerin crawled into the *hora* wagon and collapsed at dawn, but not without the Cutters and Mountain Spears raising a cheer. Elissa caught a hint of smile on his face before he disappeared behind the curtains.

Their company was doubled in size, but fear lent them speed, and they made the next station by midday.

This time, the demons had left no survivors, shattering the walls and tearing up the cobbles in the yard so they could rise inside the station when the sun set.

They pushed on instead of trying to hold the walls.

There were a dozen way stations between Riverbridge and Harden's Grove. The demons struck six, those farthest from the cities and hope of succor. Sometimes there were survivors and sometimes not. Ragen and Elissa's company swelled to five times its original size, grouped close at night to shelter within the sound of Keerin's lute.

The first nights he simply held the demons at bay, but as he became more accustomed to Halfgrip's music, Keerin's powers grew. Soon he was playing from horseback, cloaking their party like wards of unsight as they rode on through the night, eventually losing the pursuit.

The way stations closest to the city were intact, oblivious to the attacks. Even with Woron and other officers giving testimony, the commanders refused to abandon their posts without orders.

Ragen left them with warnings and kept his company moving until they came to the town of Harden's Grove.

"Night," Yon spat over the side of his saddle. "I could step right over that wall."

It was an exaggeration, but not by much. Harden's Grove was a close-knit farming community. Its five hundred residents were divided into several large families, their farmhouses clustered together behind a five-foot stone wall set with tall wardposts.

Each family tended the plots of land behind their houses, forming an outer ring to the town, protected by an even lower wall, again set with wardposts at regular intervals. Ragen could see the posts standing in neat, even rows throughout the fields, protecting them from wind demons.

"On a clear day you can see all the way to Miln." Ragen pointed at the mountains, where the great walls of Miln were tiny in the distance. "I've been to the Grove a hundred times. There are good folk here, even if you could search all day and not find two who aren't related."

It was odd, hearing an old man's cackle from Yon's young lips. "Ay, know what that's like! Any o' their ladies need new trees planted, send 'em my way."

Amon Grove, who had been Speaker for Harden's Grove since Ragen's Messenger days, was waiting for them at the gates. He leaned on a rake he hadn't pulled in years, hands spotted and shaking, but his mind still sharp.

Amon was no more receptive than the station officers. "Harden's Grove has stood for a hundred years, Ragen. We're not going to abandon everything we've built over some demon attacks a week's ride to the south."

"Then check your wards three times, Speaker," Ragen said, "and the Creator watch over you."

Amon nodded. "And you."

Keerin looked skeletal by the time they reached the city. There were great dark circles around his sunken eyes, and his hair hung in limp tangles. His motley was scorched, bloodstained, and torn.

Few of them were without some wound. One of Yon's arms was textured like melted wax after taking a splash of firespit. Lary Cutter walked with a limp. Cal Cutter lost an eye, and his wife, Nona, part of her foot. Even Elissa had three lines across her chest, the remains of demon talons that nearly laid her open.

But it was Woron who worried them the most. He was passing blood in his urine and stool, abdomen distended again. He looked more haggard than Keerin. Ragen glanced at the lieutenant and the man noticed, nodding in return. Then his eyes rolled back and he fell from his horse.

Ragen leapt from Twilight Dancer's back, checking the man's pulse. He was alive, but weak. "Take him back to the manse and summon a Gatherer," Ragen told Elissa. "I'll go to the palace and give our report to the duke."

Keerin shook his head. "Go home and rest. I am royal herald. Time I started acting like it. I'll give first report to His Grace."

Ragen smiled. "Time to tell everyone of your heroism."

Keerin shook his head. "I'm through claiming more than my due. Without Halfgrip's music and Mother Elissa's *hora* stone, I would have been worthless. And without the Cutters and Mountain Spears buying me time with their lives, it would have made little difference."

Ragen looked at him, hardly recognizing the man as the one he had ridden to Tibbet's Brook with, all those years ago. "Are you certain you wish to go alone? Euchor may not be pleased . . ."

"After this past week, there is little His Grace can do to frighten me." Keerin put out a hand, but Ragen clasped his wrist, pulling him in for an embrace.

"Creator bless you," Elissa said, hugging the Jongleur next.

"Made Halfgrip's spirit proud," Yon said, slapping the Jongleur on the back so hard he coughed. "Doubt Rojer could've done much better himself."

"Yes. Well." Keerin nodded to the others and kicked his

horse, riding for the palace with their contingent of Mountain Spears as Ragen led the Hollowers up the hill toward his great walled manse.

"Night." Yon's voice was awed. "This is where ya live? It's big as Mistress Leesha's keep."

"Bigger." The wall around Ragen's manse was fifteen feet tall and reinforced with warded glass, sheltering great gardens, Warders and smiths, Servants' housing, and stores enough to last a month.

But even as Ragen looked it over, he knew it wouldn't be enough, if Arlen's predictions came to pass.

"Mother! Father!" The Servants were pouring into the yard, but the children left them all behind, sprinting from the house as if there were flame demons on their heels.

Ragen's throat tightened at the sight. He and Elissa had been in near-constant danger in the months they were away, but he had taken solace that his children were safe, never allowing himself to question for a moment that belief. Now, seeing them full of energy and joy, he was overwhelmed with the months of worry he had bottled away.

Ragen barely had time to dismount before Marya, not yet ten and already as beautiful as her mother, leapt into his arms. He laughed, crushing her to him until she squealed. As he loosened his grip, she tightened hers in response, and suddenly his legs felt like water and he dropped to one knee, weeping as he held her to him. The last nine months apart from his children had been an eternity for him. What must it have been like for them?

Little Arlen, who had turned six while they were away, was hopping up and down as Elissa swung from her saddle. He scampered up her leg and into her arms like a rodent, burrowing into her bosom as she, too, held him close and began to weep.

"We're safe," he murmured to Marya. "And I swear by the sun, we're going to stay that way."

The rest of the household stayed back, giving them space for this moment. Mother Margrit took over the scene, putting the stable hands to work taking the animals and welcoming their guests.

"Send for Gatherers," Ragen called to her. "The best. Our escort will stay as our guests."

Margrit nodded, sending runners. The big woman came over to them just as the children relaxed their grips and slid to the ground, only to sweep Ragen and Elissa both into a crushing embrace.

"Thank the Creator you've returned," she whispered.

"I don't know how the wound healed so fully with bleeding still inside." Mistress Anet tied off the last stitch in the long line on Woron's abdomen. "I had to cut into the scar tissue and repair the damage underneath. He's lucky to be alive." Woron remained unconscious, kept under by fumes pumped into a mask over his nose and mouth.

Elissa wrung her hands. "It's my fault."

"Nonsense. How can that be?" Anet was headmistress of the Gatherers' School, perhaps the finest Herb Gatherer in Miln. Accustomed to tending Royals and the wealthy, she was not drawn from the Library campus easily, but there was prestige as well as coin in a visit to the guildmaster's manse.

"I used demon bone to close the wound," Elissa said. "I thought the magic would heal the damage beneath." The Gatherer looked at her as if she were insane, but Elissa was wealthy and of royal blood, two qualities known to foster eccentricity.

"Bandage." The old woman left her apprentices to dress the wound as she went to the basin and began scrubbing blood from her hands and forearms. A line of red streaked her otherwise spotless white apron.

"Well whatever happened, he should recover, given time. He shouldn't leave his bed for a few weeks, and it may be months before he can walk any distance."

The tolerant tone irritated Elissa. She hadn't spent the last week fighting for her life to be spoken down to by a woman who had likely never seen a coreling outside a book. "That will not do."

The old woman looked as if she was losing patience, but Elissa did not give her time to respond, taking the silver stylus from her belt. "No doubt you've heard of the effect feedback magic has on men and women who fight demons."

Mistress Anet looked at the stylus skeptically. "I don't know what notions you've brought back from the Hollow, my lady, but here in Miln we trust our healing to science, not warding tricks."

"Lieutenant Woron owes his life to your science," Elissa agreed. "But it's time you widened your perspective."

Night had fallen while the Gatherer worked. Elissa had only to flip a switch to cut power to the lectric lights and bathe the room in darkness. The stylus left a trail of silver light as she drew a quick script in the air and energized it, setting a ring of wards floating overhead to bathe the room in clean white light.

Anet crossed her arms. "It may surprise you to know that I have seen light wards before."

"Perhaps, but you've never seen this." Elissa glided to the bed, and the Gatherer's apprentices backed away nervously, wanting no part in the growing confrontation with their mistress.

"What are you doing?" Anet followed as Elissa peeled away the bandage the apprentices had been wrapping.

"Getting this man back on his feet," Elissa said.

Anet grabbed her arm. She was white-haired, but her grip was strong. "I told you—"

Elissa raised the stylus again, and Anet's words cut off. She took a step back, eyes glaring. "I won't be responsible if you make things worse."

"Just watch." Elissa turned to Woron, holding the stylus like a brush as she outlined the long row of stitches in small, silvery script, each ward feeding into the next. When the circuit was complete, she fed power into it. Gatherer and apprentice alike reflexively leaned in as the light flared.

"What in the dark of night?" Anet watched as the wound knit together. In moments there was no sign of injury—no bruising, no redness, no scar. Only a few flakes of blood and a line of stitches in smooth, pink flesh.

The old woman gave an undignified shriek as Woron took a great shuddering breath and opened his eyes.

CHAPTER 20

THE ESCORT

334 AR

"Sign here." Mother Jenya pulled another paper from her seemingly endless pile and slid it in front of Ragen. Elissa sat a few feet from him at her own desk, working through a similar pile. The children were in their corner, quietly reading.

"Back barely a day, and already buried in paperwork," Ragen groaned.

Jenya laughed. "These are just the urgent ones. I'm waiting for you to settle before we wheel in the rest."

"Night." Ragen rubbed his face.

"Serves you well, disappearing for nearly a year," Jenya said.

Ragen flipped a page and saw a familiar signature. It was coming up too often for comfort. "Vincin." The man had been guildmaster before being ousted by Cob close to a decade ago. They hadn't parted as friends.

Jenya tensed at the name, and he knew this was a conversation she was dreading. "I was going to mention it after you'd had a chance to catch up."

Ragen laid down his pen. "Let's have it, then."

"Vincin called for a special election while you were gone," Jenya said. "He is acting master of the Warders' Guild."

"Son of the Core!" Ragen barked. "Were you going to wait until we found out at court?"

"Don't blame the messenger, dear." Elissa did not look up from her papers.

He took a breath. "I assume you checked the guild bylaws?"

"Of course," Jenya said. "A master Warder of good standing is within his rights to call for a special election if the guildmaster is unable to perform his duties, in person or in writing, for more than six months, until such time as the guildmaster returns, should his term have not expired."

"So I am automatically reinstated now that I am back in the city?" Ragen asked. He had nearly a year left in his latest two-year term.

"Not precisely," Jenya said. "The guild must call a meeting wherein the absent guildmaster announces his fitness to return, ratified by a simple majority vote. Until then, Vincin remains in power."

"Call a meeting, then," Ragen said, though the problem was quickly becoming clear.

"Only the guildmaster can call a meeting or vote."

Ragen balled a fist at Jenya's words. "If I can't call a meeting, then get word to every Warder in the city that I am returned, with news that will reshape the future of the guild."

"I'll send runners immediately," Jenya said. "What news?"

"The *hora* magic of the Hollow," Elissa said. "We've learned how to use demon bones to power wards, even when the corelings are not about. Sometimes even in daylight."

Jenya stared at her in silence, as if waiting for a punch line. When none was forthcoming, she cleared her throat. "That changes everything, if true."

"It's truth," Ragen said, "but we don't expect anyone to believe it without proof."

Even Jenya looked unconvinced, but she marked her writing slate. "I'll see to it."

"Get in touch with the glasseries, as well," Ragen said. "We're doing some renovations to our manse grounds." He produced a map, showing the greatward he and Elissa had spent so many hours designing, aligned to absorb their manse and the Servants' quarters. Many of the other structures would have to be rearranged, but it could not be helped.

Jenya looked at the map, eyes widening. "You want to . . . to pave your grounds with charged glass?"

"We'll charge it ourselves with *hora*," Elissa said, "but yes."

"We'll start with paint," Ragen said. "Immediately. That will let us ensure the proper shape before we begin the glasswork."

Jenya studied the symbol, and Ragen could see her making calculations in her head. "This will be colossally expensive."

"We have a colossal fortune," Ragen said. "I don't want to debate this, Jenya. Make it happen. The corelings are growing in power, and it's only a matter of time before they attack the city. We need to prepare, and we need to do it now."

Jenya paled as she took the design. "Yes, of course."

There were sounds of commotion from the yard. Ragen looked up, but little Arlen was already bounding to the window. "Mountain Spears!" He jumped up and down, pointing.

Ragen and Elissa exchanged a look. A summons to the duke was expected. Soldiers were not. They joined young Arlen at the window, and Ragen felt his stomach tighten at the sight of fifty Mountain Spears, flamework weapons held over their shoulders in precise formation, lined up on either side from the main gate to his front door, clearing a path for a royal carriage.

"Keerin?" Elissa wondered. Perhaps the duke had sent his herald to fetch them.

"Not garish enough," Ragen said. "Jongleur carriages look like a rainbow vomited on them."

Ragen's servants and the Cutters were massing, kept back by the alert soldiers. It didn't look like things were moving toward a confrontation, but neither was the mood relaxed.

"What in the Core is going on?" Ragen wondered as a footman hopped from the carriage and put down a set of steps, opening the door and offering a gloved hand to the occupant.

Mother Jone, Duke Euchor's chamberlain, stepped out of the carriage. The old woman had a pinched face, a coreling's temperament, and a reluctance to leave Euchor's keep. If she was here, it didn't bode well.

"Jenya . . ." Elissa's eyes flicked to the children.

Jenya responded immediately, guiding Marya and Arlen away from the window with a firm hand to the shoulders. "Come along. The chamberlain is here to talk business with your parents, and has no time for children underfoot. Up to your rooms."

Ragen took Elissa's hand as they were ushered out. "It's just a show of power. Euchor loves to stroke his own ego, but he wouldn't dare threaten us . . ."

"What cause could he have?" As Elissa asked the question, another carriage pulled up behind the first, this one bearing the sigil of Morning County. Elissa squeezed Ragen's hand so tightly it hurt.

The woman that stepped down from the second carriage was Countess Tresha.

Elissa's mother.

Elissa's fists clenched tightly as she gathered her skirts to curtsy. Dealing with a small army of Mountain Spears seemed a gentle breeze compared with dealing with her mother.

Unbidden, Duchess Araine's words came to her. *Step carefully, when you return home.*

"Elissa, dear." Countess Tresha spread her arms. "Come give your mother a hug."

Elissa reflexively held her breath, and not just against the cloud of perfume her mother always wore. When was the last time her mother had wanted her embrace? Not since she was a child. The act sent alarms ringing in her head.

"Keep quiet and let me do the talking, dear," Tresha whispered. "I'm here to keep everyone on their best behavior."

Perhaps her mother meant the words to be a comfort, but Elissa found them anything but.

If Tresha was the second most powerful woman in Miln, Mother Jone was the first. The duke's aunt was straight-backed and rail-thin at nearly seventy. Her dress was conservative, with long sleeves and a high collar, the material as stiff as its wearer. She looked, as always, like she had just eaten a lemon.

She nodded grimly. "Ragen, Elissa. Welcome home."

Ragen put on a smile, always able to appear relaxed when he was anything but. "Indeed, you've brought quite the welcome. Will they be firing off a flamework salute to celebrate our return?"

"They're here as an escort only, Ragen," Jone said.

"Has Miln become so unsafe in our absence that it requires fifty Mountain Spears with flamework weapons to escort us across town?" Ragen asked.

"Of course not," Jone said. "But you are heroes returned from war. Think of it as an honor guard."

"I would have been more honored if given notice of the guard," Ragen said.

Yon appeared at their backs. He must have circled in through the back entrance. "Everythin' all right?"

"Ah, this must be Captain Gray," Jone said. "A pleasure to make your acquaintance, Captain. His Grace formally requests your presence this morning, as well."

Yon's eyes flicked to Ragen's, then he turned back to Jone and crossed his arms. Jone was tall, nearly six feet, but the burly Cutter loomed over her nonetheless. "Ay, all right."

Jone seemed unimpressed by the massive man. "You'll have to surrender your weapon to the palace guards before you are admitted to see His Grace." She indicated the great axe slung over his shoulder.

"Like night I will," Yon said, and everyone tensed.

"Duke Euchor does not allow armed soldiers from foreign duchies in his throne room." Jone's smile was pinched like the rest of her face. "Surely even you can understand that."

Yon gave a whistle and the guards took the flamework weapons from their shoulders as Lary Cutter appeared. Yon unslung his axe and handed it to Lary. "Deliverer himself warded that. Ent turning it over to anyone ent from the Hollow." He gave Jone a smile just as condescending as the one she had given him. "Sure even you can understand that."

Jone cleared her throat. "Yes, well. Shall we be off?"

They walked into the yard past the ominous line of Mountain Spears to the carriages, Elissa looking over their shoulders to the frightened faces of the household Servants. Everyone was on edge, looking for some sign from Ragen and Elissa to signal what they should do.

Any show of distress could end in bloodshed, something Ragen clearly understood as well. He might have been strolling through the garden for all the concern he showed, but Elissa knew that inside, he was coiling like a spring.

Tresha took Elissa's arm. "You and Ragen will ride with me, dear." She glanced at Jone. "It's been agreed."

Elissa tried not to flinch at the touch. "Mother, what's—"

Tresha squeezed, her bony fingers digging hard into Elissa's biceps. "Captain Gray will need to ride in back. The carriage only seats four."

"Four?" Elissa asked, as the driver clad in her mother's livery opened the door. Inside sat Derek Gold, looking decidedly uncomfortable. There were dark circles under his eyes.

"Ent a problem." Yon seemed relieved to be away from the unfolding drama as he climbed into the back bench.

"We don't have a lot of time," Tresha said when the door closed behind them. "You're fortunate I caught wind of this and arrived in time to make sure Jone and her men minded their manners. They would have searched your manse if I hadn't shown up."

"Searched for what?" Ragen demanded. "What in the dark of night is going on?"

"I tried to warn you," Derek said, "but Brayan's men wouldn't allow it. I've been under house arrest since I got home."

"They arrested you?" Elissa was incredulous. "For what?"

"Didn't call it that," Derek said. "Just locked me in with Stasy and little Jef and put guards at the doors and windows. Could've used my stylus, but the count's got his whole keep on lockdown, and all his men are armed with flamework weapons. Don't think I could've made it out without someone getting hurt."

"Wise you didn't," Tresha said. "You're in enough trouble as it is."

"Trouble for what, Mother?" Elissa was out of patience. "We've been back for less than a day. What in the Core could we possibly have done?"

"Euchor knows you've been trading combat wards on the exchange," Derek said. "And now that he knows the Warded Man is Arlen Bales . . ."

"He thinks we deliberately played him for a fool," Elissa finished.

"Did you?" Tresha demanded.

Elissa eyed her cautiously. Where were her mother's loyalties? There was no love lost between them, and her mother had never made a secret of her dislike of Ragen. Was she truly here to advocate on their behalf—if only to spare the family more shame—or was she simply a convenient way for Euchor to trick a confession from them?

Ragen shrugged. "Not precisely. This was going to get out eventually." He looked to Derek. "What else do they know?"

Tresha cut in before Derek could reply. "If you're asking if Euchor knows about the warded arms and armor you've been making and selling across the city, he does."

"If he knows, he only found out recently," Elissa said. "I reviewed those orders this morning. Deliveries have gone to the Messengers' Guild like clockwork, and all have been accepted."

"And why shouldn't they have been? We've broken no laws." Ragen kept his eyes on Derek. "How did he find out?"

Derek colored, eyes dropping.

Elissa crossed her arms. "Stasy." Mother Stasy was Derek's wife, cousin to Count Brayan. Brayan was Euchor's closest advisor and the head of the only family with a fortune greater than Ragen and Elissa's. He was heavily invested in Euchor's flamework weapons, and no doubt saw the warded weapons as competition. Brayan's son was married to Euchor's eldest daughter, Hypatia, and his grandson was widely considered likely to become the next duke.

"Ent her fault," Derek said. "It's mine. Wasn't careful in my letters. Count had the Servants reading her mail, looking for information. She's angry as a rock demon."

Ragen blew out a breath. "There's nothing for it now, Derek." He gave a subtle tilt of his head toward Tresha. "I know what it's like to shame a royal family by tracking dusty Messenger boots on their fine carpets. Once we settle your inheritance, you can start your own household."

"Ay, I'd like that," Derek said, "but the count's got Stasy and Jef locked up tight. Can't leave without them."

"You won't have to," Elissa said.

"Ent a lot I can do about it," Derek said. "Ent a magistrate in the city going to side with me over Count ripping Brayan."

"It's not just you, Derek," Ragen said. "Not ever again. Announce today in open court that you're taking your family and moving to my manse. If Brayan doesn't agree, the Warders' Guild won't take orders for him or his holdings until he does."

Derek gaped. "You would do that?"

"Corespawned right." Elissa couldn't help but throw a rebellious glance at her mother along with the words. "You're family."

"That's a hollow threat, when you're no longer acting guildmaster," Tresha noted.

Ragen gave her a cold smile. "We'll see about that."

"So you knew Arlen Bales was the Warded Man?" Tresha pressed, going back to the original subject. "You knew and deliberately withheld the information?"

"He's our son," Elissa said. "Every bit as much as if I birthed him myself."

Tresha sniffed. "You should have come to me with this."

Elissa barked a laugh. "Come to you? Mother, when have you ever taken my side in anything? Night, I don't even know if you're on our side now!"

Tresha looked genuinely offended. "Whatever you may think, you spoiled little brat, I've always had your best interests at heart."

"Even when you cast me out of the family?" Elissa could see Ragen and Derek shrinking away as she and Tresha scratched at each other, but there was no other choice. Elissa needed to know where her mother stood before the ride was over.

"I told you that was all behind us, when you graduated the Mothers' School," Tresha said.

Elissa snorted. "Only because you wanted another vote on the Mothers' Council. My interests never entered into it."

Tresha crossed her arms. "Well now you're in politics whether you like it or not. You've put yourself at the center of a whirlwind, and if you want to get out of it alive and free, you're going to need my help."

"At what price?" Elissa couldn't help but ask.

Tresha's eyes flicked to Ragen and Derek. "We can discuss that later. For today, please just trust that our interests align."

"Are you saying we're going to be arrested without your help?" Ragen asked.

"I don't think it will come to that, if you ware your words

in court," Tresha said. "The three of you are heroes in every tavern in Miln. There would be rioting in the streets."

"You don't *think*?" Elissa asked.

Tresha shrugged. "You will never be this vulnerable—this unprepared—again. If Euchor truly fears you, he might think it best to throw you in irons now, before you grow too powerful to touch."

Ragen spotted a cluster of women waiting in the entrance hall. "You're on your own for now, Ragen," Tresha said. "Try not to make matters worse while the Mothers sort this out."

With that, Tresha and Jone broke off, taking Elissa with them into the Mothers' Council chambers. Ragen wondered if the next time he saw her would be at a trial.

Keerin was waiting to escort them to Euchor's throne room. The Jongleur was back in his royal motley, tunic and loose breeches striped in blue and gray under a black velvet cloak held by a gold chain clasped with Euchor's mountain crest. The underside of the cloak was striped with bright silk, allowing him to shift from the subdued tones Euchor favored to vibrant color with a flick of his arm.

But Keerin's face was as somber as his outer garb. "I'm sorry about this, Ragen. I swear I didn't know."

Ragen clapped him on the shoulder. "Not your fault. How bad is it?"

Keerin glanced at their escort and started walking, leading them to court. He lowered his voice to a murmur. "His Grace is . . . displeased. He will try to intimidate you, but the Mothers' Council is not convinced there is enough evidence to bring charges unless you incriminate yourself."

"How do you know?" Ragen murmured in return.

"I did some snooping at home last night," Keerin said. He was married, if unhappily, to Baroness Cate, a wealthy widow and prominent member of the Mothers' Council.

"Wait here," Keerin said when they reached the great doors of Euchor's throne room. The Mountain Spears opened them just enough to admit him.

"Master Ragen, Messenger Derek Gold, and Captain Yon Gray of Hollow County!"

"Follow my lead and let me do the talking," Ragen said as he led them in at a stately pace, showing no concern at the troubling signs.

The shutters of the throne room had been opened wide, filling the room with sunlight, no doubt to counter any magic tricks they might attempt if things failed to go their way.

Atop the dais sat Euchor, overweight and gray-haired, but still looking like he could break most men with his bare hands. It was said when the Krasian Messenger came to declare Ahmann Jardir ruler of all the world, Euchor had personally beaten the man unconscious, and pissed on him as he lay broken on the floor. Euchor wore a fur-trimmed blue cloak and gray tunic, heavy chains of gold, and rings glittering on his fingers. About his head he wore a thin circlet of gold.

To the left of the throne stood Tender Ronnell, the Royal Librarian at the head of a group of gray-bearded Tenders. Euchor didn't control them outright, but the Royal Librarian, who served at the will of the duke, was Tender of the Great Library and Cathedral of Miln, and the head of their order.

Count Brayan, leader of the Mining and Lenders' guilds, stood to the right, beside the other guildmasters. His receded hair was snow white, but it had been cropped close, lines giving the angular man's face the look of craggy rock. Next to him was the sneering Vincin, his oiled goatee gone to gray, thin hair slicked straight back. Rings glittered on his chubby fingers. At his breast he wore the keyward brooch of Warders' Guildmaster.

Next to Vincin stood Ragen's most likely ally in the room, Malcum, master of the Messengers' Guild. Malcum stood a head taller than the other guildmasters, all the more imposing for the patch he wore over one eye and the scars on one side of his face, evidence of a coreling attack from back in his messaging days. The guildmaster had bandaged the wounds himself and completed his run, continuing to message for years before moving into administration.

Masters of the Waste, Merchants', Harvesters', Masonry, and Beggars' guilds stood clustered together, shifting nervously with the tension in the air. More than a few of them owed Ragen great sums of money.

"Welcome home, Ragen," Euchor said. "As you have no doubt heard a thousand times since your return, all Miln owes you a debt for your services in the Krasian war."

Ragen gave a deep bow. "You honor us, Your Grace. We knew our duty to you, and to all the people of the Free Cities, and did no less than would be expected of any in our position."

"False modesty does not become you, Ragen," Euchor said. "You should be proud of your accomplishments. They are the only reason I haven't already thrown you in chains."

Euchor meant the words to frighten them. Indeed, Yon tensed, ready to fight or flee, but Ragen relaxed. Fretting and pacing were for sunset, when the threat was still imagined. When it was dark and the demons were real, it was easier to focus.

"What reason would you have to throw me in chains, Your Grace?" Ragen asked, though he knew full well the answer. "I have always been loyal to Miln."

"Yet you conspired with that foreign stray you dragged in from the hamlets to cheat me," Euchor growled.

"I seem to recall meeting the boy while tax collecting in Your Grace's name in Tibbet's Brook," Ragen noted. "Arlen is, by definition, Milnese."

Euchor reddened, and Ragen was thankful his beard, grown thick on the road, masked the smile that twitched his lips. This was always Euchor's mistake. He wanted an audience for his scoldings, but was unprepared when someone had the stones to hit back in front of his court.

"You kept his identity secret when he came to court last year," Euchor said.

Ragen spread his hands, turning to eye the others in the room. "Who among you does not keep secrets in their family? In my years as Royal Messenger, I was privy to many of them, some far greater than this one." He looked back to the duke. "Arlen Bales preached no sedition, stole no property, and harmed no people. His worst crime was cracking Your Grace's floor, and I am happy to pay for that."

"You will," Euchor agreed, "as well as for the wards he sold me under false pretenses, made worthless by your backroom dealings."

"Worthless, Your Grace?" Ragen asked, raising his voice until it echoed off the high ceiling. "Those wards are the reason my company made it back from Angiers alive. Those wards are the reason Hollow County grew from a hamlet smaller than Harden's Grove to rival any of the Free Cities in barely two years. The reason the Krasians were able to leave the desert and invade the south."

"And your apprentice sold them to me dearly," Euchor said, "even after he had given them to you to put on the exchange."

He was sifting for information, but Ragen made no effort to deny it. "What did Arlen ask, Your Grace? After you openly threatened to have your guards hold him down while you copied the wards from his flesh? After you *ordered* me to have Warders in the shadows, sketching every symbol they glimpsed?"

There were shifting feet on both sides of the throne now, and Ragen pressed the attack. "He asked only aid for Rizonan refugees, something Your Grace no doubt meant to provide, regardless."

"I won't be manipulated into providing for every Beggar at the border, Ragen," Euchor growled. "I paid for those wards fairly."

"As did every Warder I sold them to," Ragen said.

Euchor clenched a fist. "So you admit you undercut me?"

Ragen did his best to look offended. "I admit nothing of the sort. I broke no laws, Your Grace. I came by the wards legally, and as Master of the Warders' Guild and head of the Ward Exchange, I am licensed to broker grimoires and create warded arms and armor."

"And now you are rich beyond measure," Euchor sneered.

Ragen spread his hands. "Your Grace could have traded the wards on the exchange the same as I. It was your choice to lock your grimoire away in the Library and arm your men instead with flamework weapons."

"Those flamework weapons saved Angiers and kept the Krasians from claiming everything south of the Dividing," Count Brayan cut in.

"Indeed," Ragen agreed. "The Mountain Spears are formidable against the Krasians, and Creator knows, the desert rats needed the lesson. But the demons are growing in power, and wisdom dictates warding their weapons and armor for the coming war."

"Bah!" Euchor scoffed. "By all accounts, the Hollowers and Krasians are slaughtering corelings by the thousands. It's not surprising the survivors are stirred up a bit."

Ragen shook his head. "It's more than that, Your Grace. They attack with cunning now, using weapons and tactics like I've never seen after decades on the road. Intelligence from Countess Paper of the Hollow suggests we've barely seen a fraction of what the Core can spew forth."

"The woman is a heretic," Euchor cut in. "Their Tenders have broken from Northern orthodoxy and formed their own council, and the countess exceeded her power in appointing that fool apostate Jona as Shepherd. They worship your dead apprentice as Deliverer, though all he delivered was war with the desert rats and a worsening of the Plague."

"Ent like that." Yon seemed surprised that his growl echoed so in the great chamber, but his face hardened as all eyes turned to him.

Euchor smiled. "By all means, Captain Yon. Educate us."

"Easy to call people ya never met fakes an' frauds," Yon said. "Easy to sit safe in yur warded mountain keep, thousand miles from the Hollow, an' judge. None of ya were there, when our Gatherer died and the Hollowers fell sick. When the fires started, and the demons broke through the wards. I lived in Cutter's Hollow over eighty years, knew every one of its three hundred forty-seven people. Watched as an old cripple as half the people I knew fell around me. Demons in the houses and dancing in the street."

He stepped forward, and the passion in his voice had attention rapt. Even Euchor was silent, caught in the tale. "Last building standing was the Holy House, and Jona took us all in. His leg was broke, but he never rested, hobbling around on crutches, tending the sick like a Gatherer. Tellin' us all wern't lost. That the Creator had a plan."

Yon shook his head. "Din't believe it. No one did. Thought that mornin' would be my last. But then Arlen Bales rode into town with Leesha Paper and Rojer Inn. Told us to quit feelin' sorry and sack up. That if we stood our ground, we could pull through. And because of them, we did."

His eyes scanned the room. "Don't believe all the Jongleur's tales? Ay, heard one said I was ten feet tall. But ent no denying that in two years since, we went from a town with less'n two hundred on their feet to a county with more folk than any of the Free Cities I been to."

Ragen eyed the Royal Librarian as Yon spoke, looking for some sign beneath his detached façade that Yon's words were getting to him. That he might be the ally Arlen hoped.

"Ya may not believe Arlen Bales is the Deliverer. Get that. Din't see it myself, I might not, either. But I seen it. I seen him hangin' in the air, glowin' like the sun, throwing fire and lightning at the corespawn. That ent the rippin' Deliverer, don't know what is."

There were murmurs throughout the court, and Ragen gave it time to sink in. Euchor looked at Ronnell, as if willing him to rebut the story, but the Librarian kept his eyes down, silent as the old men behind him quietly debated.

Ragen stepped into the silence. "I knew Arlen Bales as well as any, but I leave theology for the Tenders to argue, safe in their Holy Houses behind warded walls. I've spent my life out in the naked night and see the threat more clearly. Calling it a plague changes nothing. We have weapons to fight the corelings, and we should be putting them in every hand able to wield them."

"And lining your pockets in the process?" Euchor asked. "You control both ends of production, so it's in your interest to exaggerate the threat. You're lucky I don't confiscate every weapon you've made with your illegal wards."

Guildmaster Malcum cleared his throat, turning all eyes his way.

Euchor raised a brow. "You have something to add, Malcum?"

The Messengers' Guildmaster took the invitation to leave his place with the other guildmasters, striding over to stand beside Ragen. "The Messengers' Guild has bought those weapons fairly, Your Grace. You seem to forget it is *our* lives at risk in the night, delivering *your* missives, escorting *your* caravans, facilitating all trade in *your* city. We pressed Your Grace to share the wards when Arlen Bales sold them to you, and were met with delay after delay, even as demon attacks increased on the road. Now we have the tools to protect ourselves, and we will not give them up."

Euchor's visage darkened at the rebellious tone, his voice quiet, dangerous. "You admit to complicity in Ragen's crime?"

"There has been no crime," Malcum said. "We bought wards legally on the exchange, and commissioned arms and armor legally from the Warders' Guild. You have no right to confiscate anything. Attempt to do so and every Messenger in the city will strike."

A stunned silence fell over the court at that. Without Messengers, vital city services would stagger to a halt, and everyone in the room would feel it in their purses.

"The Warders' Guild, as well," Ragen added.

"You no longer speak for the Warders, Ragen," Guildmaster Vincin sneered. "You gave up that right when you abandoned your post. I am guildmaster now."

"A guildmaster who cannot call a meeting without being voted from office," Ragen countered. "I appreciate you filling in during my absence, Vincin, but you cannot prevent my return to power forever. I control the exchange."

Vincin scowled, but Ragen was right. Vincin could stall on procedural issues, but with news of Ragen's return spreading through the city, the guildsmen would soon force his hand.

"Documents were filed this morning granting Derek Gold a seat for life on the Warding Exchange, as well as twenty-one percent of my warding business, glasseries, and warehouses," Ragen pressed his advantage. "I've invited him and his family to stay in my manse until Derek can build one of his own."

"A kind offer, Ragen, but unnecessary." Count Brayan smiled, but it was strained. The news had caught him off guard. "My cousin is quite comfortable in my keep."

Derek stepped forward. "I thank you, my lord, but we have prevailed upon your generosity long enough. We'll be transitioning immediately to a place of our own."

"It isn't your decision, *Merchant*," Brayan said. "Stasy and Jef are Noble-born, accustomed to life and society you can never give them."

"They are my wife, my son," Derek said.

Brayan bared his teeth. "They are a young virgin you raped and a bastard better-blooded than his father. You may have convinced her to marry you and drag your filthy carcass from Servant class, but you are not worthy of her and never were. Where have you been, as your son was grown and raised? Off gallivanting."

Malcum crossed his arms. "Gallivanting? Is that how you see the Messengers' work, my lord?"

"Derek is no rapist," Ragen said. "The gall, to spill such lies in His Grace's court."

"I won't be bullied by an absentee guildmaster, or an absentee father," Brayan snapped. "Strike, if you must. And let all your workers know their wages are being lost over the poor Royal forced to endure silk and luxury in her family home."

"Weave whatever lies you wish, my lord," Derek growled, "you cannot keep my wife and child prisoner against their will."

Count Brayan snorted, turning to look at the duke. Euchor threw up his hand as if waving off a stench. "Spare me your family dramas. This is Mothers' Council business. Take it up with them."

"Were you part of Arlen Bales' conspiracy against the throne?" Mother Jone stopped her pacing and met Elissa's eyes.

The inquiry had gone on for hours, Mothers pressing Elissa for details on everything from Arlen's childhood to her experiences in Lakton during the war. Tresha sat quietly at Elissa's side the entire time, straight-backed and stone-faced. Count Brayan's wife, Countess Mother Cera, held the Speaker's gavel in the interim.

Now they were finally getting to the meat of things.

"Don't answer that." Tresha put a hand on Elissa's arm as if she were a child who might run into the street. "Point of order," Tresha added to the room. "No conspiracy has been proven."

There were nods from many councilors, scowls from others. For once in her life, Elissa was thankful for her mother's hand on her arm. This place was more dangerous than any busy street, and Tresha had the respect—if not the allegiance—of every woman here.

"Sustained." Cera's face was sour as she banged the gavel. Cera and Jone were of like mind, but even at synced purpose they couldn't break council rules and precedents. At least, not so long as Tresha held a narrow majority of votes.

"Of course." Jone was unfazed. The seed had been planted. "Allow me to rephrase. Did you know Arlen Bales was the Warded Man before his meeting with the duke?"

Tresha's hand tightened on her arm, but Elissa felt herself sit a bit taller. She would not lie in council, or deny her adopted son, whatever happened.

"I did," she said. "Arlen Bales was my adopted son. He revealed himself to me soon after his return to Miln."

There were murmurs in the crowd at that. Tresha did not seem pleased with the response, but she said nothing.

"You admit to deceiving His Grace?" Jone pressed.

"Deceiving how?" Elissa replied. "I am a Merchant Mother with no place on His Grace's court. If you did not see fit to properly screen a petitioner before admitting him to court, I don't see how it is my responsibility."

"Perfect." Tresha's grip eased with the whisper.

"But your husband is a member of His Grace's court, is he not?" Jone asked.

"Of course." Elissa could see where this was going.

"And was Guildmaster Ragen present when Arlen Bales revealed himself to you?" Jone asked.

"No," Elissa said.

Jone frowned. "But he was aware . . ."

Tresha's hand tightened again. "Point of order. No man or woman is compelled to testify against their spouse in council."

"Raising that point only makes you seem guilty," Jone noted, to murmurs in the chamber.

"Contesting the rules makes you seem to have no real evidence," Tresha countered, and the buzz of quiet conversations increased.

"Enough." Mother Cera banged her gavel for quiet. "Mother Elissa is not here to testify for or against her husband."

"Then we are done for today," Tresha said, her fingers pinching Elissa's arm tight.

Cera pointed the gavel at her. "You are not Speaker today."

Tresha seemed unafraid. "No, but my daughter has answered every question the Mothers have posed for over four hours. Unless Mother Jone has more than fishing attempts to add, I move we adjourn for the day and let Mother Elissa, who has only just returned to the city at great personal risk, return to the family and household she has not seen in months."

"Seconded," Baroness Cate said instantly.

There was broad consensus that they had done enough for the day. Elissa could see in the eyes of many of the Mothers that this was not close to over, but at least now there was some time.

"Thank you," she said to her mother on the walk back to the carriage.

"Thank me by coming back to Sunrise Hall for lunch," Tresha said.

Elissa tensed at the mention of the ancestral seat of Morning County.

She had been so close to escape.

"That son of the Core," Derek growled when Euchor called recess and they were released from court. "To call me a rapist, because the baron's daughter fell in love with a Servant."

"It will be all right." Ragen put an arm on Derek's shoulder. "Brayan has no reason to harm Stasy and Jef. We can sort this before long."

"Easy words," Derek said. "I can't even see them now without putting myself back in Brayan's power. Next time even Countess Tresha may not be able to spring me."

"We weren't bluffing," Malcum said. "Brayan won't be getting his mail or deliveries until the Mothers' Council makes a ruling."

"Ay, but who's to say what that will be?" Derek said. "None of those old women care about my family, only how to twist this to political advantage. Mother Cera commands a lot of votes. Together with Jone, they can overrule even Tresha."

"Whatever the politics, they can't hold a Mother against her will," Ragen said. "As soon as Stasy testifies, they'll have no choice but to free her."

"So they won't let her testify," Derek said. "I know Brayan. First she'll fall mysteriously ill and not be able to see anyone. Then he'll bribe someone 'impartial' to visit her, and press her to sign a statement. If we demand a trial he'll insist it be in his county, where the magistrates are all in his pocket. He might not be able to win a fair trial, but he can delay for months, even years, and turn every official against me. In the end, he's a Royal and I'm not, and there's no fix for that."

"If it goes that far," Ragen lowered his voice, "we'll magic the lot of them to sleep and kick in the door." It was an ugly suggestion, but Derek straightened at the words.

"Magic them?" Malcum asked.

"We've more than just wards to arm your Messengers with now," Ragen said.

"Oh?" Malcum raised a brow.

Ragen slipped the silver stylus from his jacket pocket and handed it to Malcum for inspection. "It has a demon bone core that will burst into flames if exposed to sunlight, but plated in gold or certain other metals, it retains its power. Worked into armor, the wearer can shrug away the flamework of a mountain spear or catch a rock demon punch to the chest and live to tell the tale. Embedded in a crank bow bolt, it can shoot through a stone wall."

Malcum eyed the stylus, then Ragen. "If you were anyone else, I would think you full of demonshit."

"If it hadn't saved all our lives on the road, I wouldn't believe it, myself," Ragen said. "We have Cutters at my manse as well. Expert demon fighters like Yon here, to train your Messengers in the use of warded weapons and arms."

"Ay," Yon said. "Ent no one can chop demons like my Cutters. Happy to teach ya what the Deliverer taught us."

"So it's true," Malcum said. "You Hollowers believe Arlen Bales is the Deliverer?"

"Mr. Bales always denied it, but what else could he be?"

"A good man," Ragen said. "Trying to do right by the world and rid us of demonkind."

Malcum looked back and forth between them, doubtful.

"It's irrelevant." Ragen took back his stylus. "What matters is that we can arm and train your Messengers. The road is more dangerous than ever. If you believe nothing, believe that."

Malcum nodded. "I'll put the word out. You may have a crowd tonight."

CHAPTER 21

NEOCOUNTY

334 AR

Elissa and her mother sat straight upright, chins high, staring at nothing through the carriage windows. There was peace between them, but it was a fragile thing.

Sunrise Hall loomed before them, and Elissa felt like a child again passing through its great gate. The hall was a remnant of the old world, partially destroyed in the Return and rebuilt some hundred years later by the first Count of Morning.

The servants all turned out for Elissa's arrival. First in line was Mother Soren, who had been Elissa's governess some thirty years past. Elissa remembered her from a child's perspective as a looming, powerful woman, but in her sunset years she looked small and frail.

"Mother Elissa, my darling, welcome home." Soren spread her arms, and Elissa fell into them, embracing her tightly. She had been stern, but more a parent than Tresha. There were other eager faces in the crowd, some of them childhood friends, and others beloved house workers. These people were more her family than her mother and elder sisters, married off to local barons while she was still a child.

"I've missed you," Elissa said as Tresha was helped down from the carriage by the driver. Mother Soren and the other Servants stiffened, eyes quickly out front. From there Elissa and her mother walked in silence down a solemn line of stone faces.

Moments later they were alone in the parlor. The room was just as Elissa remembered it—clean to the point of sterility, and stifling with lectric heat. Mother Tresha was always cold.

The room was empty, but Elissa could see Servants had just been there. Steam was coming from the teakettle, sitting in precise formation with two freshly filled porcelain cups. Thin sandwiches and other bite-sized food had been laid out in a pattern, each its own island on the sterile marble tabletop.

Two crystal glasses stood in triangle point with a crystal ice bucket. Vapor still curled from the neck of the open bottle of Rizonan summer wine within. The glasses were already poured. A silver bell, polished to a sheen, waited in case they need anything more.

Elissa smiled, recognizing the Head Servant's work. "Mother Kath is older than Soren but still artful and invisible."

"Servants *should* be invisible, unless you need something." Tresha went directly to her favored chair and sat down. A porcelain plate already sat on the table next to her with the countess' preferred sandwiches and a cup of milked and doubt-lessly oversweetened tea. "I don't want them hovering around me all day and night."

What a sad, lonely way to live, Elissa was wise enough not to say. She reached for the wine.

"They're not as excited to see me as they are you, of course." Tresha reached for a tiny sandwich, sitting in a bed of delicate folded paper to keep her fingers pristine. She ate it like a bird in neat, snapping bites. The paper alone cost more than most Servants earned.

"Perhaps if you bothered to learn their names." Elissa had somehow already drained her glass and reached for the other one. Her mother raised an eyebrow at her, but Elissa ignored it.

"I know their names." Tresha crumpled the paper. "Who do you think has paid their wages all these years? But what do I know? You left your own *children* with your Servants for nearly a year."

"Is that what you're mad about now?" Elissa asked. "What difference would it have made? You let the Servants raise me."

Tresha whipped a hand at her. "And look how that turned out."

"You've never seen Marya and Arlen outside of a Solstice dinner." Elissa managed to keep her voice calm, though her mother was testing her limits. "Suddenly you want them *hovering* around you, day and night?"

"Of course not," Tresha snapped. "But I know board members of all the great academies. I could have . . ."

"Taken them in only long enough to pack them off to school," Elissa said. "You've never really wanted to know them. Or me."

Tresha took her tea and blew on it. Elissa blinked. "You're letting that go? The last time I spoke like that, you broke a plate over my head."

Tresha sighed and sipped her tea. "It took you long enough, but you're a Mother now. I can't treat you like a Daughter anymore. Come and sit with me."

Elissa did, and for a time it was much like the carriage ride, sipping her wine and staring at nothing as her mother ate finger sandwiches in silence. Elissa finished her second glass and rose to pour a third.

"I can ring," Tresha said.

"I can pour wine without help, Mother. I learned all sorts of things while the *Servants* raised me." The barb came without her even intending it. She was more like her mother than she wanted to admit.

The clink of cup on saucer showed her mother's irritation. "You should be glad your father's not alive to hear you speak that way to me."

"When Father was alive, I didn't have to," Elissa said.

"Of course, your father was Creator-sent." Tresha laughed. "Just like your adopted son. Just like the Messenger you fell for. Do you think every man you care for is the Deliverer, dear?"

Elissa snorted, but then her eyes widened as she recognized the pattern on her glass. "The good crystal? I thought this was only for when Royals came visiting."

"You are Royal," Tresha said.

"That's not what you told me when I married Ragen." Elissa

raised her voice to a screech. *"Marry that dirty road rat, and I'll disown you! See how you enjoy life as a Merchant!"*

"I never did it," Tresha said.

"Eh?" Elissa stopped mid-sip.

"Disowned you," the countess clarified. "No papers were signed, no documents filed. Can you imagine the scandal?"

Elissa could hardly believe her ears. She glanced at the cup in her hand. Had she already finished that third cup of wine?

"So you're telling me that all these years . . ."

"You've lived a Merchant's life by choice," Tresha clarified. "All you ever needed to do to come home was apologize."

Elissa ground her teeth. "Apologize for what? Ragen is a good man! He's worth both the idiot barons you married my sisters to ten times over!"

Tresha set her cup and saucer on the table and stood, all rigid posture, even if she was shorter than Elissa now. "You're right."

"Ay, what?" Elissa asked.

"I apologize," Tresha said. "Ragen has proven to be a far better husband than I imagined."

Elissa stood in stunned silence for a moment, then looked around the room. "No wonder you didn't want anyone hovering to hear."

"I can admit when I am wrong." Tresha flicked a speck of dust from her dress. "Enjoy it while you can, dear. I daresay you may not live long enough to see it happen twice."

Elissa shook her head. "I should have known you'd never disown your own daughter."

Tresha laughed. "Disown? No. Disinherit? Certainly."

"I never wanted to be countess," Elissa said.

"And your sisters wanted it too much," Tresha replied. "Only they haven't a brain between them. I'd rather let the title revert to the crown to be doled out to any fool Euchor owes a favor than let one of them have it. You're the only one of my blood to make something of herself."

"Creator, Mother!" Elissa snapped. "Can you not just say you missed me? That you want to know your grandchildren? Is your pride as high as the city wall?"

"If mine is a wall, then yours is a mountain," Tresha said. "We've lost years over this little spat. Years we won't get back. Magic may be shrinking your crow's-feet, but the years continue to weigh on me. I'm a dying old woman, and set in my ways."

Elissa felt something shock through her, turning and taking her mother's arm. "What do you mean? You're not that . . ."

Tresha cackled. "Finish that thought, I beg! Tell me your heart's honest word, and I will tell you mine."

They stared at each other awhile, then mutually dropped their eyes.

"What is it?" Elissa asked. "Have you seen a Gatherer?"

"Cancer," Tresha said. "And ay, I've had the best minds in Miln marching through my gates and combing through the Library for months."

She went back to her favored chair and sat down.

"There are none in the world more learned than Milnese Gatherers," Elissa said. "But what they can do pales in comparison with the healers in Krasia and the Hollow."

Tresha shook her head. "I want nothing to do with your demon magic."

"It's not *demon* magic," Elissa said. "It's just magic. It comes from the Core. The demons have simply evolved to absorb it."

Tresha raised her brow. "Do you have proof?"

Elissa took a deep breath. "There is evidence, but not proof. We are still learning . . ."

"I won't be some gambled experiment, with my holy spirit as the wager," Tresha said. "Test your theories on wounded fighters, if you must. Test them on Beggars and Servants. But not me. I've lived my share, and I'm tired, Lissa."

She reached out, bony fingers cold on Elissa's hand. "Your names are on the lips of everyone in Miln. Rich is as good as Royal, and there are few men richer than Ragen. With a fistful of coins and a few strokes of the pen, I can announce you both as my heirs, and not even Euchor himself could stop it."

Elissa laid a hand over her mother's, trying to lend her some warmth. "My sisters would hate me."

"Hah!" Tresha said. "They hate you already! And me. Those two and their greedy husbands live on hate like it was bread. They hate everyone beneath them for being low, and everyone above for being high. They hate the sun and clouds in equal measure. Let them have their hate. I won't trust Sunrise Hall or the people of Morning County to them."

Elissa felt her legs weaken, and sat down. "I . . . I'll have to talk to Ragen."

"Of course," Tresha waved it away like a fly. "But we both know he would have to be on tampweed to turn this down."

She sipped her tea. "Trust me. It's easier to get things done when you've an entire county behind you. Take your birthright. If you truly care about this city and the people in it, you can do more for them in the duke's court than at your Warding Exchange."

Elissa looked down instinctively, stroking the silver stylus that hung from her belt. Could she, or was there another path in store for her?

Tresha noted the movement. "If not for that, then do it so I can spend my last months with my ripping grandchildren!"

Elissa smiled, and suddenly it all seemed clear. "As the countess wishes."

The organ was beginning to thrum as Ragen made it to the top of the hill to the Great Library and Cathedral of Miln. Soon it would begin the song of dusk, calling the last hour before curfew.

It would play again at sunset, at dawn, and at midday. The mountains that formed the Cathedral's backdrop provided a sort of Jongleur's shell, echoing the music back so loudly the entire city could hear it.

The Library was one of the few remaining structures of the old world. The one library in all Thesa that had survived the Return intact, protecting the knowledge within while the demons burned the old world around them.

There were ruins of the old world everywhere, if you knew where to look, but there were only a few structures still in use in the Free Cities. That the Great Library of Miln was the grandest of them was a fact any schoolchild could recite, but most of the students and Tenders moving across the great steps were used to the sight, never having seen its comparison.

Ragen had. The Great Cathedral of Angiers. The Monastery of Dawn. The Temple of the Horizon. Only Sharik Hora outstripped it in size, but even that could not match the Library's sheer aesthetic beauty, soaring up into the twin mountains at its back, a reminder to all who should approach that while knowledge was power, it was a gift from an even greater Power above.

It was said that Sharik Hora's true power was within its walls, the place adorned with the bones of fallen warriors. Ragen, a *chin,* was never allowed to see it from the inside. But how could any bones compare to the priceless knowledge protected within? Knowledge that had kept Miln the greatest power in Thesa for so many years.

A sprawling campus surrounded it, housing both the Mothers' and Gatherers' schools, as well as other institutions of science and learning. The Acolytes' School was housed in the Cathedral's cellars, which burrowed deep into the hill.

The hilltop had no walls, ringed with thirty-foot stone statues of the Guardians, dukes of Miln since the king of Thesa was slain in the Return. The shields and armor of the Guardians, as well as the great marble bases, were inscribed with powerful church wards.

Church wards were different from those the Warders' Guild traded. They were more beautiful and complex, and wove nets of incredible power. Such wards not only would bar a demon entrance but could reflect the force of any attack back upon the coreling—and in some cases reverse it. Ragen had once seen a flame demon hawk firespit onto church wards, only to have the blazing phlegm bounce back and land on its face, freezing where it touched. The demon had shrieked and run into the night. Demons had been known to literally beat themselves to death against a skilled Tender's warding.

Together the ring of statues formed the most impenetrable net in Miln. If the rest of the city fell, this place would be their last hope.

But in the moment, all that paled in comparison with the organ, rising to life. Ragen meant to go directly into the Library, but found himself drawn to its power.

The Cathedral was filled with worshippers, and there were glances and whispers at his passing. Mothers, Gatherers, and Tenders alike pretended not to stare. To escape, he flashed his guildmaster pin for access to the high balcony where the organist sat, overlooking the crowded nave. Far below he could see Tender Ronnell finishing services.

The organist was not an acolyte or even a Tender, but Ronnell's daughter, Mother Mery. Ragen watched as her skillful fingers rolled down the levels of keys as effortlessly as a stream flowed over stones. Shoes lay beneath the bench as she worked the pedals with bare, nimble feet.

The sound gathered in the nave, rising to the domed ceiling a hundred feet above, painted like the mountain sky. The song was one that had thrummed through him, from bones to balls, since his earliest memories. He felt tears welling in his eyes, realizing how close he had come in recent months to never hearing it again.

Mery finished her playing, reverently covering the organ's keys. She was putting on her shoes as Ragen approached.

"That was beautiful," he said.

"Guildmaster Ragen!" Mery gave a little hop and fell back onto the bench, one shoe flying.

Ragen caught the shoe on reflex, kneeling to hold it for her to slip her foot into. "Just Ragen, unless you insist I call you Mother."

Mery shook her head. "Of course not. We haven't spoken in many years. I didn't want to presume."

"Years make no difference," Ragen said. "You were under our roof enough when you were so young that Elissa and I will always consider you family."

Mery blushed and dropped her eyes. "Thank you, Guil . . . Ragen. That means a lot to me."

"Your playing brought tears to my eyes," Ragen said. "I did not realize it was you, all these years."

"I only play the services my father celebrates," Mery said. "Every acolyte is trained at the organ, but it does not begin until they take first orders at fourteen summers. My father taught me from his lap starting before I could reach the pedals."

"I daresay it shows," Ragen said. "I've heard the choir sing in the Temple of the Horizon, and the *dama* calling prayers from the minarets of Sharik Hora, but nothing to shake the ground and resonate in the bones like the organ of Miln with a skilled player."

"Thank you," Mery said.

"All those years," Ragen chuckled, "you listening to Jaik struggle to carry a tune . . ."

"Biting my lip." Mery giggled. "I knew then he was not serious about becoming a Jongleur. It was Arlen who wanted so desperately to believe."

The name was a cold wind blowing between them. The smile left Mery's lips. "What brings you to the Library? I've seen the private collection at your manse, and it is not lacking."

"I'm here to see your father," Ragen said. "I have a message for him."

"I can take it if you wish," Mery said. "There's only an hour before sunset, and I'm sure you're eager to return home after so many months abroad."

"Indeed I am," Ragen agreed. "But this message is of a personal nature, and addressed to your father, alone. It was entrusted to me by Countess Paper of the Hollow, and I am duty-bound as Messenger to put it in his hand and no other."

"Of course." Mery got to her feet. "I can take you to him." Ragen could see the gears turning behind her eyes. He was taking a chance, trusting even her.

Ronnell's office was high above the stacks in the adjoining Library, along a narrow balcony that let the Librarian look down over the tens of thousands of paper charges in his care.

Ronnell had not yet returned when Mery pushed Ragen inside and closed the door. "You said it came from Countess Paper in the Hollow. Is there news of Arlen? More than in the official account?"

Her sudden intensity made Ragen shift uneasily. "Of a sort, but I cannot . . ."

"Who sent the letter?" Mery demanded.

"Mery, I can't—"

"Who?!" she cut in just as Tender Ronnell entered the room.

The Tender looked at Ragen in shock. "What is the meaning of this?"

"Guildmaster Ragen has a secret message from the Hollow." Mery crossed her arms in a way that reminded him of

Elissa when she set herself. "One he did not see fit to mention at court."

Ragen's eyes flicked to Mery. "May we speak privately, Ronnell?"

Ronnell recognized the look on his daughter's face and gave a resigned shake of his head. "I have no secrets from my daughter."

Ragen sighed, pulling the sealed envelope from his jacket pocket. "It is a letter from Arlen Bales."

Mery's mouth fell open, and Ronnell rocked back a step. "How is this possible? We are told he fell from a cliff in the battle against Ahmann Jardir. Does he yet live?"

Ragen held up his hands. "I could not say. This letter was written shortly before he left to challenge the demon of the desert. I am told he wrote several such, to be delivered in the event of his death. It was entrusted to Mistress Leesha, who entrusted it to me." Ronnell's eyes widened and took on a covetous gleam as he reached for the letter.

"Night!" Mery exclaimed, causing Ronnell to snatch his hand back. "As if Arlen hasn't caused enough trouble, now he's sending letters from the grave?"

Ronnell reached out and took her arm. "Perhaps it's best you give the guildmaster and me a moment."

"No," Mery said. "Now that I know there's a letter from him, I need to see it."

"I understand." Ronnell tightened his grip on her elbow as he moved her toward the door. "But I fear your attachment to Arlen clouds your judgment. Allow us a moment to—"

Mery yanked from his grip. "Like night I will. If you try to kick me out, I'll go right to Jone." She looked over to Ragen. "No doubt she and the Mothers' Council will have many questions about why neither you nor Mother Elissa mentioned this letter while you were being debriefed at court."

Ragen scowled. "Will you reveal your own part in this so-called conspiracy, as well?"

Mery looked at him in surprise. "What?"

"I know Arlen revealed himself to you, before his meeting with the duke," Ragen said. "He told us what happened."

Ronnell looked to his daughter. "Is this true?"

Mery's eyes flicked down, staring at the thick carpet. "He

came to see Jaik, I think, not knowing we were married. He . . . ran when I answered the door."

"Why didn't you tell me?" Ronnell asked.

"I'm so sorry," Mery said. "I . . . I chased him into the streets. Knocked his hood away, and saw what he'd done to himself. He's . . . unhinged, Father. You saw him. How he . . . *mutilated* himself. How he'd rather live out among the *demons* than with his own kind. He's a madman. To think I meant to marry him . . ."

"But you didn't betray his trust," Ragen noted. "It was months before the duke got word of his identity. What do you think they will do if they discover you knew all along?"

"Are you threatening my daughter?" Ronnell demanded, putting his arms around her as she began to weep.

"Of course not," Ragen said. "But this is a Holy House of Learning, so let us speak only honest word. You said you and your daughter had no secrets, but that isn't entirely true, is it? She had one from you, and you still have one from her."

Mery looked up. "Father?"

Ronnell let go of her and stuck his head outside to scan the terrace. He pulled the thick goldwood doors shut and lifted an ancient key from the ring on his belt. The click of the lock echoed through the room.

Ronnell looked at his daughter. "He came to me, too."

Mery gaped. "What?"

"After he met the duke and cracked the floor," Ronnell said, "Arlen Bales visited me here, in this room. He told me he had already given the combat wards to Ragen, and dared me to tell His Grace, giving him time to suppress them or to rescind his offer of succor to the refugees from Rizon."

"It wasn't fair of him to put you in such a position," Mery said.

"It was," Ronnell said. "He asked me to choose between tending my flock and my liege's pride. Between standing in the Creator's light, or hiding in shadow."

"That does not make us accomplices to his crimes," Mery argued.

Ronnell shook his head. "His Grace would think otherwise. But even if not, what I did next was a crime most grave."

Mery said nothing, just staring.

"His Grace's copy of *Weapones of the Olde Wyrld* was not damaged by a leak in the ceiling," Ronnell said quietly.

"That almost cost your position," Mery said. "It took a week and a score of scribes to re-create. Father, tell me you did not . . ."

"I gave it to him," Ronnell said.

"Why?" Mery demanded.

"Because he is the Deliverer." Ronnell strode to his desk, snatching his Canon from its pedestal. He opened to a marked page and began to read. *"For he shall be marked upon his bare flesh, and the demons will not abide the sight, and they shall flee terrified before him."* He snapped the book shut.

"The Creator didn't mark him," Mery argued. "He did that to himself. Anyone could have."

"But anyone did not, until the coming of Arlen Bales," Ronnell said. "He was the first."

Mery shook her head. "I believe in the Canon, Father. I believe in the Plague, and that one day a Deliverer will come. But I will be corespawned before I believe it is Arlen Bales."

"Do not speak blasphemy in this holy place!" Ronnell barked, and Mery dropped her eyes. "I know this is difficult for you, but I have bent my every thought to it for nearly a year, and I believe it with my heart and soul. Arlen Bales is the Deliverer, sent by the Creator to end the Plague. Think of his miracles."

Even Ragen raised an eyebrow at that. "Miracles?"

"He withstood the naked night as a boy, cutting the arm from a rock demon."

"I heard that story a thousand times from his own lips," Mery said. "It was luck that saved him, and his own stupidity that put him at risk."

"He brought us warded glass, and built the exchange that Ragen sits atop," Ronnell added.

"They ward differently in the hamlets," Mery said. "All he did was write them down and sell them."

"He saved the Hollow," Ronnell said. "Flew in the sky by many accounts, throwing lightning from his hands and saving thousands."

"Demonshit," Mery said. "Those are ale stories. Tampweed tales to dress up a battle."

"He slew the demon of the desert," Ronnell said.

"The only truly good thing he's done," Mery said. "Throwing them both from a cliff."

"Enough!" Ragen barked. "You may be a Mother now, Mery, but you ate at my table when you were just a Daughter. Did I ever show you the slightest disrespect?"

Mery shook her head. "I apologize. That was . . . unkind of me."

"Unkind doesn't begin to cover it," Ragen said. "I'm sorry Arlen broke your heart when he left. He broke ours, too. But you knew the kind of man he was. I won't have you spinning lies into his life."

The words shook Mery, and for a moment she had no response, torn between loyalties. As a Mother, she was bound to the council; as a daughter, to her father. But as herself?

Ragen held up the letter again. "Do you wish to keep speculating, or do you wish to read in his own words?"

Ronnell took the letter and Mery moved close as he broke the seal. Ragen had never thought they looked much alike, but as both tilted their heads at precisely the same angle to read, the resemblance was uncanny.

Summer, 333 AR

Tender Ronnell,
I am not a believer.

I never believed the corelings to be a plague sent from Heaven. Never believed a loving Creator could inflict such horror upon people. Never believed in a Deliverer. Waiting for another to solve our problems only lets them fester.

But these last years have taught me I do believe in something. I believe it is time for humanity to stand. I believe we can cast off the demons and take back our world.

They know we are getting stronger. They know, and they are massing. There will be blizzards and quakes in the coming months. You and Ragen have magic to defend against them, but it will take more than wards. It will take belief. Belief that we must put aside our

differences and unite against the corelings. Belief that
every life matters, and that we fight not just for
ourselves, but to succor those who cannot.

My friend Rojer discovered a way to forbid demons
without wards. If the Creator exists and speaks to
anyone, it is him. Enclosed find sheets of his music to
teach your choir the Song of Waning. *With it, even the*
weak can have power. Use it when new moon comes and
times are darkest.

Tomorrow I go to battle Ahmann Jardir. I do not know
if I will survive, but I believe it doesn't matter. What's
been started is bigger than me.

Arlen Bales

"There, in his own words." Mery flicked the paper with a finger. "He is not the Deliverer."

Ronnell shook his head. "His words make no difference. The Deliverer is an agent of change. He cannot serve his function if he believes in the old ways. He is here to show us the new."

"This is nonsense," Mery said. "Blizzards and quakes? Magical choirs? Arlen has always had delusions of grandeur, but this is too much to believe."

"You think it coincidence that demons were tracking us on the road back to Miln?" Ragen asked. "That they crushed the way stations between here and Angiers, killing dozens of Mountain Spears? Ask the survivors if there was magic in Keerin's music those nights."

Mery looked at her father. "What will you do?"

"Speak to the choirmaster," Ronnell said. "Order my Tenders and acolytes to begin using the new wards I've taught them."

He looked down at the paper in his hands. "And I have a sermon to write."

"Would we have to live with her?"

Elissa laughed at Ragen's guarded response to the news. "No, but we'll need to meet with her regularly. My mother will retain her full title and Sunrise Hall during the transition. Power will not transfer to us fully until her death. We can decide then if we wish to move my family's two-hundred-year-old seat of power."

Ragen made a face. "I thought you hated the place."

"I hated my mother," Elissa said. "For a long time, she and that hall were one and the same. But now . . ."

"Do we get titles?" Ragen asked.

Elissa smiled. "You would be Guildmaster Ragen, Neocount of Morning."

Ragen let out a slow whistle. "I do like the sound of that. Can your mother leave you leadership of the council?"

Elissa shook her head. "Only a majority vote of Mothers can do that. More reason to start the transition early."

Ragen sighed. "A good thing Derek just became fabulously wealthy. He might be the only one in Miln I'd sell my home to."

Elissa put her arms around him, and he held her until there was a knock at the door.

"Yes?" Elissa called.

Margrit entered. "Begging your pardon, but the Messengers have arrived."

"Thank you for answering my call." Ragen strode down the lines of men in the yard. As Malcum warned, nearly every Messenger in Miln was there, along with the fittest men and women of the Warders' Guild.

"For too many years, Messengers have been forced to cower inside our circles at night, unable to defend ourselves if the demons broke through." There were a lot of familiar faces in the ranks, including some who had long since retired, drawn by rumors of the rejuvenating power of magic.

Ragen selected one of the spears Elissa had infused with *hora,* holding it up and manipulating the net with his fingers to make the wards glow brightly in the twilit courtyard. "Those days are over." He thumped the spear on the flagstones as gasps ran through the crowd.

"Each of you will be given a warded weapon, and training

to use it. Keep it close at night. Even when you are behind the wards. Even behind Miln's walls. Even in your homes."

There were more than just Messengers and Warders watching. A skeptical-looking group of Gatherers led by Mistress Anet stood to one side, Keerin and his apprentices to another. Even Tender Ronnell had broken curfew with a handpicked group of Tenders and acolytes to observe.

Mother Mery was absent.

"We going to be fightin' in our bedrooms?" one Messenger asked. She was gray and leather-skinned, years retired.

"I pray to the Creator not," Ragen said. "Nor will any of you be pressed to go into the night looking for trouble. I have no intention of doing that, either."

He pointed the glowing spear at his walls. "But Miln's walls were breached once not so long ago, and the demons are growing stronger. One by one, Euchor's way stations fall silent. Make no mistake, the corelings are coming to Fort Miln. There will be blizzards and quakes. We need to be ready for them."

CHAPTER 22

THE EDGE OF
NIE'S ABYSS

334 AR

Briar's tattoos had long since healed, but his palms still itched. It was a constant reminder the wards were still there beneath the dirty cloth.

As if he could forget.

He tried to resist the power they represented, keeping them wrapped and relying instead on his spear. But even through the shaft and the layers of cloth, magic still passed into his hands when he struck a demon. The wards drank it greedily, an addictive pleasure that had him seeking corie encounters he would otherwise have avoided.

And every time he thought of the tattoos, he was reminded of Stela Inn, and the night they spent in the Briarpatch. Stela Inn, naked and covered in demon ichor. Stela Inn, on hands and knees with Brother Franq behind her.

He shook his head. *Need time. Time and distance. Won't come lookin' for me this far out.*

Part of him wished she would. Hunt him down, make him hers again. Part of him would always be hers. Part of him *wanted* to.

Briar focused instead on his duty. When his family died, everyone gave up on him but Tender Heath of Bogton. After the Krasians came, Captain Dehlia of *Sharum's Lament* made them both honorary members of her crew. Told him they were family.

It was time for his family to be free. The Krasians had never truly taken Lakton, and with Jayan's forces destroyed, Docktown was greatly weakened. Captain Qeran and his privateers dominated the waters for now, but Briar knew the Laktonians had boats in reserve. If he could gather enough information, they might be able to retake Docktown.

And so Briar moved to gather as much information as possible before returning. He kept to the underbrush alongside the Messenger road south, slipping in and out of the hamlets along the way. He questioned contacts where he had them, and listened to the talk in the squares and inns.

Most of the villages on the road to Docktown were under Hollow control, with considerable traffic in goods, travelers, and Cutter patrols. Countess Paper was aggressively expanding her borders in response to raids by the Wolves of Everam.

The Wolves were a *Sharum* cavalry unit under a Krasian warlord named Jurim. They were always on the move, never staying longer than it took to sack a town. If they had a base, none could find it, and their numbers were likewise opaque. There might be as few as two hundred of them, or more than a thousand.

Even in Hollow territory, Briar saw Wolf scouts spying on the road. They were skilled woodsmen by now, but clumsy and loud by Briar's standards. He could easily have snuck up and killed them, but couldn't bring himself to spill blood when there was no immediate threat.

It was fear of the Wolves that kept the hamlets on the Krasian side of the border under Evejan law. The Laktonians now outnumbered their Krasian overseers, stripped bare after the Battle of Angiers. But those who tried to throw off the local *dama* without aid from the Hollow had been visited by the Wolves, reduced to ash and blood.

Traffic thinned in Krasian territory. Trade wagons were fewer, and the *dama* did not allow *chin* to travel between villages. By the time Briar reached the split at Northfork, the Messenger road was empty.

Briar headed east for a few days to learn what he could before reporting to Lakton. Krasian Messengers and patrols passed from time to time, but otherwise all was quiet. Hamlets east of Northfork were more firmly under Krasian control now that Prince Egar's rebels had been crushed at the Battle of Docktown.

But firmly under the thumb of the Krasians as they were, there were few *Sharum* in the hamlets. If the Laktonians struck now, there would be no reinforcements.

He turned back, heading for Docktown. There were *Sharum* blacks in his pack he could use to slip into the town and explore. Then he would head north along the shoreline until he reached a certain hidden cove Captain Dehlia favored. If he moved a certain rock, she would be sure to notice and send a boat to pick him up.

But as he was about to cut cross-country, a lone traveler caught his attention.

"The sun will set soon," Ashia told Kaji.

It was not the *Sharum'ting* way to speak aloud. For the last decade she had largely spoken in the intricate hand code of the mute eunuchs who served the *dama'ting*. She and her spear sisters were not meant to be seen or heard. Only felt.

But she was no longer simply a *Sharum'ting*. She was a mother, and a mother's duty was to teach her child to speak.

"We'll need to make camp," she advised, wondering if there were hidden ears about. If they had just revealed too much of their plans. She saw a slight movement in the undergrowth. It could have been a deer, or a shadow, or nothing at all. Her veil flared and pulled tight as she sniffed the air.

"Cap!" Kaji echoed.

"That's right, my heart!" The chatter, however unnatural it felt, only helped her disguise.

Sharum patrols are apt to force themselves on any woman caught traveling alone, the Damajah had said. *Or a shapely young mother, even with her babe. But a shapeless old woman traveling with her grandson will be invisible.*

And so Ashia had strewn rough *dal'ting* blacks over her armor to give her a shapeless figure. She hunched, adding the weight of years to her carriage. A thick black veil hid her face and hair. Makeup around the eyes added wrinkles to her smooth skin.

Her twin stabbing spears were unscrewed and sheathed in

cloth, supports for the pack Kaji rode on her back. She could have them in her hands in seconds if needed, extending the warded spearheads contained in the hollow shafts with a flick of her wrist.

The mirror finish of her warded glass shield was hidden under a coating of paint shaded to look like battered bronze. The sort of shield almost every Krasian family had at least one of, left over from some *Sharum* relative who walked the lonely path. It hung from her saddle, not worth the effort of stealing.

Likewise, her mare had been carefully chosen to appear nondescript. Rags tied about her fetlocks hid the silvered wards cut into her hooves. Even the horse's name, Rasa, meant "hidden strength."

She seemed just another of the countless Krasian women in the wetlands, widowed by Prince Jayan's foolishness. With nothing worth stealing and a child on her back, she was largely ignored by bandits and *Sharum* patrols alike.

The Damajah had used her earring to check their progress the first few nights, but Ashia had long since passed out of range. They would be in Everam's Reservoir in just two more days.

Ashia found a secluded patch of dry land not far from the road as the sun set.

"Cap!" Kaji cried, as she got down from her horse.

"That's right," Ashia agreed. "This is our camp. What do we do first?"

"Hoss!" Kaji answered immediately. They practiced every evening.

"Yes," Ashia said. "First I have to stake the horse." She did not use a hammer, driving the peg into the ground with a precise thrust of her palm, like striking a blow against Ala itself.

"What do we do second?" Ashia asked.

"Suhkul!" Kaji shouted.

Ashia smiled as she spread her portable warded circle. Last night, he responded to the second question with "hoss." The night before, nothing. Already, he understood her well enough, and every day brought a new word to his tiny lips.

She set his pack down and began laying stones for a fire.

"Cap!" he pointed at the sticks she gathered.

Ashia set them ablaze with her ruby ring, which contained a piece of flame demon horn. "Fire."

"Fir," Kaji agreed, and she felt a thrill run through her. Another new word. It was fitting, for today was a special day.

She unstrapped Kaji and lifted him from the pack to change his bido. Her eyes never left his as her practiced hands went about the task.

"It is your born day." She lifted Kaji close. "Ala has made one journey around Everam's sun since the night you were brought into this world." She opened the front of her robes to free a breast.

There was a slight rustle in the trees. Ashia gave no outward sign, cooing as she brought her son in to suckle, but all her attention homed in on that spot. Eyes like a falcon's could see no sign of anyone. Sharp ears strained, but there was no further sound.

It could have been anything. The sun had not set, so she knew it was no demon, but it could have been a small animal. A falling nut. A slight breeze.

But there was that scent again. The one she'd smelled on the road.

She waited, falling into her breath as she strained her senses, but there was nothing to indicate a threat.

"Your mother sees enemies everywhere," she told Kaji at last. The boy was not listening, eyes closed as he nursed. Ashia took her own repast, one of the small dense honey cakes the *Sharum'ting* used to keep up their strength with minimal ingestion.

When he was done, she left him on a blanket in the hollow of her rounded shield. He stretched and fidgeted, free at last of the confining pack, but the wobbling shield kept him safely confined while she tended Rasa, removing the saddle and brushing her down.

By the time the horse was settled, the sky was darkening. Perhaps a quarter hour before the rising. She lifted Kaji from the shield and set him on his feet. He held on to her sleeve, but it was for balance, not strength. For the next several minutes, he stumbled gleefully through the camp, dragging his mother along.

"Hoss!" he shouted at Rasa.

"Yes, horse!" Ashia laughingly agreed.

"Fir!" he barked at the fire.

"Yes, fire!" Ashia gave his hand a squeeze.

"Cap!" he cried to the wards.

"Wards," Ashia told him, tracing the symbols with a finger.

"Wads!" Kaji shouted.

Another rustle. Ashia kept her breathing steady, but she picked Kaji up and swung him through the air. The boy squealed with joy as she brought him back to the fire in the center of the circle.

She reached into her saddlebag for a carefully wrapped box. "I have something special for you, my son. A present, for your first born day." Inside was a soft, yellow cake. "My Tikka made this when I was a girl, and I loved it more than anything. Now she has made one for you."

She began to sing, a traditional song for a child's born day. She and her spear sisters were all trained singers. Ashia seldom had call to use the skill, but never did she feel closer to Everam than when she sang to her son.

Again, the sound from the trees. The warded coins strung about her forehead let her see in Everam's light now that the sun was setting, but even with them, there was no sign of any creature in the woods.

But it was there, and it was clever, timing its movements with the rise and fall of her song to mask the sound.

Whoever it was did not appear to wish them immediate harm. After a few moments, they began drifting away. A spy on the way to report to a superior?

The spy moved in time with not just her voice, but the crickets and birds, the cries of bats and the howl of wind. Sensitive to the night's harmony, it was no mere animal. No simple demon. One of Asome's elite Krevakh Watchers? A *dama* sorcerer?

Or was it one of the shapeless *alagai*? The *kai*. Ashia fought one of them, Asome at her side, what seemed a lifetime ago. The demon recovered quickly from even her strongest blows, doubling and redoubling its assaults, growing more and more limbs until she could not dodge or parry them all.

It had been her husband who killed it, in the end. Ashia

could not say in truth that she would have been victorious alone. Such a demon had killed her master, Enkido.

As she sang, she slipped her warded glass spear shafts from the baby pack, screwing them together into a walking stick. When the song was done, she set the cake in front of Kaji. He stared at it.

"Cake," Ashia said.

"Cay," Kaji said.

"You eat it." Ashia reached out and broke a piece off the cake. How long since she last tasted Tikka's cake? Nearly a decade. "Like this."

She popped the piece into her mouth. Soft, sticky, and sweet, it tasted like childhood. Like happiness and safety. She remembered her own private pillow chamber filled with silks and velvet and rich carpet, golden chalices and stained glass. Vapid conversations with the crowd of young women who seemed to exist only to flatter her. The life she lived before being wrenched into cramped subsistence beneath the Dama'ting Palace.

Kaji laughed, mimicking her as best he could. He used two hands, grabbing the spongy cake in gleeful fists, scattering far more than made it into his mouth. Ashia laughed again. She hated Kajivah for witlessly sending her and her cousins to Inevera, and hated her again when she was pulled away from them to marry Asome. But if all those moments were leading to this, the sound of Kaji's laughter, then every moment of suffering was worth it.

But even as she watched her son experience Tikka's yellow cake for the first time, a part of Ashia was tracking the spy. They had drawn off, but not too far. She could smell them.

Ashia cleaned Kaji's sticky hands and nestled him in a blanket inside her shield. Even if the outer wards should fail, the circle around the rim of the shield would keep him safe until she could get to him.

She lifted Kaji's soiled bido. "You may be allowed to empty yourself in the circle, my son, but I am afraid I cannot." She kissed him. "I will be back in a moment."

She moved slowly, in case the predator still watched, pretending to need the walking stick to get to her feet. She shuffled slowly out of the firelight, slipping behind a tree.

The moment she was out of sight, Ashia dropped her heavy outer robe, clad now in feather-light black *Sharum'ting* silks, reinforced with plates of warded glass. She activated her *hora* of silence, making no sound as she scampered up the tree and into the boughs.

Kaji was speaking to himself as he often did, much of it indecipherable sounds. Ashia focused on them, moving as one with their rise and fall, as the predator had. She flitted from tree to tree like a hummingbird between flowers, and soon circled around the camp and into the trees, at last getting a look at the spy.

Briar lost a day, but while his information was useful, there was no one expecting him in Lakton. The road was not safe for an old Krasian woman and her child. The *Sharum* were his enemy—he had to believe that—but his home had not been invaded by women and children.

He was impressed by the woman, and a little suspicious. Her back was stooped, as if she did not have the strength to carry herself upright, but she rode the day through with a babe on her back, stopping only to feed and change him. When the day grew late, she showed no fear, calmly finding a spot out of sight of the road and making camp.

Krasian women were hard. They did the majority of work in their communities, ran businesses, constructed buildings, slaughtered livestock, and raised children.

What they did *not* do was fight. Not against other humans, and certainly not against demons. This one didn't even have any weapons, only a battered shield, yet she faced the coming night with no sign of worry. Even Briar was filled with fear when the sun set. It was the reason he was still alive.

Who was this woman? Was the boy her son? Grandson? Or just another orphan, like Briar? Everam knew there were endless stories of broken families throughout the land. The Krasians sank or captured more than half the Laktonian fleet and kept their grip on the hamlets, but not without terrible losses. Were they headed to Docktown seeking his father?

Or perhaps the woman worked for an orphanage? A Messenger of sorts, ferrying children to whatever families would take them. Krasians always succored the children of *Sharum* who walked the lonely path, and they would need to replenish their warriors after the battles. What family would turn down a healthy Krasian son?

But from the moment she unstrapped the baby, he knew that was not it. Whoever she was, whatever she was, there was no mistaking a mother's love for her child.

He watched, basking in the sound of the boy shouting words in Krasian, and the mother's replies.

Relan insisted his children understand who they were and where they came from. He taught them to speak his language, sing his songs, dance his dances. He taught his sons *sharu-sahk* and sought to find good husbands for his daughters.

Briar heard his father's language often of late, but always in anger. This woman spoke with laughter and joy, the way Briar Damaj remembered it best.

He understood then that anyone who could love so fully and speak with such joy could never be his enemy. They appeared to be headed for Docktown, and he resolved to see them safely there, even if it cost him time. He would keep watch as they slept, luring the cories away from them.

She sat with the child, and by the time Briar realized what was happening, she had bared her breast to feed him.

Briar felt his face heat, turning quickly to avert his gaze. Too late. The image burned in his mind's eye. Even after several moments of steady breathing, it lingered. A young woman's breast. The bulk that gave her an appearance of age was due to a second robe beneath her first, the armored blacks of a *Sharum*. A rarer sight than a woman carrying the family shield, but not unheard of. It explained some of her calm before the setting sun.

Briar heard her shuffling cloth when the baby was finished, and dared to look again in time to see the boy clutch at his mother's robes and pull himself onto his feet. He hung tightly for balance, stumbling around the camp, pointing and shouting his words. Briar moved closer, not wanting to miss a moment of it.

But then the woman took her son back to the fire, and began to sing a song Briar had not heard in years. The born day song, praising Everam for giving life.

How many times had Briar's family sung that song? There were seven in the Damaj house.

The woman's voice was the most beautiful, transcendent thing Briar had heard short of the duet Halfgrip's wives performed at his funeral. He lost himself in the sound, letting it wrap him like a warm blanket.

And for an instant he remembered the sounds of their voices. The choir of his brothers and sisters. The deep tone of his father. And his mother, as always, leading the song.

He choked, swallowing the sound and squeezing sudden drops from his eyes. He tried to grasp the memory again, to hear them one more time, but it was gone like a wisp of smoke. He felt sobs building in his chest, and knew he could not suppress them for long.

Holding his breath, Briar backed away as quickly as he could without being noticed. When he was far enough away, he put his back to a tree, slid down to the wet soil, and wept.

Ashia watched the spy, unsure.

He was certainly no *dama,* years too young, and clad in filthy rags. He carried a warrior's spear and shield, but he looked like no *Sharum* Ashia had ever seen. His clothes were of Northern design, filthy with sap and soil to make him all but invisible in the underbrush, even to wardsight.

But now that she was close, Ashia could see his magic was strong, particularly focused in his hands. His face was so covered in dirt that his features were hard to make out. He could have been Krasian, or a dark-haired greenlander who spent too much time in the sun.

Who was he? What did he want? And why in Everam's name was he weeping?

Capture him and find out.

Ashia tightened her grip on her staff, keeping the blades retracted. With her other hand, she drew a few inches of silk cord from the spindle on her belt. There was a point where the lines of power converged in the back of the neck. Leaning forward, head between his knees, the spy had bared it for her. A precise strike would stun him long enough for her to loop the cord around his wrists and ankles. She would be back in the camp with her prisoner before Kaji began to miss her.

She leapt, silent as a diving wind demon, but somehow the spy noticed her. He rolled forward at the last moment and her staff struck only the wet soil where he sat.

The enemy will not wait for you to hit them, Enkido's fingers taught.

Ashia used the energy from her landing to roll after him, managing to throw a loop of cord around his ankle. She pulled, but he caught his balance mid-trip, twisting to kick her in the face with his free leg.

Ashia was knocked back, losing her grip on the cord long enough for him to slip free. The spy might have pressed the advantage, but instead he turned and ran.

Ashia moved immediately to pursue. The spy cut left, then ran two steps up the trunk of a tree and leapt to the right, grabbing a branch and pulling himself up.

Ashia wasn't fooled by the move, gaining inches on him as she ran up the trunk of the second tree, as light on the branches as he. For an instant, there was a gap in the foliage and she threw, staff striking him between the shoulder blades as he reached for another branch. His arm fell short, hand spasming, and he fell from the branches.

Ashia dropped straight down, dispersing the energy in a tumble as she pulled more cord from her belt.

But the spy landed in a roll as well, turning to face her as she rushed in. He threw a push-kick she easily slipped, trying to catch the foot in a loop of cord. He was too fast, grabbing the silk and pulling her in as he threw a punch.

Ashia parried with minimal contact and moved in to grapple, but the spy's skin was gummy with sap. He wrestled free before she could get a firm grip.

They both got to their feet, and he came at her in a straightforward attack. His kicks and punches were perfectly executed, but they were basic. *Sharukin* taught to children and *chi'Sharum.*

But what he lacked in skill, he made up for in speed and adaptability. He caught one of her return punches in a twist of her own cord, then dove between her legs. Ashia threw herself forward into a flip to reverse the hold and use it against him, but he let go and used the distraction to sprint away.

Again she raced after him, drawing farther and farther from her camp. Kaji began to cry, and Ashia grew worried. It was full dark, and the sounds might draw *alagai* to him.

But this man was too dangerous to let escape. She put on a burst of speed, snatching a stone from the muck and throwing to strike the convergence at the back of his knee. The leg collapsed on his next step, and he tumbled, trying to keep balance, as Ashia closed the gap.

This time she did not hesitate. Having taken his measure, she struck again and again, kicks and punches, knees and elbows. If she could not bind him without harm, she would force him to submit.

The spy was quick and strong, blocking or dodging the first blows of the flurry, but soon one slipped by, and then two more. He reeled, off balance. His limbs, numbed by her blows, betrayed him.

He tried to say something, but she struck him in the throat, and he choked on the words. It was not time for talk. She caught his arm and began to twist it into a submission hold.

Still coughing, the spy turned to her and spat stinking juice in her face. It stung her eyes and she pulled back, giving him space to heel-kick her away from him.

By the time her vision cleared, Kaji's cries filled the night, and the spy was gone. She sniffed at the sticky juice on her fingers. Like the spy himself, they reeked of the herb *dama'ting* used to treat demon wounds.

You must seek the khaffit, the Damajah said. *And find my lost cousin. You will know him by his scent.*

But what did it mean? Could this vagabond be the Damajah's lost cousin? It seemed unlikely. And if so, what then? Did he have information she needed? Was he a friend? A foe?

Could she afford to find out, with Kaji to protect?

She recovered her staff on the way back to camp. A bog demon had been drawn by Kaji's cries. It shambled around the circle, testing the wards.

The wards sewn into Ashia's robes made her all but invisible to the demon. She slipped behind it, extending one of her spearpoints and impaling it in the back. The demon shrieked and thrashed, but Ashia hung on as magic pumped into her, crackling around the wards painted on her nails. It made her feel strong. Fast. In moments she had broken camp and set Kaji back in his pack on her shoulders. She removed the rags around Rasa's fetlocks, revealing the wards carved into her hooves. These she painted with *alagai* ichor until they shined brightly in her wardsight.

Then she mounted and kicked the horse hard, galloping into the night. There were occasional corelings on the road, and she purposely ran a few down, activating the wards on Rasa's hooves and boosting the animal's strength and stamina. She drew upon her *hora* jewelry for the same. Kaji, soothed by the steady hoofbeats, fell fast asleep.

She reached Everam's Reservoir an hour before dawn, pausing to replace her disguise. She thought she caught his scent again, but after sniffing about, she became convinced she imagined it. No warrior on foot—or even a normal mount—could have kept pace with Rasa.

At sunrise Ashia broke camp. This close to Everam's Reservoir, the road was active with *Sharum* returning from patrol and vendors preparing for the coming day. She was just another old *dal'ting* woman with a child—invisible.

But the spy would stand out, if he tried to follow. She would either lose him or draw him from hiding.

Briar ran as fast as he could, zigzagging through the trees, over and under obstacles and through water, trying to put as much distance as possible between him and that terrifying woman.

Stela Inn had frightened him, but at least she spoke, and he understood her motivations. This woman moved like a *kai'Sharum* Watcher. Was she *Sharum'ting*? Traveling with a baby? It didn't fit.

Whatever she was, he was no match for her in a fair fight. She was too fast, too skilled.

Before he felt protective, determined to guard innocent travelers on their path. Now he was curious. Was the woman a spy? The child a ruse to draw attention from her mission? Greenlanders were known to sympathize with Krasian women, often seeking to free them from bonds they did not wish to be free of.

Given the chance, such a warrior as this could infiltrate the resistance and assassinate leaders.

When he was certain he'd lost her, he cut diagonally back to the Messenger road, trying to get ahead of her. Before long, she came thundering up the road, the hooves of her simple mare glowing brightly with ward magic.

Whoever she was, whatever, he needed to know. To warn his people before she could cause any harm.

He waited for her to pass, then set off after.

As expected, the *Sharum* in Everam's Reservoir ignored Ashia. Any woman who was not bearing food or sexually available was beneath their notice. She walked unmolested all the way to the piers.

Women and children far outnumbered the men in Everam's Reservoir. Jayan's warriors were entrenched so long that many sent for their wives and children to settle in homes doled out by the prince as spoils to his warriors.

Most of those men rode off with Jayan, never to return. Asome, not wanting to draw eyes to his brother's former stronghold, had been slow to send reinforcements. The result was a shadow of a town, missing some essential part of what made a community thrive.

Ashia's cousin Sharu, the Deliverer's fourth son, had been left in command of Everam's Reservoir. She could see his banner flying over the town hall. They had been close as children, but Ashia passed the building by. Sharu was one of the only men east of Everam's Bounty who might recognize her, and Asome had always dominated his younger brothers. Sharu would betray her without a thought.

She could see that her cousin's forces were spread thin. There were not even enough warriors to protect the town hall, should it come under concentrated attack.

The only places that seemed fully alive were the docks. A steady stream of *chin* and *dal'ting* poured on and off the ships, hauling supplies, checking manifests, cataloging spoils, selling food and drink. The Krasian fleet was so large only a portion of its vessels could dock at a given time.

Seek the three sisters, Inevera advised after consulting her dice. As with many of the Damajah's foretellings, it did not make sense at the time, but now a quick scan of the docks was all she needed.

A lone pier, large enough for half a dozen vessels, was dedicated to *Tan Spear,* the flagship of Everam's Reservoir, and its two escorts: *Tan Shield* and *Tan Armor.*

The names were a reminder that while Sharu technically ruled in Everam's Reservoir, his strength came from the *kha'Sharum* privateers under the command of Drillmaster Qeran. Scorpions and slings lined their decks, lashed in neat rows. Each of the vessels—superior to any in the fleet—flew the camel crutch flag of Abban the *khaffit.* It was said the Battle of Everam's Reservoir would have been lost without them.

The crew members all wore loose tan pants, though many were shirtless as they labored. Ashia knew it was sinful, but she let her eyes drift over their bodies. She had only lain with her husband twice. Was that the only contact she would ever have with a man, apart from fighting?

On the decks, those on duty worked efficient maintenance, while those off practiced *sharusahk* and spearwork. Ashia could not deny the warriors were skilled. Drillmaster Qeran was a legend, having trained the Deliverer, himself. Even her master Enkido spoke of Qeran with respect.

There were any number of ways Ashia might have snuck onto *Tan Spear* unnoticed, but there was no reason to risk swimming or climbing with Kaji when the boy provided the perfect cover. She walked right up to the *kha'Sharum* guard at the gangplank. He looked at her—through her. This was not one of the lax *dal'Sharum* that filled the city. He searched with his eyes, assessing potential contraband or threat.

Ashia's disguise satisfied him. Kaji lent a weight to it that no clothing or makeup possibly could. Eliminating the possibility of threat, the warrior's interest waned and his guard dropped.

"I am Hannali vah Qeran, eldest daughter of your master," Ashia lied. "My father will want to meet his latest grandson."

The *Sharum*'s brows raised slightly. He signaled a runner, who quickly returned with permission to come aboard. The Damajah's foretelling revealed Qeran's affection for Hannali.

It was obvious to Captain Qeran the moment she stepped into his cabin that she was not his favored daughter, but he said nothing, waving two fingers to dismiss her escort.

Ashia watched as the former drillmaster bounced to his feet, walking on one muscular leg and one curved sheet of metal. A wooden limb would have cost him balance, but Qeran was fully in control, using the spring of the artificial limb to propel himself around.

There were few *Sharum* Ashia felt could threaten her in *sharusahk*. Knowing he had lost his limb, Ashia did not expect to add Qeran to the list, but the captain surprised her. He would be fast, harder to unbalance, and the tense steel leg made possible moves other warriors could never attempt.

Qeran, too, gave her an appraising glance. "You're wearing armor under your robe. If you're an assassin, I thank you for the respite from my endless paperwork. Set the child aside and let us have done."

The words were casual, but she could see in his eyes the threat was real. Having sent his guard away, Qeran was fully prepared to fight and kill an assassin, alone in his cramped cabin.

"I am no assassin," Ashia said. "I am Sharum'ting Ka Ashia vah Ashan am'Jardir am'Kaji. I am here on business from the Damajah."

Hold nothing back with Qeran, the Damajah said after consulting her dice, but still Ashia tensed, ready to fight and kill should he threaten to expose her. Her eyes flicked around the room, looking for ways to use the close walls, low ceiling, and numerous support beams to her advantage.

Qeran shifted, ready for an attack, but he crossed his arms. "I knew Ashia as a child, but I have not seen her face since she was taken into the Dama'ting Palace a decade ago."

He thrust his chin at her pack. "You mean to say that is Kaji asu Asome am'Jardir am'Kaji? Heir to the Skull Throne?"

Ashia kept her breathing even. "Yes."

"Prove it," Qeran said.

"What proof would satisfy you?" Ashia asked.

Qeran smiled. "I don't know Ashia's face, but I did know Enkido. He was my *ajin'pal.*"

Ashia blinked. Her master had been such a part of the Dama'ting Palace that she seldom gave thought to his life before. Wives and children he left to serve Damaji'ting Kenevah and learn the secrets of *dama'ting sharusahk. Sharum* trained in his years as a drillmaster.

And brothers. The bond of *ajin'pal* was as strong as blood.

"The great drillmaster took one *nie'Sharum* each year as his *ajin'pal,*" Qeran said. "Drillmaster Kaval was the year before mine, a bond that made us brothers as well. I am told Kaval and Enkido died together on *alagai* talons, their glory boundless, while I trained *khaffit* back in Everam's Bounty."

His voice did not waver, but Ashia could hear the sorrow in Qeran's words. The pain. He would have gladly died at his brothers' side.

He locked eyes with her. "That is why you must fight me, Princess. If you have been trained by Enkido, I will know, and help you in any way I can. If you have not . . ." His eyes flicked to Kaji. "You have my word that after I kill you I will raise the boy as if he were my own."

Ashia felt a chill at the words, but she did not hesitate, removing the pack with Kaji and laying it on a bench as far out of the way as possible in the tiny cabin. She stripped off her thick *dal'ting* robe, standing in her silk *Sharum'ting* blacks, plated with warded glass. She drew a white silk scarf from her sleeve and wrapped it over the black scarf and veil of her *dal'ting* disguise.

She bowed. "You honor me, Drillmaster."

Qeran bowed in return. "It is I who am honored, if you are indeed the Sharum'ting Ka." He shifted his foot slightly, adding just a bit of tension to the curved blade of metal supporting the other limb. His hands came out in a *sharusahk* readiness position Enkido had drilled countless times into Ashia and her spear sisters. She flowed to mirror him.

Hold nothing back with Qeran.

"Begin," Qeran said, and she was moving, but not in the direction he expected. Ashia quickstepped from a stool onto the wall, spinning into a kick to take the drillmaster in the face.

But Qeran was quick to react, slipping the kick and catching her armpit as she sailed past. He twisted, using her own momentum to add force as he punched her in the chest.

It was as if her breastplate had been struck with a maul. She slammed down into the deck, losing her wind, but she kept balance, sweeping a leg at his ankle.

Qeran hopped back out of range of the sweep, using the sudden bounce on his metal leg to spring at her as she kicked her feet up to throw herself upright.

This time Ashia met him head-on, matching the drillmaster blow for blow. He might not have been privy to the full secrets of *dama'ting sharusahk,* but Qeran knew what Ashia was doing when she tried to drive fingers, knuckles, and even toes into convergence points on his body. Most he was able to slip or block, always with a powerful series of blows to flow in after. Ashia worked hard to honor her master's teachings, picking them off and countering, searching for an opening.

Once, he let a blow slip past his defenses and Ashia thought she had him, but when her stiffened fingers struck the hidden plate beneath his robe, Ashia knew she had been played. Like hers, Qeran's robes were lined with warded glass. She breathed away the pain, thanking Everam the fingers were not broken.

Unable to dominate the battlefield enough to strike at the convergences, Ashia shifted her focus to targets more difficult to defend against, and it became a slow attrition. She landed a punch, but it cost her a knee to the stomach. She kicked out his good knee and barely avoided his metal leg taking her head off.

Little by little, they worked out the pattern of armor plates in each other's robes, aiming blows for the weakened areas.

Ashia landed a kick to Qeran's ribs. The drillmaster was quick and caught the leg. Ashia twisted to slip his grip, but it cost her, giving Qeran an opening to strike her in the back.

But instead, the drillmaster shoved her away. Ashia did not question her fortune, rolling with the throw to come back to her feet out of range. There were bookshelves built into the bulkhead, and Ashia ran up them, readying to strike from above.

"Enough, Princess." Qeran's guard was down, his stance

unthreatening. Ashia dropped lightly back to the floor. Both were breathing hard.

The drillmaster knelt, putting his hands on the floor. "What are the Damajah's commands? Is there any word of reinforcements?"

"There are none to send," Ashia said. "Everam's Bounty is in chaos. The Majah have left the Deliverer's army. They march with their slaves and spoils back to the Desert Spear."

Qeran spat on the deck. "Majah dogs."

"They have just cause for grievance," Ashia said. "My cousins used *hora* stones to give advantage when they murdered the *Damaji,* but even with the assistance—"

"Young Maji was no match for ancient Aleverak," Qeran finished. "An outcome that should surprise none."

"The Majah had a pact with the Deliverer," Ashia said.

"I know," Qeran said. "I watched your father fight Aleverak for the Skull Throne while you were still in tan, Princess."

"You do not think the Majah have a right to their anger?" Ashia asked.

Qeran shrugged. "Murder is the *dama* way. They call us savages, but *Sharum* advance in rank when our superiors die on *alagai* talons, not when we kill them. But that is no excuse for Aleveran to steal supply and warriors from the Deliverer's army when Sharak Ka has begun, slinking back like cowards to hide behind the walls of the Desert Spear."

Hold nothing back.

"Asome tried to murder me, too, Drillmaster," Ashia said. "His own wife. The mother of his son. When Asome moved for the throne, Asukaji threw a garrote around my neck. As he did, Dama'ting Melan and Asavi joined forces in an attempt to kill the Damajah."

"Who could no more be killed by lesser fools than Aleverak." Ashia's words seemed to shake the drillmaster for the first time in their encounter. "Perhaps it is best, then, that Prince Asome's eyes are turned away from Everam's Reservoir. Has the Damajah sent you and Kaji to succor here?"

Ashia shook her head. "I am seeking the *khaffit.*"

Qeran did not need to ask who Ashia meant. "I cannot help you there, Princess. I have held hope that my master is alive, but there has been no word since the Battle of Angiers. The son of Chabin is resourceful. If there was a way to get word to me, he would have done it by now."

"Perhaps he has," Ashia said. "Everam informed the Damajah that Abban is alive, in the hands of the Eunuch."

"Hasik." Qeran balled a fist. "I should have broken that mad dog's skull while he was still a pup in *sharaj*."

"Tell me about his defenses," Ashia said.

"He will be difficult to dislodge," Qeran said. "The Eunuch Monastery is built on a high outcropping over the water, with sheer cliff on three sides and a Laktonian blockade out on the water. Only by the main road can any sizable force approach. It is narrow, with bridges the defenders can collapse, and ambush points where they can attack invaders from cover."

"Does he control the land around this stronghold?" Ashia asked.

Qeran shrugged. "He has scouts throughout the wetlands, but when not out on raids, his men only patrol a perimeter half a day's ride out, returning at sunset."

"They are not active at night?" Ashia asked.

Qeran spat. "The Eunuchs have abandoned *alagai'sharak*. Demons cluster thick in their lands, and the fools do nothing."

He sighed. "A lot of good warriors will be lost to rescue one *khaffit*."

"You will not be rescuing him," Ashia said.

Qeran's eyes went cold. "Do not mistake my demeanor, Princess. You are not in command here. The Deliverer himself named Abban my master, and I have an oath to protect him. While I breathe, I must put the safe return of Abban asu Chabin am'Haman am'Kaji above my own life, above all things short of Sharak Ka. Neither you nor the Damajah is going to stop me."

There was a threat to the words, and Ashia tensed slightly, ready to react should he renew their battle. "You noted yourself that an assault on the monastery would cost the Deliverer's army countless warriors. The Damajah has foreseen this as well, and sent me as an alternative. I will infiltrate Hasik's stronghold and find a way to secure the *khaffit's* release."

Qeran looked doubtful. "Your *sharusahk* is gifted, girl, but I see through the theatricality. You cannot walk through walls any more than my own Watchers, especially with a babe on your back."

"The Damajah has gifted me with magics," Ashia said. "No Watcher can be as silent as I can be. As invisible. As strong. As fast. Kaji can scream his loudest, and those inches away will only hear it if I will it so. Sheer walls are as broad steps to my hands and feet."

"Even so," Qeran said. "By all accounts, Hasik has over a thousand men—tortured, mutilated, and sadistic. You would take your son, the heir to the Skull Throne, into such a place?"

"We must walk the edge of the abyss together, if Sharak Ka is to be won," Ashia said. "The Damajah has foreseen it. The *alagai* are readying to mount a new offensive. We need no more red blood spilled."

"Red blood will spill in any event," Qeran said, "without reinforcements from Everam's Bounty."

"Your guard is light," Ashia agreed. "But the foe will come from the lake, will they not? Your ships have command of the water."

"For now," Qeran said. "We smashed their fleet, and my privateers have harried their attempts to resupply. They are half starved, but still have more boats in reserve. They know Prince Jayan's army was shattered, know we are vulnerable. They will attack. Soon."

"How are their spies getting through, if you patrol the lake-shore?" Ashia asked.

Qeran laughed. "There are hundreds of miles of shoreline, Princess! This is not some oasis you can see across on a clear day. In the deep, there is no sign of land in any direction."

Ashia shuddered at the thought of so much water. How could something so sacred as water make her feel such fear?

"And the Laktonians have a turncoat spy," Qeran said.

"Tell me about him." Ashia could already guess what he would say.

"Barely more than a boy," Qeran said. "Small for a warrior, but not so much as to draw attention. Moved like a desert hare, impossibly fast."

"But not faster than you." Ashia nodded at Qeran's metal leg.

"It was a near thing," Qeran said. "He moved into a fierce

attack when I drew close. Basic *sharukin,* but his speed and strength made him formidable, nonetheless. Lack of formal training makes him . . . unpredictable."

"He didn't defeat you." Ashia felt a tinge of doubt.

"In a manner of speaking." Qeran did not look pleased to admit it. "He wasn't fighting to win, only to distract long enough to resume running. He dove into demon-infested water and swam to a Laktonian vessel."

"Did you notice anything else, when you were in close?"

"He stank," Qeran said. "Like the poultices *dama'ting* place on *alagai* wounds. His skin was light, and his features muted. There was a *Sharum* deserter living in one of the hamlets north of here. Relan am'Damaj am'Kaji. He died with his family in a fire more than a decade ago, but there is rumor that one son survived."

Damaj. The name sent a tingle down Ashia's spine. The Damajah's family name.

He is the lost cousin.

Qeran went to his desk and took a sheet of paper from atop a pile, handing it to Ashia. The poster offered a hundred thousand draki for the living spy, and ten thousand for just his head. Below was stamped an artist's approximation of his face, a fair likeness to the boy she'd met on the road.

"All the more reason not to deplete your men further." Ashia folded the paper and put it in her robe. "How far north is this monastery?"

"Nearly a week's ride, through difficult terrain," Qeran said. "The road is watched, and the wetlands are thick with muck that can break a warrior's ankle as easily as their mount's. The bogs have their own *alagai.* Their spit is not as impressive as a flame demon's, but it burns and paralyzes. Many of our wetland spies, even trained Watchers, do not return."

"I will manage," Ashia said. "Can you provide me with a map?"

"I can do better," Qeran said. "My flagships are too visible, but after nightfall I can secrete you aboard a smaller, more inconspicuous vessel and sail you under cover of darkness out of the harbor. They can set you ashore just outside Hasik's patrol range."

"Thank you, Drillmaster, that is most helpful," Ashia said.

"Have you ever been on a boat before?" Qeran asked.

"On the oasis in the Desert Spear." Ashia's eyes flicked down. "Once."

"Your *Hannu Pash* celebration," Qeran nodded. "I was there. Until last year, it was my only time on a boat as well."

He leaned in. "This lake is nothing like the oasis. The water comes in waves that keep boats in constant motion. I have seen it churn the stomachs of *Sharum* and *dama* alike, leaving great men emptying their stomachs over the rail."

"My master taught me to endure worse," Ashia said.

Qeran nodded. "Perhaps. You will be given the captain's quarters. Only he will know of your presence, and nothing of your identity. A spy, I will tell him. He will not question it. Keep to your cabin and the crew will not even know you are there. We cannot risk an encounter with the blockade ships, so they will put you ashore some distance south of the monastery."

"That will allow me to scout the area," Ashia said, "and build safe warrens to hide from *alagai* and pursuit."

"Pursuit?" Qeran quirked his lips. "I thought you could walk up walls, silent as a shadow."

"On the way in, perhaps," Ashia said. "On the way out, I will be hauling a fat, crippled *khaffit* with me."

Qeran chuckled. "A weight I know well."

An hour before dawn, Briar watched the strange woman pause outside Docktown to reapply her disguise.

It was curious. Briar thought it a ploy to fool greenlanders, but it seemed it was for her own people as well.

He veered from the road to get ahead of her, finding one of the numerous streams this close to the water. He stripped off his clothes, folding them into a tight bundle and stowing it in a compartment of his satchel. He rolled away the filthy wraps on his hands, staring at the wards on his palms. Impact. Pressure. Spear and shield to the Wardskins.

Was that his tribe now? Or was it Elissa and Ragen? Lakton? The Hollow? His father's people? Pulled in so many directions, Briar was losing sense of who he was.

But for now, he could put all that aside. For now, there was a mystery.

He waded into a cold pool, breathing in the discomfort until his body acclimated. He used a bar of soap, scrubbing off sticky hogroot sap and the dirt that clung to it. When he was finished, he drew a clean set of *dal'Sharum* blacks from his satchel and changed.

He smelled of hogroot, even now. He ate so much of it the scent was on his breath, in his sweat, even his saliva. But the clean robes were thick enough to mask it.

A bazaar had been built on the edge of Docktown, and Briar knew it well. He was perusing the bread carts as she came down the road, a simple *Sharum* among many, finding a morning meal.

The spy blended as easily as he, just an older woman carting a child on her morning shopping. She chatted amiably with the *dal'ting* vendors, casual questions and leading statements that quickly informed her about the town and the Laktonian resistance.

Briar shook his head. He had never been good at that part of scouting. He preferred to lurk unseen and listen.

She moved unhurried from the bazaar to the town proper, flitting seemingly at random from shop to vendor, but it was obvious to Briar she was headed for the docks, and it was easy to get ahead of her.

Briar knew the docks as well as his Briarpatch, but there was something different, this time. Posters with a drawing of his face hung at the entrance to every pier, offering unfathomable wealth to whomever should catch him.

It was a kind of glory, seeing his face everywhere. Captain Dehlia papered the walls of her cabin on *Sharum's Lament* with waxed copies of her wanted posters. She squealed with delight whenever one of her raids netted a fresh one with the bounty raised.

Their hatred is like meat to me, Briar, she said of it. *Let them lament they cannot catch me.*

But Briar took no pleasure in being hated. Making a difference for his mother's people meant betraying his father's. He might have relatives in this very town, and it did not fill him with pride that they would know of him only as a traitor.

Still, he pulled down one of the signs and stowed it in his robe as he followed the woman toward the far pier. She was heading for *Tan Spear*, Captain Qeran's ship.

Briar swallowed his first real sense of fear since entering the town. Captain Qeran terrified Briar, on the lake and off. If a more dangerous man existed, Briar did not know of him.

Rather than answer questions, this added more. Was the woman an elite spy sent from Krasia to serve Captain Qeran? She would be underestimated by the greenlanders, as well. Given time, she could get close enough to kill almost anyone.

But those very same skills might be used in a more immediate way, to eliminate Qeran and open a path for new leadership.

Briar slipped under an abandoned pier and stripped off his clothes, stowing his spear, shield, and satchel out of sight before slipping into the water. He swam with smooth, efficient strokes, passing right under the noses of the guards patrolling the beach and flagship pier. Even *Sharum* sailors couldn't swim. Most of them avoided even looking at the waves for too long.

The spy was still waiting for permission to come aboard when Briar climbed the anchor rope in the shadow of the great vessel. Captain Dehlia had taught Briar all the common boat designs, and how best to take advantage of their weaknesses.

He was just able to squeeze through the tiny rope port into the unattended winch room. From there he made his way to the cabin below the captain's. A sailor, likely just off duty, slept soundly in a hammock, rocked slowly by the waves. He did not wake as Briar climbed a beam to press his ear to a certain spot in the ceiling.

There was a scrape of metal against the deck. "You're wearing armor under your robe," Qeran said above.

CHAPTER 23

SHARUM'S LAMENT

334 AR

Ashia's stomach had not churned this way since the first months of her pregnancy. She could spend hours perched on a ceiling beam. Execute tumbles and rolls that would leave a greenland Jongleur dizzy. Dance atop a rolling log.

But the open water was nothing like Qeran's ship, docked at harbor. The cabin rocked gently from side to side, a constant, uneven motion that made chaos of her equilibrium. The lake, like pregnancy, was an unforgiving reminder that while there was much one could control with the proper training, some things were in Everam's hands.

Her footing was the real concern. She paced back and forth, eyes closed, trying to learn the rhythm of the lake. She did not wish to be caught out of balance should she be called upon to fight during the voyage.

Thankfully, the prospect was unlikely. Qeran's men escorted her onto the ship *Evejan Justice* at sunset, when the glare on the water kept any from seeing her too closely. It was a small three-mast vessel, sleek and dangerous, with a crew of thirty hardened *dal'Sharum*. It was no great trade ship with a full hold, nor a warship of value. The sort hopefully not worth the effort of capturing.

"Captain Rahvel has already vacated his quarters for the voyage," Qeran said. "He is an honored drillmaster."

Simple words, but coming from Qeran they had weight. He

was sending some of his most trusted men to see her to her destination. Meals were to be left outside her door, but otherwise she would not be disturbed until they were close to the drop point.

Kaji had it worse than her. Ashia expected the ship's rocking to lull him to sleep, but instead the poor boy turned deathly pale and vomited on her.

"Sick," he groaned into her shoulder.

"Yes, my heart, I know." She kissed his head. "It is the motion of the waves. You will grow accustomed and feel better soon."

She could only hope.

But even that was not the worst of it. A small porthole, too small for even Ashia to squeeze through, let her see the water, glittering in the starlight. Miles of it, in every direction. There was no sign of land.

More, there were flashes of light in the water, like lightning in the clouds. Each time they flared, the ship rocked.

Water demons, testing the wards on the hull.

Ashia fought *alagai* every night, but water demons were something beyond her. Nightmare creatures of tooth and tentacle, unseen, unknowable. She had learned to swim in the *dama'ting* baths, and could hold her breath for over ten minutes, but this was different. She could not fight beneath the waves or strike the demons from afar. She could do nothing but sit as her stomach roiled and her child screamed, hoping the wards held.

Please, Everam, she prayed. *Giver of light and life, we walk the edge of Nie's abyss in your name. Grant that we make it safely to our destination and complete our mission.*

As if in answer, one of the many rings in Ashia's ear began to vibrate.

The Damajah.

Ashia froze. She had thought herself far beyond Inevera's reach, and part of her was glad. For the first time in her life, she felt in charge of her destiny, of Kaji's.

Ashia's hand trembled slightly as she twisted the earring until the wards aligned with a click. "Damajah."

"I have learned to amplify the range of your earring," Inevera said. "It requires great concentration and tremendous magic. I will not contact you often."

"I hear and understand, Damajah."

"Good," Inevera said. "Report."

"I have reached Docktown and met with Drillmaster Qeran," Ashia said. "The situation there is dire, Damajah. Without reinforcements, the greatest living drillmaster is concerned the Laktonians may retake the docks."

"I am aware of the situation," Inevera said. "I have already ordered reinforcements."

"*You* have ordered, Damajah?"

"Circumstances with your husband have changed," Inevera said. "I am fully in command of Krasia until your uncle returns."

Ashia blinked—her stomach, her sick child, the flashing of the water wards all forgotten. The news changed everything.

"So I am . . . free to return?" Ashia's voice was very small. There was no reply.

"Damajah?"

"You must complete your mission," the Damajah said. "The dice are clear. Only then may you return, or Sharak Ka may be lost."

"With the *khaffit,* or not at all." She made it sound like a *Sharum's* boast, and once it would have been heartfelt, but Qeran's words echoed in her mind.

Hasik has over a thousand men, tortured, mutilated, and sadistic. You will take your son, the heir to the Skull Throne, into such a place?

Was Sharak Ka worth her life? Even Kaji's? Of course. But if the choice to sacrifice Kaji for success came to her, she could not, *would* not, betray her son. Instinctively, she clutched him closer.

"Where are you now?" the Damajah asked.

"Aboard ship, headed for the Eunuch fortress," Ashia said. "In two days I will be dropped outside their patrol perimeter and will begin penetrating their layers of defense. I will infiltrate the monastery, confirm the *khaffit* is alive, and if so effect an escape."

"He is alive." No doubt the dice told the Damajah more

than that, but Inevera was never one to volunteer more of their futures than served her purpose.

How many had her escaping with Kaji and the *khaffit* alive? How many ended with any of them alive at all?

The Damajah would never say.

"And what of the lost cousin?" Inevera asked.

"I believe I have found him," Ashia said. "But I do not believe he can be trusted, and do not see how he would be able to assist us."

"Tell me quickly." There was a terse quality to the Damajah's normally patient tone. Reaching out hundreds of miles with her magic truly was taxing.

"Briar asu Relan am'Damaj am'Kaji," Ashia said. "His father was . . ."

"My second cousin Relan," Inevera hissed. "When he disappeared, we believed he died on *alagai* talons and was carried off."

"He was a deserter," Ashia said. "He came north with a Messenger, and died in a fire with his family a decade ago. One son is said to have survived. He works as a spy for the *chin* resistance."

"The half-breed Qeran spoke of in his reports," Inevera guessed.

"The same," Ashia agreed. "I encountered him on the road. He was following me. I confronted and tried to subdue him, but he . . . evaded capture."

"And now sees through your disguise," Inevera noted.

Ashia felt her face heat. She was not accustomed to reporting failure. "Yes, Damajah. But during our brief bout of *sharusahk,* his . . . scent was unmistakable."

"What scent?" Inevera asked.

"Alagai'viran," Ashia said. "Demon root."

Again, Inevera was silent for a time, though no doubt every moment she held open the connection was taxing. "It is a sign from Everam."

"A sign of what? I left him behind on the road. I would not know how to find him if I wanted, and still do not see a reason."

There were whispers through the connection that Ashia could not make out, followed by the clatter of dice.

"You need not seek him," Inevera said. "He is close, even now."

"And when I encounter him again?"

"I . . . cannot say," the Damajah told her.

Cannot, or will not? Ashia wondered.

"You must use your own judgment, Niece," the Damajah said. "Like you, he has a part to play in what is to come. Do not kill him until he has played it."

Caring for poor Kaji throughout the night kept her from meditating, and even Ashia drifted off to sleep before dawn.

She woke shortly after sunrise with a jolt as something hit the ship, knocking her and Kaji out of the captain's pillow bench. Instinctively she secured her son and hit the moving deck in a roll, assessing the threat.

The door to her room remained barred from the inside, and there was no scent of smoke or hint the ship was taking on water. But shouts of alarm echoed through the lower decks, along with sounds of battle.

They were under attack.

She danced as the deck rolled, keeping balance until the boat stabilized with a heavy thump. The porthole went dark.

Quickly she donned her disguise and got Kaji into her pack. He was pale and listless, needing rest and water, but there was no time for such things.

"Be brave, my son," Ashia whispered.

"Bave," Kaji agreed weakly.

Her spears were left hidden in his pack, but Ashia had other weapons—knives and throwing glass, along with other tools, subtler but no less lethal.

She opened the door to peek out, only to pull it quickly shut again as several of the *dal'Sharum* crew ran past. She could hear the commotion out on the main deck.

When the sailors passed, Ashia slipped out behind them. The walls and ceiling were too close and low for her to move with any cover, but a group of *Sharum* on the way to battle provided distraction enough for her to follow unnoticed.

There was open fighting on the deck. A Laktonian vessel had latched on to their ship, boarding them with perhaps fifty spear-wielding *chin* warriors. From the far rail, *chin* archers swept the deck, softening resistance.

Ashia glanced up, recognizing the vessel's flag. It was a woman's silhouette, looking off into the distance while a *Sharum* stood aflame at her back.

Sharum's Lament, led by the infamous Laktonian pirate Captain Dehlia.

Ashia stayed just inside the cabin as the *Sharum* rushed out onto the deck and into the bowfire. Eyes scanning, it didn't take long to find the pirate princess.

Dehlia wore a colorful scarf on the crown of her head, but it did nothing to hide her face, or her hair, spilling out to fall down her back in sandy waves.

She was flanked by two bodyguards, tall men with longer spears designed to help keep a protective zone around their mistress, who led the attack personally.

Dehlia skittered barefoot on the rolling deck, as balanced as on a training room floor. The blade of her short fencing spear was curved, allowing her to leave deep slashes on her opponents in close quarters. Her free hand held a similarly curved knife, blade glistening red. Two of the *dal'Sharum* crew already lay dead at her back.

Ashia knew now the tales of this woman were not exaggerated. If nothing, they failed to do justice. Her glory was boundless.

But Captain Rahvel, easily recognizable by the red night veil loose around his chin, was no less glorious. He batted away enemy fire with his shield and cut down every *chin* that drew near. His armor turned what few blows he allowed past his defenses.

The crew had rallied behind him, trained *dal'Sharum* who met the enemy charge and made the *chin* pay for every inch with blood. If not for the archers they might have held against twice their number, but as it was, it seemed inevitable they would be overrun despite their superior fighting skill.

Like a spear in flight, Rahvel made directly for Captain Dehlia, killing *chin* warriors who tried to slow him without missing a step.

No coward, the *chin* captain turned to meet him. "He's mine!"

"I am Rahvel asu Najan am'Desin am'Kaji!" Rahvel cried in return. His *Sharum* spread out, knowing better than to interfere. Ashia wondered if she were about to witness the end of the infamous pirate captain.

Rahvel's short spear was not curved like Dehlia's, but he moved it like a seamstress' needle—quick and precise. It was all Dehlia could do to parry the first few thrusts and skitter back from the assault. She spun her weapon into a series of deft attacks, but Rahvel picked them off, continuing to advance. She was fast and agile, no novice fighter, but Rahvel controlled the battlefield, herding her into a pool of slick blood on the deck. She stumbled, and he was upon her, readying a killing blow.

But he was stopped short as one of the *chin* bodyguards abandoned his honor, leaping forward to thrust his long spear. It was turned by Rahvel's armor, but it caught the drillmaster by surprise. Dehlia had declared single combat, and Rahvel had introduced himself. It tarnished her glory for the warrior to interfere and deny her an honorable death.

But it seemed the *chin* did not see it that way. Rahvel turned, catching the spear shaft in his shield hand and pulling the bodyguard close enough for the drillmaster to open his throat. Even as he did, the other bodyguard leapt at him. When Rahvel turned to meet him, Dehlia sprang forward, hooking the edge of his shield with her spear and pulling it wide as she put her knife into his eye.

Rahvel heel-kicked her away, but the other bodyguard found a seam in his armor, stabbing deep into the drillmaster's side with his spear. He took Rahvel's spear in the lung in return, and the drillmaster pulled the *chin* weapon free, spinning it defensively as he gripped the handle of Dehlia's knife and slowly pulled it out of his eye.

The two crews, frozen in the face of their battling leaders, resumed combat, with a new flight of arrows raining into the *Sharum* ranks. Dehlia circled Rahvel, poking at his defenses as blood poured from his face and side. All around them the fighting was fierce.

Ashia considered getting involved. There was still time for her to get to Rahvel's side, to kill the pirate captain.

But it would make little difference in the end. She might

kill Dehlia, but it would be the end of her. Of her mission. Of Kaji.

She could not fight, nor could she secure one of the dinghies without being seen. She could swim, but they were deep in the waters—no land in sight. It was tantamount to suicide for her and Kaji.

And so she waited, as the *chin* slaughtered or subdued the remaining *Sharum*. As Dehlia gave Rahvel an inglorious death.

She rushed out onto the deck then, wailing in anguish. The *chin* pirates froze at the sight of an unarmed mother and child, and she made it all the way to the drillmaster, falling to her knees beside him. "Everam!" she cried. "Guide my husband, your honored drillmaster, Rahvel asu Najan am'Desin am'Kaji, on the lonely path, that he may stand before your divine judgment!"

Whether he was truly upset or simply in tune with his mother, Kaji gave a cry as well, screaming as Ashia hugged the corpse.

Captain Dehlia hesitated, then took a tentative step forward. Ashia caught the move and flinched back.

"Don't be afraid," Dehlia said. "We won't harm you, or your son. You'll be taken to Lakton and treated fairly. Perhaps better than you're accustomed to. You won't have to cover yourself anymore."

Ashia carefully kept the fearful, tearful look on her face as she watched the honorless woman approach. Did they think Krasian women such fools they would take the word of someone who killed without honor? Just like the rest of the *chin* savages, she thought the scarf Ashia wore for modesty before Everam was some shackle to be freed of.

The safest path for her and Kaji would be to surrender to the pirate, but going to the *chin* city on the water would not allow Ashia to complete her mission.

In a moment, Dehlia would be close enough for Ashia to strike. She had already plotted the *sharukin* to disarm the pirate and put her in a submission hold before she even registered a threat. Then she would flick the blade from her sleeve and put it at the woman's throat for her crew to see.

Ashia had seen the loyalty of the *Sharum's Lament* crew. Their captain meant more to them than honor before the

Creator. They would not risk her life. She could use that to secure transport for herself and Kaji to the mainland. Just another step . . .

"Cap'n Dehlia," a voice said.

Ashia flicked her eyes to the sound, seeing Briar Damaj vault the rail. Had he been hiding there all this time?

Dehlia turned as well, and her face lit up with surprise and delight. "Briar!" She gave a great whoop and rushed across the deck, sweeping the boy into such a great hug his feet left the boards. "Briar! Briar! Briar! Thank the Creator you've returned!"

Ashia had been prepared to kill Dehlia, and owed Briar a beating at least, but the reunion left an ache in her heart. Had anyone in her life ever been so pleased to see her? Only her spear sisters, and they were as sand scattered in the wind.

"What are you doing here?" Dehlia asked.

"Qeran sent the ship on a secret mission." Briar's voice was throaty, the words a growl.

"What mission?"

Briar's eyes met Ashia's, just for an instant. "Dunno. Stowed away to see."

One of Dehlia's lieutenants returned from a search of the ship, whispering in his captain's ear.

"Nothing interesting in the hold," Dehlia said. "Only a handful of fighters, no strong armament. Do you know where they were headed?"

"Monastery," Briar said.

"Past the blockade?"

Briar shook his head. "Were gonna put a boat ashore before they reached the blockade."

"Why?" Dehlia asked.

Ashia tensed, but Briar only shrugged. "Don't know. Was waiting to see who they put ashore."

Dehlia grinned. "Sorry to muck up your sneaking about, Briar, but it's worth it to have you back. Any guesses about what they were up to? I thought even Docktown wouldn't deal with the dickless monster that rules there."

Briar shrugged again, pointedly not looking at Ashia. "Only the cap'n knew, and he's dead."

Dehlia glanced at Ashia. "Perhaps his wife knows something."

"Won't tell," Briar said. "Killed her husband. All she'll do is try'n kill ya, get too close."

The pirate eyed Ashia. "She might *try*. I think we might persuade her."

Arrogance. Even with Briar's warning, Dehlia underestimated her. Even now, Ashia could put a throwing glass through Dehlia's eye from across the deck before anyone could move. It would be fitting, after what the woman did to Rahvel.

"Like we persuaded Prince Icha?" Briar demanded.

Dehlia seemed taken aback at the words. "Briar, that was different."

"Ent," Briar said. "Any hint she might know somethin', they won't stop until she talks."

"She's a woman with a child," Dehlia said. "I won't let them—"

"Won't be up to you," Briar cut in. "Dockmasters'll give her to the little man with the screws."

Dehlia crossed her arms. "They've done far worse to us, Briar. You know it better than any."

"Ay," Briar agreed. "An' you're always sayin' we're better'n that. Ent we?"

"Fine," Dehlia said. "We'll just call her a prisoner."

"And send her to Prison Isle?" Briar demanded. "Only woman on an island with two hundred starving *Sharum*?"

"What am I supposed to do, Briar? Sail her all the way back to Docktown?" Dehlia threw her hands protectively in front of her face. "Oh, don't shoot, Qeran! We have a *woman* on board! We're bringing her back so you can cover her up and keep treating her like a slave!"

"Course not," Briar said. "Cap'n Rahvel had a horse to carry her and the babe in the hold. Put us on shore. I can get her home, then signal for a boat."

Ashia couldn't believe what she was hearing. How much did Briar Damaj know? Whose side was he on, if anyone's but his own?

"What, we're giving her a horse, now?!" one of Dehlia's crew exclaimed, to murmurs of assent.

"Shut it, Vick," Dehlia barked, and the man stiffened. Her eyes swept over the crew. "That goes for the rest of you, too! Ever want your opinions I'll kick you in the balls till they pop out!"

She looked back at him. "I like that idea least of all. You've only just returned to us . . ."

"Just a run to Docktown." Briar waved dismissively, as if penetrating the defenses of Everam's Reservoir was no great feat. "Back before you know it."

Briar eyed the Krasian woman uneasily as they waited. He didn't know her. Not really. But he had lied to Captain Dehlia, one of his few true friends, for her.

"Why?" she asked in Krasian, so the others would not understand.

The words of his father's tongue were thick in his mouth. "Seen enough torture." Briar nodded to the boy. "Deserves better'n growin' up surrounded by folk who hate him for things his people done. Know what that's like, even before the war."

"If you've been following me, you know I am not bound for Everam's Reservoir," she said.

"Ay," Briar agreed. "Got business in the monastery. Can get you there."

"Why?" she asked again. "Why are you helping me? Why would I not kill you the moment we're set ashore?"

"Someone trapped there, ay?" Briar asked. "Goin' to sneak 'em out? Good at that."

"Do you know who it is they have?"

Briar shrugged. "What's it matter? No one deserves to be a prisoner."

The woman raised an eyebrow. "Even Abban the *khaffit*?"

Briar froze. He knew the name. Everyone in Lakton knew it. The *khaffit* whispered poison in the Krasian leaders' ears. It was said he engineered the annexing of Lakton's mainland, and their naval defeat in the Battle of Docktown.

He should tell Dehlia. He should do it now. But he remained frozen. Nothing had changed. Now more than ever, they would give her to the torturers. That hunched old acolyte, daring to wear robes of the Creator even as he turned his awful screws.

But could he trust her? Briar didn't know. He'd thought he could trust Stela, but she, too, had proven more dangerous than she appeared. "Don't even know your name."

The woman's eyes crinkled, but with the veil in place, he could not guess her expression. "Ashia vah Asome am'Jardir am'Kaji. My son is Kaji."

"Vah Asome . . ." Briar said.

Ashia nodded. "The wife and child of the current leader of all Krasia. Valuable prisoners."

"Why're you tellin' me?" It was like she was goading him.

"Because I think if you were to betray me, you would have done it by now," Ashia said. "But I do not think you have it in you."

"Don't know me," Briar growled.

"No." Ashia shook her head. "I do not. But I know Everam has brought us together, cousin."

"Cousin?" Briar was confused.

"My mother-in-law, the Damajah, is Inevera vah Kasaad am'Damaj am'Kaji," Ashia said. "Your father's cousin. You are strange, son of Relan. Too much a greenlander, but with a *Sharum's* fighting spirit, and a savagery I do not understand."

She reached out, taking his hand. Briar flinched, but he did not pull from her grasp. "But you and my son share blood, and I would know you better."

It took a moment to make sense of the words. Mother-in-law cousin of his father? What did that make them? Did it make them anything?

You and my son share blood.

The words echoed in his head as he looked at the boy, hanging pale and listless in her sling. He needed rest. He needed water. He needed protection.

She was right. He was not going to betray her.

Briar felt the vessel slide onto the shoal and grind to a halt. He and Ashia were already in the hold with Captain Dehlia and her new bodyguards.

"Be careful." Dehlia held a loaded backpack. "Packed you a lunch."

"Don't need it," Briar said. "Can hunt."

Dehlia pressed the pack into Briar's chest. Instinctively he put his arms around it and she let go. "More in there than food, Briar, and you're skin and bones." She smiled at him. "Suffer for Cap'n Dehlia and eat some bread and cheese."

Briar's brows raised. "Bread?"

Dehlia winked. "The kind with the crumbly crust you like." Briar grinned and swung the pack onto his back as they opened the hold and dropped the gangplank.

"We'll be gone with the tide, but you'll want to be well south of here by then," Dehlia said. "Cories been acting strangely this far north."

Briar cocked his head. "Strange how?"

"Massing in numbers, with breeds we've never seen," Dehlia said. "Killing half our scouts, but they don't attack the monastery or the Eunuch's raiding parties."

"Scared of their wards?" Briar asked.

Dehlia shrugged. "Maybe. But I never met a corie smart enough to be scared."

Briar nodded. "Be careful."

Dehlia's hug squeezed the breath from him. "You'd better. Want you home, safe and sound, before new moon rolls around."

"I will." The lie was bitter on Briar's lips as he returned the embrace. Then he took Rasa's bridle and led the mare down the gangplank and onto the sandbar. Water splashed up to his hips as they waded to shore, but Ashia and Kaji, atop the horse, were clear of it.

"The strange behavior of the *alagai* concerns me," Ashia said when they reached the shore, out of earshot of the boat.

"Me, too," Briar said. "Maybe they mean to take the monastery?"

"That would suggest a demon princeling has an interest in it," Ashia said. "If so, we walk into great danger."

"Don't have to," Briar said. "Can walk away, just as easy. Go to the Hollow or Fort Rizon. Keep Kaji safe."

"*You* can, perhaps," Ashia said. "Kaji and I cannot. I do not think I will ever truly be welcome again in Everam's Bounty, whatever the Damajah might claim."

"Know the feelin'," Briar said. "But the Hollow—"

"Could not protect my spear sister's husband," Ashia said, "now she is a widow at eighteen. It could not protect my master, dead on *alagai* talons. I would not trust any welcome from the Hollowers, knowing what they could gain by hostaging my son."

Briar threw up his hands. "Wide world. Could get lost in the hamlets, or go into the mountains or forest and build a briarpatch to keep us safe."

"Like your namesake against the nightwolves." Ashia tilted her head as Briar started. "What?"

"Never told anyone that story." It had always been a private thing for Briar, a cherished memory of his father, kept secret and safe.

"Every child in Krasia knows the story of the Briarpatch," Ashia said. "There is a song, as well. Do you know it?"

Briar felt like he had swallowed a stone. He shook his head numbly.

"Tonight I will sing it for you and Kaji," Ashia promised. "But we cannot abandon our people and hide in the woods. That is the way of selfish *chin* who have put Everam from their hearts. We have a part to play in Sharak Ka, and that part is here. We must walk the edge of the abyss, and trust in the Creator to see us through."

CHAPTER 24

FIRST STEPS

334 AR

As soon as they put some distance from the lake, Briar guided Ashia to a marsh where a thick patch of *alagai'viran* grew around an ancient, sagging tree. The weed had even taken root in the moss on the tree's bark, growing right up the trunk.

"In here," Briar said.

Ashia shook her head. "This will not do. It is too damp . . ."

Briar smiled. "Trust."

The ground was soft, sucking at Rasa's hooves, though Briar walked atop it like an insect on water, leaving only faint markings in his path.

The soil at the base of the tree, held together by an old network of roots, was firmer and drier, but it was a cramped space. Barely big enough for the horse.

Briar tied her bridle to a branch. "Follow."

He sprang easily into the tree, climbing into the boughs and quickly out of sight. Ashia stared after him a moment, then shrugged and followed.

Briar hadn't gone far. Just above, the great trunk split, then split again, and again. The trunks were like the four fingers of a hand, their crux the palm. Briar had used them as supports for a ring of woven branches, looking like a great bird's nest. The space was large enough for the three of them to relax comfortably, sheltered by the branches, hidden by the leaves, and protected by the demon root, safe as any warded camp.

Briar smiled, setting down his pack. "An' we got bread!"

The smile was infectious, and Ashia laughed, setting Kaji down and freeing the poor child from his pack. The water sickness had abated once they were back on land, but Kaji was weak, hungry, and dehydrated.

Briar watched silently as Ashia changed Kaji's soiled bido. She covered herself with a scarf as she opened her armored robe to set the child at her breast. Briar started, realizing what was happening, and quickly turned his back. Ashia closed her eyes, and began to sing.

> *The nightwolf came to the briarpatch*
> *Teeth like knives, claws like spears*
> *The nightwolf came to the briarpatch*
> *But Briar didn't fear*

> *The thorns were long*
> *Bramble and burr*
> *They tore its flesh*
> *And caught its fur*

> *The nightwolf came to the briarpatch*
> *Teeth like knives, claws like spears*
> *The nightwolf came to the briarpatch*
> *But Briar didn't fear*

> *The wolf twisted,*
> *Flesh caught and stuck,*
> *Briar took stone,*
> *Drew back and struck*

> *The nightwolf came to the briarpatch*
> *Teeth like knives, claws like spears*
> *The nightwolf came to the briarpatch*
> *But Briar didn't fear*

Briar tried to swallow a sob and choked, clutching his knees and shaking. Not knowing what to make if it, Ashia stopped singing.

Kaji had fallen asleep on the teat, exhausted from their or-

deal. She gently pried him away and set him in her shield. By
the time she turned to Briar, he was gone.

Briar ran, but not far. He had not expected the song to affect
him so strongly, but while she was singing, he remembered.
His father used to sing that song to him. How could he forget
such a thing? It was like forgetting the sun.

"Mudboy." He punched himself in the chest. "Can't even
'member their faces."

He circled the area, cursing himself as he tended the briarpatch. When he had cooled down, he orbited closer to the
tree. Rasa was still saddled, grazing on hogroot.

Part of him was alarmed at the sight of their protection
being stripped away, but the horse needed to eat, and the briarpatch was large. The danger was minimal, and there were ad-
vantages to traveling with an animal smelling of hogroot.
Demons would shy away from her unless provoked.

The horse snorted as he drew close. Pack animals tended
not to like Briar as a rule, and in truth he cared little for them
in return. Mounts were unpredictable when cories were about.
He trusted his own two feet more than an animal's four.

"There, girl." He stroked Rasa's neck before removing the
saddle and brushing her down.

"I am sorry." Ashia's voice came from above.

Briar kept working. "Nothin' to be sorry over. Just . . . got
homesick, is all."

"I understand." Ashia's quiet words drifted down from the
sheltering boughs. "I once felt as you. But then I realized I
was longing for a home that never truly existed."

"Mine existed," Briar said. "Till I burned it down."

"The reports said your family died in a fire," Ashia said.
"But that is not your fault."

"Is," Briar said. "Laid the fire myself. Stoked it myself. Forgot to open the flue, all by myself."

"An accident," Ashia said.

"Ever kill your whole family by accident?" Briar asked bitterly.

There was a long pause above. "Not your whole family."

Briar climbed back up into the nest. Ashia met his eyes and

held them. She did not offer physical comfort, no touching or embraces like Dehlia and Elissa, no kisses and groping hands like Stela. She simply looked into his eyes, present for him.

"Safe here," he said when the silence had gone on too long. "Might want to rest." He knew Ashia was eager to get on with her mission. In truth, so was he. But there was more than the two of them to think of.

Ashia nodded. "Kaji is weak from the water sickness. He will need a day or two to rest, and some of the crusty bread, if you can spare it."

"Course," Briar said. "Can scout while we wait. Then what?"

"Then we travel north," Ashia said. "Have you other . . . briarpatches in the area?"

"Ay, lots." For months the Monastery of Dawn had been the base of operations for the Laktonian resistance, but Briar had never been comfortable behind walls.

"The *khaffit* is heavy," Ashia said. "And he is lame. We will need a series of hidden places to succor from both *alagai* and Eunuchs as we make our way to Everam's Reservoir."

Briar brightened. "Ay. Can do that. Might take a few weeks to sweep 'em off."

"Preparation is the key to success." Ashia spoke the words Enkido had instilled in her like they were her own.

Kaji clapped as Briar climbed into the boughs. The night's rest had brought color back to the boy, and returned his spirit with it.

"Smell." Kaji slapped a hand over his nose. Ashia had been mortified the first time she saw the boy do it, but she soon learned Briar had taught the move—and the word—to him.

Ashia laughed as Briar struck a pose, pinching his own nose so his voice came out as a high-pitched whine. "Smell." Kaji laughed and clapped again.

"Ready to get back on the horse?" Briar asked.

"No." It was Kaji's favorite word. It had power the others didn't, and he was tyrannical with it.

"Rather walk?" Briar asked.

"No," Kaji said.

"Mum to carry you?"

"No."

"Me to carry you?"

"No."

"Stay here?"

"No."

Briar smiled. "Hungry?"

Kaji paused. When Ashia asked the question, she meant her breast. When Briar asked it, it meant crusty bread.

He faltered. "Bread?"

Briar produced a small loaf, but held it out of reach. "Do you want it?"

Ashia could see the strain on Kaji's face as his desire to refuse battled his stomach. At last the stomach won and he reached out. "Want."

Seeing them together, Ashia felt her own throat tighten. Who would have thought the half-*chin* son of a traitor would be a better parent to her son than his own father?

The wetland was vast, but Briar knew it well, guiding them to dry ground firm enough for Rasa's hooves. Even so, the way was uneven and teeming with vegetation, making riding at speed impossible. Ashia led the horse instead, walking beside Briar. The air was hot and thick with moisture, mosquitoes active day round in the twilight beneath the canopy of trees. She kept her veil up, protective netting thrown over Kaji.

Briar was chewing on a stalk of *alagai'viran*. Ashia had become so used to the smell she hardly noticed it anymore, but the thought of eating demon root still turned her stomach.

Briar noticed her queasy look and took a fresh stalk from a pouch at his belt, handing it to her. "Try."

Ashia shook her head. "I don't understand how you eat that."

Briar shrugged and resumed chewing. "Fills your belly when huntin's bad. Keeps cories away. Sometimes keeps 'em from seein' you at all."

Ashia remembered their first encounter, when she had searched for him in Everam's light and found nothing. Had she been looking in the wrong place, or was it something more?

The darkness was not complete under the trees, but it was enough for Ashia to Draw on the stored magic in her *hora* and activate the vision wards on the helmet beneath her silk head-wrap.

The world around her lit up with magic. The glow was the root of all life, and it flourished in the wetlands. Light throbbed in the pools of water, sang in the rich vegetation, hung heavy in the ancient, stooped trees. Even the mud glowed softly, teeming with life too small to see.

But Briar, skin and hair and clothes covered in hogroot sap, looked . . . dim. Too dim for any human not close to death.

All save his eyes. They shone like a cat's at night, belying the power within. Somehow, the demon root masked the magic.

"Perhaps I will try." She reached for a stalk and took a bite. The herb was bitter, but so were many things in life. Enkido taught her to endure.

More than a week went by as they visited one briarpatch after another. Some were little more than well-positioned camp-sites with more visibility out than in. Others were master-works blended perfectly into their surroundings with security, space, and comfort.

All were thick with *alagai'viran.*

The latest was a clearing on a small rise. Like all Briar's hiding places, it was unremarkable at a glance. Just high enough to give visibility and some relief from the puddled ground below, but not so high as to draw attention by itself. From atop it, Ashia could see the demon root ringing the base, too even and perfect to be a natural occurrence.

"Normally just lie down at the top," Briar said. "Cories can't see me, but I can see 'em comin'. Never come near the hogroot, anyway."

"We'll lay my circles, as well," Ashia said. "The *alagai* are numerous in the wetlands. In Krasia, they do not cluster so thickly in uninhabited lands."

"Here neither." Briar helped her set the circle. "Never seen so many cories in these parts. Odd ones. Flamers and windies. Big rocks and woodies. But they ent doin' anything. Not even huntin'. Just . . . stumblin' around."

"In two days, it will be Waning," Ashia said. "If Alagai Ka or his princelings rise, they will have an army waiting. We would be wise to find better shelter to wait out the dark moon."

"Ay, know a place." Briar laid a fire in the pit with dry kindling from his pack. "Have to backtrack a bit, but it's safe."

Safe for us to cower from the forces of Nie, Enkido's fingers used to say of the Dama'ting Underpalace. Hiding behind wards grated on Ashia. She was bred and trained for the front lines.

A good kai *is a patient* kai, Enkido taught. Battles were won when the attacker chose the place and time to fight. This Waning was neither.

"Fight when you gotta." Briar filled a pot with fresh water and raw hogroot, setting it over the fire as Ashia freed Kaji and brought him to her breast. "Not when you wanna."

"Is it so clear in my eyes?" Ashia asked.

"Seen that look a lot, this last year," Briar said. "Folk itchin' to start a fight, because they can't stand waitin' for one that might or might not come."

"That is the *Sharum* way," Ashia said.

"Ent a *Sharum,*" Briar said. "Tenders say to always offer peace."

"Those who offer peace to *alagai* are slaughtered," Ashia said.

"Fight when I'm in a corner," Briar said. "But it's better if they don't even know I'm there."

Briar boiled it in frog meat, but the *alagai'viran* soup remained bitter. Ashia ate it anyway. They needed every advantage if they were to accomplish their mission. Already she could smell the demon root in her sweat, her breath, even her milk. She feared Kaji might refuse to nurse, but he was too hungry to question it.

This close to Waning, the demons were more active. In Everam's light, Ashia could see them prowling in the darkness, and the sight of their small campfire drew the *alagai*'s attention. Most were turned aside by the demon root, but eventually one enterprising bog demon took up a tree branch and began to whip it back and forth, cutting the stalks like a reaper's blade.

Briar grabbed his spear and shield, getting to his feet.

"Killing the demon with a warded weapon will be bright and loud," Ashia said. "It will only draw more attention."

"So will letting it scrape the wards." Briar slung his shield on his back and set down his spear. "I'll draw it off. Circle back."

Ashia did not doubt he could do just that, but an inner unease counseled caution. Something of Briar's own philosophy, perhaps.

"Let me try," Ashia said.

"With Kaji in your arms?" Briar asked.

Ashia smiled and began to sing the *Song of Waning*. She and her spear sisters had sung it a thousand times under the watchful eye of their *dama'ting* instructor, but it was different when her sister sang it for Shar'Dama Ka on the day she married the greenland Jongleur. Ashia had sensed the power even then, and learned more from her spear sister's secret missives.

Each verse of the song had its own rhythm, its own pitch, its own power. One to make them invisible to demons. Another to drive them away. Others still, to deceive or harm them. They required considerable range, but Ashia was up to the task.

The bog demon hacked through the *alagai'viran* patch and was approaching the ward circle when Ashia's song began to nudge it back. With a touch, Ashia rolled the wardstones to activate her *hora* necklace. Dialing the wards into different configurations could make her silent as death, or project her voice far and wide. Listen to something far, or silence something near.

Her song grew louder, driving the demon back the way it came. When it was clear of the demon root patch, Ashia layered another verse alongside the first, confusing the demon, then added in the cloaking verse. The demon shook its head and seemed to lose sight of them, eyes passing blankly over their camp. Eventually, it wandered away and Ashia let the song fade.

Briar stood dumbfounded. "Saw magic like that in the Hollow at Halfgrip's funeral. Two Krasian women singing."

Kaji had fallen asleep, and Ashia laid him curled in the hollow of her shield. "My cousins Amanvah and Sikvah. They and their honored husband were touched by Everam. I am only running my fingers across the surface of their power."

Something caught Briar's attention. He turned away, peering into the night.

Ashia moved to his side. "What is it?"

Briar pointed to a wood demon, bigger and stronger than those common to the wetlands. "That corie's been followin' us."

"Are you sure?" Ashia asked. The *alagai* did not appear interested in them.

"Sure," Briar said.

Ashia squinted in Everam's light, trying to study the pattern of magic in the demon's aura. It did not *appear* interested in them, but its aura said otherwise. They were its *only* interest.

"I think you are right," Ashia agreed. "We should kill it. Stay with . . ."

"No." Briar was already moving out of the circle, spear in hand. "Got it."

Ashia pursed her lips beneath her veil. She was used to commanding obedience, but Briar was his own force.

To his credit, even with Ashia knowing what to look for, Briar slipped unseen from the *alagia'viran*. She caught only the barest glimpse as he slipped into the trees. The demon gave no sign, in behavior or aura, that it noticed his departure.

But then there was a call in the distance. The demon cocked its head, then turned and ran after the sound.

A few moments later there were shrieks and flashes of light. Too far for Ashia to make out the details, but as the light and sound continued, a dread began to fill her. If Briar had surprised a lone demon, even a large one, he should have been able to kill it quickly. No warrior wanted a prolonged battle with a demon that large. Demons did not tire.

It went on, and on, and Ashia got to her feet, flicking her arms to extend the blades in her short spears. Every muscle in her body screamed for her to rush out and protect Briar. To stand in challenge against the *alagai*.

But Kaji, lying in her shield, bound her to the circle. What would happen to him if Ashia and Briar were killed?

Still the battle raged, and Ashia made her decision. She reached for Kaji's pack. If they were to go into danger, let it be together.

The night fell silent. Ashia shivered, staring into the darkness. Ten breaths. Twenty. She picked up the pack and began to pull the straps over her shoulders.

"Ashia!" Briar materialized out of the darkness, in the open ground where the bog demon had slashed away the demon root. "Ent a normal corie. Need to see." He started to turn.

Ashia glanced at Kaji, asleep in her shield. "Is it dead?"

"Ay," Briar said. "Way's clear, we're quick."

"Everam curse me." Ashia lifted her spears and followed, running low to the ground until she caught up with him in the trees. "Briar! By Everam, you will tell me . . ."

Briar turned to face her, a cool breeze at his back, and for once he did not smell of demon root.

It was all the warning she had before the mimic demon lashed out with an arm that lengthened into a tentacle with a spearlike tip. Ashia threw herself back at the last instant, but it was her armor that saved her. The overlapping plates of warded glass deflected the blow, but she felt the woven layers of silk holding them in place weaken and tear. She would not survive a second blow in the same place.

Enkido's training came to her instinctively. She stole energy from the blow, using it to roll out of the way and back to a position of balance. She felt the vibration as tentacles twice struck the ground mere inches from her, but she kept ahead of them as she circled back in, spears leading.

Another tentacle whipped out to slow her, but Ashia bent as a palm in the wind, slashing with the blades of her spears as it passed overhead. There was a spray of ichor and a lifeless thump behind her as she stepped in close, stabbing at the demon's body.

The demon howled as magic flared and rushed into her. Ashia looked up, expecting to see the light leave its eyes, but the demon only snarled and spit fire in her face.

Firespit was one of the most dangerous weapons in the *alagai*'s arsenal. It clung like sap but burned hotter than a furnace. Instinctively, Ashia pulled back, even as the wards on her jewelry warmed, turning the fire into a cool breeze.

The demon stole a moment to re-form, but Ashia knew the respite would be short-lived. She glanced at the rise and saw with horror that demons were coming out of the surrounding woods in frightening numbers. The foremost held branches, mowing down the demon root with calm efficiency. The demons hissed as they stepped onto the bed of mown *alagai'viran,* but they pressed forward, closing in on Kaji.

Ashia turned and bolted for the rise before the demons grew too thick to get past. She made several strides before a tentacle snaked around her ankle, pulling her from her feet. She caught herself with her hands, using the energy of the pull to twist into a slash of her long-bladed spear. The severed tentacle fell limp around her ankle, and she shook it free as she rolled into a defensive stance.

The mimic was still mostly in the form of a wood demon, and it abandoned water demon tentacles in favor of powerful branchlike arms.

They were formidable weapons, talons like sharpened stakes, but the large form was slow compared with tiny Ashia—her speed heightened by magic. She wove through the blows to step in past the demon's guard, stabbing with both spears. They crackled with magic, and Ashia felt some of it rush into her.

She longed to keep the feeling, but there was no time. She pulled the weapons free and rolled away from the mimic's attempt to claw her. The demon struck itself instead, howling in pain.

A few quick strides closer to Kaji before she was forced to turn and face the demon again. Already *alagai* crested the rise and were testing the wards around Ashia's circle. Magic skittered across the wardnet like dew sparkling on a web.

The mimic came in hard, and like a tree sprouting new limbs the gnarled arms split, four attacks instead of two. Ashia ducked one, slipped another, parried a third, but the fourth snaked around her guard, striking her across the back.

Her armor held, but at least one of her ribs cracked with the blow.

The demon came on again, and this time Ashia was faster, dancing past all four limbs and preparing to deliver a devastating counterblow.

But four limbs became eight. The demon spun, limbs whipping at her too fast to see clearly. Ashia worked on instinct, skittering back and trying to bat the blows out of alignment, tangling its limbs. She gave ground until the demons swarming the hill were at her back. Those nearest turned to face her, and the mimic struck.

The lesser demons did not attack, simply blocking Ashia's path. With no room to retreat, she went back on the offensive, slicing away at the demon, bit by bit. Mimics could heal most any wound that wasn't fatal, but they could not regrow or reattach mass that was severed.

She could wear it down.

A familiar squeal cut through the sound of combat. Ashia stole a glance and atop the rise saw Kaji, roused by the sounds of battle and demons at the wards, roll out of her wobbling shield in a tumble of blanket.

And then he did something miraculous.

She watched with shock and a little pride as, for the first time in his life, Kaji rose shakily on his own two feet and began to stumble through the camp, right for the flashing wards.

"Wads!" he shouted, and Ashia felt fear like she had never known.

The distraction proved too much. The mimic pounced, knocking her down and pinning her arms, spears useless. Ashia struggled against its foul weight, but even her heightened strength could not overcome the physics of it. This was no mindless *alagai*. This demon knew how to fight. Its maw opened, jaw unhinging as it grew wide enough to swallow her head. Even as she watched, rows of teeth added to the thickening gums.

Drawing a deep breath, Ashia did the only thing she could do. She shrieked.

It was not a cry of fear or a wail of pain. It was the raw essence of the verse in the *Song of Waning* that gave pain to *alagai.* Unable to sing fully, she held those harsh notes in the air, waving them like a torch.

The response was immediate. The wood and bog demons nearest to her scattered, and even the mimic loosened its grip, limbs moving instinctively to cover its head. Ashia lost one of her spears in the struggle to get free, but she managed to kick the demon off her, scrambling up the rise, using her voice to drive the demons away. With her free hand she pulled off her veil and dialed the wards on her necklace, adding power to her song.

A tree stump, torn from the ground the way a child might grasp a handful of sand, struck her hard in the back before she made it to Kaji. The heavy wood blasted the breath from her, and scattering soil choked her when she tried to draw another. The song died on her lips.

She went limp, letting her armor absorb as much of the blow as possible as she hit the ground in a roll, diffusing the impact. It only took a moment to find her balance, landing just steps from her son, toddling toward disaster.

But it was long enough for the mimic to pounce, pinning her. She gasped a breath, throat still raw, but a tentacle snaked around her mouth, silencing her. The demon drew back an arm, razor-sharp talons lengthening.

A speartip, bright with magic, thrust out from the mimic's midsection, spraying Ashia with ichor. The demon screamed, loosening its grip enough for her to draw a shallow breath, but not enough to escape.

Briar appeared, running up the mimic's back and taking its head in a *sharusahk* hold. His hands blazed with magic. The demon thrashed and gnashed its jaw, but it could not loosen the hold. Ashia could see it jolting as wards on Briar's hands sent waves of crushing magic through its skull.

The demon began to lose cohesion, the limbs holding Ashia turning flaccid. She struggled, managing to slip free. She hacked with the blade of her spear, stabbing and cutting while the demon did not have the wherewithal to heal.

But then there was a flash of light and a cry from above. A demon had struck at Kaji, slamming against the wardnet. The *alagai* rebounded, stunned, and Kaji fell back, landing hard on his bottom.

"Go!" Briar shouted.

Kaji had begun to cry, but stopped when he saw her coming. "Mama!" He got to his feet more easily this time, reaching for her and again stepping toward the wards.

And then she was there, sweeping him into her arms. "My son, my son! I am with you." She kissed his head. "Be brave, Kaji."

She tucked him into his pack and slung it over her back. Twisting the end of her remaining spear, she telescoped it to twice its size, taking her shield in her other hand.

Briar gave a yelp, and Ashia looked up to see the mimic had him wrapped in a horned tentacle, its flesh hissing and giving off some foul vapor as it gripped him. Unable to hold on for long, it flung the boy into the ward circle. Briar tangled up in the cord as he rolled to a stop, pulling the wards askew and opening a great gap in the protection.

The mimic took a moment to regroup, three demons forming a defensive wall around it. Briar's spear sloughed out of its body. Its flesh became hard and resilient once more, but Ashia could see its magic was dimmer. The demon was weakening.

Rasa gave a terrified whinny as *alagai* swarmed for the break in the circle. She pulled up her stake, rearing and leaping out into the night. For a moment it looked as if she might break away, but then the demons turned and half a dozen raced after her.

Rasa's screams sounded almost human as they tore her apart.

A pair of bog demons were first to reach the gap in the wards, but Ashia made short work of them, batting the attack of one into the other, then using the distraction to spear the second through the heart. She twisted her spear as she pulled back, making sure the organ was torn beyond the *alagai's* ability to repair before it died.

She caught the next attack from the first demon on her shield, punching her spear up through its chin and into its brain.

But it was all just distraction as the newly re-formed mimic came at them, a rock demon's body gliding on wind demon's wings. It lashed out with the horned tentacles of a water demon, its flame demon snout aglow with firespit.

Ashia felt Briar rushing her way, but without his spear she did not think he could get close enough to do the demon harm before it killed him.

Still he leapt by her, turning a circuit and hurling the soup pot at the demon. Briar's hogroot stew splashed across the mimic and it shrieked, flesh boiling and bubbling like tar.

They both rushed in, Ashia catching a thrashing mass of tentacles on her shield, severing a thick one before skittering back. Briar leapt in, and Ashia could see the large wards tattooed on his palms, shining with magic. He struck the demon in the throat with the impact ward, choking it on its own firespit, then boxed its ears.

The demon stumbled and Ashia was back in, stabbing and slicing, spear spinning.

A swamp demon managed to get behind her. She sensed its leap, but was not fast enough as it struck Kaji's pack with its talons.

Kaji cried out, but the warded glass scales woven in silk between the layers of stout cloth turned the blow. Her son's cries told her he was all right even as she opened the swamp demon's stomach and gave it a kick, watching its vital organs spill onto the wet ground.

The mimic was just getting its footing when Briar threw a pouch at its maw. Instinctively, the demon chomped down, and the pouch erupted in a cloud of demon root powder. Ashia slashed across its throat as Briar rolled down the hill for his spear.

More demons took the places of the fallen. One fell before it could reach Ashia and Kaji, Briar's thrown spear pinning it to the ground. Briar retrieved Ashia's lost spear as well, burying it in the mimic's back.

Her breath returned, Ashia began to sing, her voice keeping the lesser demons at bay while she and Briar pressed the mimic. It was slowing noticeably now. Healing and transforming its flesh took an enormous amount of magic, and in Everam's light it was growing dimmer and dimmer.

They did not let up. It tried to take flight, but Ashia slashed a great rent in its leathery wing, bashing the light, flexible bone that supported it with her shield. The wards on the rim flared, and she felt the bone shatter.

The other wing fell limp and Briar ran right up it, seizing the demon's horns in his warded palms, pulling its head back. Ashia took the opportunity to lunge, and at last managed to sever the demon's neck.

The other demons froze as the mimic fell dead, already beginning to melt like wet clay.

Ashia shrieked at them, and the *alagai* fled.

Briar had broken down the camp as the sky filled with color. Ashia patrolled the ring, her warded eyes searching the darkness and fog for signs of cories. It seemed the demons had fled the rising sun's power, but they were not prepared to break the wardnet before sunlight touched the rise.

Neither of them slept, even after the circle was restored. The power they Drew battling the mimic was more than enough to sustain them. Briar's muscles felt like ship cables, and he was jittery with energy. He felt he could throw Ashia and Kaji both on his back and run a hundred miles.

Only Kaji slept, snoring peacefully in his harness on Ashia's back. His breath was deep and even, like Briar's father, Relan, had taught his sons during their *sharusahk* lessons. Briar breathed with him, borrowing the boy's peaceful nerves to settle his own.

He made quick forays outside the circle to harvest the hogroot the cories had reaped, filling his pockets and pouches. He bruised handfuls of leaves, rubbing the sticky sap into his clothes.

He handed a few stalks to Ashia. "You, too."

He was getting better at reading her expression under the veil. Her nose scrunched slightly in disgust.

Briar was not offended. Folk were always like this around him. Some threw stones, calling him Stinky. Mudboy. Ashia was not so cruel, but he could smell the soap on her, and even after weeks in the wetlands the silks she wore remained pristine as one of Leesha Paper's dresses. She might be down in the mud, but she was raised in a palace.

Still, there was no time to coddle. Briar shook the leaves at her. "Cories got our scent. Need to do everything we can to shake the trail."

Ashia sighed, taking the stalks. "Do you think we can?"

"Got a few tricks to pull. Gonna be a long day's running, but we'll have safe succor tonight."

"We will need it," Ashia said. "It will be the better part of a week before Waning is safely past. It seems even a crescent strengthens Nie's power."

The words were serious, but Briar remained confident. "Best briarpatch I got. Cories can get us there, they can get us anywhere."

Ashia stared at him a moment, then nodded. The decision made, she was thorough and efficient, grinding the leaves and rubbing them over every inch of her silks, permanently ruining them with sticky, smelly sap. She set Kaji down, rubbing the sap into his pack, even his blanket.

Briar broke off the best leaves, mixing them with nuts and berries and a bit of oil for their breakfast.

"Why do you hide them?"

"Ay?" Briar looked up, finding her staring at his hands, again covered in their wraps.

"Your tattoos," Ashia said. "Do you cover them because you fear I will be offended?"

Briar remembered what Jarit had told him about the Krasians and tattoos. It was supposed to be an affront to Everam, but Briar could not see how.

Briar turned slightly, hiding his hands. "Don't like the look of them, is all."

"But they give you power," Ashia pressed. "I do not believe they are an affront to Everam. My master Enkido was tattooed, and I know of no man save the Deliverer himself who carried greater honor."

"Got 'em for the wrong reasons," Briar said.

He worried he'd said too much and she would press for more. He could see the desire in her eyes, but she respected his privacy. "What does the reason matter? The *alagai* cannot abide your touch, and your honor is boundless."

Briar took his hands back out, pulling the wrapping from one to look sadly at the ward beneath. "Think so?"

Ashia moved over to lay a hand on his shoulder. "I know you do not like to fight, Briar Damaj, but you leapt atop a demon *kai* for me and my son. Everam is always watching, even if I had not borne witness. You will be received in glory at the end of the lonely path."

"Won't," Briar said. "Nothin' I do can make up for what I done."

"What happened to your family wasn't your fault," Ashia said.

Briar turned away, knowing he must speak the words now if he was ever to, but fearing what he would see in her eyes. "Was. Laid the fire wrong and filled the house with smoke."

Ashia was silent for a time. Too long. Briar wanted to scream, to run off into the mist. Anything to escape the silence of her judgment.

Instead, she gently squeezed his shoulder. "That was ten years ago, Briar. You were a child. Nothing occurs, but that Everam wills it."

"Everam willed me to kill my family?" Briar was incredulous.

"Perhaps." Ashia shrugged. "Or perhaps it was going to happen, and He simply did not stop it."

Briar looked back at her. "Why?"

Ashia reached out, touching his face. "All things come second to the First War. Like me, Everam forged you in pain to be a weapon against Nie."

"What's the point of doing anything," Briar asked, "if it's all Everam's will?"

"My master used to say Everam draws power from our courage. Will is the one gift we can give to aid Him in His never-ending battle against Nie. Everam guides us, but the choice to be fearless or a coward, to fight or flee," Ashia reached out, touching his chest, "this comes from within."

The silk wrapping Ashia's sandaled feet was soaked through with water and muck from the bogs Briar led them though, zigzagging through the wetlands, sometimes wading hip-deep in water in an attempt to obscure their trail.

By midmorning he seemed satisfied, leading them onto drier ground. Ashia was completely lost, but Briar seemed at home as they picked up speed on the flatter land. By midday, they made it to the coast, and followed the cliffside up and up.

The excess magic from the demon *kai* burned off with the sun, but Ashia knew the danger they were in and said nothing at the brutal pace Briar set. She thought she and her spear sisters had endurance, but Briar Damaj put them all to shame. They covered many miles before the sun began to dip low in the sky.

"Is it much farther?" she asked finally. The reflection of the setting sun was so bright on the water it stung her eyes, but she knew it heralded darkness soon to come.

"There." Briar pointed to a seemingly unremarkable section of cliff, hundreds of feet above the waves crashing below.

Ashia was going to question, but she could see the confidence on Briar's face and trusted that he was about to produce one of his usual surprises.

He went to the edge of the cliff and knelt, reaching over the lip. "This way."

He jumped.

Ashia started, staring a moment before moving to peer over the edge. Dozens of feet below, Briar was sliding down a rope made of braided *alagai'viran* fibers, secured in a crevice just under the lip of the cliff. He kicked off the rock face to give the rope some swing, and disappeared.

Ashia sighed, tightening her pack straps to ensure Kaji was secure as she took the vine and rappelled after him. Perhaps thirty feet down the sheer cliff, she came across a small cave, invisible from above, obscured by vines of *alagai'viran* that appeared natural at a glance.

She slipped inside and found the cave larger than the entrance had led her to believe. The walls and floor were carpeted in dried demon root, softer and safer than raw stone, preventing *alagai* from rising in the cave. Too high above the lake for water demons to reach, too far below the cliff's edge for land demons to notice. The entrance was too small to admit a wind demon with its wings unfurled, even if it should see past the curtain that grew across the entrance.

"What do you think?" Briar asked at last.

Ashia smiled at him as she took Kaji from his straps. "It is perfect, son of Relan. Your skill is as boundless as your honor."

Briar grinned, walking past her to part the *alagai'viran*

vines covering the entrance like a curtain. "Haven't even looked at the best part."

Ashia turned, and the view took her breath away. The lake spread out before them, the horizon glittering with the last rays of the sun, sky brilliant in purple, white, and blue.

Kaji's eyes were wide. He pointed at the horizon. "Wud?" He wanted to know the word for what he was seeing.

Ashia hesitated. What word could do justice to such a sight? *Sunset* fell far short.

She knelt, placing Kaji on the ground beside her. She touched her hands to the floor, and he mimicked her. "It is Everam, my son. Creator of all things, Giver of Life and Light. It is for Him we live. It is for Him we fight. It will be for Him, when we die."

She began to sing *The Prayer of Coming Night* to him. Briar did not join them, but Ashia's sharp ears caught him stumbling through the words under his breath, as if sifting it from memory.

When the prayers were done, Briar pointed north. "There's the monastery."

Ashia had to lean her head out of the cave mouth to see, but there it was, a fortress alone on a high bluff jutting out over the water. Lights glowed in its tower windows and on its walls.

More lights shone out on the water, marking the fleet of Laktonian ships that held the blockade.

"More'n they need to cover the docks," Briar said.

"Do they mean to take the fortress?" Ashia asked. With their numbers, the fish men could likely take the docks and storm the fort, but seeing the long climb from the water, Ashia knew the cost in lives would be enormous.

"Maybe bait for Qeran," Briar said. "Try'n pull his ships north."

"He won't be fooled," Ashia said. She took Kaji inside, feeding and changing the boy in the warm glow of Everam's light. Briar had no wards around his eyes, but he moved about as comfortably in the near pitch blackness as he did in the light of day.

They moved in silence for a time, preparing a cold meal and eating, lost in their own thoughts. Kaji was the first asleep, and soon Briar followed suit, curling into a small nook at the back of the cave, breath calm and even.

Ashia closed her eyes, seeking the shallow sleep of her training, but tired as she was, it was difficult to find. Too many images flashing across her mind. Kaji's first steps. The mimic in Briar's form. The swarm of *alagai* tearing Rasa apart. The ring of demons closing on her helpless son.

The weight of her body seemed to double. She slumped, succumbing to the insistence of deeper sleep, where the images became nightmares filled with flashing claws and demon shrieks.

She started, coming awake. There was the cry again. It hadn't been a dream. Had the *alagai* found their hiding place? If so, there was no escape. They would need to hold the entrance till dawn. With her circle laid across the narrow threshold, it was possible.

Unless there was another mimic on their trail.

Ashia drew her spears, rolling to her feet, but Briar was already moving past her, darting to the cave mouth to seek the source of the cries. She moved close and readied herself for action as he stuck his neck out past the wards to look upward.

There was a flash of light, and Briar gasped and pulled himself inside, scrambling back as a wind demon dropped right in front of the cave mouth, opening its wings with a great *snap!* and catching itself on a current of air.

The demon was lit from below, visible without Everam's light, and Ashia realized in horror that it clutched a flame demon in its talons, the glow of the creature's eyes and mouth illuminating the carrier.

She readied her spear for a throw, but hesitated. If she threw out over the water, there would be no retrieving the weapon.

But then the demon flapped off into the night, soaring out over the water away from the cave—unaware of their presence.

Ashia and Briar returned to the entrance, watching the sky come alive as dozens of wind demons leapt from the cliff with their burning payloads, winging out onto the water.

"What in the abyss could they be doing?" Ashia whispered.

"Fightin'?" Briar asked. "Flamers don't get on with other

cories 'cept rockies. Maybe they're gonna drop them in the lake?"

Ashia shook her head. "The winds are not dropping them, and the flames are not struggling. This is some stratagem."

"For what?" The answer to Briar's question became obvious as the flight of wind demons banked with uniform precision, soaring toward the Laktonian fleet.

Ashia drew a ward in the air. "Everam preserve us."

The wind demons threw out their wings, abruptly changing direction and using the momentum to fling their charges at the sails. Flames blossomed on the canvas as the demons slid down to the deck, spitting fire on crew and boards alike. They raced across the decks leaving a burning trail, then leapt suicidally from the bows.

But they did not fall into the water. The wind demons, circling above, swept in and caught them again, winging back toward the cliffs, their part in the attack complete.

In moments it was done. Burning crew members ran across the decks of every ship, some rolling on the deck, vainly trying to extinguish themselves, others leaping into the lake, heedless of the water demons.

The remaining sailors beat frantically at the flames, but firespit was sticky, clinging to everything used to beat at it. A bucket brigade formed, but the water only made things worse. Demonfire was so hot the water instantly turned to steam that sent fire leaping through the air to stick wherever it spattered.

Soon the ships were engulfed in flames, visible for miles in the dark of night until at last the heat and smoke weakened the wards on the hulls. Water demons churned the waves around the ships, pulling them under, flames winking out one by one.

"What?" Briar's face was lit in the glow.

Ashia reached out, taking his hand and squeezing it. She did not know if the act was to comfort him, or herself.

"Sharak Ka has begun."

CHAPTER 25

THE MOUTH
OF THE ABYSS

334 AR

"Beloved."

The moon was a scant crescent of silver light as Jardir circled the night sky. He could see demons thick in the lands below, glowing like torches to his crownsight.

"I am here, my love," Inevera responded almost instantly.

"We approach the gateway to the abyss," Jardir said. "We are far from civilization, but *alagai* are thick in the area. The ambient magic is increasing. This may be the last time we speak before I pass beyond even the reach of the Crown of Kaji."

Below, the Par'chin and his *Jiwah Ka,* wards of unsight glowing softly on their skin, escorted Alagai Ka's prison. Shanvah drove the small wagon, its steel car covered in the Par'chin's wardings, containing the evil within and masking it from the evil without. Her father sat chained to the bench next to her, staring blankly into the distance.

If those protections had not been enough, Shanvah's voice enveloped them, amplified by the choker her spear sister had given her. She sang a verse of the *Song of Waning* over and over, a beautiful, tranquil melody that threatened to ensorcell even Jardir.

Watching from above, Jardir could see the wards protecting the party below. They glowed in crownsight—the limit of their light's reach the limit of their power. Shanvah's magic was subtler, but its effect was unmistakable. The movements of the *alagai* rippled as they came into her range, subtly steering away without rousing attention.

"My niece has grown powerful," Jardir said. "Truly Everam's Plan is unknowable. There are Spears of the Deliverer who fought by my side for twenty years. I have so many sons I cannot claim to know them all. Yet it is my niece, barely old enough for marriage, chosen to walk with me into the Mouth of the Abyss and bear the weight of Sharak Ka."

"Forgive me, beloved, for every unkind word I have ever spoken of your sisters," Inevera said. "From their wombs sprang three of the greatest warriors Ala has ever known."

"Everam grant they be enough."

"Have you slept?" Inevera asked.

"We rested for an hour, when the sun was high," Jardir said.

"That is not enough, husband," Inevera said. "Magic can restore vitality, but your minds need to dream, or you risk madness."

"Then I pray we can stave it off until our duty is complete," Jardir said. "After that, it does not matter."

"Of course it matters," Inevera said.

"We will sleep in the coming day," Jardir said. "Tomorrow night is Waning, when we will set Alagai Ka free to guide us on the path into the dark below. I fear there will be no sleep after that, until victory or death."

"Where are you?" Inevera asked.

"Just north of the mountain where the Par'chin and I fought *Domin Sharum*. There is power here, beloved. I understand now why the Par'chin was drawn to it."

"Your voice grows fainter," Inevera said. "Open your heart to me one last time. What do you feel as you approach the Mouth of the Abyss?"

"Eager." Jardir hesitated. It was true, but not the whole truth. "Afraid. Afraid I will fail you. Afraid I will fail all Ala. Afraid I will be weak, and Everam forsake me in my hour of need."

"These are the fears of all Everam's children, while Nie exists," Inevera said. "It is only just that the Deliverer feel them most of all. But I have watched you all your life, son of Hoshkamin. If you cannot bear the weight of Sharak Ka, then it cannot be borne."

Jardir swallowed a knot in his throat. "Thank you, beloved."

"Thank me by—" The words cut out, and suddenly Jardir heard only wind. He stopped, even flying back to try to reestablish the connection, but he could not find it again without traveling farther from the wagon than he dared.

Below, the father of demons lay thrice-bound—once on his very skin, once by silver warded chains, and a third time by warded steel walls.

The journey is long, and you are mortal, Alagai Ka promised. *The time will come when your guard grows lax, and then I will be free.*

It was a prophecy Jardir could not let come to pass. Twice, they had battled Alagai Ka, and twice the prince of Nie nearly defeated them. If he should manage to summon aid when released, there were *alagai* enough in the area to overwhelm even Everam's chosen.

"Farewell, beloved," he whispered to the wind as he flew back to watch over the wagon.

They followed ancient roads gleaned from the Par'chin's dusty maps. Through prairies and deep wood, cutting this way and that to avoid hamlets and refugee camps as they made their way up into the forested foothills. The road vanished soon after, heavily overgrown over the centuries. There were paths wide enough for the wagon, but only barely.

From his high vantage Jardir noticed something strange. The road reappeared up ahead, having seen regular use, and recently. He flew higher, and saw why.

He activated the crown, speaking to his companions below. "There is a large village ahead. Guard the father of demons closely while I investigate."

"Ay, think we can manage," the Par'chin said.

Jardir Drew hard on the power of the spear, launching himself toward the town in the distance. After so many weeks at a crawl, it felt good to flex his power.

The village, hidden in the trees, came into view, and Jardir pulled up so short the force of it wracked his body.

Surrounding the village were ancient stone obelisks, each standing twenty feet tall and weighing many tons. The wards on their pitted surfaces were still strong enough to hold the *alagai* at bay.

But what truly shocked Jardir was that they, and the village beyond, were Krasian in design. Not modern script and architecture; more like the remnants of Anoch Sun. What were a lost tribe of his people doing so far north?

And where had they gone?

Shanvah dropped to her knees when she returned from searching buildings. "There are no signs of battle, Deliverer. It looks as if everyone abruptly gathered supplies and left peacefully."

The Par'chin frowned. "Lot of that goin' around, since you folk came out of the desert, spears wavin'."

Jardir ignored the barb. "This far north, Par'chin? I doubt they even had word of my coming."

"Deliverer," Shanvah said. "Could this be the remains of Anoch Dahl?"

Renna tilted her head. "City of . . . Darkness?"

"Just so," Jardir agreed. "Kaji built Anoch Dahl to supply his army as he took them into the abyss."

You will find a piece of Kaji, Inevera said. *A gift from your ancestor to guide you in the dark.* Could that be what this was? A marker left by the Deliverer to his heirs?

The Par'chin blew out a breath. "And they survived three thousand years, only to pack up and leave for no reason . . . what? A year ago?"

"Less," Shanvah reported. "Months."

"When Alagai Ka staged his assault on Waning," Jardir guessed.

"Sure as the sun ent a coincidence," Renna said.

"We will learn soon enough," Jardir said. "We must rest now, while the sun is in the sky. It may be the last sleep of our lives, for tonight we release Alagai Ka."

———

The prison was hot under the hated day star. The metal walls acted like an oven, the inside reaching temperatures that would be fatal to the surface stock.

The heat was less a comfort than the lack of discomfort, but it remained the one tolerable thing about the Consort's captivity.

Everything else was pain. Each bump of the primitive conveyance jolted the demon, pulling the silver chains tight, their wards bringing fresh agony and shame. When his captors fed him at all, it was with the minds of animals, a diet of fat with no meat. Chained, he was forced to sacrifice the last of his dignity to crawl, each movement a new torture, to press his face against the disgusting flesh, sizzling in the heat. The prison stank of it.

And the singing!

The demon hated all his captors, but he was beginning to hate the Singer most of all. Even muffled by the thick metal walls, the sound of her voice grated, chewing a still-primitive part of even the Consort's powerful mind.

The Consort had experienced in the thoughts and memories of the Singer's sire his abhorrent feelings toward the girl—love, pride, hope. It made the demon despise her—want to hurt her—even before hearing her cursed voice.

Like the combat wards, the song was an echo of an ancient magic the mind court thought long since expunged. It tugged at the base emotions of demonkind, and magic was drawn to emotion. His kind provided the very power the song used against them.

Even knowing it for what it was, the Consort wanted to flee the sound. If the humans regained such power in force, they would be difficult to quell. Perhaps impossible, with the hive scattered.

The Consort remembered the great choirs of Kavri and shuddered.

His chains chafed and burned with the movement. He stopped trying to heal the damaged flesh, letting it die and form a barrier as he used his precious reserve of inner magic to build new layers of dermis beneath. It was a slow process, but one that would, over the weeks to come, erode the ink on his flesh, even as the wards eroded his own strength. He did not know which would give out first.

In the meantime, the Consort could only wait in darkness as the carriage jolted across the land. He could not see their route, and his bonds prevented him from reaching out with his mind.

That was the most disconcerting of all. Since he was a hatchling, the Consort's consciousness had been a thing independent of his body, able to leap vast distances in an instant. Never alone, he felt the urges of his drones, heard the voices of his brethren.

Now, nothing.

Only the coming and going of the day star's heat gave the Consort a sense of time, but it was enough. New moon was upon them. If they did not set him upon the mindless drone and begin the long trek down to the mind court now, it would be pointless. Very soon, the queen would begin to lay, if it had not already begun.

If it had, they were all doomed, the Consort most of all. If it had not, all of them had an interest in getting to the queen before it happened. If the only way to draw closer to her side was as a prisoner, it would suffice. Once they passed into the deep, where magic heightened and his drones were numerous, there would be opportunities to escape, should his captors ease in their vigilance.

With a sudden jolt, his prison came to a stop.

The Consort hissed at the glare of starlight as the heavy door to his prison was pulled open.

The Consort marked their positions even as his lidless eyes adjusted to the brightness. Even hatchling minds were taught to read the hated stars. It was impossible to gain status in the mind court without experience in the surface wars.

They were close to the path.

His captors gathered at the entrance—the Explorer and the Hunter, the Heir and the cursed Singer.

Chained beside them was the Consort's mount, the drone Shanjat.

"Gah! Stinks in here!" The Explorer made a show of contorting his face and spitting on the ground, but his aura said otherwise. It was a dominance gesture, meant to manipulate the Consort into anger, in hope he would give up some valuable piece of information.

The Explorer dared lay hands on the Consort, hauling him out of the prison by the burning chains and hurling him to the ground at the center of their ring. The night air was cold, carrying strong ambient magic this close to the path. The power was drawn naturally to the wards on his flesh, and they began to burn. He let the flesh die, tasting the magic on the wind.

One of his brethren was in the area, no doubt holding the vent. It was one of the few direct vents from the Core, and the only one for hundreds of miles large enough to march captives through. An ideal place for a hive, if a mind was powerful enough to hold it from his rivals.

The imprint on the magic told the Consort this one was of his own line. The eldest of his spawn, the Consort's most trusted lieutenant. Favor had led the Consort to let him live too long, and now he was powerful. Powerful enough to destroy the Consort's captors, if they were taken unawares.

The Consort rolled to a stop at the feet of his mount. Part of him wanted to refuse to bond with it, simply to remind the humans they did not control him. That at their most crucial hour, he could still stymie them if he wished.

But he did not wish it. Now was the time to gain their trust, and even the limited agency of the mount was better than he had on his own.

When he struck the sandaled foot, there was a moment of flesh-to-flesh contact. It was all the Consort needed to slip in and take control of the drone's body. It opened its robes, then bent and picked the Consort up, setting him on its back and covering him against the starlight with the cloth.

The demon closed his eyes against the brightness, seeing instead through the eyes of the drone. Chains attached to a thick belt kept its limbs from full extension, just enough to make the climb over the hills and up the mountainside.

They were in a human breeding ground, the one the Consort destroyed when he held the vent several turnings past. Having consumed the mind of its leader, the Consort knew the place intimately.

"You have done well," he congratulated them in the growls that passed for their communication. "We are near the entrance. I can show you the way."

"Awful eager, alla sudden," the Hunter said.

"As a fish is eager for water," the Consort replied. "As you are eager to consume the flesh of my kind."

"Ent." The Hunter's aura lit with indignation, and the Consort relished it. The humans were so easy to provoke.

"Your lies are meaningless," the Consort said. "It is written across your aura. You tell yourself you march to save your kind, but in truth you crave only the power."

The Hunter clenched a fist, ambient magic gathering to her. She would not have to feed much into the tattoos to kill the Consort, but he was unconcerned.

On cue, the Explorer intervened. "Don't let 'em rattle you, Ren. Know what they're like."

The Hunter's aura eased at the words. "Ay."

"What place is this, demon?" The Heir waved his weapon as he spoke, and the Consort watched it warily. Kavri's spear was one of many ways his captors could destroy him, but the Consort had feared that weapon for thousands of years. His own sire had fallen to it. "It bears the markings of my people. What happened to them?"

Countless lies presented themselves, but the truth was more exquisite. "It is Anoch Dahl, the city of night. Staging ground for the armies of Kavri, northern seat of Kavri's power before his empire came to ruin, leaving a scant few to guard the vent."

"What happened to them?" the Heir demanded.

"They forgot what they guarded, and why," the Consort said. "They grew lax, as you will, and their wards failed. I was able to penetrate their defenses and march their bodies down to the mind court for my personal larder." The words upset the humans. He could see it in their auras, and relished it.

"How can the demon know all this?" the Singer asked.

The Consort turned his drone's eyes toward her. "Because he consumed their leader's memories, much as he did mine, daughter. It is how he knows my shame when your ugly mother presented me with a female firstborn. I was too cowardly to strike your mother, but I found a *heasah* who looked like her to vent my frustration."

"Lies, from the Father of Lies," the Singer growled, but there was doubt and pain in her aura.

The sound of her father's laughter struck the Singer even deeper. "From that violent coupling was born a bastard I loved more than I ever did you."

She shrieked at him, the sound scraping along his aura. Shanjat fell to his knees, covering the Consort's ears, but even amid the pain he found pleasure in the Singer's anguish. Human minds were so fragile. Claw at the right moment and she would shatter.

The Heir laid a hand on her shoulder and her attack died away. The Consort used the drone to flash a grin at her in response.

It was a step too far. The Heir raised his spear and released a burst of power into the wards on the Consort's skin.

It was agony beyond even his ability to endure. The drone's robes held him in place when his grip on its back faltered, but the Consort's control ebbed, and the drone fell atop him as he writhed.

Then, abruptly, the pain stopped. The Consort reclaimed the drone's body, slowly getting it back on its feet.

This time it was the Hunter who drew a warding, setting the Consort's nerves aflame and dropping him back to the ground. There was real damage done in the assault. Damage it would take precious magic to repair. The others looked on, impassive.

At last she Drew the power back, and the Explorer stepped forward. "You'll speak when spoken to, know what's good for you. You'll answer our questions and take us where we want to go, and keep your corespawned mouth shut otherwise, or we'll leave you for the sun and find our own way."

"You will never find it," the Consort promised. "Not with a hundred of your years, and you have no such time."

"These prisoners you sent." Revulsion was slick across the Explorer's aura. "They walked the entire way by themselves?"

The Consort shook the drone's head in the human fashion. "I sent a mimic to guide them past the more . . . difficult ob-

stacles, and imprinted magic upon the stock, so all the creatures of the dark would know they were mine."

"What kinda obstacles?" the Explorer asked.

"Even when your ancestors traveled the path it was long
and difficult," the Consort said, "and it has been thousands of
years since Kavri led his legions below. Tunnels have collapsed or flooded, others worn through or since dug. Steep
drops and sheer climbs. It may be difficult for this drone to
navigate them bound."

"Cross that river when we come to it," the Explorer said.
"Wouldn't count on us takin' them chains off, I were you."

"Sooner or later, I will be free," the Consort promised.
"And when I am, I shall feast on your minds."

"Maybe." The Hunter stepped forward, aura flaring hot. "Or
maybe you'll try'n get free, and we'll kill you and feast on
yours."

She bared her teeth at him. They were not long or sharp like
those of his kind, but nevertheless the Consort felt a chill of
fear. "You think it'll work the same way with us? Suddenly
know everythin' you know?"

The Hunter drew the blade from her belt. It was an item of
considerable power, imprinted with a heady mix of emotion
that Drew magic on its own. "Night, maybe we're going about
this whole thing the wrong way. Maybe I cut you open right
now, and lead us down myself."

She took a step forward, and the Consort knew he had
taken the game too far. She meant her words, would kill him
and likely go mad consuming his ancient mind.

The thought brought no comfort. If he did not survive, the
Consort had no care for what happened between the humans
and his kind.

He looked to the Explorer, and found some sense of sanity
as the man moved between the Consort and his mate. "Breathe,
Ren. Ent got any way to know that'll work." Her aura remained
hot, unpredictable, but she eased slightly, and the Consort
drew a relieved breath.

The Consort had his drone meet the Explorer's eyes. It was
a strange sensation, looking into another creature's eyes without also being able to see into their mind. How had the humans grown so powerful with such rudimentary senses?

"There is a quicker path for you and me, Explorer," the Consort said quietly. "One we can travel in moments, sparing weeks of travel. Sparing risk to your mate and get."

"We go together," the Heir said. "Or not at all."

"He does not trust you," the Consort advised the Explorer. "It is obvious in his aura. He fears you will betray him. Betray all your kind." He had seen the strain between the two. The doubt. They were not as unified as they appeared.

He tilted the drone's head. "Is that what you fear, Explorer? What you may become, so close to the Core's power? You trust yourself little more than your so-called ally."

The Explorer raised a hand, summoning magic and suffusing the Consort's wards again. The drone collapsed, the two of them howling and convulsing in unison. The mind tasted human blood, realizing the drone had bitten his tongue.

"Warned you about speakin' out of turn," the Explorer said, Drawing back the power. "Only thing we don't trust around here is you."

"Yet you ask me to guide you below," the Consort said, still clutching his fallen drone.

"No time like the present," the Hunter said.

The Consort considered. He could lead them to the vent, walk them right into the talons of his get, and perhaps see them all brought down.

But what would his rival do, if he found the Consort bound and helpless? Rescue him? Unthinkable. He would do what any in his place would do. He would kill the Consort and consume his mind, gaining power enough to return to the Core and take his sire's place, fathering a new generation of demons.

"The vent is guarded." He growled the words.

"Guarded how?" the Explorer demanded.

"Can you not feel it? One of my get controls the vent. Even I can sense him, crippled though you have me."

The humans froze, all of them tilting their heads as if to listen. It was a moment of distraction the Consort might have used to escape, but he was too weak to attempt it, and feared the Hunter would keep her promise.

"I can hear it," the Heir said, after a moment. "A whisper on the night air."

The Explorer frowned, unused to being second when it came to magic. He had the greater skill, but the artifacts the Heir carried were no simple trinkets. The belief of millions remained imprinted upon them, even after so many years.

"There," the Explorer said after a moment. "Got it."

"Well I ent," the Hunter growled.

"The princeling hides behind wardings, even as we do," the Heir said.

"Draw and Read the flow, but don't look for anythin'," the Explorer said. "Look for emptiness, like a pothole in the road."

The Hunter closed her eyes again, face locked in an animal grimace of concentration. Finally, she opened them, turning and pointing toward the vent. "That way."

The Heir turned to the Singer. "Shanvah?"

Shame filled the girl's aura, and the Consort relished it. She bowed. "I am sorry, Deliverer. You three have six senses, but Everam has seen fit only to grant me five."

"Don't fret over it," the Explorer said. "Not like any of us warblers can sing."

It was difficult to keep the drone's face from contorting in disgust. Their understanding of the power around them was rudimentary at best. The lowliest caste of drone had greater control by instinct than the best humanity had to offer.

The Consort compartmentalized emotions, for therein lay the essence of magical control. Still, it took an effort to suppress the shame that he should have been taken unaware and captured by . . . mammals.

But there was hope in the thought, as well. If they could barely read the currents, it opened a range of subtle magics the Consort could safely work without detection.

The problem remained the power source. The wards on the Consort's skin kept him from letting his own internal magic rise, or Drawing from without. He could work through the drone, but Shanjat, while healthy and strong, was unwarded and broken of will—nearly magic-dead. To work magic he would need a repository, like the items his captors carried.

A small distraction, and the demon might reach one of the items long enough to power a warding. Defensive wards would be no hindrance, working through the human drone.

A puzzle for later. There was a more immediate concern. "You will need to eliminate my get, if we are to pass through the vent into darkness."

The Explorer turned back to the Consort. "We're supposed to believe you're gonna help kill your own son? Maybe you already warned him we're coming and are walking us into a trap."

"Do not doubt that I would, human," the Consort said. "But if my get senses me in my weakened state, he will not hesitate to kill me as well."

"His own da?" the Explorer asked doubtfully. His disgust at demonkind was palpable in his aura.

"Believe it," the Hunter said.

"Listen to your mate, human." The drone turned to smile at the Heir. "It would hardly be the first prince willing to kill for his father's throne."

It was a guess, but the Heir's aura confirmed it immediately. Much like the mind court, the Heir's proud get were making war upon one another in the vacuum of his power. The surface rebellion was ripe to be crushed.

"If he finds me bound, my get will gleefully feast on my mind, adding my power to his own. None of you could stand against him, then. He will feast on your minds, learning everything about your people and plans before returning to the Core to imprint his essence on a new generation of demons. They will mature quickly, and rise up to pacify the surface long before your crude greatwards can reach a critical mass."

The captors shared a glance, then the Heir looked at him. "Back in your gaol, Prince of Lies." He sent power into the wards, and again mind and drone fell to the ground, writhing in agony.

The Explorer came forward, hauling him free of the drone, but the Consort was barely aware of the burning of the chains against his skin. In the moment just before they were pulled apart, the demon's flailing talon touched something slung from a leather thong around the drone's neck, nestled between the thick muscles of his chest.

The Singer had made a critical mistake. She thought the vial of her tears hung around her sire's neck was symbolic, but the bottle held real power. Not much, but imprinted with her sadness, the item Drew and retained magic.

Unbound by the wards on the Consort's skin, the drone could take hold of the bottle to power a simple warding.

Enough, perhaps, to buy the Consort's freedom.

Arlen checked the wards three times as he locked Alagai Ka back in the steel car. Its protections were strong, but Arlen knew what the minds could do. If the wagon was located, its cargo discerned, it would not take this other demon prince long to penetrate its defenses.

Tension radiated from Jardir. "I do not trust the servant of Nie."

"Ent a reason you should," Arlen said.

"We've had it imprisoned for months," Jardir said. "How did it know about my sons?"

"Don't think it did," Arlen said. "It made a guess from Shanjat's memories when your guard was down, and got your aura to confirm it."

"Or maybe we ent been careful enough what we say in front of Shanjat," Renna said.

"Gonna have to start bein' extra careful," Arlen said. "Can't haul that prison car down with us. Meantime, Ren, need you and Shanvah to guard the wagon while Ahmann and I go hunt this mind."

"Ay, 'cause that worked out well the last time," Renna said. "Took all three of us to bring down a mind saw us comin'.""

"If it's a bushwhack, we ent got much chance against a demon standing on a magic vent that big," Arlen said. "If it ent, need you here."

"Why?" Renna said.

"We get hit, you need to make sure nothin's left of Alagai Ka for this other mind demon to chew on."

"Demonshit," Renna growled. "Shanvah can do that. You just don't want me coming."

"Any reason I should?" Arlen asked. "Creator, Ren. You're showing already."

"Ent," Renna said. "Put on a little weight is all. Eatin' for two."

"I can see right into your belly, Ren," Arlen said. "Baby shouldn't be growin' this fast. Same thing happened to Leesha. Gave birth months early."

He knew it was a mistake the moment he said it. No good ever came from mentioning Leesha Paper in an argument.

"Ay, kickin' *dama*'s heads in and killin' demons the whole rippin' time, to hear the Hollowers tell it," Renna said. "Sayin' I ent as tough as Leesha Paper?"

"Trouble found her, and she handed it right back," Arlen said. "Didn't go down into the Core lookin' to pick a fight."

"That's the demon talkin'," Renna said. "Tryin' to split us up. Weaken us."

"Doesn't mean it's wrong," Arlen said. "That's what they do. Smack you with the truth where it hurts the most."

"And that is where you must resist the most, Par'chin," Jardir cut in. "Your *jiwah* is too powerful to leave behind. You know it to be true. There is no one else who can go in her stead, and we have need of the help. We all must make sacrifices."

Arlen glared at him. "Easy for you to say, Ahmann. World's littered with your kids—your wives. These are the only ones I got."

"Do you think it is my wish to take my niece, barely old enough for marriage, into the abyss?" Jardir demanded. "That my only grandson is on his mother's back, walking into a nest of spears for the sake of a *khaffit*?"

"Ent the same and you know it," Arlen snapped. "Would you take Olive Paper down into the abyss with us?"

Jardir didn't hesitate. "If it shifted odds of destroying Alagai'ting Ka even slightly in our favor, then yes, Par'chin. I would take all my wives and all my children into the abyss to see it done. This is what it means to be Evejan. The First War comes before all else. Inevera cast the dice in your *jiwah's* blood. She must come into the abyss with us, or our chances to prevail will be only a fraction of the slim hope we hold now."

There was conviction in his aura that terrified Arlen—and filled him with envy. How simple life would be, if he could trust to fate.

"It's my choice," Renna said.

"Ay, but I don't have to like it. We should be on my da's farm, makin' things grow and waitin' nine months like every other corespawned fool in creation."

"Wanted that all my life," Renna said. "You were the fool who ran off and started this mess. Up to us to finish it. Your da's farm ent safe. Nowhere is, till we see this done."

"Fine." Arlen bit the word. "But I don't recall the corespawned dice saying anything about staying with the wagon this once while we open the gate."

Renna crossed her arms. "Can't stop me. You go off and I'll follow, 'less you want to lock me up with the demon."

Arlen clenched his fists. Ragen and Elissa told him many times growing up that marriage was hard and full of compromise, but he never truly understood till it happened to him.

Arlen focused power into the wards of confusion and unsight on his skin as they climbed the slope of the mountain. He could feel the coreling prince sweeping the area with its mind, but it did not seem to be seeking them in particular.

Renna did the same. When he looked at her directly, she appeared insubstantial, like a reflection on a glass window. Trying to focus on details about her person dizzied him. In peripheral vision, she melted away almost entirely.

She said it was the same when she looked at him. Their wards were keyed to affect demons, but the coreling flesh he and Renna consumed had become part of them, and they felt a portion of the effect. They kept close so as not to lose sight of each other.

Jardir, with his crownsight, had no problems tracking them. He soared the night sky above as they approached the vent cave.

It still unsettled Arlen, the way Jardir could hear the demon whispering on the night wind. The more time Arlen spent near the Crown and Spear of Kaji, the more he respected the first Damajah, who crafted them thousands of years ago. Arlen could claim with no ego to be the greatest Warder of his age, but he was a child banging on a pot compared with the orchestra of magic in those items. Jardir couldn't dissipate, but with his evolving mastery of the items, he was discovering powers even Arlen could not replicate.

They came to the edge of the mind demon's wardnet, carved by wood demon talons into the trees all around the base of the mountain. The rise was too big to hide entirely, especially with power spilling from the vent. Arlen could see into the net with his normal vision, but in wardsight it was like staring into thick glowing fog.

Arlen sensed the forbidding was keyed not to demons but humans. Anyone attempting to pass would be thrown back in a flare of light and pain, alerting the mind to their presence.

Jardir, too, stopped short. Arlen could see him hovering at the edge of the wardnet as he studied it from above.

Renna pointed upward. "Wanna see what he's seein'."

Arlen reached out and took her hand. "Careful not to mist more than a little."

"Told me a thousand times," Renna said. "Go too far an' our wards fail. Demon will sense us and it'll come down to a battle of will."

"Neither of us wants that fight, we can avoid it," Arlen said. "Especially when the demon's got a wardnet to protect his mind from us."

"I'll be careful."

They dissipated partially, retaining enough mass to keep their wards active, shedding enough to be lighter than air. Like a couple at a festival dance, they kicked off together, floating up to meet Jardir.

It was a clear night, and even with only the stars to go by, Arlen's sharp eyes could pick out the narrow road leading up to the vent. The cave was smaller than he expected, but the power radiating from it was too much for even the demon prince to hide. Around the cave were ancient stone pillars, their wards broken and marred.

"The Mouth of the Abyss," Jardir whispered reverently. "More sacred ground, marred by the *alagai*."

"You're the general," Arlen said. "How do you want to play this?"

Jardir considered. "When the coreling princes came to Everam's Bounty on Waning, they cut greatwards into the fields, much like the demon has done here. I was able to penetrate them using the powers of the crown."

"Can you breach the net without the demon sensing you?" Arlen asked.

Jardir frowned. "I am not sure. The last prince was weaker, his warding unfinished, and his attention inward. This foe is prepared. I can sense his will, reaching out from his succor."

"I could distract it," Arlen said. "Big unfocused blast of magic will light up the whole net. Time it right, demon shouldn't sense you pushing through."

"*We'll* distract it," Renna said. "Gonna strike back at you, second you touch that web. Told me yourself we can't dissipate without baring our necks."

"All the more reason for you to stand clear," Arlen said.

Renna shook her head. "I'll scatter another blast from the far side of the mountain, three breaths after yours. Give you a chance to run. We take turns, until Jardir kills it."

"Ent gonna be able to keep that up for long," Arlen said.

"You will not need to be long," Jardir promised. "I will be swift as Everam's spear."

Arlen slowly drew a breath. "Better be."

"If you cannot put your faith in Everam, Par'chin," Jardir said, "put it in your *ajin'pal*. Go now."

Arlen gave Renna's hand a squeeze. Though she was as insubstantial as a soap bubble to the rest of the world, she still felt solid to him. Their eyes met, and then Renna turned and flew off. Jardir drew his Cloak of Unsight close, blurring before Arlen's eyes. Arlen dropped away, flying a good distance in the opposite direction Renna had.

Then he hovered just above the trees before the net and Drew. Magic was thick in the area, rolling like a waterfall down from the vent. Power came to him in such strength he was sure the mind must sense it. He threw the power at the wardnet, lighting it up like a constellation.

He moved as he did, putting on a burst of speed. It was just in time, as a return blast of magic shot out from the cave mouth, centered where he had hovered a moment ago. The power splintered the tops of the trees, setting a vast swath of woods alight.

No sooner did the light die away than the wardnet lit up from another direction as Renna did her work.

A second blast shot out, this one in Renna's general direction, though doubtless she was long gone. Arlen cast again, and still the wardnet held, but this time there was no return fire. A shrieking came from the cave and he froze, forgetting even to breathe. Had Jardir struck?

But the shrieks did not die away. They grew louder and louder, high-pitched and overwhelming. Arlen's fists tightened as they burst from the cover of the demon's camouflage— hundreds of small wind demons, agile and fast. Their leathern wings slapped powerfully against the air.

More and more of them swept out, thousands now, flying with terrifying uniformity as they divided into two thick clouds, circling the edge of the wardnet in opposite directions. There were mimics among them, glowing brighter in wardsight than their fellows.

"Corespawn it." Arlen spat into the wind. If they remained in the area, a cloud that large would sweep them up in moments. The instant one of the demons bumped against them, the mind would have their position.

"Swift as Everam's spear, my bido," he muttered, putting on a burst of speed.

He needed to find Renna.

Renna was so close to the blast she felt it singe her feet, but she pulled up short a moment later, going back the way she came in case there was a follow-up strike.

The lump of power at the center of the camouflage was shining brightly now. The demon was Drawing heavily on the vent. No creature could hold that much for long, but in the short term it made the demon incredibly dangerous.

Then the wind demons swept from the cave.

From a distance they looked like the bats that roosted in her father's barn, but as they drew closer she could see they were the size of dogs, with powerful corded muscle under sharp scales, and snouts filled with sharp teeth.

She took off, but the demons were moving in both directions along the surface of the demon's warding, a rapidly expanding net that would soon catch her and Arlen—if he hadn't been swept up already. The magic from the cave mouth began to pulse angrily.

She traced quick wind wards as she flew, scattering them like tacks in her wake. Demons bounced off them as the flight began to catch up, causing chaos in their tight formation, but there were too many to be slowed.

Up ahead she saw the flight overtake Arlen. He turned and fed power to his wind wards, the tattoos flaring silver, too bright to see. Demons bounced off the forbiddance, colliding in midair. When the light died away, Arlen had dropped from the swarm and was flying fast her way.

The cloud of demons overtook Renna, as well. She powered her wind wards as Arlen had, demons rebounding away, but one of them was undeterred, colliding with her in midair and wrapping around her like a snake.

With the added weight, the two began to fall. Renna fed power to her mimic wards, pushing the creature away from her flesh, but it kept coiled around her, pulling her down.

"Ren!" Arlen screamed, but he would not reach her in time as the ground rushed to meet them. She gathered power into her muscles and bones, into the flesh of her belly, hoping to survive the impact.

But then a final throb of power burst from the cave. It rolled out like a ring in a pond, carrying a wail that could not be heard with the ears.

It was a sensation she'd felt before, the shock wave from a mind demon's psychic death rattle. It passed through the vast colony of bat demons, dropping them from the sky, and at last the mimic loosened its hold. She broke away as it careened shrieking into the trees.

There were a series of explosions as Jardir Drew upon the vent to energize massive impact wards, pulverizing clusters of trees that formed the keywords of the demon's wardnet. A moment later the forbidding dropped, and she sped for the cave, Arlen joining her as they pulled up short at the mouth. His face was grim and she readied herself to argue further, but he said nothing, his attention fully on the entrance.

The pillars to either side of the cave, battered by coreling talons and the weight of ages, were unmistakably Krasian.

Worn down over the millennia, Renna could still make out the demon's head carved into the living rock above the cave, its mouth the gateway into the abyss.

Arlen pulled up next to her. "Mouth of the Abyss ent just a name."

"Woulda been disappointed if it was just a cave." Renna alighted by the entrance, Drawing hard on the abundant magic, ready for anything as they stepped inside.

Jardir was waiting as they entered, standing with spear at the ready over the corpse of a mind demon. He lowered the weapon as they approached. "There were a pair of mimics, but they died with their master."

Arlen nodded. "Same for the bat demons outside."

"Couple mimics mighta survived," Renna said. "Out of range of the full effect."

Jardir nodded. "Let us retrieve Shanvah and the prisoner swiftly, before any survivors have time to recover."

"We should take the wagon all the way up to the mouth," Arlen said. "All a mimic needs to do is lay a claw on that mind, and we're done."

"Good thing there ent any demons down where we're going," Renna muttered.

Arlen sighed, pinching the bridge of his nose. "You got a better idea, Ren, now's the time to share."

Renna eyed the mind demon. "Just mutterin'. We're all jumpy. Both a' you go escort the wagon. I'll hold the vent."

She expected Arlen to be suspicious, but he seemed relieved not to have to argue. He was right, in any event. It was pointless to cast shade on his plan without having a better one to offer.

The two men flew off, and she turned to the demon's body. Did it really work both ways? Alagai Ka had been right. She could not risk their mission by killing their only guide on a hunch. But here was a fresh mind, its body still warm . . .

Before she could think twice, Renna had her knife in hand. The warded edge cut deep into the tough, knobbed flesh of the demon's cranium, and she peeled the skin back to expose the bone beneath. She wiped the excess ichor away with her hands, sucking her fingers clean.

She hardly noticed the putrid stench of demon ichor anymore, nor the foul taste, but she was learning to identify subtle differences of magic. She could tell stone demon ichor from rock, pick out the tingle of lightning demon from the flavor of wind. Most memorable was the mimic demon ichor she'd licked from her blade and skin, rolling the magic in her mouth like chaw.

But none of it prepared Renna for the rush of power that came from mind demon ichor. It shocked like a jump into freezing water. She shivered, feeling more alive, more alert, than ever in her life. It was all the other flavors of magic combined, and so much more.

She fractured the thick skull bone with a sharp blow from the impact ward on the pommel of her knife, then slid the blade into the gap, prising it open to expose the brain beneath.

It jiggled like gelatin, slick and glistening with ichor. In wardsight, Renna had never seen anything glow as brightly as the demon's mind. She cut a large chunk and seized it in her bare hand, shoving it eagerly into her mouth.

The power in the ichor was nothing, the crackle of a carpet compared with the bolt of lightning in her mouth. There was a rush of pleasure, the world around her opening to her senses like never before. Every moment stretched out, infinite, as the world lit up with information. She marveled at motes of dust frozen in midair, saw the whorls and eddies of the magic coming through the vent like a frozen waterfall.

But the information poured into her faster than she could comprehend. What began as a refreshing drink threatened to drown her.

Power sizzled in her veins, burned across her nerves. Not the dry, horseradish feeling of Drawing too much magic. This was being cast living into a funeral pyre. She screamed, and it felt like breathing fire.

A barrage of input followed, impossible to make out. Senses she didn't even have names for, delivering information with the roar of a river at spring melt. Images that made no sense.

There were emotions, as well, but these Renna had a name for.

Evil. It saturated her. Penetrated her. Contaminated her.

Renna fell to the floor—or rather, she felt the floor strike her, but then it was lost in the maelstrom. She sloshed up, black ichor and charcoal gelatin jiggling in the bile in front of her face. She could not think, could not feel her body, had no idea if she were still breathing. Everything was pain and cacophony, skin to soul. Her vision bounced and vibrated, and she realized she was convulsing.

Then it all went black.

"She cannot be trusted, Par'chin!"

"None of us can be trusted," Arlen said. "But like you said, ent no one to take our places."

Cold water splashed Renna's face, and she sat up with a jolt. Arlen stood over her with a pail, scowling. Behind him, Jardir had his spear at the ready, but he was not looking for outside threats.

He was pointing it at her.

Renna shivered. She tried to look around but everything was still alive in wardsight, the creatures too small to see with the naked eye glittering in the air. It was dizzying, and she put a hand out to steady herself.

"Easy now." Arlen knelt at her side, steadying her with one hand as he ladled water from the pail and brought it to her lips. "That was real stupid, what you done."

There was life in the water, too. So clear she could not believe she had never noticed it before. Millions of tiny organisms. She could feel them wriggling in her mouth and coughed, spattering Arlen. "Had to be done."

"Din't." Arlen wiped water from his eye. "Have our plan."

"Plan's crazy, and you know it," Renna said. "Told me yourself it was time for other ideas. Had one."

"Meant ones less crazy than mine," Arlen said.

"You're the one overthinks everything," Renna said. "Rest of us just do what feels right."

"Overthinkin's kept me alive," Arlen said. "Doin' what feels right lands you in hot water."

Renna looked at him, seeing into his aura as never before. "Remind me again, who the first person to eat demon was?"

"Ay, and that's worked out great," Arlen said.

"Got you where you are today," Renna said. "Mister Over-thought now, but the Arlen Bales I knew back in the Brook was reckless."

Arlen rubbed his face into a palm. "Might not be in this fix, I wern't so reckless."

"Maybe," Renna conceded. "Or maybe we just might not have as good a chance to set it right."

"It is pointless to argue," Jardir said. Renna looked at him, and could see one of the gemstones on his crown glowing brighter than the rest as he stared into her aura, trying to decide if the demon's mind had corrupted her in some way.

Core if I know, she thought. She felt like herself in some ways, but in others she was irrevocably changed.

Yet after a moment, Jardir seemed satisfied. He raised the point of his spear. "What did you see, Renna vah Harl? Your aura is . . ."

"Chaos," Arlen finished.

"Saw everythin'," Renna said. "And nothin'. Like everyone in the Hollow clustered in the Corelings' Graveyard, all talkin' at once. Too much to make out. Wasn't no sense to it."

Arlen nodded. "Was like that for me, when I touched that demon prince's mind. But I remembered a few things. Things that might mean winnin' and not losin'. There's anythin' you can recall—"

"Ent," Renna said. "Leastways, not yet. Need time."

"Time is the one thing we lack," Jardir said. "The darkest hours are already passed. If we do not release Alagai Ka and enter the Mouth of the Abyss, we will need to wait out the day here, and lose any advantage of surprise."

Renna pushed her feet under her and stood, breathing in rhythm to center herself. "Put it together on the way. Let's go."

CHAPTER 26

THE DARK BELOW

334 AR

Jardir embraced his doubts one by one as he left the Par'chin and his *jiwah* in the cave. Bad enough the woman carried an unborn child into the abyss, but she was unstable, as well. Unpredictable. Impulsive. Lacking judgment.

But what was he, to have agreed to this plan? To be led down into the abyss by Alagai Ka himself? The daughter of Harl was powerful. Fearless. Sacrificing her life and the life of her child in the First War. She was not Krasian, but she was Evejan in her heart. He shamed himself by doubting her.

Shanvah stood guard over Alagai Ka's prison, just outside the cave mouth. Her father was still chained to the bench, the demon king locked behind warded steel, but Shanvah was alert, spear and shield at the ready, scanning for threats—external and from within.

"Deliverer." She bowed when he drew close. "Is the daughter of Harl well?"

"It was foolish of her to risk herself by consuming the princeling's mind," Jardir said, "but she will recover, Everam willing."

"Did it . . . work?" Shanvah asked. "Does she have the demon's memories?"

Jardir shook his head. "It appears not. We will continue with our original plan. Now."

"Inevera." Shanvah sheathed her spear and leapt lightly

onto the bench, backing the wagon up to the cave mouth. She untethered the horses and removed their traces. The demon's prison could not go down into the abyss with them, and so it was time to set the animals free.

Jardir looked at the stallions, wondering if setting them free was sending them to their deaths. There were wards cut into their hooves, and the sun would rise in a few hours. Most of the demons in the area were dead, killed by the mind demon's psychic scream. The horses had a better chance to survive the coming days than Jardir and his companions did.

Jardir raised his spear, tracing wards in the air over the creatures. The magic clung to the horses, revitalizing them one last time even as it shielded them from *alagai* talons. The magic would fade with dawn, but for the remainder of the night they would be protected.

The stallions lifted their heads, alert once more. "Everam watch over you, noble steeds," Jardir said. "I name you Strength and Fortitude. If I live to tell of this journey, your names will not be forgotten in the holy verse."

He drew another warding in the air, setting off a harmless bang and flash that sent the stallions galloping down the ancient road.

Jardir moved to Shanjat, unlocking the chain that secured him to the wagon bench. Shanjat did not react, staring as blankly as the horses had. Jardir pulled his brother-in-law down, throwing him over one shoulder like a practice dummy.

The son of Jeph and daughter of Harl were waiting with Shanvah as he set Shanjat on his knees by the wagon door.

My sister's husband, Jardir thought. *Who trained and fought beside me since Hannu Pash. And I lay him on his knees for Alagai Ka.*

He looked down at his true friend. *I swear on Everam's light and my hope of Heaven, brother. When the time is right, Alagai Ka will pay for what he has done to you.*

With that, Jardir unlocked the wagon door and pulled it open. The demon lay in the center, staring at him with those huge, alien eyes. He strode into the circle and unchained the creature, then gripped the demon by the throat and dragged it hissing out of the circle. He tossed it from the wagon to land unceremoniously by Shanjat.

He would allow the creature its life for the good of Ala, but it deserved no dignity.

Alagai Ka made no pretense this time, taking control of Shanjat immediately. The warrior opened his robe, securing the demon underneath the cloth on his back.

The two, demon and host, stared at the body of the slain mind, its skull opened and scooped like a melon. Then they turned to Renna.

"Nice night," the daughter of Harl said, sucking ichor from her fingers.

Shanjat seemed to relax, smiling. "Your hatchling will be strong, if by some chance it survives. More akin to my kind than its weak ancestry."

Renna's aura flared so hot Jardir had to squint to look at her. She drew her knife, advancing on the demon. Shanjat retreated, but they had the demon surrounded, and there was nowhere to flee as Renna kicked him onto his knees and put the tip of the powerful blade against the demon's throat.

Shanjat looked at her. "Do it. Kill me if you dare. If your ploy had worked and your primitive brain been able to comprehend the vastness of my get's mind, you would have no need of me, and the Heir would have killed me as I lay helpless."

Shanjat's lips curled into a smile. "But you do, don't you, Hunter? To kill me is to doom your own kind."

"Maybe," Renna said. "But mention my babe one more time, and you'll be dead long before my 'kind.'"

She meant every word. Jardir could see it in her aura. He feared she might lose control and doom their plan, but it was good for Alagai Ka to fear them. If the demon king began to feel secure, he would prove increasingly difficult to control.

If they even controlled him now.

"Your life only has value as long as you are of use to us, Prince of Lies," Jardir said. "The Evejah tells us Kaji's armies marched for three times seven days to reach the abyss. Is it so?"

"To reach the abyss?" The demon laughed with Shanjat's throat. "Nie's abyss is a fantasy created to motivate drones. There is no such place."

Jardir bristled at the smug smile—had to restrain himself

from killing the vile creature once and for all. It was baiting them, whispering truths that sounded like lies, and lies that rang of truth. Even without looking into their minds, the demon had an uncanny knack for manipulating their emotions. It would seek to confuse them, to get them to lower their guard. They must be vigilant.

"How long a walk to your hive?" the Par'chin asked.

"A turning, perhaps," Shanjat said, winking at Jardir. "We travel deeper than Kavri and his dogs."

Shanjat looked at him expectantly, but Jardir only smiled.

> *"And so did Kaji*
> *Unleash his war dogs*
> *Driving evil to* Sharum *spears*
> *Like foxes before the hunter."*

"You think to insult me, demon?" Jardir asked. "To insult my people? Kaji's dogs drove your kind back underground like cattle."

"Scared, even if he don't admit it," Renna said. "Ent every day someone ets your son."

Shanjat laughed again. "An unexpected boon, to be ridden of my strongest rival. I thank you for that."

"He one of the ones that came to Anoch Sun?" the Par'chin asked.

Shanjat shook his head just as he had in life. It was unnerving. "No. He was one of two left in the mind court powerful enough to refuse my summons."

"That is nine, including you," Jardir said.

"We killed three in Anoch Sun," Shanvah noted.

"And captured Alagai Ka," Jardir said.

"This'un makes five." Renna kicked the corpse of the demon princeling. "Plus the four we killed last summer."

"Had over a dozen minds, before this all started," the Par'chin said. "How many you got now? Four?"

"Four mature enough to survive a mating without being eaten alive when it is done." Shanjat's smile spread. "Along with juvenile princelings enough to lay waste to your Free Cities. They will scatter, striking where your people least suspect, building new hives and using drones to herd your kind underground like cattle to feed their hatchling queens."

"Then why was the strongest of them here, far from any human city?" Jardir asked.

Shanjat looked at him as if he were a fool. It was a look Jardir had seen his brother make many times, but never in his direction. "There is power here. My get would have let his younger brothers fight over your territories, then taken spoils from them all when their forces were sufficiently weakened."

"How do you know that?" Renna asked.

"Because I have done it many times over the millennia," Shanjat said.

"Some other mind gonna try and claim the vent now?" the Par'chin asked.

"When they realize it is unguarded, certainly," Shanjat said, "but it is unlikely they will encroach upon their elder brother's territory enough to discover it soon."

"When will they attack?" Jardir asked.

Shanjat threw back his head to laugh. "If my get was here, they already have! Krasia. Thesa." He turned to look at Renna. "Perhaps even your Tibbet's Brook. It is isolated, with so many deliciously empty minds to feast upon."

Renna bared her teeth, but she held her tongue, and her ground.

The Par'chin wavered. "Still dark. I could skate back . . ."

"And do what, Par'chin?" Jardir asked. "Warn them of an attack that has already come? Abandon our mission to fight lesser princelings?"

"Don't know," the Par'chin said. "Might be somethin' I can do."

"Warned 'em best we could," Renna said. "Ent this what you're always preachin'? Save yourselves?"

The Par'chin blew out a breath. "Ent ever been one to stand by when trouble comes callin'."

"It would be unwise for you to enter the between-state here in any case," Shanjat said. "Even I take care when dissipating near such currents."

"Lose yourself," the Par'chin said.

"There is no return from the Core," Shanjat said. "Not even for my kind."

The Par'chin turned on Shanjat. "Why're you so chatty, all a sudden? Why tell us about the attacks at all?"

Shanjat drew a deep, mocking breath through his nostrils. "For the exquisite scent of despair it imprints on you." The Par'chin's hand closed into a fist, but Shanjat wasn't finished. "And to give you hope."

"Hope?" Jardir asked. "What do the creatures of Nie know of hope?"

"We know how you apes treasure it," Shanjat said. "How you cling to it. Kill for it. How it cuts you, when snatched away."

"And is this your plan?" Jardir asked. "To dangle hope like a string to a cat, then snatch it away?"

"Of course," Shanjat said.

"What hope can you dangle," Jardir asked, "now that you have revealed your ploy? Now that you have told us war has begun upon our homes?"

"The hope that comes from knowing the mind court is empty while my get make war on your homes," Shanjat said.

Jardir stiffened. If true, it meant their mission might actually succeed. If their people could hold back the *alagai* for another moon—two, at the most—they had a chance to cripple the hive once and for all.

But the demon already promised the hope would be snatched away. Was the claim a lie, or was there more Alagai Ka was not telling them?

Likely, it was both.

"The time for second guesses is past." Jardir went to the wagon, pulling his pack from the storage compartment. Shanvah was already wearing hers. "If we walk the road to the abyss, let us be upon it."

Jardir brought up the rear, watching Alagai Ka's back. Even with his hands chained to his waist, Shanjat picked his way down the tunnel slope with familiar nimbleness. It was a reminder that the demon had more than possession of his brother-in-law's body. It had all the skills and knowledge the man had in life.

Shanjat was a very dangerous man.

Renna and Shanvah walked to either side of the demon, eyes watching in periphery. The Par'chin was ahead out of sight, scouting the path.

Jardir lost track of time in the lightless tunnels. They had not rested, but with magic to sustain them, they might have been traveling days for all he could tell.

The path to the abyss was not what he expected. There was life even here, far from the holy sun. They had encountered no demons yet, but the damp soil teemed with insects, and other creatures too small to see with the naked eye lit up in his crownsight. There were underground streams full of fish, moss and lichen on the walls. Lizards. Salamanders. Frogs.

And sometimes, the prints of larger things. Not demon, perhaps, but nothing he recognized.

The tunnel ended at the base of the slope, coming to a ledge that opened on a chasm so vast they could not see the other side. The Par'chin waited at its edge, leaning against a pitted stone archway of Krasian design.

"Bridge collapsed."

"We will need to climb down to the cavern floor, and back up the far side," Shanjat said. "This drone will need all his limbs to manage it."

Jardir kept one eye on the prisoner as he moved to stand by the Par'chin. Together they stared out over the chasm. At the edge of his crownsight was a crumbling bridge support.

"I could fly across," Jardir said.

"Maybe, but Ren and I shouldn't," the Par'chin said. "Demon's right. Call of the Core's gotten stronger, deeper we go. Need to stay solid, much as we can." He squinted at the distant bridge support. "Too far to jump, even with a boost."

"I could ferry us," Jardir said.

"Demon, too?" the Par'chin asked. "Gonna get that close, away from backup, when you don't have to?"

"So we climb," Jardir said.

Renna joined them as they peered over the edge, the cavern floor lost in the haze of magic. "Need a meal and a rest, if we're gonna unchain Shanjat's hands for him to climb down that." She spat over the edge, watching the spittle vanish silently into the haze. "'Less we want to just kick him over and have done."

Jardir looked again at Shanjat. His fiercest lieutenant. A man whose prowess in the Maze was so great, Jardir gave his own sister for him to wed. How many times had he seen Shanjat kill with bare hands alone?

"Wise words," he said. "My warrior's heart wants nothing but to press on, but we must not let hunger and fatigue cause our vigilance over Alagai Ka to wane. It is too easy in this lightless world to forget the passage of time."

"Ent no clock as reliable as my stomach these days." Renna patted a belly that grew rounder by the day.

They gathered in the hollow of the tunnel mouth. The Par'chin and his *jiwah* striding over to Shanjat.

"Kneel," the Par'chin commanded. Ambient magic rushed into him, the area darkening even as his aura turned white with power.

Renna had her knife in hand, and she, too, blazed with magic. No fool, the demon knelt Shanjat and allowed the manacles on his ankles to be reconnected to his belt.

Shanvah set about scooping soil into large bronze bowls. She smoothed the surface with a blade in preparation for Jardir.

Like the greenlanders, Jardir Drew ambient magic through the crown, using it to power the wards Inevera taught him. The soil melted, blurring into a whirlpool of magic, and then grew calm again. One bowl was now full of fresh water—the other, steaming couscous.

Shanvah knelt, hands and forehead on the floor, saying prayers with him, thanking Everam for His endless bounty, and renewing their oaths to fight in His name.

When they were done, Jardir produced a tiny porcelain couzi cup, inlaid with gold, and a matching pair of eating sticks. With reverence and precision, he filled the tiny cup with water and held it out. "Rise, Niece, and let Everam's blessed water refresh you."

Shanvah sat up like a snake, a sinuous movement of perfect grace. She bowed her head and lowered her veil, for it was no shame to be seen by her uncle. "Thank you, Deliverer, for the honor Everam bestows through you."

She took only a small sip from the tiny cup, but drew back with new light in her eyes, her aura refreshed.

He lifted a bite of couscous with the delicate sticks. "Eat, and let Everam's blessed food fill your stomach."

Shanvah bowed again. "Thank you, Deliverer, for the honor Everam bestows through you." She took a single bite, but immediately she seemed stronger, satiated.

"Stand guard, so the greenlanders may eat as well," Jardir said.

Shanvah touched her head to the floor. "Your will, Deliverer." She took up her spear and shield, taking position to watch over the prisoners.

Renna floated over immediately. "Night, that smells good."

"It is blessed food," Jardir said. "One sip of Everam's water will quench your thirst. One bite of Everam's food will fill your stomach."

"See about that," Renna said. Jardir moved to serve with his tiny cup, but the woman didn't even notice. She had the dusty cup out of her pack in an instant, filling it with a great scoop of the sacred water. Jardir gaped as she threw the entire cup back like a shot of couzi, wiping the excess holy water from her lips with the back of her dirty hand.

Her eyes grew wide. "Oh, sweet sunshine." She tossed the cup back again, seeking any missed drops, then turned look at the Par'chin. "Arlen Bales, you get over here and try this water!" She filled a second cup, draining that, as well, before moving to the couscous.

Jardir lifted his eating sticks and coughed pointedly, but again Renna missed the cue, digging in her pack for her bowl and spoon. She scooped couscous carelessly, spilling some on the ground as she piled her bowl with enough blessed food to satisfy an entire company of *Sharum*.

The woman's rudeness knew no bounds, but she was a chosen of Everam, and a guest at his table, and so he embraced the insult and said nothing.

"Thanks." Renna put her back against the tunnel wall and slid down to sit, shoveling the food into her mouth.

Jardir realized he was staring, and forced himself to look away as the Par'chin approached.

"Sorry about that." The Par'chin knelt smoothly, and bowed. "Ren didn't . . ."

"Make no excuses, Par'chin," Jardir said. "We've been eating together for months. She knows it is polite to pray over food."

"Old habits die hard," the Par'chin said. "And she ent comfortable prayin' to Everam."

"She may replace His name with *Creator*," Jardir said. "It makes no difference to the Almighty."

"Be sure to tell her." The Par'chin glanced at his bride. "Just not now. Ent wise to get between a pregnant woman and her food."

"From Everam's lips to your mouth," Jardir agreed. He began the blessing, and the Par'chin prayed with him, as they had so many times after a night in the Maze.

Jardir scooped a delicate cup of water. "You pray."

"Ay?" the Par'chin asked.

"Heaven is a lie, you said," Jardir recalled. "Everam is a lie. Why, then, do you pray with me?"

"Mam called it mindin' your manners," the Par'chin said. "Wise old man once told me our cultures were a natural insult to each other. That we had to resist the urge to give and take offense.

"'Sides." The Par'chin shook his head. "Startin' to think it don't matter if Everam's in the sky or in your imagination. It's a voice that tells you to act right, and that's more than most folk have."

The words were blasphemy, but Jardir saw such sincerity in the Par'chin's aura that he could not help but smile. In his own way, his friend was paying his respects. When they spoke thanks over the water and food, the Par'chin followed the ritual with practiced precision.

Like Shanvah, he only required a sip and a bite to be satisfied, but Renna had finished her bowl and was eyeing the remainder hungrily.

"This drone will require sustenance as well, if you wish him to survive the journey," Shanjat said. "As will I."

Jardir's lips twisted with distaste, but when Shanvah looked at him, he nodded. She took a small tray from her pack, with a cup and bowl. Jardir poured two mouthfuls of the sacred water into Shanvah's cup and placed two bites of holy couscous in the bowl.

Shanvah went to kneel beside her father. She set the tray down with precision and grace, producing her own eating sticks.

"Now, this is the daughter I always wanted," Shanjat said. "Quiet. Obedient. You were never going to marry well, not with your mother's horse face, but you could still have been a daughter to be proud of."

"My father *was* proud of me," Shanvah said. "*Is* proud of me. Nothing you say while wearing his skin can change that."

"A flash of pride at the end cannot make up a lifetime of disappointment," Shanjat said. "Your sire's mind reeks of shame over you. Your mother may have been his *Jiwah Ka*, but he loved the least of his wives more than either of you."

Shanvah appeared calm, but her fist clenched the eating sticks as if resisting the urge to plunge them into the demon's eye.

Still, she kept her center, breathing the emotions away until her aura became tranquil. The next time the demon opened Shanjat's mouth, the sticks darted out, filling it with couscous. He swallowed reflexively.

Shanvah reached out and took the back of her father's head, pulling him in and manipulating a muscle to open his mouth for a sip of the blessed water.

The deed done, Shanvah drew back with the tray.

"I must consume as well," Shanjat said.

"Demon, you are not worthy of blessed food and drink," Shanvah said.

"I have sustained myself on scraps for many months now," Shanjat said. "But even I have a limit. If you will not feed me, I will lead you no farther."

Shanvah was on her feet in an instant, driving her spear out with a two-handed thrust. Shanjat and the demon flinched, but they were not her target. Impaled on the spearpoint was one of the blind salamanders that roamed the walls, hunting insects. They could move quickly when they sensed a threat, but not so quickly as a *Sharum'ting* spear.

This she pulled from the point, tearing the still-squirming animal in half with her bare hands. She kicked Shanjat onto his side, taking the demon down with him. When the conical head slammed against the tunnel floor, she thrust half the salamander into Alagai Ka's mouth.

"Eat it," she growled. "Or I will sing until you do."

The Consort worked his mouth as they descended the rock face, trying to rid it of the bitter taste of the low creature. The flesh and blood sustained him, but the pathetic minds of the salamanders forced him to relive every moment of their meaningless existence. He might have vomited, but despite the exquisite pleasure of torturing the Singer, he had no wish to hear her song up close.

They had freed the drone's arms for the climb, the first of many eases of vigilance. And why not? The Consort cut at them with words, but he kept the drone's body docile. Compliant.

The time to escape was approaching, but it was not now. They were still too shallow, too close to the surface. It was cold here. Dim. The humans might be impressed with the magic this far down, but it was a pale comparison with what awaited at further depth. Not even the weakest drones ranged so far from the heat of the Core without cause.

But soon the tunnels would open up into a honeycomb, dug by drones over millions of years. The humans would quickly become lost without the Consort, as unlikely to find the mind court as they were the way back to the surface. It pleased him to think of them, endlessly wandering the bowels of the world until it drove them to madness. What a feast their minds would make then! The mix of pride turned to despair and madness would combine into a flavor like no other.

For now, they watched him closely. The Hunter and Singer flanked him as they climbed, with the Explorer working his way down from above.

The Heir floated away from the cliff, spear in hand, watching the Consort descend. It was amusing, the caution with which they guarded him. It would fade soon enough. Humans did not have the patience for such things.

The drone needed no assistance for the climb. The Consort issued the command, and let the drone's learned skills handle the task while he focused his energies inward, taking the salamander flesh and making it his own, growing another thin layer of dermis to push the ink closer to the surface.

Soon.

Jardir drifted to the ground ahead of the others, watching their descent. Renna, Shanvah, and the Par'chin all kept out of Shanjat's reach, but it seemed the demon had no intent save reaching the bottom safely.

It was understandable, even for one such as Alagai Ka. Three human skeletons lay at the base of the cliff, bones picked clean by Everam only knew what. The humans Alagai Ka marched into the abyss had been forced to make the same climb, and not all were up to the task. One was female, skull crushed in a fall. Another was male, but small even for a greenlander, perhaps not come into his full growth. Multiple bones had been shattered as he bounced down the rock face, but a broken neck had done him in. Likely they had not suffered, and without reaching the abyss, Jardir hoped their souls had managed to escape the darkness and find the lonely path.

The third was a child.

Worse, her skeleton was intact, save for a single break in her leg. From the scraping of the soil and her separation from the others, it appeared she had crawled for some distance, bound to follow the demon prince's will even as her body failed. Jardir laid a gentle hand on her skull, meaning to bless her, but her pain had imprinted magic on the bone, a silent scream that shocked through him. He snatched his hand away as if burnt.

The pain was not of her body, or her loss of liberty, but a psychic wail at her inability to follow the demon's command. The others, neighbor and kin alike, had left her behind without a thought, driven by similar need.

Realizing his distraction, Jardir's eyes darted to the others, but they remained well. Renna pushed off from the cliff face, dropping the last forty feet as easily as she might skip the final step in a stair.

She, too, noticed the bones. "Think we ought to bury them?"

"Their spirits have gone onto the lonely path, leaving their pain behind." They might have been placating words once, but Jardir saw now how true they were. "We do them greater honor by pressing on in our sacred task."

The daughter of Harl grunted, but she did not disagree, watching closely as Shanvah and her father finished the descent. The Par'chin let go as well, riding a current of magic to drift down as gently as a falling leaf.

Seven columns like the pillars of Heaven guided their path as they hiked, but these were crumbled and broken, shattered stone littering the cavern floor, slick with wet, smooth from centuries of droplets from above. Stalagmites grew among them and elsewhere, some great and some small.

More bones greeted them at the far end, and Shanjat's arms had to be freed once more to climb back up the cliff face to find the path again.

They paused at the top for another meal, and this time Renna's eyes were down as she was called to the holy water and couscous. Proud like a mountain, she did not apologize for her behavior, but she made an effort—clumsy though it was—to join Jardir in prayer.

Again, she ate more than he would have believed possible, and it seemed to him that even in that short time the curve of her belly had grown more prominent.

The tunnel sloped endlessly down, the air growing so hot and humid it was difficult to abide. They drew wards in the air to provide some small comfort, but they were all of them filthy; even Jardir's fine silk raiment clung to him with sweat. He Drew power into the embroidered wards, burning away the dirt and moisture, but it wasn't long before it returned.

Again the tunnel opened up, this time into a vast cavern housing an enormous lake. The air was thick with moisture, and great stalactites hung from the ceiling far above.

More fascinating, though, was the ground leading to the water, covered with fungal vegetation glowing bright with life.

"We will need to clear a path," Shanjat said.

Jardir looked at him. "Why?" The mushroom field was thick, with some reaching as high as his elbow, but those seemed simple to push aside. Most would be easily trampled underfoot.

"Send a wind through the field," Shanjat suggested.

Jardir eyed him warily, then shrugged and drew a quick warding, sending a jet of air toward the water.

Immediately, countless spores exploded, filling the air with a dark cloud of noxious fume. Jardir drew another warding, a gentler breeze to keep the cloud from drifting their way.

"What in the dark of night was that?" Renna asked.

"It is how the colony draws sustenance," Shanjat said. "The spores emit a paralytic that cripples and infects any creature foolish enough to disturb them."

"Infects?" The hand Renna placed on her rounding belly was hardly subtle, but her aura spoke volumes. In it Jardir could see an image of her clutching a child as she bathed the area in flame.

Before Shanjat could answer, there was movement in the field, and a demon, previously invisible, raced toward them, claws leading.

The beast was like nothing Jardir had ever seen. Its aura was flat, blending perfectly with the colony around it. Fungal stalks grew from between its scales—it was being consumed from within, even as it moved with speed and agility.

Nevertheless, it was only a demon drone. Jardir concentrated a moment, activating the warding field of his crown to keep it from approaching.

The creature slowed a moment, as if running through water up to its thighs, but then crossed the barrier, picking up speed.

Jardir blinked in surprise and raised his spear, but Shanvah was faster, flinging warded throwing glass to intercept the demon. The sharpened projectiles thudded into the creature's center mass, but if it registered the impacts at all, there was no sign as it continued to race their way.

Jardir drew an impact ward, swatting the demon like an insect. It was still airborne when the Par'chin followed up with a powerful heat ward. The *alagai* exploded in a blast of fire so intense Jardir felt his face flush. Its flaming ruin fell back into the colony, setting off another cloud of spores that fed the flame into a great fireball.

Mushrooms and fungal stalks burned in the aftermath, but the ground and air were wet, and the flame did not spread or penetrate the soil as they might have wished.

"There will be others," Shanjat noted. "The spores can infect the minds of drones, turning them into defenders before their bodies are consumed past the point of use."

"It crossed my forbiddance," Jardir said. "It seems the creature is more fungus than *alagai*."

"How'd your prisoners get past them?" the Par'chin asked.

"The mimic that escorted them became a flame drone and burned a path, but not without loss." Shanjat showed his teeth. "Some of your kind may still serve the colony, if they have not yet been fully consumed."

"And that lake?" Renna asked. "How did they get across?"

"They swam, of course." Shanjat was smiling openly now.

"Don't trust it," Renna said. "Creator only knows what's in that water. Demon's led us into a trap."

Shanjat shrugged. "There is this way, and no other."

"I trust the demon no more than you, daughter of Harl," Jardir said, "but we cannot stay here, and we cannot go back."

"Creator, will you ripping people stop callin' me that?!" Renna snapped. "Harl Tanner might not have been the worst man ever lived, but he was the worst I ever met by a far sight. Killed him myself, and I'm sick of you actin' like his name's more important than mine."

Jardir opened his mouth, then closed it, taken aback. Her aura was a wild thing, and he remembered well the shifting humors of his wives while they were with child.

But then her words sank in. "You admit to slaying your own father?" It was . . . monstrous. He glanced at the Par'chin, who met his eyes as Shanvah kept watch over her father and the demon. "Did you know this?"

The Par'chin nodded. "Son of the Core had it comin'."

The words were a comfort. He knew well the value his friend put on all human life. Even so, it was insufficient explanation for such a crime. Jardir turned back to Renna and peered into her aura, seeking the truth of it.

"Want to know so bad?" Renna demanded. The Par'chin had trained them all to mask their inner auras to hide their most private thoughts and feelings, but she let down her guard for a moment, and in it Jardir could see horror unlike anything he had imagined.

Jardir raised his hands. "Peace, Renna am'Bales. Your

honor remains boundless in my eyes. No doubt Everam Himself guided your hand."

"Everam must've been sleepin' on watch, waitin' so long to do what needed doin'."

"Peace, sister," Shanvah said, not taking her eyes from the prisoner.

"Even I cannot speak for Everam's Plan," Jardir said. "Only the *dama'ting* can do that, and even they can only offer the barest glimpse."

Shanjat laughed at that, but said nothing in response to Jardir's glare. Jardir looked back to Renna, and bowed. "If our words have offended you, I apologize. I have known many warriors to enter *sharak* carrying the weight of a father's shame. Shanvah and I will not utter his name again."

Renna grunted, her aura still hot.

"Nevertheless, it does not change our situation," Jardir said.

"Ent swimming in that." Renna nodded toward the lake.

"Won't have to," the Par'chin said. "Gonna make a bridge."

Jardir looked at him. "How are we supposed to do that, Par'chin?"

"Same way we're gettin' past the mushrooms." He stepped out to lead the way. "Form up."

Shanvah wrapped her veil around her nose and mouth three times, producing a second silk and handing it to Renna.

"Got my own." Renna produced a pristine veil of white silk from a pouch at her waist, wrapping it around her nose and mouth as Shanvah had. "Wedding gift from Amanvah."

"Everam sees all ends, and guides us as He can." Jardir put up his own night veil, and the Par'chin took Shanvah's spare to cover his own face.

Shanvah pulled her father's white veil over his face, as well. He looked at her. "The drone may have this scant protection, but I—"

"Had best keep your mouth shut and stick close," the Par'chin finished for him.

Jardir took the rear, Shanvah and Renna on either side of Shanjat in a diamond formation as the Par'chin began drawing cold wards in the air, freezing spore and stalk alike. The moisture in the air only aided the effort, and a thick rime of ice formed on everything as they began.

Understanding his plan, Jardir and Renna began to do likewise, trapping the deadly spores. Their feet crunched the frost as they made their way to the water's edge.

And then they were under attack, creatures bursting from the cover of the stalks on all sides. There were demons, a nightwolf, a pair of stout, muscular lizards the size of clay demons, and even a human man, his eyes dead, skin pale and dark-veined, with mushrooms sprouting from his ears. Their auras were strong, but blank, blending in perfectly with the surrounding colony. There was no thought to their actions, no feeling.

Shanvah yanked the chain to bring Shanjat to his knees, dropping the shield off her shoulder and onto her arm to cover them both. The demon did not resist the defense she offered as she slid her glass spear from its harness.

"Don't cut them!" the Par'chin warned, but he needn't have bothered. The daughter of Shanjat was no fool. She kept her shield out, driving back the foe with push-kicks and shattering blows of her spear shaft, breaking limbs to cripple pursuit.

The others kept to their cold magic, freezing the creatures and preventing them from releasing their deadly infection.

When the first wave was driven back or frozen in place, Shanvah took up the chain again, leading the way to the water. Twice more they had to stop and fight, but they were prepared now, and the mindless foe not so great a challenge for a ready defender. Even the *alagai* were weak, their cabled muscles rotted from the inside by the consuming fungus. The water drew closer . . .

"Ware above!" Shanjat called, and Shanvah got her shield up just in time to block a great mass of slime that sloughed from a stalactite overhead. Instinctively she protected her father first, her glass shield turning the attack from him, but the spatter struck her arm and back, smoking and hissing as it burned away at her silks and seeped between the plates of her armor.

She did not cry out or stop moving, her glory boundless in the face of what was no doubt an agonizing attack. Instead they quickened the pace to the water's edge, where the fungal colony thinned and finally ended, replaced by rock covered in more of the caustic slime.

This, the Par'chin burned away, and his *jiwah* froze it after, clearing a path to the water.

Shanvah was weakening. Jardir could see it in her aura, the slime burning, liquefying her skin as it ate her alive. There was magic to it, feeding and multiplying at an incredible rate. Untreated, she would be dead in moments, dissolved to nothing in an hour.

"Guard us while I tend to her!" Jardir called, stripping away her silks. She was his niece, and there was no dishonor in seeing her unclad, but Shanvah had not the strength to resist in any event. The flesh of her arm and back was bubbling, melting away. Renna drew heat wards over Shanvah's ruined robes, killing the deadly parasite.

"You must embrace the pain," Jardir told her. "Everam is watching."

"Pain . . ." Shanvah gasped, laboring for breath, ". . . is only . . . wind."

"Indeed," Jardir said, peering deep into the muck as he summoned power and began to draw wards. Shanvah thrashed, biting her thickly wound veil, but she did not cry out as he burned the slime away, taking healthy flesh as well as infected to ensure he had it all. When he was satisfied that not a bit of it remained, he altered his warding to spells the *dama'ting* had used for centuries to regrow flesh and stimulate new blood.

Immediately Shanvah opened her eyes, aura colored in shame. "I apologize, Uncle. Again, I am the weakness your enemies exploit."

"Nonsense," Jardir said. "Without your quick action we would have lost our guide, or had the attack strike another of the chosen. Rest a moment."

But Shanvah was shaking her head, already pushing herself upright. "There is no time, Uncle. I am well enough to continue on."

It was true, though her previously pristine flesh now had the look of melted wax, angry and red. She gave no thought to shame as she retrieved the warded glass plates from her ruined robes, dressing quickly in a spare from her pack. Another fungal demon emerged from the colony, but the Par'chin drew a heat ward with such power that it flashed white with flame and was reduced instantly to ash.

Renna gave a shriek as a tentacle splashed from the water, reaching for her. It wrapped around her arm, but with a thought she powered the wards on her skin, and it loosed its grip. A slash of her knife severed the appendage, but others followed. In the commotion, they had lost the protection of their wards of unsight.

Jardir looked at Alagai Ka, wondering if this was his plan all along, but there was fear in the demon's weak aura. Trapped by the wards in its current form, it would not survive being pulled under any better than they.

The Par'chin stepped forward, pulling power away from his wards to allow the tentacles to wrap around his arms. He planted his feet and began to walk back, hauling the beast from the water. It was a thing of nightmare, slimy appendages covered in sharp horns and suction tips all joining at a center mass that seemed entirely mouth, with thousands of snapping teeth.

Jardir did not hesitate, launching himself at the creature and driving the Spear of Kaji deep into its throat, killing it.

The water was alive with demons. He focused his will on the crown's warding field, driving them back as he returned to the others.

His patience thinned, he went to Shanjat, violence barely held in check. "How could any human swim through such an infested place?"

"Because they carried my imprint," Alagai Ka said through his friend, "and had a mimic to guide them and dominate the lesser drones."

"And Kaji's armies?" Jardir demanded. "Is this the path they took?"

"The lake was not here back then," Alagai Ka said. "My kind created it to discourage further intrusion into our territory."

"You built a lake?" Renna asked.

"A simple enough task, to have rock drones open tunnels to nearby water flows," Shanjat said.

"Ent swimmin'," Renna said again.

"Won't have to," the Par'chin said. "Gonna freeze us a bridge."

"And when the water demons come at it?" she asked.

"The Crown of Kaji will keep them at bay," Jardir assured her. He took out the sacred bowls and shattered the frozen stone, drawing soil beneath to fill them and create food and water while the Par'chin summoned magic to build his bridge. Shanvah seemed much recovered, but she would need food and drink to replace the lost flesh, and there was little to be done for the scars. Magic could fade a clean cut into an invisible line, but this damage was too much for that.

When Shanvah had been fed and returned to guard her father and the demon, Renna am'Bales drifted over like a fish on a lure.

Jardir bowed. "Again, I apologize . . ."

"Nothin' to be sorry for." Renna bowed in return. "You din't know. Just snapped. Thought I'd got a handle on it, the flashes of anger that come from magic, but the babe's made it worse'n ever, and I took a big dose up in that cave. Anyone should be sorry, it's me."

"It is a . . . failing among my people, to put the father's name first in all things." The words were difficult for Jardir, in part because the truth of them gave lie to so much of his own life. "My own father died young and without glory. I spend more hours pondering how to win a place of honor for him in Heaven than I did on my mother, raising four without a husband."

Renna glanced at Shanvah. "Looks like you did all right by them in the end."

"Perhaps," Jardir allowed. "The Par'chin, too, grated at being named the son of Jeph, though it was years before I learned why."

"His da found redemption without anyone's help," Renna said. "Wouldn't be sitting here, he hadn't stepped off his porch and faced down a demon with nothin' but a plain old axe."

She sighed. "Maybe none of us would be here, my da hadn't taken up his pitchfork and shepherded Arlen and his mam and da to succor all those years ago."

"Only the Creator can see all ends," Jardir said, careful not to use Everam's name for fear of upsetting this fragile moment. "We can spend eternity questioning the past, but it is the future we must look to."

"Honest word." Renna then spoke the prayers with him, again eating more than the others combined.

By then, the Par'chin had gathered an incredible amount of ambient magic, glowing as bright to crownsight as the sun. He began his warding, and ice crystals formed on the surface of the lake, streaking toward one another and connecting, spreading out and thickening down to form a sheet of ice that extended out from the shore into the darkness.

Jardir waited, watching as the bright shine of his friend's power dimmed. When it threatened to go dark, he went to him and gently laid a hand on his back. "Enough, Par'chin. Eat and refresh yourself. Let me continue your work."

"Ay." The Par'chin put his hands on his knees, panting as if he had been in pitched battle, when he had only stood on the shore. "Might be that's a good idea."

As the Par'chin took the rare luxury of a moment's ease, Jardir gripped his spear and Drew as his friend had, pulling in as much ambient power as he could gather before stepping out onto the ice. The water did not conduct magic well, and he could feel himself cut off from the rich abundance felt on land. The lake shone dark even to crownsight, save for the glow of fish and water demons in the deep.

He raised the forbiddance of his crown to keep the latter at bay as he strode out, drawing cold wards with the tip of his spear. The bridge extended almost eagerly, the water already colder than he would have thought in the humid heat of the cavern.

The spear grew dim, but Jardir pressed on, determined to double the Par'chin's construct in length before giving in. He felt his lungs begin to burn, his muscles ache. The bit of power used to fend off the cold became too much to spare, and his sandaled feet grew numb on the ice.

When he began to Draw upon the power of the crown, Jardir knew it was time to retreat. Without it, he would be defenseless if some leviathan of the deep struck at him. His dignity would not allow him to rush, but neither did he linger in his stride back to the shore.

"My turn," Renna said. Her husband looked ready to protest, but she silenced him with a glare. She gathered power—no less than Jardir and the Par'chin—and focused a portion onto the water wards on her skin, creating a forbiddance to deter the *alagai* as she, too, moved to extend the bridge.

The Par'chin appeared to watch her calmly, but Jardir could see images of him rushing out onto the ice replaying over and over in his mind. He was ready to act in an instant should she be threatened.

Trusting in his friend's vigilance, Jardir turned his attention to Alagai Ka, bound once more while they waited, gnawing with disgust on a fish Shanvah had speared for him. Her father, she treated with greater tenderness, cleaning and binding scrapes and blisters on his hands and feet, feeding him the holy food and drink, brushing and braiding his hair. The sadness in her aura was palpable as Shanjat stared out over the water, unseeing.

"I can see the shore." Renna, too, was breathing hard on her return. "One more of us can make it, I think."

"We may not have time to wait." Shanvah nodded to the edge of the fungal colony, where the lifeless eyes of myriad creatures watched with the malice of whatever intelligence guided this collective.

Jardir turned to the Par'chin. "Do we go now, or tempt fate by sending another out?"

The Par'chin pursed his lips. "Don't like either choice."

"Could barely see you back on the shore at the far end of the ice," Renna said. "Anyone goes that far, they're going alone."

"We stay together, then." Jardir signaled Shanvah and again Alagai Ka was unchained and allowed to invade Shanjat.

Shanvah took the warded chain and first secured it around her waist, then locked the far end through the loops in Shanjat's manacle belt. "If you try to escape into the water, I will kill you, even if it be my last act on Ala."

Shanjat's eyes crinkled behind his veil. "I have spent too much time flavoring your mind to die before I consume it, daughter."

Shanvah raised her spear. "Do not call me that again."

"Daughter!" Shanjat laughed, thrusting out his chest, daring her to strike. "Daughter! Daughter! Daughter!"

The young woman bristled, and Renna laid a hand on her shoulder. "Just spit and wind, Shanvah. Don't pay it no mind."

"Indeed," Jardir said. "Leave the once mighty demon lord to his impotent barking."

Some of the tension left her, and Shanvah gave a tight bow. "As the Deliverer says. I will bend as the palm before this . . . spit and wind."

"Let's go, then," Renna said. "Those mushroom things are makin' me itch."

"Renna and I'll focus on the bridge," the Par'chin said. "You focus on keeping your forbidding up, and hold your power in reserve in case there's trouble."

"Agreed," Jardir told him, calling the field back to life as they stepped out into the bridge in their customary diamond formation around the prisoner. He kept the field small to draw as little attention as possible, but all the armies of Nie would not be able to penetrate it while he remained vigilant.

He cast a nervous eye behind them at the colony, remembering how the infected demon had ignored its protection. It was a reminder to vigilance he would not forget.

Their feet crunched on the ice as dark water lapped at the edges, raised to prevent the gentle waves from washing onto the bridge. The shore grew distant behind them, and the Par'chin, his water wards glowing powerfully, stepped beyond the range of Jardir's forbidding to complete the construction.

That was when the leviathan struck. There was an instant's warning, the glow of a powerful *alagai* coming to the surface, but it did not attack the barrier, instead slamming its great bulk against the bridge behind them. There was a thunderous crash, and cracks raced along the length, chasing them like flame demons. It would not withstand another blow.

"Run!" Jardir cried, drawing cold wards to repair what damage he could. Renna, Shanvah, and Shanjat took off, racing for the far shore where the Par'chin still worked to complete the bridge.

Again the leviathan struck, shattering the bridge and splashing out of the water like a nightmare come to life. The bridge behind was broken into great chunks of ice that flew high and rained down upon them. Jardir held his ground, drawing impact wards to deflect those that would have struck his companions as they raced away from the fissures tearing at their footing.

The demon made another pass, this time too close to Jardir's forbidding. It bounced away, but not before its great tail swatted the bridge one more time, sending huge pieces of ice into the air, blinding Jardir with smaller particles and the spray of water. One piece struck the bridge in front of him, and then he was enveloped in darkness.

Jardir learned many skills in *sharaj*. He could wrestle an *alagai* with his bare hands, leap from great heights and roll away the impact, lead men in formation, and stem wounds that might otherwise have been crippling or fatal.

But he never learned to swim.

Enveloped in the black water, there was no sense of up or down, only the battering of ice and the scream of his lungs. The Par'chin taught him that magic could do nearly anything, but it could not replace precious breath, and Jardir had not had time for more than the barest gasp.

He felt the crown loosen at his brow and reached desperately to secure it. If the precious item were lost, so were his own chances, and the hope of all Ala. His other hand gripped the spear in similar desperation. He did not have faith they could be recovered if they sank to the depths of this cursed lake.

The water demons, however, had no such limitations. They were in their element, and he could see them circling. Some were great leviathans, and others smaller, tentacled abominations, but all were focused on his destruction. They struck from all sides, buffeting him at the center of the forbidding. They could not attack him directly, but in the water he felt every blow, pounding with a force he could not believe and keeping him from his bearings.

His lungs screamed, and Jardir knew he did not have long. He embraced the impacts and fear, reaching out with his senses, seeking the power nestled in the *ala* below. He touched it for an instant, but another strike from a water demon spun him about, and he lost it.

One of the larger demons came in for another pass.

If I am to die, let it be on alagai *talons,* he thought, *not breathing water in panicked fear.* He shoved the crown down hard onto his brow and dropped the forbiddance, and the demon, expecting impact, arrowed toward him, right onto the point of his waiting spear.

He felt the beast shudder with pain as the spear bit deep, and held on as it gave a mighty sweep of its fins, breaking the surface long enough for him to gasp a breath.

He pulled the spear, trying to free it to leap away and into the air, but it was stuck fast on a bone, and an instant later he was returned to the deep. The demon corkscrewed, trying as much as he to remove the barb, and again Jardir lost all sense of up and down.

Around him, *alagai* gathered once more.

But then there was a flare of magic, and they were scattered. Jardir looked to see the Par'chin shooting for him, glowing brightly and propelling himself with powerful strokes of his arms and legs.

Jardir put his foot on the demon and tore the spear free, ripping a deep and jagged wound he hoped the demon would never recover from. His first thought was to finish it, but discretion took the better part of glory and he renewed his crown's forbiddance, driving the demons away as the Par'chin reached out and grasped his hand.

The next few days seemed an eternity, spent hiking and climbing, sliding along narrow ledges. For over a mile they crawled on their bellies in a tunnel less than two feet high. Always hot, always soaked with sweat, waiting for Alagai Ka to inevitably betray them.

For his part, the father of demons seemed as miserable and exhausted as they. Controlling Shanjat for long periods of time drained him, and no doubt the wards on his skin burned as freshly now as the day the Par'chin put them there.

The journey is long, and you will grow lax.

Jardir clenched a fist. Was this even the way to the abyss? Inevera's dice had said he would lead them there, but perhaps there were several ways, now that they were deep in the bowels of Ala. Was he deliberately taking them on the most dangerous paths, hoping to weaken them sufficiently to make his escape? There was no way to know. The demon princes had thousands of years of experience in masking their auras. Who could say what words were truth and which lies?

Jardir had first thought *alagai* would be their only concern, but it seemed the dark below held many terrors beyond the servants of Nie.

Arlen did not relax when the cavern widened, allowing them to walk without hunching, but he'd learned to take what comforts he could on this cursed journey.

The walls were braced with ancient columns of Krasian design, lending confidence they traveled the path of Kaji's armies, but the wards were long since scarred. Having taken point in their journey, Arlen took the chance where he could to repair some of them. He could not replace the mind wards if they wanted their guide to pass, but others seemed a wise precaution, in the unlikely case they survived long enough to flee back this way, likely with all the demons of the Core on their heels.

But abruptly the wide, clear path ended in a cave-in. Great stones, too heavy for even him to shift, had collapsed into the tunnel, blocking the path. Beneath them, a pool of water had formed. Arlen eyed it warily in wardsight, but saw no sign of demons. Too shallow, perhaps. There was life, though. Tube coral clung to the floor beneath the water, feeding on Creator only knew what.

He climbed the stones while waiting for the others to catch up. There were crevices that allowed the flow of magic, and if he dared dissipate, he might easily pass through and explore. But the call of the Core had become insistent as they descended, and now it thrummed in him, a summoning he was not certain he could resist save under the most dire need. If one of their lives depended upon it he would take the risk, but not before.

In any event, only he and Renna could dissipate. If they were to continue on, another way must be found. The collapse looked ancient, stones settled into one another by the constant drip of water as if cut to fit. If Alagai Ka had marched prisoners this way, there must have been a way past.

Arlen already had a sinking suspicion what it was, and soon after, Shanjat confirmed it.

"A short swim beneath the stones," the demon said with the *Sharum*'s mouth. "Even the weakest-lunged humans could manage it. The waterway to follow has a small pocket of air between the water and the stone. It continues for not more than one of your miles."

"Night." Renna's sentiment was echoed throughout the group. Even Jardir's aura colored with fear at the thought. His fall into the water had shaken him, despite his triumphant emergence.

Arlen did not hesitate. "I'll go."

Shanvah bowed. "With respect, Par'chin, it should be me. I am the most expendable."

Arlen scowled, and the fearless young woman's aura colored. "Don't wanna hear that kind of talk, Shanvah. Ent none of us expendable. If there's trouble, I'm best suited to get out of it. Worse comes to worst, I can dissipate."

Renna put a hand on his shoulder. "You been hearin' the call?"

Arlen covered the hand with his own. "Ay. More like a command than a call now."

"Like a twig in a rushin' stream," Renna said. "Don't be doin' it, 'less you ent got a choice."

Shanjat laughed. "Your mate is correct, of course. Your minds are too weak to resist, or we could have been in the mind court and ended your foolish quest months ago."

He made no mention of how that quest would end, but Arlen knew even now, the demon had something up his sleeve, a last trick to play, one it thought they would not expect. They would need to be ready for it.

Renna took the knife from her belt. "Take this."

Arlen's eyes widened at the gift. Renna hated her father, but his knife was the most precious possession she had. More than the brook stone necklace from Cobie Fisher, more than the warded wedding ring he'd made her. His throat tightened at the thought she would offer it to him.

"Ren, I can't—"

"Can and you will," Renna cut him off. "Ent gonna have room down there for your spear, things get ugly."

"Got a knife." Arlen touched the weapon on his belt, but the six-inch blade seemed woefully inadequate compared with the foot of razor-sharp warded steel Renna wielded.

Renna snorted. "Good for spreadin' butter or whittlin' a stick, maybe, but that little thing ent much use in a fight."

She winked at him. "Girls might tell boys size don't matter, but it's just to make 'em feel better."

Arlen chuckled, sliding the smaller sheath off his belt and replacing it with Renna's heavy blade.

She grabbed him by the chin, turning him into a kiss. "Want it back safe, though. And you with it."

"If there was a sun down here I'd swear by it." Arlen kissed her again, then stripped to his bido and belt. Shanvah's eyes ran over his body for a moment, but then she remembered herself and averted her gaze. Arlen glanced at Renna, but the normally jealous woman only smirked in response. She and Shanvah had grown close of late.

Arlen wasted no further time, breathing deep, fast breaths as he waded into the cold pool before holding the last and diving under. He shivered. The water was dark, seemingly magic-dead. There was no sign of water demons or marine life.

He fed power to the light wards on his skin to illuminate his way. A few strong strokes put him beneath the stone, and he tried hard not to think about the countless tons of rock wedged above him.

Been there a thousand years. Ent gonna fall just now. His mind understood the logic, but it did nothing to alleviate the growing dread.

The next minute seemed to take an eternity, but then, as the demon promised, he came upon the pocket of air.

Arlen had expected something large enough to put his head and shoulders above water at least, but in most places it wasn't even two inches high—just enough to throw his head back and put his nose and mouth above water for a few quick breaths before plunging under once more.

Still, the way looked clear, apart from murky sediment stirred by his passing, and the ever-present tubes of coral on the floor. They bent toward the light as he passed, like flowers leaning toward the sun.

He made it to a second pocket of air, and then a third. His light wards seemed somehow dimmer on his next dive, and he fed them more power.

Something caught his leg as he kicked into the next stroke, and he pulled up short, coughing precious bubbles of air and nearly taking in a gulp of water.

He turned to see that a worm had reached out from one of the tubes on the floor, wrapping around his leg. Its end stuck to his calf like the suction cup on a water demon's tentacle. The worm shone bright with magic, and Arlen could feel his own power draining.

All around him, the other tubes had perked up, turned his way. The mouths of worms worked out of their tips, sucking the water like babes for the teat. All were glowing brightly, even as his own magic dimmed.

Too late, he understood the danger. Instinctively he Drew to replace the lost power, but there was no ambient magic to be had. These creatures fed upon it, and his attempt only roused more of them to action. As one, those closest began to reach for him.

He went for Renna's knife on his belt, but the tube worms moved quicker than he would have thought possible, extending many times the length of their dens to tangle his limbs. One wrapped around his midsection; another caught his throat. They squeezed like sandsnakes crushing a mouse.

The drain on his power became like Leesha's vacuum pumps, sucking away magic like life's blood. His preternatural strength faded. His wards went dark.

He was just Arlen Bales now, drowning in black water with a million tons of rock overhead. The thought chilled him, and for a moment his struggles ceased as he was pulled down.

Then, as it often did at moments like this, Jeph Bales broke the silence.

In over your head as usual, Arlen Bales. Words from a quarter century ago, when Arlen was learning to swim at Fishing Hole. *Mean to sink, or you gonna swim?*

"Swim." Arlen angrily coughed the word into the water, as he had so long ago. He tore the knife free of its sheath, keeping the blade along his forearm to twist it through the worm latched on it.

Harl Tanner's knife was sharp as sin. He sliced through the worm and most of it fell away, save a few inches still latched to his arm. He could feel it trying to pull at his magic, but the drain was negligible now that it was no longer grounded.

There were others, though, sucking hard on his magic, and Arlen knew he did not have much left. What would happen when they stole that last spark that gave him life?

His wardsight was dimming, the water getting darker by the moment, despite the tremendous power the tube worms held. They should be glowing like the sun.

He focused his will, pulling back against their suction with a Draw of his own. It was like swimming upriver, but the drain ebbed.

He freed his other arm next, pulling the grasping worm taut and slashing through its body. Another drain ceased, and he even Drew a touch of power back from the length still stuck to him.

He gripped the worm wrapped around his chest with his free hand. It was all slimy muscle, thicker than he could wrap his fingers about, stronger than he could pry away. The touch gave him a target, and he slashed again, the knife cutting through the worm. He felt the steel pass through and cut into his flesh as well, but there was no way to know how deeply, no point in worrying over it.

Half of the creature fell away, and he Drew hard on the wriggling other half, taking back some part of the power it had drained as he tore it free of his skin.

Wardsight returned, and the other worms now shone like paper lanterns, illuminating the silty bed. The water around him was cloudy with his own blood and the slime that seeped from the severed worms.

Arlen dove down, feeling the worms slacken, then kicked off against the water's bed. He struck the rock ceiling so hard he heard the familiar sound of his nose breaking, but before the worms pulled him back under, he managed to blow out his breath and draw a fresh one.

He went back down with a vengeance, slashing at the

brightly glowing worms, easy targets now that they had revealed themselves.

He freed his legs, but as with the others, the worms did not seem to die, still squeezing and sucking even after they'd been severed from their bases. The severances closed before his eyes, the base worms growing new mouths to replace the old, even as the ends he'd sliced off sank to the bottom and implanted their hind ends in the silty bed.

Night, I'm spawning more of them.

In the time it took to shake them off, others were taking their places. Arlen was forced to yield his defense to rush to the surface for another gasping breath, and three more of them latched on to him in that instant. This time he began slicing the worms vertically, shaking himself free and forcing them to use power to heal without multiplying.

It was still a losing battle, and an unnecessary one. Gathering what strength he had left, he kicked off back the way he'd come. He would pull himself from the water, replenish his lost magic, throttle the mind demon, and form a new plan to get past these underwater parasites.

The worm beds were slow to react as he swam by, not fast enough to catch him save in those moments he needed to steal breath.

Even then he was ready, eyeing the hunters and slashing when they got too close. He began to feel he would make it to safety, until by the third breath he realized he could not have been going back the way he came. All that twisting in the dark had turned him around.

A mile, the demon said. Had he gone more than half that? Was succor closer ahead than behind?

There was no way to tell, and he had little desire to turn back and face the worms he had roused into frenzy. At least these he was passing were only just sensing his presence, their slimy lips poking from their hard tubes to taste the magic in the water. He put on speed, swimming as quickly as his screaming lungs would allow.

He roared when he broke the surface on the far end of the collapse, gulping air as he trod the last few steps to the shore. Worms grabbed at his ankles, but they were smaller in the shallow water, and the air in his lungs and the sight of dry rock ahead gave him new strength. He strode on, tearing the worms, tube and all, from the silt and up out of the water.

They writhed madly as he pried them off his legs, flopping like fish out of water, bright with the magic they stole, even as his own glow was a last dying ember.

Before he realized what he was doing, he pulled one of the worms taut and bit hard into it. The outer layer of muscle was tough, but underneath the boneless flesh gave easily, and he gnawed at it even as he Drew its magic. He left its tough husk drained beside him like the rind of a citrus, and took up another, his hunger only growing.

It was an animal moment, eat or be eaten, unlike anything Arlen had felt since that night in Anoch Sun when the primal needs of his stomach had overruled his sense and forced him to make a choice that changed his life—and the lives of everyone in Thesa—forever.

The meal was all-consuming, replenishing not just his magic. His stomach had been empty for weeks, save for a daily bite of Jardir's holy couscous.

There was no food in all the world to match that bite, but a single mouthful, no matter how potent, could never truly fill an empty belly. Only Renna was eating a real share, and she ate for two.

Arlen was left unsatisfied, and when he'd sucked the last of the flesh from the worm's hide, he waded back into the water, ripping more of the corespawned things free. The tubes were hard, sharp-spined shells that tore at his hands, but he ignored the pain, crushing them to hold the worms tight inside as they were uprooted from the silt.

He hurled the worms out of the water to land in a wriggling pile, too far inland to find their way back to the water before they suffocated.

"See how you rippin' like it," he growled, tearing another shell free. He worked until the lagoon at the far end of the cave-in was clear.

Then he set to feeding, and the world fell away in the gush of flesh and the taste of magic in his mouth.

It was some time before he came back to himself, gorged on worm meat and magic. The excess power throbbed in his aura, barely contained. He felt as strong as he had ever been, short of standing on a greatward.

And so it took a moment to feel the tingle of one particular group of wards on his ear.

His friends were trying to contact him.

Arlen drew a quick warding in the air, needing to power it with considerable energy to break through the ambient magic in the air and through the collapsed tunnel to create a firm link with Renna, Jardir, and Shanvah.

"You all right?" Renna's voice came the moment contact established.

"Ay." Arlen went back to the water to wash the sticky slime from his hands. "Demon wasn't lyin', but he din't tell all."

"Are you in danger, Par'chin?" Jardir's voice was like a crank bowstring, ready to loose.

"Not anymore." Arlen splashed water on his face, washing away the worm juice that clung to his lips and chin. "Bad news is, the whole swim's full of giant worms that come at you like water demon tentacles and suck the magic out of you like leeches."

"Night, what's the good news?" Renna asked.

Arlen stood and stretched his back. "They're rippin' delicious."

Renna barked a laugh as Arlen turned to survey the area.

"Creator," he breathed.

"Ay?" Renna asked.

"What was that, Par'chin?" Jardir pressed, when he hadn't answered after a moment.

"Arlen Bales, you—"

But Arlen wasn't paying attention, his eyes wide.

The lagoon stood at a high bottleneck, overlooking a vast cavern. Down from the rise, the cavern wall was riddled with tunnels and pathways, great and small.

But that was not what took Arlen's breath away. Atop the rise was a great *csar,* a walled Krasian fortress filled with stone buildings. In the desert, a *csar* might house a great family, or perhaps an entire village, protecting them from *Sharum* raiding parties.

But this was no simple village. The pillared walls rose high, wards cut deep into the polished rock, still strong after all this time. Just peaking the walls Arlen could see the tips of the great minarets and domed ceiling of a Sharik Hora.

And its walls . . . Arlen's legs went weak, and he fell to his knees. The walls were a greatward, not unlike those he and Leesha had designed for the Hollow. But their warding was a crude thing compared with the elegant flow of the *csar.*

The place sung with magic, a symphony of power that brought tears to his eyes.

"Ahmann." Arlen tried, and failed, to keep his voice from trembling. "I . . . think I just found the Spear of Ala."

CHAPTER 27

BEDFELLOWS

334 AR

"They have arrived, mistress," Arther said.

Leesha fidgeted on Thamos' throne in the receiving hall. She hated the monstrous thing, using it only when ceremony demanded. It made her feel like a girl sitting in her father's chair.

Angierians were on average the shortest people of the Free Cities, and their nobility had compensated in the size of their furniture. The solid piece of polished goldwood was so heavy even Gared could not move it without a grunt, expertly carved with the ivy pattern of the Rhinebeck family. A fortune in scrollwork, and not a ripping ward to be seen. The throne was designed for one thing—to loom.

But Leesha could not deny it did that admirably, and to-night she was thankful for it. She put a benevolent smile on her face and set it in porcelain. "Send them in."

Wonda signaled the guards at the doors, and they opened to admit the Krasians. The delegation had arrived at midday, and it was well after dusk. She could delay them no longer.

Making guests wait for an audience was another game of nobility Leesha didn't care for, but she played it all the same, sending Gared to escort them into the Hollow. Krasians loved Gared. A warrior of renown—the kind of man they understood.

As agreed in advance, they were escorted to the manse

Amanvah built for Rojer. The servants were already Krasian and did not object as *dal'Sharum* warriors secured the walls and ran down the Jongleur's fiddle crest. In its place they raised the Krasian flag—crossed spears over a setting sun— marking the soil as their own.

The move made many of the Hollowers—refugees from Krasian conquests in the south—uneasy, but there was nothing for it. Leesha would no more let her own people bully her into breaking the bonds she had sacrificed so much to forge than she would let Euchor or the ivy throne.

She allowed the Krasians a few hours to settle and explore, delaying the meeting until sunset. It was enough to show her power without causing offense. *All men are brothers in the night* was the Krasian mantra. To meet in darkness was a sign of truce, a reminder of the common foe.

It also let the Krasians witness the Hollow's greatwards as they rode in their palanquins to Leesha's palace. Another show of power.

There were five in the delegation, not counting the *dal'Sharum.* Three *dama'ting,* one *kai'ting,* and, most vex- ing, a *dama.* Leesha scrutinized their auras as Gared led them into the nearly empty chamber.

Wonda and Darsy stood to the right of the throne, Jona and Hayes at the left. Arther hovered just behind the throne, near a ward circle on the floor. The words of any who stood in it would be for her ears alone.

Auras on both sides were flint and tinder, ready to burst into flame at the slightest abrasion.

In Krasian custom, the dominant male always spoke first in a group, but Leesha was surprised to see him hang back with the others while an ancient *dama'ting* took an additional step.

The crone reminded Leesha of Bruna, withered by time into wiry, wrinkled flesh pulled tight over sharp bone. But her back was straight, her eyes piercing. Her aura was as old as any Leesha had ever seen, but it was strong. Age had taken none of this woman's strength.

"Greetings, Leesha vah Erny am'Paper am'Hollow, Mis- tress of the Hollow Tribe." The *dama'ting's* bow was respect- ful but not deferential. The bow of a powerful woman in a lesser woman's home. "I am Dama'ting Favah. The Damajah was a student of mine."

"You honor us with your venerable presence, Dama'ting Favah." Leesha's nod was deep enough to avoid insult, barely. She did not wish to antagonize the woman, but neither would she be looked down upon.

"These are Dama'ting Shaselle and Jaia, and Kai'ting Micha." Favah swept a hand in the direction of the women. "Sent as promised by Damaji'ting Amanvah to support your Gatherers and household."

The introduction was abrupt, even offhand, but Leesha could see how it grated at the *dama*'s aura. Not only was a woman speaking before him, she was introducing other women first!

She smiled, breaking in before Favah could introduce him. "Your delegation is most welcome. It is my hope that a permanent embassy will help promote peace and cooperation between our . . . tribes."

His patience at an end, the *dama* stepped forward. His bow was barely a twitch. "I am Dama Halvan. I trained with Shar'Dama Ka in Sharik Hora."

"Ahmann never mentioned you," Leesha said, "but I imagine he trained with many in his years there."

The *dama* blinked. Not only did the words steal the wind from his sails, but Leesha's intimate use of Jardir's first name was a reminder that she was no simple *chin,* and that his affiliation with Ahmann would not impress her.

Follow the medicine with something sweet, Bruna used to say. "Please accept my condolences for the loss of the Andrah. Before ascending to the Skull Throne, Damaji Ashan fought beside my people against the *alagai,* and shared a blessing with Shepherd Jona," Leesha swept a hand at Jona, "before breaking bread at my table. I was saddened to hear of his death."

"Indeed." Halvan's bow was more respectful now.

"Dama Halvan is to minister to the Evejans in Hollow County," Favah said. "He will also serve as translator and *sharusahk* instructor to exceptional *dal'Sharum* seeking the white veil."

"You are welcome, Dama." Leesha could see Jona's and

Hayes' auras seething in her peripheral vision, but she ignored them. "Most of the *Sharum* that came to the Hollow last year were killed on Waning, when the mimic demon set Drillmaster Kaval and Enkido on the lonely path."

Halvan drew wards in the air at the words, and all bowed their heads a moment.

"The rest have been absorbed into the Cutters, under General Gared." She nodded to the Baron. "Many of the widows and children have assimilated, as well. Some attend services by Shepherd Jona, our . . . *Damaji,* and his second, Inquisitor Hayes." The men bowed in turn with the introductions.

Dama Halvan's nod to the other clerics was barely tolerant. "I will bring them back to Everam, if they have strayed." His aura made clear he intended to give them little choice in the matter.

"They are Hollow Tribe now, Dama," Leesha said, putting a touch of steel into her voice. "Free folk. Their choice of worship will be respected."

"The only freedom is in submission to Everam's will," Halvan growled.

"Not in the Hollow," Leesha said. "We do not force faith on our people. If that does not agree with you, you are welcome to return to Everam's Bounty."

Jona's and Hayes' auras were smug as Halvan's mouth opened, searching for a response. She turned to the men. "As you, Tenders, will respect the choices of those Hollowers who have taken an interest in becoming Evejan."

It was the Tenders' turn to gape as Halvan suppressed a smile. "I see you are constructing a new temple, Countess. I will need to consecrate the land and structure in order to hold services there."

Shepherd Jona took a step forward. "Now, just a corespawned minute! If you think . . ."

Jona had been Leesha's childhood friend and confidant, but she whipped a hand up and he silenced instantly.

Inquisitor Hayes was less well trained. "If our cathedral is not suitable for the heathen, let them return to their own."

Leesha turned her glare on him, and the Inquisitor met it with his own stony gaze. "Did you become count in the last few minutes without my knowledge, Tender?"

"Of course not—" Hayes began.

"The Creator is the Creator," Leesha cut him off. "Whether he is called Everam or not. The cathedral of Hollow County will serve as Holy House to Krasian and Thesan alike."

She turned to Halvan. "The land was consecrated in Evejan fashion, with the blood of our people in the night. It is called the Corelings' Graveyard for good reason. Ahmann himself declared it sacred ground. Is that enough to satisfy you?"

Halvan bowed. "If the Shar'Dama Ka named ground holy, then it is so. The temple, however . . ."

Leesha sighed. "What does your consecration require?"

"Prayers," Halvan began, "incense, and the bones of heroes."

"This, too, has been done," Leesha said. "Damaji'ting Amanvah blessed the temple with the bones of her honored husband, Rojer asu Jessum am'Inn am'Hollow."

Halvan bowed. "That is a beginning, mistress, but it is not enough. A temple's blessing increases with every hero's bone."

"Barbaric!" Hayes growled. "To suggest we defile both the honored dead and our temple with some gruesome display—"

"Dun't sound so bad." All eyes turned to Gared, who blushed at the attention.

Hayes blinked. "Surely, Baron, you cannot mean that."

Gared shrugged. "Why not? We keep graveyards on Holy House grounds, an' crypts beneath. I seen Sharik Hora when we went to Everam's Bounty. Standin' there, surrounded by the bones of folk like me, who fell fightin' corelings, I felt part o' somethin' bigger'n myself. Ent that what it's all about?"

Leesha blinked. Gared Cutter had been a woodbrained boy, but Baron Cutter surprised her anew every day.

"Bones have magic, Countess," Favah advised. "Demon, and man. Did you think we built a temple of heroes' bones for aesthetics alone? *Hora* Draw and bind magic to the beliefs of the departed souls they housed. If they died defending their people from demons . . ."

". . . the building will Draw magic and focus it to the same purpose," Leesha finished, her mind racing at the prospect.

She turned to Arther. "This is Lord Arther, my first minister. Dama Halvan and the Tenders will sit down with him and come to terms acceptable to both sides on the consecration of the ground and the sharing of the cathedral."

"Just how are we supposed to . . . !" Hayes growled.

Leesha ignored him, turning to Jona. "Figure it out. I don't care if you divide the hours, or argue scripture and find common ground for a service you can perform together. Just get it done. Next time I hear about it, every one of you had best be satisfied. Am I clear?"

Jona bowed deeply. "Perfectly, Countess. Think no more on it."

Leesha breathed a sigh of relief, turning back to Favah. "May I interest the rest of you in some tea while the men argue?"

Favah's aura was hard to read, her face hidden behind her veil, but her bow was deeper now. "Thank you, Countess. That would be most acceptable."

Leesha's heart stuttered as she turned the corner to find Elona, heavy with child, waiting outside her office door. Just steps behind, Wonda and Darsy escorted the other women.

"What are you doing here, Mother?" Leesha quickstepped to Elona's side, her voice a harsh whisper.

"Honest word?" Elona asked. "You really thought I was gonna sit in my room and miss this?"

Leesha had begged her to do just that, had even posted guards and servants to deter it, but she should have known none would stop her mother. Folk were always more scared of Elona than she was of them.

"Hurry now." Elona winked. "Don't want to cause a scene in front of the guests."

Leesha had little choice but to play along, nodding to the guards to open the door. The moment it closed behind them, she grabbed Elona by the arm, squeezing hard. "I swear to the Creator, Mother, if you undermine me in this meeting, you can go back to living beside Da's paper mill."

Elona didn't flinch. "Don't you threaten me, girl. I'm one of the only ones you trust to change your baby's nappy. You ent fool enough to send me out of your sight."

Out of the corner of her eye, Leesha caught sight of Tarisa, gliding silently around the room after setting the service. Her aura was one of complete discretion, but there was no doubt she heard.

Tarisa heard everything.

A moment later Wonda entered the room, eyes scanning it like a battlefield, looking for threats. Her gaze lingered on Elona a moment, but she said nothing, moving to take up a position between Leesha's favorite chair and the entrance to the nursery.

Favah paused on entry, studying the wards around the nursery door. They glowed bright in wardsight, drawing both from the greatward and from powerful *hora* hidden around the room.

"Impressive," Favah allowed, "if clumsy. It pleases me to see Princess Olive so well guarded, but I would look upon her with my own eyes to ensure she is well."

"Perhaps," Leesha said. "When I am satisfied."

Favah tilted her head. "And what will it take to satisfy you?"

"Can start by showing our faces," Elona cut in. "All women here, ent we?"

Leesha grit her teeth. "Favah, this is my mother—"

"Elona vah Erny am'Paper am'Hollow." Favah's bow was deeper than it had been for Leesha. "Your name is known throughout the palaces of Krasia."

"Is it now?" Elona put her hands on her hips, managing to appear humble even as her aura seethed with satisfaction. "Ent that a thing."

"Indeed, you are correct. If we are to trust one another, lowering our veils is a good place to begin." Favah gave her scarf a precise tug, and her white silk veil collapsed like smoke to drape at the base of her throat. The crone's face was all sinew and bone. "How else could we enjoy our tea?"

The other women relaxed, lowering their veils as Leesha crossed the room, taking a seat first in Bruna's ancient rocker. Still draped with the old woman's frayed shawl, the chair was the one piece of furniture Leesha kept when she moved into the palace for good and gave Bruna's cottage over to Darsy. It was a chair very much *not* in the Angierian fashion, the wood plain, smoothed more from use than polish. There was no cushion, and it creaked as Leesha rocked it.

The sound comforted Leesha sometimes when she was alone, reminding her of her mentor. Of how she could turn that creak into a steady rhythm to relax—or unnerve—patient and petitioner alike. The creak could break a silence gone on too long, or interrupt speakers before they had a chance to build their oratory.

"Welcome." She spread her hands, beginning the *dama'ting* tea ritual, which was, in truth, not so different from the Angierian way. The order of seating meant everything. Leesha and Darsy had rehearsed it over and over. Darsy would sit next at her right, then Favah and her group to her left. It would make clear Darsy's position in Leesha's esteem, while still giving the Krasians a strong position by which they could claim no offense.

But before Leesha could finish, Elona strode right in and sat herself at Leesha's right. To the Krasians, it was an open declaration that she was the second most powerful woman in the room.

Leesha hesitated, meeting Darsy's eyes. Seating too many before her guests would be a grave insult. She gestured to her left. "Favah."

The ancient *dama'ting* took the offered seat beside Leesha, snapping her fingers at Shaselle and Jaia, who flocked to the couch beside Favah's chair. The couch was big enough to seat three, but the two of them spread out to fill the space.

Only Micha was left standing when Darsy finally took the center of the couch beside Elona, the big woman filling much of it herself, looming over the *dama'ting*.

Still Micha kept her feet, eyes down, the very model of humility, but her aura, calm and focused, told a different tale.

Right now, Micha's focus was on Wonda. Leesha could not tell if she was deferring to the woman, unwilling to sit before her, or eyeing her like a target. Wonda seemed to sense the attention, shifting her feet like she was readying for a fight.

"Enough." Leesha clapped her hands. "I won't have a princess of the Kaji standing while the rest of us sit. Pull up a chair, girl. You, too, Wonda. If we're going to get along, we're going to have to take off more than one veil."

Leesha gave a slight gesture as Tarisa filled her teacup. It was all the lady's maid needed to smoothly move to fill Favah's next. A sound formed in Elona's throat, but she was smart enough to swallow it. Tarisa served Elona and the Hollowers before getting to the other Krasians. She set milk and sugar out, but only the Hollowers reached for it. The Krasians watched Leesha. When she left her tea black, so did they.

"We are strangers this night," Leesha said. "But it is my fervent hope that by the time these cups are cleared, we will be as friends. Waning approaches."

Favah lifted her cup. "On that cursed night, friends will not be enough. We must be as sisters."

Leesha lifted her cup to precisely match the old woman's. "Sisters."

The silence as they sipped went on a touch too long, and Leesha broke it with the chair's creak. She caught Favah's eye and looked deep into the old woman's aura. "Are you or any of your party here to harm my child?"

"That depends." If Favah was surprised by the sudden, invasive question, she gave no sign, face and aura placid. "Do you plan to use your child's lineage to make a claim on the Skull Throne and attempt to supplant the Damajah?"

Leesha was horrified. "Of course not!"

Favah squinted, and Leesha realized the old woman had been reading her aura right back. "Then your child has nothing to fear from the *dama'ting*."

There was truth in her, but the qualifier stuck with Leesha. "And the *dama*?"

"Halvan is arrogant," Favah said, "but he loved Ahmann Jardir like a brother. The dice say he will not harm the child of his friend."

"The *Sharum*?" Leesha pressed.

Favah shrugged. "I cannot vouchsafe every man, woman, and child in Krasia. I can only tell you the *dama'ting* will protect your . . . *daughter* like one of our own."

Leesha rocked her chair back. Again, a qualifier. "I think it time for proper introductions. Amanvah promised a single *dama'ting* to come in her stead. Instead we are sent three."

"Damaji'ting Amanvah advised the Damajah to send a minimum of one," Favah agreed. "The Damajah in her wisdom decided the Hollow Tribe would be better served by three."

The old woman indicated the young *dama'ting* next to her with a bony finger. "Dama'ting Shaselle trained in the *dama'ting* underpalace with the Damajah."

Not young, then, Leesha thought. Inevera was older than Ahmann, in her forties at least. Leesha once thought it was paint that kept the Damajah's skin smooth. She realized now it was the *hora* that kept *dama'ting* young.

Her eyes flicked back to withered Favah. Just how old *was* the woman?

"Shaselle will teach at your Gatherers' Academy," Favah said. "She will be given a title commensurate with her status and the importance of the material, and she alone will determine who she instructs. The secrets of the *dama'ting* are not some *dal'ting* herb lore to bandy about."

Leesha's nostrils flared as she drew a deep breath. "I will make her mistress of Krasian studies. She will have a clerical staff and her pick of the women Amanvah had begun instructing to apprentice."

Favah nodded.

"She will also prepare curriculum for general education classes on basic Krasian medicine, warding, and *sharusahk*," Leesha said.

"*Sharusahk* was not part of the agreement," Favah said. "The secrets of . . ."

Leesha rocked her chair forward, cutting the old woman off with the squeak. Ire rose in the old woman's aura, but Leesha began rocking back and forth in a soothing rhythm, making it difficult for her to claim insult.

"I'm not interested in the horrid ways you've designed to cripple and kill humans," Leesha said. "I've felt it firsthand. What I want is for my Gatherers to have the skills to evade harm if they must draw near the battlefield to tend the wounded."

Favah held Leesha's eyes a long moment, her aura cooling. "Very well. Shaselle will see to it."

Leesha nodded. "She will be answerable only to myself and Headmistress Darsy."

"Nie take me before I take orders from that uneducated cow," Shaselle hissed to Favah in Krasian. The words were too fast for Elona, Wonda, and Darsy to follow, but Favah, whose eyes never left Leesha's, could tell she understood.

"Unaccept—"

The old woman was again cut off by the creak as Leesha resumed her rocking. She turned to Shaselle, locking eyes with the woman, but her words, spoken in Krasian, were for Favah. "She will report to Headmistress Darsy, or she will march her silk-covered bottom back to Krasia and tell Amanvah she thinks too much of herself to keep her *Damaji'ting's* promises to me."

There was indignation on Shaselle's unveiled face, but her aura blanched with fear at the words. "You may petition me, if you have concerns," Leesha shifted smoothly back to Thesan so the others could hear, "but you will find I have little more patience than I did with the men. We have less than a week before new moon. Sharak Ka comes first."

In their custom, the Krasian women all bowed at the words. The Thesans, even Elona, mirrored them and repeated the phrase.

"Sharak Ka comes first."

"Dama'ting Jaia." Favah gestured to the youngest priestess.

Jaia bowed. "Damaji'ting Amanvah and I were in our bidos together in the *dama'ting* underpalace. She has told me much of her love and respect for your people."

Perhaps twenty, then, Leesha guessed. Jaia's face was soft with real youth, not the unnatural thirty of Shaselle and Inevera. Like Amanvah, her aura was calm—even. A woman who was never truly allowed to be a girl.

"Like Dama Halvan, Jaia is here to provide healing and guidance to the Krasian women living in the Hollow. She will report to me alone."

Elona snorted. "Got her work cut out for her." Leesha shot her a glance, but the damage was done.

Favah nodded. "I am to understand there have been some . . . irregularities?"

Leesha wondered if it was the dice or the servants at Rojer's manse that informed her. "Many of the widows of new moon witnessed Arlen Bales rise into the sky and smite the demon princes with lightning. Bereft after the loss of their husbands, many have come to name him Deliverer. They have taken their children to an . . . enclave of like-minded folk."

"The so-called Warded Children," Favah noted. "One of the

more . . . spectacular failures of your reckless experimentation with magic."

"Perhaps," Leesha conceded. "But I cannot say I would have done much differently, given the choice again. The Warded Children are powerful, and have pledged to protect us when Waning comes. Sharak Ka comes first."

She expected the women to bow and repeat the phrase, but it seemed that trick could only be played once. Favah lifted an eyebrow. "Perhaps."

Leesha couldn't argue. Renna said the Children could be counted upon come new moon, but she remembered the wild look in Stela's eye and still had doubts.

"The remaining Krasian women in the Hollow look to Shamavah," Leesha told Jaia. "Her Krasian bazaar and inn employs most of them."

"The *khaffit's* wife and her uses are known to us." Favah gave a dismissive wave of her hand before pointing to Micha. The girl was short for a Krasian, with wide hips. The youth on her face was real. "Micha vah Ahmann vah Thalaja is half sister to your daughter. She is here to care for the child."

There was a clink of porcelain as Tarisa busied herself at the tea station, but it might as well have been a shattering clash from the normally silent woman. Every Thesan woman tensed at the mention of Olive.

Leesha turned to meet Micha's eyes, but the girl avoided her gaze, slipping from her seat to kneel, head down, hands on the floor.

Leesha did not hide her annoyance at the dramatic show of submission. "How old are you, child?"

"Old enough to marry, should a worthy suitor be found," Favah said.

"Speak to my mother if you want to discuss marriage peddling." Leesha kept her eyes on Micha as she switched back to Krasian, her words a sharp command. "Sit back in your seat, girl. Look me in the eye, and speak for yourself."

Micha immediately returned to her seat and met Leesha's eyes. The submission was gone, replaced by a flat stare that would do any house cat proud. "Sixteen, Countess."

"Call me mistress," Leesha said. "Do you have experience in childcare?"

Some of the confidence in Micha's aura drained away. "No, mistress, but I learn quickly."

"You are *Sharum'ting*?" Leesha asked. Micha hesitated, glancing to Favah, but Leesha checked the move with a creak of her chair, switching back to Krasian. "Don't look at her. Look at me. If I am to allow you near my child, *I* am your mistress now, Micha. Not Favah. Not Inevera. Me. Is that clear?"

Micha slipped back to the floor, but there was no performance in the submission now. "It is clear, mistress. I swear it by Everam and my hope of Heaven. I am *kai'Sharum'ting*."

"You trained with Sikvah, under Enkido," Leesha guessed.

Micha nodded. "My cousin is Sharum'ting Ka now, and selected me personally for this task. My half sister will come to no harm."

"Corespawned right," Wonda growled. "That's my lookout, not yours."

Micha looked up at her, the focus back. She bowed. "Even you cannot protect our mistress and her child day and night, Wonda vah Flinn am'Cutter am'Hollow, First of the *Sharum'ting*. It would be my honor to serve you in this."

Wonda had been leaning in aggressively, but the words seemed to mollify her, as the truth in Micha's aura did for Leesha.

Leesha nodded. "When I am not present, you will report to Wonda and Tarisa."

Favah could not contain herself. "The slave?!"

Tarisa arched her back, and there was steel in her eyes as well. "I beg your pardon?"

"No slaves in Thesa," Elona said. "Before that girl is allowed anywhere near my grandchild, she'll need to know how to change a nappy with one hand and hold a bottle with the other while singing and rocking a cradle."

"Tarisa is the head of my household staff," Leesha added. "If you do not meet her standards, I will ask Sikvah to send another of her spear sisters."

Micha touched her forehead to the floor. "Yes, mistress."

"You will not report doings in my private chambers to anyone," Leesha said. "Not the *dama'ting,* not the Damajah herself. If I find you have done so, you will be ejected from service immediately."

Micha made no effort to mask her aura. She did not like the conditions, but she would abide by them. "Yes, mistress." She bowed again. "I am also commanded to seek out Kendall Demonsong."

This was a surprise. "You can sing like Sikvah?"

Micha smiled. "We used to call Sikvah the warbler. None could have foreseen the day her singing would be the standard to which Everam's spear sisters are held."

"I'll take that as a yes," Leesha said. "Kendall is my herald; you'll see her often enough. If your singing is anything near your boasts, you may find your song is more powerful than your weapons in the night."

Leesha turned back to Favah. "So it falls to you to instruct me in the use of the *alagai hora*."

All the Krasian women had been trained to veil their emotions, but the auras of the younger women went cold at the words. Favah hadn't told them this part.

"I instructed the Damajah in the Chamber of Shadows," Favah said. "There is none in all Krasia who has spent more years pondering the mysteries of the dice."

"Excellent," Leesha said. "We will pick up immediately where Amanvah and I left off. I have read the scrolls of prophecy, and have questions about . . ."

"I advised against training you," Favah went on. "Amanvah exceeded her authority."

Leesha felt her fingers tighten on the teacup. "Nevertheless, your *Damaji'ting* and I have a pact."

"A pact the Damajah is well within her rights to overrule," Favah noted. "The *alagai hora* are not some puzzle box for idle women; they are a glimpse at the infinite. *Dama'ting* train entire lifetimes just to scratch the surface of their divine power."

Leesha set down her cup, resisting the urge to cross her arms.

"The Damajah, in her wisdom, has decided to honor her daughter's oath," Favah said, "and so I will teach you, but we will begin where all *nie'dama'ting* do. You must destroy your dice and begin carving a set from clay."

Leesha smiled. "And then a set of wood? A set of ivory? And then months in darkness, carving them in bone?"

Favah nodded. "I see we understand each other."

"I'm afraid not." Leesha slid her cup and saucer out of the way, spreading her spotless white napkin on the table. She reached into a pocket of her dress, pulling out seven carved pieces of demon bone.

She produced a surgical blade and made a small, precise cut on her hand, rolling the dice in the blood. "Creator, giver of life and light, your child needs answers." She looked at Favah. "Will Dama'ting Favah am'Kaji honor my agreement with Amanvah, in spirit and letter, or will she take her ripping delegation back to Everam's Bounty at dawn tomorrow?"

The dice began to glow, and when the magic built to a flare, Leesha threw. All three *dama'ting* looked aghast to see an outsider perform the ritual, but none could resist leaning forward as the dice spun to unnatural stops.

"I think I can read the answer, honored Dama'ting," she said. "But pray, tell me what you, in your venerable wisdom, can see?"

Favah grit her teeth, eyes flicking to the younger priestesses. "Very well . . . mistress. We will begin instruction after I have seen the child."

Leesha studied the old woman's aura for a long time before nodding.

Her riding trousers creaked as Leesha called a halt. She knew many of the Cutter women adored the things, but Leesha had never cared for them, or even the divided skirts many of the Hollow women had taken to wearing.

But the outer edges of the Hollow's greatwards were too far to walk any reasonable amount of time, especially with ancient Favah in tow. Pestle—one of many gifts of friendship Amanvah sent with the delegation—was a sleek purebred Krasian charger. The battle-trained stallion was confused by skirts, but in trousers was responsive to the slightest squeeze of her legs, ready in an instant to leap or run.

Leesha's blue riding coat was long, and worked with thin plates of warded glass. It was a bit stiff from high neck to tapering waist, then flared broadly to cover the back of her horse. Its many pockets were sewn with the unbreakable glass as well, housing herbs and *hora*. Her wand was secured to her belt in easy reach.

Sitting atop Promise and Rockslide, Wonda and Gared towered like thick trees at her back. Next to her, Darsy rode Pestle's mate, Mortar. The mare was half a hand shorter than Pestle, but Darsy Cutter still sat a head taller than Leesha.

Nonetheless, the Krasians to her left made her nervous. Favah was not one to wear trousers or sit atop a horse. She was carried across the Hollow on a palanquin borne by six muscular eunuchs in *Sharum* black, their wrists and ankles bound in golden shackles. The men ran in perfect unison, easily keeping pace with the horses. None was breathing hard as they set the palanquin down and opened the curtains for the ancient *dama'ting*.

The six slaves were a gesture of defiance from Favah, a reminder that she would not be bullied, even if she had agreed to Leesha's terms.

There is no slavery in the Hollow, Favah had been told, but she paraded the men before the Hollowers, daring a confrontation.

Leesha knew better than to take the bait. The men, mutilated and conditioned by the *dama'ting,* did not wish for freedom. Indeed, their auras sang with pride. In addition to their mistress' weight, the men carried spears and shields of warded glass, and Creator only knew how many other weapons about their person. If Leesha or anyone else tried to free them, there would be blood.

She breathed, letting the insult drift away as she swung down from the saddle. Up ahead, a group of engineers worked on the new armament, scorpions and rock-slingers of Krasian design.

"Your people adapt quickly," Favah noted. "Everam's Bounty fell easily, for lack of scorpions."

"As did Prince Jayan's army, for lack of flamework weapons," Leesha reminded her. "Wars have a way of escalating the worst in us."

Erny, working with the engineers, caught sight of them and waved, wiping ink-stained fingers as he moved to join them.

"Father, this is Dama'ting Favah am'Kaji," Leesha said.

Erny's bow was smooth and respectfully deep. "Welcome, Dama'ting. I am honored to meet you." His Krasian was progressing rapidly.

"The honor is mine," Favah said, again bowing deeper than she deigned to for Leesha. "Your name is spoken with honor in Krasia, Erny am'Paper am'Hollow."

Erny puffed at the flattery, and Leesha gave him a moment to enjoy it, chatting amiably in Krasian with the dama'ting.

"Your honored daughter tells me we are here to witness some new adaptation of your wondrous greatward," Favah said.

"Ah, well," Erny shuffled his feet, "most of the credit for that goes to my Leesha and Arlen Bales, who plotted the first greatwards."

"My father is being modest," Leesha said. "Tonight's display will be of his work alone."

"Explain," Favah said.

"When the demons attacked on Waning, they threw great stones and trees to crush resistance and to mar the shape of the greatward, weakening it enough for them to cross the forbidding."

"A benefit of walls your 'greatward' lacks," Favah agreed.

"Lacked." Erny's voice hardened. He easily tolerated personal condescension—a lifetime with Elona had burned that from him—but never about his work. "We can now resist most bombardment."

"Most?" Leesha asked.

Erny turned, signaling to a sling team stationed outside the forbidding. A company of Cutters surrounded them, eyes facing the woods, searching for demons fool enough to draw this close.

The engineers signaled back and loosed the counterweight, the sling arm whipping about to pitch a boulder the size of a woodshed in a high arc, aiming for a cleared section of land inside the greatward.

But the greatward flared on impact, and the stone shattered against it.

Favah blinked. "You added impact wards." The ancient

woman squinted. "The men cross the forbidding easily enough. What is the equation?"

Now it was Erny's turn to blink. He was used to struggling to explain even the basics of warding. He recovered himself and produced a slate, plotting out the equation that sized and spaced the impact wards to only affect large objects moving at certain speeds.

"Useless against stingers," Favah noted.

"We don't anticipate demons using scorpions, even on new moon," Erny noted. "Bigger worry is the debris." He pointed to where there was still a settling cloud of dust from the shattered stone, and large chunks of it lay on the cleared ground inside the ward.

"It will be confined to the outer edges of the forbidding," Leesha said. "We can evacuate those areas."

Erny nodded. "Brigades of Warders and engineers will be on call to clear any debris that threatens to weaken the wards."

Favah continued to study the equation. "The power drain is enormous."

"Ay." Erny blew out a breath. "The greatward can handle the drain, mostly."

"There's that word again," Leesha said.

Erny took back the slate and drew another equation beneath the first. "This is the calculation for how many stones an hour it would take to drain the ward completely."

Leesha felt a throbbing pain begin to build behind her left eye. "And if that were to happen?"

Erny threw up his hands. "All the magic in the Hollow winks out. Maybe for a second, maybe a minute, or longer if the corelings keep up the attack."

"Creator," Leesha said.

"Ent gonna happen, Leesh," Gared said. "Fire teams have warded stingers and stones. We'll have Hollow Soldiers to take down any rock or wood demons big enough to toss a barrel."

He raised his axe as the Cutters escorted the engine back onto the ward, and the men came over, led by Dug and Merrem Butcher. "Got some new recruits to show you. One of 'em's bigger'n me. Practically a rock demon himself."

The Cutters formed a line at sharp attention as Leesha and

her group passed, punching fists to the breasts of wooden armor. There were folk of all kinds in the group—short Angierians, lanky Rizonans, bowlegged Laktonians, and . . .

Leesha broke stride, coming up short when she saw the giant Cutter, carrying an enormous mattock like a straw broom. Her heart clenched.

"This is the one I was tellin' you about," Gared said, oblivious. "Quiet Jonn dun't say much, but he's got more kills than any five in his squad combined."

The huge man had been looking straight ahead, but at the sound of his name, the man turned and caught Leesha's eye.

She knew him instantly, his face etched forever in her mind. The mute giant who'd raped Leesha on the road—who'd sat upon Rojer while his friends did the same—was here in the Hollow.

Leesha froze, suddenly shaking with fear. It was ludicrous. She, who had stared down a mind demon, felt helpless before this man. And yet . . .

The other bandits who attacked her were dead, slaughtered by corelings after Arlen and Rojer reclaimed the portable circle they had stolen. But the mute had not been among the bodies. Leesha thought she had seen him a hundred times since, hiding in this shadow or that grove, his face reflected in firelight on a windowpane.

Recognition blossomed on his face, too, followed by fear and horror. He turned and ran.

"Wonda, stop him!" Leesha shrieked. It was a desperate, fearful wail, but in the moment, Leesha didn't care.

Wonda was a blur of movement, reaching the man in two great bounds. She caught his wrist and gave a wrench, causing the mattock to fall from spasming fingers. The giant roared, shoving at her with his other arm, but Wonda's feet were already at work, tangling the giant's legs and tripping him to the ground.

Gared and the other Cutters rushed forward, but Wonda needed no help, working her way steadily into a hold that kept the man prone, unable to strike back at her as she squeezed, slowly cutting off the flow of blood to his brain. The giant's face reddened, and when his struggles eased, just before he lost consciousness, Wonda relaxed, letting him draw a breath.

"Night," Gared muttered. "What'd he do?"

Leesha realized she had been holding her breath. She forced it out and pulled another in, feeling her heart restart with heavy beats.

"He was one of the bandits who . . ." Leesha's throat went dry and she swallowed hard, ". . . robbed me and Rojer on the road, before we returned with Arlen."

"Din't meana hurt!" the giant cried. The words were atonal, slurred, and Leesha realized the man wasn't mute at all. Just . . . simple.

"Jussa quick squirt!" the giant cried. "Dom said s'what they're made for." He began to weep. "S'what they're made for." He began to rock back and forth, repeating the words until Wonda tightened her hold, cutting them off.

Leesha froze again. She had kept the details of the attack secret, though there were always rumormongers in the Hollow whose guesses were uncomfortably close. Now they were laid bare before Favah and her *Sharum,* not to mention Leesha's most trusted allies, teams of engineers, Warders, and new recruits.

Eyes and auras grew dark as the words sank in, coloring in a way Leesha had never seen before.

Wonda produced a long knife in one hand. She looked up, meeting Leesha's eyes. "Want I should kill him, mistress?"

She meant it. Looking around, Leesha realized they all did. Darsy, Favah, the Butchers, the *Sharum* and the Cutters, the engineers. Even Erny had no mercy in his aura. Any of them would kill for her, and not just demons.

The thought sickened her, even though her own hands were not without their share of blood. She had poisoned her own *Sharum* escort on the road, and dropped thundersticks on Jayan's army as they rammed the gates of Angiers. She still remembered the way Dama Gorja's spine felt as it whipped and shattered beneath her foot.

But those had all been moments of life and death. Her decision to harm had been for the direct protection of others, not the murder of a simpleton, helpless in Wonda's iron grasp.

Leesha looked back to the man, meeting his eyes, remembering what he did to her. The casual way he had brushed aside her resistance and pinned her. The savagery of his last moments before spending himself in her.

Had women endured that horror from him since? Would others in the future, if she let him live? Simple or not, the giant was equipped to take such things, and even the large women of the Hollow would be like children against one of his size and strength. Her roiling stomach brought bile to the back of her throat, and the pain behind her eye roared to life.

Wonda would do it. She would kill him then and there, and none in the Hollow would judge either of them for it. Wonda would sleep easy after, and Leesha could not deny she might do the same, knowing the last of those wretched men was gone from the world.

Her hand hurt, and Leesha looked down to see it clutching her *hora* wand. "Let him up."

Leesha expected Wonda to argue, but the woman disengaged immediately, rolling to her feet and stepping away before Quiet Jonn had time to recover. He might have gone for his mattock, but instead he remained on his hands and knees, shaking, tears streaking the dirt on his face.

She pointed the wand at him. "I wish the corelings had taken you, too."

Erny looked up at the words, and something changed in his aura. Some hint of mercy. Leesha still remembered what he'd said years before, the night she wished for the corelings to take her mother: *Don't ever say that. Not about anyone.*

"Do it." Gared had his axe in hand. "Or let me." Quiet Jonn was not so large compared with Gared Cutter. He was more than willing. He *wanted* to do it, to kill anyone who would dare lay a hand on her.

Leesha lifted her wand further, but her hand shook.

"The man owes a blood debt," Favah said. "It is death to strike a *dama'ting.*"

The word triggered another memory, the day Arlen confronted Kaval and Coliv, men who had tried to murder him. *We have a blood debt. I could have collected today, but I kill only* alagai.

How many times had Arlen repeated those words to her, as

they shared kisses in the night? *It's us against the corelings, Leesh. Anything else is a losing fight.*

But even he had broken that promise, for her.

"No." Leesha dropped her arm, letting the wand fall to her side. "This is no gibbet, and we are no hangmen."

"I'll get chains," Wonda said. "Throw him in the cells."

The thought of the man who attacked her, bound and screaming in the tunnels below where Leesha slept, was no comfort. She lifted her wand slightly, making the giant flinch as she stepped close, examining his aura.

"Do you want forgiveness?" she asked.

"Ay!" the giant moaned.

"New moon is coming!" Leesha shouted, drawing a quick ward that caused her voice to boom through the night. "Do you swear to stand for the Hollow when the deep dark comes, and the demons come for us?"

"Ay!" the giant moaned. "Ay! Ay! Ay!" His aura was as simple as he was, clear and easy to read. He meant the words.

She turned to face the Cutters, veteran and raw wood alike. "The corelings do not care what we have done. They will come at us, united in our destruction. We must stand together, united in theirs!"

"Ay!" the Hollowers boomed, raising fists and weapons. Even Favah's eunuchs, divested of their tongues as well as their trees, clattered their spears against their shields.

Leesha looked back to Quiet Jonn, still shaking in fear. She dropped her voice, releasing the magic that amplified it. "You will report to Headmistress Darsy thrice a week, to discuss what women are . . . for."

Jonn nodded eagerly as Darsy pushed up the sleeves of her dress and put her hands on her hips. "And you'd best keep your hands off 'em until I'm satisfied."

"Ay," Jonn said again in his toneless voice.

Leesha clipped the wand back onto her belt, bending to lift the giant's heavy mattock. "Now get back in line."

The giant hesitated, then snatched the weapon, hurrying back to the position he had fled. The recruits to either side shied away from him now, but none protested.

It's us against the corelings. Anything else is a losing fight.

Leesha drew a deep breath and arched her back, striding to the horses with grace that would have done Duchess Araine proud.

Favah inspected Leesha's dice closely. Leesha knew the ancient *dama'ting* would seize on any flaw, no matter how slight, that she might demand they be destroyed and carved anew.

In the end she only grunted, handing them back and choosing three cards from a deck. These she laid facedown. "Cast, and tell me what you see."

Leesha sliced her hand, coated the dice, and felt them warm in her hands as she shook, flaring with light as she threw. She felt a thrill as she watched them jerk out of their natural spin and come to a stop.

Favah looked less impressed, having seen the trick countless times. "Well? What do you see?"

Leesha did not need a lot of time. "Three of Water, five of Spears, *Sharum* of Shields." She spoke with confidence, the reading clear. It was the most basic skill of dice lore. She was reading her own future looking at the cards, and that future was locked once the cards were laid.

Favah turned the cards, offering no comment as Leesha's predictions came true. She shuffled the cards again, putting the deck on the floor in front of her. "Now tell me which three I shall choose next."

It was a harder test. There was no way to know if Favah would pull from the top of the deck or the bottom, choosing the first three in line, or selecting from the deck at random. Leesha cast the dice, searching more than a hundred thousand possible outcomes.

"Damaji'ting of Skulls," she said after long moments. "Seven of Spears. *Khaffit.*"

Favah's eyes flicked down, studying the dice herself, then chose from the deck at random, producing the cards Leesha predicted. She grunted. "The permutations of cards are in the thousands. The futures of the living are infinite."

Leesha nodded. "Would that I had the luxury to spend years in the Chamber of Shadows, but Sharak Ka is upon us."

Favah put away the cards. "Ask a real question now."

Leesha took a tiny vial of blood from Elissa and coated the dice. "Creator of life and light, your children seek answers. Reveal to me the fate of Elissa vah Ragen am'Messenger am'Miln."

They had gone weeks without word from the city in the mountains. The regular envoys of Miln had ceased, and no Messenger who ventured more than a day's travel north of Riverbridge returned.

Leesha cast, and this time Favah was paying close attention as the dice jerked to a stop. They both leaned in, studying the result. Rock and wind wards intersected, and Leesha pointed. "Mountain."

Favah tilted her head. "Facing north they are inverted. Valley."

"The city of Miln is nestled in the valley between two mountains," Leesha said.

"Are you studying the pattern, or searching for justification?" Favah asked.

Leesha knit her brows, focusing again on the pattern. "So you do not subscribe to the teachings of Dama'ting Corelvah, who says the dice should be read from north to south, and follow Dama'ting Vahcorel, who believed they must be read from the center outward?"

"You deduce that from a single word?" Favah made a spitting sound, though no moisture left her dry lips. "The Damajah did not exaggerate when she said your arrogance was boundless."

Leesha pulled back. "I meant no offense." The woman's tone reminded her of Bruna.

"Corelvah was my grandmother," Favah said. "Vahcorel her sister. I listened to them shouting at each other when I was a child."

Night, how old are *you?* Leesha wondered. Again she thought of Bruna, wisdom piled like weight upon her years.

"Both so sure they'd unlocked a mystery of the universe," Favah went on. "So sure Everam spoke only to them.

"And why not? None could deny both had the Sight. My great-aunt predicted the time and date of her own death a hundred years before it happened, and my grandmother stopped an attempted coup by the Majah simply by tripping a man on the street. She'd known since she was a girl to be there at that precise moment. Each had staunch supporters. Partisan fools who refused to even consider the other's work. Yet both schools of thought produced seers who walked with one foot on Ala and the other in the infinite."

Favah raised a sharp finger. "You think the mysteries of the universe are an equation to be solved. But the future is not an equation. It is a story. And there are many ways to tell a story."

Leesha bowed, lower than she had allowed herself to honor the woman in public. "You are correct, Dama'ting. I apologize. I am simply . . . eager to learn."

Favah sniffed, flicking a finger back to the dice. "Read, girl."

"Air over water," Leesha said. "A cloud . . . no, there is lightning. Storm cloud."

"Storm clouds gather like fog around the city in the . . . mountain valley." Favah winked so quickly Leesha thought she might have imagined it. She clawed a hand through the air over a group of demon symbols on the edges of the dice. "The *alagai* are thick about their walls. But the Northerners are . . ." She pointed to a symbol.

"Arrogant," Leesha translated. She put her hands over her mouth. "They don't see it coming! We must . . ."

"Perhaps there is nothing we can do." Favah pointed to another symbol.

"Island," Leesha said. "They're alone? Cut off?"

"In nearly every future," Favah said. "A pillar in the river of time."

"I can't just not send help because the island symbol is pointed toward the mountain valley," Leesha said. "What's the point of seeing the future if you can do nothing about it?"

"What's the p . . . !" Favah's eyes bulged. "Arrogant, idiot girl! You spend five minutes staring at the puzzle, guess a few pieces, and move on to conclusions? Do you think my grandmother made all her prophecies at a glance? She often spent a week, meditating without rest or sustenance, to examine every permutation of an important throw."

"I don't have a week to starve myself, staring at a set of

dice," Leesha said. "New moon comes tomorrow night, and I have a county to run."

"So there can be no middle, between five minutes and a week?" Favah asked. "Surely even the great Countess Paper can spare an hour between pardoning *Sharum* rapists and suckling that hungry babe."

Leesha glared at her, but the woman's aura was serene. Favah swept a hand over the dice. "Sharak Ka is upon us, and there are a thousand stories of blood in this throw, Leesha vah Erny. They deserve more than a passing glance."

"Mistress, will you not reconsider returning to the capital?" Arther asked for the thousandth time. The first minister looked awkward in his wooden armor, defter with a pen than a spear.

The alagai *will strike at nightfall in the north of the Hollow,* Leesha and Favah agreed, after staring for hours at Leesha's final throw of the dice. Shaselle and Jaia were brought in to study the dice, and reached the same conclusion with no hint from Leesha or Favah.

Leesha stroked the *hora* wand at her belt, feeling a pulse of magic. "I am needed here."

Pestle stood like an obsidian statue, but Leesha could feel the tension in the powerful stallion, ready to leap to action. His silver horseshoes were worked with demon bone and powerful wards. He would be swift. Tireless. His kick could crush a wood demon's skull.

The horses of her captains and the Hollow Lancers were similarly equipped, a mix of giant Angierian mustangs and sleek, fast coursers. They stamped and paced, echoing the agitation of their riders.

Leesha was in Stallion's Ranch, the northernmost great-ward of Hollow County. While it was the least populous of the boroughs, Stallion's Ranch sat upon vast acreage for grazing and training the powerful mustangs and fast coursers the Hollow's cavalry depended upon.

But while large, the Stallion greatward was one of the Hollow's weakest, shaped mostly by wooden fences and the few buildings at its center. Baron Stallion employed hundreds of hands now, but they all still gathered in the town hall for communal meals, more family than barony.

It made sense the demons would strike here. A few well-thrown rocks and the sweep of full-sized trees rock demons favored as clubs would open too many holes in the greatward to guard. A loss here would deprive the Hollow of one of its most important resources.

Leesha ordered the Stallion civilians evacuated to the inner boroughs, along with the horses too young or wild to take a saddle. The rest of Jon's people were mounted and patrolling the edges of the greatward, or hidden in the grass with bows, as the sun dipped in the sky.

Gared waited next to her on the hilltop vantage Leesha had chosen. His best Cutters and the Hollow Lancers waited at the base, ready at his command to reinforce any breaches.

"Means a lot to have you here, mistress." Jon Stallion loomed at her side atop his massive brown mustang. "Hope it ends up a waste of your time."

Blood will flow in rivers tonight, the dice predicted.

Leesha touched her wand again. "I hope so, too."

Tensions grew high after sunset. Leesha walked Pestle in circles around the hilltop, staring into the night through her warded spectacles, but there was no sign of gathering demons, or anything out of the ordinary. The patrols rode the perimeter unmolested, and scouts sent beyond the forbidding checked in regularly.

"Ent right," Gared muttered.

Leesha agreed. Last time the demons attacked on new moon, they began by constructing greatwards like engines in a siege. It wasn't something that could be done quietly or without drawing attention.

Instead, there was silence, save for the call of birds and the chirping of insects. Even the casual demon activity of any given night was absent.

Leesha gave one of her earrings a twist. Their reach beyond the greatwards was minimal, but in Hollow County contact was instantaneous.

"Mistress," Darsy said in her ear.

"Report," Leesha said. "There is no sign of demon activity near Stallion's Ranch."

"Nothin' happenin' in Gatherers' Wood," Darsy said. "Captain just checked in. Ent heard a peep elsewhere."

It was the same as Leesha checked in with the other boroughs, one by one. They patrolled, paced, fretted on the edge of battle, but when the dawn came, there was nothing.

The alagai *will strike at nightfall in the north of the Hollow,* they had all agreed. What went wrong? Were Leesha's dice indeed flawed?

She thought back to the pattern, cemented in her mind from hours of study. Had they truly said that? Or had they all instinctively assumed the Hollow would be the demons' target?

The alagai *will strike at nightfall in the north of the Hollow.* Night.

"Arther." Leesha felt a pain building behind her eye. "Be a dear and send Captain Gamon and the Hollow Lancers north."

Arther raised an eyebrow. "Mistress?"

"Wonda, go with them. Take Kendall with you."

Wonda gaped. "Mistress?"

Leesha clenched her fist, angry at her own arrogance, but she kept her voice placid. "I fear Angiers may be under attack."

CHAPTER 28

ARAINE'S TALE

334 AR

Arther and Darsy fell in behind Leesha while she inspected the preparations in the Corelings' Graveyard. "Report."

"Triage tents are stocked and ready." Darsy waved toward the white pavilions filling the old town square. "Surgeries in the hospit and academy are standing by."

Leesha nodded. She'd traded the gowns she favored as countess for the blue dress and heavy pocketed apron that had served her for so many years as Gatherer. There would be no tea politics today. Only scalpels and needles and blood to her elbows.

"Supply wagons are ready with food, water, soap, and clothing," Arther said. "Temporary privies are assembled."

"I want teams sanitizing and swapping the buckets regularly," Leesha said. "We can't have . . ."

Arther looked down his nose at her, and she drifted off. He already knew. Of course he did.

"The Cutters . . ." Leesha began.

Again the look. "Already at work, clearing land for the settlement."

Leesha blew out a breath. "Seems like just yesterday, we had no idea how to handle thousands of refugees pouring into the Hollow."

"Practice makes perfect," Darsy said.

"Only . . ." Arther began.

Leesha and Darsy looked at him. "Yes?"

"I fear it may not be thousands," Arther said. "The Messengers report considerably less."

"Impossible," Leesha said. "Gamon's report said the city was lost."

Arther nodded. "Indeed."

The pain in Leesha's head grew. "Fort Angiers was home to more than forty thousand souls. The surrounding hamlets held half again as many."

"At least," Arther agreed. "But reports say the group led by Gamon's Lancers numbers in the hundreds. We must prepare for the worst."

Leesha looked out at her people, hurrying to and fro in the Graveyard, preparing to give succor to an endless stream of survivors. "I thought we were."

Darsy put a hand on her shoulders. "Wasn't the Krasians this time, Leesh. Demons ent got mercy for those that come out hands-up."

Leesha put a hand to her mouth, and it was all she could do to will back tears. So much death.

Soon after, Gamon and his Hollow Lancers—battered and bloody, their numbers thinned—rode into the square. Behind them, a caravan of refugees stretched down the road and out of sight, guarded by a handful of Wooden Soldiers and Mountain Spears, most of them sporting bloody bandages.

Gamon himself had his arm in a sling, and when he took off his warded helmet, his head was wrapped in bloody cloth, yellow from sweat.

Wonda and Kendall flanked him, looking equally filthy but none the worse for wear. All three were stone-faced.

"They have gazed into Nie's abyss," Favah said.

The three escorted what had once been a grand carriage. Now its wheels were mismatched, one of the doors replaced with a nailed board painted with wards. The slumped driver pulled up. An equally haggard footman dropped to the ground and set a stair.

"Night," Leesha said. It had not occurred to her until this moment that Duke Pether himself would be among the refugees. The Hollow was still technically his domain. Could he claim it right out from under Leesha? Would the Hollowers let him?

She imagined Gared's reaction, and knew that would never happen. If Angiers had fallen, then the Hollow was free, no matter what the Rhinebeck family thought.

But Duke Pether did not emerge from the carriage, nor Duchess Lorain. Only Minister Janson's young son Pawl. The boy hopped down and readied the stair, climbing back up to assist the Duchess Mum, her eyes sunken and hollow.

"They didn't even bother attacking the walls." Araine's hand shook as she clutched her cup and saucer. Leesha had put a mild sedative herb in with the leaves. "They came up through the boardwalk. Tunneled right under our noses."

"Pether?" Leesha asked. "Lorain?"

"Dead." Araine's gaze was distant. "All dead."

She sipped her tea, then grimaced and delicately spat it back into the cup. "Drugging my tea? You really are Bruna's brat."

"You tasted half a skyflower leaf through all that honey?" Leesha asked.

Araine looked down her nose. "The fact Leesha Paper served tea already honeyed was evidence enough."

"Drink it," Leesha said. "You've been through an ordeal. It will help you relax while you tell your tale. Afterward, you'll have a good sleep and be the better for it."

"Thank you, but no." Araine looked to Pawl. "Bring a fresh cup. Make it yourself."

"Yes, Mum." The boy moved to take her tea, but Leesha froze him with a raised finger.

"Drink." Leesha met Araine's steely gaze. "Gatherer's orders."

"Pfagh!" Araine broke the stare and drank the tea, but the victory was unsettling. The woman Leesha knew wasn't so easily bullied. She waited until the cup was empty before signaling Wonda, who opened the door to admit Favah.

"What is this?!" Araine looked like a hissing cat.

"Dama'ting Favah is the ranking Krasian ambassador in the

Hollow," Leesha said. "Having her here will save me having to tell the story again. We're all on the same side in this."

"It is as the daughter of Erny says," Favah agreed. "Whatever . . . disagreements our people may have in the day are as nothing in the face of Sharak Ka. Krasia will offer safe succor to your people, and lend our spears to your vengeance, if it is to be had."

"I had four sons, Dama'ting," Araine said. "One was killed by corelings, the other three by Krasians. If you want to lend spears to my vengeance, you can start by turning them on yourselves."

She turned to Leesha. "I won't give away state secrets—"

Leesha smacked the arm of her chair as she had seen Bruna do so many times, when the woman was tired of suffering a fool. It hurt her hand more than expected, but the crack that echoed through the room was worth the sting, cutting the Duchess Mum's words short.

"Angiers is lost," Leesha said. "There is no state to protect. If the corelings are moving to exterminate humanity, we can't afford to keep fighting among ourselves."

Araine blew a breath through her nostrils, but whether from plain sense or the skyflower, she deflated and made no protest as Favah moved to the couch across from her. If anything, she seemed calmer, more herself, with an enemy in the room.

"At first we thought they could be contained," Araine said. "The Mountain Spears surrounded the breach, but rock demons emerged, and the flamework weapons had no effect. The rocks smashed through them and secured the breach.

"That was when it began to happen."

Leesha felt a chill pass through her. "What began to happen?"

"Mutiny," Araine said. "Workmen in the gatehouses attacked the guards and opened the gates. Peasant brigades with warded weapons mustered, then turned on the soldiers. At first it seemed as if the peasants were in revolt . . ."

"But they weren't," Leesha said. "There were mind demons inside the city walls."

Araine nodded. "A company of Wooden Lancers was mowing down demons by the dozen on the narrow streets, until their captain removed his helmet to wipe the sweat from his brow. He'd killed both his lieutenants before his own men pulled him down. They were struggling to pin him down when a copse of wood demons swept in."

Araine tapped a nail against her teacup, and Tarisa immediately filled it. "Reports like that kept on through the night. Most of the city shelters remained intact, as if the people weren't the demons' true goal."

"The palace," Leesha guessed.

"Our walls were thick, strengthened by magic, above and below," Araine said. "No tunneling this time. They came up the Messenger road with reaps of field demons and copses of wood demons, but it was nearly dawn, and we were sure we could hold out until sunrise.

"The wood demons all carried small stones." The duchess held her hands apart, no larger than a melon. "But they threw precise as Jongleur's knives. Not to break the wall . . ."

"To mar the wards," Leesha said.

"Every guard in the palace wore a mind-warded helm," Araine said. "As did the Royals and most of the servants, but it didn't matter. A scullery maid with a knife killed three Wooden Soldiers, and the guards came to take us to the palace keep. On the way I saw a kitchen lad with a rolling pin storm a guarded stairway. Boy couldn't have been more than eight, but he moved like a *dama,* dancing around the guards' blows and between their legs, leaving a trail of crippled men in his wake.

"By then we'd figured things out, drawing wards on the brow of everyone we encountered. The keep was secured, and Pether, Lorain, and I were placed in a thick-walled room that could only be opened from the inside. The guards fed us reports through a slot in the door."

Araine drew a deep breath. "Pether was raving and pulling his hair when suddenly he just . . . calmed. I took the moment's peace as a blessing, but when I looked up, he wasn't wearing his crown. He walked over to Lorain like he was strolling the garden, then pulled a knife and tried to cut her throat."

Leesha could not keep from drawing a horrified breath.

"She took a deep cut, but caught his arm," Araine said. "Lorain outweighed Pether by more than a little, and they struggled. And as they did, Pether, my pious boy, began to say . . . the most terrible things."

"What things?" Leesha asked.

"I'll cut my own cock off before I stick it in your rank hole again," Araine's voice was a deep rasp, *"or see that rotten egg growing in your belly sit the throne.*

"And then," Araine breathed, "he kicked her in the stomach, and kept on kicking until she was coughing blood. I swung my walking stick at him, but he caught it in his free hand and kicked me in the hip. By the time I recovered, he'd already cut her throat and turned on me, still holding the knife."

Araine's voice turned back into the rasp. *"Why should I stop there, Mother? I'm rid of the woman Euchor sent to bully me, but not the one who's done it all my life."*

"Night," Leesha whispered. "How did you escape?"

"I've learned a Gatherer's trick or two in my time, girl," Araine said. "Blinding powder in a hollow bracelet. I let him have the whole dose. Pawl tripped him to the floor while he choked, and helped me limp away. At the door I spared a last look, and saw my son plunge the knife into his own throat."

"Everam protect us," Favah whispered.

"The hall guards were all dead, but there was no sign of corelings," Araine said. "Helms littered the floor. They killed one another."

Araine finished her tea, eyes distant. "I suppose the mind demon didn't consider me threat enough to kill."

"A mistake the *alagai* prince will come to regret," Favah said.

"I doubt it," Araine said. "We used a secret passage to return to the women's wing, where a handful of my house guards remained. There was fighting in every hall, and we were forced to flee through the brothel tunnels out into the city.

"Dawn came, driving the demons back to the Core, but the remaining guards in the palace closed the gates, locking us out. When I demanded entry, they posted Mountain Spears who fired on us."

"Even in the day?" Leesha gaped.

"It wasn't long before we learned the guards at the gates

were compromised as well," Araine said. "They closed the gates and broke the winches, saying it was the only way to keep the demons out, never mind that it kept us *in*.

"It wasn't all the guards," Araine said. "But the affected showed no signs. They walked in sunlight and donned helms with mind wards, cared for themselves and their weapons, acted normal in every way—until someone tried to leave. 'Duke's orders,' they would say, barring the way as if it were routine, hearing no argument that His Grace was gone. It wasn't until a Messenger tried to scale a wall, and the Mountain Spears shot him in the back, that we realized how much danger we were in. We tried to storm the gatehouses, but they barricaded themselves inside, manning the wall with Mountain Spears."

"Trapped, like *alagai* in the Maze," Favah said.

"We did what we could," Araine said. "Everyone in the city had mind wards painted on their foreheads by then, and we used thundersticks to collapse the tunnels the corelings used for entry, but it didn't seem to matter. The palace guards drew every curtain, painting the windows black, and we knew. The demons didn't need to get back in the city. They never truly left.

"The next night the demons began carving the boardwalk around the palace into a greatward, and more and more folk began turning on their fellows. A few peasants here and there—just enough to make everyone look crosswise at their neighbors—and the numbers of guards on inner and outer walls grew."

"I do not understand what the *alagai* gain in this," Favah said.

"They cut us off from our allies," Leesha said. "They keep aid from Miln."

"I am not a fool," Favah said. "But mercy—restraint, these are not the ways of the *alagai*. What point in taking the city and leaving the people alive?"

"Because they don't want to destroy the city," Leesha said. "They want a larder."

Neither woman had a response to that, and it was just as well. Leesha had no reason to think Inevera brought Favah into her counsel regarding the swarm, and the fewer people who knew what Arlen and Jardir were doing, the better.

"How did you get out?" Leesha asked.

"Pawl." Araine patted the boy's hand. "He knows all the royal passages and had . . . contacts in the city that were able to smuggle us past the wall guards."

Leesha looked at the boy, who seemed to shrink from her scrutiny. "If you got the duchess out, could you smuggle people back in?"

"A handful, perhaps," Pawl said. "Not a sizable force."

"*In?*" Araine asked. "Are you mad?"

"I won't leave thousands of people to the mercy of a mind demon," Leesha said. "If we're to have any hope of saving them, we'll need to break through before the next new moon."

Araine sagged in her chair, skyflower and exhaustion finally setting in. "Perhaps. It's your fight now. The Rhinebeck line is ended."

"Nonsense," Leesha said. "The Duchess Mother yet lives."

"Ancient, and heirless," Araine said.

"You are still young, in my estimation," Favah said. "Will you abandon your people to wait for the lonely path to open to you?"

Araine looked at the *dama'ting,* but the fight had gone out of her. She appeared broken, and every day her age.

"A question best left until you wake." Leesha rang a bell, and Melny entered, the exiled young duchess still clad in her simple housekeeper's apron and dress. Favah's eyes flicked over her, taking in the servant's garb and dismissing her.

"This is Melny, one of the Gatherer's apprentices," Leesha said. "She'll serve as your lady's maid. She's got a strong, healthy boy growing in her belly, but the babe is still months from birth. You'll find she's a hard worker."

Araine's eyes revealed nothing as her daughter-in-law went to her. Pawl helped the old woman to her feet and the two of them lent her their arms on the way to the door.

Araine turned to give Leesha a last look, and there were tears in her eyes.

"Thank you, Countess."

CHAPTER 29

WOLVES

334 AR

Inevera watched through the warded glass window of the carriage as *Sharum* in filthy blacks flitted through the scrub and hills to either side of the road.

The Wolves of Everam had been following them for hours.

The strain of conversing with Ashia over so many miles left her head spinning for days, but the resulting throws of the dice proved worth the pain, yielding some shred of the *alagai* princelings' plan.

—The reservoir is weaker than the bounty.—

Everam's Reservoir. The name encompassed all the wetland territory Krasia claimed. Its forces were depleted, its leaders killed. If the *alagai* took the wetlands, they could begin building greatwards right on the doorstep of Everam's Bounty.

It meant Docktown was the next—the only—line of defense remaining. If the *alagai* crushed Docktown, there would be nothing to prevent them from slaughtering the wetlanders in the hamlets and claiming vast territory.

—Alagai Ka are watching.—

Are watching. Not *is*. The demon princes would rise in numbers come Waning. Even now, they watched the surface through the eyes of their drones.

—Committing too many warriors risks divergence.—

There were times Inevera hated the vagaries of the dice as

much as Ahmann. How many warriors was *too many*? How much could she reinforce Docktown before the demons sensed it and changed targets?

—The Damajah must bait the trap.—

And so she had come personally. Every future where Inevera remained in Everam's Bounty cast a shadow over the Reservoir's future. Amanvah was left to sit atop Inevera's bed of pillows in her absence. She and her brother shared power uneasily, but the dice promised balance.

Inevera brought three of her sister-wives with her—Umshala of the Khanjin, Justya of the Shunjin, and Qasha of the Sharach—a handful of *shar'dama* and *dama'ting,* and a personal guard of five hundred *Sharum'ting* trained personally by Ashia and her spear sisters. The women were untested in pitched battle, more embassy caravan than troop reinforcement. Too small a force, Inevera prayed, to draw notice.

Amanvah was not pleased to be separated from her sister-wife, especially while both were with child, but it could not be helped. The Sharum'ting Ka was needed. Sikvah was not yet halfway into the cycle—her belly still slim, the slight rounding unnoticeable in her armored robes. She and Asukaji rode in Inevera's carriage.

Her nephew was sullen, his aura filled with shame and regret since his healing. He stared out the carriage window, knowing he was there more as hostage against Asome's good behavior than for any great need of his leadership in Docktown.

"They have us surrounded," he noted.

"Jarvah said to expect this," Sikvah said. "The Wolves of Everam have grown fat off greenland plunder, feral as their namesake. Jurim will not show himself without the protection of his men."

—The Wolves have gone unleashed too long.—

"Jurim is a lost soul," Inevera said. "The last *kai'Sharum* from Ahmann's original Spears of the Deliverer. His honor among the *Sharum* is boundless."

"A warrior so honorable should meet us on his knees with hands on the ground," Asukaji said, "not threatening us with his men."

Inevera shook her head. "To a woman? To a boy in white he

hardly knew? Jurim is a true child of the Maze. His loyalty is to his *Sharum* leaders. Ahmann and Shanjat, gone to the abyss. Jayan, dead. Hoshkamin, unproven. He was submissive to Hasik, now a eunuch outcast. What warrior, then, carries greater glory than him?"

"I am his *Damaji!*" Asukaji clenched a fist.

"A boy he watched suck his mother's breast," Inevera said.

"Then perhaps I will prove myself to him today," Asukaji said.

"You will not," Inevera said. "I will handle Jurim."

"Damajah," Sikvah said, when Asukaji lapsed back into sullen silence, "Jurim has over three hundred elite *dal'Sharum* with him. It is dangerous for you—"

Inevera's eyes flicked to her, and the girl fell silent. Ashia was gone, but it seemed her assertiveness had passed with the white headscarf to Sikvah.

"We cannot bring more warriors from Everam's Bounty without alerting the *alagai* to our plans," Inevera said, "and there are no other reinforcements to be had. We need Jurim and his men if we're to have any hope of surviving the coming Waning."

"Hasik is said to have over a thousand *Sharum* at the Monastery of Dawn," Asukaji said. "Perhaps our time would be better spent there."

"Perhaps we should visit Hasik now," Asukaji said, "before Waning comes, to remind him of his oaths."

"Your sister is handling that," Inevera said. "But that information is not to leave this carriage."

Asukaji gaped. "Ashia? You sent her north?! Where is my son?!"

Inevera slapped him. He blinked at her, stunned. Had anyone ever slapped the boy in his entire privileged life? Sikvah studied the wards painted on her nails, affecting not to notice.

"Your *nephew* is with his mother, walking the edge of the abyss because you tried to murder her and set the dice of her fate spinning. Even now, she draws close to Hasik. She will free the *khaffit* from him."

"The *khaffit*?! You risk my sister and the Deliverer's only grandson—*your* only grandson—for that fat pig-eater?"

"I risk them for Sharak Ka," Inevera said. "The dice foretell the *khaffit* has a role to play, still."

Asukaji collected himself, sliding off the bench to kneel on the carriage floor. "Perhaps I do as well. Send me, Damajah. I will go north to save my sister and . . . nephew."

Inevera laid a hand on his shoulder. "You show respect at last, *Damaji,* and so I tell you, respectfully, that you do not have the training or skill for such a task. The wetlands are vast, with little food and fresh water, even for those who know how to look. They teem with swamp and bog demons, who blend invisibly with the muck and rot, spitting acid on unsuspecting prey."

Asukaji looked up, meeting her eyes. "That is where you sent my sister and an infant?"

Inevera nodded. "And they need no saving by the likes of you. You would be lucky if Ashia did not kill you on sight. The Deliverer would not have healed you if you did not have your own part left to play in Sharak Ka. Have patience, and Everam will reveal it to you."

Asukaji centered himself, bowing. "As you command, Damajah."

Around the next bend, the road ran straight for nearly a mile uphill. Inevera could see Jarvah waiting at the top with Jurim and his lieutenants. Perfect ground for an ambush. The Wolves closed in as they climbed, barring the other carriages and ranks of *Sharum'ting* from the hilltop.

Asukaji and Sikvah exited the carriage first, standing guard to either side of the stairs as Inevera descended. Her silks were the red of blood.

Jurim and his men towered over tiny Jarvah on her small courser. As expected, the Wolves largely ignored the girl, focused on Inevera, her eunuch guards, Asukaji, and Sikvah.

"Damajah." Jurim's bow was respectful, but short of the obeisance the title demanded. Inevera knew to expect it, but the arrogance and disrespect grated on her every bit as much as they did her nephew.

"Jurim." She did not bow. "I am pleased to see you."

"You're lucky I agreed to this meeting after your *Sharum'ting* bitch cut the hand from one of my men."

Inevera smiled behind her veil. "If that is so, then he put it in a place forbidden by Everam." Jurim brayed like a camel, and did not contest the point.

"You are needed in Everam's Reservoir," Inevera said. "Take your men north as if we are parting ways, then circle back overland to join us there. Report to Drillmaster Qeran when you arrive."

She turned to go, praying for one of the rare futures where her command was enough.

"And if I do not wish it?" Jurim asked, stopping her midway in her turn.

"What do your wishes matter, in Sharak Ka?" Inevera asked.

"Sharak Ka!" Jurim shouted. "A myth to cow warriors into obeisance. Is it for Sharak Ka that we bleed and die in the greenlands? For Sharak Ka that Jayan was smashed against Angiers? Or was it simply for the glory of men?

"I've never been as interested in Sharak Ka as Ahmann." Jurim turned, pacing the hilltop. "Not that he ever asked what I was interested in, or showered me with glory, as he did Hasik and Shanjat. I was one place in the gruel line short of greatness."

"There is time for glory still, Jurim," Inevera said.

"Glory is a wisp of lantern smoke, Damajah. It slips from fingers that grasp for it. It cannot be held, cannot be spent." Jurim swept an arm out over the hilltop view. "The greenlands are vast. Their men are weak and their women soft. Their villages rich with plunder. So tell me, why should my men and I come back to fight and die for glory?"

"If you disobey, your Wolves will have no welcome in Krasia or the Hollow," Inevera said. "How long before you are crushed between us?"

"There are other powers in the greenlands," Jurim said.

"Hasik?" Inevera laughed. "How will the Wolves enjoy soft greenland women as eunuchs?"

Jurim leaned on his spear. "Better I should make obeisance to the drunken, crippled drillmaster who threw me twenty feet from the Maze wall for laughing at a *khaffit*?"

"Abban was not *khaffit* at the time," Inevera noted. "He was one of your *nie'Sharum* brothers."

Jurim spit on the ground at her feet. "*Khaffit* are always *khaffit,* even if their nature is yet to be revealed."

"*Sharum* dog!" Asukaji shook his fist. "Kneel and beg forgiveness of the Damajah or I will . . ."

Jurim gave his camel's honk as his lieutenants raised crank bows. Once the Kaji *Sharum* found ranged weapons dishonorable, but honor was in short supply among the Wolves.

"You would order your men to shoot their own *Damaji*?" Asukaji asked. Inevera marveled that the boy remained naïve enough to be shocked.

Jurim brayed again. "I was killing *alagai* in the Maze with the Deliverer, boy, before Ashan held his nose and stuck your ugly mother. I don't need my men to kill a sniveling *push'ting* like you."

"Then tell your men to lower their bows," Asukaji growled, raising his whip staff.

Jurim snorted. "Your commands carry no weight here, boy. Crawl back home to your mother's teat."

Inevera glided toward the warlord. Graceful as a pillow dancer, she accented the natural turn of her hips just enough to draw Jurim's eye.

"Ahmann may have been under your spell, Damajah, but I am not," the warlord said, "and your demon magic will not work in the day."

Inevera spread her empty hands. "There is no one in the gruel line before you anymore, Jurim." She continued her slow approach, pacing her stride to pull her silks tight around her curves. "Ahmann and Shanjat have disappeared. Hasik is gelded and living in exile. Qeran is crippled and beholden to a *khaffit*. The *Sharum* need a true leader, if you can muster ambition beyond raiding *chin* villages."

Inevera sauntered close, and for the first time in his life Jurim dared eye her openly. "Everam curse me that I didn't see the truth back when you wore transparent silks to tease the Shar'Dama Ka and tempt his court."

"What truth, Kai'Sharum?" Inevera asked.

"We all thought you ensnared Ahmann with demon magic, but perhaps it was just a woman's magic after all." Jurim reached out to touch her hair.

Inevera caught him by the thumb, pulling this arm straight

and twisting, locking the bones in place as she flowed into scorpion, bending forward and kicking back over her head to strike him in the chest.

Jurim hit the ground hard, but he was a Spear of the Deliverer and adapted quickly, using the impact to bounce back to his feet, spear at the ready.

Inevera made no move to continue the fight, straightening her robes to conceal the curves she had moments ago displayed. "There is still this one chance, Jurim, to fall to your knees and put your head in the dirt."

Jurim brayed again, looking to his lieutenants with their crank bows.

Inevera inclined her head and Jarvah crouched nimbly atop her horse, then sprang across to one of his men. Her kick shattered his hip and knocked him from the saddle as she snatched the weapon from his hands.

Before the others could react, Jarvah raised the crank bow and fired, sending a bolt into a second lieutenant's unarmored groin. He howled and dropped his own weapon, clutching the feathered shaft pinning him to his saddle.

Sikvah was moving then, loosed like an arrow. Her throwing glass embedded in a warrior's hand and his crank bow fell, the bolt loosing harmlessly. Another warrior fumbled his bow toward her. Jarvah skipped across three horses' backs and kicked the man's foot from one stirrup as she shoved him from his horse. His remaining stirrup caught, and his leg broke with an audible crack. He hung suspended, his head inches above the ground as Jarvah touched down next to him.

The remaining lieutenants shouted and waved their weapons, trying to get the swift-moving women in their sights. Jarvah ran between the horses and disappeared as Sikvah threw her spear, taking another in the shoulder. One man had her in his sights, but with a crack of his alagai tail Asukaji relieved him of the weapon.

Another shout, and a warrior in back dropped into the stamping group of horses, his saddle girth cut.

The last *dal'Sharum* was frantically searching between the horses for a sign of Jarvah when she came up behind him, scaling his horse's hindquarters as easily as she might sprint up steps. She had him in a submission hold, glass knife to his throat, before he even knew she was there.

"Point it at your *kai,*" she hissed.

Eyes wild with fear, the warrior pointed the shaking weapon at Jurim. After a moment, Jurim turned back to Inevera.

"Your fate is committed to this course now, Jurim. Your men are all watching." Inevera began an old *Sharum* proverb. *"The only way out of the Maze—"*

"—is through it." Jurim bared his teeth and leapt forward with a thrust of his spear.

He was good, reading Inevera's defense and countering before first contact. Inevera managed to divert the swing, but the shaft cracked painfully across her forearms. Jurim was ready for her scorpion kick this time, slipping to the side as he rolled the shield off his back and onto his arm.

Jurim was not boasting when he spoke to Asukaji. Ahmann trained his lieutenants personally, and Jurim's *sharukin* were masterful. Between the reach of his spear and the coverage of his shield, he presented few openings.

But like most warriors, Jurim had never fought a *dama'ting* before. She moved in close, where his long spear was a liability.

He was quick enough to block her kicks and punches, sacrificing small areas to cover those he considered vital. Inevera struck stiffened fingers into the convergences as they presented themselves. Tiger's rib. Snake's rattle. Pain lanced through him, but the warrior embraced it quickly, turning his shield to shove her back.

Inevera threw herself into the blow, rolling across the curved shield to come around behind him. There was a gap in his armor at the base of his helm. Inevera locked her fists together and struck with divine fury.

Done precisely, the blow cracked the spine like a whip, a shock that left an opponent paralyzed for several minutes, with a slow return to mobility.

Done imprecisely, it might kill outright, or leave the victim paralyzed.

Jurim gasped a breath and fell onto his side on the ground, unable to so much as twitch. His spear clattered away, the heavy shield pinning his lifeless body.

Inevera kicked off his helm and caught the *kai'Sharum* by the oily curls of his hair, twisting his head to meet the eyes of his lieutenants, lying similarly broken on the ground, but very much alive to witness his defeat.

She bent close to his ear, speaking quietly. "Do you remember what Ahmann did to Hasik in front of the men, all those years ago?"

Jurim swallowed, the sum of movement he could muster. "Yes, Damajah."

"Do you need the same lesson?" Inevera asked.

Spears of the Deliverer were taught to ignore pain, but there was no training to prepare a man for the numbness of a body that had always obeyed him. There were tears in Jurim's eyes as he struggled desperately to move. "No, Damajah."

"What will you do?" Inevera asked.

"I will take the Wolves of Everam north as if we are parting ways," Jurim said. "Then circle back overland and join you in Everam's Bounty, reporting to Drillmaster Qeran."

"Good," Inevera stroked his hair like a pet. "Then there is only the matter of your laugh to attend."

Jurim's eyes grew fearful again. "My . . . laugh?"

"That disgusting camel's bray has gotten you into trouble before." Inevera pushed him onto his back and lifted his lifeless leg, bracing it onto her shoulder so the warrior could see. "I treated your leg when Drillmaster Qeran threw you from the wall and shattered it. The break was right . . . here."

She struck, and Jurim howled. He could feel nothing, but that did little to dispel the horror as he once again saw bone jutting from his thigh.

"I could heal this in moments," Inevera dropped the broken limb with a thump, "but in your wisdom, you insisted we meet with the sun high in the sky."

Jurim had stopped howling, but he grit his teeth, unable to keep back a groan.

"You have the daylight hours to reflect," Inevera said. "At nightfall, you will make obeisance and swear your oaths to me anew. Then, perhaps, I will heal your broken bones."

Jurim and his lieutenants crawled on broken limbs to make obeisance to her at dusk, and Inevera kept her promise, healing Jurim's leg and signaling her sister-wives to do the same for his injured men.

Her wards kept the *alagai* from approaching too close, and moments later Jurim and his lieutenants fled, taking the Wolves of Everam with them. They skirmished with her *Sharum'ting* as they went, but it was a ruse that left only minor injuries on each side from overzealous actors.

"The *alagai* spies will see only another failed alliance from a fractured people," Inevera said.

"Do we know otherwise, Damajah?" Sikvah asked. "Can Jurim be trusted to return?"

Inevera put her hand on her *hora* pouch. "The futures are infinite. In some he returns, and in others he does not. I have influenced events as much as I dare. Whether they come or not, Everam's Reservoir must hold."

CHAPTER 30

EVERAM'S RESERVOIR

334 AR

Jarvah was waiting as the walls of Docktown came into sight. This time she sat beside her brother Sharu—Ahmann's fourth son—and Drillmaster Qeran. Flanking the road were rows of *Sharum,* too disciplined to show they had just been pulled from their posts and bunks to escort the Damajah, who none had known was coming. Many sat their mounts uncomfortably, more used to rolling ship decks than the saddle.

The procession pulled to a halt as Sharu, Qeran, and Jarvah rode out to Inevera's pillow carriage. Eunuchs opened the doors to reveal Inevera on her pillows.

Despite his metal leg, the drillmaster leapt as nimbly from his horse as young Jarvah and Sharu, all three landing on their knees with his hands on the ground, head bowed. "Damajah."

"Welcome to Everam's Reservoir." Inevera did not need to see Sharu's aura to know he was afraid. It was in his voice, the slight tremble in his limbs. "When you sent word of a delegation, you did not mention you meant to lead it personally."

Inevera smiled, letting him dangle on the hook. Sharu supported his half brother when Jayan defied the Skull Throne in his attack on Angiers. Now that plan lay in ruins, and Asome was Shar'Dama Ka. Blood gave Sharu command in Docktown, but he was inexperienced, and it was Qeran who made the real decisions. The boy was expendable and knew it.

"I did not wish it known," Inevera said at last. "Your drill-master would have sent too many men to secure the road."

"It would have been wise," Qeran agreed.

Inevera smiled. Qeran was as prideful as any *Sharum*, but he had earned it, and remained loyal. "It would have shown our hand to the *alagai*."

"Of course." Qeran glanced dubiously at the five hundred *Sharum'ting* marching in formation behind them. "Though I am only a low *Sharum*, and do not see how five hundred . . . warriors changes our hand."

He did not mention that the warriors were women, but Inevera knew he and Sharu were thinking it. And indeed, five hundred was but a fraction of Docktown's force.

"I have brought more than warriors," Inevera said. "As of this moment, I am in command of Everam's Reservoir."

The men hesitated. This was more than a simple visit. They quickly recovered, putting their heads to the ground. "Your will, Damajah."

"What passes for a palace in this wetland shipyard?" Inevera asked.

"After the *chin* burned Jayan's palace, the *khaffit*'s warehouse became his base," Qeran said. "It is the safest and most richly appointed building in the city, with a view of the water and the road."

Sharu coughed. "I have been staying there since my brother left, but if you—"

"I do," Inevera said.

Sharu bowed again. "Your will. I will send runners to have my possessions removed and ready the warehouse for your arrival."

Abban's "warehouse" was much like the man himself. A squat, ugly building, full of industry on its sprawling main floor. But the floors above, where the *khaffit* lived and worked, exceeded even the most audacious *Damaji*'s palace décor.

There were fountains, colored silk, cashmere, and gold. Thick curtains that would aid in *hora* casting. The windows and walls were strengthened by magic already, a last gift from

Asavi before she returned to Everam's Bounty and tried to kill Inevera.

The largest room, great windows overlooking the city and docks, was a fitting place for the pillowed throne Inevera's eunuchs bore up the steps on their backs. The heavy frame was built of the bones of heroes and *alagai* in equal measure. The skulls of Andrah Ashan and Damaji Aleveran adorned the headrest, flanking the skull of a demon prince. The entire frame was warded and coated in precious electrum set with gemstones.

The pillowed throne was not as ancient or powerful as the true Skull Throne, but with the mind's skull to power it, the throne would cast a forbidding over a mile in radius. Enough to cover the docking bay and most of the city proper. Farther than a demon could throw a stone, or drop one with any accuracy.

"We have more than seventeen thousand *Sharum* stationed at Docktown," Sharu said. Qeran unrolled a great carpet before the pillow throne, woven into a map that showed the reservoir and its environs.

As he spoke, Sharu's eyes kept drifting to the white head-scarf tied over Sikvah's helm. His aura had a familiar cast—the confusion of a man who had yet to understand women as equals first encountering one his better. Sharu was a son of the Deliverer, but as with his sister Jarvah, only his veil was white.

"Seventy-three *kai'Sharum,* two thousand two hundred and six *dal'Sharum,* six thousand one hundred seventy *kha'Sharum,* and some nine thousand *chi'Sharum,*" Qeran said, nimbly pulling from a pouch on his belt meticulously painted figures symbolizing groups of warriors, placing them on the rug where Docktown was marked.

"In addition, we have a standing fleet of thirty-two fighting vessels, fifteen cargo ships, and some sixty smaller vessels." Qeran placed tiny painted ships on the great blue section of carpet.

"I see why you and the *khaffit* got along, Drillmaster." Inevera gave Qeran a hint of smile.

"Everam willing, my master will return," Qeran said. They

had not spoken of Ashia. It was doubtful Sharu even knew his cousin had passed through the city.

Inevera nodded, looking to Sharu. "More than half your warriors are *chin*. Are they loyal?"

"In the night, absolutely," Qeran answered, when Sharu hesitated. "During the day . . ." He shrugged. "The levies from Everam's Bounty are a different tribe than the fish men of the Reservoir. They have no love for each other, and will fight if commanded, but neither craves war."

"Do these . . . fish men have the resources to retake Docktown?" Inevera asked.

Sharu shook his head. "The Laktonians cannot commit to an attack on Docktown so long as they maintain the blockade."

Qeran walked easily on his bladed leg to squat where Hasik's monastery was marked, placing more ships, these painted with the flag of Lakton. "More than half the Laktonian fleet surrounds the docks. We believe their plan was to retake the monastery before converging upon us, but Hasik's coming stymied them.

"The fish men control the waters close to their city." Qeran pointed to a small island at the center of the lake, the weave depicting what appeared to be hundreds of ships, lashed together. He placed tiny models of sleek, armed vessels patrolling the water.

"The rest of the lake belongs to us." Qeran spread ships marked with the crossed spears of Krasia hemming the Laktonians in. "Our privateers keep the fish men from bringing sufficient supply from the mainland to their floating city. We have discovered their other ports around the lake and destroyed them. They have nowhere to run."

"You've given them no choice but to attack," Sikvah said.

"We were only meant to hold the enemy over the winter, while Jayan went north," Sharu said. "He was to return and fill the ships' holds with *dal'Sharum* to storm the floating city and force their tribe to kneel before the Skull Throne."

"You admit to abetting Prince Jayan's treason, cousin?" Asukaji asked.

"What were we to do?" Sharu seemed eager to defend himself. "Abandon the post assigned to us by the Deliverer's firstborn? Stand back and let the fish men escape our carefully laid nets?"

"Indeed, not," Inevera said. "You have done well under difficult conditions."

Sharu let out a breath. "Then why have you . . ."

"Come to your town, without enough soldiers to take the city on the lake?" Inevera asked. "The dice foretell a dark Waning over Docktown."

The fear that had left Sharu's aura returned tenfold. Inevera wanted to be forgiving of it. He was young and untested. But he was the Deliverer's son. The other warriors would look to him.

"Effective immediately, you will report to the Sharum'ting Ka," Inevera told him.

Again Sharu looked to Qeran, but the drillmaster held up a hand, straightening to his full height at last. "Do not look to me, boy. Bow and tell the Damajah you understand."

Sharu turned, and both men bowed. "Your will, Damajah."

They turned to regard Sikvah, who was still studying the map. She produced a braided gold cord, laying it in a precise circle on the map, encompassing much of the bay and half the town. "The pillow throne will cast a forbidding in this circle. Drillmaster, arrange to move your best ships into this part of the bay before Waning to protect them."

"That will leave openings to the fish men to regroup and slip our nets," Qeran noted.

"It cannot be helped," Sikvah said. "I have seen firsthand what the mind demons are capable of. If one of Alagai Ka's princelings rises near Docktown on Waning, the water *alagai* may begin using tools."

Qeran gaped. "We'll be helpless as they scuttle the ships. It will be done, Sharum'ting Ka."

"Triple the wall guard by Waning," Sikvah said. "But we should assume it will fall." She pointed to the gold braid. "We'll build a second defense at the forbidding."

"If the *alagai* get that far, won't the throne hold them back?" Sharu asked.

"It will not prevent them from hurling stones or burning brands," Qeran said. "They can still destroy the city without entering."

"The power of the throne is not infinite," Inevera said, "nor powered by the demons themselves, as with the outer wards. If enough *alagai* strike at once, the field will weaken, and they will slowly press inward, like swimming against the tide. The demon princes will know this and move to exploit the weakness."

"We must delay, trap, and kill as many *alagai* as possible before they reach the forbidding, to ensure it remains strong." Sikvah studied the area of the map between the gold rope and the town walls. "We have a week to turn these streets into a new Maze."

"The tide is low," Qeran said, as night fell on Waning.

Inevera had strengthened the city's defenses as best she could, but the preparations seemed woefully inadequate if the *alagai* brought their full strength to bear. Below, much of the warehouse level had been cleared and scrubbed clean, laid with white cloth as she and her sister-wives waited for the wounded to come.

And still Jurim had not shown himself.

"Eh?" Inevera asked.

Qeran pointed out the window to the dock below. "Those markers should be covered with water at this time."

"If the *alagai* break through, the shallows will be to our advantage, making water demons easier to strike." Inevera gave one of her earrings a twist. "Sikvah. Report."

"The walls are clear, Damajah," Sikvah responded immediately. "Every inch is under *Sharum* eyes, with reserves waiting to reinforce any breaches. The Maze is set and ready to be sprung. A third defense waits at the forbidding."

"The *alagai*?" Inevera asked.

"None sighted yet, Damajah," Sikvah said. "But the evening fog is thick. They could be using it to draw close. I could order a volley . . ."

"Everam's beard," Qeran said.

"Hold, yet," Inevera said.

"Your will, Damajah."

"We must get out," Qeran said.

"Eh?" Inevera turned to regard the drillmaster, pointing out the window again, this time at the horizon.

"We must get out, now!" Qeran shouted.

Inevera focused her eyes in Everam's light, seeing beyond the limits of her natural vision. Water was drawing rapidly from the bay, moorings squealing as the boats began to sink. But in the distance, she could see the water rising in a wave that threatened to crush the docks like the Hand of Everam.

Inevera touched her earring as she allowed Qeran and Jarvah to usher her toward the door. "Sikvah. Sound the horns to evacuate the docks."

"Your will, Damajah."

The horns were already sounding by the time she made the hall. Qeran was waving them toward the stairs to exit the back of the building. Inevera turned to her sister-wives and eunuch guards. "Go with Qeran to the city center."

"Where are you going?" Qasha asked.

"Too long have you been in my shadow, sisters," Inevera said. "This night, you must shine on your own. Go. Now."

"Your will, Damajah." Qasha, Umshala, and Justya bowed as one, then turned and fled with the eunuchs down the stairs.

Inevera went up instead. Behind her, she heard Qeran curse, but he and Asukaji followed. Jarvah kept silent pace with her, moving ahead to open the access door and secure the roof.

The wind was fierce, whipping Inevera's veil from her face. She made no move to secure it, facing the vast shadow of water rising in the twilight and raising her *hora* wand.

Wrist straight, the wand was an extension of her arm, and she worked it like a brush, trailing silver magic in the air as she traced a pyramid of linked impact wards. The wave was too great to break or destroy, but as in sharusahk, perhaps its force could be diverted. The shape grew exponentially as she fed it power and sent it streaking toward the wave.

The impact was deafening as the magic cut into the water, splitting the wave like a scalpel split flesh.

For a moment, at least. The flows divided, but the water kept pressing, and even the massive power she spent—half the wand's charge—could not hold back millions of gallons of water. The wave flowed back together before it struck the docks, but its power was much blunted.

Perhaps the extra moment saved a few lives as men and women fled the docks, but it did not save the ships, or the skeleton crews aboard. It did not save the Mehnding scorpion crews stationed on the far piers.

The boats that had been sinking a moment ago rose into the air, shattering as their hulls smashed together, fusing into a massive battering ram of wood and water that splintered the docks and tore through buildings like castles of sand.

Even Abban's warehouse rocked, but its foundation was deep, inlaid with a skeleton of magic and warded glass. Inevera bent as a palm in wind, keeping her feet as she watched the destruction of the fleet. In one stroke, the *alagai* princes had reached through her wards and smashed Krasia's budding naval power in its infancy.

Water exploded all around, drenching and knocking all of them back as it flooded across the roof.

"Damajah." Qeran sprang to her side, not daring to touch her, but she could see the need in his aura. "We must get out now."

Inevera shook her head. "The building can withstand . . ."

"It does not matter." Qeran pointed to the horizon. Already the wave was receding, waters flowing back to build anew. "We will be trapped. Caught in the enemy's net."

"Everam's balls!" Inevera spat, but she wasted no more time, running for the stairs. All of them Drew on *hora,* moving with inhuman speed and grace down the flooded steps.

Inevera's earring began to vibrate, and she clicked the wards back into alignment without breaking stride.

"Damajah!" Inevera could hear the crashing stone and screaming warriors surrounding Sikvah. "The demons are at the walls!"

"How many?" Inevera demanded.

"All of them!" Sikvah shouted. "We cannot hold!"

"Tell the men on the walls Everam is watching," Inevera said, "and bring the *Sharum'ting* to the town center. I will meet you there."

Asukaji made the landing first, the splashing water up to his thighs. There was a wreckage of cargo and white cloth swept in from the warehouse blocking the doors, but the young dama raised his *hora* staff and blasted a path through.

Inevera splashed out onto the streets of Docktown, purple silks soaked and clinging to her body. Her veil was lost in the wind.

The city was in chaos. Men, women, and children they had thought ensconced in the safest part of the town were a wild press trying to flee uphill. The water was knee-deep, a sucking current pulling at her center, sweeping flotsam, jetsam, and bodies through the streets.

So many dead, and the sun had barely set.

"Make for the town center!" Inevera used the warded gem anchoring her bodice to amplify her voice, sending it resounding in the streets. "Aid your neighbors! Take no possessions! Everam is watching! Everam will protect us!"

And then she Drew, people and buildings blurring as she sped past, leaving water in a slashing wake for the others to follow. She feared for Qeran with his bladed leg in the water, but there was no time to waste. If the drillmaster could not keep pace, he would find another way to assist.

Moments later she was in the town center, the square already filling with people. She had barely come to a halt beside her sister-wives when Asukaji, Jarvah, and Qeran appeared beside her.

She heard Sikvah before she saw the woman, her voice amplified by the choker at her throat as she sang the *Song of Waning* at the head of five hundred singing *Sharum'ting*.

"Sing, Children of Everam!" Inevera boomed. It was not hard for the quivering, fearful people of Docktown, Krasian and *chin* alike, to let themselves be swept up in Sikvah's song, sung every night in Sharik Hora. Their voices were tentative at first, growing in strength as they desperately clutched at hope. "Sing, for Nie is listening!"

Sikvah leapt down from her horse, but her warriors continued to sing, leading the crowd. Each woman had a *hora* brooch, less powerful than the ones Inevera and Sikvah wore, but enough to cut through the cacophony.

"Damajah." Sikvah's voice was calm, but her aura betrayed her. Her first real command, and already she had failed.

"The walls have fallen," Inevera said.

"The breaches were contained when I left," Sikvah said,

"but more *alagai* penetrate the outer wards every moment. It is likely there are already demons in the Maze."

Inevera nodded. "Then that's where we're going." She turned to her sister-wives. "Take your *Sharum'ting* east, west, and south. Hold the Maze."

"Your will, Damajah," the women said, signaling their warriors as they strode away.

"I will go to the north section of the Maze," Inevera said. The most direct approach, where the *alagai* would be thickest.

Inevera drew a ward with her wand as the field demon kicked off the wall and leapt at her.

But even the wand, its core the ulna of a mind demon, had limits. Its power spent, Inevera barely had time to slap the demon's jaws aside and roll with the impact, keeping hold of the *alagai* to stay in close and out of reach of the creature's scrabbling claws.

From her belt Inevera pulled her curved knife, slashing open the demon's vulnerable belly. Black ichor spattered her grimy silks, and she thrust the wand into the wound before the demon's magic could knit it closed. He fingers danced across the wards carved into the bone, Drawing hard.

In Everam's light, it seemed the creature turned inside out as the magic was sucked from the ichor in its veins, refilling some of the wand's reserve. She left it twitching on the cobbles as another demon came at her, this one neatly speared by Drillmaster Qeran, who advanced to cover her with his mirrored shield.

Jarvah had the opposite flank, methodically hacking at the arms of a bog demon like she was pruning branches from a tree. It spat at her, but Jarvah batted the globule aside with her shield. It struck a stone wall, smoking as it burned.

All around the ambush pocket, battle raged. A Push Guard of *Sharum'ting* drove a group of demons into a makeshift demon pit, a circle of one-way wards. Demons trapped inside would be held until dawn, if the circle was not broken.

Asukaji spun his thick *hora* staff like a whip staff, crushing demon heads with the impact wards on the heavy end. His knuckles were covered in warded silvers, and his blows fell like thunderclaps upon the enemy. A wood demon broke through the Push Guard, but Asukaji was there, drawing wards in the air to force it back into the pit.

This group contained, Inevera reached out with her senses, pulling at the flows of magic on the air. Tasting them.

"This way." She pointed with her wand. Astride her black charger, Sikvah fell in beside her, she and Jarvah weaving their voices together. The effect their song had on the ambient magic in the air was different from that of warding, but no less pronounced. She felt the spellsong weave invisibility about her as the *Sharum'ting* who followed did to themselves.

Many of the demons flooding the town were of the common variety, seemingly moving without guidance beyond their own violent lusts. But there were others, *alagai* plucked from deep in the abyss, ancient and full of magic. Two such giants were tearing through an entire company of *chi'Sharum* in a small square ahead.

Cloaked by Sikvah's song, Inevera and her company were invisible to the demons until they struck. Cobbles exploded as Asukaji drew wards with his staff, knocking the demons off balance. Sikvah lowered her long spear and galloped at one of them, taking the demon full in the belly in an attack timed precisely to add to its stumble.

Indeed, the twenty-foot demon went down on one knee, but the blow, which might have killed a common rock demon, seemed little more than an annoyance. Sikvah tried to pull the spear free, but it resisted her, and in that instant's hesitation the demon swiped, taking the horse from under her.

Sikvah leapt clear in time, landing in a roll and coming back up with her shield and short stabbing spear raised. She was a blur as she moved back in, dancing around the demon's heavy blows. Again and again she struck with her glass spear, sending flares of magic and pain through the demon, but the attacks only seemed to anger it.

Asukaji kept hammering the other demon with impact wards until it fell, the *chi'Sharum* casting chains to tangle its legs. Wards flared and strained as the powerful demon flexed and tested their strength.

Jarvah and Sharu swept in, brother and sister side by side as they hacked at the demon's chest. The demon swiped a great arm, throwing *Sharum* from their feet. Its legs kicked, and the warriors desperately pulling the chain were rung like bells on a ribbon.

Still Jarvah and Sharu worked, protecting each other with their shields as they timed their precise blows.

Like Sikvah's, the attacks seemed to do no lasting damage, until Sharu made the last stroke and the rock ward cut into the demon's breastplate activated, drawing on the *alagai's* own power to form a forbidding. The ward grew brighter and brighter until the lines blended together and the demon's chest shattered.

The remaining warriors fell on the last demon like ants on a melon rind, hacking the powerful creature into less powerful pieces. Inevera went to the corpse of its fellow, putting her wand in the ruin of its chest and Drawing, refilling the reservoir.

Her arm burned, wand hand aching. There was only so much magic a body could channel and survive. Already, her eyes were dry, throat and sinuses burning, muscles aflame.

But there was no time to ponder limits. Bog demons poured into the streets, the walls all but gone now. How long had they been fighting? How many hours until dawn? Time was lost in the battle, in the hunt. It seemed like days since she led two hundred singing *Sharum'ting* from the town center. The time before felt like another life.

There were too many demons.

"All forces disengage and fall back to the forbidding!" Inevera used her earrings to send the call to her sister-wives to pass to their *kai'Sharum*.

Sikvah lifted her head as horns sounded. "Three *Sharum* units trapped in the third layer."

Inevera pulled her wand, near fully charged, from the demon's chest with a squelch. "Lead the way."

Inevera's arm was leaden, *hora* wand drained. Her throat burned as she shouted commands, muscles screaming as she fought and ran.

The warriors didn't feel it—energized every time their

warded weapons struck the enemy—but the *hora* users spent something of themselves every time they channeled the power. Asukaji leaned on his staff, aura dangerously dim.

"You cannot keep this up," she said to him. "Use your staff and your silvers, but draw no more wards."

"What about you?" Asukaji asked. "I can see your aura dimming as well, Damajah."

"I have been doing this far longer than you, nephew," Inevera said, but she knew he was right.

"We won't turn the tide fighting hand-to-hand," Asukaji said.

Indeed, their situation was steadily worsening. On a small rise overlooking the battle, Inevera could see the shattered gates, demons crowding to push through. The Maze was lost, *alagai* slowly pushing the defenders in toward the weakening pillow throne. The bay churned with water demons.

But then a horn cut through the night, accompanied by the sound of thunder. Magic began to flare beyond the wall as three hundred spears tore into the demon ranks from behind.

Jurim had arrived with the Wolves of Everam to nip their heels.

The *dama'ting* oversaw harvesting the lifeless but still magic-rich bodies of the *alagai* before the dawn burned them away. They were dragged into barns and warehouses, hacked to pieces as their ichor was collected in slurry vats.

Traditionally, the demonflesh was burned away with acid and the bones treated to prepare them for warding, but there was no time for such luxuries. The Pillow Throne's weakened power had to be extended. *Sharum* Pit Warders were using the raw demonflesh to power new traps in the Maze.

The throne would recharge naturally, Drawing ambient magic in the night, but its reserve was nearly depleted, and it might be months before regaining full power in such fashion. Inevera ordered the windows of the throne room blocked and had Asukaji's *dama* using *hora* to speed its restoration.

The *dama'ting* set up a new surgery in the basement of Jayan's burned-out palace, working in utter darkness as they cut and stitched in Everam's light. They painted wards around the wounds with the ichor slurry, speeding healing of injuries that might otherwise take longer than the Pillow Throne to recover.

Inevera herself worked the tables, advising her sister-wives and taking the most difficult cases upon herself. All of them were drained and exhausted, moving from battlefield to surgery with time for little more than to scrub and put on fresh robes.

However much she tried to focus on the patient in front of her, Inevera could not help but see auras in her peripheral vision. The dim glow of the exhausted *dama'ting*. The fluttering light of the wounded. The hollow emptiness in the air when one winked out forever. Many of them were former Spears of the Deliverer, warriors who had slain *alagai* alongside her husband for twenty-five years.

The Wolves of Everam had taken heavy losses. Jurim's charge at the head of three hundred fresh *dal'Sharum* warriors made the difference in finding the dawn, the chaos of the Wolves' mad assault upending the careful, even press of the *alagai ka*.

But the *alagai* would return at dusk for the second night of Waning, having already broken their outer defenses beyond repair, and devastated their fighting number. Even if some survived until the dawn, the third night of Waning would be their undoing.

There was a feather brush against the entrance curtains, a series of layers of thick velvet to prevent the slightest hint of sunlight in the room where the *dama'ting* worked their healing spells.

"Speak," Inevera said.

"Damajah, you are needed on the docks." Sikvah used the magic of her choker to deliver the words to her ears alone.

Inevera handed off her patient and moved through the curtains to the scrub room, where she immediately began stripping her bloody robes. "Report."

"The fish men have come," Sikvah said, handing her a cake of soap.

"Everam's balls." Inevera spit blood into the drain of the scrub sink. "How many?"

Servants were already rushing to towel her dry and help her into fresh robes of deep blue silk.

"All of them," Sikvah said.

Inevera blinked in the bright daylight as she stepped from the makeshift Chamber of Shadows. The sun was high in the sky, glittering off the water.

Or what little water there was. Hundreds of ships crowded the bay, floating amid the wreckage of the Krasian fleet. More boats than Inevera had ever imagined could exist.

"Should not the dice have warned of this?" Asukaji asked.

"They might have, had I bothered to ask. The *alagai hora* volunteer nothing, nephew. The focus of my castings this past week has been the *alagai* and our defenses, not the doings of the fish men."

She volunteered much with the words, piercing her own aura of infallibility, but the boy had earned the lesson. The *dama* already experimented with the wards of foretelling.

"Even battered and exhausted, our warriors can make them pay a bloody price for the beach," Sikvah said, "but against such numbers, the fish men will overwhelm us."

Asukaji spat in the water. "They are no better than servants of Nie, striking when the *alagai* have weakened our defenses."

"It was no less than we did to them, in the Battle of Docktown," Qeran said, "letting the *alagai* thin the enemy before pressing the attack. We might manage such a victory again, if we can keep the Laktonians bottled up in the bay until nightfall . . ."

Inevera shook her head. "No. Not ever again. Everam will judge that night against you when you walk the lonely path, Drillmaster. You had best provide much in the balance."

Qeran knelt and put his hands on the dock. "I am prepared to face Everam's eternal judgment, Damajah."

"Indeed." Inevera knew that while Qeran had carried out the plan, it was born in the mind of the *khaffit*. Not for the first time, she wondered why she was risking so much for such a wretched creature. "If it comes to that, we will abandon the wetlands and retreat to Everam's Bounty." The words were bitter on her lips. "I will not let our army be destroyed for the sake of a ruined town."

But the Laktonians did not send their ships to storm the docks. Instead, two great vessels separated from the rest, sailing in close and releasing boats flying the white flag.

Inevera's makeshift palace still stood, an island amid the wreckage. The warehouse floor was ruined by flood, but the upper levels remained dry and secure.

She curled upon the Pillow Throne, pleased to see it glowing brightly once more. Enormous amounts of *hora* were drained to restore its well of power.

The enemy fleet sent two emissaries, a man and a woman, to treat with them. The woman was easily recognizable from her wanted posters. "Welcome, Captain Dehlia. It is an honor to meet you. The name *Sharum's Lament* carries boundless glory on the water."

Her eyes flicked to the man, his aura burning hot under finery that seemed too heavy on him, as if he were unused to their weight. "And you are?"

The man strode forward. "I am Duke Isan of Lakton, elected this morning by the council of captains."

"Duke Reecherd is dead?" Inevera asked.

"Killed in the night," Isan said.

"My people speak of you fish men as cowards, but it is bold of you to come in person, Duke Isan." Inevera gave him a respectful nod. "Are you so confident in your numbers?"

"I had to come," Isan said. "Had to look you in the eye."

Inevera raised a brow. "Oh?"

"The mother of the demon of Docktown," the duke said in Krasian. "Jayan asu Ahmann am'Jardir am'Kaji, who slaughtered my family."

"Isan . . ." The name was familiar.

"Isan asu Marten," the duke said. "Your son stripped my father and forced him to the ground, kicking his manhood to a bloody pulp before executing him in front of my mother and her court.

"Isan asu Isadore. My father's body was not yet cold when Jayan asu Inevera forced a marriage contract upon my mother, and took the pen in his eye. He ran her bloodied ruin up the flagpole for all to see.

"Isan brother of Marlan. Your drillmaster," the duke jerked his head at Qeran, "cast tar upon my brother's ship, and water demons dragged him and more than a hundred men down into the deep."

Qeran's aura blossomed with shame at the words, but he stood silent.

Inevera rose to her feet. "My drillmaster sinned against Everam when he exposed you to the *alagai*," Inevera said. "The Creator will judge him."

She began to descend the steps. "My son committed grave crimes against you, for which Everam judges him, even now."

She reached the floor, walking toward Isan, and everyone tensed. "But it was I who ordered the attack on your people."

"To capture the tithe," Isan said.

"To capture *you*," Inevera said. "To join your forces with ours in the battle against Nie."

She was close now. Isan looked as if he wanted to back away, but he stood his ground, meeting her eyes. In Everam's light, she could see the blade concealed beneath his coat.

"It is I who bears the ultimate responsibility for what was done to you and your people." Inevera spread her arms, vulnerable in her thin silk. "Do you mean to strike the first blow for them, and cast our people into battle anew, even as Alagai Ka walks the night?"

Isan's eyes were wild, hand twitching toward the blade. Even now, Inevera could stop him—break his wrist before he had the weapon free of his coat—but the duke seemed to find his center, hand moving back to his side.

"You have now looked into my eyes, Duke Isan of Lakton," Inevera said. "What do you see?"

"I see that you are not a coreling," Isan said. "I see you have the only succor on the lakeshore large enough to protect my people. And so I have come personally to test your claim. Do you truly want to join with us?"

"Everam my witness, I do," Inevera said. "We will negotiate the terms in good faith, but in the coming night, our succor is yours as well."

Isan bowed stiffly. "Thank you . . . Damajah."

"Tell me what happened," Inevera said.

"Demons been quiet for weeks," Dehlia said. "But the deep water began to churn at sunset last night. At first, we thought it nothing out of the ordinary, but then the leviathan demons began leaping and diving in the water, creating wave after wave, each building in intensity over the last.

"By the time we saw it coming, we barely had time to sound the alarm. The *Lament* sped to the city, but what could we do to defend against such a thing?"

"The island was flooded," Inevera said.

"Drowned," Isan said, "but the island was only a tiny fraction of Lakton. Three-quarters of the city was made of hundreds of ships, lashed together around its center, connected by planks and bridges.

"We hacked at the moorings desperately, freeing as many of the heaving vessels as we could. We were scattering when the worst of the waves hit."

"How many were lost?" Inevera asked.

Isan threw up his hands. "Who can say? Some were simply docked, and able to fill with refugees and sail in short order—others had not floated free in a hundred years or more. Those that survived the waves were hunted by water demons through the night."

"You've burned every other port," Dehlia said. "The demons destroyed the blockade and presumably took the monastery in the night. We have nowhere else to go."

CHAPTER 31

HARDEN'S GROVE

334 AR

"The last way station has fallen," Mother Jone announced.

The last, Ragen thought. The wording implied the others had fallen and the news kept from court. There had been no news from the south since Ragen's return. Any Messenger traveling into the region of the lost stations was never heard from again.

The courtroom filled with the chatter of private discussion, but when no one spoke out, Ragen took a step forward and bowed. Euchor sighed, but he waved a hand. "Speak."

"His Grace recognizes the Neocount of Morning." Jone thumped her staff, and the chatter fell silent.

"Were there survivors?" Ragen asked.

"None." Euchor's mouth was a hard line. The way stations were instrumental in extending his reach fully below the Dividing. Angiers was his in all but name, and the Krasians were retreating before his flamework weapons. The dream of becoming king of Thesa, so close to being realized, was slipping away.

Ragen chose his next words carefully. "Your Grace, it may be time to consider evacuating Harden's Grove."

"Preposterous." Count Brayan stepped out into the aisle beside Ragen. "With the road south closed, Harden's Grove is the biggest food producer in Miln, and their crop has barely sprouted. You would have us simply surrender it?"

"Is the crop more important than the Grovers' lives?" Ragen knew that to many at court who had investments in the Grove, the answer was yes, but as suspected, none dared voice such a cold thought. "New moon is just a few days away. If the corelings need to press to the city walls by then, they will not let the Grove stand. We must evacuate."

"Nonsense," Brayan said. "The Grove has survived a thousand new moons. Its wards are strong."

"Not so strong as His Grace's way stations," Ragen said. "The Mountain Spears had no women and children with them, no crops to protect, yet they fell. What hope do the Grovers have?"

"What hope do any of us have if we give up our winter stores?" Brayan asked. "And who will take them in? The Grove is home to more than five hundred souls, Neocount. Will you fill Morning County with them?"

Tresha crossed her arms, and Ragen knew it was above his authority to make such a promise, but Elissa stepped forward and gave her a pinch.

Countess Tresha eyed her daughter for a moment, then cast an equally dim gaze over the room. "If the other counties are too greedy to take in their share, Morning County will see it done, and let the Creator judge."

"The Countess of Morning is generous," Euchor said. "But this is premature. The Count of Gold is correct. We cannot give up the Grove without a fight."

Brayan crossed his arms in satisfaction and Ragen grit his teeth. "Your Grace, Count Brayan's words would seem like sense, but I do not think any who have not witnessed it can appreciate how dangerous the corelings become at new moon."

"Agreed." Euchor thumped his bracer against the metal arm of his throne, sending a clang through the room. "The Neocount of Morning will lead the defense of Harden's Grove."

Ragen looked from Euchor to Brayan as he felt the jaws of the trap close. This had been their plan all along, and he'd walked into it. "I am no soldier, Your Grace."

"You are Neocount of Morning," Mother Jone said. "Oath-bound to raise your spear when called upon by the throne."

"Perhaps the neocount is considering sending his aged mother-in-law in his stead," Brayan said, and there was laughter in the court.

Ragen gave a stiff bow. "How many Mountain Spears will I command?"

"You may have two hundred," Euchor said.

"Your Grace . . ." Ragen began.

"Levy your own countymen if you need more," Euchor said. "Or better yet, the Grovers themselves."

"Indeed," Brayan said. "Rally the peasants like your adopted son did the Angierians. He defended Cutter's Hollow with less than a hundred men, it is said."

Ragen drew a deep breath, thankful Yon was not there to hear. "As Your Grace commands."

Yon was waiting by their carriage as they exited the duke's palace.

"I'm coming with you," Elissa said, the moment the carriage pulled away.

"The Core, you are," Ragen said.

"You need me," Elissa said.

"Comin' where?" Yon asked.

Ragen ignored him, keeping his eyes on Elissa. "Miln needs you more. This is just the beginning. The demons will lay siege to the city. Someone has to stay here and prepare."

"Ay!" Yon cried. "Someone want to tell the rest of us what's goin' on?!"

"The way stations have all been destroyed," Elissa said. "With new moon three days away, Euchor has sent Ragen to hold Harden's Grove."

"Hold?" Yon asked. "Ent no way to hold a place like that on new moon. Got to get those folk out."

Elissa glared at Ragen. "Don't you ripping die out there."

Ragen blew out a breath. "What do you want me to say, Lissa? I'm not the Creator. Someday something's going to kill me. Or you. It can't stop us from trying to live right. The Grovers need me right now, and Morning County needs you. The law says we can levy a militia. Yon and his Cutters can stay and train—"

"Piss on that," Yon cut in. "Ent lettin' ya go off to Harden's Grove without us."

"This isn't your fight, Yon," Ragen said.

"Is," Yon said. "Everyone's fight. Deliverer said so himself. Don't care if ya ride down to the Core itself. Long as I'm around yu'll do it with Cutters at yur back."

Ragen wanted to argue further, but he knew there would be no swaying the man, and he could not deny he felt safer knowing Yon Gray would be at his side when the fighting started.

"It isn't going to be enough," Elissa said. "You cannot hold Harden's Grove with two hundred Mountain Spears and less than twenty Cutters."

"I've already called reinforcements," Ragen said as the carriage pulled into the courtyard of their manse.

Guildmaster Malcum was squeezed into armor he hadn't worn in twenty years, standing at the head of fifty Messengers and another hundred caravan guards. All wore polished armor and carried long spears of warded steel.

Derek stood with a score of Warders. More used to a quiet workshop than the open road and naked night, these carried spears awkwardly, but Ragen knew their contribution to the defense would be greater than the warriors', if they did their work well.

Lieutenant Woron was waiting with Sergeant Gaims.

"Are you sure you're up to this, man?" Ragen asked. "You barely made it back alive."

"We're alive thanks to you," Woron said. "Euchor called for volunteers among the Mountain Spears. Every man you brought back is coming with us."

These men, Ragen had spoken to at court recess and expected.

He hadn't expected Keerin.

But the herald was there in the yard, surrounded by a knot of apprentices as they struggled through the complex progressions of Halfgrip's music. Ragen went over to him, and Keerin called a halt to the playing. "We don't have a lot of time to rehearse, Guildmaster."

"Euchor will fire you, if he learns . . ."

"I resigned," Keerin said. "I'm going with you."

Ragen felt a lump form in his throat. Less than a month ago, he'd despised this man. Now . . . He glanced at the apprentices. More than a few had fear in their eyes. "Are they ready?"

"I can't say with honest word that *I'm* ready," the Jongleur said. "My wife thinks I'm mad. But for fifteen years, I've been taking credit for the deeds of Arlen Bales. Night, I had my apprentices beat him for daring to speak the truth of it to a crowd." A few of the apprentices looked at their feet at the words, but did not deny them.

"I saw what you saw on the road," Keerin said. "The demons are coming. We started this together when we brought Arlen Bales here from Tibbet's Brook. A good story demands we end it together, as well."

"Nothing is ending," Elissa said. "If you don't think you can hold after the first night of new moon, you get those people out of there and bring them to Miln. I don't care if they eat us out of house and home."

"I'm no martyr," Ragen said. "I've no intention of dying for Euchor's pride."

"Ragen," Amon Grove said. "Thank the Creator you've come. Demons are nipping at the wards like they're on tampweed. Half the town's ready to desert after what happened to Way Station One."

Ragen nodded, but he did not dismount, turning Twilight Dancer this way and that, surveying the area. "It may yet come to that, Amon."

The old man gaped. "You brought almost as many soldiers as we have folk in the whole corespawned town. Sayin' that ent enough?"

"I'm saying it would be smart to start packing bags in case we need to leave in a hurry," Ragen said. "Nothing heavy. Just food and clothing. If we need to go, they'll need to make the walk in a single day."

"Night," Amon muttered.

"That's not the worst of it." Ragen slipped down from the

horse and pulled a map from his saddlebag, opening it so Amon could see.

"Crops've barely sprouted," Ragen said. "Makes our job easier. We'll need your plowmen to cut greatwards into your fields."

Amon leaned in, rheumy eyes squinting, and then they suddenly widened. "That will ruin half the crop!"

"Twenty-seven percent, by our estimate," Derek said.

"Ay, only twenty-seven?" Amon threw up his hands. "That makes it all sunny, don't it?"

"We don't lose that twenty-seven percent, there won't be anyone to eat those crops, Amon," Ragen said. "I'm not here to petition the town council. I've a writ from Euchor himself to levy your men and fortify this town. Do us both a favor and make it easy for me, ay? Daylight's wasting."

Amon eyed Yon and the column of soldiers. "Ent got much choice, do I?"

"There's a good man," Ragen said.

The evenly spaced wardposts in the fields and orchards were a perfect grid to work off, and the Warders quickly plotted the greatwards, directing the Grovers' plows. Malcum's caravan guards followed after with shovels, filling the furrows with powdered limestone, the white stone a sharp contrast to the dark soil. They took what care they could, but Ragen could tell their estimates of crop loss to trampling were low.

Lieutenant Woron had the Mountain Spears digging trenches inside the outer fence so they could fire from relative safety and succor. The inner wall was just high enough to shoot over, should they be forced to retreat.

For three days they worked, waiting at the ready each night, expecting a demon to strike that never came.

They're waiting for new moon, Ragen realized.

The third night was the beginning of the cycle, and as the sun dipped low in the sky Ragen and Yon climbed the bell tower of the Grovers' Holy House to look out over the defenses. The greatwards were sharp and clean, a powerful forbidding, but would it be enough?

"Know the feelin'," Yon said as he watched Ragen pace back and forth.

"Ay?" Ragen asked. "I'm not sure I know myself."

"Like you got an itch you can't scratch," Yon said. "Dreadin' what's to come so much yur eager to be on with it."

"A bit," Ragen conceded. "But what if the corelings don't care about Harden's Grove at all? What if they're about to strike the walls of Miln while we're off chasing fairy pipkins?"

Yon shrugged his heavy shoulders. "That kinda talk ent gonna help anyone. Know yur worried, but folk are lookin' to ya right now."

Ragen looked down again. Not at the defenses, but at the men and women working them. More than one set of eyes glanced up at him.

He straightened, forcing himself to look more confident than he felt. "What would Arlen be doing about now?"

Yon chuckled. "Givin' one'a those speeches o' his, tellin' folk they're all Deliverers or some demonshit like'at."

"You don't believe that?" Ragen asked.

Yon shrugged again. "Mr. Bales was always a humble feller. Folk 'preciated that. Liked bein' told they could make a difference, 'cause Creator knows they can. But there's only one Deliverer."

The last of the light slipped away, and the wards on Ragen's helm activated, his eyes slipping into wardsight as the demons began to rise.

"I've never been one for speeches." Ragen turned and headed for the stairs. "Everyone knows their part."

"Dive!" Ragen cried.

As the Mountain Spears scattered, a young Warder's apprentice drew an impact ward that shattered the boulder before it could roll over the greatward and mar the lines. Several defenders could not get clear in time, caught in the shock wave and pummeled by stone.

Ragen did not see what else the young woman could have done, but she stood staring in horror at the men her spell had injured, too transfixed to see that another demon had gotten a bead on her.

"Cara!" Ragen raised his stylus, but she was crushed before he could form his first ward. The Warders were increasingly adept at using *hora* magic, but they did not yet have experience on the battlefield.

Something bashed into Ragen then, blowing the breath from him as he was borne to the ground. There was a rush of air as a stone flew past.

Yon eased off him, easily pulling Ragen in his steel armor back to his feet. "Might be best you step away from the front. Demons got ya marked."

Indeed, every time Ragen revealed himself, the corelings seemed to fixate on him. They knew to focus fire on the Warders, but not even Derek drew the attention Ragen did. He let his warded cloak fall around him and backed slowly away until he reached the area of protection Keerin and his apprentices cast in front of the inner wall.

Three of the greatwards circling Harden's Grove were destroyed, each next to the one before it. The demons were dismantling their defense deliberately, opening a wide field of attack instead of narrow, defensible corridors. They weren't ready to make a full-scale push for the wall—yet—but already the defenders were hard-pressed.

The Mountain Spears had stopped firing, conserving ammunition for defense of the inner wall. Half had affixed bayonets and joined the close fighters while the rest took position at the wall.

Hundreds of Grovers followed in the fighters' wake, using farm tools painted with wards to aid in finishing off the coreling wounded.

Already, the feedback magic had begun to tell upon some of them. Amon Grove no longer leaned on his rake. The old man swung it into a prone field demon as smoothly as his younger self might have into tough ground. Piercing wards on the tines tore through the demon's belly.

Younger Grovers were growing overconfident as the night strength took them, stepping into active combat. Ragen might have called them brave, but he knew it was a mix of fear, adrenaline, and demon magic. A mixture that could get folk killed if they weren't strong enough to master it.

A shock wave of magic knocked over a group of defenders. None was seriously injured, but as they struggled back to their feet a few of them stiffened, then began turning weapons on their fellows. Mountain Spears, mostly, firing flamework at Messengers on horseback, but regular folk as well began to turn rakes and hoes on people they had known all their lives.

Ragen could see the victims had lost the warded headgear that protected their minds. He scanned the area, but there was no sign of a mind demon. Just looking made him dizzy . . . confused.

He shook himself, raising his stylus and drawing wards to summon a wind aimed at the powdered limestone that had been shoveled into the furrows of the now inert greatward. The wind kicked up a cloud of dust, and there in the middle of it was a humanoid shape, no larger than a young man, with a bulbous, conical head.

"Mind demon!" he boomed, and drew a lectric ward, powering it with as much of his stylus' reserve as he dared.

The bolt of lightning struck the demon dead center. The mind was knocked onto its back, the distortion field around it falling. Derek and three other Warders joined the bombardment, but a field demon scampered forward, growing with every stride. Its scales thickened into the hard carapace of a rock demon as it stood over its master and took the blows while it recovered.

"Concentrate fire!" Ragen shouted. Arrows and crank bow bolts gave the mimic a hedgehog's spine as Warders drew freezing wards. Bullets from the Mountain Spears sent cracks spiderwebbing through the frozen armor.

Ragen emptied his stylus with one last impact ward, shattering the tortoise shell the mimic had formed, but by then it was too late. The ruin of the mimic revealed no sign of its master.

The mind had fled the field.

The change was immediately apparent in the demons—tactics shifting back to animal ferocity over organized assault, even as their resistance to Keerin and his players waned.

The Jongleurs cast an air of confusion over the compromised fields, and Yon, Malcum, and Woron were quick to capitalize on it, surging beyond the protection of the great-wards in brief sallies that left the vulnerable demons crippled or killed.

The move bought them time, but it was not enough. Before long the mind recovered, and organization returned to the enemy ranks. Another hour, and they were forced to fall back to fortify the inner wall.

Derek found him as he passed through the gate. "I sent the Warders to rest. They can't take much more of this." He held up his stylus in shaking fingers. "Neither can we."

Ragen nodded. He, too, was feeling the burn of channeling too much magic. He pulled out his watch. Another hour and the sky would begin to lighten, sending the minds fleeing. Two, and even the boldest demons would begin to dissipate.

"Hold the wall!" he shouted, drawing wards to echo his words throughout the town as he raced back to the front. "Dawn is coming! Stand fast for your homes, for your families, and we will all see the sun!"

"Rock!" one of the guards cried. Ragen ran up the stairs to the walltop, seeing the rock demon readying a throw. He raised his stylus, but a wave of dizziness overtook him and he mangled the warding. The stone smashed into the gate, bending steel and shattering one of the hinges. The gate hung partially suspended, crumpled on one side.

Mountain Spears opened fire as corelings rushed the gap in the wards, but they would not hold for long.

"To the gate!" Ragen cried. He shoved the stylus into a pocket beneath his armor as Twilight Dancer was brought forward with his spear and shield.

Keerin and his apprentices appeared, but the rushing demons were not deterred by their music. They struck the weakened gate, tearing it from its remaining hinges under their combined weight.

They switched instead to another tune, this one peppered with jarring, discordant notes that left the demons off balance as the defenders charged.

Ragen lost track of time as the battle wore on. More breaches opened in the wall, and he raced Twilight Dancer from one to the next, rallying the men.

The sky was beginning to lighten when they were forced to abandon the wall and retreat to the town square where the wards still held. The Jongleurs' music was overwhelming in the small space, and the demons, funneled between warded buildings, were easy targets.

But then a stone demon grabbed a piece of rubble and threw, hitting Ragen squarely in the chest. His armor held proof against the blow, but he was thrown from Twilight Dancer's back, and felt his shoulder pop from the socket as he hit the ground.

His ears were ringing as he struggled to rise, the great war-horse rearing protectively over him. But then, through it all, he heard a sound more beautiful than anything he could have imagined.

A rooster crowed.

Dawn had come.

Ragen bit down hard on leather, thrashing in Malcum and Derek's grip as Yon gave a sharp pull and twist, popping his shoulder back into its socket.

Ragen spat out the wadded glove, tasting oil and sweat, blood and ichor. "Night, Yon! How long ago was your Gatherer's training?"

Yon shrugged. "Never had *trainin'*. House full of boys learns ya a thing or two about bones."

"Creator," Ragen groaned.

"And you're lucky to have him," Malcum said. "The Grove's Gatherer and her apprentices are a little busy at the moment."

"How soon can we be on the road?" Ragen asked. "There isn't a moment to spare." A Messenger on horseback could leave the Grove at dawn and reach Miln in time for a late lunch, but the Grovers were exhausted, battered, and mostly afoot. They would be lucky to reach the city by nightfall.

"We're loading the wounded onto carts now," Malcum said. "Think you can ride?"

Ragen nodded. "I'll manage."

"Good man," Malcum said. "That monstrous stallion of yours looks strong as ever. If you set a hard pace, you can get back . . ."

"No," Ragen said. "I won't leave these people on the road without me. Twilight Dancer isn't the only stallion charged from trampling demons on warded hooves. Set a pair of Messengers to take the road at a gallop. One to the duke, and one straight to Elissa. Tell them we're abandoning Harden's Grove."

Ragen led the ragged procession up the road, carrying little more than water and the clothes on their backs. Behind them, the town that had been their home for generations lay trampled, broken, and burning.

Children too young and elderly too slow to keep the pace clung where they could to carts carrying the wounded. Ragen pushed the folk as fast as they could go, but still twilight had fallen before they had a clear look at the city.

The walls of Miln still stood, but they were battered, with rubble strewn about the base. Warders hung on harnesses from the walltop, repairing damaged symbols. The air stank of corelings left to burn in the sun.

In the distance, Ragen heard the Evening Bell. He turned back to the weary refugees. "Double-time now. They aren't going to keep the gates open for any that aren't in the city by dusk!"

"Gates closing!" the wall guard cried down as Ragen rode into the city at the head of the Grovers.

"You close it on these people, and I'll pitch you right over the side!" Ragen shouted back. The Grovers were pouring through the gate, but the weary column still stretched down the road. The sky was darkening fast.

"Euchor's orders, Neocount," the guard said.

Ragen spat. The slowest and most vulnerable were in the back, but with the bottleneck at the gate, there was no getting back out to help astride Twilight Dancer. He forgot himself as he swung from the saddle, and his injured arm exploded with pain, losing its grip.

Yon caught him with one giant arm. "Easy, now."

"Get the Grovers back to my manse," he told Derek and

Yon. "It will be cramped, but we can hold them all for the night and figure things out in the morning."

"Where ya think yur goin'?" Yon asked.

"Back out to help," Ragen said.

"Gonna make much difference with that arm?" Yon asked.

"Maybe not," Ragen said, "but seeing the Neocount of Morning outside might make the guards think twice about shutting the gates with folk still coming in."

Ragen forced his way through the press to the gate. The guards tried to bar his way, but Yon was there, shoving them aside like children.

There was panic outside among the Grovers. The mounted troops, Malcum's Messengers, Derek's Warders, and Woron's Mountain Spears had ridden through first, carrying as many of the women and children as they could manage. The carts, overloaded with few designed for a long journey, moved at a crawl. One poor mare, pulling a cart of wounded alone, had collapsed, holding up the line.

Yon cut the harnesses, sparing a moment to mercifully drop his axe on the poor beast's head. Then he wrapped the straps around his chest and, incredibly, began to pull the cart himself.

Ragen moved along the line, hurrying folk as best he could. A graybeard was lying on the road, a boy no more than six pulling at him, begging him to rise.

"Go on," the man told the boy. "Find your mother and sisters inside."

"That won't do, Graybeard," Ragen said. "We're not leaving anyone behind."

"Ankle's twisted," the old man said. "Get my grandson inside, I beg."

Ragen frowned, looking at the boy. He didn't trust his arm to carry him and hold the old man. He squatted, shifting his accent to speak like a Grover. "Up my back, boy. Quick as a squirrel, now."

"Ent leavin' Gramp!" the boy shouted.

"Neither am I, but we'll all get et you don't mind me!" Ragen barked. The boy jumped and scampered up his back. Ragen put his good arm under the old man's armpit.

"Don't think I—" the graybeard began.

"Shut it and get up," Ragen cut him off with the same tone he used on the boy. It worked equally well with the old man, and with a grunt Ragen stood, lifting them both.

"Ay!" the old man cried, wincing as he took a step.

"Collapse when we're inside," Ragen said. Others were rushing to help, but the sun was below the horizon now. Any moment the rising would begin. He looked at the gate, but his men, even Woron and the Mountain Spears, were blocking it open as the last of them limped forward.

Mist began to seep from the ground, gathering. "Run!" Ragen cried, sheer terror bringing new strength to his failing limbs. He broke into an awkward lope, half dragging the man until Cal and Nona Cutter reached him. Cal plucked the boy from his back, and Nona threw the old man over one shoulder like a bag of apples.

The wall guards were blaring horns and struggling to close the gates. Ragen spared a glance back as he ran—the smaller corelings were fully formed now, field and flame demons racing for the open gates. He pulled the stylus from the hidden pocket in his armor and stopped running just long enough to draw a quick series of wards in the air.

It was his first warding of the night, but already the magic was like boiling water across his skin. He grit his teeth and powered the wards fully, knowing their lives depended on it.

The demons slammed against the barrier like a brick wall. It wouldn't hold, but it bought enough time to get the last of the Grovers inside and slam the gates shut behind them.

Ragen sent the others ahead and climbed the wall with Woron, Gaims, and Yon. The view from the top was grim. Rock demons were fully formed now, searching the rubble for stones large enough to throw. The wards strengthened the stone walls, but their strength was not limitless. Sufficient bombardment would erode the protection.

The Mountain Spears didn't give them the chance. Approaching within throwing distance put the corelings in range of the heavy cannons on the wall. The iron cannonballs had been cast with wards, and Ragen watched one punch through the chest of a rock demon and put it on its back. The creature still glowed in wardsight, but its aura went flat—dead.

Ragen looked at the stockpiles of ammunition. The piles

were not high, and many of the balls were battered and scorched, obviously recovered from the previous night's battle.

Another rock demon drew an arm back to throw, but the cannon team aimed hurriedly and missed their shot. Ragen waited until the demon was mid-throw, then drew a careful impact ward, powering it just enough to knock the stone from its talons. Still, the power jolted him like a punch to the stomach.

The demon stumbled, then turned to retrieve the missile, giving the next cannon team plenty of time to put twelve pounds of warded iron into its back.

Still the demons massed, rising in numbers that dwarfed those sent to crush Harden's Grove. Ragen turned to Yon. "Back to the manse."

Twilight Dancer and Yon's giant mustang easily caught up to the refugees. Corelings could not rise through worked stone, and wards on the rooftops formed an effective net against wind demons. They should have been safe on the cobbled streets, but horns began to sound from all sides.

"What's goin' on?" Yon asked.

"Demons in the city," Ragen said.

"How can that be?" Gaims asked. "We were just on the wall, and it was holding."

"I don't know," Ragen said, "but keep your men at the ready."

Woron nodded, shouting commands. His men were as exhausted as the Grovers—their ammunition spent. It would be bayonets and muscle, if they encountered resistance.

More and more horns sounded, flashes of light here and there as demons tested the wards of individual homes and buildings.

"What in the dark of night . . ." Ragen did not have a chance to finish the sentence as the street in front of them caved in. Grovers and soldiers tumbled down with cobbles, mortar, and dirt. Ragen, Yon, and Woron pulled up just in time, horses rearing to avoid the pitfall.

Corelings swarmed inside the hole, falling on the unfortunate folk and tearing them to pieces.

"They're in the old sewer system!" Ragen cried.

"Aren't they sealed and warded?" Woron asked.

"Ay," Ragen said. "After the last time the demons tried this trick. Either Euchor's been skimping on maintenance, or the mind demons found a way around the defenses."

Derek and Malcum were across the divide with the bulk of the refugees. "Keep moving!" Ragen called. "We'll catch up!"

Demons began to emerge from the sinkhole, and Ragen pulled hard on Dancer's reins, cutting down a side street to circle around and catch Derek's group. There was a sinkhole on the next street as well, corelings pouring out of it.

Ragen wrapped the reins around the wrist of his injured arm, trusting in Dancer to respond to his legs. He pulled his stylus and drew wards to create a temporary seal across the top of the sinkhole. The effort made him woozy, but he kicked Twilight Dancer and the stallion leapt ahead, trampling a pair of field demons from their path with his warded hooves.

Demons were attempting to breach the wards on individual buildings, but Ragen's guild had done their work well. Without the rock and wood demons—too large to enter through the sewers—to batter through walls and doors, the lesser demons were stymied.

It was scant relief, for the corelings quickly realized the futility and went after easier prey—the refugees racing up the hill toward what Ragen prayed was the safety of his walls.

There was no sign of a mind, at least. The demons hunted with animal frenzy, not cold calculation. The coreling princes seemed reluctant to risk themselves while so many of the city's defenses remained intact.

A squad of Mountain Spears appeared, firing their flamework weapons in staggered bursts to give their fellows time to reload. Their unwarded rounds tore through the demons, killing a few, but most corelings were more angered than injured. These men had not been tested against the corelings as Woron's shooters had. They wasted shots on non-vital areas, and more than a few of them hit refugees with stray fire.

"Head shots and center mass!" Woron cried. He signaled his own men to skewer injured demons with their bayonets before they could heal and rise again.

But the flamework had driven the demons into a frenzy, and the Mountain Spears were unprepared for their savagery. The soldiers wore helmets, but their flamework weapons made conventional armor obsolete. Their blue-and-gray uniforms turned red with blood.

Field and flame demons ran up walls, spitting fire and leaping into the midst of a squad of soldiers. The men had no time to affix bayonets, and screamed as they were clawed and bitten. One man had his entire leg torn off; another was set ablaze, the intense heat of demonfire setting off the ammunition on his bandolier. They were thrown apart, landing bloodied on the ground, but while the flame demon shook it off and got back to its feet, the soldier did not.

Ragen spared a moment to draw a moisture ward and send it flying at the demon. The magic made his head spin and his stomach roil, but it was worth the pain when the demon's scales started to hiss and cloud as the magic drew water from the surrounding air. Ragen kicked his horse, riding off as the demon began to writhe and shriek.

They raced through the streets, circling back to the route Derek was leading the refugees along. They spotted mounted Messengers herding folk together, leading the Grovers around the worst of the collapsed streets. Keerin covered them as best he could with a shield of music. Many of the adjacent buildings were damaged, and the demons took full advantage of the weakened wards.

A man and a woman ran screaming from one of the buildings, each carrying a small child. At their heels ran a reap of slavering field demons.

"Yon!" Ragen cried.

"On it!" Yon called, kicking his horse. Cal and Lary followed, and the three Cutters chopped through the reap, giving the family time to join the refugees.

And so it went, until at last Ragen's manse was in sight. Demons clawed at the walls, but were thrown back again and again by the powerful wards. Even from the back of the procession, Ragen could see Elissa on the walltop, glowing bright with magic as she drew bright silver wards in the air with her stylus, breaking the coreling ranks and clearing a path for them.

The gates opened, and Ragen's Servants came pouring out with long warded spears. They kept the formation defensive, driving demons back with jabs of the spears to clear the way for the refugees to flow into the courtyard.

The Grovers, Messengers, Warders, and soldiers filled almost every inch of the space inside the walls, but as the gates clanged shut behind them, they were finally safe.

Ragen allowed himself to fall from his horse.

"They're still coming!" one of the wall guards called.

Ragen tried to shake off the blackness and push himself up, but Elissa, drawing wards to mend his arm, pushed him back down.

"No time to baby me, Liss," Ragen said. "I've got . . ."

"You've got to rest or you're no good to anyone."

Much as he hated to admit it, Elissa's words were true. The yard was spinning, and his muscles were aflame from channeling so much magic. Still, Ragen resisted. "The wards may not hold against so many. If they collapse a street outside . . ."

Elissa shoved him down hard. She was flush with magic, handling him like a child. "I'll handle it."

She called for Margrit. "Linens. All of them. The whiter the better."

Margrit didn't question the strange request, though Ragen could not see what good they might do.

Elissa drew a sound ward with her stylus, amplifying her voice a hundredfold. "Everyone look at your feet! Do not straddle the painted lines on the ground! If you are inside a painted section, put your hands in the air! If not, sit on the ground!"

The terrified fold did not question the commands, and quickly the greatwards painted on the cobbles took shape again. Elissa and the Warders roamed the yard, pushing and shoving folk into position.

The ward was already beginning to flicker to life when the Servants filtered out of the manse carrying white linens.

"Those standing, take linens and hold them overhead!" Elissa cried.

With that, the greatward quickly flared, Drawing ambient power and brightening the auras of everyone along its lines.

Fatigue washed away from them, and they straightened, sharpening the lines further.

Outside, the demons howled as the magic brightened, then were driven back by the forbidding until they fled into the city in search of easier prey.

CHAPTER 32

BLIZZARD
AND QUAKE

334 AR

Again Ragen was pulled from darkness, this time with a gentle shake. He opened his eyes to see Elissa, bathed in dawn light. He smiled despite the pounding in his head.

"How long?"

"You've been asleep all night, love." Elissa reached out and stroked his beard. "I wish you could stay that way, but we've been summoned to court."

Ragen's muscles were still stiff and sore, but he managed to roll out of bed and push himself up onto his feet. He still wore the padded jerkin and leathers from beneath his armor, stinking of sweat and blood.

"Do I have time for a bath?"

"There's no water, I'm afraid," Elissa said. "The Grovers have already eaten the larder bare and drunk the wells dry."

"There was nowhere else to go, Liss."

Elissa put a soft hand on his cheek, kissing him. "Of course not. You did the right thing, but we can't succor so many without aid."

"We can do another night if we must," Ragen said, "even if we all do without food, water, and baths."

Elissa nodded, gesturing to a small tray by the door. "Margrit did manage to set aside something for us. Eat."

Ragen set himself in front of the tray, drinking right from

the pitcher and shoving bread into his mouth. He turned as Elissa headed for the door. "Where are you going?"

"Euchor has ordered the Mothers' Council to gather apart from his court," Elissa said, "so they will not be trapped in one place come nightfall."

"Where?" Ragen asked.

"Count Brayan's manse."

Derek was waiting in the courtyard of Euchor's keep with Malcum when Ragen and Yon arrived.

"They won't even let me in to see her," Derek growled. "My own ripping wife! My own corespawned son! Brayan's got his keep locked tighter than Mother Jone's arse."

Ragen and Malcum looked around, but it seemed no one heard. Ragen leaned in as Yon and Malcum blocked them from view. "Keep your voice down. I know you're worried about your family. I would be, too. But there's nothing we can do about it right now. Brayan's walls are some of the strongest in Miln. Stasy is as safe there as anywhere, and Elissa is on her way there even now to meet the Mothers' Council. She'll find Stasy and ensure she and Jef are well."

Derek scowled, but he kept his mouth closed and gave a tight nod. Ragen clapped him on the shoulder.

Uncharacteristically, Euchor left the throne room empty, receiving only the most powerful lords and guildmasters from the head of his small council table.

"Neocount," the duke grunted as Ragen and Derek took seats. "You can have your . . . assistant wait outside."

"I've appointed Derek vice guildmaster," Ragen said. "He'll be coordinating Warders throughout the city today. It's best he receives your commands directly."

"Now, just a minute!" Vincin said. "You can't—!"

"I can and I have." Ragen produced a scroll full of signatures. "Since you've refused to call a meeting of the guild, the masters voted without you. I've been reinstated as master of the Warders' Guild."

Vincin turned to Euchor. "Your Grace! This man should be in irons, not commanding the defense! The guards say he nearly let corelings in the gate last night!"

"And where were you last night?" Ragen asked. "Locked tight in your manse while I fought demons on the street?"

"Enough!" Euchor banged his bracer. "The guild voted, Vincin. I don't want to see that oily goatee twitch again unless your guildmaster commands it."

Vincin's face fell slack. Ragen knew he should relish the look, but he took no pleasure in it. They would need every Warder in the city unified today if they were to survive.

"Vincin does have a point, Ragen," Euchor said. "Your heroics put us all at risk last night for a handful of peasants."

"Seven hundred souls, including Warders, Messengers, and Your Grace's own Mountain Spears," Ragen said. "And what does it matter, when the demons came in through the sewers?"

Count Brayan opened his mouth but Euchor gave a wave, silencing him. "A problem for another day, as you say. This . . . Waning will continue tonight?"

"At least," Ragen said. "The mind demons may only rise during new moon, but their generals, the mimics, do not seem so bound. They will attack where we are weakest, and continue to erode the defenses. Even if Miln does not fall this moon, we may not make it to the next."

Euchor sat back, steepling his hands. "Can we collapse the sewers? Block them from getting in that way again?"

"In the inner city, perhaps," Brayan said. "But it would deplete flamework we need for cannons."

"The explosions would weaken the wards on the walls and foundations of the buildings," Ragen said, "and it won't work in any event. Rock demons may not be able to fit in the tunnels, but clay and stone demons can. They can burrow through rubble like voles in a garden."

"What, then?" Euchor demanded. "We can't just leave them access into the city."

"Of course not," Ragen agreed. "We'll need to send men down into the dark to put in fresh wards. I sent word to my workshops to make stencils and collect every drop of paint in the city. We've a limited supply of *hora* collected from the bodies of demons before the sun burned them away. It should help reinforce the forbiddings and form a seal."

"Will it be enough?" Euchor asked.

Ragen shrugged. "The Warders who first sealed the tunnels did their work well. Hopefully we can shore up the weaknesses and seal off the fresh breaches. The greater concern is whether the tunnels are empty."

Euchor paled. "What do you mean, empty?"

"Many of the sewer passages have not seen daylight in a hundred years," Ragen said. "Who can say how long the demons have been planning this, or if they have fled to the Core for the day or linger just beneath the surface?"

"Night," Euchor said. "If they're infested . . ."

"We can use mirrors," Malcum said.

"Eh?" Euchor asked.

"An old Messenger trick," Ragen said. "Reflect light into the tunnels to drive them back."

"That will take every mirror in the city," Brayan said.

"And then some," Ragen said. "We'll need Mountain Spears as well, to provide an armed guard for the Warders."

"I need those men to hold the wall," Euchor said.

"They held the wall last night," Ragen said, "but there were still demons in the streets. We'll need to evacuate as many as possible. Not just to the inner city, but to the strongest-walled manses and keeps. Here. My manse. Count Brayan's and Countess Tresha's fortresses, the Library."

"I'll be corespawned before I have Beggars in my Library and walls, Neocount," Euchor said.

"We can bar the Library doors, Your Grace," Ronnell said. "The stone Guardians will keep the corespawn from the hilltop. Should they breach, we can shelter in the Cathedral. If we need to flee to the Library . . ." He shrugged. "Fingerprints on the pages will be the least of our worries."

"We have less than sixty thousand in the entire city, Your Grace," Ragen pressed, when Euchor did not respond. "The able-bodied should be armed with whatever's to hand. There's no reason the rest can't squeeze behind the walls of the royal keeps and manses for a night."

"Fine, fine." Euchor turned to his page. "Send a runner to Jone. She's to organize the evacuation of the lower city. Everyone with a private wardwall is to take in as many as they can hold. No exceptions."

"Your Grace . . ." Brayan began.

Euchor turned an angry glare his way. "Was there a *yes* before that, Count?"

Brayan drew back and blinked, but he was quick to recover and bow. "Of course, Your Grace. It will be done."

"I won't yield the walls without a fight," Euchor said. "My family has guarded this city against the corelings for three hundred years. I won't cede it in a single moon."

"This is an outrage," Tresha groused as their carriage climbed the great hill through the capital of Gold County. At the top, across a wide chasm, sat Count Brayan's keep. "My walls are every bit as strong as Brayan's. What right does Jone . . ."

"What does it matter, Mother?" Elissa snapped. "This isn't the moment for politics."

Tresha looked down her nose. "Don't make me regret naming you my heir, girl. It's always the moment for politics, times of trouble most of all."

"Then let's start with freeing Mother Stasy and her son," Elissa said. "They belong with Derek behind my walls."

"Your walls barely held last night, by all accounts." Tresha pointed to the thick walls of Brayan's keep, sitting on a bluff with great wards carved into the living rock. A single arching bridge of crete and steel was the only access point, the supports forming the lines of a powerful warding. "They're safer there for now."

"I pray you're right," Elissa said. "Are your Warders—"

"Thrice checking the sewers and laying paint all over my beautiful courtyards and gardens," Tresha cut in.

"They'll still be beautiful," Elissa said, "once you've laid gravel paths through the lawns to hold the shape of the great-wards."

"They'd best be," Tresha said. "There's enough stone in this ripping city already. The gardens were my last escape."

"We all make sacrifices in war." Elissa looked out over the chasm as they crossed the bridge.

The keep gates were open, and they were greeted in the courtyard by Servants in Count Brayan's livery. Tresha and Elissa were immediately escorted into the meeting room where the other Mothers waited.

Mothers Jone and Cera moved to greet them, but Elissa spotted Stasy across the room and slipped around the other women to intercept her. It was a snub—one all three of the elder women would likely make her pay for—but it was worth it to catch the young woman alone.

"Elissa!" Stasy cried, throwing arms around her.

"It's good to see you, dear," Elissa said, squeezing warmly. In happier days when Derek worked in Cob's warding shop, they had been frequent companions. Even out of favor with her mother, Elissa's breeding had been enough for the two women to spend time as equals without causing a scandal. "Have you been treated well? Derek is beside himself with worry."

Stasy sighed. "They've treated me no differently than before, save now I cannot cross the bridge."

"And it is your wish to leave?" Elissa asked. "To take young Jef and come to live with Derek?"

"Oh, Mother Elissa, you know it is," Stasy said. "It's all I've ever wanted, if Father and Cousin Brayan would only allow it."

"I know, dear, but I needed to hear you say it aloud." Elissa squeezed her shoulder, noticing Mother Cera gliding swiftly their way with Jone and Tresha at her heels. "We can fix things now. Derek has been appointed vice guildmaster in addition to his seat on the Warding Exchange."

"I couldn't believe it when Derek told me Arlen Bales left him a seat," Stasy said. "That man's been looking out for us since the beginning, all for the price of a few thundersticks."

"Arlen's loyalty isn't a thing you can buy," Elissa said. "The two of you earned it." Cera was nearly upon them. "Will you swear your desire to leave before the council with your aunt looking on? They've been using you as a check on Ragen's power, and won't let you go easily."

"I'll shout it from the towers, if need be," Stasy said, but her voice had dropped to a whisper as her royal cousin came within earshot.

"There you are, dear," Mother Cera said, laying a firm hand on Stasy's shoulder. "Perhaps it's time you were getting back to your chambers. The Mothers' Council is about to be called to order."

Elissa bared her teeth at the woman, but it was in her most innocent smile. "Mother Stasy is a baron's daughter, and has a right to a vote on the council." Her voice was not loud, but it carried for other women to hear.

"Of course she can stay," Tresha cut in quickly. "Every voice must be heard today."

Cera's eye twitched, but she was trapped and she knew it. It might be her house, but Tresha led the council. Elissa knew better than to press the advantage—yet—but she kept Stasy close as the council gathered and was called to order.

Hours passed as they studied reports of losses in the night, organizing evacuations and supply. They moved money and resources without the usual rancor and debate. Notes were written to allow the guilds to lend and borrow without interest money that did not exist. A steady stream of runners came and went across the bridge.

The sun was low in the sky when Elissa finally straightened from the papers she had been hunched over, putting a hand to the small of her back to relieve the strain. No doubt the roads were choked. If she wanted to return to the manse, it would need to be soon. She got to her feet but stumbled and lost her balance, sprawling to the floor.

At first she thought her legs must have fallen asleep, but then she saw women on the floor all around the room. The walls rattled, and the air was filled with a tremendous roar.

"What—?!" Elissa's words choked off as she saw Tresha lying unmoving on the floor, blood pooling about her head. "Mother!"

She rushed to Tresha's side, reaching for her silver stylus, but there was nothing she could do while sunlight still streamed in the windows. "Someone fetch a Gatherer! The Countess of Morning needs immediate aid!"

Baroness Cate, looking out the window, screamed. "The bridge collapsed!"

The words barely sank in as Elissa lifted her mother's head back, clearing the passage of air for her weakened breaths. She wadded a kerchief against the bleeding gash on her mother's temple. Tresha's pulse was slow and erratic, but it was there.

"Mother!" she cried. "Mother, can you hear me?"

Tresha's only reply was a groan, and there was no telling if it was a response to the words or the movement and pressure against her wound. Cera ushered her personal Gatherer to attend them while apprentices went among the other Mothers to triage.

"Is she dead?" Cera demanded.

Elissa glared at her as the Gatherer took Tresha's wrist. "Alive, but I wouldn't expect her to be leading the council anytime soon."

"Then it falls to me," Cera said.

Elissa lifted her chin. "I am Tresha's heir."

Cera snorted. "That you may be, child, but you've barely been part of the council a month. You've no authority."

Elissa wanted to argue, but Cera was right. There was nothing to gain in fighting over it.

"A little lower, easy, now." Ragen watched Yon and Cal tilt the heavy silvered mirror to cast sunlight into the sinkhole where another mirror team caught the beam and reflected the light deeper.

"Looks clear!" Derek called.

"You're up," Ragen said to a group of workers waiting with hand mirrors. They looked nervously at one another, then climbed down into the hole, lifting their mirrors to catch the light and send beams into the tunnels. When nothing happened, more men were sent in, angling the light even further. Warders readied their equipment and went in after to begin their work.

And then the screams began.

The workers just inside the hole dropped their heavy mirror and scrambled up to the street, leaving those inside the tunnel in darkness.

Ragen didn't hesitate, his exhaustion lost in a rush of adrenaline as he leapt into the hole, skipping off a chunk of rubble to land beside the mirror. It had an ornate brass frame that protected it when the workers dropped it, but the thing weighed well over two hundred pounds, and he strained to lift it alone.

Cal and Lary Cutter jumped down after him, catching the frame and easily lifting it to catch the light once more.

Bodies littered the tunnel, bleeding in the fetid water. One was clutched in the talons of a demon that burst into flames when the sunlight struck it full-on. There were shrieks as other demons fled the light, and a few workers managed to scramble back out.

"Corespawn it," Ragen cursed. They had found and sealed the tunnels the demons used to get past the walls, but apparently many demons had never left the city, and clearing them from the dark, cramped tunnels seemed an impossible task, even as daylight faded.

"Guildmaster!" a voice cried from above, even as a team of guards braved the tunnel to haul out the survivors, and the bodies.

Ragen climbed from the tunnel, catching Yon's hand. The giant Cutter easily hauled him out of the hole where the runner was waiting.

"Guildmaster!" the boy cried.

"What is it?" The adrenaline was already fading, leaving Ragen even more tired than before. He didn't think he could handle more bad news.

"Trapped?" Derek demanded. "What in the dark of night is that supposed to mean?"

"It looks like the demons tunneled beneath the bridge supports," Ragen said.

Derek punched the heavy desk, but if the blow pained him, it didn't show. "Corespawn it! I should have blown the doors off that ripping place!"

"And left everyone defenseless when the demons came?" Ragen asked. "They wouldn't have knocked out the bridge if they thought they could easily breach the walls. They wanted to cut off the Mothers' leadership."

"Maybe," Derek said. "Or maybe they want to hit the place tonight and don't want help coming."

Ragen grit his teeth. The same thoughts were running through his mind, but he needed to project calm, now more than ever. Night would fall soon, and if the demons could hit Gold County while the sun still shone, then nowhere was truly safe.

"Can't we, I dunno, throw 'em a rope or sumthin'?" Yon asked.

"If you've got a Krasian scorpion handy, perhaps," Ragen said. "Not even you can throw a rope across that chasm, and even if you could, what then? Ask old women to climb a quarter mile hand over hand?"

"Guess not," Yon said. "Can't just sit here, though."

Ragen was silent a long time. The evacuations had only increased the number of souls behind his walls, their blankets bleached and dyed to reinforce the greatwards as they huddled on the grounds. He was the Neocount of Morning now, not Ragen Messenger, not the Warders' Guildmaster. His responsibility was to his people.

But the demons had Elissa trapped.

"No," he agreed at last. "We can't just sit here."

"Was it the demons?" Countess Cera asked as they looked down from the walltop at the ruin of the bridge below. The cloud of dust was still settling over countless tons of shattered crete.

"There were a lot of people running back and forth over that bridge today," Elissa said, "but I don't think we can accept it as coincidence on new moon. We have to assume the minds will come for us tonight. Somehow they knew we were meeting here. They want to take out our leaders to weaken the resistance."

Mother Jone grew pale. "His Grace—"

"Is likely in terrible danger," Elissa cut in. "But we have our own problems." Tresha had been moved to a darkened chamber where Elissa could mend her wound, but she remained unconscious, and there was no telling when—or if—she would wake, or what she would be like when she did. She remembered Mistress Anet's words. Magic by itself was not always enough.

She turned to Countess Cera, tightening her jaw as she spread her skirts and curtsied. "Mother. I apologize for challenging your leadership. This is your home, and the council is yours to speak for until my mother recovers. But I beg of you, allow me to take control of your Warders and the defense preparations. Your household complement is no doubt skilled, but I have practical experience they cannot match."

Cera glanced at Jone, the two women seeming to hold an entire conversation with their eyes. After what seemed an eternity, Cera turned back and gave a brief nod. "What can we do?"

"Gather the Servants and any council members who remember their wardcraft lessons from the Mothers' School," Elissa said. "We'll need ink, paint, every strip of white cloth in the keep, and anything that could be used as a weapon. Broomsticks, fire pokers, rolling pins, whatever you can find." As she spoke, her eyes were running across the walltop wards. The keep was high above the city wardnet, and there were additional wind wards to keep those demons from swooping into the keep at night. An idea began to form—grisly, but perhaps effective.

"What good will broomsticks do against demons?" Jone asked.

"Feedback magic strengthens items," Elissa said. "A broomstick might snap if you strike a man with it, but one with impact wards along its length will be strong as steel while the wards are charged. Anything long enough can be sharpened to a point with piercing wards to hold demons back."

"You expect Mothers to fight hand-to-hand?" Cera was incredulous.

"Let's hope it doesn't come to that," Elissa said, "but hope is in short supply. If they break past the outer defenses, we don't have time to pretend women can't swing their arms to save their own lives. Now, can someone take me down to the cellars?"

Elissa leaned over the wall of Gold Manse to look down the sheer drop as the sun set. Mother Cera, Stasy, and Jone leaned over the crenellations next to her.

In wardsight she could see demons appear on the chasm floor below as soon as the shadows were deep enough, but they did not rise from mist. They poured from fissures in the ground around the collapsed bridge supports.

"They've been in the city all day." The thought made Elissa's chest tighten, and she labored to keep her breathing even.

"Night," Stasy whispered.

"If your adopted son really is the Deliverer, Elissa," Cera said, "now is the time for him to appear."

"I would be happy to be proven wrong, in that regard," Jone agreed.

"I wouldn't count on it," Elissa said.

Still the corelings continued to pour through the fissures, dozens becoming hundreds, until the chasm floor was filled. The demons swarmed the base of the cliff, but the rock face was cut deep with wards that sparked and flared, throwing them back.

Last to climb from the tunnels below were half a dozen full-sized rock demons. These wasted no time snatching up huge chunks of bridge masonry and hurling them at the cliff. They shattered against the rock, weakening the wards, and again the demons swarmed, this time scrabbling at the stone before the wards repelled them.

"We have to stop those rock demons," Elissa said, looking to the house guards manning the nearest of the heavy cannons Brayan and Euchor took such pride in. "Can you shoot them?"

"Begging your pardon, Mother, but no," one of the guards said. "Cannons are meant to take aim across the chasm, not down into it. They'll flip right off the wall if we try to aim that low."

Elissa eyed the sixteen-pound warded iron balls stacked by the wall next to the powder keg. She lifted one of the heavy things and eyed one of the rock demons below. She took a few steps back, then got a running start, pitching it over the side.

Elissa watched the ball drop out of sight, picking up speed as it fell hundreds of feet into the demon ranks. She caught sight of it again when it struck and the wards activated, smashing through a cluster of field demons. She had missed her mark by a fair margin, but the throw was satisfying nevertheless.

She looked to the guard. "Gravity need not be our enemy."

The guard coughed. "Ay, Mother. We'll pass the word."

"None of that is going to stop those rock demons." Jone's voice had an uncharacteristic edge. Fear. Despair. Elissa looked and saw the same on the face of Mother Cera. Stasy. The guards on the wall.

Elissa slipped her silver stylus out of her pocket, looping the chain at the end around her wrist. "I'll handle the rock demons." Her words were loud enough for several cannon teams to hear.

All eyes were on her as Elissa drew a series of wards in glowing silver script that hung in the air. When the final symbol was linked, she opened the nib to feed the spell, aiming at a pair of rock demons.

The line of wards flew like a blade, growing larger and brighter as it went until it cut through the demons like a spike through stone. Their armor shattered, and the pair were thrown down, dead.

"Creator above!" Cera cried.

Elissa's satisfaction was short-lived as a wave of dizziness came over her. She'd used too much power to make sure the demons were killed on the first strike. She teetered, but Stasy caught her belt, pulling firmly back before she pitched over the wall.

"Are you all right?" Stasy kept her voice low.

"I'm fine." Already, the dizziness was fading. Thankfully, only Stasy seemed to notice. The others near them on the wall stared at her, dumbfounded.

From farther off there was pointing and shouting, and Elissa knew word would spread quickly. It was worth the risk, to give the defenders hope, but she could not continue to cast spells like that.

"Back to your stations!" She sketched a ward to amplify her voice, and the men turned their attention below with renewed vigor, lifting heavy iron balls and pitching them into the demon masses.

"Mothers," Elissa said, looking to Jone and Cera. "You've seen all you need to see from the wall. I think it best you head back inside."

The women hesitated a moment, then Cera shook herself and nodded. "Of course. Come along, Stasy." She turned to go.

Elissa caught Stasy's arm. "I'll need the young Mother to assist me, I'm afraid."

Cera looked like she wanted to protest, but she'd just seen

Elissa tear two rock demons in half with her stylus. Jone tugged at her arm, and the two women hurried down from the wall.

Stasy looked out over the edge again. "I don't know whether to thank you, Mother."

"I don't want thanks." Elissa produced a second stylus, plainer than her own, but nevertheless powerful. The Warders' Guild had a template now, and used the pens to great effect in Harden's Grove. "I want your help. You're the only person in this keep I trust with one of these."

Stasy started to reach for the pen, then drew her hand back, rubbing her fingers together. "It's been a long time since I worked in Master Cob's warding shop."

"I'm sure you recall the basics, dear." Elissa pressed the stylus into Stasy's hand, meeting her eyes. "Everyone in this keep is going to die if we don't stop those rock demons. I need you. The Mothers need you. Your *son* needs you."

Stasy nodded. "Ay, Mother. How does it work?"

Elissa quickly showed her the wards to open the nib, and how to adjust the flow of power. "Try something simple."

"An impact ward?" Stasy asked, eyeing a rock demon illuminated in the wardlight.

"I think not, until you've practiced more." Elissa eyed a guard as he pitched an iron cannonball over the wall, and had a thought. She chose the nearest rock demon to the throw and drew a magnetic ward.

They lost sight of the projectile, but then it flared with magic, yanked from its natural trajectory to smash the rock demon in the chest. The demon staggered back, alive but not unscathed.

Stasy nodded, drawing a magnetic ward of her own. She fed it too much power, and from along the wall half a dozen cannonballs were drawn to a single demon, bashing it to death. Elissa readied herself to catch the young woman, but she did not seem harmed by the spell.

"Oh, to be twenty-five again." Elissa sighed.

"What's that, Mother?" Stasy asked.

"Nothing. Come along, dear."

They walked the wall aiming shots for the guards, but for every rock demon they put down, more appeared. Little by little, the corelings were gaining ground, slowly scaling the cliff. Soon they would reach the keep walls in numbers that threatened to overwhelm the wardnet.

"Wind demons!" one of the lookouts cried.

The flight of demons swooped from the sky carrying smaller bits of masonry to rain down upon the defenses. A few smashed against the battlements, or knocked guards from the wall. The lucky ones fell twenty feet to land on the hard courtyard cobbles. The unlucky ones fell to the demons.

The deaths were incidental, Elissa noted. "Creator. They're aiming at the wards! Shoot them!"

Guards raised mountain spears, and the flamework weapons went off like festival crackers, tearing through the wind demons. Corelings soaring with grace and ease suddenly yarped and spasmed, some dropping their stones prematurely, others losing altitude and crashing into the keep's wardnet.

Just a few hours before, wind wards had formed a barrier that would have left a dead demon lying in midair atop the wardnet until the sun burned it away. A live demon would have skittered off, pained and angered but relatively unharmed.

Elissa had since added cutting wards to the net. When the wind demons struck the forbidding, they were sliced to pieces. Ichor, leathery bits of wing, and still-twitching chunks of flesh rained down upon the courtyard, sending shimmers of power through the crude greatwards painted on the cobbles.

A demon caught sight of Elissa, veering from its course to focus on her, a heavy stone in its talons. She raised her stylus and drew an impact ward, keeping it small, like the head of a hammer. It smashed into the thin shoulder joint of the coreling's left wing, and the wind demon lost control of its flight, flapping awkwardly before the wardnet tore it apart.

Guards in the courtyard rushed out with warded halberds to finish off anything still kicking. These were followed by Warders who spread the remains to power the greatwards evenly, and harvested *hora* to power wardings of their own. It was grisly work for men and women used to ink and carving tools, and the sour stink of vomit mixed with the stench of demon ichor in the air. Elissa wet a scarf and pulled it over her nose and mouth, but her own stomach roiled.

Buckets of demon guts and ichor were collected and carried to the cellars to strengthen the sewer wards. If the demons had been able to knock out the bridge supports, it was likely they were already in the tunnels below the keep, looking to break through.

The demons' progress on the cliff was steady, if not quick. Even the mighty rock demons couldn't throw stones the full height of the cliff. They began to climb, tearing chunks one-handed from the rock face and hurling them upward. It was slower work, but only a matter of time before they reached the top of the cliff and began to assault the walls.

Elissa looked to a cannon team, their store of ammunition rapidly diminishing. "Pitch the powder keg over the wall."

"Flame powder don't work like that, Mother," one of the guards said. "Won't go off."

Elissa raised her stylus. "I think I can encourage it."

The guard grinned, and he and his men heaved the barrel up and over the side. Elissa watched it fall, then drew a heat ward just before it fell from sight. The keg exploded, knocking demons from their purchase to plummet to the chasm below. Corelings could recover from enormous damage, but Elissa doubted even they could survive a fall from such height.

The defenders cheered, daring to hope once more, but then there was a rumbling like a quake and part of the courtyard collapsed. Demons, unable to reach the wall, had tunneled beneath it. Greatwards crumbled in huge sections of the yard, their power winking out.

"Breach!" Elissa felt the wall teetering beneath her as the foundation crumbled. Soldiers and Warders were rushing for the stairs, but whether by luck or design, Elissa and Stasy were far from an exit as their section of wall began to tip toward the chasm.

Elissa froze, but Stasy kept her head, drawing wind wards in front of them as she grabbed Elissa and pushed both of them off the wall into the courtyard.

Stasy's wards activated, cushioning their fall, but still they struck the cobbles hard, breath knocked out of them. Elissa would be a mass of bruises by morning, if she lived that long.

She would have lost her stylus if not for the chain about her wrist. She caught it again and Drew just a little, restoring her strength.

A pair of stone demons were pulling themselves from the foundation of the broken section of wall. These were followed not by field or flame demons, as Elissa might have expected, but something she had only heard of in stories.

Snow demons, their white scales scintillating in the ward-light, came in a blizzard. Elissa raised her stylus to draw heat wards, but the demons ignored her and the other defenders, running to hawk coldspit onto undamaged sections of wall. The crete turned white with hoarfrost even as Elissa began burning the demons alive.

Guards armed with flamework weapons formed firing lines, and many of the snow demons yelped and dropped to the ground, but the damage was done. The stone demons ignored flamework and heat wards alike as they charged the wall, hammering the frozen stone with blows that shook the entire keep.

Blizzards and quakes, Arlen said. The words proved prophetic as the stone demons smashed through the walls, opening the courtyard to the night. Corelings shrieked as they came streaming through the gap.

"Back to the manse!" Elissa used magic to strengthen her voice, but she needn't have bothered. The few soldiers who managed to reload laid down fire as their fellows stampeded through the courtyard to enter the house proper.

It was chaos like Elissa had never seen as the nimble snow demons set upon the fleeing men and women.

"Keep to the greatwards!" Elissa boomed. Indeed, the wards still glowed in sections of the yard, and demons chasing those who reached their succor were swatted away.

Elissa and Stasy were not so fortunate, having landed on a section of the damaged cobbles.

Stasy caught movement out of the corner of her eye and turned just in time to draw an impact ward and knock away a wind demon that soared through the gap in the wardnet. It would only be moments before others took similar advantage.

A group of snow demons turned in unison, black eyes fixed on Elissa. She drew a heat ward at them, but the demons scattered, converging on them from several angles.

"Run!" Elissa lifted her skirts with her free hand, and she and Stasy ran for the manse doors. The demons were faster, but they drew snow wards, knocking them from their path. It looked as if they would reach the house when a stone demon stepped into their path.

They pulled up short, raising styluses, but at that moment one of the pursuing snow demons hawked coldspit, striking Elissa across the legs. She screamed, falling to the cobbles, the limbs burning with pain unlike anything she had ever known.

"Elissa!" Stasy screamed.

"Run!" Elissa struggled to one hand, raising her stylus to draw a shaky heat ward that scorched her own face even as it burned the nearest snow demons.

"Like night I will!" Stasy held the stone demon off with a quick ward of protection and ducked to throw Elissa's free arm over her shoulder. She heaved, and managed to get them both to their feet. One of Elissa's legs burned but held her weight. The other was numb, and managed little more than a jolting limp.

They stumbled onto one of the greatwards, but the stone demon tore free a cobble and threw it their way. Stasy turned, swinging Elissa in her haste, but she wasn't quick enough to stop the projectile. It smashed into her chest, knocking her and Elissa both to the ground.

"Stasy!" Elissa drew an impact ward, using much of her remaining magic to power it. The stone demon was knocked onto its back, armor spiderwebbed with cracks.

Elissa felt for a pulse. Half the woman's chest was caved in, her face red with blood.

There were screams all around them, men, women, and demons dying, but many of the injured corelings were already recovering. They scratched at the forbidding of the greatward, talons trailing silver light as they search for the gaps in the protection. Not far off, Elissa saw the other stone demon pick up a piece of rubble and take aim at her.

All around the courtyard, demons were turning her way.

She felt hundreds of eyes on her, and knew a mind must be close.

With a wail of anguish, Elissa pushed herself to her feet. One leg shook and the other was little more than a peg to balance against. She threw an impact ward to knock away the demon's missile and limped for the manse doors.

A pair of guards reached her, ducking under her shoulders and lifting her right off her feet as they ran for the house.

Demons charged, but the greatwards were only growing in power, feeding the wards on the manse walls. They were flaring brightly now, pulling power from the swarming demons. A rock demon threw a hunk of masonry at the manse, but the ward flared and it shattered, leaving the wall intact.

The greatwards had reached critical mass with so many demons to Draw upon, fields overlapping one another around the manse. The demons tried to surge through, but it only made the forbidding stronger. They pressed up against the magic like children putting their faces against glass as guards fired cannons and flamework weapons from the manse roof, turning the courtyard into a kill zone.

"Quickly now!" Mother Cera herself was at the door, holding a spear in one hand and stretching the other toward Elissa. She was pulled inside, and the doors slammed shut behind her.

Elissa was dimly aware of being dragged to a couch. She was wrapped in blankets in front of a roaring fire, but couldn't seem to stop shivering and sobbing. Stasy's crushed breast was frozen in her mind's eye.

A cup was pushed into her hands and she drank, ignoring the burn of the hot tea on her throat. She lay there shaking as the Gatherer lifted her dress, but she felt nothing.

"Night," the Gatherer gasped.

And then the tea took hold, and Elissa let her eyes close, welcoming oblivion.

It was still night when Elissa was started awake. She was bathed in sweat, head pounding, throat dry. Every movement brought burning pain. Outside, the bombardment continued.

"What time is it?"

"She's awake!" someone cried. "Fetch Mother Jone!"

Elissa shook herself, trying and failing to sit up. She pulled the arm of the couch until her head was raised when the Gatherer came to her. "Easy, Countess."

Countess? The word struck her. Had her mother died?

Jone appeared a moment later. "Elissa. Thank the Creator." Mother Cera was at her back, looking less pleased. And why shouldn't she be? Elissa had taken Stasy from her and gotten the young woman killed.

"My mother?" Elissa asked.

"Alive," Jone said. "But she hasn't woken, and the Gatherer says every hour that goes by makes it less likely that woman who wakes will be the one we remember. Until she recovers, you are Countess of Morning."

"The demons?"

"Your greatwards and my remaining guard have them stymied, at least for now," Jone said. "But there are sounds of digging below the keep, and we don't know what to do."

"I need to see for myself." Again, Elissa tried to sit up, and failed. "Gatherer . . . I can't feel my legs."

The Gatherer's blank stare was telling, and Elissa fumbled at the blankets. Pulling them away from her legs.

"Countess!" The Gatherer reached out to stop her, but Elissa slapped her hand away, at last revealing her legs. They twitched as she flailed, but she could not feel it. The skin was pale, mottled with sunken patches of gray and stark white.

Elissa felt her tears returning and ground her teeth, forcing them back. "Is there anything you can do?"

Again the blank stare, but Elissa met it with a hard one of her own. At last, the Gatherer threw up her hands. "The flesh is frozen, Countess. Dead. In time, you may heal in part, but I do not expect you will walk again."

Elissa searched herself, realizing her own clothes were gone. "Where is my stylus?"

"You're in no condition—" Jone began.

"Give it to me," Elissa cut in. "Unless you want corelings swarming from the basement."

Jone looked pained, reaching into a pocket of her gown for an item wrapped in a silk kerchief. She handled it like a hot iron pan.

Elissa snatched it from her hands, unwrapping her silver stylus. Its charge was largely depleted, but she prayed enough remained as she slid fingers over the wards to allow her to Draw directly on its power.

She inhaled as the magic jolted through her. The aches and pain in her skull receded, and she felt clearheaded for the first time in hours. Something of her strength returned. She moved to put her feet under her, but her legs did not obey as they should, tangling each other and leaving her awkwardly twisted.

"Countess . . ." the Gatherer warned. Elissa ignored her, taking the stylus and drawing wards directly on her legs, opening the nib to release whatever power remained.

The wards flared and some feeling returned, the white and gray mottling receding slightly, but it was nothing like the total healings she had effected in the past.

But as with Woron's wound, sometimes magic alone was not enough.

Elissa shoved the thought aside, again trying to get to her feet. She managed to get her right leg under her, but the left dragged, and when she stood it could not fully support her. She balanced on one shaking leg a moment, then fell back.

"Don't just stand there gawking," she snapped. "Someone fetch me a cane."

Elissa felt her nerves clench every time she heard the rumbling sound. Dust shook from the walls and ceiling, choking air thick with the stench of ichor.

Elissa's Warders had drawn greatwards on the floor and charged them with coreling remains. Elissa refilled her stylus the same way. Mother Jone lent her a steadying arm as she stared at the wall, *hora* pen at the ready.

It was an old, sealed-off sewer entrance where the breach seemed imminent. Demons should not have been able to approach the powerful forbiddings, but the sounds of shattering rock continued.

Then, suddenly, all grew quiet. Elissa held a breath as the wall turned white with rime. It made a high-pitched whine as the moisture inside turned solid, then an impact sent everyone lurching. Elissa's legs buckled, and she banged her hips as she hit the stone floor. The wall was shattered, and from the rubble stepped . . . Derek.

"I'm through!" Derek's eyes scanned the room, lighting on her. "I see Elissa! She's alive!"

Ragen came rushing past, shoving confused Warders aside as he fell to his knees beside her. "Lissa, are you all right?"

She wanted to tell him the truth, but in the moment it didn't seem to matter. She threw her arms around him and squeezed tight. "I'm all right. How did you get here?"

"The same way the demons have been getting around. The sewers." Ragen nodded to Yon and Woron, who came out of the rubble followed by a group of Mountain Spears. "Flamework proved quite effective in the cramped tunnels."

Derek spotted Mother Cera standing with Jone. "Where is Stasy?" He strode in close. "Where is my son?"

"You don't—" Cera began, but Derek raised his stylus, pointing it right at her nose.

"No more hiding behind your title, Countess," Derek growled. "Not tonight. You will take me to my wife. Now."

"Or what?" Jone snapped. "You'll murder the Countess of Gold in front of everyone?"

Derek waved the stylus at her as well. "Don't test me, old woman."

"Stasy is dead," Cera said. "Killed by a stone demon."

Derek stumbled back at the words, face twisting in pain. But then he rushed back in, *hora* pen leading. "Because of you!"

Mother Cera stumbled back, falling to the floor as Derek stalked in. "No. Because of her." She pointed to Elissa. "Because Mother Elissa had her fighting demons on the walls when she should have been safe inside with the other Mothers."

Derek's eyes flicked to Elissa, and she could not lie to him. "Stasy saved countless lives tonight."

Derek gaped at her, then squeezed his eyes shut and shook his head to clear it, turning back to Cera and pointing his stylus. "She wouldn't even have been here had you not been holding her prisoner. Now take me to my son."

"I'll do no such thing while you're—"

Derek drew a sharp warding, and the stone floor beside the countess cracked. She jumped, getting to her feet.

"Go with them, Yon, ay?" Ragen said. "Make sure Derek . . ."

". . . dun't do anythin' stupid," Yon finished. "On it."

"I'll see that fool in irons," Jone said when they were gone.

"You've bigger problems than a man who just lost his wife wanting assurance his only child is well," Ragen said.

"Euchor's keep is in flames."

CHAPTER 33

EVIL GIVES BIRTH

334 AR

"Push," Leesha said.

"Idiot girl!" Elona was legs-up on the birthing table, hair slick with sweat. "What in the Core do you think I've been doing?!" They were hours into labor, and no closer to crowning.

"Leesha is only trying to help, dear." Erny tried to take Elona's hand, but she slapped it away.

"Get out."

Erny's face fell. "But . . . !"

"Shut it!" Elona snarled. "You're as useless here as you are in my bed! Ent no way this babe came from your limp little stump, and we both know it!"

"Dear!" Erny turned bright red, glancing around the room. Darsy and Favah kept their eyes down and affected not to notice.

"Get out!" Elona screeched. "Get out! Get out! Get out!"

Leesha took her father's elbow. "Da."

Erny needed no further instruction, allowing her to lead him from the room.

"She doesn't mean it."

Erny slumped on a bench just outside. "Oh, Leesha. Of course she does."

Leesha sighed. There was no point in pretending she hadn't seen the truth of it in vivid detail. "Why don't you go back to your chambers? This may take hours yet. I'll send for you when it's done."

Erny shook his head. "Maybe that babe's mine and maybe it isn't, but for better or worse your mum is. I'll wait right here."

Leesha squeezed his shoulder. "You're too good for her, Da."

Erny chuckled. "Too good, yet never good enough. I've made my peace with it, but it never stops stinging."

"Nonsense," Leesha said. "Mother uses the truth to hurt you so you don't see that for the lie it is. You gave her the chance to leave you for Steave and she didn't take it. She never would. You were always the better man, and you've a right to demand she treat you like you deserve. There's more to a man than the size of his tree. If she can't see that, perhaps she should try raising that babe on her own."

Erny shook his head. "I love her, Leesha. Always have, always will. There's never been another woman in the world to me. I'm not going anywhere. Not from this bench, not from this marriage. We said our vows . . ."

"But only you keep them," Leesha said.

Erny looked at her. "Is that the only time we should keep our promises, Leesha? When others do? I taught you better than that."

"Ay, Da. You did." Leesha smiled, bending to kiss the top of his balding head before she went back into the birthing chamber and shut the door.

"Push." Darsy had taken up Leesha's place between her mother's legs.

"I am pushing, you stupid cow!" Elona barked.

"Well you ent doin' a good enough job of it, you mean old witch," Darsy muttered.

"Like you'll ever know what this is like," Elona growled. "The sight of your sour mash face is enough to wilt any man's tree."

Darsy reddened but wisely bit back her retort. She was used to cowing others, but no one could escalate a fight like Elona Paper. Whatever she said, Leesha's mother would come back with worse.

"Be as the palm, and bend to let this wind pass over you,"

Favah advised. "Everam does not judge women for words spoken in the birthing chamber."

"You don't know my mother well, if you think these words limited to labor," Leesha said.

Favah looked ready to say more, but Elona growled like a bear, and Darsy gave a cry. "I can see the head!"

Leesha rushed over, gently pushing a grateful Darsy aside. There it was, the child's tawny-haired crown, visible at last. She began massaging it free. "This is it, Mum, one last . . ."

"If you say push, I swear to the Creator, I'll—!"

"I don't care what you do, so long as you push," Leesha snapped. Elona grit her teeth, blood vessels breaking across her face as she strained. Then the head slipped free, and the rest came in a rush.

"I have it!" Leesha reached to clear the babe's mouth and nose, but it wasn't necessary. The child thrashed in her arms and gave a mighty cry.

She found herself in accord, her own eyes tearing. "I'll never tire of that sound."

"Give it . . ." Elona gasped a breath, ". . . a little time," she panted again, "and we'll all be . . . sick of it."

Leesha ignored her, running sensitive fingers over the child, checking the beat of its heart, the tone of its skin, the strength of its movements, the rate of its breaths. Favah moved in, tying knots in the cord with a practiced hand and slicing it with a sharp curved blade.

Leesha looked deeper, seeing the child's aura in wardsight. She sobbed. Whatever horrors Elona had said and done, this child, her sibling, was a soul yet unburdened with the weights of life.

"What is it?" Elona demanded, seeing the tears. "Something wrong?"

Leesha shook her head. "Oh, no. Everything is . . . beautiful."

"Don't keep me in suspense," Elona said. "Is it a boy?"

Leesha shook her head. "A girl, strong and perfect."

"Night, not again!" Elona smacked a fist against the table, but Leesha's mind was far away, remembering Amanvah's words, months past, when she cast the dice for Gared's bride.

She will bear him strong sons, but it will be his daughter who succeeds him.

Whatever her disappointment, Elona reached for the child. Leesha tied a clean nappy on her and laid her skin-to-skin on her mother's chest.

"What will you name her?" Favah asked.

"Selen, after my mum." The look on Elona's face was something Leesha had never seen before. Could it be love?

"A strong name," Favah said, moving away to dispose of the cord. Leesha watched her, and followed when the woman turned her back by the table and she saw a telltale glow.

She reached Favah as the old woman cast the dice, wet with blood from the umbilicus. It was a violation of privacy, but Leesha's curiosity outweighed her offense, and she leaned in to see as the dice spun to a stop and the symbols aligned.

Wood intersecting a cutting ward.

"Woodcutter," she breathed, too low for Darsy and her mother to hear.

Favah nodded. "The baron's *Jiwah Ka* will be pleased it is a girl child."

Not so pleased, Leesha thought, but she kept it to herself, studying the rest of the throw.

"Ay!" Elona barked. "Don't think I'm stupid enough not to guess what you're doing over there! I want a look!"

Favah snatched the dice up and thrust them back into her pouch. "Bad enough for one *chin* to look upon the sacred dice. I will not suffer another."

"Well?" Elona demanded when Leesha returned to her side. Erny opened the door unbidden as Leesha answered.

"She's Gared's."

Leesha returned to her office to find Araine at her desk, attended by Lord Arther, Pawl, and Tarisa as she bent over a mound of papers. Melny sat on the couch across the room with Olive.

Was this the loyalty of her inner circle? Two days into Araine's return, and she'd already taken Leesha's place. She opened her mouth to shout when Olive, barely three months old, reached up and took a firm grip on Melny's décolletage, pulling herself to stand up on her lap.

"Creator!" Leesha rushed to them, her anger forgotten.

"I know!" Melny beamed. "She's been doing it all morning!" Olive turned, eyes meeting Leesha's, and gave a joyful laugh.

Leesha knew she should be concerned at Olive's unusual development—most children could not stand until nine months at least—but she could not help laughing in return. There was nothing usual about Olive Paper.

The girl let go her grip before Melny's great bosom slipped free of her dress, reaching for Leesha. For a moment she kept her feet, but then her little legs buckled and she fell back on her bottom, laughing again.

Leesha swept her up and kissed her. "I met your aunt today. At this rate you'll be running before she learns to roll over." Olive replied by reaching out and tweaking her nose.

There was a shuffle of paper, and Leesha looked back across the room. Araine continued reading through the papers, murmuring to Pawl who took careful notes. Arther and Tarisa at least had the sense to look guilty.

"Mistress." The first minister bowed as Leesha stormed their way, babe in hand. "We did not expect you back so soon."

"Is that your only excuse for breaking your oath to me?" Leesha demanded. "The Hollow's ledgers were closed, you swore."

"Pfagh!" Araine looked up at last. "You said yourself there were no state secrets anymore."

"*Your* state," Leesha snapped. "This is mine."

"I haven't shown her anything sensitive," Arther said defensively. "The Duchess Mum asked to help with requisitions for her refugees . . ."

Araine whisked a hand, and Arther fell silent. "You can't expect me to sit around all day rubbing Melny's belly, Leesha. I can't help you on the battlefield. I can't ward, heal the sick, or deliver babes. But this, I can do."

Leesha blew out a breath. She had a right to be angry with all of them, but she could not deny she needed the help, and there were few in the world with more experience in running a city than the Duchess Mum. "And what have you surmised?"

"That your heart is far larger than your coffers," Araine said. "It's a wonder you've kept the Hollow afloat with all the entitlements you hand to every beggar who comes to town."

Leesha's eyes narrowed as she turned to Arther. "Nothing sensitive, you say?" The man looked like he wanted to sink into his starched collar. It was true Leesha needed the help, but she had little desire for Araine to know just how fragile the Hollow's economy was with war on all sides.

"It doesn't take a genius to see the larger picture from how much you've done for my people in just two days," Araine said. "You're spending klats faster than you can stamp and lacquer them."

"We stopped lacquering them months ago." Olive pulled at her dress, and Leesha freed a breast, bringing her to suck. Arther made a strangled sound and turned his back so fast, she thought he might give himself whiplash.

"Even so—" Araine waved at the papers.

"What would you have me do?" Leesha demanded. "Let your people starve on my doorstep, like you did when the Rizonans came begging to your gates?"

"Of course not," Araine said. "I'm trying to compliment you, girl, if you'll stop interrupting long enough to let me. You've danced a razor's edge, and yet there are no empty bellies in Hollow County."

The old woman shook her head. "The first Rhinebeck drove Angiers into bankruptcy to assure the lords of Angiers would grant him the throne when my father died, did you know?"

"Rojer said something of the sort once," Leesha said.

"Leave it to a Jongleur to spin tales out of turn," Araine said. "What did he tell you?"

"That Rhinebeck the first invented the machine to stamp klats," Leesha said, "and kept one in five for himself."

Araine snorted. "It was a lot more than that. Even so, after the bribes were all paid to keep his throne, the old fool died and left his son and me with a vault filled with little more than ledgers of debt and the smell of must. My Rhinebeck was more interested in hunting and bedding harlots, leaving Janson and me with a demon of a time keeping our empty coffers secret until the city got back on its feet."

The old woman reached out, her withered hand clutching Leesha's with surprising strength. "You've done better than I ever could have, girl. You should be proud. My city is lost—perhaps forever. I don't want your throne, for myself or Melny's child, but I can help you here, if you'll let me."

With sunlight streaming into the room, Leesha could not read the Duchess Mum's aura, but the sincerity in her eyes was enough.

"Alagai Ka," Leesha said.

"Do not be so distracted by what you hope to see that you miss the adjacent symbols," Favah said.

Leesha squinted, tilting her head to look from all angles. "New." She pointed. "Birth."

Leesha considered a moment. "Hatchlings? Young mind demons?"

Favah nodded. "What does this throw tell you?"

Leesha knew the old woman had already formed her own opinion. It was a test, as always. Sometimes they saw the same things in a throw. Sometimes Leesha made mistakes.

And sometimes, they saw completely different things that might both be right, depending on divergences.

Leesha studied the scattered symbols, fitting them together like a puzzle. "The mind that controls Angiers is sending hatchlings to the Hollow to pen us in while it consolidates power." Already attacks along the outskirts of the greatward had increased, focusing on the boroughs with the weakest wards. What would happen when minds came and could direct those savage attacks into surgical ones?

Favah bowed. It was not so grudging for her as it was a few weeks ago. "I agree. If you are to get a force of any size out before Waning . . ."

"It must be soon," Leesha finished.

CHAPTER 34

SPEAR OF ALA

334 AR

"Is the Spear intact, Par'chin?" Jardir demanded. "Does it still stand?"

"Ay. Gates still closed." The words were choked. Could the Par'chin be weeping? "It's perfect, Ahmann. Creator, it shines like the sun."

"I must go," Jardir said. "Now."

"Of course, Uncle," Shanvah said. "We will watch over the prisoner. Alagai Ka will not escape our captivity."

Jardir nodded, and she turned back to the demon and her father as he began to remove his excess robes for the swim.

"Now, wait just a corespawned second!" Renna shouted. "'Fore you run off and leave me and Shanvah alone with Alagai rippin' Ka, someone mean to tell me what's the Spear of Ala?"

"The greatest *csar* ever built," Jardir told her. "The Evejah teaches us it was the fortress Kaji himself built to stage and supply his assault on the abyss."

Renna blinked. "Oh."

Jardir continued to disrobe. "And so you see why I must go."

"Don't see," Renna snapped. "Said yourself we don't get lazy. Said yourself we stay together. No one gets left alone with the demon."

"Sister," Shanvah said. "This is the Spear of Ala . . ."

"Ent an idiot, Shanvah. I get what it is. I get why it's important." Renna turned her gaze on Jardir. "But it's stood there three thousand years. Ent goin' anywhere in the next couple hours, if that's what it takes to play this safe."

Jardir blinked, his eyes flicking to Alagai Ka and Shanjat. The demon looked smug, even in its chains. He blocked their words from the demon with the powers of the crown, but no doubt the creature could read lips, and guess much from their position.

Was this the moment Alagai Ka had been waiting for? For Jardir to be so focused on the Spear of Ala that his guard over the prisoner might lessen? Jardir remembered the demon's last escape attempt. It was sudden, and though they were prepared, he took Shanjat and nearly had the better of all four of them.

He turned to Renna, and bowed deeply. "I apologize. Of course you are correct. Alagai Ka is our greatest charge. Thank you for reminding me to place the First War above my personal desires."

"Ay." Renna's aura had been smoldering for a fight, and his sudden agreement unnerved her. "Welcome, I guess."

Shanvah wore only her headscarf, veil, and bido as she swam deeper and deeper into the pool, harvesting the worms. Jardir could not help but be impressed at the amount of magic the creatures held, but he paced the water's edge impatiently as she worked.

Shanvah's aura was the dimmest and least likely to draw the worms' attention. Wisdom dictated she be the one to clear the path. He and the Par'chin's *jiwah* watched over the prisoner, but Jardir's muscles were knotted, screaming at him to smash through the countless tons of rock and stand before the Spear of Ala.

"Creator," Renna growled as she gnawed on one of the worms. "Tastes even better than your couscous."

Jardir believed her. Her aura brightened as she ate, absorbing the worm's stored power. It might be wise for all of them to feed when the way was clear, but even if Jardir could stomach the thought of eating these subterranean creatures, tainted by the abyss, he had no desire to eat. Only to reach the Spear.

One of the worms, desperately trying to return to the water, wriggled free of its shell and slithered toward Alagai Ka, who eyed it hungrily.

Shanvah had left most of her weapons in easy reach on the rocks, and Jardir snatched one of her throwing glasses, pinning the worm to the rock before the magic-rich creature could come close to the demon's talons. Alagai Ka's aura was weak, and for all their sakes, they must keep it so.

There was a splash, but it was not Shanvah who surfaced. The Par'chin gasped air as he waded out of the water. There were shallow lacerations on his skin, puckered redness, but his magic was strong, and already the marks were fading.

Jardir looked to his friend, but the Par'chin only had eyes for the demon, stalking Alagai Ka like prey. Roughly, he gripped the demon by the throat, dragging him to where Shanjat was chained and leaning the demon against him.

"Still alive," the Par'chin growled.

Shanjat's eyes flicked over his wet form. "Obviously."

"That an attempt to kill me?" the Par'chin demanded. "You knew those worms were in the water."

Shanjat smiled. "I answered your every question truthfully, Explorer. Blame yourself if you did not ask enough. I am your prisoner, not your friend."

"Demons don't have friends," Renna growled.

"And we're stronger for it." Shanjat eyed Jardir. "No wasted sentiment leading to foolish action."

"I was saved from foolishness by a friend, demon," Jardir said. "And so your words hold no poison for me."

Shanjat winked at him. "This time."

The Par'chin straightened his back and took a deep breath, unclenching his fists as he let it out. He turned to Jardir.

"Move quick enough through the water, the worms that are left won't have time to latch on to you. It's a straight shot from here."

Jardir nodded. He removed his cloak and stepped into the pool wearing only his crown and his bido, clutching the Spear of Kaji in both hands.

The moment he touched his spear to the water, he could

feel it—the pull of the great *csar,* resonating with his very soul. He gathered power in his spear and dove, thrusting with his magic to fly through the water as easily as he did the air.

Jardir walked dripping from the pool, mindless of the spiny shells of the Par'chin's harvest crunching beneath his bare feet. He knew nothing, felt nothing, but the Spear of Ala. It shone in the darkness, singing with glorious power. He fell to his knees at the sight.

It was true.

The holy scripture of the Evejah had guided the lives of his people for millennia. No doubt the clerics added flourishes over the years, inflating what was already glorious, or serving some political agenda, but the heart of everything he and his people believed was true, and before him was the proof. Kaji had been here, to this very place, and built a bastion against the darkness that had stood for more than three thousand years.

It called to him, in much the way the Par'chin had described the call of the Core. The Crown of Kaji throbbed at his brow, a key hungry to enter a lock too long bolted. Inside those walls, his power would be like the Hand of Everam Himself, and woe befall the foe that should try to stand against him.

Shanvah broke the surface soon after, coming to kneel beside him, mindless of their unclad bodies. "Deliverer." Her voice was a whisper.

Jardir took her hand, squeezing gently. "Niece." He would have said more, but what words could convey what their senses were telling them? Her lips moved in silent prayer, and he joined her.

Everam, if ever I was your chosen servant, grant me strength and worthiness in the days to come. Give me the power to succeed where even great Kaji could not. If not through force of legions . . . He squeezed Shanvah's hand again. *. . . then through the trust and support of the companions beside me, Your chosen ones.*

There was a ripple in the water behind them, and both were on their feet in an instant as Shanjat emerged, carrying Alagai Ka on his back. The demon hissed and averted its eyes at the sight of the Spear of Ala. The demon was not so bold now, in the face of Everam's power.

Moments later Renna am'Bales appeared in the pool. "Arlen's haulin' the baggage. Be along shortly."

Jardir nodded, advancing on Alagai Ka. "What do you know of this place?"

"It is cursed," Shanjat said. "Haunted. You will find no respite here."

"Spare me your lies and dissembling," Jardir growled. "The gates remain locked. I can sense it from here. The fortress still stands. How can this be so?"

"We waited," the demon said. "Waited for the One, your Kavri, to return to the surface to levy more drones to the fight."

Jardir gripped his spear so tightly his knuckles whitened. "And then?"

"Our workings could not touch the greatward of your ancestor's *csar,*" Shanjat croaked, "but we gathered our magics and collapsed the tunnel he marched his forces through. Smashed the bridges. Destroyed his supply. By the time Kavri's armies returned to the vent, the way was shattered and we cut them apart, leaving his warriors trapped below.

"Oh, how he railed against us! How he struggled to return to them, to . . ." Shanjat's smile was evil, "*deliver* them. But it was doomed to failure."

"And the men inside?" Jardir asked.

Shanjat shrugged, as if it were of no import. "Cut off from support, it was a simple matter for the drones to retake or collapse the lower tunnels, whittling away their sallies until they were too weakened to fight on, and sealed the gates forever."

Jardir's chest constricted, and he realized he was holding his breath. "So there may yet be survivors."

"They starved to death long ago, or were eaten by the war dogs." Shanjat showed his teeth. "An ugly, honorless death, either way. Perhaps they were wise enough to simply fall upon their spears."

"They could have eaten holy couscous." Jardir knew he was grasping at sand, but he could not help himself.

Shanjat snorted. "For five thousand years?"

"If there were women . . ." Surely the *csar* had priestesses to cast foretellings, at least.

Shanjat gave a cruel laugh. "Even the legendary whoring of the *dama'ting* would not be up to such a task."

Shanvah tightened her grip on her spear at the blasphemy, but Jardir embraced his anger. "Only words, Father of Lies. We will see for ourselves."

The Par'chin emerged from the pool at last, dragging their packs. He looked around, taking in the scene. "Night."

His tone gave Jardir a sense of unease. "What is it, Par'chin?"

The Par'chin was scanning the rocks. "I left gnawed worm hides all over these rocks not two hours ago. What happened to them?"

Jardir looked around in confusion, realizing that, indeed, there were only shells to be found. "Scavengers?"

As if on cue, there was a howl in the distance that made his blood turn cold.

Shanjat was not smiling any longer. "We would be wise to flee this place, before the war dogs are upon us. Unlike your warriors, the dogs survived, feeding upon fallen drones before turning on their masters."

"Nightwolves, we can handle," Arlen said.

"Not these, Explorer," Shanjat said.

Jardir shook his head. "We are not going anywhere until we look inside the Spear of Ala."

"Place is warded better'n anything I've ever seen," Renna said. "Ent gonna drag a demon in there without killing him, and we can't just chain him up and stick him in a hole out here."

The Par'chin sighed. "You go, Ahmann. But not alone. Take Shanvah. Renna and I will stand guard over the prisoner."

Quiet Shanvah bowed deeply. "Par'chin, it should be you to go with my blessed uncle."

"Ent gonna lie and say I don't want to." The Par'chin shook his head sadly. "But it ent my place. Learned my lesson with Anoch Sun. More than anyplace in the world, this is holy ground to your people. The first feet to touch it after all this time should be Evejan."

"They will be," Jardir agreed. "For you and your *jiwah* sacrifice all in the First War. You are as Evejan as any, whether you see it or not. Shanjat as well, even if his feet are moved by the Father of Evil."

Alagai Ka hissed. "It will be my death to enter your great-ward. There are many miles to go, Heir. You need me, yet."

Jardir smiled. "Be full of fear, Father of Evil. I can protect you with the crown, but you will know that every moment of your existence is at my sufferance."

"And if your sufferance wanes, even for an instant, I will be dead," Shanjat said. "Incinerated by the greatward."

Jardir shrugged. "If so, it is *inevera.*"

The howling grew closer as they approached the *csar.* The creatures had been circling them for some time, ensuring they were alone—vulnerable.

And then the dogs grew silent as death. Jardir could still sense them like demons in the Maze, but despite his crown-sight, the creatures remained invisible.

Alagai Ka hissed and squirmed as they approached the *csar.* It was rare for the creature to give much information in his aura, but his fear was palpable now.

Jardir felt exhilarated. Every step strengthened the link between the city and him. It spoke to him, telling a tale like the layers of rock in a desert mesa.

He turned to the Par'chin. "Was this what you meant, Par'chin, when you said Anoch Sun spoke to you?"

He expected his friend to join in his wonder, but the Par'chin paused, tilting his head, then gave it a shake. "Felt like I was part of something, at Anoch Sun. I can sense the power here, but it ent speaking to me."

Jardir scanned the others, but it became clear the connection was his alone. He felt the gemstones of his crown puls-ing, and knew that somewhere in the heart of the *csar,* gems cut from the same stone, focused by bones taken from the same demon prince, were pulsing in return.

The moment they stepped onto the greatward, Jardir felt its power wrap around him like a raiment, bending to his every whim and will.

"How're we supposed to get inside?" the Par'chin asked, eyeing the great barred gates. "Climb the walls?"

"That will not be necessary, Par'chin." Jardir gave a casual wave of his spear and the great gates began to rumble, swinging open to admit them.

A clattering sound echoed in the cavern behind them, like talons on rock. Jardir looked behind but saw nothing.

The demon gave a low growl. "Quickly," Shanjat said. "They are almost upon us!"

Jardir did not trust the demon, but his tone spoke truth, and they rushed into the city, Alagai Ka hissing in pain as they crossed the threshold. Jardir signaled for the gates to close, but not before faces materialized just outside.

Twisted canine visages, but Jardir recognized them. Even now, Krasian warriors favored the breed—*gwilji,* desert runners—as hunting companions and protectors of wells and women.

But these were larger by far than the *gwilji* in Krasia, snapping and slavering like starved dogs thrown in a fighting pit.

Most chilling of all, they had no bodies, all claws and jaws, floating in the darkness as the gates slammed shut.

"What in the dark of night were those things?" Renna asked.

"What Evin Cutter has to look forward to," the Par'chin said, "he keeps letting Shadow eat demon meat."

Shanjat shook his head. "You have no idea what you face, Explorer. These creatures have been feeding and breeding far from the sun for the rise and fall of millennia. Powers you barely grasp are as simple to them as breathing."

"It does not matter," Jardir said. "They cannot touch us here. Nothing can."

Indeed, power suffused him as he led them through the silent streets. He could see the greatward in his mind's eye, knew its every contour, felt every door and wall and rooftop. Without ever having seen the place before, he knew it as intimately as the streets where he had come of age. He knew no life remained in the *csar,* and knew, too, where to find its last remain.

He guided them to Sharik Hora.

The giant doors opened with a thought. The temple was the pulsing center of the *csar,* focusing the power that kept its streets and buildings pristine, its walls inviolate. Alagai Ka hissed and squirmed on Shanjat's back as they entered, crawling deeper into the warrior's robe.

Like its namesakes in Everam's Bounty and the Desert Spear, the inside of the Temple of Heroes' Bones was covered in the bodies of fallen *Sharum*. Their bones formed intricate latticework on the walls. Carpets and tapestries, woven of dyed human hair into elaborate designs, seemed untouched by the millennia, colors still vivid and bright.

The benches, chairs, and tables were built from human bone, stretched and padded with leather from human skin.

Everything was warded with breathtaking beauty—wards etched into bone, woven with hair, painted in blood. All of it tied together, linked to the heart of the *csar*—linked to him. Jardir could feel it all flowing in harmony with his spirit.

Even the others were stunned. The Par'chin's eyes roamed everywhere, trying to take in everything at once—an impossible task. His *jiwah,* similarly overwhelmed, took the opposite tack. She flitted from one thing to the next, examining closely for a moment, crying out wonders, and moving on.

But Shanvah, faithful Shanvah, watched only her father. In her aura, he could see how Shanjat hovered over her like a specter.

She carries his honor, Jardir realized. *Holding herself to account for her father's actions, even now, under the demon's control.*

"Be at peace, Niece. In this place, even Alagai Ka cannot bring harm to us." He could see the words pass through her aura, the words of Shar'Dama Ka. She allowed herself a few furtive glances around the great temple, but her attention remained fixed upon her father and the demon atop him.

The eyes of heroes stared down at them from the great chandeliers, glowing with light that filled the halls. They brightened when Jardir took notice of them, but a thought dimmed them back down. The temple had woken when the crown drew near, responsive to his every whim as if it were the Holy Word.

Fountains still danced, arcing sacred water from hollow bones, the pools clear and pure even now. Jardir and the others drank of them, instantly refreshed.

In crownsight, Jardir could see the power of the bones, pulsing and throbbing in time with the heart of the temple, in time with the gems at his brow. These untold thousands had died with Everam and Sharak Ka in their hearts, and that unity, that truth of purpose, had imprinted upon their remains.

Unlike the Sharik Horas of the surface, where much of this power burned away with the sun, these bones had been locked underground, accruing power for millennia.

"Everythin' looks shiny and new," Renna said. "So where is everyone?"

"I fear we are looking at them," Jardir said, continuing a steady stride toward the great domed hall where the faithful gathered for prayer.

Outside the great doors hung cages of bone, meant to hold prisoners awaiting Everam's justice.

Jardir turned to look at Alagai Ka, cowering in Shanjat's robe. In his enhanced crownsight, he could see the demon's link to his friend as never before, an infection that spread wherever their flesh touched, making the two as one.

But here in his place of power, Jardir broke the demon's hold effortlessly with an act of will. A flick of his finger and Shanjat's robes opened; with a clawing motion of his hand the horrified, terrified demon king was peeled away from his friend like a dirty bandage, held aloft with nothing but a raised finger.

"You cannot enter the inner temple, Prince of Nie, nor can you sully the sacred ground of Sharik Hora." A flick of Jardir's wrist and the demon was thrown toward the hanging cage. It responded to his will, opening to receive the prisoner, then snapping shut.

"That gonna hold him?" the Par'chin asked.

Jardir snapped his fingers. Bones peeled away from the walls, forming into warded spikes that surrounded the cage from every angle, their deadly points facing inward. The demon hissed, but there was nowhere to retreat, and he stood frozen in the center of the cage.

"There is no prison on Ala stronger, Par'chin." The weave tightened like a briarpatch until the demon was out of sight. "The Father of Evil is beyond all sense of what goes on outside his cell. Should he make any attempt to escape, I will know, and the *csar* itself will rise against him."

The Par'chin looked at him a long time. "Glad we're friends, 'cause sometimes you scare the piss out of me."

Jardir smiled. "And you, my *zah'ven*."

The Par'chin looked up as the great doors to the prayer hall swung open. "Outside, maybe. In here, ent no denying you're Shar'Dama Ka."

The Par'chin fell short of calling Jardir Deliverer, but it was on his aura, calling into doubt all the beliefs he held dear, and those he scorned.

Jardir laid a hand on his shoulder. "Be at peace, my friend. If I am Deliverer in this place, there can be no doubt I would never have reached it without you."

He gave a last squeeze, and turned to face the doors.

Shanvah took Shanjat's arm, his hands still bound. "Walk with me, Father." The warrior followed her, and at last her eyes began to take in the marvels around her. They grew wide, and wet.

So much was becoming clear to Jardir as the *csar* continued to speak to him. He peeled back the years of Shanvah's life in her aura effortlessly. He saw her being raised—as he was—in a dark underpalace; saw her taught only the joyless lessons of war. Saw the flash of glory when he named her *Sharum'ting,* stolen soon after by her defeat at the hands of the Par'chin's *jiwah.* Another glory, as they struck their blow against the minds that came to Anoch Sun, robbed not long after as the prince of Nie took her father.

But now, with Alagai Ka locked away, there was wonder in her face again, and Jardir paused a moment to remember it before turning and leading the way inside. Behind him, the doors thudded shut, sealing them in the holiest place in all Ala.

There was room for thousands to sit and kneel on benches of polished bone, surrounding the altar on all sides. The altar itself contained a Skull Throne like the one in Everam's Bounty, coated in electrum and affixed with gemstones that reached out to those upon his crown like reunited lovers.

And as in Everam's Bounty, a bed of pillows sat next to the

throne, and there lay an ancient woman, curled as if in sleep around a scroll tube of bone, capped with a great ruby.

The others fell back as Jardir ascended to the altar. He could see from across the room that she was long dead, but her body had been preserved by this holy place. Her wrinkled flesh was gray but untouched by time. She might have let out her last breath a moment ago.

She was clad all in white, save for a black headscarf, the mark of a *Damaji'ting*. This woman had been a leader to these people when she died. Perhaps their last.

Jardir knelt, reaching out a hand reverently to take the scroll. For a moment, their hands touched, and her life flashed before his eyes. She was born in the *csar*. Had never left its walls. Had never seen the sun or moon. Her life was spent in prayer and labor, crafting the monument that surrounded them, painstakingly adding bones and hair and skin to Sharik Hora as, one by one, everyone around her died. Her last years were ones of utter loneliness, trapped within the beautiful prison of Sharik Hora.

He sobbed at her sacrifice, feeling her essence so strongly that for a moment, he felt he could reach through her and up the lonely path to retrieve her spirit.

He heard his mother's voice in his head. *You would pull a woman, a Bride of Everam, from Heaven?*

He embraced the words, and let them fall away. Yes. For the First War, he would sacrifice even a woman's place in Heaven. It was no more than they asked of the son Jardir could see growing in Renna am'Bales' belly.

But perhaps it was not necessary—if such a thing could even be done. Jardir let go of her hand and slid the scroll tube from her hands.

It was the hollowed thighbone of some massive warrior, polished and etched with warding as exquisite as anything Jardir had ever seen. He could see the lines of power, and knew the tube was nearly indestructible, the gemstone locked in place so that none could ever open it.

None, save the wearer of the Crown of Kaji. The ruby on Jardir's brow throbbed as his fingers clasped the cap and twisted through the threads of magic binding it closed.

Inside was a single sheet of parchment Jardir knew well from his time in Sharik Hora. Human skin.

There, written in blood on a hero's skin, were this woman's last words to him.

Shar'Dama Ka,

I am Kavrivah, your great-granddaughter. Though we have never met, I have felt you in my heart since I was a little girl.

This is the last parchment in the csar. *All the rest have been used to record the history of the Spear of Ala since we were severed from you. They are in the library, protected, like this last letter, against the glorious day when you shall break the walls and reclaim what is yours, in this life or another.*

Know, Deliverer, that while we have failed you, we have not forsaken you, or our duty to Everam.

The histories tell of ten thousand Sharum left to garrison the Spear of Ala in your absence, led by your son Sharach and daughter—my namesake—Kavrivah.

But then the alagai *collapsed the tunnels, and filled the cavern in a seething mass. Again and again, Sharach led sallies to retake the collapsed tunnel, but the excavation was hard, and slow, and the warriors vulnerable while they worked. Every attempt cost lives, including your son. It is said he died on* alagai *talons, Deliverer, with Everam's name on his lips. Others were dragged into the darkness beyond Everam's sight. We have prayed for the* alamen fae *ever since.*

There were less than a thousand left when Kavrivah ordered the gates sealed and began her rule. Less than a thousand warriors, and only seven dama'ting.

They took multiple husbands, desperate to preserve the seed of the strongest and wisest among them, but no wisdom or throw of the dice foresaw the day the gwilji *turned on their masters, and found their way into the nurseries. My mother was the only female to survive, and I her only daughter.*

I bore many children, Deliverer, but in the end it was

inevera *that I outlived them all. Now, after two hundred and eleven years, even the holy couscous can sustain me no longer.*

Know, Deliverer, that I love you with all my heart.

Everam speak through you always,
Kavrivah vah'Ajasht am'Kavri am'Kras

Kras. The fabled one tribe in the time of Kaji, before the Deliverer died and his followers' factions came to define the Krasian nation.

"Everam bless you, ancestor," he whispered, "as you sup in His great hall in Heaven. Your sacrifice will not go unsung."

He put the parchment back in the tube, tucking it into his belt as he rose and strode for the Skull Throne. The crown felt like it was aflame as he sat upon it, feeling the full power of the *csar*—the greatwards, the spirits of the fallen, Everam Himself—flowing through him.

He reached out, not along the path that separated Kavrivah from the living, but along one that seemed more distant still, the path back to the surface of Ala. Through all the noise of rushing magic, over the miles, and out the Mouth of the Abyss. It was night on the surface, and his power traveled with the speed of thought, covering the distance instantly.

"Jiwah."

Inevera's voice came to him instantly. "Husband, is it truly you?"

"I did not know your name until our wedding day," Jardir said, "only to realize I had known it all along."

"I have missed you, beloved," Inevera said.

"And I, you, Sun of my Life," Jardir whispered. "But I must speak now with the Damajah. We are linked with Shanvah, the Par'chin, and his *Jiwah Ka.*"

"Damajah." The Par'chin bowed, though the woman was a thousand miles away. "I apologize for throwing your husband from a cliff."

Inevera laughed ruefully, but it was a welcome sound. "I begged my husband to let me poison your tea, Par'chin, the day you came to us with the spear you stole from Kaji's tomb. Did you know?"

The Par'chin nodded. "Ahmann told me."

"Many times, have I regretted staying my hand, Par'chin," Inevera said. "No longer. Everam wills as Everam will. What has happened is what was meant to happen."

"What's the point of anythin', we ent got a choice?" Renna asked.

"There is always choice, Renna am'Bales," Inevera said. "It is the ultimate power, what makes the infinite futures finite. But Everam guides us to the right ones, like pieces on the board."

Renna rolled her eyes but said no more.

"Kneel with me before the throne," Shanvah whispered to her father, and the two of them knelt together.

"Shanvah?" Inevera asked. "Niece, is that you?"

"Go with your father," Shanvah quoted. *"Obey and protect him on his journey. Do not return without the Deliverer, or reliable news of his fate, even if it take a thousand years."*

She placed her hands on the floor and bowed forward to touch her forehead against the bones of heroes. "I have kept my mission, Damajah, and will stay true, even if it take a thousand years."

"Your glory is boundless, Niece," Inevera said, and silently Shanvah began to weep.

"There is another who must link with us," Jardir said.

A slow, steady exhale was Inevera's only response. "Leesha Paper."

"That gonna be a problem?" the Par'chin asked. "Because this is Sharak Ka."

"Your words are truer than you know, Par'chin," Inevera said. "All across Thesa, fires rage and cities fall."

The Par'chin's eyes widened, but Jardir did not give him time to speak again. He reached farther, finding Leesha's familiar aura across hundreds of miles and creating wards of resonance around her.

Was this what it was like for the minds? To never be apart from one another in thought? It was an alien concept.

"Countess Paper." He kept his words formal. In his heart they were anything but. Leesha Paper had borne him a child. She would always be a wife to him, and everyone knew it.

They all heard the gasp. "Ahmann?"

"Ay, and me," the Par'chin cut in.

"Me and Shanvah, too," Renna said.

"And—" Jardir began.

"—Inevera," his *Jiwah Ka* finished, her voice a razor cutting silk.

"Night," the Par'chin said when they were caught up.

"The Long Night of Sharak Ka," Jardir agreed. "Angiers and Docktown are the least of the losses we will suffer, if it lasts long enough to darken the heart of our power."

"Only one way to stop it." Renna gripped the handle of her knife.

"Ent heard anything from Miln?" The Par'chin could not hide the desperation in his voice. "Not even ale stories?"

"The demons have severed contact with the North," Leesha said. "Short-range scouts report a series of *alagai* greatwards in the foothills of Miln. Thus far, no Messengers can get through. Whatever is happening in Miln, they are alone."

There was the familiar clatter of Inevera's dice. Everyone fell silent.

"I see a city in the mountains," Inevera whispered. "Nie is strong there."

"Need dice to tell us that?" Renna snapped. Shanvah looked horrified, but Jardir had been a prisoner to the dice all his life, and understood the sentiment.

He put out a hand. "Peace, Renna am'Bales."

Inevera did not respond to the outburst, continuing to sift secrets from the dice. "The *alagai* have shattered the great wall and entered the city."

The Par'chin clenched a fist, and Jardir felt his instinctive pull on the greatward. With hardly an effort, he resisted the pull, drawing his friend's eyes. "Breathe, Par'chin. Embrace the pain."

His *anjin'pal* nodded, staring at nothing as his coiled and corded muscles relaxed.

"I see a city become a *Sharum*'s Maze," Inevera said. "I see demon and man, wrestling for a throne."

Renna took the Par'chin's hand. "So they're still fightin'."

"Nie expected them to fall easily," Inevera said. "But Everam has not abandoned them."

"Lots of walls in Miln," the Par'chin said. "Built in tiers right up into the mountainside. Whole city's warded. Lots of places for ambush pockets and succor . . ."

"Trust in your people," Jardir advised.

"Know Messengers are in short supply, Leesha." Renna's voice was unusually timid. "But if you could spare one for Tibbet's Brook . . ."

"We sent one immediately after the attack," Leesha said. "But Tibbet's Brook is a long journey, even on warded horseshoes."

Renna grunted. "Even on a straight round-trip, it will be new moon again by the time you get an answer."

Again the dice clattered, and this time Renna am'Bales held her breath, but after long moments, Inevera said nothing.

"What?!" Renna cried when it went on too long to bear. "What do you see?"

"Some futures cannot . . ." Inevera began.

"Cut the demonshit!" Renna barked. "Pickin' up more'n words along this link. Know you're lyin'. You saw somethin' and don't want to say it."

Inevera breathed. "You are correct. I apologize for my attempt at deceit. It shames us both. I beg your forgiveness."

"Don't care about any of that," Renna said. "Tell us what you saw."

Inevera breathed again. The Par'chin's *jiwah* was a trial, but she was also correct. "I see a village entire, dancing like puppets to a demon's strings. I see brother killing sister, father killing son.

"I see an empty cradle."

The council continued for hours, but without a word from Leesha and Inevera, Jardir sensed the approach of dawn on the surface. A gentle push against his magic that would soon be an irresistible force.

"The night grows long, and dawn approaches," Jardir said at last. "This may be the last time we speak before the end, and I would have a few words in private with my *Jiwah Ka*."

They made their goodbyes quickly, and one by one Jardir broke them from the link as easily as he might blow out a candle.

"Are Asome and Asukaji behaving?" Jardir asked when he was linked to his wife alone.

"The boys are proving fine leaders now that they have remembered their place," Inevera said.

"That is well," Jardir said. "It seems in my effort to keep you from the abyss, I have sent the abyss to you."

"We will stand fast as you pierce the heart of Nie, beloved," Inevera said.

"Never in my adult life have I been without your counsel," Jardir said. "I did not realize how much I had come to depend on it."

"Is that your way of saying you miss me?"

"It is my way of saying I am afraid, *jiwah*. And that when you are near, I am less so."

"Oh, beloved," Inevera whispered. "Everam Himself could speak no truer words."

"Deliverer." Shanvah pressed her forehead against the floor. At her side, Shanjat mirrored her.

"Rise, Niece." Jardir already knew what she would ask. He'd watched with quiet dread as she gathered the courage to speak.

"Here, as in no other place, we are cut off from Alagai Ka's influence," Shanvah said.

Jardir nodded. "That is true."

"And your power is greater than it has ever been."

"Yes," Jardir agreed.

"Then perhaps here, as in no other place, you can heal my father," Shanvah said.

Jardir said. "Perhaps. And what of our plans, if I do? Who will speak for Alagai Ka to guide our way?"

"I do not know," Shanvah said. "I am not the Deliverer. But I know that with Everam's blessing, all things are possible."

"All things are possible," Renna agreed. "But that don't make 'em likely."

"If he is healed, and Alagai Ka still needs a voice, I will volunteer," Shanvah said.

"Niece—" Jardir began.

"It will be my choice," Shanvah dared to interrupt. "A choice my father did not have. He was a great man. Kai of the Spears of the Deliverer. I am a girl, drowning in the sea of his glory."

"Your words are false, Shanvah vah Shanjat," Jardir said. "Your glory is boundless as your father's. I do not believe he would wish you to rob him of such a sacrifice."

Shanvah took her father's limp hand. "Then let it be his choice."

"It's a bad idea," Renna said. "Shanvah's got our secrets . . ."

"What secrets, Renna vah Arlen?" Shanvah asked. "That we are a candle dropped into a bottomless well? That we are afraid? The demon knows these things already. He mocks us with them. Let him have my secrets, if it will free my father from this . . . living death."

Jardir looked to the Par'chin, and his *ajin'pal* gave a nod. "Think you can do it, we owe it to Shanjat to try. We'll find another way to make the demon talk."

"Thank you, Par'chin," Shanvah said.

"But it ent just a matter of power, Shanvah," the Par'chin said. "It's a puzzle, and we ent got all the pieces."

"But you will try again?" Shanvah pleaded.

Jardir nodded. "Rise, Shanjat."

Jardir watched Shanjat's aura as he stood. In this state, without Alagai Ka to control him, his brother-in-law could resist no direct commands.

Jardir saw his words ripple across the otherwise placid pool, triggering more than just muscle memory. Shanjat's entire faculty engaged in a flare of brilliant color.

"Recite the Fourth Dune of the Evejah," Jardir commanded.

In life, such a command would have tested Shanjat greater than any combat, but with no will to resist, his mind produced every word in perfect recitation. As the colors flashed in his mind, though, they cast shadows.

"There." Jardir pointed.

The others had kept distance, but at the invitation, the Par'chin stepped in to examine. "See it."

Renna moved to stand next to him. "Ay. Like clouds on a blue sky."

"I do not see," Shanvah said.

"It is as we feared," Jardir said. "Alagai Ka has done more than crush your father's will. He has . . . infected his mind."

Shanvah bowed her head. "Even here, in the heart of Everam's power, the demon's spirit remains?"

"Ent the demon's spirit," the Par'chin explained. "More like . . . little notes left around his mind. *If* this *happens, do* that."

"So he has made a *gwil* of my father." An image flashed over Shanvah, her atop Alagai Ka, beating him savagely as ichor arced the air. "A dog taught tricks for his master."

"You demanded this, Niece," Jardir reminded. "You must steel yourself."

Shanvah removed her veil and nodded, aura relaxing. "I am centered, Uncle."

Jardir turned back to Shanjat. "Whom did you wrestle, at the festival after I first took the Skull Throne?"

"Qeran," Shanjat said. Lights flickered in his mind, but the shadows remained dark.

"Why?" Jardir asked. "You would have had a better chance if you had chosen Hasik, who had been at the couzi."

"Because victory is not enough for Hasik," Shanjat said. "He would not relent until he had shamed me to the onlookers. I knew Qeran would let me keep my honor."

They were truer words than the proud man would ever have spoken aloud, but with his will removed, he spoke them as easily as he recited scripture. The darkness in his mind remained dormant.

"Who would you choose now?" Jardir asked.

Shanjat's aura absorbed the question and color flared for an instant in a small part of his mind, but it dissolved away without igniting a response.

"Shanjat," the Par'chin said. "Do you think we should press on into the Core, or go back to the surface?"

Again Shanjat's mind considered the words, and dismissed them. "There." Renna pointed, but whatever it might have been vanished before Jardir could focus upon it.

"Father, does the demon make you lie to hurt me?" Shanvah asked.

A spark leapt across that gray chasm. "No."

Shanvah kept her center, aura placid, but Jardir knew the words would sting her for years to come.

"Do you want to die?" Renna asked.

The question flared, but dissipated against the gray wall.

"Right there," Renna said. "That's where the demon severed his will."

Shanvah's aura remained uncomprehending. She, too, could see magic's glow, but had not learned to read more than the most unguarded of feelings. "What does that mean?"

"It means your father's spirit has not traveled the lonely path," Jardir said. "Everything that made him who he was remains. His memories. His skills. The demon left them intact to tap into. But without will."

"His body is a prison to his spirit," Shanvah finished.

"What would you do if Alagai Ka was threatened at this moment?" Jardir asked.

The words did more than bridge the gap. The web of the demon's infection lit up like lightning rolling across the clouds.

"Interpose myself and protect him, unless he is threatened by one of you," Shanjat said.

"You are not to harm us?" Jardir was surprised.

"Not without the command," Shanjat said.

"What command?" Jardir pressed.

In response, Shanjat let out a sound that came from deep in his chest, something caught between growl and hiss, resonating from his very center. The air rumbled with it.

"And if given that command?" Jardir asked, already knowing the answer from the crackle of the demon's web.

"Kill any in my path, take the demon, and flee."

Jardir reached out his hand, touching his friend's head. His fingers drifted across the neat, tight braids Shanvah had tied, touching the skin between. The contact was like a spark, and he sent his will leaping into Shanjat. He could feel his friend's mind, his body, much as he imagined Alagai Ka must. A puppet to control.

But Jardir had no interest in peering into his brother-in-law's private memories, no desire to desecrate his body by making it dance. Instead he leapt across the gap in Shanjat's mind and attacked the demon's corruption.

This was not something he would have dared attempt before. Mere hours ago, he would have been hacking into his friend's brain with a spear. Now he moved as delicately as a *dama'ting* scalpel, cutting away rotten flesh.

But the demon had been too clever. The threads wove into Shanjat's mind like palm fronds in a basket, and even as Jardir began to cut, he saw how too much damage threatened to unravel the weave. He would need to replace them with something else.

But what? Could he create commands and place them in Shanjat's mind? How would that be different from what the demon had done? How would that restore the man he had been?

He pulled back, leaving the demon's corruption much as it was, focusing instead upon the gap. He had bridged it easily enough with his own will, and there, at its edges, he could see Alagai Ka's influence, like a scum of oil atop clear water. When Shanjat was issued a command, or one of the demon's conditions was met, the scum bubbled to life, bursting aflame to bridge the gap.

It was complex magic. Not beyond Jardir's capabilities, perhaps, but certainly beyond his skill. He was trying to rewrite a book written in a language he could only read a few words of.

He wished Inevera were here. Healing was a *dama'ting* art, and there was none better in all the world than his first wife.

But could even she tell him how to create will from nothingness? Where desire originated, and how it was transformed into action? These were questions for Everam Himself.

On sudden inspiration, Jardir gathered his power, reaching up into the heavens, he knew not where or for what. Just reaching, as high as he could.

Everam, Creator of all that is, he begged. *Show me the path to cure my brother from the infection Nie has set upon him. Give me the strength to rid him of her foul taint.*

But for all the vaunted power of the Spear of Ala, it gave him no direct communication with Heaven. Everam, locked in His eternal struggle with Nie, had no time for the prayers of men.

If He is listening at all.

The thought crept in like a thief, fleeing like a coward when he turned to it. He wanted to blame Nie. Blame Alagai Ka. Blame anything but his own mind, but in that moment he knew the truth of his doubts.

What if the Par'chin is right? What if Heaven is a lie?

He pulled his will back into himself, turning to Shanvah.

"I cannot help him, Niece. I can drive out the demon's influence, but without anything to replace it, he would be left even more lifeless than before. If his will is trapped somewhere, I cannot find it, and only Everam can create will out of nothingness."

If Everam exists, the voice whispered in his mind again.

He lowered his spear, feeling tired, even as near-limitless power coursed through him. "Let us be gone from this empty place."

CHAPTER 35

SEVERED

334 AR

Every moment in the prison of human bone was agony. The religion of the sun dwellers was a sad fiction full of inconsistencies and contradiction, but the shared emotional conviction of Kavri's faithful imprinted powerful magic on their relics.

Their Unifier, their *Deliverer,* had been first in the thoughts of every human, focused by a lifetime of hopes and prayers. Undiminished after thousands of years, it was why the demons had never truly conquered the hated fortress. It was time that killed the enemy. Time, and the war dogs. For centuries, this place had lain dormant—a sleeping giant too near the hive for anyone's liking.

Kavri's witch queen bound the belief of the people upon the wielder of the relics of power, the Spear and Crown of Shar'Dama Ka. Now, with his coming, the Heir had woken that power.

His might was terrifying in the *csar*—greater even than Alagai Ka at the center of the mind court. His drones, all but mindless, could not focus their magic in joint cause as the humans could.

From the Skull Throne at the *csar*'s center, the Heir could crush the hive, if only he could reach so far.

There were limits, even here.

Every moment on the greatward was agony for Alagai Ka, even with the protection of the Heir.

Worse, the Heir, drunk on power, might at any moment decide the Consort was no longer needed and slay him outright. Or perhaps grow in his understanding of his power to attempt to link with the demon's mind. Anywhere else, and Alagai Ka would welcome the attempt, confident no human will could match him. But here there would be no defense. The Heir could strip away his memories like a talon flaying flesh.

But even that might not matter, if he died in this cage. There was no food, no drink, no air. Alagai Ka Drew on his dwindling reserves of power to meet those needs, but his supply was nearly exhausted. The bone spikes, scraping at every angle, were anathema, sucking power like mosquitoes.

And so Alagai Ka, who had held iron-fisted primacy over the mind court longer than any Consort in the memory of the hive, knew fear. Stark terror that should be the suffering of lesser creatures.

Better to have attempted his escape early and taken his chances with the war dogs than suffer like this, slowly poisoned by the idealism of lesser beings.

There was a sound. Alagai Ka stiffened, muscles tense to avoid touching any of the bone spikes with enough pressure to prick his skin.

The prison walls parted, and for a moment relief flooded him, but then it was replaced again by pain as he was unceremoniously dropped to the ground, eyes burning from the light.

It baffled the demon why the primitive creatures took such comfort in the limited spectrum of light, depriving themselves of information more than if they volunteered to blindfold themselves and stuff wax in their ears.

Alagai Ka coughed, gasping air greedily to spare further drain on his power. His skin had turned pale, his muscles gelatin. He struggled weakly to rise, to present himself with dignity before his captors, but this time it was beyond him.

"Pick him up," the Heir ordered, and Shanjat reached down, lifting Alagai Ka like a hatchling and using his robe as a sling to hold him against his bare back.

On contact with his skin, Alagai Ka attempted to slip into the human drone's mind.

For one terrifying moment, the effort was beyond him. Alagai Ka wondered if he was already past the point of no return, and the void was inevitable.

He wondered which of the remaining minds would outlast the others, and realized he didn't care. What matter, if it was not him?

Fear gave him strength to try again, and this time he made the connection, putting on the drone's body like a raiment. The humans had attempted to tamper with the drone's mind, but their damage was minimal and easily repaired.

The gesture told Alagai Ka much. They had attempted to circumvent his aid, and failed. They still had need of him, at least until they exited the cavern.

The rules would change then, as they entered the outskirts of the hive.

"No insults?" the Heir asked. "No half lies to cut at us?"

"Finally learned his place, maybe," the Hunter said. Alagai Ka glared at her. When the time was right, she would be the first to die.

The drone Shanjat smiled behind his veil, eyes flicking lower.

Her hatchling will die first, the demon amended, *seasoning her mind with anguish that will be exquisite to taste.*

Renna couldn't stop thinking about the look Shanjat had given her. Pure hatred. And the way his eyes flicked to her belly. It was all she could do not to kill the creature.

But much as she hated to admit it, they needed him. Consuming the mind demon's brain had given her no insights into their journey, and even Jardir in his seat of power had not produced a better way to the demon hive.

The howls resumed when they exited Sharik Hora, sounding close. Too close. They were far from the walls that kept the *gwilji* at bay, yet the sound echoed through the streets of the *csar,* stiffening the close-cropped hair on the back of her neck.

"Quickly, now." Jardir was holding tremendous power as he led them toward the city gates.

"What're you plannin'?" Renna asked.

"You and the Par'chin had the will to resist the . . . seduction of power when you fed on demon flesh," Jardir said, eyes ahead. "The war dogs did not, and my people paid the price for it. When we open the gate, I plan to cleanse them from Ala, and let Everam be their judge."

Renna thought of Shadow, Evin Cutter's wolfhound, who had eaten demon meat and grown to the size of a bear. The dog was terrifying in battle, but still licked his master's face, and guarded Evin's family with loyalty to do any canine proud.

She thought of the Warded Children, and how they grew violent and dangerous when left unchecked. Of all the times she herself had struck at Arlen—the love of her life—in a fit of magic-fueled rage.

"Maybe they ent all gone," she said. "Maybe there's still a way to reach 'em. Remind 'em what they were trained to fight."

Jardir shook his head. "With the original *gwilji,* perhaps. But these are generations removed, born in darkness, never having known the light of the sun. Our mission is too important to let them hinder us."

The howls sounded again, seemingly all around them, and Renna ceased her arguments, putting a hand to her belly. There was time for mercy, and time to protect oneself.

There was a clatter behind them, as of claws on stone. The others heard it, too. But when they turned, there was nothing to be seen. A moment later it sounded off to the side. Ahead of them. Above. Renna strained her wardsight, but still she could see nothing.

"All around us," Arlen said. "Bein' hunted. Herded."

"How can that be?" Jardir asked. "The walls hold them outside the city."

The *gwil* that leapt from a low rooftop, claws swiping at him, gave proof to the falsehood. Even right before her eyes the creature seemed insubstantial. It didn't roar, nor did the roof creak or shift with its leap. It was silent as a shadow.

Even taken by surprise, Jardir whipped his spear up in time

to block, yet the *gwil* passed through shaft and wards alike, a creature of smoke.

But its claws were solid enough. The war dog's blow slipped his defenses and cut deeply into Jardir's robes. He staggered, and blood struck the ancient cobbles.

"They have us surrounded." Shanjat could have been talking about the weather. All around, Renna could hear the clacking of those hard, obsidian claws. The *gwilji* were hard to look at directly, but in her peripheral vision, she could glimpse them.

And they stank. The scent more than anything told her where they were. Dozens of them, stalking like cats in a field.

Jardir recovered quickly, raising his spear and letting forth a blaze of magic at the creature as it tamped its claws down for another swing. The blast struck the demon center mass, but it passed harmlessly through and the creature leapt again.

Another pounced from an alleyway. Shanvah got her shield up in time, and there was an earsplitting whine as its claws scratched against the metal. She batted at it with her spear, but the creature scrabbled at the shield tenaciously, even as her blows passed through it like smoke.

Three more sprang from above, going after Renna and Shanjat. Renna drew a wind ward that slowed the dogs long enough for them to dodge aside, but the creatures had too little mass, and they resumed their attack the moment the wind stopped.

Two leapt at Arlen, but safe on the greatward, he misted along with them, catching them by the throats in the between-state, where strength was meaningless and only will mattered. He dominated the creatures, forcing them to solidify, then broke their necks with a sharp shake.

"Back-to-back!" Arlen called, sliding in close to Renna. Shanjat complied immediately, taking up her other side. Renna would rather have had one of the war dogs at her left.

Shanvah gave a shove at the next scrabbling attack from the *gwil,* knocking it back long enough for her to join the formation at Shanjat's left. The Spear of Kaji was a blur as Jardir quickstepped to complete the ring between her and Arlen.

"The crown!" Arlen shouted as he seized another dog, forcing it to solidify so he could tear its jaw off. "Drive them back with the crown!"

"Do you think me a fool, Par'chin?!" Jardir shouted back. "The crown no more repels them than it does you!"

"That explains why they weren't stopped by the walls," Shanvah said.

"Haunted, I warned you," Shanjat said. "This drone requires a weapon."

"Not on your life," Renna said.

Shanjat blew out a breath, an expression so human it was easy to forget there was a demon at the reins. "His shield, then."

Jardir frowned, but he slipped his brother-in-law's shield from his back, flinging it to Shanjat.

The demon immediately had Shanjat put the item to work, slapping aside black talons flashing in the air. "Sever the talons! They are the war dogs' only remaining link to the corporeal world. Without them they . . ."

"Can't resist the call of the Core," Renna finished, stepping into the next attack with a front kick, misting her leg enough to connect and stop the *gwil* short. She slashed with her father's knife, and bloody talons clattered to the cobbles. The war dog howled as it dissipated fully, sucked down into the Core like dust into a bellows.

Jardir sliced the talons from his attacker and watched it similarly dissipate. More war dogs raced at them, silent but for their clattering claws. Jardir raised his spear, and the very cobbles of the street responded, leaping into the air to form a wall too solid for their claws to pass through. They howled, but Renna did not think it would delay them long. All around, *gwilji* were gathering.

"We have to get out of the city!" the demon shouted through Shanjat. "The war dogs fear to hunt in the deeper tunnels."

He left the reason unsaid, but it was obvious to all. There would be demons in the lower tunnels, likely in numbers the surface dwellers had never seen. Drones the demon prince might, even now, be able to influence.

"Lot of ground to cover just to get to the gates, much less out of this cavern," Renna said.

"Leave that to me." Jardir grit his teeth, and his aura brightened, its normal crackles and whorls flat with concentration.

There was clattering from all around, and Renna thought there must be thousands of the dogs in the *csar*, slowly closing for the kill.

The sound grew into a cacophony—a clash of steel, rapping of wood, whooshing of air.

Windows and doors burst open all over the *csar*, spears flying out to answer Jardir's call. They spun though the air, gathering in clouds as they swept the streets.

"If the war dogs cannot be slain by magic," Jardir watched the spinning blades sever the claws from a pack of *gwilji* and send them to the Core, "let them fall to the spears of the very masters they betrayed."

With spears dancing around them in an impenetrable cloud, Jardir resumed a steady march through the *csar*. *Gwilji* howled and yelped, the streets littered with bloodied black talons. The clatter of their claws was growing fainter as they fled the storm.

Jardir opened the gates with a wave of his spear, and they stepped out into the cavern. War dogs were gathered before the gate, and the cloud of spears cut them apart. Some, clinging to stalactites and stalagmites, tried to leap at them from above, but Jardir sensed them and spears spun to catch them in midair, shearing away the talons that let them cling to the physical world.

Alagai Ka heard the sound the moment the doors of the *csar* opened, but it was not the howls of war dogs.

The queen was crooning.

The humans heard nothing. Felt nothing. But even in the demon's weakened and warded state, the sound was unmistakable, reverberating in every stone. The queen had begun to lay, sending out an endless stream of drone eggs. Not enough to lure back the other minds, desperately trying to establish hives of their own, but by the next turning she would begin to lay a few valuable mimics, a smaller group of minds, and six queens, deadly from the moment they hatched. They would begin sucking magic from the queen, growing more powerful by the moment as they fought one another with talon and stinger for primacy.

Unless a Consort was there to kill them before they grew too strong—as Alagai Ka had done many times in the past—or if his strongest brethren each stole one and fled. If that should happen, it might be millennia before the Consort could regain primacy, if he could manage it at all.

He could delay no longer. He needed to escape and return to the mind court now, while it remained deserted, restoring his power before his brethren returned. His greatest rivals were already destroyed. There was none who could stand against him once he regained his greatward.

He kept the drone focused, showing nothing as his insides clenched. Still, the demon breathed a sigh of relief with his own lungs when they stepped off the greatward of the *csar*. The pain squeezing him for the past day dissipated, and options that were unavailable a moment ago moved back into reach.

But he had to be careful. The Heir's current display of power was terrifying. Even the inanimate objects of the *csar* leapt to his command by the strange magic of human faith. Setting so many weapons spinning in unison was a measure of the Heir's will, and that had grown into something formidable. The spinning spears worked like a wardnet, protecting them from all sides at once.

The surface dwellers had grown powerful, and power emboldened.

The Heir did not ask for direction as he led the way across the cavern, headed for the correct tunnel to most quickly reach the hive. They had learned something, at least, during their time in the human temple. Perhaps too much.

The howls of wounded and fleeing *gwilji* died away, and the Heir, his ability to Draw upon the *csar*'s power diminishing with every step, began sending the summoned spears soaring back over the *csar* walls, no doubt to the very spots they had lain for thousands of years.

When the last of the spears had been sent home, the Heir took a moment to breathe, the others focused outwardly in defense.

And in that moment, covered by his shield, Shanjat reached

into his robe and took up his daughter's tear bottle. He broke the seal with a thumbnail and spilled the tears—infused with emotion magic—onto his fingers, drawing a quick warding onto his chest, and a few others onto the chain that bound them.

The wards glowed briefly, fading as the tears evaporated. Shanjat's eyes flicked back and forth, but there was no sign his captors noticed. It was unlikely they would, for the magic that now radiated from him stank of humanity, of love and emotion and all the vile weakness of his captors. They might sense the magic, but they would not see it as a threat.

Indeed, it wasn't a threat—to them. It was an invitation and a trail, singing of human frailty, inviting a mimic demon to attack Shanjat.

It was a plan not without risk. The Consort had not been able to grow enough layers of flesh to force the tattoos from his skin, and an attacking mimic could accidentally kill him with a stray slash of talon.

But even an instant's physical contact would be enough to take control of the mimic. With such a powerful drone, he could flee to a safe space long enough to flay the wards from his skin. Then nothing could prevent his dissipating to an empty mind court.

By the time these insects found their way down without him—if they even could—the Consort would be back in power, healed, and have an endless army of drones to stand guard as he imprinted upon the new generation.

It was two days in the lower tunnels before Alagai Ka sensed the mimic.

Two days of cautious descent, using wards and the Singer's wretched voice to slip unnoticed past hundreds of drones that hunted—and sometimes fell prey to—the subterranean life in the higher tunnels.

The Heir kept the warding field of the crown in close, lest the demons sense its presence. They put their backs to the tunnel walls when packs of demons passed through, using subtle magics to divert the herding drones from brushing against the field.

The stupidity of drones was an asset in dominating them, but in times of war with the humans, it could be a liability. The hive's defenses were weak.

Ahead, the mimic waited, wrapped around a great stalagmite mound. Its body blended perfectly with the surrounding rock, down to the layers of sediment and the slickness of dripping water. Its magic was drawn in close, hidden beneath its outer layer where even the Heir would miss it at a casual glance.

It was close. So close. But whether by instinct or sheer luck, the Heir led them on a path that put the mimic just out of reach. Even this more intelligent drone could not pierce the cloak cast by the Singer and his captor's wards, save for the human stench the tear bottle painted on Shanjat. The mimic could sense the prey was close, but not see or hear it. Not yet.

The Consort slowed, and the Heir and Explorer, senses focused ahead, did not notice as they pulled ahead until they were just out of sight.

The mimic hid just a few short strides away, but Shanjat's daughter was positioned between them. The Consort had Shanjat stumble slightly as they passed another stalagmite, cut off momentarily from the others' line of sight.

He shattered the weakened links on the chain, freeing the drone's hands and feet. Shanvah reacted quickly, but not quickly enough. The drone's fighting skill and muscle memory were undiminished.

With the element of surprise, the drone quickly established a dominance hold, leaving a free hand to hammer precise blows, shattering bone and breaking joints. In seconds he cast her aside, a broken thing, and sprang for the mimic.

His sudden movement negated the cloaking wards, but the mimic gave no sign as he approached, continuing to lie in quiet wait, like a spider in his web. When he got in close it would strike, and the demon might have only seconds to slip free of Shanjat's mind and into the mimic's. He readied his last reserves of power for the transfer.

The Hunter noticed him bolt from cover. She was a blur of movement as she ran to cut him off, unwittingly putting her back to the mimic. Her knife was in her hand, and her aura was without mercy. She would kill him, if she could.

The woman was a fool, facing him with her body. Her knife. She could have drawn wards where she stood, powering his tattoos and killing him. The humans had power, but their primitive minds had not come to trust it more than steel.

She lunged, but for all her magic-enhanced strength and speed the Hunter did not have skill to match this drone. He caught her wrist in a turn that set her blade shaking in nerveless fingers. She turned her attention to keeping the grip, letting the drone hold her in place long enough to kick hard off a ridge in the tunnel floor, adding power to the already mighty blow as he struck a fist into the rounded egg sac bloating her belly.

The Hunter screamed, knocked from her feet. The Consort followed her down with a rain of swifter blows, all aimed at the same, vulnerable spot.

Renna cursed silently, lungs emptying as she landed hard on her back. Shanjat was atop her immediately, continuing his heavy blows. It was not the fluid grace of his daughter's *sharusahk*. The *sharukin* of the *Sharum* were cruder, but no less effective. Renna thought herself a skilled fighter, but he took her as easily as a cat took a mouse.

But while the demon had full control of Shanjat's skills, it did not seem to care much for his sense of pain. By the time he noticed his mistake, Shanjat's hand was shattered to pulp.

"Think I'm stupid?" Renna had used powerful magic to strengthen the muscles of her stomach. Her child floated in a suit of armor hard as warded glass. "Saw you eyein' my belly back in the *csar*."

The demon's hesitation gave her an instant, and Renna punched Shanjat in the chest, the impact wards on her fist flashing. She felt ribs crack. He was knocked several steps back, landing with surprising grace.

Renna was already back on her feet, charging in. The bone handle of her knife was hard in her hand, throbbing with power.

"I would tell you it is not personal," Shanjat said. "That it is survival, my race against yours, that forces my hand."

She was faster, stronger, but still Shanjat picked off her attacks until he locked on to her knife arm, twisting until he had control. Slowly, he pressed the knife in Renna's hand toward her belly. The magicked blade was one of the few things Renna did not trust her belly against.

"I would tell you that," Shanjat whispered, "but it would be a lie."

Renna remembered the first time that knife cut her. She was five, and Harl made her clean it after a kill. The blade, sharp as a razor even then, slid through the cleaning cloth like it was nothing, cutting a thin line across her palm.

Her mother gasped, but Harl only grunted, holding up a hand to keep her from rushing to the girl. He caught Renna's tiny hand and pressed it in her face, forcing her to look at the reddening wound.

Knife's like a mean old hound, Harl used to say. *Bite what you tell it to, but you ent smart, it'll bite you, too.*

Renna grit her teeth, forcing the blade back. She could hear Arlen and Jardir rushing to her, but they would not be in time.

She breathed, visualizing her movements as Shanvah had instructed her. Then, in a sharp jolt, she broke the hold and reversed it.

The ground is the true battlefield, sister, the Sharum'ting taught. *Bring your opponent to it, establish control, and force submission by blood or air.*

Now Shanvah lay senseless, perhaps dead. It was time to put an end to Alagai Ka, even if it meant finding the Core on their own.

But that didn't mean Shanjat had to go with him. Renna pinned his struggling limbs and curled up, putting her foot between Shanjat and the demon. She kicked, tearing his robes and throwing the demon far enough away to power its tattoos without killing Shanjat.

"Gonna burn you like the sun," she growled. Arlen and Jardir were rushing back to the scene, bright with readied power. There would be no escape for the demon king.

Alagai Ka tumbled less gracefully than Shanjat, coming up hard against a stalagmite mound. Renna readied her attack when the movement stopped, but her concentration was broken when the stalagmite reached out of its own accord to wrap around the demon.

"Mimic!" she shouted, though it was obvious to all by now.

Idiot girl, she cursed herself. *Demon was plannin' that all along. Played right into his talons.*

All three of them, Renna, Arlen, and Jardir, unleashed powerful blasts of magic, but the demon sloughed them off even as the stalagmite was destroyed in a cloud of debris. None of them hesitated, bulling forward through the screen.

"I have him in the crown's bubble!" Jardir cried. "He will not escape!"

The demon was only out of sight for an instant, but when Renna's vision cleared, the mimic had swollen, with the spiked armor of a rock demon and the horned tentacles of a water demon. Rows of four-inch teeth grew from a mouth large enough to swallow her head and shoulders.

"Mind's still bound by the tattoos!" Arlen shouted. "It's in there somewhere, wearin' the mimic like a suit of armor."

He drew a mimic ward, smashing the demon hard against the edge of Jardir's bubble. The creature flattened, and Renna glimpsed a lump in the middle. She leapt, knife leading. She would not hesitate again.

The mimic flowed away faster than she could move, tentacles shooting out to knock them all back. Renna and Jardir were ready, slicing at the tentacles. Mimics could heal instantly, but they could not regrow what was severed.

Alagai Ka knew this as well. The tentacle was thicker than her blade, the demon accepting the cut to whip around and strike her from behind. Knocked to her knees, she glimpsed Arlen from the corner of her eye.

Arlen could have dodged, or warded his tentacle away, but he caught it instead, holding the long powerful muscles with his bare hands as he shocked killing magic down the limb. He caught sight of her then, and his eyes widened. "Ren!"

The demon took advantage of the distraction. A second limb split off from the one Arlen held and drew a quick ward, knocking him sprawling. Another quick ward collapsed part of the ceiling onto him.

Renna did not have time to watch things unfold. The demon continued to press the attack, tentacles merging, dividing— turning hard and sharp, then soft as jelly. She fought to draw a ward in the air, but it slapped her hands, foiling the attempts while it searched for a submission hold.

Renna wanted to dissipate. It would be so easy. But this deep underground, the call of the Core—a song once like the seductive burble of a brook—was now a river roaring with spring melt. Could she swim that? Could she trust that she could pull herself—her baby—back out?

No. She needed to stay solid.

Jardir did not appear to be faring better. He was fast, picking off attacks and delivering the occasional blow of his own, but he was a shadow of the infinitely powerful man he had been in the *csar*.

The demon had a score of limbs now. Jardir's spear was a blur, but more than one slipped past his defenses. With the power of the crown focused on keeping the demons in, he could not use it to turn the demon's blows. He was stripped to the waist instead, the wards scarring his skin bright with power. The demon could not touch him, but he was battered and bruised by the rebound as it pummeled the wards. Jardir shrugged the blows away, but soon they would begin to tell.

Then one tentacle, appearing from the midst of half a dozen just like it, folded back at the last instant to produce a hidden stone. The rock shattered against Jardir's brow, knocking the crown from his head. It flew through the air, clattering to the tunnel floor several feet back.

The instant the item slipped free, the demon's attacks ceased. Tentacles retracted and the mimic leapt, shifting in midair to a large field demon. It hit the ground running, racing down the tunnel.

Jardir glanced at the crown, but there was no time to retrieve it. He lifted his spear and took off after the demon.

Renna shook herself, focusing magic to strengthen her stride as she gripped her knife and bolted after them.

Jardir was gaining on the demon, and she on him, when a tentacle extended from the demon's back, drawing a ward in the air. There was an explosion, and the tunnel ahead collapsed. Renna lost sight of Jardir, unsure if the falling stone had missed him or buried him alive.

"Ahmann!" She was surprised at the passion in her voice. She stuck her knife in its sheath, coughing at the falling dust, but did not hesitate to reach for the nearest stone and tear it away. And the stone after that, and the one after that. But with every stone, her fears grew. The demon's magic was precise. Even with her strength it would take too long to dig through.

Shanjat and Shanvah were likely dead, and perhaps Arlen with them. Was Jardir buried under all this stone? Was she the last one left alive?

"Sorry, love." She put a hand on her belly as she prepared to dissipate. "Whole world's countin' on us." It was just a short hop through the rubble. Too quick to pull her down to the Core.

She hoped.

"Ren, wait!" Arlen caught her arm, and relief flooded her. He held the Crown of Kaji gripped in his fist. "I'll go after him. Shanvah's alive, but she ent gonna be for long. Do what you can and I'll be back."

"You better be!" she screamed, but he was already mist, flowing through the barrier.

Renna hesitated. Every instinct in her body screamed at her to follow, to help Arlen. But the babe was shifting in her belly, and Shanvah's aura was dim and flickering.

Gotta trust him to save himself. Like he done for me.

Renna rushed over to Shanvah, laying the young woman flat as she pulled magic through her and Read it. There were breaks and bleeding everywhere—it was a miracle she had lasted so long.

"I . . ." Shanvah gasped.

"Don't try'n talk," Renna said.

"I am . . ." Shanvah breathed again, "ready for the . . . lonely . . . path . . ."

Renna spat. "Core, you are. Got work to do, girl. Dyin' ent no excuse for shirkin' chores."

Renna wished she had a Gatherer's training, or Arlen's skill at healing magic, but there was no time for lament. Power rushed into her as she Drew, holding Shanvah's hand as she extended her magic into the *Sharum'ting*.

Her hands worked along with the power, massaging bones and flesh back into place as infusions of magic sped the body's healing. She focused on Shanvah's chest first, securing her heart and lungs, then repaired the fractures in her skull, drained the swelling from her brain.

She worked outward from there, losing track of time as she worked. She blinked, eyes dry and burning, and knew it was time to stop. She had seen how healing drained Arlen. If she weakened herself too much . . .

Shanvah's eyes were closed, but she was breathing comfortably now, her broken body whole, if still weak. Renna drew back, still holding an excess of power despite the burn that was beginning to seep into her muscles. At any moment, Arlen, Jardir, or a thousand demons could burst through that cave-in.

She waited long, tense moments, straining her senses, but there was nothing, no sign of life up ahead.

A wheezing startled her, and she whirled, knife in hand, to find Shanjat, lying exactly where she had left him in the struggle. With no one to tell him to rise, the warrior would lie there until he died.

It wouldn't be long. Renna's punch had shattered his sternum, and his hand was a crumpled ruin. The mind had been heedless of Shanjat's injuries, interested only in escape.

She could save him, even now. His injuries were not as extensive as Shanvah's. But to what end? Jardir at a dizzying height of power had not been able to fix the man. If Arlen did not return with the demon, then what use was Shanjat? And if Arlen did bring Alagai Ka back, would it only give the demon another chance to use Shanjat to escape? To try to kill her child?

Renna's hand found the comforting grip of her knife. Her gaze flicked to Shanvah and found the girl watching her, eyes wide behind her scarf and veil. They locked stares, and no other words were needed.

Shanvah struggled onto her side, pushing onto an elbow, working a knee under her. "If it must be done, sister, I should be the one to do it."

Renna moved to help her, but the girl waved her off. She struggled to her feet, wobbling slightly until she found her balance. A knife of curving glass appeared in her hand, and she stalked forward.

She stood over her father a long time, then knelt beside him, cradling his head in her lap.

"Is your soul prepared for the lonely path?" she whispered.

"Only Everam can judge a soul." Shanjat's voice was devoid of emotion.

Shanvah blinked, pain and confusion in her aura. The question had been rhetorical.

"Do you wish to go?" Shanvah asked. Renna saw tears in her eyes but made no move to try and catch them. This moment was too private. Again she turned her senses outward. How long had Arlen been gone? Minutes? An hour? More?

There was no way to tell, and no way to ignore the last words of father and daughter.

"I no longer wish anything," Shanjat said in the dull monotone.

"What would you have wished, before?" Shanvah asked.

"To serve Shar'Dama Ka, who will deliver us from Nie," Shanjat said. "To protect my daughter, greater than any son."

The words were cold, but Shanvah sobbed, clutching him to her.

"Sister," Shanvah begged, and Renna rushed to her side. "I cannot bear this burden. You must . . . must . . ."

Renna gently took the glass knife from Shanvah's limp hand. Their eyes met, and Renna slid the knife unused back into its hidden sheath in Shanvah's robe.

"You heard the man." Renna ignored the burn as she Drew more power to heal Shanjat. "Dyin' ent no excuse for shirkin' chores."

It was hours before Renna could clear the rubble enough to squeeze through, but there was no sign of the others on the far side.

They were buried, woulda been signs, she told herself. *Woulda sensed it.*

They were alive. Or had been, when they passed this point. But had the demon killed Jardir? Had Arlen been sucked down into the Core? Was Alagai Ka on his way back right now with an army of demons?

She climbed back to the chamber where Shanvah and Shanjat lay. Their bodies had been repaired, but food was required for full healing.

For her, as well. The baby kicked and squirmed as it often did when too much time passed without a meal. She found their packs, producing the bowls Jardir used and filling them with soil, packing it down and smoothing the surface.

"Sister, what are you doing?" Shanvah asked.

"Makin' food," Renna said.

"That is one of the most difficult wardings of the *dama'ting*," Shanvah warned. "To prepare the holy food and drink incorrectly is said to create a poison that can kill with a single crumb or drop."

Renna felt a churning in her gut, but she forced a shrug to her shoulders. "Ent gonna let us starve down here."

She drew the wards as she had seen Jardir do so many times. The magic burned as it passed through her, but it seemed to work. The soil in one bowl became steaming couscous, and in the other, clear water.

Still, she looked at them doubtfully, Shanvah's warning repeating itself endlessly in her mind. But what alternative was there? Finally she grunted, reaching out.

"Sister, let me!" Shanvah cried. "You are with child. There is no need to risk two lives. I should taste the food."

"What difference does it make?" Renna asked. "If it's poison, we're both dead anyway."

"If I die you could make for the Spear of Ala," Shanvah said. "The wards for food and drink remain there, and the temple is secure."

"Great," Renna said. "Fight through Creator only knows how many war dogs to die of old age in some forgotten fort."

"Only if the Deliverer does not return," Shanvah said.

"Ent waitin' out the war," Renna said. "Meant to do that, would've stayed home. Got a better reason why I shouldn't eat the food?"

"I am more expendable." Shanjat's voice was flat as he answered the rhetorical question.

Renna and Shanvah exchanged a look. At last, Shanvah nodded, taking the tiny bowl, cup, and eating sticks from her pack. She knelt with her father as she had so many times before, and they prayed together before Shanjat, at her command, drained the cup and took up the eating sticks, swallowing a mouthful.

Renna realized she was holding her breath. She blew it out, and when Shanjat did not drop writhing to the floor, she fell on the food like a demon over a fresh kill.

Later, refreshed by the food and drink, the three of them shouldered their packs and squeezed through the rubble, following the tunnel down until it came to another cavern. A great hole had been blown in the floor, with a drop of hundreds of feet to a great underground canyon below.

Had they all fallen through? Was it a trap Arlen or Jardir avoided? A shortcut to the Core? There was no way to know. Renna tried Reading the currents of magic, but there was too much information for her to sort out.

"Demonshit," she growled, her legs dangling over the terrifying drop. In addition to the hole, there were several tunnels branching off from here, and she didn't remember the map they had seen. The only copy was in Arlen's notebook, gone now, along with her husband. "Even if they didn't fall, which tunnel leads to the hive?"

There was a shuffling of feet, and Shanjat began walking away from them. The warrior picked the third tunnel to the left with no hesitation, and began making his way down it.

Renna and Shanvah met each other's eyes for a long moment, then turned and followed.

CHAPTER 36

SMOKE AND MIST

334 AR

Leesha looked back from atop Pestle, seeing her mother holding Olive, receding in the distance. Not for the first time, she wondered if she was making the biggest mistake of her life.

Wonda noted the movement as Leesha shook her head to banish the thought. "All right, mistress?"

"I'm fine," Leesha said. "Just wasting thoughts on death and failure."

"Such thoughts are not wasted, mistress," Micha said. Leesha glanced at the girl, usually so silent it was easy to forget she was there. Even now, she refused to doff her disguise, dressed in common *dal'ting* robes. She rode sidesaddle behind Kendall, her spears and shield hidden in their baggage.

"What is there to gain, dwelling on failure?" Leesha asked.

"My master taught my sisters and I to visualize our deaths every day in meditation," Micha said. "Glory on *alagai* talons, murdered in the night, poisoned by a rival. Thrown from a cliff. Pulled under to drown by a water demon. Every possible death we can imagine."

"That's horrid," Leesha said. "Why would you do such a thing?"

"A *Sharum* must always be ready to die, mistress," Micha said. "We keep thoughts of it close to remember to always be prepared, to keep our spirits pure. To know that life is a fleeting gift of Everam, and death comes for us all. *Inevera,* when the lonely path opens to me, I will walk it without looking back."

"There is wisdom in what you say," Leesha chose her words carefully, "but I prefer to visualize success, and strive to make that vision reality."

Micha bowed. "Of course, mistress. We are your instruments. The blade does not question the carver."

Leesha blinked. Was that what she had become? A carver of fate? She thought back to her foretellings, and the plans she formed from them. Plans that put thousands of lives in danger for what was never more than a slim chance of success. "Is that all you wish to be? A knife in someone else's hands?"

"Better the knife than the wood." Young Pawl rode beside Kendall and Micha on a nimble pony. "Father always said true power came from working in unison as part of something bigger."

Gared was waiting for them as they rode down from Leesha's keep to Cutter's Hollow proper, along with Headmistress Darsy, Captain Gamon, and Inquisitor Hayes.

"Any word from Stela or Franq?" Leesha knew the answer but needed to ask.

"Ent been sign o' any of the Warded Children in days," Gared said. "Camp's deserted."

Wonda spat. "Knew we couldn't count on 'em."

"Don't need 'em," Gared said. "Got two hundred lancers, five hundred Cutters, and near ten thousand Hollow Soldiers. Warders and Gatherers, too. Ent nothin' the demons can throw at us we can't handle."

"Aw, Gar," Wonda said. "Why'd you have to go and say a thing like that?"

Angiers was close to a week's ride by Messenger, but the Hollow Soldiers were on foot and could only march as fast as the supply trains. They sang *Keep the Hearthfire Burning* to lock their steps in daylight and guard the camp at night.

But the demons did not attack the first night. Or the second.

"We're cutting it too close," Leesha said over dinner after a week on the road. "Waning is just four nights away."

"Makin' good time," Gared said. "Trip's been quiet. Too quiet, you want honest word. Demons been gatherin' at the edge of Hollow Country for months, but then we walk off the greatward and they just leave us be?"

"Maybe they weren't expecting us to advance so aggressively," Darsy said.

Minds're selfish, Leesha remembered Arlen saying. *Never in a million years occur to them you might risk your own neck for someone else.*

"Gar's got a point, mistress," Wonda said. "You ever know demons not to attack somethin' right in front of 'em? On new moon, ay, but they been like this a week."

"There's a mimic with them," Leesha said.

"So what're they waitin' for?" Wonda asked.

"Rather be fightin' than waitin' for it," Gared said.

"Well I ent complaining," Kendall said. "I'll take waiting over fighting any day."

"I expect we'll all have our fill of fighting soon enough." Leesha sniffed the air, acrid and thick from cookfires for ten thousand men and women.

Darsy noticed it, too. She went to the tent flap, and her eyes widened just as cries of alarm began to ring through the camp. "Night."

"What is it?" Leesha rushed to the flap, seeing smoke thick in the air, an evil orange glow coming from the woods. "Creator. Gared! They've set the woods on fire! Give the order to pull stakes and move before it runs through the camp!"

Gared was out of the tent in moments barking orders, but Leesha knew it would not be enough. They kept underestimating the cunning of corelings. Why waste drones attacking their forces when a handful of flame demons could do the work with smoke and fire?

"Darsy, round up as many *hora* users as you can, and be quick about it."

The Hollowers stumbled down the road for half the night.

Leesha felt dizzy and her lungs burned, but not from smoke. She and the other *hora* users depleted much of their supply of demon bone creating firebreaks and wind to keep the worst of the smoke and embers away.

The strain was telling. More than one fainted, and others were forced to stop channeling when the pain became too great. Only Leesha and Darsy managed to keep on, and it was hours before the sun.

Greasy ash smudged everything, weakening wards up and down the line. Leesha passed a ragged squad of Hollow Soldiers, out of step with their company. Some soldiers still sang *Keep the Hearthfire Burning,* but choked with smoke and ash, it was hard to keep the beat.

Kendall worked Rojer's fiddle instead, using the *hora* embedded in the chinrest to amplify the sound a hundredfold. She still wore the headscarf Amanvah had given her, and kept the silk veil pulled over her mouth to filter the smoky air.

"Wind demon!" Wonda raised her bow, loosing an arrow. In an eyeblink she had another nocked and drawn.

Leesha looked up, seeing the flight of demons descending on them. The lead demon banked, dodging Wonda's first arrow, and her second. The third struck, and the demon veered off, crashing to the ground beside Kendall's horse.

Raising her *hora* wand, Leesha drew a powerful wind ward that flared in the air as the other wind demons struck it.

But then Kendall screamed, and Leesha turned to see the wind demon had become a rock, rising before her horse. Before she or Micha could react, the coreling spun and lashed out with its heavy tail, smashing the legs of their horse out from under them. Fiddle and bow fell from Kendall's grasp as they tumbled to the ground.

The mimic gave a distinctive cry, and from all around demons rushed out of the smoky haze to attack the road. Some of the wards flared, throwing them back, but many were compromised, and demons penetrated the exhausted ranks of the Hollow Soldiers.

The ragged squad nearby rushed in to help Leesha and the others, but she didn't like their chances against a mimic. "Stay back!" she cried as Gared charged the demon.

The mimic lashed out with an arm that extended to a whipping tentacle, but Gared was ready, hacking the limb free with his machete, never losing speed in his charge. Over his shoulder, Wonda kept firing, heavy wooden arrows thudding into the demon.

The demon struck at Gared, but his armor was strong, deflecting the blow as he got in close and buried his axe in the mimic's side.

"Mistress, look out!" Pawl pointed over her shoulder.

Leesha was so occupied watching the battle she didn't notice the squad of soldiers until they were almost upon her, charging with spears pointed at her breast. When she saw their faces, she knew something was wrong. She fumbled with her wand, scattering the men with an impact ward.

Spears and shields clattered away as they fell, their uniforms melting into scaled armor as they grew claws and great sharp teeth.

Mimics. Nearly a dozen of them. How had they gotten so close?

"Mimics on the road!" Darsy lifted her own *hora* wand. "Protect the countess!" There was no flourish to her warding, the mimic wards tight and blocky, but they were strong, and the demons were held back.

Gared's personal guard were the first to answer the call. Cutters Leesha had known all her life. Samm Saw and Tomm Wedge, Linder Cutter, Evin and his great wolfhound Shadow. A dozen others, including Quiet Jonn. Hard men in warded armor who had killed corelings by the hundred.

But these were no ordinary corelings. Shadow leapt on one of the mimics, five hundred pounds of tooth and claw, strong as a nightwolf. The demon caught the dog by the head, flinging it to the ground. Shadow yelped and lay still.

Evin and Linder used the distraction to get in close, but the demon's flesh turned thick and viscous, catching their axes and holding them fast as it slapped Evin away with a horned tentacle and lifted giant Linder like a doll, throwing him at Leesha.

The armored man sailed through the mimic wards and smashed into Pestle's legs. Leesha heard bones break as she was pitched from the saddle. Darsy screamed as she, too, lost her seat atop Mortar. Demons flowed around Darsy's wards, but the remaining Cutters met them head-on.

Samm could cut a wood demon's head off with a few

strokes of his great two-handed saw, but it was a slow weapon against a mimic. There was a seam in his armor at the elbow, and the demon's talons found it, severing the limb as it knocked him across the road. Tom Wedge swung his heavy sledgehammer, but the demon flowed around the weapon, snatching one of his own spikes and thrusting it into the eyeslit of his helmet. His sons screamed and charged the creature.

Leesha Drew power from her wand, recovering her strength as she got to her feet. She reached into a pouch at her waist, scattering warded klats that flashed and sparked, buffeting any demon that drew close to them. She drew impact and mimic wards, keeping the demons off balance, but there were too many of them, and her wand was already depleted.

A mimic spotted a gap in the silver wards hanging in the air, growing wings that beat two powerful strokes, taking it over the protection to drop on Leesha from above.

She fell back but could not bring her wand to bear in time. The demon would have had her, but there was a dissonant cry, and a great mattock swatted the mimic aside. Leesha watched numbly as Quiet Jonn charged past, driving his mattock home again and again.

The mimic squealed, form losing cohesion, but then it snaked a tentacle around the giant man and yanked him from his feet. Leesha hit the demon with a mimic ward, but two others spotted the gap and were already above her.

Kendall and Micha appeared, fiddle and song as one. Micha's fingers were at her throat, manipulating the wards of her choker to amplify her voice to match the power of Kendall's playing.

The demons scattered briefly, but they were wise to the trick, taking earless forms that could withstand the brunt of the music's power.

Leesha cast about for Wonda, but the girl was working in tandem with Gared, her attention fixed on the mimic demon. Both she and Gared had lost their weapons, Wonda punching with knuckles painted with blackstem wards and Gared with his heavy warded gauntlets. When the demon struck at one, the other charged in. Leesha warded their armor personally, and the creature's blows could find no purchase. Slowly, impossibly, they were pummeling the coreling to death.

Not that it would save her, as three mimics rushed Leesha, sweeping talons to tear up the road, hitting her with great clumps of packed dirt and choking soil. She was not injured but, momentarily blinded, she couldn't get her wand up in time as a tentacle wrapped around her. Immediately the demon grew wings and gave a great beat, attempting to carry her away.

There was a blur of mist, and something struck the demon, knocking it from the sky. The tentacle holding her turned white, and a warded fist shattered it.

"Ay, sorry we're late." Stela yanked the still-twitching tentacle from around Leesha and cast it aside. The demon attempted to regroup, but again there was a misting and Brother Franq appeared, smashing into the mimic and knocking it back. He drew a ward in the air, and lightning shocked through the creature.

All around, her Warded Children appeared. Callen Cutter. Keet Inn. Jarit and her *Sharum*. The mimics were unprepared for the new assault and attempted to flee, but the Children gave them no avenue to escape, encircling the demons with mimic wards as they moved in for the kill.

Stela offered a hand and Leesha took it, letting the girl pull her to her feet. "Hung back like you said, but it looked like you were in trouble."

"You did the right thing, dear," Leesha said. "This was precisely why I asked you to follow us."

"Didn't get the flamers until after they started the fire. Sorry about that."

"You kept it from getting worse," Leesha said. "Thank you."

All along the road, the Hollowers were regaining the upper hand. Exhausted soldiers had night strength now from killing demons, and without the mimics, the other demons fell into disarray and were scattered.

Scouts found them the next morning.

"Farmer's Stump is gone," Gared said. "Looks like some of the folk got out, but the town's destroyed. Demons are massing at the Angiers River. We won't make it through easy, or quick. They destroyed the bridge. We'll need to find a crossing, and they'll be waitin' come sunset."

"Keep moving," Leesha said. "Let them see you coming."

Gared looked at her. "No rippin' way. I'm goin' with ya."

"We already discussed this," Leesha said.

Gared shook his head. "*You* discussed it. I din't say spit."

"I am not asking, *General,*" Leesha said. "It's an order."

"Don't care about that." Gared balled his giant fist. "I took orders and left ya in Angiers and now Rojer's dead. Give all the orders ya want, I'll be corespawned before I let ya march into a nest of mind demons without my axe at yur back."

Leesha felt her throat tighten at the heartfelt words. For as long as she could remember, Gared Cutter had always been there to protect her. For all that he vexed her, the world felt a little safer when he was near.

But now was not the time for it. "You're not cut out for this one, Gared. Favah and I cast on this. Any men, and the mission will fail."

"Yur takin' Pawl!" Gared cried.

"He's just a boy," Leesha said, "and the one with contacts in the resistance. We need him to sneak us in, but a seven-foot-tall Cutter in wooden armor is going to be noticed. I need you here, leading the attack. I'm counting on you to smash in the gates before I get myself into too much trouble."

Wonda put a hand on Gared's shoulder. "Ent nothin' gonna happen to Mistress Leesha while I'm around, Gar."

Leesha could hear Gared's teeth grind. "Better not, or there'll be the Core to pay."

CHAPTER 37

JESSA'S GIRLS

334 AR

For two days and nights, Leesha, Wonda, Kendall, and Pawl hiked cross-country through virgin woodland, resting only when exhaustion demanded it.

All wore Cloaks of Unsight, but the protection was seldom needed. Demons grew scarce away from human settlements, and the ones they encountered were nudged away by Kendall's music. When she looked away from the girl, Leesha could pretend it was Rojer playing, and felt her friend watching over her on this last, desperate mission.

They made camp by a stream just south of Angiers. There was a small pool Leesha warmed with heat wards, that they might take it in turn to wash and put on fresh clothes to pass unnoticed in the city.

"You go first, mistress," Wonda said. "Won't let anythin' bother you."

Leesha didn't protest, letting the hot water soak her aching muscles as she expressed milk into the pool. Miles to the south, Olive was suckling at Elona's pap, and the thought brought a tear to her eye.

The sun was coming up as Leesha put on a fresh dress in the Angierian style. Kendall wore the motley pattern Angierian Jongleurs favored, and Pawl dressed as a common street urchin. Wonda kept her armor on, covering the breastplate with an Angierian tabard.

"This way," Pawl said. "The rendezvous is just over the next hill."

They kept to the shelter of the woods as the city came in sight, and Leesha gaped to see her apprentice Roni leaning against a tree, chewing on an apple. It was only a few months since she'd last seen her, but Roni looked years older. Well beyond her eighteen summers, especially with the low neckline of her dress and powder on her face.

"Mistress Leesha!" Roni kept her voice a harsh whisper, but she gave a little squeal and leapt into her arms, squeezing tightly. "Thank the Creator you've come."

"Gotten yourselves into a bit of trouble?" Leesha asked.

"Night, that's undersaid," Roni agreed.

Leesha reached out and tugged one of the carefully curled hairs framing Roni's painted face. The hair straightened and then sprang obediently back into shape. "What's all this?"

"Ent it lovely, mistress?" Roni struck a pose and gave her hair a flick. "Jessa's girls been showing us how to paint and preen."

Leesha turned to regard Pawl, who shrank under her glare. "Jessa? As in Weed Gatherer Jessa, who poisoned Duke Rhinebeck?"

Pawl shifted his feet. "Her Grace expected you would take the news amiss."

Leesha crossed her arms. "So she had you keep it from me until we were committed."

"Her Grace was no more pleased than you, Countess," Pawl said, "but the brothels were the only safe place to hide until we smuggle her out of the city."

"Mistress Jessa ent so bad," Roni said. "She and Jizell have been taking good care of folk since the . . . changes."

Leesha blew out a breath. "I look forward to seeing her. Can you get us inside?"

"Ay, mistress. There's a few small gates—just big doors, really—with only a handful of guards." Roni grinned. "Lonely men with nothing to do all day since the gates were shut. We bring them meals and give them someone to talk to."

Leesha nodded to Roni's low neckline. "And while they're talking . . ."

Roni giggled. "We take turns slipping out the gate. The girls'll open it a crack when they bring supper tonight, and I'll sneak us back in."

"The guards won't notice three extra women and a boy passing through?" Leesha asked.

Roni reached into her cleavage, producing a tiny wooden box. "Smell."

Leesha opened the box, filled with soft red wax. It smelled of roses, but beneath . . . "Tampweed and skyflower. Another trick Jessa's girls taught you?"

Roni winked. "Sometimes talk ent enough. A few kisses with that on our lips and they'll be seeing double."

Leesha wanted to disapprove, but she needed a way into the city, and Roni had always been boy-crazed. She seemed to think it no hardship to tease her way through the gate.

"Well done, Roni," she said instead, and a smile lit the girl's face. "I'm proud of you."

The shadows grew long as they waited in a small stand of trees by the gate, giving Leesha ample time to worry over her plan. Would the sun set with them still outside the city? It was the first night of Waning, and like a spider at the center of a web, the mind demons might sense a tremor in the wardnet if the gate opened at night.

She wondered where Gared and the others were—if they were all right. If her ruse worked and the minds did not realize she'd left her forces, all their attention would be focused on her friends.

But then there was a heavy click, and the door opened just a few inches.

"That's my cue." In a move that Leesha had seen Elona do countless times, Roni stuck a finger in her neckline, pulling down even as she used the heel of her hand to push her bosom up. She tugged the laces and tied a quick bow to hold things in place. "Wait here."

With that, she flitted off and slipped through the gate.

The wait was interminable. Leesha watched the shadows and guessed it was no more than a quarter hour, but it felt like days. She could feel her heart thumping in her chest.

At last, the gate opened wide enough to emit a familiar face. Mistress Jizell, Leesha's former teacher, reached out a meaty arm, waving them toward the door. "Quickly now."

Hurriedly they filed through. Jizell locked the heavy door and pulled the warded steel gate shut. She locked that as well, shoving the key into her cleavage.

A guard was passed out at the gatehouse table, Roni wiping the red from his lips. She took a half-empty mug of ale, spilled a bit on the table and his shirt, then arranged it into his hand. Through the next door Leesha could hear laughter.

Leesha held out her arms to embrace her old teacher, but Jizell took a full platter of mugs off the table and shoved it at her instead. "We can hug when we're safely away, girl."

Leesha took the tray reflexively, and while her hands were full, Jizell shamelessly reached in and adjusted Leesha's bosom in much the same fashion as Roni. Leesha hadn't ex- pressed in hours, and didn't need much propping to give a man an eyeful. "Walk out like you belong there and start serv- ing."

Leesha looked over and saw Roni giving Kendall the same treatment. The young Jongleur's scars made her cleavage too memorable, so they shortened her skirt and gave her hair a fluff. Pawl had already disappeared. Wonda stood awkwardly, not knowing what to do.

Jizell pinched Leesha's bottom, giving her no time to pon- der the problem. She yelped in surprise as she was shoved through the door.

Leesha quickstepped to regain her balance, putting on a wide smile as she swept into the guardroom. "Who's thirsty?"

There was a cheer from the men, some swaying a bit on their stools as Jessa's girls, several of whom Leesha recog- nized, worked the room. In one corner, Leesha's old appren- tice Kadie was propping a guard who could barely stand against the wall while he drowsily attempted to paw at her.

"Party got a little wild." She winked. Leesha shook her head and started passing out full mugs and collecting emp- ties.

Jizell strode to the front of the room. "Got a surprise for you this evening, boys. She's the prettiest Jongleur in Angiers, or I'm a coreling."

While all eyes were on Jizell, Kendall slipped from the gatehouse and sauntered up, all legs and hair. She did a back-flip and put bow to string, playing a lively tune. The men gave a cheer.

Wonda attempted to leave the gatehouse next, but the sergeant happened to turn his head and noticed her. "Ay!" He pointed a swaying finger.

Leesha froze. She was behind the man with a heavy clay mug in her hand. She could . . .

"Yur shift ent over for another half hour, Ames!" the sergeant bellowed. "Back in the gatehouse!"

"Ay," Wonda dropped her eyes and attempted to deepen her voice, hunching into her armor. "Yessir." She scuttled back into the gatehouse.

The sergeant grunted, returning his eyes to Leesha's neckline. "Freakish, how corespawned tall that boy's gettin'."

They kept to the crowded market streets on the way to Jizell's hospit. At a glance, it could have been a normal day as folk bustled about making final purchases and sales before curfew sounded.

A closer look showed disheveled, fearful faces. Produce carts were half empty, the remainder poor specimens sold dear. Folk shifted nervously when Wooden Soldiers and Mountain Spears stomped past.

They made it to the hospit just as the sun set. Jizell opened the door to her private staircase. "Hurry, now. The corelings will rise any moment, and we don't want to be caught on the street when that happens."

Leesha heard a great din on the far side of the staircase wall. "I used to be able to count the number of full beds from the noise through this wall alone, but I've never heard it like this."

Jizell huffed. "Ent surprising. Got two to a bed, and folk on the floor between."

"Night," Leesha said.

"Lot of men were cored that first new moon," Jizell said. "We know our business and didn't lose many who made it this far, but we've had to be careful not to draw attention, especially at night. We wait for daylight and use magic in a dark room for the worst wounds. The rest are left to heal naturally. We're running out of *hora* as it is."

She opened the door to her office and hurried them in, locking the door behind them. A woman rose from behind the desk, coming around to greet them.

"Countess." Like her girls, Jessa's face was painted, her hair immaculate. She spread the skirts of her silk gown, dipping in a perfect curtsy. "What a pleasure—"

Leesha gave her no chance to finish the sentence, punching the Weed Gatherer right in the nose.

Every jaw in the room dropped. Leesha couldn't blame them. She'd expected to find the woman there, and had no intention of striking her, but her anger had risen quick when she saw Jessa's smug face.

It's the magic, she told herself. She had Drawn heavily of late, and knew how it enhanced the passions. But was it truly the magic? Leesha could not deny her satisfaction as Jessa's bottom hit the floor hard.

Jessa clutched her bloodied nose, words slurring. "Whad id da Core dib yud do thabt for?!"

Thamos' words came to her. *There are times a leader must remain firm, even when they are in the wrong.* Leesha hadn't agreed at the time, but she saw the wisdom in it now. "That was for Bekka, who you nearly killed, and everyone else who paid the price for your scheming."

Jessa pulled out a cloth, blowing bubbles of blood and examining the nose with skilled fingers to see if it was broken. She pinched at her brow to stem the blood flow.

"You've got some stones, girl. If Bruna were here, she would rap your knuckles with her stick. She could never suffer a hypocrite."

"Ay, you can't talk to Mistress Leesha like that!" Wonda took a step forward.

Jizell laid a gentle hand on Wonda's breastplate, but it was enough to stop Wonda short. "Stay out of it, girl. This was a long time coming, and needs to run its course."

"You're the one Bruna cast out, Jessa," Leesha said. "Not I."

Jessa threw up her hands. "I admit to all of it. I tried to steal the secret of liquid demonfire. Do you know why?"

"Because you're selfish and power-hungry?" Leesha guessed.

"Because Araine ordered me to!" Jessa snapped. "Just like she ordered Bruna to train me. You think that was an accident?"

Leesha blinked. It made an uncomfortable amount of sense, and explained why Araine so trusted the woman. "You weren't so loyal to her when you were drugging her son."

Jessa put her hands on her hips. "You want to blame me for every bad thing that's happened, these last months. I can see it in your eyes."

"And why shouldn't I?" Leesha said. "I never would have come back to this cursed city if not for your scheming. Euchor would never have sent his flamework weapons south. Rojer would be alive."

Jessa slapped her, hard on the face. The sound was like thunder inside Leesha's head, and she stumbled back from the blow, cheek burning. "Don't you talk to me about Rojer. That boy was like a son to me. You think I wanted anything to happen to him? That I wanted to be forced to hide rather than attend his funeral?"

She raised an angry finger. "I drugged Rhinebeck seedless, ay. That son of the Core had it coming. But Rojer and Jasin had blood between them long before you brought him back from the Hollow. Euchor's wanted to be king since before you were born.

"But you, you had the demon of the desert out of his armor. You could have poisoned him, or slipped a knife between his ribs, and stopped his advance. Instead you let him curl your toes before going on to murder half of Lakton, and enslaving the rest.

"You think you can judge *me*, Leesha Paper? My girls? You're as much the whore as any of us, though at least my girls are smart enough to remember their pomm tea."

The words were harsher by far than Jessa's slap; they were all Leesha's deepest fears laid bare. Countless lives had been lost, but she would not change what happened with Ahmann. Not now. Not since Olive.

And in the end, it was Ahmann's son who attacked Lakton. She couldn't be blamed for that.

"We make our choices, Leesha, and we live with them,"

Jessa said. "But none of it matters anymore. It's us against the demons, now."

How many times had Leesha said those same words, or watched Arlen shout them from a bandshell? They were everything she believed, and here Jessa was, explaining them to her.

And she was right.

"You're right," Leesha said. "I'm sorry."

"There have been some changes in Angiers in your absence," Jizell said. "Herb Gatherers and Weed Gatherers decided we had more in common than we thought. We are the resistance."

"The mind demons have hypnotized half the men in Angiers," Jessa said. "Made it so you can't trust your own brother, but they've left the women alone. So long as no one attempts to escape during the day, or gets too close to the wards men are building around the palace, they go about their business and leave the women to ours."

"And at night?" Leesha asked.

"The demons stopped attacking the walls," Jizell said. "Some field and wood demons still rise in the city, and they'll kill anyone out at night, but they don't attack the wards or the men on the walls."

"They want you alive," Leesha said.

"Why?" Jessa asked. "For what?"

Leesha didn't answer. "What do you think the wall guards will do when Gared's army appears?"

"They'll treat you as invaders, and fire upon you with flamework weapons," Jessa said. "There are already Jongleurs spreading tales of the Ward Witch of the Hollow coming north to claim the rightful throne."

"Rightful?" Leesha asked. "Pether is dead. Who sits upon it?"

"No one can prove he's dead," Jizell said. "The palace has been sealed since we smuggled out the Duchess Mum. They say it is for the Duke's protection. Heralds speak in town square of Duke Pether's curfews and new laws, designed to keep us away from the walls and the greatward they're building."

"Night." Leesha took out her wand, drawing wards to silence and mask their presence. "Are any of your patients affected by the minds?"

"Not many," Jizell said. "The apprentices question every new admission to probe for their influence. We're blessed that the mind demons ent interested in hypnotizing the wounded, so there were none in that first attack. The stricken are new arrivals, guards injured preventing escapes, or the workers injured when part of the boardwalk collapsed while working on that new greatward. We have them quarantined."

Leesha nodded. "We'll need to question them. Particularly the ones that worked the greatward."

"You may not get much out of them," Jessa said. "They act open enough but get lockjaw when asked about their work. You need to circle the topic and infer."

Leesha nodded, looking to Pawl. "Are you sure you can still get us into the palace? The brothel tunnels have no doubt been sealed."

"They are . . . compromised," Pawl agreed. "But they connect to others, known only to the royal family, that run the length of the palace."

"What are you planning, girl?" Jizell asked.

Leesha ignored the question. "Do you have flamework?"

"This is a hospit," Jizell said.

"I have it." Jessa winked. "The Duchess Mum liked having a personal supply."

"Which no doubt disappeared after her Weed Gatherer committed treason and fled her service," Leesha guessed.

"Finally keeping up with the dance," Jessa said. "How much do you need?"

"All of it," Leesha said.

"That much flamework will draw a lot of attention," Jessa warned.

"Waning has already begun," Leesha said. "Who knows what the minds are doing at this very moment? Gared and the Hollow Soldiers might be fighting for their lives. We can't afford to play this quietly."

Jizell crossed her arms. "Play *what*?"

"At daybreak the girls are going to blow up the greatward," Leesha said. "And while everyone is focused on that, we're going to sneak into the palace and kill the mind."

Demons still prowled the streets of Angiers in the twilight before dawn, but Leesha knew the minds would have long since retreated from the brightening sky. They moved quickly under the cloak of Kendall's music, visiting Jessa's hidden cache of flamework then setting the girls in position.

"Got maybe fifteen minutes between the last demon turning to mist and the morning work crew arriving," Jessa said. "All the time in the world to plant a thunderstick, light the fuse, and walk away."

The rest of them made their way to Jessa's abandoned school—now a garrison for Wooden Soldiers. Roni and some of the girls were already there, charming the guards as they delivered morning pastries and coffee heavily laced with tampweed and skyflower. Leesha and the others joined in while Wonda, an Angierian tabard over her armor, took up a post and kept her helmet low.

"What . . . !" one of the guards gasped as his men began to drop to the floor. He stumbled toward Wonda. "Quickly, man! Sound the alarm!"

Wonda moved as if to steady him, then shoved a rag in his mouth and twisted him to the ground.

"Quickly now." Jessa pulled the hidden latch that slid a bookcase aside, revealing a twisting stair down.

Just then the ground shook, and there was a great roar as the thundersticks blew apart the boardwalk greatwards.

"What's going on up there?" a voice demanded.

Leesha poured two chemics into a flask and stuck in the cork, giving it a brisk shake. This she threw down the stairs to shatter on the landing. The mixture hissed and gave off an ominous steam. There were muffled shouts and coughing.

Wonda led the way down. She wore a filter mask, the wards on her helm allowing her to see clearly through the haze in wardsight. She was fast, and Leesha could hear bones breaking as she cleared the path. Even if they managed to wake, many of the men would not be able to follow.

Leesha slipped the wand from her belt and held her breath, stepping into the darkened stairwell. She drew air wards, and a gust of wind cleared the fog from their path as they descended.

"Kendall." The young Jongleur tucked her fiddle under her chin and began to play as Jessa opened the secret tunnel nobles had used for two generations to access the brothel from the palace.

Leesha nodded to Jessa and Jizell. "Get out now. Gather the girls and keep them safe."

Jizell gave her a quick hug. "Creator go with you, girl."

"Ay," Jessa said. "Good luck."

And then Pawl led them into the darkness.

Kendall's music wrapped around them like a Cloak of Unsight as she, Leesha, Wonda, and Pawl slipped by the corelings patrolling the catacombs. At one unremarkable wall, Pawl opened a hidden door that took them out of the demon-infested tunnels and into a narrow, carpeted passage that led up into Araine's office in the women's wing of the palace.

But the place was not what Leesha remembered. The windows were painted black and covered with heavy curtains, leaving them in darkness save for their wardsight. The walls and floors had been stripped of wards, scoured with deep claw marks.

"We have to cross the hall to the next passage," Pawl said.

Under the cover of Kendall's music, they slipped from the office to find the wide hall equally devastated. Demons slept on the floor, and Leesha discovered she was holding her breath as they tiptoed past. Pawl led them to another room where the cold fireplace opened to a new corridor.

"Almost there," Pawl said, pointing to a doorway at the end of the narrow passage.

There was a growl behind them. Leesha looked back, seeing nothing. "Quickly now."

Pawl nodded, hurrying to the door and opening it. Just then, the walls and floor behind them came alive, paint and carpet distending and turning to hard scales, molding into demonic form.

"Run!" Leesha cried, dashing through the doorway into the throne room. She felt the mind wards on the silver netting in her hair grow warm, and knew the trap was sprung even before wards lit up in a circle around them.

Wonda fired an arrow at the approaching demons, but it skittered off the wards and fell back at their feet. Kendall, still running, ran into the wardnet. It flared to life and she gave a cry of pain as she was thrown back, fiddle skidding across the floor.

Leesha lifted her *hora* wand, but an impact ward appeared in the air, knocking it from her grasp and out of the circle. There was a tug at her belt, and her *hora* pouch was yanked away. Wonda gave a shout, hammering the meat of her fists against the wards. With each strike she cried out in pain. Leesha could see in the magic spiderwebbing through the air there were no holes to exploit.

Pawl sauntered into the throne room even as the mimics began to circle, flitting half seen through the darkness.

"You little pissant!" Wonda continued to hammer at the wards, seemingly oblivious to the pain. "When I get my hand on you—!"

Pawl threw back his head and laughed. The sound sent a shiver down Leesha's neck. When he spoke, his voice had grown colder—older. "For all your arrogance, you are no better than the lowliest rock drone, beating yourself to death against the wards."

"Pawl?" Leesha asked.

"The boy's mind is rich, for one so young," Pawl said. "We will feast upon it, when we have no further use for him."

Leesha tilted her head. "How did you get in? I painted the mind ward on him myself."

One of the mimics shimmered, and as it walked up to the wards, Leesha's heart caught in her throat. It looked for all she could tell that Rojer was standing right before her. "How delightfully stupid they are."

Another mimic shimmered, taking the form of Thamos so precisely Leesha's eyes grew moist. "Even now, they do not see."

"You were always in," Leesha realized. "From that first night. Araine didn't escape. You let her go."

"It would have been difficult to unseat you from your center of power," Pawl agreed.

"Easier to dangle a carrot, and lure you like a mule," Rojer said.

"The boy himself did not know he was ours, even as he led you to us," Thamos said.

"And now what?" Leesha asked. "You kill us? Eat our minds?"

Pawl showed his teeth. "When you are of no further use to us."

"Still they do not see," Thamos repeated in wonder. "Pathetic."

"We're pathetic?!" Wonda shouted. "Yur the ones hidin' behind kids and changelings!"

In response, the room brightened in wardsight, and Leesha looked up to see a demon lounging on the ivy throne, watching them with bulbous eyes. The coreling shone so bright with power, Leesha had to squint.

Two other mind demons stood at the base of the steps. Their thin bodies were no larger than Kendall, supporting great conical heads, ringed with vestigial horns and ridges that throbbed and pulsed.

Thamos lashed out an arm that became a long tentacle, wrapping around Leesha.

"Mistress Leesha!" Wonda grabbed her, but the demon was too strong. It yanked, pulling Leesha from the circle even as Wonda fetched up painfully against the wards and was thrown back.

Thamos pulled her in close, smiling in that way he had when they were alone. He caressed her cheek with his hand, feeling—even smelling—like Thamos. His hand slid up, gently sliding out the pins that held the warded silver hairnet protecting Leesha's mind in place.

She thrashed, but Thamos only grinned. "Do not struggle, my love. Soon you will have such a headache you will beg for my caress." He bent in and kissed her, so like Thamos, down to his breath. Leesha tried to hide her revulsion, but no doubt they could see it on her aura.

"When you leave this place, it will be with tales of our defeat," Rojer said. "You will believe them. Remember them as if they truly happened. You will be regarded as saviors, and take command of your armies once more."

"You will walk in day, and ward your mind at night, even as you weaken your defenses from within," Pawl said.

"And the Hollow will be ours," Thamos said.

It was Leesha's turn to smile. "I don't think so."

"You are helpless to stop it." Thamos pulled the last of the pins.

The boy with the blood debt will lead you into the spider's web, Leesha's dice had said. *Only then may you strike.*

"Now, dears," she said into her warded earring.

The demons paused, but for a moment nothing happened.

Then there was a deafening boom that knocked human and demon alike from their feet. Even the demon atop the dais clutched the ivy throne tightly. There were more explosions, muffled by the ringing in Leesha's ears.

And then, through the choking haze of dust, morning sunlight streamed through blown window frames to crisscross the throne room. The mind demons shrieked, scrambling for the shadows, but even there, the light touched them, their limbs smoking.

Micha appeared in one of the windows, pitching a spear of warded glass that punched through the chest of the mimic demon in Thamos' form.

Stela Inn bounded through another, kicking the Rojer mimic into a sunbeam that burst it into flame. She snatched up the struggling Pawl before he could cause any mischief.

Leesha pulled free of the tentacle as Kendall snatched up her fiddle and Wonda charged from the now disabled circle.

The remaining mimics and minds could not mist and find a path to the Core in sunlight. They ran for the exits, but Stela Inn was faster, moving to block one hall. They scattered, but Brother Franq appeared at the next. Ella Cutter at a third.

"I'd like to introduce you to my Warded Children," Leesha called to the demons as they shrieked and batted at the flames beginning to spark on their skin.

"We don't like the way you've been treating Mum," Stela said.

CHAPTER 38

SHARAK KA

334 AR

"Damajah. Your holy mother has arrived."

Inevera turned. Lost in thought, she hadn't even sensed Jarvah entering. That sort of carelessness could get her killed. "Show her in."

She turned back to the window as Manvah entered and came to stand beside her. Jarvah closed the doors, leaving the two of them alone, staring out at the rebuilt docks where Laktonians and Krasians worked together to salvage what ships they could, and strip the remainder for parts.

"Never in my dreams did I imagine an oasis so vast, or a fleet so great," Manvah said.

"It will still not be enough, if we are forced to flee the city on Waning," Inevera said.

Manvah looked at her. "You would give in to Nie so easily?"

"Not easily," Inevera said. "If by my death we can hold Everam's Reservoir, my glory will be boundless. But if at the cost of my dignity I can preserve our people to fight another night, I will take that deal and call it a bargain."

Manvah nodded, turning back to the window. "That's the daughter I remember."

"The journey was uneventful?" Inevera asked.

"The *alagai* tested us," Manvah said, "but it was nothing ten thousand *Sharum* could not handle."

Inevera nodded. Now that the *alagai* knew they meant to hold the Reservoir, she was free to bring in reinforcements, but she did not dare bring so many that the Bounty defenses were weakened. Amanvah and Asome reported fighting on the outskirts of the city proper, demons increased in number, led by hatchling minds, but as in the Hollow, Everam's Bounty's wards were too strong for the demons to yet threaten their center of power.

"What word of the *chin* rebellion?" Inevera asked. "Asome and Amanvah say it has remained quiet, but you hear things in the bazaar they do not."

"With the *alagai* slashing and burning at the wards," Manvah said, "and the Messenger from the Hollow reporting Angiers' fall, the *chin* have little desire to continue fighting those best equipped to defend them."

"Sharak Ka brings with it an end to Sharak Sun," Inevera quoted.

"It would appear so." Manvah gestured to the Krasians and Laktonians laboring side by side at the docks. "These *chin* fed the rebellion, but now they are yours."

Inevera dropped her eyes. "That is not . . . entirely truth."

"Eh?" Manvah asked.

"I needed an enemy to keep the *Damaji* in line with Ahmann gone," Inevera whispered. "A scapegoat for the *chin* rebellion. Abban pressed to attack Docktown and take their winter tithe of grain and supply to the city on the lake, and so I—"

"Sat on your pillowed throne and lied," Manvah finished. "Using Everam's name to cast these people prematurely into Sharak Sun to serve your own interests."

Inevera nodded. "And for that, I lost my eldest son and much of Everam's army to gain a foothold in this fetid swampland."

"Sometimes a foothold is all one needs to make a leap," Manvah said. "I can hear in your voice that you expect me to chastise you, but it is not for me to say what is right and wrong. You are the one Everam burdened with power, and from what I have seen, you have used it with great wisdom." She turned and smiled. "Most of the time. Who can say what would have happened last Waning, had you not come to the Reservoir?

Lakton may have been lost in any event. At least now there is a chance for their island city to be restored."

"Did you bring the shipping manifests?" Inevera asked.

Manvah nodded, producing a sheaf of papers from her robe. "Food, lumber, tar, and other supplies. Enough to rebuild Docktown, and thousands of *dal'ting* engineers and craftswomen to do the work, if they can find their way from the maze of tents you have them building."

"We cannot house fifty thousand inside Docktown's walls," Inevera said. "The tent configurations will form greatwards to hold the *alagai* at bay while we construct new defenses."

"I will see it done." Manvah had risen in power quickly, when it was revealed to the people that one of the most powerful businesswomen in the Great Bazaar was in fact the Damajah's mother. There was no one Inevera would rather have at her side.

A knock at the door, and Jarvah escorted Asukaji into the room. He flinched at the sight of Manvah. "Holy Mother, I did not realize you had come . . ."

"Close your jaw, boy," Manvah said. "You're going to be seeing a lot of me."

Asukaji dipped lower in acknowledgment, then straightened. He had been a cripple when Asome kidnapped her and killed Kasaad, but they all knew he'd supported the plan.

"It is time, Damajah," Asukaji said. "The fish men wait before the throne."

Inevera nodded, then swept out of the room with Manvah, Jarvah, and Asukaji at her heels. They joined the Krasian delegation of Inevera's sister-wives, Sikvah, Sharu, and Qeran as Inevera ascended to the Pillow Throne.

Across from the Krasians stood Duke Isan, Captain Dehlia, and the surviving dockmasters. Isan strode out to stand before the throne when Inevera was seated, giving a shallow bow. "Damajah. This is an auspicious day for both our people."

She could not see his aura, but no doubt he was angry still—resenting her presence, resenting his bow. Nevertheless, his words seemed sincere. He produced two rolls of parchment, written in neat, identical hand in both Krasian and Thesan. "The contracts are ready."

"All that remains, then, is the blood." Inevera rose and glided down the seven steps, drawing the curved blade from her belt. Isan eyed it warily, even as he produced a keen blade of his own. Jarvah appeared with the pot of ink, opening it on the small signing table between them.

"We have shed blood together in the night, Isan asu Marten asu Isadore," Inevera said as the two leaders pricked their fingers, each squeezing seven drops to mingle with the dark liquid. "Let our mingled blood usher in a new age of peace between our people."

When it was finished, Jarvah mixed the blood into the thick ink and stepped back. As one, Inevera and Isan lifted quills not unlike the one Isan's mother had used to blind Jayan, and dipped them in the ink.

"I name your people Lake Tribe, the fourteenth tribe of Krasia," Inevera said as she signed her copy, "and you Damaji Isan. You will have sovereignty over these lands and peoples, subject only to the throne of Krasia. When Sharak Ka is ended, if we be victorious, I will return with the bulk of my people to Everam's Bounty, leaving only those who will coexist in peace. This I swear before Everam, by His light and my hope of Heaven."

"Inevera vah Ahmann am'Jardir," Isan's Krasian was heavily accented, but understandable, "I name you Damajah, who sits upon the Pillow Throne of Krasia. I pledge my loyalty to you and the Shar'Dama Ka who sits upon the Skull Throne of Krasia. We will fight as one in the night." He signed his name, and Jarvah smoothly switched the scrolls for them to sign.

When it was done, Jarvah whisked powder across the surface to quicken the drying, then sealed and pocketed the ink jar. The mixed blood of Inevera and Isan might grant a powerful foretelling.

"And now, Damajah," Isan gestured to the great window, "a gift from the Lake Tribe to cement our alliance."

A large Laktonian galley Inevera had never seen before entered the bay, making for the docks at speed. Armament covered the deck, and Inevera looked back at Isan, expecting him to put his quill in her eye. "What is this?"

Isan offered no threat, backing toward the window. They watched in silence as the boat slid in to the dock and was moored in place. The sailors opened the hold, emptying hundreds of *Sharum* warriors onto the docks. The men looked filthy, but strong. Healthy. Fit to fight.

"After the city was lost, I sent a ship to retrieve the captured crews from Prison Isle," Isan said. "The dockmasters argued against risking a ship for the sake of those who invaded our waters, but to abandon them to the corelings was to risk becoming demons ourselves."

Inevera, shocked, took a moment to react. Then she bowed, sending the other Krasians in the room scrambling to do the same, longer and deeper. "Your honor is boundless, Damaji Isan. We are all the Creator's children in the night."

—Alagai Ka do not swim.—

Inevera pondered the symbols. It explained much about how the Laktonian fleet survived after their city was broken into pieces. The Evejah'ting taught that water was a poor conductor of magic. The minds sent their leviathans as blunt weapons to destroy the city, but they did not oversee the destruction personally.

If there was a limit to how far a mind could control its drones, then the deep waters of the lake might be safer than the shoreline. Somewhere between Docktown bay and Lakton was likely where the demon's influence ended, or the water demons would have scuttled the entire fleet.

The leviathans were the greatest threat to Docktown. Even with additional *dama'ting* and *shar'dama* with *hora* to work spells, it was easier to fight *alagai* than the water itself. The Pillow Throne was more powerful now than the previous Waning, but it offered no defense against the waves.

"Summon Qeran."

"Your will, Damajah." Jarvah made no sound as she slipped from the room.

"Your will, Damajah." Qeran put his forehead on the floor.

"You do not approve." Inevera could see it in his aura.

"It is not for me to approve or disapprove *inevera*," Qeran said, "but the Damajah need not risk herself. You are needed here, to guide the battle in town."

"We have the blood of the Deliverer for that, Drillmaster."

There had been fighting enough for all, but night after night, wherever battle was thickest or there were hints of the presence of the *alagai* generals, the grandchildren of Kajivah appeared, reaping glory like grain. Sikvah, Asukaji, Sharu, and Jarvah. Blood of the Deliverer. Their names were whispered among *Sharum* and *chin* alike.

Still Qeran looked unsatisfied. "Speak."

Qeran put his face to the floor. "The deep water is . . . unforgiving, Damajah. It cares nothing for Everam's children. If flung to the Maze floor, warriors can breathe—can cry for help. They know up from down. The ground does not try to kill them. Not so, the lake. It seeks our deaths, Damajah."

"As do the *alagai*," Inevera said. "Your words are wise, Drillmaster. Your counsel noted. But our new defenses cannot hold if the demons cast waves at us again. I have foreseen it."

"I will go in your stead," Qeran said. "I will take *Tan Spear, Tan Shield,* and *Tan Armor,* the finest ships in the fleet, to trawl for the leviathans. I will hunt them and send them to the deep."

"*We* will hunt and send them to the deep," Captain Dehlia said. "I volunteer *Sharum's Lament.*"

"And the *Isadore,*" Damaji Isan said. Inevera looked at the man curiously.

"I never asked to be a dockmaster," Isan said, "nor a duke, nor a *Damaji.* I have always been a better captain than any of those things. If the water demons are the greatest threat to my people, then it is my duty to face them."

Inevera nodded. "It is all of our duties." She looked to Sikvah. "You and Damaji Asukaji will command *sharak* on land, Niece. Umshala will command the *dama'ting.* I will ride with Qeran on *Tan Spear.* Qasha will sail with Dehlia on *Sharum's Lament.* Justya will join Damaji Isan on the *Isadore.*"

It was a strange feeling, walking the rolling deck as they set sail into the gloaming on Waning. The *alagai* dare not yet approach the surface, but already the water seemed to chop and kick, the boards in constant motion beneath her feet. It was simple enough to keep her balance, but Inevera's stomach churned at the sensation.

She closed her eyes, envisioning a palm tree, swaying in the wind. The deck was a constant. She reached into it with her center as if planting roots, becoming one with the boards. Her stomach calmed, and she opened her eyes, walking the deck to inspect the armament. *Sharum* sailors, unaccustomed to so lofty a presence, dropped what they were doing to prostrate themselves as she passed.

"Tell them to stop that." Qeran nodded and turned to shout at the men as Inevera looked over the gunwale, seeing the lines of scorpion stingers on the lower deck. Below that, dark water loomed.

The deep water seeks your death.

Inevera knew how to swim, but as land faded behind them, she began to realize how meaningless that was. A fall overboard at night in churning water would be the end of any of Everam's Children. Even her.

Pulling her thoughts from grim notions of drowning in the dark, she let her eyes drift over the larger scorpions on the decks, firing giant barbed stingers her sister-wives had warded personally for their prey this night. The giant spears had cores of warded glass with an eye at the butt end. These were attached to strong cables connected to great capstans the crew could bend their backs to. Mehnding archers stood ready on the fore and aft castles. Beneath the bowsprit, the ship's beak cut the water, warded glass, sharp and hard. Those wards Inevera had attended personally.

Tan Spear was flanked by its twin guardians, *Tan Shield* and *Tan Armor.* These were nearly identical in make and armament, but lacked the beak of the flagship.

Up ahead, the Lake Tribe waited, Damaji Isan aboard the *Isadore* and Dehlia captaining *Sharum's Lament.* They patrolled a carefully calculated line, one Inevera believed was just beyond the mind demons' control.

She watched the sun set on the water, beautiful and terrifying. Waning was upon them.

As darkness fell, wards began to glow all over the ship: the gemstones in many of the *Sharum* turbans, water demon wards along the hull, and wards of sight and protection on the helms of the crews. They would see in Everam's light, fighting as easily in the darkness as bright day.

But so, too, did the water begin to glow as the *alagai* rose from the deep. Some were quick, fleeting things, barely glimpsed. Others . . .

They did not have to wait long. The enemy was eager to crush Docktown's resistance once and for all. The entire lake began to glow, brighter and brighter, until it seemed the surface of the water was aflame. Waves surged and the deck rolled, but Qeran and the other captains knew their business and kept the ships pointed right at them, riding the swell as the first leviathan demon burst from the water, leaping high into the night sky.

It was beautiful and terrible, a giant, ancient thing, bright with magic. Its great maw could swallow half their ship in a single bite. Its tail could smash a building to splinters and rubble. The sharp bone edge of its flukes could tear through a galleon's hull without slowing.

But it could not see them. The wards of unsight on their ships hid them from the swirl of demons gathering below. The crew held their breath, waiting.

The leviathan seemed to hang in the air a moment, then twisted with a snap of its tail as it descended.

"Fire!" Inevera screamed, and the scorpion crews of the other ships fired, giant stingers piercing the colossal beast from all sides. They let the cables whip slack as the demon stuck the water, creating an enormous upsurge, then bent their backs to the capstans, steadying the ships against the wave even as they held the creature in place.

Only *Tan Spear* did not fire. With its sails furled, powerful eunuchs strengthened by *hora* magic pulled at the oars, climbing the swell. They reached the crest and rode down at terrible speed.

Inevera slashed cutting wards into the air, weakening the demon's thick, ancient hide as they rammed the leviathan with the ship's beak.

The jolt was terrible, knocking even skilled crewmen from their feet, and more than a few overboard. They had lashed themselves to the deck in preparation for the strike, but even the tough silk cable and steel hooks were strained. More than a few broke loose, sending warriors screaming into the water's cold embrace.

Ichor burst from the demon's wound, bathing the crew in the forecastle, but it only fed the wards of the beak and hull, making the ship stronger as the demon thrashed and let out a high-pitched wail that reverberated through the water.

The crews were not idle, peppering the demon with bowfire and stingers from the lower scorpion decks. Qeran himself aimed the great scorpion on the deck of *Tan Spear* and fired a monstrous stinger into the demon's black eye, bursting the orb in a spray of ichor.

The eunuch rowers pulled, but the beak held fast in the demon's hide. Inevera rent at the wound with cutting wards from her wand, widening the gash faster than even so ancient a demon could heal. Then she drew water wards, using the forbidding to push the ship away.

The creature thrashed again, threatening to pull the other ships under. Qeran gave the signal and the lines were cut, but the demon flopped one more time on the surface, twisting and opening its maw to bite at the ship.

Inevera Drew on the energy flooding the ship's deck, using the demon's own magic to power heat and impact wards sent down its throat. The demon's belly distended, then burst like an overfilled bladder, and it sank into the deep.

The crews cheered, but there was little time to celebrate. Along the line between Lakton and Docktown, more of the leviathans were rising into the night sky and slamming back down, building the waves to critical mass.

The tentacle, big as a city street, slapped against the hull, horned suckers grasping for purchase. Water wards flared and held, but the ship was spun about like a child's toy. Inevera danced to keep her feet, but her stomach roiled and she had no choice but to give in to it, grasping the gunwale and retching over the side, her wand dangling from the electrum chain manacled to her wrist.

There was no time to wipe her mouth or finish her heaves. Three more massive tentacles burst from the water, grasping for the ship more by feel than sight. Archers turned the limbs into pincushions, but they came on unhindered. The scorpion teams, unwilling to waste stingers on fast-moving targets, concentrated fire into what seemed to be the demon's center mass in the water.

Inevera severed one tentacle just before it struck, but could not stop the next. The wards on the mainmast, weakened by torn sails and tangled rigging in the constant waves and spray, gave way, and it shattered, toppling.

The tentacle was stopped by the wards on the rails, but it skittered along the forbidding, sweeping the deck. Inevera and the *Sharum* were forced to throw themselves to the boards, losing weapons and grips on rigging in the desperate move to duck the horned appendage. The slowest were swept screaming from the ship to begin their journey on the lonely path.

Masts snapped and sails fell over the deck, adding to the chaos and further weakening the wards. Inevera herself, rolling to keep some sense of control on the bucking planks, was covered as a mass of canvas fell over her.

She swept the knife from her belt, slicing the tarp in one smooth motion, but it still left her too tangled to raise her wand in time as she saw the third tentacle looming above them, blocking out the stars.

Everam, your Bride is ready to meet you, she thought, but it was premature.

Sharum's Lament cut across the water between *Tan Spear* and the demon, severing the tentacle with her ship's beak. They were at hard row, but still only barely avoided the fallout as the massive appendage came crashing down into the water.

Inevera watched the glow in the water fade as the dying creature sank back into the depths.

There was a sudden lull. The waters still churned, but already it was lessening. For a blessed moment, no *alagai* threatened.

Tan Shield was lost, sinking beneath the waves like the tentacled demon. *Tan Spear* and the *Isadore* were forced to flee the battle, limping back toward Docktown with smaller water demons at their heels. Inevera had lost sight of them, and did not know their fate.

Qeran bounded over to her. "Damajah—"

A glance at his aura was all Inevera needed to read his mind. He wanted permission to call a retreat. "I have eyes, Drillmaster."

Inevera twisted an earring, signaling Qasha on the *Lament*.

"Damajah," Qasha responded immediately.

"We must retreat," Inevera said. "*Tan Spear* cannot sustain more damage and remain afloat."

"Captain Dehlia agrees, Damajah," Qasha said after a moment. "The glory of the *chin* sailors knows no bounds this night, but the *Lament* cannot continue the fight without fresh ammunition and repair."

Inevera nodded at Qeran. "Give the order."

As the captain darted off, steadier on his metal leg than the sailors with two, Inevera broke the connection and twisted the earring that would signal Sikvah.

For long moments, there was no reply. At last, Inevera broke the connection, summoning Asukaji.

"Damajah," her nephew replied immediately.

"I cannot reach Sikvah," Inevera said.

"You must come quickly, if you can," Asukaji said. "Sikvah has fallen."

Inevera shouted at the eunuch rowers to bend their backs, using *hora* to leap to the docks before the ship even pulled in. The streets blurred as she ran to the Chamber of Shadows, where Asukaji was waiting. "Is she alive?"

Her nephew bowed, but there was anger in his aura. "She was not breathing when we brought her to the *dama'ting*, but still they work their spells over her. Her fate is . . . *inevera*."

Inevera steeled herself, pushing past. *Dama'ting* and acolyte alike looked up as she entered the chamber, but none dared speak.

Inevera saw why, looking into the aura of the woman on the operating table. The spirit of Blessed Sikvah, Sharum'ting Ka of Krasia, had gone down the lonely path, but Umshala had used magic to keep her body alive, for the sake of the life within.

I will bend, Inevera swore silently, glancing at her sister-wives; the *dama'ting* and *nie'dama'ting* working to heal the wounded. *I am the Damajah. I must be the ground beneath their feet.*

But even the supplest palm could break in high wind, and what sacrifice was worthier of the Damajah's tears? "Bottle."

A girl still in her bido appeared with a tear bottle. Her lip quivered and her own eyes were wet, but her hands kept steady as she scraped the tears from Inevera's cheek.

Inevera cupped the girl's chin when it was done. "What is your name?"

"Minnah vah Shaselle, Damajah," the girl said.

"We must all take Minnah's example," Inevera said loudly. "The sacrifices are countless in Sharak Ka. We shed tears for all of them, but ever our hands must be steady."

As one the women bowed, and Inevera strode from the chamber to where Asukaji still waited. He clutched Sikvah's spear, stained with demon ichor and bright with magic, staring at the blade as if there were secrets it might reveal.

"Report," Inevera said.

"Jurim yet lives, but few of his Wolves remain," Asukaji said. "The tent greatwards were overrun after Sikvah fell. I took command of the evacuation and held the *alagai* at the wall until their offensive broke. Sharu is in command now, but I do not think the demons will press again with dawn so near."

Inevera nodded. "You have done well, *Damaji.* Until further notice, our forces are yours to command. Return to the wall and hold it until dawn, then report back."

She was about to turn away when she caught the defiance in his aura. She paused, shifting her feet slightly to offer him only her profile, casually moving her hand closer to her *hora* wand. "Was there something more, nephew?"

"Did you know?" Asukaji asked quietly.

"Know what?" Inevera asked.

"The Deliverer commanded I obey you, *Aunt,* and so I will." Asukaji leaned close. "But you dishonor us both by pretending ignorance of what I speak. Did you know my cousin was with child when you gave her the command?"

Inevera raised her jaw. "I did."

"All these weeks." Asukaji spoke as if he could not believe it. "Battle after battle, in the Maze, on the wall, out beyond the wards. Again and again you put her on the edge of the abyss with an innocent in her belly, just like you did to my sister and Kaji."

"Shall we speak at last, Asukaji, about which of us has more wronged Ashia?"

Asukaji bared his teeth. "I know what I did, Aunt. I attempted to kill my sister out of jealousy, and Everam smote me down for the crime. But the Deliverer healed me. Forgave me. Yet still you seek to punish me."

"Punish you?" Inevera was incredulous.

"You would not let me aid my sister and nephew. You put Sikvah and her unborn child on the front lines, rather than give me command of Sharak."

"You have an exaggerated sense of your own worth, nephew," Inevera said. "You were raised in Sharik Hora. What do you know of leading troops in the Maze? Of *sharak*? A few weeks of fighting in the night, and you think yourself equal to your sister and cousin, who spent years in *Sharum* training with Drillmaster Enkido. Your father was a great man, and you assume you must be the same, even as you helped your lover murder him. Sikvah was more qualified than you. That is why she was given command."

It was her turn to lean in, advancing as Asukaji shrank back. "Sharak Ka is not about your pride, boy. Your cousin, your sister can see that, but it seems you cannot. The *alagai* do not simply come to kill warriors. They come to kill the corrupt and the innocent alike. The First War asks sacrifice of us all."

"Yet it falls to me even so," Asukaji says. "While Sikvah is doomed to half life, in the vain hope we can save the child."

"Inevera," the Damajah said. "Will you stand here and bemoan that fate as well, or will you go and hold the wall?"

"If the *alagai* come at it again in force, there will be multiple breaches," Asukaji said. "We cannot hold another night without significant repair and reinforcement."

"Repair what you can," Inevera said, "but there is no reinforcement to be had. We cannot risk pulling more warriors from Everam's Bounty, and the Hollow Tribe has its attention turned to the North. We must trust in ourselves, in Everam and the Shar'Dama Ka, to deliver us a miracle."

CHAPTER 39

WHISTLER'S MIND

334 AR

The sound of Dawn's scream jolted Abban awake on the hard bench of his cell.

It was like this every morning, now. Hasik had seen the value in keeping Abban in good health. He needed the *khaffit* for his tallies, but never let him forget the unpayable blood debt between them. Abban had not escaped his punishment. As they agreed, he was leasing it to another, one day at a time.

Soon after, Dawn entered his cell, bearing the breakfast tray. Her face was a scarred ruin, with a gaping hole where her nose had been, jaw swollen from the teeth Hasik had pulled. A ragged bit of cloth covered her missing eye. The littlest fingers of both hands were gone, and she shuffled, favoring one foot.

The woman kept her eyes down, and Abban was thankful for that. She had been nothing but kind to him, and he repaid her with treachery. Hasik knew how it cut at him, which was why he had her bring Abban's breakfast each morning. So Abban could look upon the woman and be forced to accept that he would rather she suffer instead of him.

"Feeling hungry, *khaffit*?" Hasik asked, appearing at the door to the small office that was Abban's work space and cell combined. There was a writing desk, a sleeping pallet, and a small privy—little more than a curtained alcove containing a board with a hole in it that opened to a pit that went Everam only knew where.

Abban was not allowed to leave save in Hasik's company, and the guards outside the door had proven impossible to influence once Hasik cut the ear from a *Sharum* who dared bend to listen to a whispered word from the *khaffit*.

Hasik ate meals with him, ensuring he was the only personal interaction Abban was allowed.

Which, of course, was the greatest torture of all.

Dawn set the trays and quickly shuffled from the room.

"If I cut much more off that one, she won't be much use as a servant," Hasik said.

"You are master here," Abban said. "You could always show mercy."

"Bah!" Hasik said. "Easier to kill her and start fresh with one of her daughters."

Abban shuddered, and Hasik laughed, shoving the tray at him. "Eat up, *khaffit*! You're barely fat anymore!"

The food was not much to look at. A cup of sour, watered wine, a crust of hard, gritty bread. A cut of meat left overlong in the coldhouse, a green apple picked too early from the tree. And yet Abban ate better than many in the monastery, if the tallies were true.

Hasik ate like a greenland prince, his plate piled high with boiled shellfish in melted butter. The smell of it was maddening as the brutal warrior gorged himself.

"Nie's tits, it never ceases to amaze me, how well the *khaffit* eat," Hasik said. "The *dama* told us you were a cursed people, but for centuries now you have feasted on swine and bottom feeders, drinking couzi and laughing at your betters."

"The *dama* want control," Abban said. "What better way to get it than denying pleasure to their followers, save that which they claim Everam allows?"

Hasik burped, tossing another empty shell into the pile. They only had one boat left—the rest destroyed by the Laktonians and demons—but rather than use it to scout or expand his power, Hasik had the crew casting nets and laying traps for bottom feeders.

"Have your scouts had any success finding the tunnel to the *chin*'s secret cove?" Abban asked. Hasik's warriors killed the *chin* attacking the basement, but never found how they got in, reporting a maze of natural caverns beneath the monastery.

"I do not trust them with the search," Hasik said. "Whoever controls that tunnel controls my fortress. I will find it myself."

Abban looked up, his food forgotten. "You search the tunnels below the keep alone?"

"I find . . . peace in the solitude," Hasik said.

Abban blinked. "Peace is good, when it can be found, but the tunnels may be rife with *alagai*."

"If so, they have not been fool enough to challenge me," Hasik said.

"*Alagai* are not known for their wisdom," Abban said.

"What do you care, *khaffit*?" Hasik asked. "If the demons have me, you will be free at last."

Abban sniffed. "You'll forgive me if I do not trust in the mercy of your *kai*."

Hasik laughed. "Nor should you! At best, they will keep you here, chained to the tallies, but some of the men have new appetites to replace the loss of their manhood. I have heard them speculating on what a man grown fat on rich *khaffit* food would taste like."

Abban tried to suppress his shudder, but Hasik caught it, his grin widening. He sucked the last bit of meat from the shells, then stomped around the room while Abban ate, shuffling papers with greasy fingers as if he had any idea what the symbols upon them meant.

Abban pretended not to notice, eating quickly. Hasik delighted in knocking food to the ground just to torment the crippled *khaffit*. When the meal was finished, Hasik rang the bell and Dawn limped back in to take the trays. A guard appeared in the doorway with Abban's wheeled chair.

Hasik took the chair and brought it to Abban's side. "Come, *khaffit*, bring the tallies. We have a meeting."

Abban knew better than to question it, thankful simply for a brief release from the cell. He slung a small satchel with his writing kit over a shoulder, took his crutches and pushed himself upright, limping into the chair Hasik deliberately kept out of easy reach.

The cruel warrior was known to pull the chair away suddenly as Abban tried to sit, but had no patience for the game today. Abban eased himself down and before he was even settled, Hasik was pushing him swiftly out of the room.

It was a bright summer day, almost pleasant, save for the ever-present stink of the fortress' dirty inhabitants. Foremost was the smell of piss. Fifteen hundred men continually wetting themselves within the walls raised an abysmal stench. Hasik promised Abban would grow used to the smell, but it struck him anew whenever he was allowed a brief excursion from his cell.

But the reek of the Eunuch Monastery was more than just urine. The warriors trained hard, kept their weapons sharp, but discipline was not a hallmark of Hasik's men. Freed as they were from the need for pleasures of the flesh, few of the men bothered to bathe, trim hair and nails, or clean their clothes. *Sharum* and slave alike were uniformly filthy, eyes sunken as supplies waned.

Hasik had taken the Shepherd's chambers from Dama Khevat when they claimed the monastery, locking Abban in one of the smaller offices. Khevat had been relegated to the back room of a smaller chapel on the far side of the compound.

As they made their way into Khevat's sphere of power, Abban saw something closer to discipline. Gelded men still stared blankly into the distance when there was no task before them, but Khevat had forced the warriors to keep their uniforms in some semblance of order, grimy though they were.

Guards hopped to open the doors, bowing to Hasik as he wheeled Abban into Khevat's office, where the *dama* waited with the Deliverer's son Icha.

Careful that Hasik should not see, Abban touched a hidden fold in his pantaloons, where a tiny paper lay concealed. He would need to be quick, if he dared deliver it. He had tried to find the courage many times in recent months. As yet, it remained beyond him.

Of late, Hasik had kept his torments and indignities to small things, inflicting the worst of it on Dawn. Abban had his uses, especially to a leader who could not read, write, or count past his fingers and toes. But if Khevat betrayed him . . .

Abban broke into a sweat, wondering what the brutal warrior would cut off next.

Khevat glanced at Abban. The *dama* had always terrified

him, looking down his nose at Abban like a beetle crawling on shit. An insect he could crush at will, should the whim take him.

But the prideful disdain had left Khevat's gaze since Hasik cut his manhood away.

It was the great equalizer among them, that every male in the monastery, from *dama* to slave, elder to child, suffered that ultimate indignity—a permanent reminder of Hasik's power. Pride was a distant memory for most of them. Only the most savage *Sharum* adapted—just the sort of animals Hasik wanted in his band.

"Thank you for meeting with me, Eunuch Ka." Khevat gave a polite bow.

Hasik grunted in amusement. Khevat had lorded over him as a child as well, and he never tired of the man's submission. "Of course, Dama. How may we help you?"

"You have heard the scouts sent to Docktown," Khevat said. "The *alagai* press them hard."

"What of it?" Hasik scoffed. "They are days of hard ride to the south. We are safe here."

"I would not be so sure of that," Khevat said, "but in any event, they need assistance."

"They have it," Hasik said. "The Damajah herself has come to Everam's Reservoir, and with Ahmann gone, she has invited the fish men into her pillow chamber."

Khevat's jaw tightened, a vein in his neck throbbing. The words were blasphemy, but Hasik was provoking him purposely, and the old *dama* knew not to take the bait.

"Where was Docktown when these walls were under assault from the *chin*?" Hasik demanded. "Where was the infinite mercy of the Damajah when the *khaffit* shamed me before the Deliverer's court? We owe them nothing."

"If not from loyalty to the throne, we might still consider a more . . . mercenary arrangement." Khevat's voice was tight. "They are well supplied, Eunuch Ka, and we could use the stores before the cold comes."

Not long ago, the *dama* would have shouted the words, calling Hasik a fool and punctuating it with a touch of threat.

After the cutting, no one was stupid enough to shout at Hasik.

"Bah!" Hasik spat on the floor. "The cold is months away! It cannot be so bad. Tell him, *khaffit*."

Khevat's knuckles whitened at his counsel being summarily dismissed for the word of a *khaffit*. Abban knew he must tread carefully. He made a show of spreading his writing kit on Khevat's desk, giving the tension time to diffuse. He set the inkwell and licked the end of his pen before dipping and opening the ledger.

Even then, he made a show of scanning the tallies, though he knew them all by rote. Slowly, the tempers in the room began to cool.

"The honored *dama* has a point, Hasik. Your men have raided these lands too well. The few *chin* hamlets that remain barely produce enough to fill their own bellies, let alone ours."

"I'll speak to the men," Hasik growled. "The *chin* do not eat before us."

Irritation flashed across Khevat's eyes, but he kept his voice calm. "If the slaves starve, there will be nothing for any of us to eat, Hasik."

Hasik's eyes narrowed, perhaps considering if he should take umbrage at the use of his name. "I will not spend Eunuch lives on the Damajah, nor will I crawl before her Pillow Throne and beg for the scraps off her table."

Abban cleared his throat. "Perhaps there are answers closer to home."

Hasik put the back of his hand to his forehead. "Have I sunk so low that the only voice on my side is that of a *khaffit*? Come, Abban, tell us your brilliant plan. Perhaps you think we should sack Angiers, again?"

Abban took a deep breath. Of the many failures of his life, the attack on Angiers had been by far the costliest, for him, and for the Krasian empire. "Nothing so bold, Eunuch Ka. I have simply found that healthy slaves with security to work produce greater tithes than those who get gruel and the whip."

"There is no security in this world, *khaffit*," Hasik said. "Not for men and certainly not slaves."

"I believe Abban means the *alagai*." It was strange to hear Khevat use his name and not his caste.

"Eh?" Hasik asked.

"It is summer," Abban said. "The *chin* should have crops

ripening in their fields, but your Eunuchs took them all, and burned the farmhouses for good measure."

"They can plant more," Hasik said.

"Indeed," Abban agreed. "But without proper succor, the *chin* are too preoccupied with surviving the night to focus on the fields."

"How is that my concern?" Hasik asked.

"They are your thralls," Khevat said. "It is written in the Evejah that we must defend our thralls from the *alagai* as we do ourselves."

"The Evejah?!" Hasik laughed. "Where has the Evejah gotten us? Ahmann brandished the Evejah as he led us on his fool demon-killing quest. Now he's thrown from a cliff, his son shot dead in *chin* land, and the rest of us cockless and filthy, fretting over cold months that would freeze our balls off, if we had any. I am done with *alagai'sharak.*"

"You are correct, of course," Abban said. "There is no profit in following the sacred text simply for Everam's sake. But there is some wisdom in the proverbs. It would not be difficult to send out bands of Eunuchs to scour the *chin* fields of *alagai,* with full bellies our reward."

"Your belly remains full enough," Hasik growled.

Abban bowed his submission. "A suggestion, only."

"Refused," Hasik said. "The *alagai* have not attacked us since we stopped attacking them."

"But they have grown thick in these lands," Khevat said. "They prey upon the hamlets and Docktown now, but who can say what will happen if their numbers continue to increase? You saw what they did to the fish men."

"What of it?" Hasik laughed. "Should I lament the destruction of my enemies?"

"Yes," Khevat said, "if it comes as victory for Nie."

"Nie!" Hasik barked. "Everam! You clerics know two words, and work them into everything! There is no Nie! There is no Everam! No light and void in eternal combat. The *alagai* are animals. If anything, they deserve their heads scratched for setting the fish men and their ships aflame."

The words seemed madness. Abban did not understand how Hasik could have seen the cold, efficient way the demons dispatched the Laktonians and not fear them.

Khevat, too, seemed flabbergasted. He threw up his hands. "Very well then, Eunuch Ka. How shall we handle the supply shortage?"

"I'll call for more raids," Hasik said. "And tell Jesan, Orman, and the other *kai* that the one with the smallest haul will lose his left hand."

"Brilliant." Abban felt nauseous.

"Wise." Khevat grit his teeth.

Hasik smiled. "And we'll send fresh scouts to the south. If the Damajah's hold on Docktown grows weak enough, perhaps we can take it from her."

"Everam's beard," Icha whispered.

"Do not be so shocked, boy," Hasik said. "Did not your brother attempt the same when he sent Melan and Asavi to kill that shameless *heasah*? If you ask me, it's time the Damajah learned some humility. Perhaps I'll sew her cunt shut and keep her as a slave."

Khevat and Icha paled at the words, and Hasik got to his feet, his patience worn thin.

Abban reached to collect his writing kit and pretended to slip, knocking over the ink bottle. The black liquid ran across the table, staining the *dama*'s faded white sleeve.

"Watch out, fool!" Khevat growled, snatching his arm away.

"Apologies, Dama." Abban produced a kerchief that was passably clean, blotting Khevat's sleeve. As he did, he slipped the tiny paper into the old cleric's hand.

Khevat stiffened slightly, but he did not betray the confidence. He palmed the paper and made his hand disappear into the robe as he made a show of examining the stained cuff. "Just go, *khaffit*. I will tend to it."

Hasik snorted, pulling Abban's chair away from the desk. "A pleasure as always, Dama."

Abban caught the *dama*'s eye as the chair swiveled away, and they shared a knowing look.

"I am surprised," Abban ventured carefully as they walked back across the compound.

"By what, *khaffit*?" Hasik asked.

"That you trust your men to lead the raids instead of going yourself," Abban said.

Hasik laughed. "Eager to be rid of me, Abban? Do not think I would leave you here to scheme. You would join the raids slung over the back of my horse, just as we started."

"I miss those times," Abban lied, and Hasik chuckled. "But I am pleased to have a roof over my head. It is only that you always seemed to take such . . . satisfaction in the conquest."

"I take my satisfaction in pig now," Hasik said. "In bottom feeders, and in the pain of those who displease me. Remember that, *khaffit*."

Abban nodded. "Always, Eunuch Ka."

A well-nursed Kaji napped on Ashia's back as she and Briar watched the warriors ride from the monastery.

"They're sending out raiding parties," Ashia noted. "Their supplies are low."

"Gonna come up empty," Briar said. "Nothin' left to raid."

Ashia began unwrapping the silks that bound Kaji's pack to her. Briar looked confused as she pressed it into his hands. "Kaji will sleep for hours yet. Take him back to the briar-patch."

"What are you doing?" Briar asked.

"The keep is as empty as we have ever seen it," Ashia said. "There is no better time to scout within."

Briar made no move to strap on the pack. "I can do that."

"Your honor is boundless, Briar asu Relan," Ashia said, "but I have contacts among my people that you do not. It must be me."

Briar hesitated, and Ashia moved to help him sling on the pack before he could argue. "If they catch you . . ."

"They will not," Ashia said. "I can scale the wall now amid the commotion, and will return before nightfall."

"Be careful," Briar said.

Ashia kissed his cheek. "You have my word, cousin." She patted his bottom, and the boy took off running for the safety of his hidden cave on the cliff face. They had made improvements, so much that all three of them began to think of it as home, and had little eagerness for their mission.

But the Damajah was counting on her, and Sharak Ka was in the balance.

Ashia took a black scarf from her robe, twisting and wrapping it over her white headscarf in a proper man's turban, a black veil loose around her neck.

Seek the khaffit *through the father of your father.*

It could only mean one thing. Dama Khevat, who had ruled this place before the coming of Hasik, was still alive within.

It was a simple matter to circle around and scale the keep wall on the western side with the lake at her back. The morning sun cast her in shade, and all eyes were fixed on the warriors departing the gate. *Hora* in her boots and fingerless gloves allowed her to climb the sheer outer wall as easily as a spider.

She kept to the shadows as she slipped over the wall, dialing the *hora* stones of her necklace to put a cushion of silence around her, blending her to her surroundings to appear little more than a diffuse blur.

It was a needless precaution. The guards on duty were lax, thinking their walls great and high. She slipped by them and down into the courtyard easily.

The place was filthy with refuse, stinking of urine and unwashed bodies, but the clutter provided ample places to hide as she scouted the keep. The few times she needed to cross a sunlit street, she seemed just another underfed *dal'Sharum,* her *alagai'viran*-stained clothes just as filthy as everyone else's.

It didn't take long to find her grandfather's chapel and slip past the guards, but he was not alone when she found him. Her cousin Icha was with him. She settled in to listen and wait for her cousin to leave before making contact.

"He is a *khaffit,*" Icha was saying. "Do you trust him?"

"Of course not," Khevat said. "Abban would not hesitate to lie if it served his ends."

"Then you cannot know it is truth," Icha said.

"But I believe it," Khevat said. "Your brother, the Deliverer's firstborn son, was not shot down in the Battle of Angiers. He was murdered by that . . . that . . ."

"What if he was? Would that finally be a crime great enough for us to resist?" Icha laughed bitterly. "Hasik was right about one thing. We left Everam's sight long ago. What does it matter, who killed who?"

"What, indeed." Khevat sighed.

It was painful, listening to the broken spirit in their voices. Her grandfather had always been a huge, terrifying figure in her life. The patriarch, the final arbiter in their family. His words were sacrosanct.

Now he was just a man, the front of his white robes stained yellow and smelling of urine. It seemed the rumors were true. Hasik had cut the manhood from every male in his fortress.

The shame to her family was enough to make her weep, but there was no honor in filling tear bottles for the living. Before this was done, she would find Hasik and collect in blood.

Icha left soon after, and she stalked her grandfather into his inner chamber. She was about to make contact when he sighed. "If you mean to kill me, *Sharum,* you may find it more difficult than you believe."

Ashia blinked. He had sensed her? Impossible.

"Grandfather." She unwrapped the black silk to reveal her white headscarf and veil.

"Ashia?!" Khevat whirled to gape at her. "Everam's beard, girl, what are you doing here?"

"I was sent by the Damajah," Ashia said. "*Seek the khaffit through the father of your father,* the dice said."

What little life had returned to Khevat seemed to leave him then, his aura diffusing as his shoulder slumped. "I do not know what purpose Everam might have, sending you to this forsaken place."

"They say the monastery had fallen to Nie," Ashia said. "That is reason enough."

"I do not deny it," Khevat said. "Hasik has given up *alagai'sharak.* He does not fight for Nie, perhaps, but neither does he resist. He lets Her grow unchecked like a greenland coward."

"What of the *khaffit*?" Ashia asked. "The dice foretell he yet has a part to play."

"Alive," Khevat said, "but you will not get to him easily. Hasik keeps him close, attending him personally. The *khaffit* is precious to him. He is seen with Hasik, or not at all."

"I am here to rescue him, if I can," Ashia said. "Will you help me?"

"The dice sent you here, to ask my help in rescuing the

khaffit?" Khevat's aura flared again. "A lifetime I have served Everam, but sniveling Abban is worth more to the Damajah than I?"

"Abban is a *khaffit,*" Ashia said. "*Hannu Pash* branded him a sniveling coward, and so he is. Tell me, Grandfather, what is your excuse?"

Khevat's eyes widened. "How dare you, girl . . . ?!"

"How dare I what?" Ashia said. "Hasik murdered my cousin. He cut your manhood away, and broke pact with Everam, abandoning *alagai'sharak* with Sharak Ka already begun. Yet you do nothing but cower and serve him."

"To stand against Hasik is to die," Khevat said.

"Was it not you who taught me that there was no path to Heaven, but to die in Everam's name?" Ashia asked.

Khevat blew out a breath. "Even if I wished to help you, rescuing Abban will be nigh impossible. The *khaffit* is still fat, with one leg lame and the other foot mangled. Even if you could use *hora* to bear the weight, you would find the man . . . unwieldy, and Hasik would be close on your heels."

"Then perhaps it is time to put an end to Hasik," Ashia said.

"Hasik is powerful, child." Khevat spread his hands sadly. "And I am . . . not what I once was."

"What you were was the voice of right and wrong in our house," Ashia said. "In our tribe. Now you will let the man who murdered the Deliverer's son walk free because you fear death?"

"I hope you never understand that there are fates worse than death, granddaughter."

Ashia spat on the ground. "I was trained by Enkido. My master's spirit was undimmed by the loss of his cock, nor his *sharusahk* slowed. If you have not the heart to kill this rabid dog, then I will do it."

Khevat's aura crackled to life again. "Do not speak down to me about Enkido, girl. I knew your master long before you were born. I knew him when he was a skinny boy in a tan bido. I selected the drillmasters to train him in *Hannu Pash,* and when he lost his bido, I took him into Sharik Hora and trained him myself. I knew him when he ran the Maze with his spear brothers, howling at the moon and glorying at every kill. I gave him counsel when that glory faded, leaving him unfulfilled."

He reached out with sudden swiftness, grabbing Ashia by the arm. She attempted to block, but her grandfather was more skilled than she credited him for, and he twisted her into a submission hold, smashing her face-first into the stone wall of the chapel. "So trust me when I tell you, beware the Eunuch Ka. If you underestimate him, even for an instant, you will die."

Ashia put a foot against the wall and kicked off, striking a convergence point in her grandfather's arm that weakened the hold enough for her to break free.

"Then help me," she said.

Something of the man she had known crept back into her grandfather's eyes. "The *chin* had a secret way into the fortress from below. Hasik has been seeking it in the maze of tunnels. If the Damajah's dice can divine its location . . ."

Ashia shook her head. "The dice cannot help here, but I know someone who can."

For a brief time, the briarpatch was a place of laughter. Briar and Kaji might only be distant cousins, but already they had taken to each other as brothers. Briar doted on the boy, chasing him around the cave, teaching him new words, delighting in his innocence.

But he knew Ashia was in terrible danger every moment she scouted the monastery. When Kaji finally fell into a second nap, Briar paced the cave like a nightwolf, clenching and unclenching his fists.

Was this what Dehlia felt when he went off scouting? The worry Ragen and Elissa spoke of? It was painful. Intolerable. He didn't understand how they bore it. He glanced at sleeping Kaji. Could he leave the boy? Just for a short time while he made sure . . .

"Made sure what?" he growled to himself. Ashia was like him. She was fast, and quiet, and knew how to pass unseen. She was as strong as he was, and a better fighter. Either she was safe, or she was in trouble enough that Briar was more likely to get captured himself—leaving Kaji alone and defenseless—than he was to effect a rescue.

So he paced.

It was growing dark when a rustle of the hogroot vines alerted him. He was at the cave mouth in an instant, watching Ashia rappel down.

"Briar. All is well?"

Briar nodded. "What did you find?"

"My grandfather lives," Ashia said. "And my cousin Icha. They will help us, but we must act soon, for Waning is upon us. The *khaffit* is confined to a wheeled chair, held in one of the Shepherd's acolyte cells. Do you know them?"

Briar nodded. "Have to cross the yard to get to the wall. Won't be easy with a wheeled chair. Can your grandfather open the small gate?"

"Not without drawing attention we would be better to avoid," Ashia said. "He spoke of a hidden tunnel into the keep."

"Ay," Briar said. "Know it. Few parts ent friendly to a chair. Might manage, but not if we've got spears after us."

"Grandfather says they have failed to find the path," Ashia said. "If we can get to the tunnels unseen and cover our tracks, they'll never catch us."

Briar frowned. "Don't make sense. Tunnels're a little confusing, but if the *Sharum* know it's there, they should have found it. Only thing really protecting it was that no one knew it was there."

"It seems Hasik wants the knowledge to die again," Ashia said. "He won't let his warriors explore the tunnels."

"Or he's found it, and your grandfather's leading you into a trap."

Ashia opened her mouth as if to argue for her family's honor, then closed it again, unsure. She crossed her arms. "Waning comes tomorrow night, Briar. If we don't rescue the *khaffit* tomorrow while the sun shines, we may not have another chance."

Briar shrugged. "So what? Wouldn't have this mess if not for him. Why's his life worth risking the three of ours?"

"My mission—" Ashia began.

"Core with your mission!" Briar barked. "We can—"

"We can what?!" Ashia cut him off. "Flee to the Hollow? To Miln in the mountains where they make weapons of fire to slaughter our people? There is nowhere to flee Sharak Ka, Briar. It will find us if we flee to the ends of Ala. You saw what the demons did to the fish men and their boats. They will come for us all, in our turn. You can hide in your briarpatch and wait as they burn the world around you, but that is not my way. The Damajah says rescuing the *khaffit* will deal a blow to the *alagai* and that is worth risking my life. Kaji's life."

Kaji stirred at the sound of his name. "Mama?"

Ashia went to him, loosening her robe to free a breast, but her eyes did not leave Briar. "It is up to you to decide if it is worth risking yours."

Dawn twilight had chased the *alagai* away as Ashia and Briar picked their way down the cliffs. Kaji was in his pack on Ashia's back, and she kept her breathing steady and even as she glanced down at the dizzying drop. Alone, she would not have given thought to the height, but with her son on her back, she was thankful the cliff face remained in shadow and she could use the *hora* in her boots and gloves to cling to the surface.

There was a tiny scrap of beach at the bottom, and, hidden behind scrub and some thick vines of *alagai'viran,* a small cave.

"Is this it?" she asked. "So close, all this time?"

Briar shook his head. He'd been even quieter than usual since their words the night before. He pulled away the vines, revealing a small boat hidden in the shallow cave. He dragged it onto the beach, checked it over, and slid it into the water.

"Climb in." He held the boat steady as Ashia nimbly hopped in, her feet in perfect balance as the small craft rocked from her weight.

Briar shoved off and jumped in, no less nimble even without Ashia's training. She'd been teaching him *sharusahk* and he took to it quickly, but it was astounding how much the night had taught the boy.

He took the oars and began to pull, falling into an easy rhythm that sent them gliding smoothly through the water.

Ashia knew there were no demons swimming beneath the morning sun, but still she cast a wary eye over the side, praising Everam that Briar kept the shoreline in sight.

"Is it far?" she asked. Above them, the monastery loomed atop the cliff, but they were far enough off and close enough to shore that the small craft would be difficult to spot.

Briar shook his head. "Almost there. Gonna get our feet wet the rest of the way."

Ashia looked at him curiously but did not let her face betray the fear in her heart as Briar dropped an anchor in deep water.

"This way." Briar leapt from the boat into the water, and Ashia's breath caught. Did he expect them to swim all the way to shore?

But Briar did not sink as he struck the water. It splashed around his ankles, but he remained standing.

"What magic is this?" Ashia asked.

"Ent magic," Briar said. "Nowhere to dock in close to the cave. Tenders built crannogs to get to deep water. Know where to step, you can walk from here to shore. If not . . ." He took his spear and thrust it into the water just a few inches from where he stood, sinking the shaft—taller than he was—all the way into the water. "Step only where I step."

Ashia nodded, keeping her breathing steady and letting fear pass over her as she pulled off her boots and followed after Briar. The water was cold, but there was firm footing beneath, a stone pathway hidden under the dark liquid. Briar moved quickly along and she kept pace, watching closely to mirror his steps precisely. A single misstep could send her plunging into the water with Kaji on her back.

It was a twisting route meant to send pursuers into the water, but Briar did not hesitate in his steps, and the cliff approached rapidly. There was no shore to speak of, just sheer rock, jagged with patches of dirt and scrub. Briar leapt, catching a snag with his fingertips and hauling himself up into a shadowed crevasse.

Ashia followed and saw that the crevasse was deeper than it appeared from the water. Inside they made a steep climb into darkness. It might have been a natural formation but for the soft glow of protective wards cut into the tunnel walls.

She caught up to Briar at the rear of the tunnel, blocked by a heavy, warded stone. Briar put his back to it and heaved. Even with his considerable strength it was slow to move. Ashia lent her arms to the task, shifting the stone away. It opened into a larger cave, raw and natural, with no wards on the rock face.

They moved the heavy stone back into place, and Ashia had to admit it fit the cave wall so perfectly she might never have known it was not a natural formation.

It was daytime, but the dark tunnel made her wary. She slipped the glass shafts of her short spears from Kaji's pack, extending the blades with flicks of her wrists. She began to sing the *Song of Waning,* searching in Everam's light for *alagai* as Briar led the way upward.

"Breakfast, *khaffit*!" Hasik cried, opening the door with a slam.

Abban jolted, slamming his face on the hard bench as Hasik strode into the room, tray in hand.

"Where is Dawn?" Abban shook sleep from his head, pushing to sit up.

Hasik threw something that struck Abban's chest with a wet smack. He caught it instinctively, looking down to see a bloodied scalp, the locks of gray-streaked hair unmistakable.

Dawn's.

Abban cast the thing to the ground in horror, and Hasik threw back his head, roaring with laughter.

"Your *chin* friend did not cling to life as desperately as you, *khaffit*," Hasik said. "I found her hanging from the ceiling beam in her cell."

Abban looked sadly at the scalp. *Everam, giver of life and light, I have never been your most faithful servant, but neither am I an* alagai *like this one. Give me the power of life and death over him, even for an instant, and I will never again be such a fool as to let him live.*

But if Everam were listening, He gave no sign. "Come, *khaffit*," Hasik beckoned. "Your breakfast will get cold."

"I am surprised you brought the scalp yourself." Abban

tried to sound nonchalant as his stomach churned. "The Hasik I know would have sent her daughter in with it."

"I think I will leave her daughter be, for now," Hasik said.

Abban raised an eyebrow. "Growing soft?"

Hasik chuckled, pulling his small hammer from his belt. "Of course not. I simply think you should return to bearing your own punishment for a time."

Abban felt his face go cold. "Eunuch Ka. If you spare me I will . . ."

"Now you beg and bargain again!" Hasik laughed. "Oh, *khaffit*, how I have missed this! Whatever flicker of emotion you had for the *chin* woman, it was not worth offering bribes for!"

Abban swallowed. The words bit hard, but he could not deny the truth of them. He fancied himself better than Hasik, but was he truly?

Hasik lifted the hammer. "So, *khaffit*. What can you offer me, in exchange for your thumb?"

"I . . ." Abban hesitated. What indeed? He had nothing, trapped in this tiny cell. His fortune was with Jamere in Krasia, with Shamavah in the Hollow. And even if he could access it, what in Ala might appease this man, who only truly felt alive while Abban screamed.

"Come, *khaffit*, you must play the game." Hasik grabbed Abban's wrist, pinning it to the table with an iron grip as the little hammer twirled in his fingers.

"Please!" Abban squealed. His feet, his legs, he could endure. But what was he without his hands? "If . . . you spare my hands, I will tell you the location of the Deliverer's electrum mine."

Hasik looked up. "You lie."

Abban shook his head. "I was the one who first brought knowledge of the sacred metal to Ahmann, Hasik. The mine is remote, with limited guards. Your Eunuchs could take the place easily, and hold its canyon indefinitely with a small number of warriors."

Hasik sat up, putting the hammer back on the table. Abban felt a burst of hope. Electrum weapons could make the Eunuchs a dominant force in the wetlands. "How far?"

"Perhaps a fortnight of riding." Abban shrugged as if the journey were inconsequential.

Hasik spat. "Too far to easily trust the truth of your words. Too far to send warriors on the promises of a *khaffit* desperate to keep his fingers."

"Kill me, if I am lying."

Hasik eased again. "That is new."

"This is not some honeyed dissembling, Hasik," Abban said. "If I cannot buy my way from torture with *chin* slaves, then I will do it in precious metal."

Hasik studied Abban, tapping the hammer lightly against his jaw. He tilted his head as if listening to an invisible advisor. At last he stood, his breakfast of steamed shellfish forgotten. "Bring the *khaffit's* chair!"

"I can draw a map—" Abban was cut off as Hasik hauled him up and shoved him into the wheeled chair. Something in the warrior's eyes frightened him even more than the hammer.

"Where are we—" This time his words were cut off as Hasik cuffed him on the back of the head.

"Silence," the warrior growled. "There is another way to test the truth of your words."

Abban wondered if he'd made a terrible mistake, but knew better than to continue his protests. He was wheeled out of the cell and through the halls to a guarded door. There, they abandoned the chair, Hasik throwing Abban over his shoulder like a sack of grain. The door opened into a stair that looked like a pit to the abyss, descending deep into the catacombs beneath the monastery.

At last they reached the bottom, where a heavy door was guarded by a number of Eunuchs. They stood sharply to attention as Hasik and Abban entered the chamber, and readied spears as they pulled open the door as if expecting all the abyss to spew forth.

The guards looked at Abban warily, but they said nothing as Hasik carried him through. On the far side, dim light from the guard chamber showed man-made supports and flooring giving way to natural tunnel formations. There had been wards on the supports and floor, but they were broken and scuffed. Then the guards closed the door behind them, and they were left in darkness.

"Hasik," Abban began.

"I've heard enough of your words these past months, *khaffit*." The gem on Hasik's turban glowed softly, granting him sight in the dark, but Abban was swallowed by the black, able to see no more than his captor's dimly lit face. "Now it is time for *you* to listen."

"I'm listening," he said, when the silence went on too long for him to bear.

"Not to me." Hasik dropped Abban heavily to the hard stone floor. "To the true master here."

"And that is?" Abban asked.

In response, a light ward flared to life on the chamber ceiling. Abban squinted in the glare, seeing there was another figure standing right in front of them.

He was even more afraid when he realized it was himself. "Everam preserve us!"

Not a true reflection—this Abban was fit, pacing the room on two feet. It was what Abban might have been, if he hadn't fallen from the Maze walls.

Not-Abban circled, looking at him like a cat eyeing a mouse. Abban began to shake, feeling himself break into sweat. He lifted a hand to draw a ward in the air.

Hasik slapped the hand down. "Do that again, *khaffit,* and I will cut off your arm. The master has no need of your body. Only your mind."

"Master?" Abban looked up, seeing another demon blur into sight, silhouetted in the shadowy chamber.

"Alagai Ka." Hasik dropped to his knees, putting his forehead to the floor as the demon stepped into the light.

The demon was small, shorter even than Abban, with spindly arms and legs and a torso that looked like coal-black leather pulled tight over a skeleton. Its huge, conical head was ringed above its giant black eyes by a crown of vestigial horns.

The knobbed flesh of the demon's cranium pulsed.

Not-Abban shifted, melting away like a water reflection after a stone was cast in the pool. It re-formed a moment later as Hasik—or as Hasik imagined himself before the cutting. The not-Hasik was naked, manhood swinging between his legs like a child's arm.

"I don't think you have it quite right," Abban noted. "Hasik's limp spear was far less impressive when my wives and daughters held him down and cut it from him."

Hasik glared at him, but as Abban expected, he did not dare rise unbidden.

"You speak boldly, *khaffit*," not-Hasik said, mimicking the real Hasik's voice and mannerisms with eerie perfection.

"What does it matter?" Abban laughed, surprised to find his fear and panic fading. This was not a battle that required his body, only his wits. He looked at not-Hasik, speaking as if to the genuine article. "If I am here, Hasik, it is because your master has need of me, and my fate is no longer in your hands."

"Do not be so sure, *khaffit*," not-Hasik growled. "You may be returned to my care when the master is done with you."

"May," Abban noted.

"If he does not consume your mind in the flesh after he has stolen your thoughts," not-Hasik agreed with a smile.

Abban shrugged. "It does not matter anymore, Hasik. You may dream of being master, but we both know you have never been more than a dog. I saw it in *sharaj* with the drillmasters and Khevat. Nightfather Jesan. Ahmann. When there's a larger cock in the room, you've no ambition past sating your own lusts."

"You lie, *khaffit*!" Not-Hasik thrust his chin at him, but Abban did not flinch. "I am loyal to Alagai Ka, and will be rewarded."

Abban met his gaze. "Rewarded with what? Bottom feeders and pig? Me to torture? A new spear between your legs? You have always lacked imagination, Hasik."

The real article would have struck him for such words, but the mimic rippled again, turning back into not-Abban. "What would Mother say, to hear you antagonizing the customer before the bargaining begins?"

"You obviously know very little about my mother," Abban said.

The mimic demon rippled again, taking the form of Abban's aged mother, Omara. Unlike not-Hasik and not-Abban, this illusion was perfect, down to the wrinkles about her eyes and the perfume she favored.

"Be proud, my son. You are worth more than any *Sharum*

dog." When she spoke, it was with Omara's voice, her gestures. Her inflection.

But Omara was a thousand miles away, and Abban had made sure Hasik had never been near the woman. How could the demon mimic her so perfectly?

And then he felt it, the demon's will, tingling through his mind. He wasn't here to be questioned with words. The interrogation had already begun.

But now that he sensed the demon's will, the outside world fell away as he focused inward. He followed the demon into his memories, visions from his past that were so vivid he felt he was living them all over again. Being pulled from Omara's arms and thrust into *sharaj*. The beating Hasik had given him that day, and in the days that followed. The humiliation. The pain.

These the demon seemed to drink like couzi, giving off the mental equivalent of a contented sigh.

It was an unspeakable violation, and Abban shoved at the *alagai*'s will, trying to drive it from his mind.

Alagai Ka barely noticed, slapping his clumsy resistance aside as easily as Hasik did his return blows when they were children.

Again the demon plunged him into memory, this time of the fall from the wall that left him with legs shattered on the floor of the Maze. The humiliations that followed, as his body failed him, and he failed his only friend time and again, forcing Ahmann to choose between friendship and duty until he could do it no longer.

What could have been, if Abban had not fallen? Might Ahmann be at his side even now? If he had never returned to the bazaar, never given the Par'chin the map . . .

Suddenly the swirling will seemed to stiffen in his mind, beginning to coalesce as the demon focused sharply on these memories, pulling so hard at Abban's recollections that he felt dizzied. His body twitched spasmodically as the *alagai* drew forth every scent and sound, every texture from his memories of the Par'chin.

Abban knew then this meeting was about more than just the electrum mine. It was about something infinitely more dangerous—for him, and all Ala.

The demon wanted to know about Ahmann. It wanted to know about the Par'chin. And somewhere in his soul—if there was such a thing—Abban knew that he must not allow it, even if it meant his own life.

The thought freed him as he gathered his will. Abban loved his wives and children, loved his wealth and comforts, but none of it more than his own life. If he was willing to sacrifice that on the bargaining table, then there was no reason to fight with less than everything he had.

In that moment, he understood Ahmann and the Par'chin in a way he never had before.

Oh, my friends, how I have wronged you. You were right all along.

And with that last thought, Abban threw his will against the alien presence in his mind.

The demon was not prepared for his renewed assault. It thought him weak, cowed. Abban burst through its defenses, jarring it from his memories. Then, slowly, he began to force the demon's will from his body.

The creature looked at him in surprise. Not the mimic, still wearing Omara's form, but the *alagai* prince itself. It tilted its head and regarded him with those huge eyes, puzzled as if an ant should presume to step upon him.

Abban saw himself reflected in those giant black eyes, body shaking, drool running from his mouth, but none of that mattered. Only the demon, and its will.

What do you want? his mind demanded, and suddenly he was following the creature as it withdrew into itself.

In its alien mind he saw her, Alagai'ting Ka, the Mother of Demons. He heard her lowing, smelled the hormones in the moist, hot air. Eggs were spilling from her, and soon, queens. Queens that would feed in a frenzy after hatching, growing rapidly in size and power.

They needed humans, close at hand, in numbers, to sate their needs.

Like thousands of fools trapped in a monastery.

All of the walled cities. They were not safeholds. They were larders.

The demon struck back, and Abban realized he had become distracted by the new knowledge. He was ejected from its mind, but the battle was not over. There, in the space between them, their wills wrestled for advantage.

Abban understood his adversary now. Like a mark in the bazaar, he read the demon's desires. And when you knew what the customer wanted—needed—it was a simple thing to reel them in and make the sale.

The demon struggled, no simple mark. It knew his weaknesses as well, and its will was enormous.

But Abban relished a tough sale.

The struggle wore on, and Abban found himself losing ground. The demon's will matched him move for move. Abban had nothing to lose, but the demon had everything to gain. More, it had skill at mental combat, the rules of which Abban was only just beginning to grasp. Slowly, inexorably, the demon dominated the space between them, forcing Abban's will back into his body.

It did not even need to defeat him. If Abban allowed it the slightest opening, the demon would signal Hasik or the mimic to choke Abban unconscious, and then work its will on his insensate mind.

But then Abban heard a familiar song, and he realized that neither did he need to defeat the demon, only hold the creature in place a few moments more.

Ashia kept her voice steady, cloaking them in the *Song of Waning* as she, Briar, and Kaji crept up on Alagai Ka.

Enkido had taught detachment in battle, the emotional distance that allowed warriors to keep their minds outside a battle to study it from all angles. Ashia could approach a quake of rock demons with cool confidence.

But this was Alagai Ka, father of demons, who had stood against Kaji himself. What was her pitiful singing, her short spears, against a foe such as that?

Nonetheless she continued to creep slowly forward, spears at the ready, while the demon had its attention focused on Abban. Hasik remained on his hands and knees. The old woman—whoever she was—stood limply, like a puppet with its strings cut.

Briar was only a step behind as they crept from the cover of one of several tunnels that converged at this cavern. Still the demon did not notice them.

Swiftly now, Ashia's fingers said to Briar. Then she broke into a sprint, weapons leading.

Hasik sniffed, glancing up. "Master!"

The demon caught sight of her just as Ashia struck with a double thrust of her spears. The creature twisted, and her speartips struck only air. It drew a ward in the air, flinging her away like backhanding a child. She nearly stumbled into Briar, but the boy was fast, quickstepping around, raising his waterskin.

The demon, expecting another physical attack, was unprepared when Briar squirted hogroot tea at it. The creature shrieked and fell back, skin and eyes sizzling with chemical burn.

The demon landed on its back, glaring at them, but then its eyes turned with surprise back toward Abban. Whatever connection they shared remained unbroken, and the *khaffit* was pressing the attack.

Ashia leapt in the moment of distraction, but she was tackled before she could reach the demon by the old woman, faster than a *Sharum'ting,* stronger than a rock demon. They hit the ground in a roll, and the woman flung Ashia like a doll against the cavern wall.

Briar got the woman's attention with another spray from his waterskin. Her wrinkled flesh rippled, and the woman became a field demon, a sleek fast form well suited to the small underground chamber. The creature puffed, growing the armor plating of a rock demon, spiked and sharp. Its eyes and mouth glowed with flame.

The mimic swiped at Briar, who dove aside just in time, rolling to avoid the spatter as the demon hawked a glob of burning firespit at him.

The mimic's face melted, becoming the long beak of a lightning demon that shrieked a bolt of electricity at Briar.

Briar had his shield up in time, deflecting the worst of it, but Ashia saw pain jolt through his aura. He screamed, and Ashia snarled, charging the creature.

She struck first with her voice, a vibrating shriek she could maintain indefinitely, amplified by the *hora* stones of her necklace. The sound cut through the chamber, and the mimic stumbled, crying out in pain. Even the mind demon put its thin, skeletal hands over its earholes.

She snapped the ends of her short spears together, now six feet of spinning, razor-sharp warded glass. She battered and sliced at the mimic's limbs, severing as much as she could before the creature regained its wits.

But the stumps didn't bleed, the mimic melting into a larger, even more menacing form.

Ashia paid the form little mind, focusing on the magic in the creature's aura. Healing and shape-shifting Drew heavily on that power. Their only chance was to wear it down quickly.

The demon lashed out at her, a tentacle growing from nothing as quickly as a cracking whip. It would have had her, but Briar hit the creature from the side in a shield-rush, stunning it with the mimic wards etched into the steel.

Ashia used the distraction to stab the creature in the heart, jolting it and causing another drain on its power to grow a new one.

Briar stabbed next, piercing that new organ, and as one they let go of the weapons, leaving them to continue sending waves of killing magic through the creature.

Ashia fell into the *sharukin* she had studied all her life, driving stiffened fingers into the convergence points in the demon's aura. Her nails, painted with wards and lacquered hard, struck its armor like a hammer to a nutshell. Each blow sent feedback jolting through her, filling her with strength and speed as the demon's aura waned. Even Kaji took a portion of it, the boy laughing gleefully, unaware of the danger they faced.

Briar turned to bare hands as well, his pressure and impact wards strong as any spear and shield as he batted aside the demon's blows, striking with short, fast, open-hand counters. An eyeblink could miss one, but Ashia could see the damage throb and build in the demon's aura.

They hammered at the weakened and stunned creature again and again until Ashia saw her opening. She tore her spear from its body and spun it in an arc, striking the demon's head from its body.

She completed the circuit with another spin, turning and

hurling her spear at the mind demon. But before it could strike, a shield deflected the weapon, sending it clattering to the floor on the far end of the chamber. Hasik interposed himself.

"Everam has granted me another day," Hasik said. "None will stand against me."

"You have left Everam's sight, Uncle." Ashia took another of the supports from Kaji's pack, warded glass laced with electrum by the Damajah herself. She snapped open the blade of a short scythe as she rolled her glass shield onto her arm. "There is nothing He would grant to one such as you."

"We shall see, little girl."

Hasik came in hard. Ashia caught his blows on her shield, or hooked them away with the scythe, but she was unprepared for his ferocity. For a moment, it was all she could do to block the rapid thrusts and spinning slashes of his spear. With Kaji on her back, she could not commit to moves that exposed the boy to a counter, so she gave ground, desperately seeking a weakness in the Eunuch's defenses.

Briar saw her distress and charged at Hasik's back. Ashia gave no sign, but Hasik dropped beneath the blow at the last instant, delivering a crushing kick that put Briar on his back.

Ashia pressed, but Hasik was not distracted, never lowering his defense even as he all but crippled Briar. They clinched, and he bashed her in the face with his forehead, laughing wildly as she stumbled back.

She dropped beneath his next blow, hurling her shield at him as she dove into a tumble, popping the weighted end off her scythe and drawing out the slender chain hidden in the shaft. She threw, catching Hasik's ankle as he dodged the thrown shield.

Ashia pulled, but Hasik was wise to the move, using the leverage and strength of her pull to throw himself at her, kicking her hard in the face. A snap of his armored ankle yanked the scythe from her hand and sent it skittering away.

Ashia hurled throwing glass at him as he rolled to regain balance, but Hasik's shield was in place, catching all but one. This last struck his robes with a *plink!* and dropped, stopped short by his glass breastplate.

With no time to ready another weapon, Ashia fell into a *sharusahk* pose to meet Hasik's next charge.

The move made the Eunuch stop short. He glanced at Briar, but the boy was still on his back groaning. She could see in his aura that Hasik had broken Briar's hip. He was holding it in place as his magic knit the bones, but he would not heal quickly enough for her to count on his aid.

"Put down the child," Hasik offered. "Give me a real battle."

"Never," Ashia replied.

Hasik pulled the scarf away from his throat. "Put down the child and I will put down my spear and shield."

"Why would you do that?" Ashia asked.

"Because I want to see what Enkido made of you," Hasik said. "What he made of my daughter."

"Your daughter was ashamed of you," Ashia said. "Even before the *khaffit* cut you, Sikvah said you brought shame upon your house daily, outspending even the pay of a Spear of the Deliverer to cover your gambling and *heasah*. Striking everyone from slaves to your *Jiwah Ka*."

Hasik threw down his spear. "Show me what Enkido made of you before I kill you with my bare hands."

"And my son?" Ashia asked.

Hasik smiled. "If you fail, I will do the same to him and your foul-smelling friend."

"Then I will not fail." Ashia stepped slowly around to where her shield had rolled against the chamber wall. She flipped it over with her foot and slipped off Kaji's pack, laying it in the protective circle. She was loath to take him from her, but there was no denying the advantage Hasik offered. She could not afford to refuse the opportunity.

"Do not thrash, my son," she whispered. "Let my shield protect you until I return. I love you always."

A tear slipped free to land on his cheek before Ashia realized she was weeping. She squinted and the drops fell like rain on the boy's face.

Kaji only smiled. "Mommy fight."

Ashia nodded, using the motion as she brushed away the tears to slip the last support from Kaji's pack into her sleeve. "Yes, my love. Be brave."

"Mommy brave," Kaji agreed.

As she stepped away from her son, Hasik kicked his spear and shield aside, assuming a *sharusahk* stance. Behind him, Abban and the demon stared at each other, locked in some unholy battle. The aura between them was alive in a way Ashia had never seen before. There was no way to make sense of it, or to guess how much longer the *khaffit* could hold the creature at bay.

She assumed a stance of her own, skittering in to face him.

Hasik bared his gap tooth, blowing out a whistle. "Begin."

Briar wanted to scream as he watched Ashia stalk in to face Hasik, but he knew what happened if you let a bone heal wrong. He had to keep still, putting pressure on his hip until it knit straight.

When the fighting began, it was almost too fast to follow. They looked like dancers with a practiced routine. Many of their moves were identical in form and execution—economical and precise.

Hasik had the advantage in height, weight, and reach. Ashia had greater speed, balance, and flexibility, but it was not enough to make a telling difference. She was holding her own, but Hasik was landing more blows than her. Most were just bashes against the armor plates in her robes, but such strikes still hurt, stunned, and bruised. In time, they would wear her down.

There was a growl, and Briar turned to see a sand demon stick its head from one of the tunnels leading into the caverns below. Letting go of his hip with one hand, he snatched his spear and threw it, taking it in its thinly armored belly. The demon yelped and fell, letting out a cry that was echoed farther down the tunnels.

He crawled on three limbs to keep the injured hip straight, untying the strings on small pouches of hogroot powder. These he flung into the tunnel entrances, putting up a cloud the demons would find noxious and difficult to pass. The effect would lessen over time, and from the sound of the howling in the tunnel, the sheer press from behind might force them through. "Ent got a lot of time, Ashia!"

Caught up in battle with Hasik, Ashia made no reply. By

the time Briar dragged himself to his spear, he was feeling stronger. He gripped the shaft, point still embedded in the dying sand demon, and felt a jolt of power through the ward tattooed on his hand.

He lifted the spear, driving the point in deeper and out the demon's other side, hastening its death as he used the spear as a cane to pull himself upright. He tested his weight on his broken hip and found it would hold.

He looked from Ashia's battle to the *khaffit* and the mind demon, then pulled the spear free and drew back for a throw.

Something struck his arm as it came forward. When he tried to loose, Briar found the spear stuck to his hand with what looked like spider-silk. He glanced up just as the cave demon dropped on him from above.

Ashia caught a punch on her forearms, turning her thigh to block a kick without costing her balance. The move left her unable to guard against Hasik's second punch, a powerful hook to the ribs.

The glass plates in Ashia's robe took the brunt of the blow, but it knocked the breath out of her, bruising muscle and cracking bone. This was not the first time Hasik had struck that precise spot.

Still, she left another opening a moment later. When Hasik struck, she caught the blow, twisting under his wrist and keeping the hold as she ran up his thigh and scissored her legs around his throat.

It was a perfectly executed takedown, but Hasik was heavy, and strong as a rock demon. He danced about, keeping his feet and hooking punches into her. Ashia landed a few blows to his head, but was forced to relinquish the hold when she could not get full control.

"I never met the legendary Enkido," Hasik said. "At least not before he cut off his own cock and tongue. But even then his name was honored, and feared." He spat blood on the chamber floor. "He would be ashamed of you."

Ashia growled and came back at him, but she was beginning to fear he was right. She glanced about for Briar, and found him fighting for his life against an eight-legged demon shaped like a giant, armored spider.

She and Hasik traded blows again. Hasik's breastplate was impenetrable glass, and did not absorb blows like her own armor plates. Punching it was like punching a wall while Hasik laughed on the other side.

But there were seams, and gaps in the joints, to allow freedom of movement. She struck at these, weakening his lines of power, but it was a slow attrition compared with the teeth-chattering, breath-stealing blows he dealt in return, looking—as she was—for opportunities to deliver a crippling move.

At last one came. Hasik snaked an arm around hers, locking her elbow and pulling tight as he pivoted into a throw. Ashia felt her shoulder snap from its socket and she struck the ground hard, stunned.

Hasik would have had her then, but there were sudden cries and sounds of battle on the far side of the door to the keep. Ashia heard her grandfather's voice shouting above the din.

In that moment of distraction, Ashia flicked the scythe from the sleeve of her good arm. Snapping the blade open, she slashed it along the narrow seam at the waist of Hasik's armor.

Hasik's grip weakened as she opened his intestines, and Ashia twisted free, turning a full circuit into another slash, this one meant for his throat.

"Don't!" a familiar voice commanded. Ashia looked to see Kaji standing just a few feet from her, holding her other scythe to his own throat.

Ashia gasped and stumbled back from Hasik without a killing blow. One arm hung limp, shoulder snapped like a twig, but she kept hold of her weapon.

"Drop it, Mommy," Kaji said. "Or I drop."

"Put the blade down, my love." She choked out the words.

"No." It was Kaji's favorite word. The most powerful one in his vocabulary.

"Kaji asu Asome am'Jardir am'Kaji," Ashia sharpened her tone. "Put that blade down this instant."

The boy hesitated, and Ashia took a tentative step forward.

"No." Kaji lifted the scythe higher, pressing the razor edge against his skin.

Ashia pulled up short, close enough to see her tears still streaking the boy's face, but too far to stop him before he could cut his own throat. She lowered her own blade, even as Hasik, holding his intestines in with one arm, pushed himself to his feet.

"Please, my son," she begged. "Be brave."

She watched his aura, saw his pure glow and the darkness that had infected it. The demon had a hold on him that she could not break with words.

But then the lines on Kaji's face began to glow, Ashia's tears binding the ambient magic to her wish to keep him safe. The glow spread, driving away the demon's shadow.

Even the palm weeps, when the storm washes over it, Enkido once told her. *The tears of Everam's spear sisters are all the more precious for how seldom they fall.*

Kaji turned to look at the mind demon, scythe dropping from his tiny hand. "No."

The word seemed to have a physical effect on the demon. It shook with effort, ichor running from its nostrils and ears, much as blood ran from Abban's as they locked stares.

Hasik lunged, a long knife in his hand, but Ashia was ready, hooking his wrist aside with her scythe as she delivered a kick to his wounded midsection. Still he bore into her, taking her down to the ground where they both struggled for control.

Briar rolled this way and that, contorting himself to avoid the rapid strikes of the cave demon's legs, covered with sharp spikes to grip and hold in sheer stone walls. It reared back, legs beating a drum rhythm on the floor as it struck.

Briar managed to get his shield on his arm. He caught the demon's blows more easily now, but the corie had greater reach, and his return strikes at its bulbous abdomen fell short.

Across the chamber, he saw Kaji lift the blade to his throat. Briar froze, and the demon nearly had him. He barely managed to scramble away from its next series of blows. Sensing the advantage, the demon began snapping at him with the thick pincers around its maw, dripping venom that sizzled against the wards on his shield.

"No," Kaji said, dropping the scythe as he turned to look at the mind demon. Briar followed his gaze for an instant, and saw the demon shaken.

With his shield hand, Briar pulled the waterskin from his belt, hurling it at the cave demon's maw. The corie caught the skin in its pincers, popping it in a spray of hogroot tea. It fell back shrieking, and Briar rushed in, knocking the demon back with his shield's forbidding.

Then he turned and hurled his spear as hard as he could at the mind demon's head.

He didn't wait to see if it struck, darting forward in the weapon's wake. It blasted through the mind's thick cranium, and Briar was there an instant later, slamming the impact ward on his palm against the demon's throat. He pinned the corie with a knee as he fell atop it, taking hold of the spear on either side of the demon's head. With a mighty flex, he turned it like a capstan and heard the demon's neck snap.

The mind demon gave a last shriek, cranium throbbing as its body bucked and thrashed. The cave demon gave a shrill cry and collapsed on its back, legs curling.

Hasik, too, gave a shout, going limp long enough for Ashia to establish a controlling hold. Abban groaned, putting a hand to his face.

Moments later, Khevat and Icha burst through the doors, robes wet with blood.

Hasik shook his head to clear it, even as Khevat, Icha, and their men surrounded him. He was on his knees, propped on one hand while the other tried to hold in his intestines, but he was still dangerous and everyone knew it.

Ashia moved to collect her spears. Her arm was still numb, hanging limp at her side. Kaji stumbled to her, wrapping his arms around her leg, oblivious to the blood soaking the silk. "Mama."

"You were very brave, my son," Ashia said.

"Bave like Mama," Kaji agreed.

Abban had collapsed on the floor. Briar went to him, dragging him to the wall and propping him against it. "You all right?"

Abban sniffed, wrinkling his nose. "The spy."

"Saved your life," Briar reminded him.

"What is the meaning of this?!" Hasik demanded. "Fetch the *chin* Gatherer. I need . . ."

Ashia put her spear to the nape of his neck. "You need nothing, servant of Nie."

More men were pouring into the chamber. Not all were Khevat's warriors, and many looked ready to continue the fighting and free their leader.

But then Briar took hold of the body of the demon prince and threw its ruin beside Hasik. The men looked on in horror at the creature, the symbol of everything they had been taught from cradle to *sharaj* to fear and hate.

"I am Ashia vah Ashan, Sharum'ting Ka of Krasia!" Ashia shouted. "You have been duped, warriors of Everam, but I have come with an offer of redemption. Even now, the *alagai* press the Damajah's forces at Everam's Reservoir. Many of you have friends there. Family. Ride with me there now, and your crimes will be forgiven. Remain behind, and when Sharak Ka is over the victorious armies of the Deliverer will hunt you down."

"If they are victorious," Hasik sneered. "The Deliverer is dead. His son . . ."

"Was murdered by you!" Khevat shouted.

Ashia nodded. "Hasik, shame of his family, for the murder of my brother-in-law Prince Jayan, and desertion from the Deliverer's Army, I sentence you to death."

Hasik had been gathering his strength. He whirled quickly, but he was not quick enough. Ashia thrust her spear, severing his spine at the neck. The eunuch's body went limp, and he collapsed. Before anyone could move, she drew back and slashed her spear, severing his head.

"Bring it," she commanded, "and the demon's head as well. Let those above see who they were following as they make their choice."

CHAPTER 40

ALAMEN FAE

334 AR

The mimic grew legs as long as the tunnel would allow, sprinting hard from the collapsing ceiling. The stones would delay pursuit only a short time, but it would be enough for the mind to lose them in the maze of the depths.

Yet the Heir was fast. Soaring past the worst of the collapse, he batted the last of the stones, knocking it into the mimic's back. The drone's armor held, but it was knocked from its feet.

The Consort looked back. The Heir was alone, trapped on the far side of the cave-in. He had his spear and cloak, but not the hated crown. It was a rare opportunity to rid himself of the scourge of the Mind Killer.

The Heir was unprepared as the mimic bounced off the wall and used the force of his own attack to spring back at him. As the Consort surmised, the Heir did not have the focus to sustain flight while fending off a concerted attack. He dropped back to his feet, that he might better access the repetitions that formed the basis of human combat.

The Consort had studied *sharusahk* in the human drone's mind, learning its strengths and weaknesses, and watched the Heir's style closely.

It was all the human could do to block the mimic's attacks. His aura was filled with aggression, but he did not lose focus. He knew he was divided—weakened. He gave ground as the mimic pressed in, shedding his armored robe to bare the wards scarred into his flesh.

The mimic spat the thick, sticky acid of a swamp drone at the. Heir's face. His defensive wards would have protected him, but as expected he flinched, losing a moment's focus as the drone grew multiple limbs, each ending in a sharp, chitinous spike. The Consort Drew from those spikes, leaving them magic-dead and immune to the defensive wards.

The Heir dodged the acid, taking a spike in the side. He rolled away from the blow, too shallow to kill, and somehow managed to block the next three attacks before the fourth pierced clean through his thigh.

Still he fought, hacking off the next spike and drawing a mimic ward that knocked the drone hard into the tunnel wall, creating fighting space. The Heir rushed past to cut off escape, pinning the Consort between himself and the collapsed tunnel.

His spear came alive with cutting wards as he spun it at the mimic, and this time it was the Consort desperately trying to defend. Any appendage that came near the spinning weapon was lopped off, weakening the drone and robbing the Consort of the magic stored in that flesh.

But while there was little defense against the spear, the Heir was all but blind without the crown. The Consort shifted the drone's armor to blend into the tunnel, melting into a sinuous shape as it flowed up the wall and onto the ceiling to regain favorable ground.

It was too much for the Heir's weakened vision, but he responded on instinct, guessing the plan and drawing great mimic wards at the ceiling. The drone was bashed against the stone and lost purchase, dropping to the tunnel floor.

The Consort shifted the glands in the mimic's throat to those of a specialized water demon, producing a thick, viscous black ink. He Drew from the liquid until it was magic-dead, and spat.

This time the Heir did not flinch, catching the blinding ink right in the face. Shock ran through his aura, but he did not lose focus, driving his spear right through the mimic's midsection, inches from where the Consort hid.

The Heir was no longer trying to keep him contained. He was there to kill.

The Consort realized how foolish, how arrogant he had been. True, the Heir was weakened, alone, but he was still the Mind Killer, and the Consort was hardly at full strength.

He sent out a vibration, Reading the stone around them. He sensed a cavern not far below, vast and sprawling. There would be countless places to hide long enough to flay the wards from the Consort's flesh that he might dissipate back to his place of power.

The Heir opened his eyes and they were alive with magic, burning the ink away with a hiss. Already his wounds were closing. He sent a jolt of magic through the spear, shocking mimic and mind alike before tearing the spear free to draw back for another thrust.

The Consort blocked the blow and pressed the attack, stabbing with magic-dead spikes and forcing the Heir to give ground.

When there was enough space, the Consort grew a sinuous limb and siphoned magic into it to draw wards even as the other limbs attacked. With no power to waste, each ward was precisely placed to drive cracks into the stone supporting the floor.

But before he could complete the task, the Explorer dissipated through the still-settling stone of the cave-in. It was a dangerous move. Magic moved in tides in the deep, and could sweep the unwary into the Core, from which there was no return.

More, the between-state would have opened the Explorer up to psychic attack, if the Consort still had his powers. Mimics were effective at duplicating the skills of lesser drones, but they could not replicate the complexity of a prince's mind.

The Explorer took no chances, solidifying the moment he was on the far side of the collapse, the hated crown in hand.

If the Explorer had donned the relic, it might have been the Consort's undoing, but human weakness saved him.

"Ahmann!" The Explorer threw the crown at the Heir even as his other hand began drawing wards to keep the demons contained.

The Heir caught the crown, but before he could place it on

his brow, the Consort drew the last ward, and the floor collapsed beneath them.

The Consort was prepared, snapping the mimic's arms out into wind demon wings as he elongated and streamlined the body. It caught an updraft and glided away into the cavern as his enemies fell.

Arlen tumbled amid shattered rock, wind rushing in his face as he was buffeted by the stones. He glimpsed Jardir in similar free fall while the demon soared off.

For the second time, he risked dissipation. On the surface, ambient magic flowed across the ground in subtle whorls and eddies, like low fog. There the call of the Core was a distant thing, like the great horn in Tibbet's Brook. Here it was a thunderous roar, the flows of magic like great storm-waves threatening to drown him and drag him into its depths.

He watched the currents, finding one flowing upward and latching his will to it. He rode the draft of magic, solidifying enough to maintain cohesion and resist the call of the Core while remaining light enough to stay aloft.

Jardir let go of the spear, picking up speed as he struggled with the crown. He managed at last to get it onto his head, and summoned the spear with a quick sketching of wards. It returned almost eagerly to his grasp, and he, too, took flight.

Arlen scanned the air, catching sight of the mimic as it glided through the cavern. He pointed and saw Jardir change course after it. Without another word, Arlen focused his magic in a concentrated burst, hurling himself at the demon like one of Leesha's flamework rockets.

Jardir spent magic recklessly as he raced after Alagai Ka. There was a limit to what the Crown and Spear of Kaji could store, but the past months of sacrifice were meaningless if the demon escaped, to the doom of all Ala.

But the Par'chin was with him now, and the crown was back on his brow. He'd kept his wits when the abyss broke loose and now Everam stood with them again.

Miles sped by as they pursued, slowly closing the gap until

the demon was nearly in range of the crown. Aware of the gain, the mimic furled its wings and fell like a stone into a deep canyon, momentarily dropping out of sight.

The Par'chin dove after it as Jardir arced into the canyon, putting on speed instead of letting gravity do the work. The Par'chin was floating in midair, turning desperately to search for the father of demons. The ambient magic was thick this far below the surface, and Jardir knew the demon could hide in it like a Watcher in the shadows.

But while Alagai Ka might hide from the Par'chin, he could not escape Jardir's crownsight. Jardir pretended not to notice it cowering against the canyon wall, the mimic's body perfectly blended with the stone. He turned his head, giving the creature a moment's hope before he spun, bashing mimic and mind against the wall with wards of forbidding.

Stunned, the demon was slow to react as Jardir rushed in close, throwing the crown's bubble around it at last. The Par'chin tackled the demon in midair, more than willing to grapple as mind and mimic wards flared on his skin. They fell into the canyon, battering and bashing at each other.

Jardir followed them down, drawing in the bubble. The demon had little room to maneuver when they hit the ground. The Par'chin broke the clinch and rolled back, bleeding from deep punctures from magic-dead spikes the demon had grown.

But the wounds of his *ajin'pal* were already closing as he and Jardir stalked in. The weakened mimic was no match for them together. The Par'chin caught a spike-tipped tentacle and tore it clean off the demon's body. Jardir blocked stabbing spikes and spun the spear to slice a deep cut of meat from its back.

Ichor splattered them both, but it only made them stronger. Jardir lost track of time as they fought, slowly wearing down the foe.

At last, the mimic grew too weak to sustain a transition, locked in a crippled form. Then it lost cohesion entirely, sloughing away to coat the floor in a reeking ooze, revealing the mind within.

Jardir charged, spear leading, but then the demon did something unexpected. It knelt in the Krasian fashion, hands on the ground, eyes lowered.

"Enough," it rasped, voice harsh and cutting. "I surrender."

"Since when can you talk?!" The Par'chin gaped, pulling up short even as Jardir checked his attack.

The demon gave an almost human shrug. "When I dissipated in your tower but failed to escape, I re-formed with a throat and tongue that could form your primitive grunting sounds."

Jardir lifted his spear. "So Shanjat . . ."

Another shrug. "Was a useful drone."

Rage gathered in Jardir's spirit and he Drew magic to power the killing wards still tattooed on the demon's flesh.

"Would you have done differently, child of Kavri?" the demon asked. "When has your kind ever shown mercy toward mine?"

Jardir shook his head. *Do not let Alagai Ka speak,* the Evejah taught, *for he is the Father of Lies whose silver tongue can convince men night is day and friend is foe.*

But the Par'chin stepped forward. "Plan ent changed, Ahmann. Still need him, we want to see this through."

"Perhaps," Jardir said, "but is that truly what we want, Par'chin?"

"Ay?" the greenlander asked.

"He is the Father of Lies, Par'chin," Jardir said. "He has deceived us at every turn, never as helpless as he seemed. He hollowed Shanjat like a melon rind, killed Shanvah . . ."

The Par'chin shook his head. "Shanvah ent dead. Renna's with her."

"And where are they, Par'chin?" Jardir asked. "Where are we, for that matter? We have come a long way from the tunnel where this began."

His doubt was mirrored in the Par'chin's aura as he stared back the way they came. "Might be able to trace our path across the currents . . ."

"And if we can?" Jardir demanded. "Slowly hunt our way back over a hundred miles away from our goal?"

The Par'chin frowned. "All the more reason we keep the demon alive."

"I can still take you to the mind court," the demon said. "It is close. The drone and your females will only slow you now."

There was no lie in the demon's aura. Jardir found he could read it better now that the demon did its own speaking instead of projecting through Shanjat.

"He will try to escape again," Jardir said.

"Of course I will," the demon agreed. "As would you, in my position. But I will guide you to the hive."

"And into traps along the way," Jardir said.

"The mind court is not without defenses," Alagai Ka said. "Whether you can survive them is, as you say, *inevera*."

Jardir raised a finger, sending power into the demon's tattoos until it shrieked and writhed. "Do not speak that word, slave of Nie."

He let go of the power and the demon looked up at him with its massive black eyes. "I am no one's slave."

"What will your *jiwah* do when we do not return?" Jardir asked as they marched through the canyon and into deeper tunnels beyond.

Arlen's thumb ran across the wards of his wedding ring. "Don't know. She'll be mad as spit, half with worry and half at me. Like to think she'll take Shanvah and head back to the surface, but . . . Ren's stubborn."

Jardir laughed. "Something you have in common."

"Easy for you to say," Arlen snapped. "Ent your baby in harm's way."

"Do not condescend to me, Par'chin," Jardir growled. "I have already lost my eldest son to Sharak Ka, and you fought alongside my eldest daughter in the Hollow. Is your sacrifice greater than mine?"

"Jayan and Amanvah are grown," Arlen said, a lump forming in his throat. "Made their own choices in life. My son . . ."

Jardir reached out and put a hand on his shoulder. "A father's fear for his children does not fade when they grow, Par'chin."

Arlen nodded. "Ay, reckon that's so. Din't mean . . ."

Jardir squeezed his shoulder. "Of course, Par'chin."

"Your sentiment is pathetic," Alagai Ka rasped as he matched their pace on his spindly legs. "It will be your undoing."

The words were meant to cut, but Arlen found they had no edge. "Seen your kind fight. When I killed one, its brothers didn't lift a claw to help. Rather die for sentiment than live in a world without it."

The ambient magic grew stronger as they marched, until Arlen felt he was swimming in it. His tattoos formed a constant Draw that suffused him with power. Jardir, too, shone with magic. Only the demon was dim. It kept a tight hold on its power, lest the wards on its flesh activate.

Arlen spent the power freely, tracing wards in the air as they walked—silence, confusion, unsight—masking their passage to the many demons whose paths they crossed.

The glow of their auras was not the only light. Arlen began noticing that he could see, however dimly, in natural sight. The walls were glowing softly green. On closer inspection, he found lichen clinging to the damp rock, alive with magic and emitting the faint light.

As the light grew brighter, the air lost the stink of demons but quickly became something altogether worse.

"Gah!" Arlen said. "What's that corespawned awful smell?"

"We have entered the larder," the mind demon said.

"Alamen fae," Jardir whispered, remembering Kavrivah's letter. The phrase meant "those below Everam's sight." "Kaji's warriors, taken prisoner five millennia ago."

"How many generations is that? Two hundred?" Arlen shook his head. "After just a year living on a greatward, Hollowers who didn't even fight were stronger than regular folk. What does five millennia this close to the Core do to people?"

"You will soon see," the demon teased. "We've wandered too close to the warren of one of their rut tribes. They've surrounded us."

"Could've warned us," Arlen muttered.

"You knew this was coming," the demon said. "It is your own fault if you did not prepare."

"You ent worried you'll get ripped in the crossfire?" Arlen asked.

"The stock know the futility of resisting my kind," the

demon said. "But we seldom intervene in their dealings with other stock. You, they will kill and eat."

"They eat their own?" Jardir asked, just as an arrow whistled through the air and caught Arlen in the shoulder.

"Corespawn it!" Arlen cried, wrenching the bolt free. The shaft was some tough, fibrous plant, tipped with obsidian, sharp as a razor.

Stooped creatures materialized out of the stones around them, walking as much on four limbs as two. In the rocks above, others leapt and climbed like monkeys. Their teeth and nails were thick and sharp. They were naked and filthy save for a few pouches and straps of leather, some carrying crude bows of bone and gut, others with obsidian-tipped spears and clubs.

Their stringy muscles were hard, auras bright with magic.

Jardir expanded his warding bubble, but the creatures passed harmlessly through the barrier. Likewise, Arlen's wards of unsight had no effect as the tribe's fighters stalked in, heading straight for Arlen and Jardir.

Arlen glanced at his friend's aura. It was twisted with indecision and guilt. Were these truly the descendants of Kaji's army, and what did he owe them, if so? Rescue? Death with honor? Or were these creatures forever below Everam's sight?

Arlen stepped into the lead position. "Keep your eye on the demon. Got this."

"Par'chin . . ." Jardir's voice held a warning.

"Ent gonna kill anyone," Arlen said. "But ent gonna be pushed around, either. Need to set the tone."

"Very well." Jardir's aura still churned. He welcomed a few moments to simply observe.

The biggest core dweller roared a challenge at Arlen, lifting a giant bone club studded with obsidian chips. The auras of the tribe showed this one was their leader, and his aura thrummed with primitive need to establish dominance over newcomers. He thumped his chest.

Arlen kept his wards dark, thumping his chest in return and stepping forward. The provocation worked, and the leader attacked. He outweighed Arlen, long arms giving him dangerous reach, and his strength and speed were almost a match for Arlen's.

Almost. The core dweller's attack was as crude as his weapon. Arlen easily slipped the blow and struck back, hooking a punch into the dweller's ribs.

The punch might have felled a surface man, but the core dweller accepted it with little more than a grunt, backhanding his club Arlen's way.

Again Arlen ducked the blow, snaking his forearm around the thick, hairy wrist. He locked the arm, establishing control over the weapon as he drove his knee into the core dweller's midsection once, twice, a third time.

The dweller took these blows as well, bending in and biting his shoulder. Arlen screamed and stopped pulling his punches as sharp teeth ripped into his flesh. The core dweller clawed at him with sharp, filthy nails, but Arlen slapped them away. His uppercut cracked the dweller's jaw. A push-kick sent the brute tumbling back until he hit hard against stone.

The dweller shook even this damage off, more interested in the taste of the blood in his mouth. He wiped it from his lips, sniffing like an animal. His aura was confused, but he knew the taste of blood. Their crude weapons had never made a demon bleed.

He held up the hand, yelping, and a shower of arrows came at them. Arlen drew a ward in the air and they were batted away.

There was a cry from above, and one of the core dwellers dropped at Jardir, spear leading. Instinctively, Jardir dodged the blow and stabbed it in midair, twisting to slam it into the floor.

Jardir's aura filled with horror. It was a girl, barely more than a child. He pulled his spear out, meaning to save her, but he had struck true. The girl coughed blood, and her aura snuffed like a candle.

"Everam's beard." Jardir reached out with shaking fingers. "It is true."

The dweller girl had overlarge ears and eyes. Long fingers and toes for gripping and searching dark places. But with her aura gone, Arlen could see the distinct Krasian turn to her features.

The leader was already recovering, his magic strong. He gave a howl that was quickly echoed by his fellows. The entire tribe, males and females, closed in with clubs, spears, and bows.

Several carried children on their backs, but their eyes were no less cold than the fighters'. One held a suckling babe to her breast with one hand and waved a jagged, obsidian-studded club in the other.

"Enough!" Jardir boomed, stamping his spear with a thunderclap of magic. His crown flared with power, filling the cavern with light.

The core dwellers froze, wide eyes squinting tears in the light. They turned back to Jardir, and Arlen tensed.

"Erram," the leader grunted, dropping to his knees and putting hands and forehead to the floor in the Krasian fashion.

"Erram." The others immediately followed, the entire tribe falling to their hands and knees, chanting the name.

"Erram?" Arlen asked. "You don't think . . ." A glance at their auras killed the words on his lips.

"They think I am Everam," Jardir whispered.

The mind demon hissed in amusement. "This is your faith, Heir. It has always been animals grunting in the dark at what they cannot understand."

The females moved in, some carrying children as they moved to sniff at Arlen, still too afraid to approach Jardir. They started purring, and Arlen caught the scent of their arousal. One bent to present her sex to him.

"Ay, that's enough!" He let the wards on his skin flare.

"Erram." Again the tribe fell to their knees. "Erram. Erram."

"Ay, great," Arlen muttered. "Now we're both Everam."

"Or neither," Jardir said quietly. Arlen glanced at his aura and began to worry.

He is the Father of Lies, Jardir reminded himself.

But what did that mean if the Evejah was just a book?

War is, at its crux, deception, Dama Khevat taught. *A great leader must hold his deceit so close that even he himself does not think on it until the time to strike.*

Yet Abban taught Jardir that the best deceptions were mostly true. The demon was trying to hurt him, yes, but that did not mean it was lying.

"Erram," the *alamen fae* chanted, and Jardir wondered if his primitive ancestors had done the same, making a deity of the sky and spinning tales to comfort themselves in the night.

Jardir knew to praise Everam before he took his first steps. At times he doubted Inevera's dice spoke Everam's will, but he never questioned the existence of the all-powerful Creator. Never doubted He was looking down upon His children from Heaven, guiding their paths and waiting for them at the end of the lonely road.

Not until Alagai Ka began to whisper his poison.

But Jardir searched for Heaven when he held the full power of the Spear of Ala, and found nothing.

"Erram," the animals chanted.

"How could Everam allow this, Par'chin?" he asked. "His children, fighting His war, dragged below his sight by the *alagai*. Abandoned for hundreds of generations, left to live and die as . . ."

". . . livestock." The Par'chin shrugged. "Been makin' this argument with folk since before we met, Ahmann."

"And perhaps you are right." Jardir felt cold as he said the words. Alone and vulnerable as never before.

The Par'chin looked at him, but there was no satisfaction in his aura, no righteousness. "What does it matter, Ahmann?"

"How can you ask that?" Jardir said.

"Does it change the job we gotta do," the Par'chin asked, "if we're striking a blow in some cosmic proxy war, or just killin' a nest of animals that like to eat on us and ours?"

The words were a lifeline, and Jardir clutched it. "Indeed not."

"And that means we got a choice right now," the Par'chin said.

"What do you mean?" Jardir asked.

"Ent got time to save these folk right now," the Par'chin said. "But we can teach them to save themselves."

Arlen pointed to the rocks above, where stone demons were gathering.

"Shepherds saw the lights and came to check the flock."

"We must kill them immediately," Jardir said. "We cannot let them give word of our passing."

Arlen shook his head, studying the auras of the demons. "They can't see us. Our wards don't work on the dwellers, but the demons just see a light."

He and Jardir both let their wardlight fade, Jardir pulling his bubble tighter around the Par'chin and Alagai Ka.

Arlen stepped up to the hulking male that led the dweller tribe, reaching out his hand. "Give me your spear."

At first the man seemed not to understand, but Arlen pointed with his other hand to the weapon. "Spear."

The chief took a tentative step forward, quickly slapping the weapon into Arlen's hand and falling back to his knees. The entire tribe watched closely.

"Piercing ward." Arlen lifted a glowing finger and drew the symbol in the air. It hung there in silver light. He used his magic to harden a fingernail until it could carve the symbol into the spear's obsidian tip.

He fed the ward power and held it up for all to see, the symbol reflected in their great wide eyes. "Piercing ward."

Then he turned and launched the spear at one of the small stone demons moving in to investigate the tribe. The weapon blasted through the creature with a flare of magic, sending it tumbling down to land at their feet. Arlen powered the stone ward on his foot, pinning the squirming demon as he pulled the weapon free.

The ward needed no power from him now, sizzling in the demon's ichor. Arlen thrust it back into the chief's hand, then pointed to the demon. "Kill."

The core dweller froze. Arlen could see it understood his meaning if not his words, but even this savage brute knew better than to attack a demon. He looked at the creature, writhing under Arlen's heel.

Bleeding ichor. The dweller touched the wetness on the tip of the spear, bringing a finger to his mouth.

"Kill," Arlen said again, this time in Krasian.

A wild look came into the core dweller's eyes then, and he thrust the spear into the demon. The warded obsidian punched through armor once thought impenetrable, and the dweller let out a wild cry as magic shocked up his arms.

Arlen turned to a female, pointing at the three obsidian-tipped arrows she kept slung over one shoulder. She handed them over, and again Arlen used a nail to ward them in front of her.

"Piercing ward," he said again.

"Peesing wad," she grunted reverently, watching the lines of silver light he drew on her arrowheads.

He handed one back to her, and she took his meaning, searching the stones above and spotting another demon. She drew back carefully and fired. The demon yelped and fell from its perch.

"Peesing wad!" Others stormed forward, holding forth their weapons, chanting the words over and over as Arlen scratched wards into the obsidian, arming them against their gaolers for the first time in millennia.

"What do you think to accomplish?" the mind demon hissed. "Teaching animals to draw crude wards on rocks will not be enough to defeat the guardians of the hive."

Arlen smiled. "Probably not. But it'll sure get their attention."

"Peesing wad!" The crone thrust the spear into the air, and the new tribe roared, raising their own crudely warded weapons into the air.

"Erram!" they chanted. "Peesing wad!"

The elder females of the *alamen fae* spun stories for the tribe like *chin* Jongleurs, communicating with a mix of pantomime, mimicked sounds, and a broken form of ancient Krasian that Jardir could almost follow.

With each tribe they met, the number of women spreading the tale of Erram's coming with the holy wards increased. Already, hundreds of core dwellers had crude wards etched, painted, or carved into their weapons. They were quick to put them to use, growing stronger with every *alagai* they killed.

Alagai Ka had gone quiet, displeased at the turn of events, but Jardir still had doubts.

"They cannot win against the enemy," Jardir said. "Are we saving the *alamen fae,* or dooming them?"

"Core if I know," the Par'chin said. "Never believed in

Heaven, but I always wanted to die with a spear in my hand. Owe them the same. Maybe that's Everam's will, maybe it ent."

"You used to be certain He did not exist," Jardir said.

The Par'chin sighed. "Ent certain of much these days. These folk can help us—keep the hive distracted while we do what we came to. We manage it, and they'll be better off. We fail, and they'll likely get et when the laying's done."

Jardir looked at him, and it seemed the gap that had stood between them all these years closed. "Indeed, what does it matter, if Everam is watching or not?"

"You used to say for certain that He did," Arlen said. "Were willing to kill me over it."

"I am not certain of much, these days," Jardir echoed the Par'chin's words. "But I see I have wronged you, my true friend."

"Ay, maybe." The Par'chin turned his eyes away. "Or maybe it's the other way around. Past is past. Ent worth dwelling on."

CHAPTER 41

LIGHT OF THE MOUNTAINS

334 AR

The fires in the duke's keep were extinguished from within, but the gates did not open with the sun. Mountain Spears manned the flamework weapons atop the walls, firing on any who approached. Warders hung from the wall on slings, altering wards into strange new configurations. Ragen had no doubt that, in the courtyard, a greatward was forming.

The sewers were infested with corelings, with little the Milnese could do save track their movements. The concentration increased the closer the tunnels came to Euchor's fortress.

There were a thousand places Ragen should be, a thousand things he should be doing, but instead he was pacing in a waiting room with a group of men who hated one another.

Derek and Count Brayan glared daggers at each other over the head of ten-year-old Jef. His fate would be decided today, one way or another, but for his own part the boy didn't seem to want to go with either of them.

Brayan waited with his and Euchor's grandson, Princess Hypatia's son Toma. Tender Ronnell watched over young Symon, Princess Aelia's eldest. Barely in their teens, the boys were known troublemakers, but now they sat soberly staring at the carpet.

All around the room, Royals of sufficient blood waited with quiet dread. This was a day they'd all dreamed of, now become nightmare.

"What is taking so corespawned long?" Ragen smacked his open palm with a fist. "I've got more important things to do than stand around while they deliberate."

"Arrogant," Count Brayan's lip curled. "You think you've already won."

"I don't care who wins," Ragen said. "What does a vote of the Mothers' Council matter when there's a gateway to the Core like an open wound at the center of Miln?"

The door to the chamber opened. Keerin kept his gaze on the floor, refusing to meet Ragen's eyes. "They will see you now, my lords."

Inside, Mother Jone held the council floor. She'd never liked Ragen, and the feeling was mutual. Hypatia and Aelia glowered from where they stood with a blank-faced Mother Cera. Elissa rested upon a stool next to her mother's wheeled chair, her face like porcelain.

Half of Tresha's body was lifeless, leaning heavily against the side of her wheeled chair. The other half looked positively smug.

"The council has reached a decision," Jone announced. "Ragen Messenger will be the next Duke of Miln."

"Ragen the First, Duke of Morning, Light of the Mountains, Guardian of Miln."

Thousands had gathered for the ceremony, filling the Cathedral and spilling out down the hill. There were somber faces, many filthy, most fearful, holding their breath as the words were spoken.

Derek was conspicuously absent.

Ragen knelt as Tender Ronnell set the crown on his brow. Ragen's own Warders made the piece, a custom helm of warded glass with two simple points at the temples, symbolizing the twin mountains of Miln.

A second crown was brought forth, this a narrow, warded circlet. Unable to kneel, Elissa kept her seat as the Librarian set it on her brow. "Mother Elissa, Duchess of Morning, Light of the Mountains, Chamberlain of Miln."

"Creator save the Duke and Duchess of Morning!" someone cried, and the somber crowd erupted in thunderous applause. The sound rolled through the pews and out the door, continuing through those gathered in the streets.

Ragen rose to his feet, giving the crowd this moment of hope, but every second worked against them.

"Brothers and sisters of Miln." The Cathedral acoustics took his words and reflected them clearly through the din of the crowd. The folk fell silent again, hanging on his words.

"For over three hundred years, Fort Miln has stood as the greatest of the Free Cities. Our walls were strong and so, too, was our resolve to protect our Library, the greatest collection of human knowledge since the Return. Miln is the light that keeps humanity from slipping back into the Dark Ages.

"But that light is fading. A black heart of evil grows at the center of Miln, pumping demons like infection into the veins of our city. If we are to survive, it must be lanced and purged. We cannot—*must* not—let our light go out."

Elissa raised her voice to join his. "Until the danger is past, no longer will the safe succor of the Guardians and the Library campus be denied to those in need. The young, the old, the infirm, and their caregivers are welcome to shelter in the Cathedral, where the Creator Himself may watch over them behind mighty church wards."

"But those of you who can wield a spear," Ragen said, "or simply hold a crank bow steady, if you can play an instrument, or sing, or draw wards with an even hand, Miln needs you, if we are to see morning."

Ragen saw fear in many eyes, and he raised his hands for silence. "I will not command you to fight from atop a throne. I will not watch from on high as others die in my name." He lifted his spear. "I will fight to keep Miln alive, but I cannot prevail alone."

Ragen set the butt of his spear on the dais and got down on one knee. "And so I beg you to join me, for only together do we have a chance."

There was a pause, every second seeming to stretch into minutes. Ragen realized he was holding his breath.

Then a man cried, "Ay, we're with you!" Others, scattered through the Cathedral, shouted agreement.

Ragen rose to his feet. "Will you stand for Miln?"

The *ay*s came faster this time, along with cheers and a stomping of feet.

Ragen thrust his spear into the air, voice booming. "Will you stand for one another?"

The responses were drowned out as the crowd gave a thunderous roar.

Behind him, Yon gave a snort. "Ent one for speeches, my arse."

Elissa had once loved the great marble steps dominating the main hall of her manse. Any visitors would be forced to pass beneath them, so that she could speak to them from on high, or glide down to embrace them. Only family and select Servants were allowed on the highest level, an escape when the day grew long.

But now, every step was torture. She managed to keep the worst of it from the public, but Ragen and the closest servants knew. She could not even attempt the climb without help.

"Easy now." Margrit supported Elissa with an arm that felt like stone. "Ent in a hurry."

But in Elissa's heart, they were. Already she had put this off too long, and it was nearly too late. At last, they made the top floor, Margrit bearing much of her weight as they went to the visitors' wing.

"But I don't want to live in a warding shop!" Jef cried. "I want to go home!"

"I'm your home," Derek said. "I'm your da."

"I want Mother!" Jef said.

"Ay, you think I don't?" Derek snapped. "But she ent coming back, and we can't join her."

Elissa turned the corner, and the boy looked up, seeing her. He turned to his father. "I hate you!" Then he stormed into his room and slammed the door in Derek's face.

"That will be all, Mother," Elissa said.

"I don't think—"

"That will be all." Elissa deepened her voice, and she did not need to say it a third time. Margrit made sure she was steady on her cane, and took her leave as Derek looked up, noticing her. He looked like he, too, might run to his room and slam the door, but he stood impassively as she slowly limped over to him.

Derek made a leg, eyes down. "Your Grace. I apologize for the shouting."

"You needn't be so formal, Derek. If anyone has the right to call me by name, it is you." She waved a hand at Jef's room. "And you needn't live behind the warding shop. You and Jef are always welcome here."

Still Derek refused to meet her eyes. "You are kind, but Jef and I have spent too many years living as the guests of others. It's time we made our own way."

"Derek . . ." She reached for his shoulder, but he flinched, stepping back. Elissa overbalanced and needed to catch herself on her cane. "I'm so sorry."

Derek put his hands up to keep from looking at her. "I know how this must weigh on you. I know you were doing what you thought best to protect those in your charge." He waved a hand at her legs, her cane. "And I know you paid a heavy price."

At last he looked up, meeting her eyes. "But I also know that every Mother on the council was taught wardcraft in the Mothers' School. Cera had house Warders. Yet it was Stasy you gave that pen to."

"I know." Elissa felt her eyes grow moist. "Every moment since I have asked myself why. Perhaps there were Warders more skilled, but she was the one I knew. The one I trusted. Perhaps it was selfish, but I can't think of another who could have done as well. I would be dead, perhaps everyone in that manse, if not for her."

Derek drew a great shuddering breath. "I understand, and for the love I have always borne you, I forgive. But Jef has a right to grow as more than a guest in the house of the woman who got his mother killed."

"No use." Yon spat on the cobbles. "Weeks o' fightin', and we're still losing ground."

"And Waning tonight," Derek reminded, as if Ragen could possibly have forgotten. The man looked haggard, but they all did, and he fought as hard as any when night came. Too hard, some said—taking foolish risks.

"I mean to break the keep open before the sun sets," Ragen said.

"How?" Yon asked. "Can't get close enough to attack or fortify without them firing on us, and the tunnels are packed with demons, even with the sun up."

"A trick I learned from Briar." Ragen led them down the street to where a Gatherer and a group of apprentices were overseeing large, boiling vats.

"Every child in Miln has been out collecting hogroot," Ragen said. "We're going to dump it into the sewers, and storm the keep from below."

Derek stepped forward, an eager gleam in his eyes. "I'll go."

The demons shrieked as the hogroot tea was poured into ancient runnels that flowed into the sewer tunnels. The mixture burned coreflesh like acid, and Ragen could hear the splashing as the demons fled.

The Mountain Spears didn't give them time to escape, following in with their flamework weapons and warded rounds, devastating in the narrow passages. Keerin's Jongleurs provided support, playing from the rear, their instruments magicked with *hora* to echo through the tunnels.

For a time it seemed to work. The demons thinned as they advanced to the tunnels nearest the keep walls.

But then they turned a corner and found the way barred by Euchor's Mountain Spears, their flamework weapons leveled.

"Fall back!" Ragen cried, but it was too late. The Mountain Spears opened fire, and the narrow tunnels his own flamework forces used to such great effect suddenly proved a liability.

Hundreds were cut down in the chaos of those first moments. Bullets whined off Ragen's warded armor, and one that struck his helmet nearly knocked him senseless.

"Ay, I got you." Yon caught Ragen's arm, pulling him back and shielding Ragen from the press of fleeing soldiers.

They made it back to the streets as night was falling. Ragen's forces, waiting for the sewer teams to open the gates, looked on in horror at the rout.

Then the streets around the keep collapsed, and it seemed all the Core poured forth, scattering into the city streets.

"Headmistress! She's choking!" a triage apprentice at the Gatherers' School shouted.

"What happened?" Anet rushed to a guardswoman who lay thrashing and gasping, face darkening as she struggled for air. Elissa bit her lip to keep from crying out in pain as she struggled with her cane to keep pace.

"We were fighting down on Moon Street," a young guardsman said. He was pale, sweating, and filthy, but seemed uninjured. "Stone demon hit sergeant in the chest, but her armor held. We thought she was all right, but she just started gasping, and coughed blood . . ." He broke off with a sob. "Please, you gotta save her."

Elissa lifted her stylus. "I can . . ."

"No!" Anet snapped. "Heal that woman and you'll only kill her quicker. Get her armor off."

Apprentices cut the straps of the breastplate and lifted it away, then cut away her padded jacket and the blouse beneath. The guard gasped and turned his back.

"Just breasts, boy," Anet said. "You nursed at a pair yourself. Have a look. You need to see what a demon can do, even if your armor holds."

The young guard turned and looked at his sergeant, but then he slapped a hand on his mouth and ran away to retch.

The guardswoman's thrashing was greater now, her face turned purple as she strained to draw air through her blackening chest.

"Hold her still." Mother Anet swabbed alcohol over a spot and took a long, thin blade, driving it down into the woman's chest. There was a geyser of blood, and the woman pulled in a ragged breath.

"Blow broke ribs and drove them into her left lung," Anet said. "If you'd magicked them—"

"Her lung would have closed with bone still inside." Elissa covered her mouth in horror.

"I'll need to cut her open to clear the way before you can begin healing," Anet said. "Can you keep her alive? Give me time to work?"

"I'm not sure," Elissa said, "but I can try."

"I'm not sure I can save her in any event," Anet said. "Trying is all a Gatherer ever has."

Apprentices fed the woman air from a pump while Anet cut and Elissa traced and powered wards to keep the woman's aura strong, to keep her heart beating. The bone was pulled from the lung with forceps and held in place as Elissa healed her way out of the wound, layer by layer.

"Incredible," Anet said. "The power of life and death, all in that little pen."

"Believe me, Gatherer," Elissa put her cane under her, gritting her teeth against the pain as she stood up straight, "even magic has limits."

Anet stiffened. She had examined Elissa's legs personally, and offered no more hope than Cera's Gatherer. "I apologize, Your Grace. I did not mean . . ."

"Let us not dwell on it." Elissa turned to the young guard. "Return to your unit."

"Ay, Your Grace." The man bowed and shouldered his Mountain Spear, heading back to the front.

More bodies, more shouting, coming from all sides. The air was thick with smoke and the scent of blood, making Elissa dizzy. She sipped at magic from her stylus for strength, but while it could ease the constant pain and weakness in her legs, neither retreated entirely.

"Your Grace, are you well?" Anet's tone shifted from supplicant to command. "When was your last meal? Have you had enough to drink?"

"I'm fine," Elissa said. "I just . . . need some air."

"Of course," Anet said. "I'll have one of the girls—"

"That's all right," Elissa cut her off. "I need a moment alone."

"As you command, Your Grace."

Elissa turned away quickly, that the Gatherer might not see her grimace in pain as she put her cane out and shuffled that first, agonizing step. She found a rhythm after that, keeping a slow but steady gait that retained some modicum of dignity.

She exited the halls of the Gatherers' School into the Library campus courtyard. It was summer, but a chill crept in at night as a gust pulled pins from her hair.

Women lingering outside flocked to her immediately. All had been waiting for her to emerge, clamoring for a moment of the duchess' time to approve this list or that, answer messages, settle disputes, solve problems.

"Not now, ladies." Elissa put the tone back in her voice. "Head to the Library and check in with Mother Mery. I will see you all in turn there shortly."

The women glanced at one another for a long moment, but then Mother Jone appeared, cracking her hands together. "You heard Her Grace!"

The women stumbled over themselves to curtsy and hurry toward the Library in hope of getting a good spot in the petition line. Already they were arguing the importance of their business with one another, jockeying for position.

"Thank you," Elissa said.

Jone nodded, offering her arm. "Of course."

Elissa accepted the arm gratefully, leaning on the woman as she moved toward the Guardians. The giant statues surrounding the hilltop campus around the Library and Cathedral formed the most powerful wardnet in the city.

Library guards patrolled the perimeter stiffly, able to hear demon shrieks, the sound of Keerin's players, and fighting echoing through the streets.

The sounds were close. The demons had given the campus a wide berth, fearing the power of the Guardians, but it was new moon, and Elissa knew better than any what that meant.

No sooner had the thought crossed her mind than a flame demon came running up the street, heading for the forbidding. One of the guards shot it down with a warded crank bow. Before it stopped twitching, a stone demon appeared on another street, lumbering toward the wardnet. Guards fired upon it, but its stone armor was thick and the bolts did little more than anger the demon. It bashed against the Guardians' wardnet and was swatted back like a child.

All around, more demons were appearing. They had little more success than the first at breaking through the forbidding, yet suddenly Elissa found herself wondering just how powerful the Guardians were. If there was a vulnerability, the demon princes would find it.

Her hand itched to take up her stylus, blasting corelings away from the forbidding, but it was no longer her place. If the demons breached the wards, she would—with her crippled legs—be more liability than asset to the defenders.

She was duchess, now, and could save more lives in the Library answering those women's questions than she could on the front lines.

"Call for reinforcements," she told Jone. "Have the guards arm everyone strong enough to hold a spear." Jone nodded, moving off, and Elissa slowly made her way back to the Library, taking private halls to Mother Mery's office suite.

There was a shout just before she rounded a corner, and there Elissa found Mery and her husband, Jaik. Elissa had not seen Jaik in years, since the days when he and Mery and Arlen were young and inseparable. Too caught up in their own drama, they did not notice her approach.

"I *am* helping!" Jaik snapped. "I've been carrying water to the injured all night."

"Duke Ragen didn't ask for the able-bodied to carry water," Mery said. "He asked them to pick up a weapon and fight. The Library guards are calling for aid."

"Me, fight a demon?" Jaik was incredulous. "Are you insane? I'd be cored for sure."

"Boys half your age are lining up to volunteer while you hide under my father's robe," Mery said. "You won't even join the Jongleurs."

"My music's no better than my spearwork," Jaik said. "You know how hard it was for me."

Mery crossed her arms. "Ay, because you never bothered to practice."

"Easy for you to say!" Jaik shouted. "We weren't all given organ lessons in the Cathedral from birth."

"You always find something to blame," Mery said. "I'm starting to realize . . ."

"What?" Jaik demanded. "What are you suddenly realizing?"

"That Arlen was right about you," Mery snapped. "That

you've no ambition. You just show up and do the least you can."

Jaik flinched. "Always comes down to that in the end, doesn't it? Measuring me against the perfect Arlen Bales. Night, I'm lucky you were always too holy to open his pants."

Mery sneered. "I rubbed against it enough times to know you don't measure up there, either."

Jaik bared his teeth. "Ay, and he left you, anyway. What's that say about you?"

"That is enough!" Elissa barked, cracking her cane against the floor.

Mery and Jaik whirled at the sound. "Y-your Grace!" Mery spread her skirts and dipped while Jaik bent an awkward knee.

Elissa pointed a finger at Jaik. "If carrying water is what you're good at, Jaik, there are plenty of wounded in the Gatherers' School who need it."

"Ay, Your Grace." Jaik seemed relieved as he scurried off.

"I apologize, Your Grace," Mery said. "That was . . . unseemly."

"It sounds like a conversation long overdue," Elissa said. "But best saved until the moon waxes."

There was a scream from down the hall, and Elissa was forced to grab at Mery, biting the inside of her cheek to keep from crying out in pain as she stumbled as quickly as possible to investigate.

They caught up to Jaik on the wide balcony overlooking the Library stacks. Below, acolytes raced up from the lower levels.

"Demons!" one robed boy called. "Demons in the catacombs!" Acolytes, Mothers, and scholars scrambled, scattering papers and spilling inkwells in a panicked stampede across the floor. Nimble flame demons burst from the lower halls, chasing folk into the stacks.

"Night." Elissa felt the pincer snap shut. The demons massing outside the Guardians did not need to break through— only to prevent escape while the mind demons struck from within.

Flame demons spat fire, but the wards Arlen carved all those years ago flared, turning firespit into a cool breeze. Field demons leapt at fleeing librarygoers, but again Arlen's net flashed, throwing them back from people hiding between the shelves or under the tables. Demons bounced about like balls as Arlen's warding hurled them from one shelf into the next, leaving them battered and dizzy while scholars made their escape.

The danger was greater out in the open, but Elissa had her stylus out, freezing flame demons and knocking field demons into one another with impact wards.

"Quickly!" She sketched a brief forbidding over the nearest access to the catacombs. "To the Cathedral!" The wards of the Holy House were some of the strongest in Miln, but more than warding bound magic to the stones. Faith gave strength to the walls.

Elissa looked at Mery, seeing Stasy all over again, but nevertheless she took a *hora* pen from her pouch and pushed it at Mery. The young mother shrieked and recoiled. "I cannot touch demon bone! The Creator forbids it."

"The Creator forbids you let all these people die because you're too holy to touch a pen!" Elissa shoved the stylus into Mery's hand. "Shut up and ward."

Mery looked at her in fright, but she took the pen. The Librarian's daughter proved a competent Warder as they descended to the main floor, sweeping up the terrified Library staff as Elissa led the way to the Cathedral.

But more demons were coming up from below, finding the gaps in Elissa and Mery's hastily drawn forbiddings. They were not able to start fires, but they circled around the fleeing humans, attempting to cut them off.

A demon leapt down from the balcony, and Mery barely drew a forbidding in time to keep it from landing on Elissa's shoulders. The demon bounced off the magic, landing amid their group. It opened an old Mother like a butchered cow then sprang on Jaik, who fell back, curling into a ball as sharp teeth sank into his shoulder.

Elissa hit the demon with an impact ward, but it took a great chunk of Jaik's shoulder in its jaws as it was knocked away.

"Mistress!" Mery called. "He needs . . . !"

"To keep running!" Elissa barked. "Everyone! If we don't make it to the Cathedral, we're dead!"

Perhaps even if we do. She kept the thought to herself as Mery pulled Jaik to his feet, blood spurting from his wound. The two of them stumbled even more slowly than Elissa as the corelings massed behind them. More than just flame demons now, there were iridescent snow demons, dull gray stone demons, and sleek green-scaled field demons. These last raced ahead, cutting off their escape into the Cathedral.

But then the Cathedral doors opened, Tender Ronnell standing with ranks of faithful in flowing robes. The choir.

"Run!" the Librarian cried, waving an open path into the Cathedral as the choir began to sing. The demons, focused on Elissa and her charges, were caught off guard by the *Song of Waning.* They shrieked and recoiled from the sound, those standing on two legs covering their ears.

"Don't stop!" Elissa shouted as some of the scholars gaped. "Into the nave!"

The choir kept their voices strong, but up close Elissa could see sweat on the brows of the men and women, uncertainty in their voices as they looked upon the approaching horde. For most—if not all—this was the first time they had ever seen corelings up close.

The song held back the tide—barely—but Elissa did not think it would last. A snow demon hawked coldspit down from a balcony, striking one of the singers in the thigh. He stumbled in shock, and there was a crack as his leg struck the marble floor.

The singer screamed, breaking the harmony, and the demons were quick to strike. Cold- and firespit rained into their ranks as field demons leapt in, claws leading.

Some of the choir were protected by the wards on their robes, but others were not. One acolyte caught flame, flailing into his fellows and spreading the fire. Two more were laid open by coreling talons, others slipping on the bloody marble.

"Fall back!" Ronnell cried. Elissa drew sound wards over the singers' heads to amplify their music, and they managed to drag most of the wounded inside and slam the Cathedral doors shut.

Thousands already filled the pews, taking succor after their homes and neighborhoods were evacuated. They looked on in terror, but for the moment the wards held.

Jaik lay on the floor, Mery weeping as she cradled him in a growing pool of blood. Elissa fell to her knees beside them, drawing wards to lend Jaik strength, but he had lost too much blood already, and Elissa could not simply create more, or regrow what the demon had bitten away. She managed to slow the bleeding, but Jaik's breaths grew quicker and more desperate, then went still, his eyes staring at nothing.

Mery wailed, clutching at him. The Cathedral doors boomed and shook as demons hammered the wards. Dust clattered down from above and Ronnell looked up at the massive pipes of the organ.

"Keep singing!" He raced for the stairs to the organist's loft, and seeing his intent, Elissa put her cane under her and stumbled after.

Again the doors rattled with the impact of some unseen force. Magic might hold the corelings back, but they could still hurl great chunks of marble at the heavy doors until they shattered.

Ronnell sat at the organist's console surrounded on three sides by controls. The Cathedral organ had thousands of pipes controlled by five keyboards, each with its own stop pedals.

He wrung his shaking hands, cracking fingers to limber them for the task. Rojer's music sheets were open on the rack in front of him. Elissa tried to read them, but the symbols Jongleurs used to write music were gibberish to her.

Slowly, the Tender began to coax the great organ to life, grinding through a semblance of the *Song of Waning*. But the music was written for singers and string instruments, not the massive pipe organ with its hundreds of keys. The instrument had more power and range, but Ronnell struggled to match the agility of Keerin's lute or the choir's voices. Though the music was recognizable, it seemed to have no effect on the demons crashing against the Cathedral doors.

Elissa looked out a window, seeing demons streaming from the Library to run down civilians around campus and flank the Library guards at the perimeter. There was fighting in the streets and blood on the cobbles.

Ronnell's thinning hair was damp with sweat. His hands shook, but still he played, hoping to find something of Rojer's magic in the unwieldy instrument.

Mery appeared at the top of the steps, her dress soaked with blood, tears running lines through the red smears on her cheeks.

"Are you all right?" Elissa asked, but Mery ignored her, pushing past to lay a gentle hand on her father's shoulder.

Ronnell turned, his eyes wet with tears. "I cannot do it, daughter. I haven't the skill. The Deliverer's gift is beyond me."

Mery looked at him sadly. "What if Arlen isn't the Deliverer, Father?"

"Then the corespawn are going to win," Ronnell said. "So this once, you must have faith that he is. That he could see when our night would be darkest, and send us a light."

"How can he be the Deliverer if he's dead?" Mery asked.

Elissa leaned in, her lips close enough to kiss Mery's ear. "He is alive. Even now he fights for us all. So if you can play this ripping song, now's the time."

Mery looked at her, eyes probing. At last she nodded, handing her father the *hora* pen as Ronnell gratefully yielded the bench. Mery kicked off her shoes and sat at the console, snatching up the sheets of Rojer's music. She left bloody fingerprints as she flipped the pages, head cocked to listen to the choir.

The doors boomed again, and Elissa heard a crack. "They're coming."

"Then hold them back," Mery growled, studying the pages like a Warder's grimoire.

It was no tone for a young mother to take with the Duchess of Miln, but Elissa was comforted by the determination in the words. Ronnell drew wards of protection in the air around the organ console as Elissa stumbled to the edge of the loft, looking out over the nave.

Thousands crowded against the wall across from the Library doors, struggling to get as far as possible from the demons. Those up against the wall groaned and cried, crushed by the pressure of the unthinking mob.

"Back away!" Elissa amplified her voice, and it was doubled by the acoustics in the domed Cathedral. "Crushing your fellows will not save you! Step back and join the choir! Sing as if the world depends on it, for tonight it surely does!"

The remaining members of the choir, battered and bloody, had returned to their own loft, the vaulted ceiling magnifying their ragged song. Tentatively, the crowd began to sing, mumbling unfamiliar words as they tried to match the harmony of the skilled men and women.

A handful of campus guards with warded spears and shields formed a crescent a few paces from the door, waiting for the imminent breach.

Elissa drew pressure wards to shore up the doors just as another projectile struck. The wards flared and caught the impact, but the reinforced wood still splintered and cracked. They would not hold much longer.

But then the organ thrummed back to life. Mery began gently, a sound felt in the air more than heard. She began by following the choir, but as her playing gathered strength, it began to transcend. The pipes rose in power and volume, resonating in everyone present, in the very stones of the walls.

Mery took the lead now, the choir and the faithful becoming harmony for the pipes even as the volume continued to rise. Outside, Elissa could hear corelings shrieking in agony, and then the sounds drew away. The thumping at the doors ceased.

Elissa limped back to the window, watching as corelings poured like rats from a fire into the campus streets. They charged the perimeter guard, whose eyes were focused outward at the demon horde, unaware of the enemy racing toward their backs.

But the Guardians flared, and the corelings were swatted back. The circles worked in both directions, creating a pocket where their defenders were safe.

Only then did the demons turn their heads back to look in terror at the Great Cathedral, the trap slowly dawning on their primitive brains.

The power continued to grow as Mery's confidence built. Jaik's blood left streaks on the keys and pages as she turned to verses that could shatter a rock demon, melt a snow demon's heart. She wove each with separate pipes, playing multiple keyboards simultaneously as her feet held notes with the pedals.

All around, demons collapsed to knees or bellies, writhing

and shrieking. Elissa could see the ichor running from their eyes, ears, and noses. It was a slow death, but no less certain than a spear in the heart.

Still the power rose. Miln was nestled in a valley where the roots of two great mountains met. Like the vaulted ceiling of the Cathedral, the mountains picked up the music and echoed it back, carrying the sound all over the city.

Horns blew in the distance, sounding charges as men and women roared. The shrieks of demons echoed in the streets.

CHAPTER 42

THE HIVE

334 AR

"Ten minutes." Renna stopped at the most defensible spot she could find, but the tunnels all glowed with dim light from some fungus on the walls. It meant she could see with her eyes for the first time since the Spear of Ala, but it also left her feeling exposed, even with her warded cloak and Shanvah's singing.

"Of course." Shanvah reached out to halt her father, and the two of them knelt facing outward, on guard as Renna prepared the couscous.

"Want some?" Renna asked when it was steaming in the bowls.

"Thank you, no." Shanvah spoke the words quickly, never missing a note of her concealing song.

"I require nothing." Shanjat's voice was cold.

The two of them could easily last a day on a single bite of the couscous and a sip of the water, but despite the race to catch up with Arlen and Jardir—if they were even still alive—Renna could not ignore the needs of her rapidly expanding belly.

The deeper they went, the stronger the ambient magic became and the faster her son grew. Renna once wondered how the demon queen could hatch so many, but now she began to understand.

Renna was putting away two full bowls of couscous at a

sitting, stopping to eat thrice as often as Shanvah and Shanjat required. By that rough measure, it had been over a week since Shanjat began silently leading them into the bowels of the world.

When questioned, Shanjat could answer little about the route, as if the mind had simply sketched a map in his brain. He did not know what the glowing moss was, where it might end, or how much farther they had to go before they reached the hive.

If they weren't already in it.

Renna ate in silence, feeling the inside of her belly come alive with the repast. The hard outer muscle she formed to protect the child did nothing to diminish the shock and discomfort of his powerful kicks and punches. He shoved against her bladder, and Renna moved quickly behind a stone for a privy break. He had gotten so big, she feared he might come any day.

Hold on, just a little longer, she begged. What would happen if the child came now? Could she hope to protect him?

They moved on quickly when she was done eating. Up ahead, Renna heard familiar sounds of battle—the shriek of demons, the sizzle of combat wards. Could it be Arlen? She pulled her knife and raced down the tunnel toward the noise.

"Father, keep pace!" Shanvah called as she followed. "If attacked, defend us and yourself!"

It was simple for the *Sharum* to match Renna, whose run had become something of a waddle. She used magic to put on speed, and the three of them were a blur as they rushed into the tunnel junction where the sound originated.

A group of wild-looking humans had surrounded a cave demon, stabbing from all sides with obsidian-tipped spears. Their auras were hot with core magic, and their weapons flared with battle wards.

Renna could tell Arlen's script at a glance, and her heart leapt. "They been this way."

Shanvah nodded. "The Shar'Dama Ka and Par'chin have armed the *alamen fae.*"

Several feet away, the corpse of another cave demon lay with legs hacked off, oozing guts and ichor from its bulbous belly. Two of the core dwellers lay nearby, auras cold save for the venom still in their veins. Another was stuck to the wall with silk, half her head bitten off.

The core dwellers hooted and howled as they brought the second demon down. Magic crackled along the lengths of their weapons, and they shivered, absorbing even more power.

Their eyes were wild when the *alamen fae* caught sight of Renna, Shanvah, and Shanjat. They closed in from all sides, much as they'd surrounded the demon, huffing and beating their chests.

But then they took note of Renna's belly, and their aggression faded. They circled, chattering in a rudimentary language that sounded vaguely like Krasian. The crowd parted, and an elder female crawled forward. Her body remained strong but her hair had gone white, and Renna could taste the weight of years on her aura.

The female reached for her. Renna wanted to flinch back, but she could see the elder meant no harm. Her hands were rough with calluses, but surprisingly gentle as she ran them over Renna's belly. She put her ear to it, and laughed aloud, a cry that made the core dwellers take up a cheer. She pulled some of the glowing fungus from a pouch in her belt, mixing it with water and drawing a heat ward in the thin skin of soil over the stone of the tunnel floor.

"Renna," Shanvah said warily, when the old woman presented her with the steaming cup.

"Stay calm," Renna said. "Don't mean any harm. Near as I can tell, they think I'm good luck." Whatever tea this subterranean Herb Gatherer was serving smelled awful, but she held her breath and quaffed it. The female nodded and gave an approving grunt.

The *alamen fae* next moved their gaze to Shanjat. No doubt the powerful male seemed to present the greatest threat, but when one of their males moved up to him, grunting and thumping his spear, Shanjat gave no reaction. The male went so far as to poke Shanjat in the chest. At a word from Renna or Shanvah, he could have broken the core dweller's arm, but without it he stood impassively, and the core dwellers lost interest in him.

Shanvah, however, drew the attention of several males. They

knuckle-walked around her, sniffing the air and grunting. Renna looked their way, and her eyes bulged.

"Corespawn it!" She averted her gaze. More than one had a visible erection.

One of the core dwellers reached to touch Shanvah, and she had enough. She caught his wrist and twisted into a *sharusahk* throw that sent him tumbling head over heels. She snapped a kick into the erection of a second core dweller who moved too close, and he dropped to the slick tunnel floor, moaning.

The next male backed off when Shanvah hissed. The two she put down collected themselves, and all the males retreated into the forming crowd.

Renna looked at the others—females, children, and less aggressive males, many holding weapons warded by Arlen and Jardir—and wondered what she should say.

Before she could open her mouth, one of the males returned with a haunch of meat from some unknown subterranean beast. He offered it to his Gatherer, gesturing at Shanvah and grunting.

Shanvah gaped. "Is he . . ."

"Marriage tradin'?" Renna asked as the Gatherer turned with the haunch to open negotiations. "Sure as the sun looks like it. Must think I'm your mam."

"I am flattered." Shanvah's voice was flat. "But please refuse."

Renna was about to attempt just that when another came forward, offering the Gatherer some scaly pelt, also pointing at Shanvah.

"Want to wait and see how high they go?" Renna asked Shanvah.

"That is not funny, sister," Shanvah said.

"Ay, guess not." Renna powered the wards on her skin. They flared to life, filling the tunnels with light. She turned her gaze on the males. "She ent for sale, you randy bucks!"

The males cowered at the display and went quickly to their knees, followed by the rest of the core dwellers.

"Erram," they began chanting. "Erram."

The collective aura changed, and Renna pulled at it, absorbing a taste to Read. Images of Arlen and Jardir flashed in her mind, and she knew they were not far behind. She could sense the tunnel they had taken.

But there was something new in the air now. A vibration that was almost like sound, so loud she wondered how she had never sensed it before. Then she thought back to the mind demon's brain she'd consumed and instinctively understood the source.

"Sister, what is it?" Shanvah asked.

"Know where to go," Renna said quietly. "Can hear the queen moanin' in my head as she lays."

Jardir and the Par'chin watched the *alamen fae,* perched high on the stone walls, waiting in silence as the clutter of spider-like cave demons approached.

Cave demons were the most common breed of *alagai* the minds employed as sheepdogs in the larder, herding Jardir's distant cousins like camels. The demons were wary now, the territory of the *alamen fae* suddenly become dangerous. The camels had begun to kick.

Still, the *alagai* were unprepared as the core dwellers dropped on them from above, roaring as their spears struck.

The core dwellers were strong, and their enthusiasm for the fight was impressive once they had weapons that could bite at the *alagai.* For centuries, the demons had herded them, killed them, dragged their fellows off to butcher. No longer.

The cave demons twisted, but their long segmented legs were not designed to strike at creatures on their backs. The *alamen fae* were too quick, hopping back from the demons' swipes, keeping them distracted as their tribe rushed in to attack. Men, women, and children entered the fight, crude wards scrawled on their obsidian weapon tips and the shields Jardir taught them to make from leather and bone.

Sparks of magic flew wildly through the tunnel as spiked clubs rose and fell. They had only a fraction the power of properly warded weapons, but it did not stop the *alamen fae.* Blows from the weakest kept the demons disoriented as the stronger tribe members broke limbs and slowly beat in skulls.

Their glory was boundless.

One demon managed to leap away, clinging to the tunnel

wall and skittering out of easy reach. Obsidian-headed arrows skittered sparks across its armor until one stuck, followed by another.

Knowing it could not escape, the demon turned to fight, tensing to spring back down among the tribe. They would still bring it down, but not without the cost of lives.

Jardir raised his spear to blast the life from the creature.

"Ahmann, no!" the Par'chin cried, grabbing his arm.

Jardir scowled. "Remove your hand, Par'chin. I must help them."

"Can't." The Par'chin withdrew his hand.

"Why not?" Jardir saw the demon drop into the knot of *alamen fae*.

"Because, fool, the queen knows everything her drones do," Alagai Ka sneered. "Unruly livestock will not concern her. The Heir of Kavri will."

"He's right, Ahmann," the Par'chin said. "Right now, the crown and my wards have us hidden. But we start throwin' real power around, ent no missin' that."

Jardir gripped his spear so tightly his hands ached, and the demon gave its hissing laugh. "It pains you to sacrifice drones. Even pathetic savages like these."

"They were my people, once." Jardir saw blood spatter the tunnel wall and knew it was too late to help.

"Queen knows the thoughts of drones this far from the hive?" the Par'chin asked.

The demon turned his head-tilting stare the Par'chin's way. Jardir was coming to recognize the look as more derision than curiosity. As if Alagai Ka was wondering how they could be so utterly stupid.

"We have been inside the hive for days, Explorer," the demon said, and Jardir felt his blood turn to ice. "The queen keeps her larder close. When the laying is done, she will feast on them by the thousand to replenish her strength. The losses in your petty uprising are meaningless."

"Not meaningless," the Par'chin said. "They serve something greater."

"Do they, Par'chin?" Jardir asked.

"You're the one always talking about fate," the Par'chin said. "About Everam's Plan. Well maybe He's got one, after all. Maybe He didn't abandon these folk. Maybe He set 'em here to help us when we needed it most."

"At what cost, Par'chin?" Jardir asked.

"Don't matter the cost," the Par'chin said. "Victory is worth any price. Ent that what you always said? Ent that your excuse for killing your way across Thesa? But now, when victory is so close you could touch it, you suddenly grow a conscience?"

The greenlander's words gave Jardir pause. He looked at his old friend, trying to peel away the years to see the innocent young greenlander beneath the hard, painted man.

"Do you remember the first time we argued, Par'chin?" Jardir asked.

The son of Jeph nodded. "In the Maze."

Jardir nodded. "When the Pit Warder was ravaged by *alagai* talons and readied himself for the lonely path."

The Par'chin's eyes flashed. "He had a name, Ahmann. Zaji asu Fandra am'Hessath am'Kaji. He was my friend. The man who taught me one-way wardings and pit magic. The man I could have saved, had you not murdered him."

"Do not condescend to me, Par'chin," Jardir said. "I knew Zaji far better than you. He had in his grasp what every warrior dreams of—a glorious death. But you would have snatched it away, forced him to live for decades as a crippled shell of the man he had been, heedless of his wishes, all because Arlen asu Jeph would give the demons nothing."

The Par'chin's aura spiked, and Jardir knew his words hit home.

Arlen felt like he'd been slapped.

Give the demons nothing. A childhood oath that had become the defining lens of his life.

He'd broken it before.

Arlen looked at the core dwellers, bringing down the last cave demon. Some clutched wounds already beginning to heal, but two lay cooling on the tunnel floor, auras snuffed.

Jardir was right. The man he had once been would never have stood by and left anyone to the demons—corespawn the greater good. Leaving folk to the demons wasn't the man his mother taught him to be.

"You told me on that day that Heaven was not true," Jardir said.

"It ent." Arlen's answer was a reflex, but his thoughts did not match the conviction in his voice. Who was he to say? "And if this world's all we got, I'm going to do whatever's needed to save it."

"Including spending the lives of the *alamen fae* in a feint," Jardir said.

"Ent forcin' 'em to fight, Ahmann," Arlen said. "Doin' it of their own free will."

"Because they think us gods," Jardir said.

Arlen laughed. "You been calling yourself the Deliverer without irony for years now, Ahmann! These folk ent fighting demons for us. They're fighting because they're sick of being slaves."

"They are savages," Jardir said. "Are we empowering their will, or manipulating it to our ends?"

The mind demon made his hissing laugh—a dark, eerie sound. "You are barely less savage than they. Both clinging to fictions you do not understand."

"Used to feel that way," Arlen said, "but the deeper we go, the more I see things I thought fiction are real enough to touch." He met Jardir's eyes. "Demon said it himself. We ent successful, most of these folk are gettin' et anyway. Better they go down with spears in hand."

"They might not have gone down at all, had we pointed them toward the surface and not the center of the hive," Jardir said. "If you have the heart to sacrifice their lives, give them the honor of admitting it."

It was an unexpected lash from his old friend. Indeed, their roles had reversed, for his friend had always been able to see the Creator's Plan in everything, while Arlen was plagued by doubt every day.

But now . . . Now his whole body was thrumming with the call of the Core, a song that roared through him like a hurricane. It was power incarnate, the source of all life in the world, and it spoke to him, whispering of greater truths. The world was out of balance, and there was only one way to set things right.

"Ay," Arlen spat. "That what you want to hear? Know they

can't win against the hive, but they can hold its attention while we do what we came to. This ent stealing wells, Ahmann. It's Sharak rippin' Ka. Either we win, or everyone loses."

Jardir looked at the fallen sadly, but he nodded. "Of course, you are correct, Par'chin." Doubt clouded his aura.

Arlen looked at him, confused. "Can't you hear it?"

Jardir cocked his head. "Hear what?"

"The Core," Arlen said.

Jardir closed his eyes a moment. "I hear nothing."

Again, the mind demon gave his hissing laugh.

"Don't listen with your ears," Arlen said. "Not really hearing anything. More than that. Sense we ent got a word for. Shifts in the way the magic feels when it flows through you, telling more than words ever could."

Jardir fell into his breath, aura going calm as he reached out with his crown. "I can sense the abyss—feel its power. I can Draw its magic, shape it to my will, but it does not . . . speak to me."

"Maybe you just ent listening," Arlen said, "because it's got a lot to say."

Jardir crossed his arms. "And what is the abyss telling you, Par'chin?"

"That it ent the abyss," Arlen said. "Life flows from there, Ahmann, not the other way around. Every livin' thing's got a touch of magic in it, and the sun burns magic away."

"What are you saying, Par'chin?" Jardir asked.

"Maybe there's a Creator, after all," Arlen said. "Just been looking for Him in the wrong place."

They followed silently in the wake of the *alamen fae,* hidden by wards of unsight and silence that even the core dwellers could not penetrate.

Jardir welcomed the quiet, still reeling from the Par'chin's words.

Could it be true? Everam and Nie, Heaven and the abyss, all lies? It was blasphemy. It was madness. And yet, when he searched the Heavens, they were empty, and the demons knew nothing of Nie.

More and more tribes joined them as they approached the tunnels that led to the center of the hive. The core dwellers adapted quickly, and the crude but effective wards Jardir and the Par'chin taught them spread like stones in an avalanche to every bit of sharpened obsidian in the larder.

Jardir could not deny the glory of the sight. These tortured souls, hundreds of generations born into a captivity they could not possibly understand, finally rising up against their gaolers.

They did well, at first. The drones were unprepared for their sheer ferocity, or the speed with which the masses armed themselves. They came with insufficient numbers, and were slaughtered.

They entered a great cavern, dotted with stalagmites. Some were just a few feet high, others larger than the minarets of Sharik Hora. All were hot with magic. Were they vents from the abyss?

The *alamen fae* did not seem to notice, advancing into the cavern as if they had been here many times before.

"Par'chin," he said.

"Ay," the son of Jeph agreed. "Place ent right."

Suddenly demons clinging to the stone on the far side of the stalagmites sprang from hiding, striking at the core dwellers. Rock demons appeared behind them, moving to cut off any retreat.

"Alagai'ting Ka has taken notice," Jardir said.

"There." Alagai Ka pointed upward to a small cave high on the far cavern wall. "My brethren use that vantage to overlook the larder and choose savages for culling."

"For eating, you mean," the Par'chin said.

The demon hissed. "Do not feign superiority, Explorer. You are hardly above eating my kind."

"Ay, and don't you forget it." The Par'chin looked to Jardir. "Wait here. Follow me up when the mind is dead."

Jardir nodded, watching the Par'chin's essence drift apart just enough to lighten his body. His wards of unsight throbbed as he went aloft, flying like an arrow for the cave mouth.

The cave was too far for the demon's psychic death to kill the drones fighting the *alamen,* but it was immediately apparent when the demons lost the mind's guidance and became animals once more. The rock demons left their positions guarding the exit and charged, eager to join in the killing, even as the core dwellers regained footing against the enemy. There were shouts and flares of magic, human screams and piercing demon shrieks.

Jardir could not guess how the battle would end now, but there was no time to ponder. He gripped his spear and took to the air, the crown's bubble carrying Alagai Ka along behind.

They landed at the lip of the cave to find the Par'chin holding the head of a juvenile mind demon. It looked as if he had twisted it off with his bare hands.

"This way." Alagai Ka affected not to notice the body of one of his brethren. He pointed into the darkness of the cave, out of reach of the luminescent moss and lichen that grew on the larder walls. "We will progress quickly now."

Jardir tensed as they entered the narrow tunnel. He could still could hear the battle as the *alamen fae* fought—died—to draw attention away from them.

He felt a crushing pain at their sacrifice, wondering again how Everam could have left them here to suffer in the abyss for thousands of years.

If there was an Everam. If the abyss was not just molten rock below the surface, hot with magic, as the Par'chin and the demon both believed.

The tunnels were smooth-walled with sharp turns, sometimes narrowing or widening abruptly. Jardir could sense the magic flowing through them, linking with countless other tunnels to form a three-dimensional greatward.

The ward was not one of forbiddance—as Jardir encountered from the mind demons that attacked Everam's Bounty—preventing humans from approach. The demons would not forbid entry to their livestock. This ward simply focused power, Drawing it like a whirlpool down to the center of the hive where the queen lay.

As the Father of Lies promised, they moved at speed for a time, but Jardir began to notice something amiss. Mimic demons patrolling the tunnels were pausing, sniffing the air. Searching for something they could not fully perceive.

"Sensing us," the Par'chin said.

"How is that possible?" Jardir asked. The crown and Leesha's cloak protected him, and the Par'chin's wards of unsight glowed bright with power. Alagai Ka was trapped in the crown's bubble, unable to reach beyond the forbidding.

"Your wards are keyed to lesser breeds," Alagai Ka said. "Even my brethren and I are only a flickering reflection of the queen's power."

"Ent got queen wards on the crown?" the Par'chin asked.

"Not even Kaji faced one and lived to tell," Jardir said.

"So she senses something, but doesn't know what it is," the Par'chin said. "And the mimics only know what she does. Maybe we can still tiptoe by."

"With every step you take, her power grows," Alagai Ka said. "Soon there will be no hiding from her."

Indeed, not long after, a seemingly empty tunnel came alive with tentacles tipped with magic-dead spikes. The tentacles slapped against the crown's bubble, but the spikes penetrated and fired like arrows. Jardir spun his spear, scattering them, but one thudded into his thigh.

Unarmed, Par'chin moved with incredible speed, plucking two of the spikes out of the air even as he twisted and wove around the others. These he threw back at the tunnel wall near the base of the tentacles. The spikes sent up spurts of ichor as they struck. Mimic demons sloughed off the wall to loom before them.

Jardir embraced the pain as he tore the spike from his thigh, focusing his magic to heal the wound. He tried to push the attackers from their path using the crown's forbidding, but too much of the power was focused on holding Alagai Ka in for him to project it outward with any force. The demons clustered at the end of the tunnel, and the bubble prevented him from approaching.

"I can clear them," the Par'chin said.

"No," Jardir said. "We must do it together."

"You lose focus and drop that field, Alagai Ka escapes," the Par'chin said.

"Then perhaps the Father of Lies has led us far enough," Jardir said, pointing his spear at the demon.

"You cannot hope to find—" Alagai Ka began.

"Think you're right." The Par'chin turned a cold eye toward the demon. "Reckon we can find our own way from here."

The Consort read their auras and knew the game could go no further. Steeling himself, he summoned his last reserves of power, burning his own flesh from the inside out to sear away the killing wards tattooed on his skin.

A flash of agony, hot and raw, and he was able to molt off the ruined dermis, free at long last.

Free, but crippled. The act nearly killed him. His body was in desperate need of repair, his aura dimmer than the lichen on the larder walls. He was too weak to fight.

Immediately the Consort took to the between-state, becoming too diffuse for physical attack. He remained trapped in the Heir's bubble, but they could no longer touch him.

It was a risky ploy. With so little magic left, the Consort did not have the strength to rebuild his body. But only the Explorer could dissipate after him, at the cost of the wards protecting his will. The Consort hoped the Explorer was so foolish, but even human stupidity had its limits.

The Consort spread himself thin across the field, casting shadows that made him appear to be gathering in one place. His captors took the bait, sending great blasts of energy at the spot. Most of it ran along the edge of the forbidding, though some of the current jolted painfully through the Consort.

His captors paid a heavy price for the assault, revealing themselves fully to the mimics at last. With visible targets, the demons renewed their attacks, hurling stones and sending magic-dead spikes in a killing spray.

Again the Explorer and the Heir were too quick to take serious harm, but they were distracted, fearing what the Consort could do if they lost track of him for even an instant.

But the Consort was not where their attention should have been. This close to the queen, she had direct control of her guardians. The mimics drew impact wards in the air, knocking his captors from their feet. They kept the press, adding heat and pressure wards, buffeting the humans about the tunnel until at last the Heir's crown was knocked askew, and the bubble flickered for an instant.

The Consort's first instinct was to go to the drones, but touching any of their minds would be the same as contacting the queen. She would see the failure in his memories, the treachery and betrayal of the hive. Most of all, she would sense his weakness. It would be the end of him.

He could not return to the hive until his power was restored. Instead he reached for the nearest path to the surface he could find and took it without considering where it went. Thousands of miles passed in an instant. He found another path down, and another up, swimming along through the planet's crust until he himself did not know where he was, and the Explorer could never follow.

"Corespawn it, he's gone!" Arlen cried.

"So are we, if we do not focus," Jardir snapped.

He was right. There was no way to tell where the demon had gone, but the mimics pressing in were powerful and could not be ignored. Individually, none was as powerful as Arlen or Jardir, but collectively they had the advantage.

The mimics surged forward while the forbidding was down, closing to just a few feet before Jardir managed to right the crown. The field he raised now was smaller, barely more than the reach of his spear.

Arlen tasted the magic on the air, Reading the current the way he might translate a scroll. The queen was nearby. He could sense her power, hear her lowing in his mind. She was clawing at their mind wards, attempting to break through, but the protections held. These demons were her last line of defense.

"Almost there, Ahmann," Arlen said. "We can still win this if we press."

Jardir raised his spear. "Then let us hold nothing back, my true friend." He slammed a mimic up against his warding field, then dropped the forbidding to rush forward and impale the creature, sending waves of killing magic through the Spear of Kaji. The demon burst into flames, shrieking as it burned to ash.

A mimic reared up before him, and Arlen drew a cutting ward, cleaving it in two. Mimics could heal most any injury, growing back even severed limbs, but there was no regrowing half its body. For a moment the split halves tried to reconnect, but Arlen kicked one away, drawing a mimic ward at the other to knock it in the opposite direction. The distance too great, the halves lost cohesion and melted away.

A heavy stone struck him in the chest, but Arlen wrapped his arms around it and planted his feet, skidding back. He hurled the stone back the way it had come, clearing a path through the demons. He ran into the gap, Jardir at his back, gaining several yards before the demons managed to block the way once more.

Magic-dead spikes thrust at him. Arlen dodged and parried what he could, but one dug into his side, another his shoulder. The mimic came in close, wrapping itself around him, suffocating.

Arlen powered the mimic wards on his skin, tearing the demon to pieces that showered its fellows in ichor and gore.

Jardir dropped the crown's forbidding as a mimic charged, then raised it right between the demon's legs, trapping one half on either side of the bubble. He sent a blast of magic from his spear, incinerating the half on the inside.

Arlen Drew more and more power, but the magic seemed without limit here. He felt like Jardir in the Spear of Ala, sweeping powerful demons out of his path like unruly vines before the machete.

Unburdened by Alagai Ka, Jardir began experimenting with the crown's warding field, using it to trap mimics in with him where he could destroy them in the enclosed space without fear of others coming to their aid.

Slowly at first, they made gains to the deeper tunnels. Arlen could hear the queen with his own two ears now—partly the lowing of an animal birthing, and partly a moan of panic and fear at their approach.

Realizing they could no longer hold them back, two of the mimics turned and drew heat and impact wards, trying to collapse the tunnel. Arlen countered with wards to turn the falling stone to mud as he and Jardir gave a final push. They smashed through the last of the guards and sprinted down the tunnel as it opened into a vast chamber.

There lay the demon queen, bloated and pulsing.

She had a conical cranium not dissimilar in shape to her princes', but huge, with a mouth like a barn door, big enough to swallow Twilight Dancer whole. Her body filled the room, little more than a massive and distended abdomen, scaled and slimy, expelling what seemed an endless stream of eggs. Her legs were short, vestigial things that had obviously not been used in many years, unable to support such bulk.

At the end was a long reticulated tail tipped with a two-pronged stinger dripping venom that glowed hot with magic. Unlike the limbs, the stinger looked limber and strong. The queen would use it to kill her female offspring before they could usurp her.

Arlen did not want to know what a strike would do to a human.

Small worker demons collected the eggs, carrying them away for hatching. The workers were not combat drones, lacking armor and talons, but they froze as Arlen and Jardir entered, then turned and attacked.

The demons smashed against the crown's warding field, but in that moment Arlen felt the queen's psychic scream vibrate through him, piercing out into the world.

The response was immediate. All around, mists flowed into the room, forming into mind demons and their mimic body-guards, almost a dozen in all, the last princes of the hive.

Mind demons were cowards by nature. Not given to acts of bravery or altruism, it seemed even they could not deny the demands of the queen and the survival of the hive.

They were weakest in the shift from the between-state to solid, and Arlen and Jardir both struck in that moment. Arlen fed power into the impact wards on his knuckles, punching through a mind demon's chest, even as Jardir parted another's head from its shoulders with a slash of his spear.

Before, the death of a mind demon had always sent out psychic waves of agony that killed other demons in the vicinity, but here in the presence of the queen's overwhelming dominance, that effect was nullified. The mimic forming beside the mind Arlen killed struck back hard, magic-dead ridges on its tentacle tearing deep grooves in his chest as it knocked him back.

Arlen rolled with the blow, already healing the wound as he powered the mind and mimic wards tattooed all over his body, and drew others in the air, scattering his enemies.

Jardir's warding field was expanding and contracting like a beating heart, finding harmony with the pumping of his spear. He pushed demons back to create striking space, then pulled it in close to stab the point of his weapon out of the field while keeping his hands and body protected.

And all the while, the queen lowed and flailed her stubby legs, distended body quivering as it continued to expel eggs.

A mimic pitched a heavy rock at him, but Arlen caught it, meaning to hurl it right back. Instead, one of the minds drew an impact ward and it exploded in his hand, smashing him onto his back.

A mimic pounced on him, growing plates of thick, magic-dead armor his mimic wards could not repel. Arlen curled back, rolling up his feet and powering the impact wards on his heels to kick out and knock the creature back. But the demon's horned tentacles dug into the stone floor, body stretching like a bowstring.

When Arlen's kick reached full extension and retracted, the demon snapped back at him, growing spikes that punched through toughened layers of muscle to ricochet off hardened bones.

He was aware that he was screaming, but barely heard it as he poured power into his mimic wards, finding the demon beneath the magic-dead armor and throwing it back. Again it stretched, but this time Arlen drew quick cutting wards and the tentacles that anchored it were severed. The demon flew back into its master.

There was no respite, Arlen already rolling and leaping away as the ground where he lay exploded with fire and concussion. The floor he landed on was suddenly slick with ice, and he lost his footing and had to roll again as a stream of acid glanced off his back, burning.

Jardir was faring little better. The demons could not pass through his warding field, but it was scant protection against their magic and projectiles. Small stones flew from all sides of the room, drawn unerringly to the crown.

Jardir threw up an arm to protect his face, jamming the crown down tight as he weathered the barrage. He dropped the field and re-energized it to trap a mind and its mimic within. He let out a huge blast of power from the spear, incinerating them before they could escape, but the attention cost him as a heavy stone hit him hard in the back.

As he hit the ground, a mimic put a spike through his right forearm, and his grip on the Spear of Kaji was broken. He smashed the spike before the demon could yank back and sever his hand, but before he could free his arm, an impact ward kicked the spear out of reach. Jardir leapt for it, but other minds took up the game, bouncing the weapon across the chamber as their mimics blocked his path. He attemped to trace wards to summon it back to his hand, but the demons countered the magic, and the spear resisted his call.

It was hand-to-hand with the mimics then, Arlen and Jardir focusing power through the wards on their fists and feet, knees and elbows, as they dodged, absorbed, and weathered blasts of magic from the minds. All along there was a tickling in Arlen's brain, the demons trying to claw past his defenses and attack his will.

Slowly, the tide began to tell. Arlen was breathing hard, his blows slowing, defenses sluggish. He began taking more hits than he blocked, and they were increasingly difficult to heal. Even this close to the Core, in the center of the hive's great-ward where the current was so strong, he felt his magic waning. The demons were Drawing on the power from all sides even as the queen continued to feed, and his internal reserves were dwindling.

He could see Jardir's aura dimming as well, his scarred flesh bleeding freely from a dozen wounds, chest heaving as he drew great gulps of air.

They were losing, and the world would lose with them.

A mimic spread out like a blanket to envelop him, and Arlen let it, snuffing his mimic wards to embrace the creature, touching his tattoos directly to its amorphous flesh. Before it could grow layers of magic-dead protection to trap him, he Drew hard against his wards, sucking magic from the demon like juice from an orange. His strength restored, he tore through its lifeless husk.

Before the minds could react, Arlen turned to the growing pile of slime-covered eggs. Demon larvae pulsed and writhed within their translucent shells. Arlen had to swallow his nausea as he drew a line of impact wards and imparted much of his remaining strength into them.

Eggs shattered, scattering in every direction with a spray of hot sticky fluid and squirming larvae. Before gravity could pull it back to the floor, Arlen added a line of powerful heat wards. The symbols flared hotter than firespit, setting fire to fluid and flesh. Larvae squealed and writhed, kicking and thrashing as they burned. Greasy smoke billowed up to the high ceiling of the chamber.

The minds shrieked at the sight, but it was nothing compared with the demon queen. Her lowing became a roar and she found new strength, rolling onto her stub legs and scrabbling until she was close enough to lash out with her stinger.

Arlen tried to dodge, but the queen's strike was faster than he believed possible. He powered the wards of forbidding on his skin, but the wards were no protection against a queen and the two prongs of the stinger caught him in the side, pumping hot venom into his body.

It was like swallowing boiling acid. His insides screamed and melted as the poison worked its way into him. His legs went limp, and he collapsed.

"Par'chin!" Jardir was by his side in an instant, chopping his hand like a hatchet into the reticulation beneath the stinger. Cutting wards scarred alongside his little finger and palm blazed with magic, severing the demon queen's tail. He pulled the stinger free of Arlen's body, the organ still spurting venom that smoked and hissed as it struck the stone floor.

Arlen summoned the last of his magic to neutralize the poison, but the venom fought him, bringing its own dark magic to bear.

He could see in Jardir's aura the desperate need to help him, but his friend's attention was split, working to defend them against the tightening ring of enemies.

"Fight, son of Jeph!" Jardir shouted. "All Ala hangs in the balance!"

But Arlen felt his fight draining away. He forced venom from the wound, but the dark liquid ran down his body like firespit, melting flesh into a putrid ooze. Still more coursed through his veins, using his own heart against him as it spread through his body.

Arlen propped himself on one arm, and Jardir let him go to focus on driving back the surrounding demons alone. Arlen tried to rise, but the chamber was spinning. He could barely tell up from down, and knew even getting to his feet was beyond him.

"Quiet, now." Renna pulled her Cloak of Unsight tight around her as she, Shanvah, and Shanjat crept into the birthing chamber.

Shanvah had been singing for hours, but still her voice continued, pure and unbroken, making them a part of the tunnels, part of the darkness, part of the stone. The demons, focused on the melee with Arlen and Jardir, took no notice of them as they hugged the wall, circling the mammoth chamber.

Every fiber of her being screamed at her to go to their aid, but Renna knew it would be a losing battle against so many. She and the two *Sharum* were powerful—they might hold back the minds a bit longer at Arlen and Jardir's side—but it would only delay the inevitable.

She shuddered as the queen's stinger struck Arlen, but she bit her tongue and kept moving, eyes on the only prize that mattered.

The Spear of Kaji lay forgotten on the floor, far from the fighting. Jardir could not get to it, and the demons could not touch it, so it had fallen from attention as the battle raged on.

Renna swallowed, forcing herself not to run. The queen and minds were focused on Arlen and Jardir, but the cloak and Shanvah's song were scant protection here in the center of the hive. Their magic worked best when standing still, or moving at a slow, deliberate pace.

The baby writhed in her belly, and she wondered if she was about to doom the child, herself, her husband and friends, all for a fool's chance.

The spear was a dozen yards away. Then ten. Five. One.

Renna scooped it up, feeling power surge into her from the mighty artifact. She broke from her slow stride, putting magical speed into her run and leap.

At the last moment the demon queen's eyes flicked to her. She lashed out with her tail—so fast. It struck Renna a glancing blow and would have been the end of her, but the stinger was severed. The stump gave her a painful smack, spraying her with ichor. She twisted in midair, never losing sight of her target.

The queen's cry echoed through the chamber as Renna buried the Spear of Kaji deep into her eye.

The orb burst, spraying Renna with fluid. The demon queen's head swung wildly, gigantic maw snapping at her. Renna caught hold of one of the many spiked horns and held fast, kicking against the giant teeth in a desperate scramble as she tried with one hand to force the spear in deeper.

The Spear of Kaji seemed to come to life. Its wards glowed brighter and brighter as it Drew the queen's power and turned it into killing waves of magic. The shaft grew hot, and Renna was forced to let go, the imprint of the spear seared into her flesh.

"Inevera!" Jardir shouted, but whether he was calling out to his wife or to his deity, Renna could not say. He lashed out with his crown, scattering demons with the forbidding as he took three great running strides and leapt. He struck a mighty blow against the butt of his spear, driving it like a nail all the way into the demon queen's skull.

The queen's entire body thrashed in response, and Renna could feel her psychic scream, echoed by the shrieks of the minds and mimics in the chamber. They attempted to retreat, but Shanvah and her father were waiting, spears thrusting into dark, cold hearts. Renna leapt clear of the queen's convulsions, landing in a crouch and drawing heat and impact wards to scatter the remaining corelings.

Jardir began warding as well. He shattered the entrance to the main tunnel to bar escape as the terrified and disoriented demons were cut down by Renna and his *Sharum*. Arlen still propped himself on one arm, but Renna could see him Drawing power, working to burn away the queen's poison.

For a moment, she thought they had won.

But then the queen gave a last moan and collapsed. Her cervix opened wide, expelling eggs in a great, shuddering flood. They ran over the floor with slime and fluid, reeking and steaming in the open air. It seemed no threat, until the last.

Six eggs the size of nightwolves burst from the womb, shattering the moment they hit air. Renna knew immediately these were the hatchling queens Alagai Ka spoke of. Unlike the mature, bloated creature Renna killed, these were sleek and battle-ready, crouching on powerful limbs, reticulated tails moving as if with minds of their own, prongs dripping venom.

The remaining minds hissed in delight. One, bolder than his brethren, rushed forward, talons clutching, as if hoping to snatch one of the demon queens and abscond.

She stung him instead. The mind threw his head back, mouth foaming, and fell to the cavern floor, twitching and convulsing.

The juvenile queens were still small, barely larger than Renna herself. They were disoriented by their sudden hatching— vulnerable. Renna pulled her knife, stalking forward to finish things once and for all.

But then the queens began to glow.

Auras already bright with power, the hatchling queens sucked at their mother's magic like babes at the teat. As they did, they started to grow. In seconds, they were the size of horses. Then rock demons. Still the power flowed into them.

They turned as one to face her and Renna backpedaled in sudden fear. There was intelligence in their eyes to match the power in their auras. Alagai Ka had said the first thing juvenile queens would do was fight and kill one another until only one remained, but it seemed that came second when there was a threat to the hive.

One of the queens leapt at her, slimy wings unfurling on her back, beating furiously as she cleared the distance. Renna Drew magic to fight back, but the baby began kicking wildly, and she stumbled, the power slipping away.

"Kill!" Shanvah pointed with her spear, and Shanjat launched himself forward, meeting the queen in midair before she could reach Renna.

Shanjat's spear punched a hole in the juvenile queen's side, but she seemed to take no notice of it. His shield was made of thick, powerfully warded steel, but the queen clawed through it like paper, tearing his arm away with the blow. Her maw darted forward, snatching the warrior up and swallowing him in three, quick bites.

Shanvah shrieked, not the sound of a daughter in mourning, but the full force of her magically enhanced voice, attempting to drive the queen back as she herself charged in.

But the sound did even less to deter the hatchling queens than Shanjat's shield. If anything, it angered them. One flew at her, and Renna could only watch as Shanvah was torn in two.

CHAPTER 43

THE CORE

334 AR

Arlen felt another wave of nausea and hawked, trying to clear his breath. Something gathered in his throat, burning and choking. He coughed violently, expelling thick black fluid that hissed and smoked on the stone. Everything began to spin. Renna, Jardir, the remaining demons.

"To me!" Jardir shouted, raising the crown's warding field. Renna stumbled back into its protection, but Arlen knew the crown's magic would do no more good than Shanjat's shield, Shanvah's song.

There are no queen wards. If just one of the minds escaped with a queen, or they established a new order here, all Thesa would suffer. If more than one managed it, everyone he knew and loved was doomed.

Alagai Ka was still missing. Had the demon planned this? Known what would happen when they killed the queen? Was it his intention all along to end the last queen's reign and begin a new dynasty? Arlen looked around as if expecting the demon king to appear, but there was no sign of him amid the maelstrom.

Time seemed to stretch. The world floated around him, a Jongleur's show he had ceased to pay attention to. Was this the end?

He shook his head violently, trying to return to the present, but instead his thoughts drifted to the past.

I don't pretend to see the path, Tender Jona told him before the Battle of Cutter's Hollow, *but I know it's there all the same. One day, we'll look back and wonder how we ever missed it.*

Arlen had thought them the words of a fool, but now, looking back, everything in his life led inexorably to this moment as if cast by fate. The death of his mother, finding the Spear of Kaji, Jardir's betrayal, the fluxing of Cutter's Hollow. Each moment, a stepping-stone leading him here, now.

And all of it was meaningless, if they did not win.

One of the queens nosed experimentally at Jardir's warding field. It glittered like sunlight on water, sending forth rings of concentric light as she pushed her snout through. She drew back, still competing with her sisters to Draw power from the old queen's bloated body, but soon the ancient queen would be drained entirely, and there would be no stopping them.

"Ren."

Renna fell to one knee, putting an arm around Arlen to ease him up to a sitting position. "Hold on. Gonna be all right."

"Ent." He clutched at her arm, hand shaking and weak. "Venom's got me."

Renna put her other arm around him. "Find a way to stop it. To stop 'em all. Always do."

Arlen coughed again. His body began to shake, muscles seizing, but he grit his teeth, forcing out the words. "Got a way. I can still hear it."

Renna paused. "The Core?"

"Ay," Arlen gasped. "Think it's time I touched it."

Jardir turned to him. "Par'chin . . ."

"Don't be crazy," Renna said. "Ent no comin' back from that."

"Know it," Arlen said.

Renna squeezed him, but he was already growing numb and barely felt it. "You're goin', I'm coming with you."

"No," he begged.

"Swore I would," Renna growled. "Ent gonna let you leave me behind, Arlen Bales."

"Ent just you." Arlen slapped clumsily at her belly, his limbs no longer obeying. He saw his hand make contact but could not feel the touch. "Ent right to make that choice for our son." His eyes blurred, tears sizzling as they ran down into the venom on his lips.

"Can't lose you," Renna said. "Won't."

"Ent losin' anything," Arlen said. "Core'll draw you back down when it's your time, and I'll be waitin'. Till then, need you to love our son for two."

It was a lie. Arlen knew no better than Renna or Jardir about what lay on the other side. But perhaps it was true, and in that moment they all chose to believe.

Renna sobbed, taking his face in her hands. "Love him enough for everyone in the world his daddy saved."

"If you are right, Par'chin," Jardir said, "and Heaven is below rather than above, you will soon be with Everam, and sup at His great table."

"Set things right." Arlen heaved a breath. "Promise."

"I swear it, Par'chin. Sharak Sun is ended."

Arlen felt himself slipping away. His senses faded, leaving him blind. Numb. Deaf.

But still he could feel the Core roaring through his body, resonating with the magic at his center.

The true Arlen Bales, not the flesh he inhabited.

The Core pulled at him, offering him everything and nothing, just a feeling of warmth, safety, and infinite possibility.

For years, the Core had called to him every night, and each time, it grew harder to resist.

Now, at long last, he gave in and answered, dissipating and letting it take him down.

Down, down, he went. The queen's nesting chamber had taken weeks of travel underground to reach. Now it rose above him like the sky as he fell into the Core, Drawing its power in even as it threatened to pull him apart.

There was no pain, only an urge to relax, to let the current sweep him away to become part of the whole.

And in that moment, Arlen wanted nothing more than to be part of that beautiful harmony of power. It was the essence of life itself, raw and omnipotent, radiating out into the world above.

He reached out, Reading the magic flowing on those countless paths to and from the surface—the lifeblood of Ala.

The world was bigger than he ever dreamed. The lands he

traveled his entire life were but a minuscule fraction of its wide grandeur. Oceans and islands and far wide continents. For a moment, his mind was everywhere at once.

He felt the Core pulling at him, drawing his consciousness still further apart, attempting to dissolve it into the single, omniscient whole.

It all became clear in that instant. He understood what life was, the simple beauty of its creation, the fragility of its existence. Magic was raw power, but it did not have consciousness, a will to bind it. It flowed out from the Core seeking those things, and when they were not to be found, it created them.

First simple creatures too small to see, then more complex life-forms, and finally true consciousness that could imprint itself on the world in lasting ways.

The Creator did not give humans wards. Humans created them out of unified need. Alone, the symbols had no power. It was the resolve of their makers, the hope and prayers of the masses huddling behind them.

That collective will Drew the magic and gave it structure, and in turn that imprinted magic fed back into the Core, becoming part of the whole. Could any will shape such vastness? Easier to take a rake to shape the Krasian desert. A bucket to empty the ocean.

The queen's venom vanished when he dissipated, but Arlen was still melting. The Core pulled at his will from all sides, relentless. Eternal. It was pointless to resist.

There was no pain here, no suffering. Always Arlen had fought death, struggling to keep himself and others from the lonely path. Now he was walking it, and with a lightening heart. He let it begin to overwhelm him, nestling him into the heart of Ala.

Don't you leave me, Arlen Bales!

The words jarred his consciousness, a slap that ruined the perfect seduction of the Core.

Had he truly heard Renna's voice without his ears—felt it without his body? Was it something Read on the current, or simply a memory?

Did it matter?

A moment ago he had been ready for the lonely path, ready

to meet Everam, or the Creator, or the oblivion of omniscience. But as if remembering a dream that had been lost on waking, his thoughts turned to Renna. Jardir. His son.

How long had it been since he dissipated? Seconds? Days? Years?

He gathered his will, pulling back into himself. One, drifting in infinity. There was no escape. He might resist a few moments more, but then the Core would have him.

He reached out, cautiously this time, Reading the currents coming down from the hive. Barely an instant had passed, and as if watching through a window, he could see what was happening miles above in the laying chamber.

Jardir again tried to draw wards to summon the Spear of Kaji, but the weapon remained trapped within the body of the queen, unable to return to him.

The hatchling queens had drained their mother's corpse of all its magic now, looming over the other demons as they approached the crown's warding field. They pushed through from all sides. The magic stung and angered them, but they were not slowed.

One leapt at Jardir, and he caught her foreclaws in his hands, twisting to turn her momentum against her as he narrowly avoided the stinger. His punches were fierce and powerful, but the queen accepted the blows and swept him aside with a lash of her tail.

Jardir rolled with the blow, leaping just in time to avoid the stinger again.

Everam, he began, but no words came to him. What did prayer matter? Either the Creator existed or He did not. Either He would help them in their hour of need, or He would not.

Arlen Drew power through the queens, Reading them—Knowing them. Their nature was so clear to him now, so basic. He felt like a blind man, seeing for the first time.

He could not return to his friends, but enough of his will remained to shape the magic flowing up from the Core into the chamber.

There are no queen wards. But that did not mean they could not be made.

Renna threw her knife, setting it quivering in a queen's eye. The handle shone bright with power as the Spear of Kaji had, Drawing the queen's power and turning it into killing magic.

But the blow was not enough to slow the queen, who lashed out with her stinger. Renna slipped the blow, wrapping her warded brook stone necklace around the venomous appendage. It sank into the ridge between reticulations and she pulled hard.

But the queen's strength was beyond anything Renna Bales could match. Necklace cord wrapped around her fists, Renna was thrown to the ground, the demon's maw opening wide.

A sudden flare of light drew the queen's attention, a symbol forming in the air, drawn in silver fire. The lines shifted and blurred like a mimic demon at first, but then they began to firm. The queen gave a shriek and took a step back.

More of the strange wards appeared, circling the chamber. They linked to mind and mimic wards, creating a circle of killing magic that closed inward.

Arlen tightened the ring and the demons shrieked, writhed, and burned. Like crushing ants in his fist, he killed every demon in the chamber from egg to queen.

Renna and Jardir were safe for the moment, but it wasn't enough.

He expanded the power throughout the hive, cleansing it of drones, and into the hatchery, killing an entire generation of demons in the shell.

Still, it wasn't enough. For in that moment of infinity, Arlen had been connected to everyone in Thesa, fighting amid the swarm. He reached for it again, finding his friends, his enemies, as he worked his will upon the endless magic of the Core.

In Miln, where demons had taken root beneath the city to hide from the power of the great organ, his wards purged the corelings from the tunnels.

By the River Angiers, where Gared Cutter's army fought desperately against a demon horde, wards appeared in the air, burning demons on the field.

In the Hollow, where corelings clustered at the edge of the greatward, he mowed the creatures down like grass. In Tibbet's Brook, he swept the boroughs clean.

Inevera was fighting on the streets of Docktown when Arlen smote ruin upon the foe.

Even in Everam's Bounty, where Amanvah and Asome led the *Sharum* against legions gathered by the demon princes, he extended his reach, creating wards the corelings could not abide. They fell to the ground, curling up as their flesh smoked and blood boiled.

Still it wasn't enough. There were yet more demons in the world. He reached out farther, seeking to destroy them all.

But as he did, Arlen realized he had expanded too far. His essence continued to dilute into the Core as he spread himself thinner and thinner, and now he found almost nothing left.

Forgot to breathe, again.

He inhaled the current one last time, tasting the essence of Renna, of his unborn son, and then he let the magic claim him.

CHAPTER 44

BORN IN DARKNESS

334 AR

"Arlen!" The wards circling the room began to fade away, leaving echoes in Renna's eyelids. "Arlen Bales, you come back to me! Can't do this without you!"

Adrenaline still pumped through her, making her feel dizzy, sick. The chamber was empty save her and Jardir and the bodies of her friends, the ruin of their enemies. The air was rank.

Jardir went to the ancient queen and thrust his hand into her burst eye. He had to reach nearly to his shoulder before he drew out the Spear of Kaji, slick with ichor and glowing brightly.

He returned to Renna, laying a hand on her shoulder. "The son of Jeph died in glory. Your husband's honor was boundless."

"Don't care about any of that," Renna said. "Want him back."

"I do not think he is coming back," Jardir said, "and we cannot stay."

Renna knew he was right, but the floor seemed to tilt, the weight of the countless tons of stone above pressing down on her. She fell to her knees, nauseous, chest constricting. She struggled to breathe.

And her thighs were wet.

"Creator, no," she whispered, touching the fluid, seeing it pooling on the floor. "Not here. Not now."

Jardir looked at her, one of the jewels on his crown glowing softly, and he knew. His warding field, collapsed by the assault of the queens, reactivated around them, sealing off the birthing chamber.

He knelt beside her, laying the spear on the floor and taking her hands. "Be at peace, Renna vah Arlen am'Bales am'Brook. Your husband was my *ajin'pal,* my blood brother. I am not him, but I am honored to stand for him. You are not alone."

His words were gentle, his aura sincere. He would protect her like his own bride, her child like his own son.

She tried to reply, but then the first real contraction came, and her words were lost as she grit her teeth and moaned.

He squeezed her hands until it passed, saying nothing, but breathing in loud, even cadence, encouraging her to do the same.

"You got lots of kids, right?" she asked when the contraction passed. "Done this before?"

Jardir shook his head. "Never. Birthing is the purview of the *dama'ting.* But I do not believe Everam and the Deliverer could see us through such darkness only to abandon us now."

Renna squeezed his hands. "We get through this, you'll be the rippin' Deliverer, Ahmann."

Weeks later, Jardir emerged from the Mouth of the Abyss. A step behind was Renna, Darin Bales bundled at her breast, sleeping contentedly on a full belly of milk.

The weight of the ever-present stone over their heads lifted away to open sky, the sun shining overhead. Jardir stood taller, breathing deeply of his first taste of fresh air in months.

Renna straightened as well, squinting and stretching her hands up to embrace the sun. "Wish the core dwellers could see this."

Jardir thought back to the thousands of *alamen fae,* free for the first time in millennia. "The lost souls of Kaji's army are not yet ready to see the sun, but the day will come. I will send forces to reclaim the Spear of Ala and dispatch envoys to return the *alamen fae* to our fold the moment I regain the Skull Throne."

Renna nodded, gentling the top of Darin's head. "Baby steps."

"Where will you go?"

"Home, I reckon, if it's still standin'. Boy's got family that'll be eager to meet him. After that . . ." Renna shrugged. "Meant to build a new life in the Hollow with Arlen, but I dunno if there's a place for me there, now."

"There is always a place with me," Jardir said.

"As what, your sixteenth wife?" Renna asked.

"If you wish it," Jardir said. "Among my people, it is honorable for a man to marry the widows of his *ajin'pal*. You need not fear I will touch you, but the oath will give you permanent protection and a place among my people."

"Ent worried about you touchin' me," Renna said. "You've already seen enough to wilt any man's spear. But don't you need your *Jiwah Ka*'s permission to make an offer like that?"

"Inevera has always known the Par'chin was special," Jardir said.

"Ay, that's why she had you try'n kill him," Renna agreed. "Don't think she'd take kindly to having me as a sister-wife, and I don't reckon I'd want to be anyone's *Jiwah Sen*."

"It does not matter," Jardir said. "You are First Wife of the Deliverer, who put the Spear of Kaji into the eye of Alagai'ting Ka. You will have a place of honor among my people, now and forever."

"Still don't buy this Deliverer business," Renna said. "Arlen did what he needed to, but that don't mean he was Heaven-sent."

"Perhaps," Jardir agreed. "Heaven. Everam. The Deliverer. Such words have different meanings now, but I cannot look at all that has happened and explain it away as coincidence."

"Ay." Renna nodded. "Offer means a lot to me, Ahmann, but I think it's time I made my own way in the world."

"Of course." Jardir reached out, gently stroking the sandy hair from the sleeping child's face. "But I pray that path intersects with mine, from time to time. I would see your child grow, and grant you any boon within my power, now or decades hence."

"Think it's over?" Renna asked. The hive was purged, and

the handful of demons they encountered as they wandered the maze of tunnels back to the surface fled before them.

"Light will always war with darkness," Jardir said. "Substance will ever be the enemy of the void. But we have this chance to strengthen our ties, expand our wards, and usher in a new era of peace."

CHAPTER 45

THE PACT

335 AR

They came to the Hollow from all over Thesa and Krasia, royal carts lining the road to Leesha's palace as they dropped off their charges.

First to arrive were the Angierians. Duchess Araine, accompanied by Melny and her infant grandson, Rhinebeck the Fourth.

"Boy wails night and day," Araine grumbled, but Leesha could tell it was only a façade. Araine looked better than she had in months, and Angiers was slowly recovering under her steady hand. Pawl accompanied the duchess as always, and Leesha could not help but feel a mild discomfort, remembering the boy's words under the demons' control.

Next came the Laktonians, Isan accompanied by his most powerful dockmasters and Captains Dehlia and Qeran.

"Welcome, Duke Isan."

"*Damaji* Isan," Isan corrected. "At least until the new pact is signed."

Duke Ragen and Duchess Elissa arrived a few days later. Leesha knew what to expect, but it pained her to see Elissa's lurching steps, even on Ragen's steady arm.

"I can have a wheeled chair brought," Leesha said in her ear as they embraced.

"No, thank you," Elissa said. "I spend enough of my time sitting these days."

"If you'll allow it, I'd like to examine you after the ceremony," Leesha said. "Perhaps there is something I can do that your Gatherers could not."

Elissa gave her arms a squeeze. "Perhaps. But I have come to see that there are some hurts even magic cannot heal."

Abban arrived before his master to prepare for Jardir's arrival. The fat *khaffit* walked on two camel crutches now, but he was smiling. "Everam's beard, it is good to see you, daughter of Erny!"

Leesha bit back a scowl at all the pain he'd caused, but Abban's advice to her had always been honest, and he paid a heavy price for his failings.

"I am glad to see you recovered, son of Chabin," she said in Krasian.

Abban bowed as much as his crutches allowed. "I am nothing short of amazed at how quickly you have mastered our language."

Leesha winked. "I've had a lot of practice."

"I am to warn you," Abban said, "the Damajah will arrive with my master."

"Of course." Leesha expected as much. "It would not be proper for Shar'Dama Ka to visit without his *Jiwah Ka* to chaperone."

Abban bowed again. "I see you have come to understand our ways as well as our language."

The rest of the Krasians arrived soon after, their honor guard of *dal'Sharum* met by Gared and an equal number of Hollow Soldiers. Leesha met their delegation in her receiving hall, but she stepped down from the throne to greet them in friendship. Wonda and Stela flanked her, eyes alert.

Briar was with them, looking almost unrecognizable in *Sharum* blacks, bathed and groomed. He carried a toddler on his shoulder, accompanied by a *Sharum'ting* in a white turban.

"Who's she?" Stela asked.

Leesha did not reply, tightening her throat against the forming lump as Amanvah appeared, carrying an infant girl. Kendall was with her, carrying the boy.

Finally, Inevera and Ahmann were presented. The Damajah's eyes were cold, but her nod was respectful. Jardir, look-

ing handsome and regal, beamed and embraced her under
Inevera's watchful glare.

"Intended."

"Will you ever stop calling me that?" Leesha asked, but she
was smiling.

"Of course." Ahmann bowed. "As soon as you agree to my
proposal."

"You may be waiting a long time for that," Leesha said.
"You are here to sign something greater than a marriage contract."

Jardir felt Inevera bristle at the words.

"Only if we agree on the final—"

"Peace, *jiwah,*" Jardir said. "There will be no further negotiations. My gift to bless this day."

"You give away too much," Inevera hissed, too low for the
Hollowers to hear.

"I must agree with the Damajah," Abban said.

"I made a promise to the Par'chin," Jardir said loudly. "Let
it be kept, and without delay."

The ceremony was short. Leesha's minister produced five
copies of the newly penned Pact of the Free Cities, formally
calling an end to the Daylight War. The signatories recognized
one another's sovereignty, including the newly independent
duchy of the Hollow and the restored duchy of Lakton. Everam's Bountry was ceded as Krasian lands, but with new laws
governing trade and the treatment of *chin.*

There were pledges of unity against the demons, but it
seemed a distant thing, now. The few demons that remained
were leaderless, pushed farther and farther from their territories by the growing greatwards.

When copies were all signed and witnessed, General Cutter
approached, slapping Jardir on the back in that overly familiar way the greenlanders had. Jardir's bodyguards stiffened,
but he gave them no signal to interfere.

"Men are all goin' to the parlor for a drink and a smoke,"
Gared said, "you and Abban want to join."

Jardir's eyes flicked to Inevera.

"Go, husband." The whispered words were carried to his

earring alone, but he could see the quirk of a smile behind her translucent veil. "I will not kill the daughter of Erny before your return."

Abban, watching the exchange, caught Jardir's subtle nod and turned to Gared to facilitate. "Of course, son of Steave. We would be honored. Please, lead the way."

The greenlanders were informal; men of various station mingled amid the haze of pipe smoke in the parlor. But even among the *chin* true royalty stood apart. Dukes Ragen and Isan were an island amid the crowd.

Isan drifted a step back at their approach, but Ragen returned the gesture when Jardir reached out to clasp wrists in the Northern fashion.

"It is an honor, Duke Ragen," Jardir said. "The Par'chin spoke to me of you many times. If you carry a fraction of the honor he lauds upon you, your place in Heaven is assured."

"The honor is mine." Ragen's aura was wary, but mention of the Par'chin helped put him at ease.

Gared gave a signal, and a tray of Nothern ale was brought over. "Thought we'd have a toast to Mr. Bales."

Jardir held up a hand. "Forgive me, son of Steave, but the Evejah forbids . . ."

"Nie's black heart, Ahmann!" Abban cried, startling everyone—Jardir most of all. Abban had never dared speak to him so in front of others.

"You are Shar'Dama Ka." Abban's tone was the kind reserved for a child. "You can edit the Evejah with a word. If a fraction of the honor you laud upon the Par'chin is truth, then this once you can honor the customs of his people and drink a toast in his name."

Jardir blinked, speechless as Abban reached into his vest, producing a small clay bottle and a handful of tiny porcelain cups. "And I have brought just the thing."

Ragen's eyes glittered. "Can't remember the last time I had couzi."

"Horrible stuff." Gared seemed eager nonetheless.

Abban passed out the cups, filling them from the small bottle. "The Par'chin visited my pavilion often, and we would drink three times before conducting business."

Jardir said nothing as Abban filled his cup. The last time he drank couzi had not gone well for him. That, more than Eve-jan law, had stayed him all these years.

Abban raised his cup. "To the son of Jeph, a hard negotiatior who never once tried to cheat me."

They all laughed at that, touching cups and drinking in one smooth motion. Jardir grimaced as the liquid burned his tongue and throat like boiling water. Around the circle, other men did the same.

Abban filled the cups again, and Ragen lifted his. "To Arlen Bales, who was as much a son to me as any of blood."

Again they touched cups and threw them back. There was no burning this time, Jardir's mouth still numb from the first. He relaxed, and knew his friend had been right. The pact wasn't the only thing he owed the Par'chin.

Abban filled the cups a third time, and this time Jardir was first to raise his. "To the Deliverer, who sits with honor at the table of Heaven."

Jardir did not hesitate as the other men gaped, clicking the nearest cup and tossing back his third cup of couzi.

This time, it tasted like cinnamon.

Safely ensconced in the women's wing, Leesha reached eagerly for the child. Olive seldom suckled anymore, eating solids as voraciously as she had her mother's milk. She was little more than a year old now, Darin barely ten months, but already the two of them and young Kaji were chasing each other around the room.

But Rojer's son Arick, not yet six months old, was still hungry for the teat. Leesha sobbed as he latched on to her, looking down at her friend's face in perfect miniature. Arick's skin was darker than his father's, but the shock of red hair atop his head was unmistakable. His eyes closed contentedly as he sucked.

Amanvah handed her daughter Rojvah to Inevera and produced a tear bottle, gently scraping the wetness from Leesha's cheek. "You honor my husband with your milk, mistress."

Leesha shook her head. "The honor is mine."

"Sikvah would have been proud to see this moment," Amanvah said. "Perhaps from Heaven she can."

"It must have been difficult, nursing two," Leesha said.

"At first," Amanvah agreed, "but Ashia helped."

"It was the least I could do for my spear sister's child," Ashia said.

Leesha bent to kiss the top of Arick's head. "You will grow up strong, nursed by a *Damaji'ting* and the Sharum'ting Ka."

"Not to mention the Duchess of the Hollow," Elona said, rocking young Selen, who had only just drifted off to sleep.

Inevera watched the others with a hawkish eye, but then Araine whispered something to her, and the Damajah's laugh was deep and genuine.

"Nice, seein' the kids all together like—!" Renna left the sentence unfinished, crossing the room in an instant to catch a vase the children knocked from a side table. "Ay, you scamps! Settle down!"

"Sorry, Auntie Ren!" Olive called, but then Darin poked at Kaji and he shrieked, setting all three off running again.

"Swear to the Creator," Renna muttered as she returned to the couches, "that boy's more likely to give me a heart attack than his da."

"Of course, none of that wildness comes from his mum," Leesha noted.

Renna winked at her. "Course not."

"Kaji is no innocent," Ashia said. "No crib can hold him now. The boy climbs like a Watcher, sneaking off in the middle of the night to find Briar."

"Olive just breaks the slats now," Leesha said. "Not fifteen months, and strong as a mule."

"If she is anything like her father, she is twice as stubborn," Inevera said, and Leesha laughed. She and Ahmann's *Jiwah Ka* might never be friends, but they were no longer enemies, and that was a start.

"Darin doesn't even bother breakin' slats," Renna said. "Boy's already mistin' through 'em at night. Scared half to death he's going to skate all the way to the desert, or down to the Core to look for his da."

"He can dissipate?!" Leesha tried to hide her alarm. Renna was right to be worried. She glanced at Olive, praying her daughter never learned the skill.

"Just a little at a time," Renna said, "like a mouse squeezin' through a crack. Ent gone all the way to smoke yet, but it's only a matter o' time."

"Night," Elissa said. "And here I thought Arlen was a handful."

They all laughed at that, and amid the sounds of babies crying and children scampering about, Leesha found hope for a lasting peace.

ACKNOWLEDGMENTS

In the decade since I first sold *The Warded Man,* countless people have helped make the Demon Cycle series a reality. Editors, agents, publishers, marketing and publicity, booksellers, and you, the reader, all deserve more thanks than I can possibly convey, but if I may call out a few . . .

Special thanks to Dr. Bill Greene for the herb lore, and Lauren Greene for bringing a perfect little girl into my life the day after this book went to the publisher. Sirena has made every moment since a treasure. Cassandra Brett, who is becoming a great little writer herself.

Myke Cole, who believed in my work before anyone, and pushed me to submit to Joshua Bilmes, whose team at JABberwocky Literary Agency has been a bedrock of support.

My editors, particularly Tricia Narwani and Natasha Bardon, who tackled a rough 1,043-page first draft and helped me polish it down to a gem, and Laura Jorstad, my copy editor, who does more heavy lifting behind the scenes than you might realize.

Larry Rostant, whose cover art catches eyes from across the store, and the cover models, as well as Millennium FX, who sculpted a real-life Alagai Ka. Lauren K. Cannon for her ward designs and Dominik Broniek for his haunting illustrations. Narrators Pete Bradbury, Colin Mace, and the cast and crew at GraphicAudio. The international publishers and translators whose work introduces me to new readers all over the world.

My assistant Karen, who takes care of so much so I can focus on writing.

And to everyone in previous acknowledgments whom I didn't have space to mention again. Thank you all—I couldn't have made it through this journey without you.

WARD GRIMOIRE

DEFENSIVE WARDS

Defensive wards Draw magic to form a barrier (forbiddance) through which demons cannot pass. Wards are strongest when used against the specific demon type to which they are assigned, and are most commonly used in conjunction with other wards in circles of protection. When a circle activates, all demonflesh is forcibly banished from its line. A mixed group of demons is referred to as a host.

BANK DEMON

Description: Called frog demons or froggies, these demons appear much like common fly frogs, but they are large enough to swallow humans whole. They lie in wait in shallow water, springing only when prey comes within range. One hop puts them up onto land, and they lash out with long, powerful tongues, catching victims around the midsection or limbs and dragging them into the corelings' wide maws. Bank demons will then return to the water, drowning their struggling prey. A group of bank demons is called an army.

CAVE DEMON

Description: Cave demons, also known as spider demons, have eight segmented legs and can run at great speed. Cave demons excrete a sticky silk that is magic-dead—invisible to wardsight and immune to wards of protection. They will prepare traps and lie in wait for the unwary. These demons seldom rise to the surface unless summoned by a mind; they are more commonly found in deep caves and the tunnels of a demon hive. They are the guardians of the larder. A group of cave demons is called a clutter.

CLAY DEMON

Description: Clay demons are native to the hard clay flats on the outskirts of the Krasian desert. They are about as big as a medium-sized dog, with compact bunched muscle and thick, overlapping armor plates. Their short, hard talons allow them to cling to most any rock face, even hang upside down. Their orange-brown armor can blend invisibly into an adobe wall or clay bed. The blunt head of a clay demon can smash through nearly anything, shattering stone and denting steel. A group of clay demons is known as a shattering.

FIELD DEMON

Description: Sleek and low to the ground, with long, powerful limbs and retractable claws, field demons are the fastest thing on four legs when they have open ground to accelerate. Tough scales on their limbs and back can turn aside most weapons, but their underbelly—if exposed—is more vulnerable. A group of field demons is known as a reap.

⚜ FLAME DEMON

Description: Flame demons have eyes, nostrils, and mouths that glow with a smoky orange light. They are the smallest demons, ranging from the size of a rabbit to that of a large cat. Like all demons, they have long, hooked claws and rows of razor-sharp teeth. Their armor consists of small, overlapping scales, sharp and hard. Flame demons can spit fire in brief bursts. Their sticky firespit burns intensely on contact with air and can set almost any substance alight, even metal and stone. A group of flame demons is known as a blaze.

⚡ LIGHTNING DEMON

Description: Though lightning demons are nearly indistinguishable from their wind demon cousins, their spit is charged with electricity that can paralyze a victim. They spit as they dive, snatching up their helpless victims to devour them alive. A group of lightning demons is known as a thundercloud.

⚗ MIMIC DEMON

Description: Mimics are the elite bodyguards to mind demons. Less vulnerable to light than their masters and more intelligent than the lesser breeds, mimics serve as lieutenants and are able to summon and exert their will upon coreling drones. Their natural form is unknown, but they are able to assume the form of nearly anything they encounter, from inanimate objects to creatures, clothing, and equipment. One of their favorite tricks is to learn the names of their prey and take the form of a friend, feigning distress and calling to their victims to convince them to leave the safety of their wards. A gathering of mimic demons is known as a troupe.

⬡ MIND DEMON

Description: Also known as coreling princes, mind demons are the generals of demonkind. The only male-sexed caste among demonkind, minds are physically weak and have little in the way of the natural defenses of the other corelings, but they have vast mental and magical powers. They can read and control minds, communicate telepathically, and implant permanent suggestions. They can draw wards in the air and power them with their own innate magic. Coreling drones follow their every mental command without hesitation, and will give their lives to protect them. Sensitive to even moonlight, mind demons only rise on the three-night period of the new moon cycle, in the hours when night is darkest. A gathering of mind demons is known as a court.

ROCK DEMON
Description: The largest of the coreling breeds, rock demons can range in height from six to twenty feet. Hulking masses of sinew and sharp edges, they have thick carapaces knobbed with bony protrusions, and their spiked tails can shatter stone. They stand hunched on two clawed feet, with long, gnarled arms ending in talons the size of butcher knives and multiple rows of bladelike teeth. No known physical force can harm a rock demon. A group of rock demons is called a quake.

SAND DEMON
Description: Cousins to rock demons, sand demons are smaller and more nimble, but still among the strongest and best armored of the coreling breeds. They have small, sharp scales that are a dirty yellow almost indistinguishable from gritty sand. They run on all fours but can rise to two legs in combat. Their short snouts have rows of sharp teeth, with nostril slits just below large, lidless eyes. Thick horns curve upward and back, cutting through the scales. Their brows twitch continually as they displace the ever-blowing desert sand. Sand demons hunt in packs known as storms.

SNOW DEMON
Description: Similar to flame demons in build, snow demons are native to frozen Northern climates and high mountain elevations. Their scales are such pure white, they scintillate with color if caught in the light. Snow demons are nearly invisible in the snow, and spit a liquid so cold it instantly freezes anything it touches. Steel struck with coldspit can become brittle enough to shatter. A group of snow demons is called a blizzard.

ⱱⱫ STONE DEMON
Description: Smaller cousins of rock demons—who form through faces of pure rock—stone demons feature armor with the mottled appearance of conglomerate rock. They tend to be squat and slow, but are among the strongest and most indestructible of demons.

Requiring less specialized environments to rise, stone demons are more common than rocks. A group of stone demons is called a conglomerate.

ⱦⱬ SUCCOR
Description: The succor ward is a general ward of protection taught to children. Not as powerful as wards keyed to individual breeds, succor wards create a general field of discomfort that is enough to drive most corelings away unless prey is in sight. Very large or powerful wards can form a forbiddance. The ward is used in the Thesan dice game Succor, as well as its Krasian variation, Sharak.

ⱳ SWAMP DEMON
Description: Swamp demons are native to swamps and marshy areas and are an amphibious form of wood demon, at home both in the water and in the trees. Swamp demons are blotched in green and brown, blending into their surroundings, and will often hide in trees, mud, or shallow water to spring on prey. They spit a thick, sticky slime that rots any organic material it comes in contact with. A group of swamp demons is called a muck.

ⱶ WATER DEMON
Description: Water demons are seldom seen. They come in various forms and sizes. Some are man-sized, sleek and scaly, with webbed hands and feet, tipped with sharp talons. Others are large enough to pull three-mast ships beneath the surface with their thick, horned tentacles. Others are bigger still, leviathans able to leap above the water and splash down to create tremendous waves. Water demons can only breathe underwater, though they can surface for a short time. A group of water demons is called a wave.

☙ WIND DEMON

Description: Wind demons can stand as tall as six feet at the shoulder, but have head fins that rise much higher, topping eight or nine feet. Their great sharp-edged beaks hide rows of teeth. Their skin is a tough, flexible armor that can turn most any spearpoint or arrowhead. It stretches out from their sides and along the underside of their arms to form the tough membrane of their wings, which can span three times their height. Clumsy and slow on land, wind demons have tremendous power in the sky. The thin wing bones are jointed with wicked hooked talons. Their preferred attack is a silent dive; they then open their wings with a great snap just before impact, severing a victim's head. They grab the body in their hind talons and fly off. A group of wind demons is called a flight.

☙ WOOD DEMON

Description: Wood demons are native to forests. Next to rock demons, they are the largest and most powerful demons, averaging from five to ten feet tall when standing on their hind legs. They have short, powerful hindquarters and long, sinewy arms, perfect for climbing trees and leaping from branch to branch. Their claws are short, hard points, designed for gripping through the bark of trees. Wood demons' armor is barklike in color and texture, and they have large black eyes. Wood demons cannot be harmed by normal fire, but will burn readily if brought in contact with hotter fires, such as firespit or liquid demonfire. Wood demons will kill flame demons on sight, and often hunt in groups called copses.

OFFENSIVE (COMBAT) WARDS

Combat wards repurpose magic for various effects. Some Draw power directly from the demon they strike, while others are powered by batteries such as demon bone, also known as *hora*.

☩ COLD
Description: Cold wards reduce thermal energy, rapidly reducing the temperature of their target area to below freezing. Powerful cold wards can shatter steel or even rock demon armor.

₡ CUTTING
Description: Cutting wards, when etched along the length of a blade, can enhance its sharpness, allowing the weapon to cut cleanly through even coreling armor and flesh. Cutting wards siphon power from the demon as they strike, weakening armor, strengthening the blade, and sharpening down to a near-molecular level.

₤ FIRESPIT/COLDSPIT
Description: These wards are used as defense against flame demons, turning their firespit into a cool breeze. When drawn in reverse, they turn the coldspit of a snow demon into a warm breeze.

℧ GLASS
Description: When etched on glass and charged with magic, these wards effect a permanent change, making glass harder than diamond and stronger than steel without changing its weight or appearance. Warded glass is widely used to create near-indestructible windows, vials, weapons, and armor.

₩ HEAT
Description: Heat wards increase thermal energy, converting magic directly to heat. Objects painted with heat wards are consumed when the wards activate unless highly resistant to temperature extremes.

IMPACT
Description: These wards turn magic into concussive force. They can be used alone, or to augment the blow of a blunt weapon. When used to strike a demon, they siphon magic like cutting wards, weakening armor even as they multiply force. The stronger the original impact, the more power is generated.

LECTRIC
Description: These wards convert magic directly into electricity that can be directed at an object or creature. The wards can also be linked to form circuits.

MAGNETIC
Description: Magnetic wards charge their target area, drawing iron like a powerful magnet. They are sometimes used to increase the accuracy of iron cannonballs.

MOISTURE
Description: Moisture wards attract moisture from the air or nearby bodies of water. They can be used to ensure that plants get the necessary water without human care, to fill a small reservoir, or to quench a flame demon. Powerful moisture wards can drown or, if reversed, dehydrate a victim.

PIERCING
Description: Piercing wards Draw from the point of impact on a demon's body, weakening coreling armor even as they focus magic into a weapon's point for maximum penetrative power.

PRESSURE
Description: Pressure wards exert a crushing force that builds in heat and intensity the longer they remain in contact with a demon. The Warded Man has one on each palm, and has been known to squeeze a demon's head with them until it bursts.

PERCEPTION WARDS

Perception wards create magical effects that can alter the senses of demons and sometimes humans.

BLENDING
Description: Blending wards pull from their surroundings to camouflage their target area. Unlike unsight wards, which only work on demons, blending wards can hide things from human senses, as well. Sudden or quick movement can negate a blending ward's power.

CONFUSION
Description: Confusion wards radiate a field of disorientation that can cause creatures to become dizzy and lose their sense of direction. Unless prey is in sight, affected coreling drones will often forget what they are doing, wandering away harmlessly.

LIGHT
Description: Light wards convert magic to pure white light. Depending on the power source, the light can be anything from a soft glow to a blinding glare.

PROPHECY
Description: Carved into the *alagai hora* of the *dama'ting,* prophecy wards read the currents of magic to make predictions about the future. Their magic pulls the demon bone dice out of their natural trajectories to answer questions spoken in prayer to Everam. The processes used both to make the dice and to read them are closely guarded secrets of the Krasian priestesses; it is death to share them with outsiders.

UNSIGHT
Description: Rediscovered by Leesha Paper, wards of unsight can make objects invisible to demons, provided those objects keep relatively still. Hundreds, even thousands of wards of unsight are used to make Cloaks of Unsight that protect humans in the naked night.

WARDSIGHT

Description: When worn around the eyes and charged, these wards can allow surface creatures to see in the magical spectrum. As a result, the creatures can see in complete darkness as easily as clear day, watch the flow of ambient magic, judge the relative power of wardings, and see the auras given off by all living things. A skilled practitioner can "Read" these auras to tell what others are feeling or thinking, and sometimes to gain a sense of their past or even their future.

EXPLORE THE WORLDS OF DEL REY BOOKS

Read excerpts from hot new titles.

Stay up-to-date on your favorite authors.

Find out about exclusive giveaways and sweepstakes.

Connect with us online!

Follow us on social media

f Facebook.com/DelReyBooks

📷 🐦 @DelReyBooks

Visit us at UnboundWorlds.com

f Facebook.com/UnboundWorlds

🐦 @unboundworlds

DEL REY